SHADOW'S SEVENTH STEP

A FANTASY LITRPG ADVENTURE

DIVINE APOSTASY
BOOK SEVEN

A. F. KAY

Shadow's Seventh Step, Divine Apostasy Book 7 by A. F. Kay

afkauthor.com

Published by Black Pyramid Press, LLC

blackpyramidpress.com

Book Cover by Magnetra's Design

Editing by tctunstall@comcast.net

❀ Created with Vellum

For Liam
your laughter fills my heart.

PROLOGUE

[*A*uthor's Note - Summaries of books 1 through 6 along with a glossary of people, places, and things can be found at afkauthor.com. In addition, the glossary can be found at the end of this book.]

LALQUINRIAL STEPPED out of the portal and into an ancient ring of stones. He savored the humid air that held a hint of salt from the waves that crashed into nearby cliffs. A solitary moon hung like a lantern in the sky, bathing everything in soft light.

The Darkness had seeped into this galaxy before Pen had stopped it, which made this planet a perfect location for further exploration into this part of the Universe. The Infernal Realm had gained a strong foothold here because of it, and Lalquinrial had visited many times.

Five days had passed since Lalquinrial had trapped that problematic boy in an Infernal Bubble. It had taken that long to coordinate this meeting. Too impatient to walk, Lalquinrial teleported to the door of the lone structure. It stood out like a

1

wart on the short grass of the field, but the isolation suited his needs.

Lalquinrial reached for the doorknob and paused. For just a moment, it had felt as if someone's gaze had crossed his back. The others had agreed to come alone, but perhaps they'd brought protection, or, unlikely as it might be, helpers to spring a trap.

Turning, Lalquinrial pushed his Divine Authority outward, hoping to trap whoever had triggered his senses. With the ease that comes with thousands of years of experience, he filtered out everything from the microorganisms in the soil to the fish in the nearby ocean, leaving nothing behind.

Lalquinrial could count on one hand the beings capable of concealing themselves from his Divine Authority. Perhaps it had been the Companion, as she proved almost impossible to hide from. This felt different, though, and the touch so light he began to doubt his recollection. Perhaps meeting his brethren after so long had made him jumpy.

Lalquinrial frowned and turned his attention back to the thick oak door, made to withstand harsh rain and howling winds. Opening it, he found his two guests already present.

The men sat at a table in the center of an otherwise empty bar, a half pitcher of dark beer between them. That the bar had no other patrons didn't surprise Lalquinrial. It took a special type of person to risk the dangers this building and its surroundings held. Now, with three of the most powerful gods in the Universe together, it would terrify anyone.

Naktos smiled at Lalquinrial and slowly filled an empty third glass from the pitcher. Lalquinrial returned the smile, genuinely happy to see his spiritual brother. He had kept himself apart from the others, perhaps for too long, but that would soon change. Only two pieces remained.

Izac stood and Lalquinrial grasped the red-haired god's forearm. All the Disciples had their flaws, including himself, but Izac combined impatience, power, and anger. The trifecta made long-term relationships difficult. Izac wanted to rule this Universe, while Lalquinrial knew it only served as a stepping stone to true power.

Eiru, Izac's sister, worried Lalquinrial. Unlike Izac, her power had paired with patience and piercing Intelligence. Thankfully she had isolated herself from the other Disciples with her talk of throwing away Grave's Spirit. Why would anyone wish to redistribute such a concentration of power?

Lalquinrial turned to Naktos and flashed a sincere smile. White-grey hair like granite blended into sun-deprived pale skin. A scarf hid the two sacks on his neck that gave his kind power over poisoned air. They clasped forearms and bumped shoulders.

"It is good to see you, Lal," Naktos said. "I enjoyed meeting your daughter last year."

Lalquinrial grinned. "Liar. She is too much like her mother, and as she grows into her power, I'm beginning to worry for my safety."

They all laughed as they sat, and Lalquinrial took a sip of the dark beer, enjoying the balanced sweet and bitter smoothness of the drink.

Naktos, with only seven connected Meridians, lacked brute Spiritual power. He compensated for this weakness with knowledge, planning, and alchemy. His scientific approach to problems appealed to Lalquinrial, and they had become friends during the eons they traveled with Pen.

"I have the boy," Lalquinrial said.

Izac leaned forward, and Naktos went still as he prepared to absorb every detail of Lalquinrial's report.

Lalquinrial leaned back and pursed his lips. "Our problems are greater than I feared, and we are fortunate I captured him now. If he had transitioned to Divine, I worry our plans would quickly unravel."

"It's true then?" Naktos asked. "He is an Axiom?"

Lalquinrial shrugged. "I could not penetrate whatever cloaks his Core, but I watched him destroy an entire army, and then five of my Aspects at the same time. He still powers his spells with his own essence—"

"What?" Izac asked, interrupting Lalquinrial. "Does he lack a mentor? Has my sister abandoned him?"

Lalquinrial pushed his irritation into the third sphere and continued. "I do not know. But remember the timeline. He has reached Peak Diamond in less than two years. What progress had we made our first two years?"

Naktos chuckled. "I hadn't even formed a Core yet."

"None of us had," Lalquinrial said. "So we should not fault a missing window when viewing the palace he has created."

"You sound as if you like him," Izac said.

"I will come to that," Lalquinrial said. "To finish my earlier thought, after he somehow escaped the trap we'd set, he proceeded to destroy the army I'd assembled. A hundred thousand followers died in minutes. I studied his attacks and believe he used pure essence combinations for each. He didn't combine any essences to create a missing third. I now believe Simandreial that the boy is a true Axiom."

Izac hissed and Naktos leaned back in shock.

"There is so much more to tell you, I don't know where to begin," Lalquinrial said.

"How about starting with how he's still an Axiom," Izac said. "I thought you were a God Killer."

Again, Lalquinrial felt enough irritation to use the third sphere. He had forgotten how quickly Izac got under his skin. "I tried and failed. In addition to reaching Peak Diamond in under two years, he has reached Grandmaster status in the Bamboo Viper Clan's secret forms."

"He is only Diamond," Izac said in disbelief. "I thought you were good."

Lalquinrial took a sip of beer to stop himself from attacking Izac. Starting a fight here would likely only result in destroying this world, and Lalquinrial needed this planet more than he needed to defend his Step skills reputation.

Naktos placed a hand on Izac's shoulder. "Perhaps we should hear all the details before rushing to judgment."

Izac shrugged, grabbed his beer, and leaned back.

Lalquinrial continued. "My Divine Fortification gave me a clear physical advantage, but he has mastered Probability Waves, which gave him enough clarity to defend himself. That is only one reason he can never reach the Divine levels. A Divine level Grandmaster with his skills could destroy all of us. He could destroy a Meridian every time he got close enough to touch you. If you do not fear me, know that I fear what he will become."

Naktos spoke into the silence. "You mentioned this was only one reason he shouldn't be allowed to reach the Divine levels. What are the others?"

Lalquinrial shook his head and took a sip of beer. He picked up the pitcher and refilled all their glasses. "You will not believe me."

Thoughts of the dark apparition Lalquinrial had witnessed as it destroyed his most powerful psychic demon, bled into his mind. A creature of pure Nihilism. It resonated so strongly with him that he'd thought of nothing else since discovering its existence.

For the first time in millennia, Lalquinrial desired something other than the power to escape the prison of this useless Universe. Regardless of what happened to the boy, Lalquinrial would claim that specter, and find a way to harbor it himself. Now that he had seen what was possible, he'd begun strengthening his own mind.

"Well?" Izac said. "Are you going to tell us?"

Lalquinrial pulled himself away from the memories of that perfect being. "Right, sorry. He has created an entire world inside his mind."

"What do you mean by world?" Naktos asked.

"His mental island is a mountain, topped by a grand citadel and surrounded by a multi-walled fortress. The walls protect a literal city. Hundreds of *thousands* of fully actualized mental constructs reside there. A mass of raw letters surrounds the mountain like an ocean, and he has somehow," Lalquinrial paused and shook his head. "He has somehow recreated Kholy."

Both gods leaned forward.

"What?" Naktos whispered. "He has a Divine fragment in his mind?"

Lalquinrial shook his head. "No Divine fragment. I doubt even his mind could tolerate that. Somehow his mind is generating self-aware constructs that seem highly focused on a particular topic. I talked to the Kholy construct, and I recognized her."

"None of that is possible," Izac said.

"I know, but I witnessed it myself," Lalquinrial replied.

Naktos remained very still. "The leaps in physical ability, the mental impossibilities, the hidden Core, maybe you aren't as crazy as I thought."

"What are you talking about?" Izac said.

Naktos faced Izac. "You know Lal's interest in the Darkness and the people who sent it. What if this boy is one of these outsiders? Or discovered some of their technology."

"Regardless," Lalquinrial said. "Imagine if we could learn how to advance our followers to Peak Diamond in two years, train them to be Step Grandmasters at the same time, and create mental fortifications capable of resisting a god. That kind of power would break us free from this shell of a Universe and allow us to face what exists outside from a position of strength."

"Or we should kill him," Izac said. "I'm only interested in this Universe and his abilities destroy all semblance of balance."

Lalquinrial immediately dropped into the third sphere and stayed there. His urge to protect the phantom in the boy's mind had overwhelmed him, and he'd almost attacked Izac. Lalquinrial would not allow anyone to kill the boy until he'd extracted that apparition.

"There is no rush to kill him," Naktos said. "He is trapped, and he holds so many secrets, they warp the mind with desire."

"What about the sixth rune?" Izac asked. "Just before you arrived, I felt Pen's Itch."

Lalquinrial narrowed his eyes. "Pen's Itch?"

"Yeah," Izac said. "Every time Pen Smeared, I felt it on the back of my neck, as if he stood behind me. I haven't felt that in over ten thousand years."

Lalquinrial took this information seriously. Izac, just like his sister Eiru, had ten connected Meridians, making the twins the most powerful Disciples. And while Lalquinrial didn't remember feeling anything like the itch when Pen had lived, he had grown in power and understanding since then. He had felt Pen's Itch tonight, too.

"Smearing with a Gem body?" Naktos said. "You saw what it did to Pen, and we all remember poor Kholy. Both of them had reached peak Deity."

Lalquinrial considered if the boy could have accomplished such a thing. He did have some version of Kholy in his mind, and she might have explained to him the process. A process that had destroyed his beloved mentor, vaporizing her body as he watched.

Of course the boy would look for ways to escape the Infernal Bubble, but using such a method was like destroying a galaxy to kill an ant. He had felt something before entering the bar, just like Izac, but it must relate to something else. The boy had accomplished impossible things, but from painful experience, Lalquinrial knew the price of such a path.

Lalquinrial rubbed his chin. "The boy would never survive the attempt. If he did try to embrace the universe, then he is surely dead." Along with the precious construct, he didn't add. "Then what is your plan?" Izac asked. "Did you just worry us for no reason?"

Lalquinrial shook his head. They had finally come to the crux of the problem. Izac and Naktos would hesitate to enter the Infernal Realm and he needed them motivated to risk entering his domain. "I need help subduing him long enough for me to destroy six of his Meridians. Once he transitions from Diamond to Angel, our chances of facing him alone disappear. Together, we can still prevail. But every step he climbs toward Deity makes stopping him less likely. We must first and foremost, keep him from reaching Divinity."

Naktos tilted his head. "What is his purpose? Did he ask for anything?"

Lalquinrial drained his glass and wiped his lip with a hand. He looked at Izac. "You asked me earlier if I liked him. He warned everyone, multiple times before he attacked. Even then, when possible, he left enemies alive."

"That is foolish," Izac said.

"Or at least, very dangerous," Naktos added.

Lalquinrial nodded. "He is powerful, noble, naïve, and merciful. He reminds me of our Master before the Darkness took him. Do I like the boy?" He shrugged. "But I do admire him. He is a younger version of all of us."

"You never answered the question," Izac said. "What does he want?"

"I almost manipulated him into revealing that, but a construct interfered. It doesn't matter, though, we need only look at his protector to guess at motives."

Naktos nodded.

"He's going to take Grave and smear it across the Universe?" Izac asked. "Why won't she let that go?"

"Because, unlike us, Eiru is also noble," Lalquinrial said.

That angered Izac, but Lalquinrial didn't care. He only needed the god for a short time. Once they had crippled the boy, he would slowly peel back the layers until he'd learned all the boy's secrets. Then he would take the precious dark phantom from the boy's mind, and nurture it himself.

Lalquinrial sighed. "The three of us might not be enough."

Izac laughed, but Naktos looked concerned.

"He may not have revealed his true strength," Lalquinrial said. "If that is the case, we need another plan."

Naktos nodded knowingly and took a sip from his beer.

"What are the alternatives?" Izac asked.

"We target his friends and family," Lalquinrial said. "We capture them and use them as leverage against him."

"Now that is something I finally agree with," Izac said.

"I will coordinate," Naktos said. "I already have assets there encouraging the civil war. It's ironic how Eiru destroyed her country by trying to save it."

"She was never too bright," Izac said.

Lalquinrial held his tongue. He knew better than to underestimate the goddess. She, like Pen and the boy, shared the ability to inspire. It stemmed from their goodness, and it even resonated with him. And that is what scared him the most. Because the boy had almost reignited a spark of hope in Lalquinrial. If that power grew and combined with Divinity, there is nothing in the Universe that could stop that boy.

Lalquinrial pushed himself away from the table and stood. "I propose we do this now."

Naktos and Izac stood as well, and the three of them left the bar. They walked toward the ring of stones, a cool breeze urging them along.

Lalquinrial felt a sliver of sadness for the miracle they went to destroy, but he knew delaying gained them nothing.

And deep down, a part of Lalquinrial worried they might already be too late. That while they all strolled through life, Ruwen Starfield sprinted.

CHAPTER 1

*R*uwen sat cross-legged on the packed dirt of the unfamiliar tent and grinned at Sift's shocked expression. "What did I miss?" he asked again.

Sift's shock turned to relief before mirroring Ruwen's grin. He leaned forward from his sitting position and hugged Ruwen. "I worried the worst had happened," Sift whispered.

Ruwen returned the hug, his throat tight. He let Sift go and whispered back. "The worst? No. Although I did see Blapy."

Sift winced. "Ouch."

Ruwen shrugged and rubbed his right wrist. "Actually, it wasn't that bad. You could say I saw a new side of her."

"Meditate," a voice hissed from Ruwen's left. "You're going to get us in trouble."

"Ignore them," Sift said. "We've been meditating here all night."

Which probably meant twenty minutes, Ruwen thought. He rubbed his right wrist again. Sift saw the movement and pointed at Ruwen's hand.

"You can't have jewelry," Sift said. "That will get you in trouble."

Ruwen looked down. The black ring he wore had small white runes swirling across the surface. He had gotten it just moments ago, and the details were still fresh in his memory.

Tring!
Pen has gifted you...

Name: *Apocalypse Hoop*
Quality: *Legendary*
Durability: *90 of 100*
Weight: *0.12 lbs.*
Restriction: *Divine Aura*
Description: *Plain black dimensional ring. When worn, white esoteric runes circle the Apocalypse Hoop detailing events from the past, present, and future. The end is inevitable.*

Pen had left this dimensional ring for Ruwen. It contained the items that Pen had wanted Ruwen to have. The Apocalypse Hoop had sat in the Third Secret, along with Blapy and all the Spirit from the Universe, for over ten thousand years.

Because of the restriction, only a Divine aura could open it. That meant Ruwen had to wait until he transitioned from Diamond to the first level of Divine, Angel, to view the contents.

A minimized notification sat at the bottom of Ruwen's vision and his display had nothing greyed out. That meant this place sat in a nearby galaxy or maybe even the same one as Grave and his connections to Uru and the Black Pyramid worked.

Ruwen pulled the ring off his finger, and the itching on his right wrist intensified. He opened the Void Band a fraction and dropped the ring into the dark portal. Now the ring sat deep under the Black Pyramid, safely out of his enemy's reach. He looked up and found the source of the itching on his wrist.

Echo sat across the room. Ruwen's passive *No Lies*, gained from Rami's last Codex of Evolution, painted a red outline around her. The red Disposition meant she viewed him with hostility. She stared intently at Ruwen's left wrist and the now closed Void Band.

Echo slowly looked up until their gazes locked. He could see the confusion on her face, and something that looked like shock. Likely both emotions originated from his sudden appearance here.

Ruwen kept his face neutral, but anger made his thoughts swirl. He needed to make sure Echo didn't leave the Master's trial. Trapping her here would stop her from causing more problems.

Echo had sent Ruwen from the Black Pyramid's kitchen to the Infernal Realm by using her own aspect, Death, to activate the Scarecrow Aspect's set bonus: *Infernal Embrace*. While in the Infernal Realm, he'd discovered that concentrating on *Infernal Embrace* allowed him to reset the bind point.

Ruwen focused on *Infernal Embrace*, terrified Echo might use the same trick again, sending him back, and making all the damage he'd done to his Core and Meridians pointless.

A notification appeared across Ruwen's vision.

Unable to set Infernal Bind Point. Infernal Realm required.

Ruwen continued to focus on the set bonus and a second later, another notification appeared.

Remote trigger: Enabled
Enable or *Disable*

With a mental finger, Ruwen smashed *Disable*.

"Where did you go?" Sift whispered. "My parents went a little crazy when you disappeared."

Ruwen rubbed his temples. How did he explain the last week?

The taste of maple syrup filled Ruwen's mouth, and he glanced at his debuffs.

Unworthy Vessel: *5 Damage per Second, Migraine, Synchronization Suspended.*
Uneven: *Everything you eat or drink tastes like pancakes smothered in maple syrup.*

Ruwen's Unworthy Vessel debuff stemmed from carrying around a divine fragment of Uru in his mind. A fragment that had fled into his Core and hadn't yet returned. Overlord had followed to retrieve her but had also not returned. Ruwen pushed his worry for the pair into the third meditation. Overlord could take care of himself. Ruwen had lived with the migraine pain for so long, he barely noticed it now.

The Uneven debuff came from the quest *That's Not a Number* and had triggered from Ruwen's poor choice of words. Because Sift had rescued Ruwen from the vastness of the Universe, Ruwen had to do one of three things every day to make the taste of maple syrup disappear: compliment Sift, aid him, or get him to accept a gift.

This would continue until Ruwen could get Sift to say they were even.

The faint scent of citrus filled the tent, and Ruwen forced his heartbeat to remain steady. He would need to try and get Sift to say "even" later. That smell meant he'd run out of time to talk.

Ruwen met Sift's eyes. "I did some group sparring and could have used your superb skills."

Sift smiled and the taste of maple syrup faded from Ruwen's mouth. Before Sift could respond, Ruwen spoke again. "We'll have to catch up later. We're not alone anymore."

Sift looked around at the other meditating students. "No kidding."

Ruwen shook his head. "That's not who I mean."

That citrus scent had accompanied Thorn the first time Ruwen had met the Founders. He had only smelled it when she had come within inches of his body. But he'd transitioned into Gem since then and Fortified to Peak Diamond. His senses had become vastly better.

Ruwen closed his eyes and concentrated on his senses, and a moment later picked up the incredibly faint vibrations of the three Founders. He opened his eyes and found their location, which looked empty. They must have some sort of soul magic that kept them invisible.

"I don't sense anyone new," Sift said.

One of the Founders stopped causing vibrations and Ruwen wondered if she'd quit moving. A moment later, a pressure wave appeared behind him, as Dusk used her Shadow Step ability to teleport to his location.

Ruwen kept his body posture neutral, although he desperately wanted to take a more defensive stance than sitting on his butt. Now wasn't the time to reveal the extent of his progress, and he kept his heartbeat steady.

Dusk moved invisibly and squatted to the side of Ruwen. He tracked her movements without looking in her direction.

Sift stretched and quietly yawned. "This place needs a suggestion box, because the food is terrible."

As Sift returned his arm to his side, he flashed Ruwen Shade Speak. *Sense. Close. Now.* While Sift's Metal-Fortified body didn't have the power yet to sense the Founders across the room, at least he noticed them when they neared.

"You should offer to open a branch of the Divine Sage here," Ruwen whispered.

Sift looked at Ruwen, carefully ignoring the invisible Dusk. "Wherever you went, I'm glad you found some sense, because that is an amazing idea. Unfortunately, these old women are more interested in their games than pastries."

Ruwen hid a smile. Sift obviously, with his "old women" phrase, wanted to get a rise out of Dusk, who remained near them. "You've already tried to convince them, haven't you?"

Sift returned his gaze to the platform. "Only twice. I'm sure they'll see reason eventually."

Ruwen smiled. "It sounds like they've already found reason."

"Bite your tongue."

The invisible Dusk disappeared and reappeared a moment later next to her still invisible sisters. Ruwen kept his gaze away from the left side of the platform.

Two dark-skinned women appeared on the platform, and Ruwen recognized Mist and Thorn. Dusk remained hidden near them. Everyone stood and bowed to the two women.

"Good morning, Adepts," Mist said. "Today begins your seventh day of the first trial."

Thorn pointed at Ruwen. "One of your brothers has arrived late, and you will determine his fate."

Everyone turned and stared at Ruwen. He had never liked attention and did his best not to squirm under all the scrutiny.

Mist pointed at Ruwen. "Since our brother missed the ranking ceremony, he will assume the rank of thirty-three. This places him in the Fourth Rung, so they will decide."

The tent remained silent, and Ruwen wondered what the Fourth Rung meant.

"Good," Sift whispered. "They really need the help."

Mist continued. "Tardiness cannot go unpunished, however. Your brother will lose one hour of daylight for every day he's missed."

"Ouch," Sift whispered. "That's going to hurt. You only get twelve to begin with."

Thorn locked gazes with Ruwen. "Be seen by your Clan."

Ruwen raised his arm for a moment, keeping his stance neutral.

"If the fourth rung does not accept you," Mist said. "You will have forfeited your opportunity to partake in these trials."

"As explained on your first day," Thorn said. "Not finishing results in expulsion from the Bamboo Viper Clan."

"Harsh," Sift murmured

Ruwen had expected to face this possibility, but not within moments of arriving.

Thorn continued. "The Fourth Rung should know, if they accept their brother, they share his seven-hour penalty."

Sift groaned. "Now you're in trouble."

CHAPTER 2

"*R*ungs One, Two, and Three may begin today's attempt at the first trial," Mist said.

Sift raised his hands above his head, the palms touching.

"Yes, Adept?" Mist asked.

Sift bowed to the Founders. "Rung One will take him."

"Absolutely not," Echo said from across the room.

Sift turned toward Echo and pointed at her. "It's your fault he's late. You can't cause the problem and then ignore the consequences."

Echo smiled, the tips of her fangs visible. "He only has himself to blame."

"I've heard that before," Ruwen whispered.

"Tell them," Sift said to Ruwen. "I know it had to be her."

Telling the truth about Echo's involvement with Ruwen's disappearance would require explaining the Scarecrow Aspect and why the gods wanted him in the first place. And he believed it wouldn't change a thing. The Founders had rules, and he'd broken more than one of them.

Still, it wouldn't hurt to make sure.

"Will the truth change anything?" Ruwen asked.

"The truth is that you arrived seven days late to the summons," Thorn said.

Ruwen bowed. "Then the cause is irrelevant."

Sift frowned, clearly frustrated. He scanned the other adepts and raised his voice. "Rung Four, hear me. You saw me fight and easily claim the top spot in Rung One." He pointed at Ruwen. "He trained me, and his Steps are better than mine. You would be foolish to pass up his help."

"We are already at a disadvantage," a man said. "Taking him would leave only five hours to locate the trial token. It would doom us."

Sift stood up straight. "We are not here to collect tokens like wretched street vendors. You arrived to prove your worth as Masters of the Bamboo Viper Clan. I reject this trial token and the material weight it represents."

A different voice, this time female. "That is easy for you to say. You are the best of us."

Sift shook his head and pointed at Ruwen. "No, he is the best of us, and he deserves the chance to advance." Sift's voice grew serious. "If you need the crutch of a token, you don't belong here."

Echo laughed. "How can you say that? You don't even know what it's for."

"Exactly my point," Sift replied. "None of us do. It's a distraction, and no different from all material things."

"Not everyone has your advantages," Echo said. "This trial token, whatever its purpose, might mean the difference between success and failure for Rung Four."

"Enough," Thorn said. "Rung Four, discuss and provide your verdict."

A group of eight people formed on the other side of the

room. Ruwen withdrew his senses, not wanting to eavesdrop on the private discussion. Echo remained in the tent and from the smile on her face, it didn't look like the initial discussions favored him.

Ruwen leaned toward Sift. "Impressive speech. I haven't heard that tone in a long time."

"Yeah, well, if you get thrown out and they erase your brain or whatever, you'll have to start over from scratch," Sift said. He smiled and continued. "And we both know you're my worst Sijun. I can't bear the thought of holding your hand to Master again."

Ruwen smiled at Sift's comment, and then grew serious. "You can't blame them. The Founders have divided everyone and used the mystery of this trial token to create fear of the future. This is all done to weaken those with doubts."

Sift tilted his head. "You're right. I hadn't put that much thought into it."

"Shocking."

"Hey, careful. I'm like the only guy on your side in here."

"Shade's first rule: a drowning man has no friends."

Sift nodded. "That's true, and an excellent idea."

"What do you mean? That was Lylan's saying."

"No, I hear you loud and clear. We don't need Rung Four as friends, but the opposite."

"Wait, how did you get to that conclusion? I'm not sure—"

"Rung Four?" Thorn asked.

The group of eight continued to discuss, voices growing louder, and even without Diamond hearing Ruwen heard it all. Many of the eight, rightfully so, worried about the seven-hour delay. But others argued the previous six days proved they'd failed to make progress on their own, and even though they didn't know him, they also didn't want the guilt of expelling him from the trial.

The tallest male turned to Thorn and bowed. "We—"

"Excuse me," Sift said, interrupting the man. He faced Thorn. "Despite our Clan oaths, during our Journeyman's trial we could attack and even injure other Clan members."

"That is correct," Mist said. "Your Bamboo Viper Step journey is like a path. You have safely walked this road for many years. Trials and tests are obstacles that block your progress. You must leave the path and its safety, successfully pass the barrier, and rejoin the road on the other side."

"Killing a member of our Clan remains forbidden, and the only oath still in effect," Thorn added.

Sift's face grew serious, and he turned toward Rung Four.

Ruwen stepped in front of Sift and whispered. "What are you planning?"

"I'm going to threaten to break their arms and legs."

Ruwen placed a hand on Sift's shoulder. "Thanks, buddy. I appreciate the support, but let's give them the chance to do this without fear."

Sift nodded and Ruwen stepped back to stand next to his friend.

The tallest man from Rung Four swallowed hard. He had argued the hardest against keeping Ruwen. After a moment, he faced Thorn and Mist. "We accept our brother along with his penalty."

"So be it," Thorn said. "Rungs One, Two, and Three, you are wasting sunshine. Rung Four, we will return for you after the penalty expires."

Thorn and Mist disappeared, and everyone but Ruwen, Sift, and the eight members of Rung Four filed out of the tent.

Ruwen glanced at Sift. "I'm glad you didn't need to use your scary voice."

Sift sat down, crossed his legs, and responded. "I've lost patience with my parents and even the Founders. This all seems meaningless. If the point is to learn the Steps, they are doing everything wrong."

That statement resonated with Ruwen, as he held the same thoughts. He looked down at Sift. "Aren't you going out with your team?"

Sift frowned. "Why would I do that when I could sit in the shade."

Ruwen sat as well. "Shouldn't you be searching for this trial token?"

"What would I do with a token?" Sift asked. "I only have two pockets and Io goes in one and Shelly the other."

Ruwen glanced at the small of Sift's back to see if the Elder Dagger Io hid there.

"Sadly, I don't have Io as we went right from the Black Pyramid's kitchen to the summoning stone," Sift said. "I didn't even have time to put Shelly somewhere safe. Not that she would stay where I put her. She always ends up back in my pocket."

"She's here?"

"Yeah, there's a field around the tower and she likes the grass there."

"There's a tower? Why don't you start from the beginning."

"Okay. We stepped through the summoning stone portal into this town. My parents immediately took off, leaving me with that monster, Echo. There are twenty-three places to eat, but only two dessert vendors. The first one bakes mostly cake donuts and you know how I hate heavy pastries. The frosting is—"

Ruwen held up a hand, interrupting Sift. "Let's talk about pastries after you tell me about the trial token and where we're supposed to go. Do we climb a mountain like the Journeyman's trial?"

Sift shrugged. "I don't know, because they didn't tell us anything. They threw us into a large sparring circle to fight and then ranked us by how long we stayed in the circle. Then they divided the thirty-two of us into four groups of eight, lumping the best together into one, all the way down to the worst eight which went into Rung Four."

"Then what happened?"

"Nothing. They said we would stay in this area until a team found the trial token."

"And you don't know what the token is for?"

Sift smiled playfully. "According to you, it purchases fear, uncertainty, and doubt."

"I know, but did they say anything about it?"

"Nope. They said we could only look while the sun shone. Continuing after sunset is automatic expulsion. Same with Soul, Mana, or Spirit use."

"And no directions?"

Sift shook his head. "Nothing."

Ruwen thought for a moment. "This differs a lot from the Journeyman's trial. Why wouldn't they provide directions?"

Sift shrugged. "Because, just like my parents, they enjoy wasting my valuable time."

Ruwen looked at Sift. "Your valuable time? You were snoring when I got here."

"That's how the ninth meditation works, Sijun."

"Right, well I hope to reach that someday," Ruwen replied. He leaned forward and tapped the hard-packed dirt floor. "It could also mean if they didn't give any directions, that they expected you to already know what to do."

"That's stupid."

"Probably, but it gives me an idea. Tell me about the tower."

"It's windowless and tall."

Ruwen waited a few seconds but Sift didn't continue. "And?"

"And what? Everyone thinks the trial token is at the top because there are things in the tower that stop you from advancing upward."

"Can you climb the outside?"

"The surface is smooth, and I heard it shocks you."

Ruwen glanced at the eight members of Rung Four. They all sat cross-legged and looked miserable. The vibrations he sensed from outside the tent told the truth of Sift's words. The tent sat in the middle of a small town.

Light and sound poured through the open tent flap as the town woke up. Ruwen had seven hours, and he hated wasting time. Leaning toward Sift, he lowered his voice. "I have an idea."

Sift sighed loudly. "Do you ever just sit? Calm water reflects the sky."

"I thought you hated your dad's sayings."

"I do. Fine. What's your idea?"

"I think we should make some new friends."

Sift groaned. "I hate the ones I have now."

Ruwen smiled. "All the more reason to find new ones. Trees planted in Spring, bear fruit in Winter."

"That's dumb. Trees don't bear fruit in the winter. I'm not a farmer and even I know that."

Ruwen patted Sift's knee. "For the record, you would make a terrible farmer. Come on, let's go make them feel better about their decision."

They both stood.

"I would make a great farmer," Sift said as they walked toward Rung Four. "You're the one who can't even handle a few chickens." Sift jumped around, swinging an invisible stick.

Ruwen winced. It had been over a year and a half since he'd thought of the Savage Seven and his disastrous first battle with them. "Fine, we should both stay away from farms."

Sift swung his invisible stick wildly and continued to stumble around. "We could make our own Steps." He jumped fifteen feet and shouted. "Chicken Style!"

The eight members of Rung Four looked on in confusion and worry.

Ruwen stopped in front of the group as Sift continued

leaping around the tent. Placing a palm over a fist, Ruwen bowed to them.

"Thank you for allowing me to join your group," Ruwen said.

A few glanced upward and made brief eye contact, but most remained motionless, their misery impossible to hide.

Ruwen would change that.

CHAPTER 3

$\mathcal{T}$he group had three women and five men, all looking like they'd reached their thirties. They all stood over six feet tall with skinny bodies. The top of their ears didn't come to a point, but they angled more than usual. Ruwen wondered where they'd come from, as he'd never seen them in any books or in person.

Ruwen sat down six feet from them and crossed his legs. "I'm Ruwen."

Silence greeted him. The only sound in the tent was Sift as he continued to make up Chicken Steps.

A blonde woman pointed at Sift. "Is he okay?"

Ruwen didn't turn. "Not in any way."

The tallest man that had spoken earlier for the group glared at Ruwen. "You've doomed us."

Sift landed softly next to Ruwen and sat. "No, you doomed yourselves. You are barely ready to be here. Why did your Sisen rush you all to the Master's trial?"

The man looked down. "Demons overwhelm us. With more Masters, we can open more temples and train more fighters." The man looked up. "This is the last effort to save our lands."

The blonde woman spoke again. "Now the trial token from this level is out of our reach."

Ruwen leaned forward. "What did the Founders say about the trial token?"

The man replied. "We would stay here until someone located it."

"Yes," Ruwen said. "Sift said the same. The Founders never specified they had value or were necessary. You assumed that, but they just as likely could be harmful."

"Are you saying we shouldn't find the token?" the man asked.

Ruwen shrugged. "I don't know, but it has affected everyone's focus. We aren't here to collect a trial token, but to pass this level and continue to the next."

The blonde spoke again. "But we need the trial token for the trial."

Ruwen shook his head. "Another assumption. The Founders only said the token would trigger the next stage." Everyone sat silently for a few seconds.

The blonde woman stood and held her hand out, palm down. Either she knew enough to recognize Ruwen's mastery by his movements, or she had taken Sift at his word, but the gesture signified Ruwen's rank over her. Had she placed her fist out, it would have signified she wanted to challenge him.

Ruwen stood and placed his fist under her palm.

"I am called, Nymthus."

Ruwen bowed. "Well met, Nymthus."

Nymthus kicked the tall blond man, and he glared up at her. He sighed and stood. Slowly, he held out his hand, palm downward. "I am known as Prythus."

"Well met," Ruwen said again.

In quick succession, Ruwen met the other six members of Rung Four. Eight fighters from their world had come to the trial, and they had all ended up at the bottom of the rankings.

"Tell me about the tower," Ruwen said.

27

"Not much to tell," Prythus said. "The other groups cleared the first level on day one, advancing to the second floor. We have yet to pass it. And now, with seven fewer hours, it will be even harder."

"Why even try?" Ruwen asked. "The other teams already have an incredible head start and now you carry my penalty. It seems hopeless."

All eight stood up straight as if Ruwen had insulted them.

Nymthus spoke. "If we quit every time we faced a hopeless situation, none of us would be here."

Ruwen smiled. "Excellent answer. Now tell me what stops you from advancing to level two."

Prythus looked embarrassed. "There is a massive tree. The branches hang down like vines and they move in odd ways. When a vine touches you, it teleports you to the entrance and paralyzes you for fifteen minutes."

"Interesting," Ruwen said. "Are the vines' movements random?"

"They look that way to us," Nymthus replied.

Ruwen felt the pressure waves and tiny vibrations from the three Founders as they returned to the stage. He turned and looked down at Sift, glancing at the stage to verify the Founders remained invisible. Sift sat with his eyes closed and Ruwen nudged him with a foot.

"Okay," Ruwen said to the eight fighters. "We have over six hours before we can leave. I wish to repay your kindness by offering feedback on your Steps. Perhaps we can make some small gains that will aid us in the tower."

Prythus frowned. "But you aren't a Step Master. Aren't you forbidden from instructing us?"

Ruwen shrugged. "I believe our Clan forbids teaching Steps to others that you have not mastered yourself." He touched his chest. "I promise to only instruct on those Steps I have mastered and take full responsibility for any consequences. Anyone interested can join me near the platform."

The members of Rung Four formed a tight circle to discuss, and Ruwen turned to the platform.

"You coming?" Ruwen asked Sift.

"I guess," Sift replied as he stood. "Are you sure this is a good idea?"

Ruwen started for the platform. "All my ideas are good."

The three Founders remained invisible on the wooden structure, and Ruwen ignored them. His confrontation with them would arrive eventually, but he doubted it would take place today. Not over helping a group of Adepts. He had already done far worse.

Ruwen flashed Sift directions in Shade Speak. *Only. Basic. No. Hidden.*

Sift nodded, and they turned to find the entire group had followed them. Sift pointed at them. "Warm up, we will join you shortly." He turned to Ruwen and whispered. "You smell terrible. Like rotten eggs mixed with week-old garbage."

Ruwen smelled his armpit. He still carried his fight in the Infernal Realm with him and had grown accustomed to the smell.

Sift pointed to the back of the tent. "There are bathrooms back there. You should change."

"Thanks," Ruwen said, now feeling a little self-conscious.

Ruwen strode to one of the curtained rooms and stripped off all his clothes. Scattered across his garments he found numerous blood stains and patches of Infernal soil. He ripped the clothes apart, placing the scraps in either a blood or soil pile. He would Analyze these later. They might even be useful to Fractal. Opening his Void Band, he added the scraps to his Inventory.

Naked now, Ruwen walked to a bowl fed by a small pipe. He could have used *Scrub* to clean himself in just a moment, but he didn't know the consequences of using magic, so he decided to wash up the old-fashioned way.

Carefully he unwound the Ink Lord's Wrap armor from around his right wrist. His shirt had covered it from view, and he figured he should probably add it to his Inventory as well. But having it available if something unexpected and dangerous appeared felt wiser. Plus, if he lost it, the passive *Lost and Found* would teleport the armor to his right wrist as soon as he traveled more than fifty feet from it.

Using the water basin, he quickly washed and then dressed in a set of Black Pyramid attire taken from his Void Band. He carefully folded his Ink Lord's Wrap into a tiny square and placed it in a small hidden hip pocket of his pants.

Feeling like a new person, Ruwen left the bathroom and headed for Sift near the platform.

Sift noticed Ruwen and spoke to Rung Four while pointing at the platform. "Two at a time," Sift said. "Show us your Steps."

The platform didn't have space for all eight to perform the Steps at the same time, but for two it served perfectly. Prythus and Nymthus stepped onto the stage, as Ruwen joined Sift.

Ruwen listened to their rapid heartbeats and realized how nervous they were. While they had reached the pinnacle of fighters in their world, coming here had opened their eyes to actual mastery, and their nervousness showed the doubt that had grown in their minds. None of them now believed they should be here.

Their world sent them here in desperation, but if they failed, none of them would keep the knowledge of the Bamboo Viper Steps, leaving their world in even worse shape.

"Begin when you wish," Ruwen said.

The two bowed and began. Prythus started with the Bamboo Steps instead of the Viper, and Nymthus had, in three Viper Steps, already moved so far out of alignment that the power of her strikes would significantly suffer.

Ruwen kept his face neutral as he studied their technique. They shared many of the same issues, which pointed at their Master having those issues and passing them down to his students. Before his experience in the Spirit Realm, he would have marveled at their movements. Now he knew the truth, and the immense amount of work needed to fix all their problems.

Ruwen didn't need to fix all their issues, though, just the most blatant and grievous ones.

When they finished, Nymthus stood a full foot from her starting location, and Prythus trembled with all the stored energy ending with Viper Steps caused. The entire sequence had been difficult to watch and barely merited an Adept's skills, let alone a Master's.

Ruwen bowed to the pair. "Honor your Master when you see him again, for he has taught you well."

Sift glanced at Ruwen but remained silent. Prythus and Nymthus relaxed, and their heart rates steadied.

Ruwen had a terrible feeling but wanted to confirm it. "Are you both the most advanced in your group?"

Prythus bowed. "Yes."

Sift let out a soft sigh and Ruwen felt the same. If they were quick learners, it would take months, possibly years, to correct all the issues with their basic Steps. It would take far longer to teach them the hidden patterns. But they didn't need all that knowledge right now. What they needed was a proper foundation, and that Ruwen could do.

Ruwen pointed to the center of the tent and spoke to the group. "Please spread out and in a moment, I'll ask you to begin your Steps. Sisen Sift and I will rotate among you, fixing issues as we see them."

Ruwen waited until they'd all repositioned themselves. The eight looked up at him, and he felt a kinship with them. They had told him they battled demons, and that they faced hopeless odds. To make a difference, they had come here, risking what had likely been a lifetime of training, so they could form their own schools and create more fighters.

"A secret is something you only tell a friend," Ruwen said. "And I will tell you one now. Everything you have learned. Every Step you have mastered. All of it represented a single ideal. It is the guiding principle of every movement, every breath, and every decision. The entirety of the Bamboo Viper Steps circles this single concept."

Ruwen paused and let the tension build.

"The secret is...balance," Ruwen said into the stillness of the tent.

Stepping off the platform, Ruwen moved among the group. "It is why we start with Viper and end with Bamboo." He jumped to the front of the group and brought his arms down sharply in the shape of a "v." "It is why Crashing Butterfly," he raised his hands, palms pressed together, upward, before spreading them wide, "is countered by Hungry Leaf. It is why we end in the exact place we begin. All of this, and everything in between, obeys this law of balance."

They all stood in silence and Ruwen let this fundamental aspect of the Steps sink into their minds. It would help them in the future, as they worked their way through the lessons he had already learned.

Into the quiet, Prythus spoke. "There is a beach on the south shore of Dreaming Lake with perfect skipping stones. My record is seventeen. Even now, I can see those seventeen perfect circles, spreading outward, their rings combining until the lake calmed and reclaimed the stillness for itself."

Nymthus spoke as soon as Prythus stopped. "In winter the snow drifts to my second-story window. The white powder reflects the moonlight like a giant mirror, and the ice wyrms would dance in the sky glowing like comets."

One after another, each member of Rung Four spoke. When

they'd finished, all eight began the Viper Steps and Sift moved away from the platform to fix the worst issues with their Steps.

Ruwen sensed the surrounding Founders but didn't react.

Dusk spoke but remained invisible. "Those eight have experienced great suffering as demons ravaged their world. To remember what is lost, and to show gratitude, they offer their memories. It is an honor to hear these remembrances."

"Thank you for explaining the significance," Ruwen said. "I will treasure them."

Ruwen hid a smile as he watched Sift move among the group, using the same tone he had used when instructing Ruwen. The memories of being a terrified Sijun felt like yesterday.

Ruwen had important business back home on Grave, but staying here a few extra days likely wouldn't matter. Especially when contrasted with the impact he and Sift could have on this group with just a few days of effort.

As Ruwen moved toward the group to help, he made a decision. He felt confident he already knew the location of the trial token for this stage, but instead of ending this phase when he stepped into the sunshine, he'd wait until this group had completed the tower's tests.

CHAPTER 4

Six townsfolk appeared and erected a long table behind the platform. They filled it with bread, cheese, meat, and fruit. Eight large urns of water sat along the table's edge, and someone arrived every hour to refill anything requiring it.

The Founders had never left the tent but dropped their invisibility at the seventh hour to inform Rung Four they could now leave. Ruwen smiled as every single member of the group decided to stay and train instead. As he'd hoped, the Founders didn't interfere.

When Ruwen had initially trained Sift this way, Sift had made incredible progress. That was a testament to his amazing Step skills and natural abilities. Rung Four didn't make such vast improvements, because they didn't immediately see how one change affected others as Sift had.

Ruwen and Sift patiently walked among them, providing guidance on minor changes so they wouldn't overwhelm the Adepts. As twilight approached and the other teams returned, Ruwen and Sift stopped their instruction. Rung Four moved to the back of the tent and continued to train, everyone sharing what they had learned with their teammates.

The other teams looked on in amusement at Rung Four's efforts. Ruwen's Diamond-Fortified ears allowed him to hear every conversation, and he determined Rung One had remained stuck on level three today. Rung Two and Three remained trapped on level two, and from their body language and conversation, they had hindered each other there.

Tomorrow, after their seven hours of practice, Ruwen would take Rung Four to the tower. They had all made visible progress and he and Sift had corrected most of the cringe-inducing mistakes. Rung Four could see the difference as well because they hadn't stopped smiling.

As the night wore on, everyone either slept or meditated, and Ruwen sat next to a softly snoring Sift. Ruwen closed his eyes, but instead of meditating, he opened his notifications. He immediately missed Rami's ability to summarize the vast number of notices.

The first notification made his head swim at the amount.

Your body has entered the Infernal Realm!
You have gained 1,000,000 experience (333,333.3*(3 Realm Count))!

Ruwen had now traveled to the Spirit Realm, Uru's Divine one, and the Infernal. Opening the log, he scrolled back to find another huge experience gain.

Your body has entered a Divine Realm (Pen)!
You have gained 1,333,333 experience (333,333.3*(4 Realm Count))!

Just after that entry, another one caught Ruwen's eye.

Gong!
You have increased your Knowledge!
***Level:** 151*

The intelligent know true power is held by knowledge. The wise know knowledge can be dangerous. Greatness is found between them.

Ruwen's experience in Pen's Realm, along with learning the true meaning of the third secret, had boosted his Knowledge by fourteen points.

Just like Ruwen's notifications, his log contained what felt like an endless list of details about all the demons he'd killed in the Infernal Realm. Interestingly, he only received fifty percent of the experience. Whatever process calculated the experience, likely a portion of Uru herself, or Lir, the protector of Uru's Third Temple, considered Overlord his own being.

Ruwen wondered how they could calculate all this. Did they access his memories somehow? But since he never detected that, he wondered if it was somehow related to the grip they had on his soul.

You have defeated a Fungus Owl, Infernal (Level 53)!
You have gained 35,675 experience (71,350*(50% Group Modifier))!
You have defeated a Screaming Siren, Infernal (Level 8)!
You have gained 800 experience (1,600*(50% Group Modifier))!
You have defeated a Rotting Corpse, Infernal (Level 29)!
You have gained 10,775 experience (21,550*(50% Group Modifier))!

Scrolling through the details, the vast majority of deaths came from low-level demons.

Ruwen closed his log and reopened his notifications. Immediately after the Infernal Realm experience, his favorite notification appeared.

Ding!
Uru's Blessings, Worker! You have reached level 27.
You have gained +1 to Strength!
You have gained +1 to Stamina!

You have 2 unassigned points.

Uru's Blessings, Root! You have reached level 27.
You have 2 unassigned points.
New Spells and Abilities are available to you. Choose wisely.

Two identical notifications followed this one, for levels twenty-eight and twenty-nine. The level advancement felt good, and Ruwen wondered how many more might hide in this endless stack of notifications. It would take days of clicking to get through all these details.

Ruwen opened his notification settings and accepted them all at once. The lightly glowing yellow box in his lower vision disappeared. Moving to his Profile, he opened it, wondering how much experience destroying an entire Infernal army would provide.

When Ruwen had left Shelly and arrived at the Black Pyramid, he'd remained at level twenty-six. The experience needed to move from level twenty-six to twenty-seven was three hundred fifty-one thousand.

Ruwen glanced at his current level.

Level: *58*
Experience: *1,420,331/1,711,000*

Ruwen stared at the value. He calculated the experience needed to move from level twenty-six to level fifty-eight and arrived at a staggering value of over thirty-one million. Traveling into two new realms had given him over two million experience, which meant he'd gained around twenty-eight million experience fighting Lalquinrial's demon army.

But jumping thirty-two levels made Ruwen's skin flush with excitement. He glanced down his Profile. His Strength and Stamina had increased by thirty-two each from the automatically assigned Worker Attributes. He looked at his unassigned values.

Before the ordeal in the Infernal Realm, his unassigned points had looked like this.

Attribute Points: 8
Spell Points: 13
Ability Points: 4

Now they had increased to these values.

Attribute Points: 136
Spell Points: 61
Ability Points: 36

Ruwen didn't know how to spend his Spell and Ability points. He didn't have any information on advanced magical capabilities. He had learned to mirror his current Mana-based spells and Abilities with Spirit, and while he couldn't use Spirit right now, it wouldn't always be like that. Adding points to spells he'd already mastered seemed a little pointless. It would be better to save them and find out what advanced things he could learn. That would make creating essence recipes in the future easier.

But that still left one hundred thirty-six Attribute points. Those he needed to spend, or at least assign a significant portion of them.

Ruwen didn't know how much longer he would keep Fighter assigned to his Root Class. Even if he wanted to change right now, he couldn't, because he held a Divine fragment of Uru. This not only gave him the Unworthy Vessel debuff but also made synchronization to the Temple impossible.

That meant if Ruwen died now, he would reset to the version of himself from the time he'd last synched with Uru, and that had been sitting in the underwater safe house the night before their final match in the Step Championship. An unbelievable amount of things had happened to him since then, and dying now would prove catastrophic.

Since, for the foreseeable future, Ruwen planned on keeping Root assigned to Fighter, he re-stepped through the logic of how to distribute his Attribute points.

So much had changed with Ruwen's body and skills that he reconsidered maximizing a couple of attributes at the expense of the other four. Unlike most people who encountered similar challenges every day, he never knew what might happen. His life since Ascendancy had been a whirlwind; having a weakness would almost certainly be deadly at some point.

Even though Ruwen had mastered spells from all the Classes using Spirit instead of Mana, he couldn't rely on those right now because of his damaged Meridians and pathways. That meant maximizing one or two attributes to gain an advantage in some situations would also make him vulnerable as soon as his opponent identified his weaknesses.

Ruwen had spent a massive amount of time and effort to Fortify his body to Peak Diamond, and that provided a huge gain for each attribute. Every time he increased his Fortification level, those points went into every attribute, which automatically kept him somewhat balanced.

Because of the Fortification bonuses, Ruwen decided, like before, to stay with a more hybrid approach. He could emphasize his essential attributes while not letting the non-critical ones fall too far behind.

Ruwen created four attribute lists in his mind: critical, important, minor, and occasional.

Under critical, Ruwen placed Stamina since it kept him alive and added to his Energy, Resilience, and Endurance.

For important attributes, Ruwen listed Intelligence and Dexterity.

Many of his Fighter spells, while powerful, consumed a lot of Mana. This would be even more critical now that he couldn't rely on his Spirit. Until he could use Spirit to cast spells, he needed to bank on his Mana. Intelligence also increased his Perception and Cleverness. Cleverness in particular had benefited him many times.

Dexterity helped Ruwen's Unarmed Combat, Step training, Energy, Armor Class, Critical Chance, Dodge, and Perception.

The two minor attributes were Wisdom and Charisma.

Wisdom almost made it to important because it directly affected Cleverness and Resilience, both of which had saved Ruwen's life. The days after his Ascendancy, when he'd suffered from the Wisdom debuff Foolish, had been truly painful. But unlike Intelligence, Wisdom didn't affect his Mana pool as it did for Hamma and the Order Class.

Wisdom would remain the most important of the minor attributes since Ruwen couldn't always rely on others for common sense. He needed Wisdom of his own to balance out his Intelligence.

That left Charisma, which Ruwen had to admit he still cared about more than he should. It mattered how he looked and how people reacted to him. The truth was he couldn't ignore Charisma because it affected his Persuasion stat, and if he meant to lead, he'd need that.

Strength Ruwen decided to ignore. It received a point at every level automatically because of his Worker Class. With Diamond-Fortified strength already, he probably wouldn't gain any increases with additional points anyway. His Void Band made Encumbrance a nonissue, and while Strength benefited Endurance, so did Stamina, which he preferred to emphasize for the obvious benefit of Health Points.

The balanced logic from before still held up, so with every level, after the automatic points in Stamina and Strength, Ruwen would add another point to Stamina, one to Dexterity, one to Intelligence, and alternate the last point between Wisdom and Charisma.

After another moment of thought, Ruwen decided to add a point to Wisdom twice as often as Charisma. Common sense really helped balance the tendencies of his high Intelligence.

That meant he would add the following amounts to each Attribute:

Strength: *0*
Stamina: *+34*
Dexterity: *+34*
Intelligence: *+34*
Wisdom: *+23*
Charisma: *+11*

That spent all the unassigned Attribute points. Even though Ruwen didn't wear any armor or jewelry and had zero buffs, he studied his Profile, curious how the additional levels had impacted his stats. He focused on the parts that had changed the most.

General
Level: *58*
Experience: *1,420,331/1,711,000*

Available Points
Unassigned Ability: *36*
Unassigned Spell: *61*
Unassigned Attribute: *0*

Pools
Health: *1,610/1,610*
Mana: *1,914/1,914*
Energy: *2,440/2,440*

Spirit: 7,527,309,664

Attributes
Strength: 104
Stamina: 161
Dexterity: 101
Intelligence: 191
Wisdom: 158
Charisma: 66

Ratings
Knowledge: 151
Armor Class: 3,509

Regeneration
Health Regeneration per second: 24
Mana Regeneration per second: 25
Energy Regeneration per second: 180

Effectively naked, Ruwen still had an Armor Class over twice that of a plate armored warrior with a tower shield. The battle in the Infernal Realm coupled with the healing to survive the Sixth Rune had cost almost seven hundred million Spirit and decreased his total to seven and a half billion.

Resistances all hovered around one hundred eighteen percent except for Ruwen's Mind Resistance, which had grown to six hundred seventy-one percent. He guessed whatever process Uru used to measure mind resistance didn't know the full extent of his mental constructs. In his current state, he didn't think much could penetrate his mind.

Ruwen studied the modifiers for his Wisdom calculation to understand why it had increased so much. It resulted from the combination of his thirty-six levels in Tactics, which increased his Wisdom by eighteen percent, and Rami's second Codex of

Bookwyrm Evolution which gave him a passive that doubled the effectiveness of all mental abilities, raising the value to thirty-six percent. It nearly made Wisdom his second-highest attribute.

Adding buffs and jewelry would vastly increase Ruwen's Stats, but even his current Regen Rates would refill his Health bar in just over one minute, Mana in eighty-two seconds, and Energy in twelve.

The combination of Ascendant leveling bonuses combined with Ruwen's body Fortifications had destroyed any sense of balance when compared to anyone his level. Unfortunately, he would need all those benefits for his upcoming Divine conflicts.

Thinking about the future made Ruwen uncertain, and for a moment he considered just jumping to the end of the Master's trial so he could go home and address the issues there. The endgame here also worried him as he didn't know if he'd prepared enough. Worse, some things he'd planned on, like using Spirit and having Overlord present, were no longer possible.

Ruwen pushed everything into the third meditation and let his mind rest in blissful emptiness. The future needed to wait its turn because the present needed his entire focus. The end here would come soon enough.

It only took seconds for Ruwen's empty mind to rebel, and his thoughts, as they did so often lately, returned to a conversation in Malth's library, the night before the Step Championship's quarterfinal match.

Ruwen now believed the words spoken to another had contained a warning for him. A warning that warred with his plans and sense of justice, but one he knew he dared not ignore.

Instead of meditating peacefully through the night, Ruwen wrestled with the words of an ancient wyrm.

CHAPTER 5

*T*he next day, after seven hours of training Rung Four, they all left the tent together. Ruwen's skin warmed from the red-tinged sun shining through a blanket of white clouds. Their tent sat at the edge of a courtyard a hundred feet long. In the center of the square stood a thick pillar fifteen-foot high.

Ruwen strode to the twelve-sided pillar and slowly walked around it. The roughly hewn granite had five smooth circles in a line down the center of each side. Every circle contained a gate rune, making each side a portal to another world. He memorized them all, assuming they led to all the worlds the Adepts had arrived from.

Food vendors and merchants lined the perimeter, and Sift already stood next to the closest dessert cart. Everyone here wore short-sleeve shirts and either shorts or summer dresses. After Fortifying to Diamond, Ruwen didn't care about the weather anymore. He could regulate the temperature of his body and his surroundings if things became uncomfortable.

Other than the clothing and red sun, Ruwen could have been standing in a small village outside Deepwell. He turned again,

44

scanning the horizon this time, and found the tower Sift had mentioned.

Sift, a donut in each hand, joined Ruwen and they strode through town toward the tower, the members of Rung Four following.

Ruwen glanced at the donuts Sift carried. "How did you pay for those?"

"Everything is free."

Once they left the village, it didn't take long for the tower to come into complete view. The smooth windowless cylinder climbed into the air, just as Sift had described it. Ruwen hadn't known if the sky here appeared whitish grey naturally or if it just had a lot of clouds. Now he knew the color came from clouds as they covered the tower past two hundred feet.

The tower stood twenty minutes from town. Somewhere in the thousand-foot circle of grass surrounding the tower, Shelly happily munched away. The blue-tinged blades reached Ruwen's knees and small flowers the size of his thumb covered portions of the field, poking up above the grass and giving the field a beautiful multi-colored look.

Kneeling, Ruwen used the knowledge he'd gained from the *Collector Novice Manual* to carefully remove both a clump of grass and a handful of flowers. He opened his Void Band only long enough to drop them into his Inventory.

A new notification appeared.

Notice: *A living entity has entered your Void Band. Estimated energy consumption to sustain additional life: 0.10 energy per second. You are currently consuming 0.26 energy per second. You have 10 seconds to make one of the following choices:*

Choice 1: *Remove the entity.*

Choice 2: *Select Yes, incur the energy cost, and sustain the entity's life.*

Choice 3: *Select No, and the entity will perish*

Remove or Yes or No

Ruwen selected *Yes*, and the notification disappeared. The Mobile Alchemy Lab the Black Pyramid had loaned him consumed point twenty-five Energy and the Burning Wheat he'd taken from the Mist Wraith Talker's level consumed point zero one Energy. His current Energy Regen had reached two hundred and three Energy per second, which more than covered the new cost.

"You really might be worse than Hamma," Sift said, looking down at Ruwen.

Ruwen looked up, skepticism covering his face.

"Fine, but admit you have a problem. You take stuff from everywhere we go. Once you hit Divine, they'll probably name you the God of Thieves."

Ruwen stood. "My parents always brought me back small things when they traveled. I'm doing the same for Fractal. I'm just being a good Dungeon Master. Besides, the God of Thieves is better than the God of Pastries."

Sift closed his eyes. "Imagine that. A God devoted to desserts. That is truly a way to make the Universe a better place. If I could become a god, I would fill the Universe with custard and cover it in chocolate."

"The Universe is pretty empty. It would take you a while." Ruwen thought about Lalquinrial and his willingness to destroy this Universe as a steppingstone to leaving it. "But to be honest, I've heard worse plans."

Sift glanced at the somber group of Rung Four behind them. "They look nervous."

Ruwen marched forward without looking back. "Yeah. Facing your failures is always hard. Think about how difficult it is for your parents to see you every day."

Sift threw a punch at Ruwen's back, just over the kidney, aimed at a nerve bundle that would paralyze Ruwen's right leg for ten seconds. Ruwen stepped to the left and backward, allowing Sift's punch and his body to pass. Ruwen snatched the pastry Sift held in his left hand and took another step back, holding up the donut.

Sift quickly turned and stared at the donut Ruwen held. "Don't do anything stupid."

"Stupid is your job," Ruwen said with a laugh. He glanced at the sweet. "Gross, did you lick the frosting off of this?"

"Don't judge me. I'm trying them different ways."

"You act weirder every day."

"Give me back my donut, or I'll spend the rest of the day collecting centipedes."

Ruwen swallowed, the taste of maple syrup strong in his mouth. He held up the donut. "Taking this is a punishment for trying to paralyze me. But because I am fair and benevolent, I'll give you this disgusting thing back. You could say we are—"

Ruwen paused, praying Sift would say they were even.

"Yeah, we're equal," Sift said.

Ruwen hid his disappointment and flicked the donut to Sift.

Sift caught the donut and brushed it off as if Ruwen had made it dirty. "Wise man." Sift faced the tower again, and they continued forward. "We should make everyone shuffle their feet through the grass. What if one of them steps on Shelly?"

Memories of Shelly rolling slowly in joy as she dived into a blazing star filled Ruwen's thoughts. "I'm going to guess Shelly would survive that."

"Maybe," Sift said. He turned to Rung Four, following twenty feet behind. "Keep your eyes open for a little white turtle. I don't want anyone to step on her."

"Tortoise," Ruwen said.

"What?"

"Nothing," Ruwen replied. He glanced at his Uneven debuff and gave up for the day. "Shelly is really lucky to have you. You display great honor in how you care for her."

Sift smiled and Ruwen's Uneven debuff disappeared.

"It's like every day you have a single moment of clarity," Sift said.

Ruwen glanced at Sift, surprised by his word choice. "Clarity?"

"One of Lylan's made-up words. It either means *idiot, understanding*, or *I'm-about-to-stab-you*. All those things happened during that conversation."

"Right. Well, Lylan is a woman of many facets."

Sift nodded. "Most of them sharp."

They approached the tower entrance and slowed. The tower didn't have a door, just an archway that led into darkness. Five seconds later, the members of Rung Four arrived.

"How do you feel?" Ruwen asked them.

Prythus stood straight and bowed. "Much better now, Sisen."

Ruwen shook his head. "I told you not to call me that." Ruwen pointed at Sift. "He's the only Sisen here."

Prythus bowed again, and Ruwen knew they wouldn't listen. Yesterday's all-day training, the night spent trading knowledge, and this morning's training had provided significant gains for every member of Rung Four. Ruwen and Sift had purged the most terrible habits from everyone. They'd probably made more progress in the last twenty-four hours than they'd experienced in years. If the situation hadn't been so serious, they'd all be jumping for joy.

"Today is different," Ruwen said. "I'm proud of the gains you've made, and confident together we will master this level."

As one, everyone's heartbeats steadied as Ruwen's reassuring words smothered the fear, uncertainty, and doubt they felt. He needed to take advantage of every opportunity to work on his leadership skills. The future would force him to lead, and that required practice. Some of this felt dangerously close to manipulation, but he soothed his conscience knowing that while he might have overstated things a little, the seed of the message held truth.

"Ready?" Ruwen asked Sift.

Sift raised a fist and shouted. "Onward into the Tower of Doom!"

Rung Four's heart rates all increased and Ruwen pinched the bridge of his nose. "Doom? Really?"

"Since this is a trial, I'm naming things for more impact."

They entered the darkness.

"What would you name it?" Sift asked.

Ruwen shrugged and thought of the beautiful field that surrounded the tower. "Tower of Flowers. It even rhymes."

"Ugh, that is horrible. Who wants to go into a flower tower?"

The darkness deepened, but the light from the room they approached bled into the tunnel and kept the smooth walls and floor visible. Ruwen felt the air movement from the challenge before he entered the room.

Hundreds of green vines hung downward, their tips scraping the ground. Thin roots poked upward, and the entire tree appeared to move as the branches, vines, and roots swayed, each one in a unique pattern. On the other side of the tree, an arched doorway revealed the stairs to level two.

The tree's motions appeared chaotic, but Ruwen's brain itched, and he narrowed his eyes in thought. Something about the movements looked familiar and a moment later, he smiled.

"What do you think?" Ruwen asked Sift.

"The movements are strange but regular."

Ruwen strode toward the tree. "Tell me when you see it."

Everyone followed Ruwen into the room which spanned thirty feet. The tree touched each wall, making the only way to the level two stairs through the tree's odd movements.

They all studied the tree for another twenty seconds, observing quietly until Sift sighed loudly. "I see it."

Ruwen nodded. "That took too long."

"I know."

Ruwen didn't bother to wait for anyone in Rung Four to answer. While they had all made great progress, they had a long way to go before they'd internalized the Steps enough to recognize their patterns in the natural world.

The tree had already cycled through three-quarters of its pattern, and Ruwen waited for it to start again. It would be more recognizable to Rung Four if they saw it from the beginning.

Ruwen marveled that something like this tree existed. It had obviously taken magic and a Master Arborist to create it. A true marriage of crafting, botany, and magic.

The cycle's beginning approached and as it passed in front of Ruwen, he stepped into the vines and roots, performing the first Viper Step. Keeping his cadence in time with the tree's flow, he moved through the Viper Steps. As he reached the far side and the end of the Viper forms, the tree had maneuvered him into the inner branches near the trunk, making it impossible to reach the level two stairs. He transitioned into the Bamboo Steps, and continued around the tree, wondering how they reached the stairs.

When Ruwen completed the final Bamboo Step, the location matched his exact starting spot. The vines stopped weaving and formed a crisscross barrier behind him. A path opened to the trunk, and he hurried forward, sliding around the tree, and continuing to the level's exit.

As soon as Ruwen stepped out of the vines, they began to weave again. Prythus entered next, and when he'd completed the test, another member of Rung Four started. The last day-and-a-half's practice showed its value when not a single person triggered the vines stun and reset.

When the last member of Rung Four stepped out of the tree limbs, the group grinned and laughed in joy. When the vines froze again and Sift came down the tunnel, the Adepts bowed to Ruwen and Sift.

Ruwen waved his hands. "No, your hard work bore this fruit."

Sift strode toward the stairs. "Like I always say, 'spring seeds for winter needs.'"

"That's my saying," Ruwen said. "And you ruined it."

Sift shook his head. "No, mine's better. It rhymes, and it fits on a pastry. Twice as better."

"Twice as good," Ruwen corrected.

"That, too."

Ruwen rubbed his forehead and sighed. "Let's see what level two holds."

Rung Four eagerly climbed the stairs, and Ruwen followed.

CHAPTER 6

$\mathcal{T}$he ten of them stepped onto level two and immediately found a wall twenty feet away with an arched entrance on each end.

The floor glowed faintly leaving the ceiling in darkness. Ruwen glanced up, feeling a small air disturbance above them. He immediately returned his focus to the doors, not wanting to ruin the point of the level before everyone began.

This level appeared even more on the nose than level one, and he wondered how long, or even if, any of his companions would see the pattern. Like many things with the Steps, the clues were obvious once you understood their meaning.

Prythus strode to the entrance on the right and with only a slight pause stepped through. When nothing happened he turned and disappeared down a hallway.

Nymthus strode to the opposite door and disappeared down a different hallway. After a moment, the other six members of Rung Four followed, three to each door.

Ruwen turned to Sift. "Are you going?"

Sift sat. "Not after I saw you glance at the ceiling and look guilty."

"I'm not guilty."

"Well, you looked weird. Weirder than normal anyway. Then I felt the air shift." He nodded at the wall in front of them. "That's probably some sort of maze?"

Ruwen sat as well. "That's my guess."

"Are you going to tell them?"

"Not right away. This level is very relevant to our situation and might be their best chance at understanding what the tower is trying to teach them."

"We're supposed to learn something?"

"That's a good question. If an Adept doesn't immediately understand the purpose of this place, what value do the Founders believe comes from the Tower and its challenges? It almost feels too late."

"Unless the lesson is for later," Sift said.

Ruwen raised his eyebrows at Sift's statement. After Ruwen had figured out some of the hidden patterns the hard way, he'd realized the Journeyman's trial had placed many clues in plain sight. They hadn't meant anything until later when he could understand them.

"What's the plan after we get back home?" Sift asked.

Ruwen leaned back on his hands. His newly enhanced Wisdom brought one issue forward immediately. "Find Hamma and Lylan. I want to make sure they're safe and explain why I disappeared. Echo couldn't have struck at a worse time. I just spent six months agreeing and promising Hamma not to disappear and then I immediately vanish. That doesn't look good."

"I knew it was that demon," Sift said. "How did she do it?"

Ruwen looked at Sift. "It's basically your fault."

"Mine? Impossible."

"Remember when we left the Spirit Realm and you needed to wear that aspect? And then you cried like a baby until I wore mine too."

"Crying like a baby doesn't sound like me. I might have suggested wearing it though."

Ruwen closed his eyes for a moment. "Uru give me patience," he whispered and looked at Sift again. "She triggered the recall for the Scarecrow Aspect's bind point."

"I hope you fixed that issue. I'm not sure they'd let you back here."

"I did. Only fools are stabbed with the same knife twice."

"Oh no, now you sound like Lylan."

They laughed and sat for a minute in silence.

"What was it like there?" Sift asked.

"The details need to wait for somewhere private, but I met Echo's parents. Both of them. Along with a few of their friends."

"Echo looked shocked to see you."

"I know," Ruwen said.

"Enough about your vacation. What are we doing when we get back home."

"First, we find Hamma, Lylan, and Rami. Then I need to talk with Big D, neutralize some crime lord in New Eiru, and stop a civil war. I also need to catch up with my parents, Bliz, and Fractal."

Sift frowned. "Can't you ever relax? We need a proper vacation. There's an island chain in the Sea of Tears that grows peppers so hot they use them as weapons. They have a pepper-flavored ice cream that is famous. I want to try that."

Sift continued describing all the pepper-seasoned food he wanted to try, and how he hoped to make a spicy frosting for his bakery. Talk of the massive inland sea caused Ruwen's thoughts to drift to the geography of their continent. Mountain ranges ran down the east and west coasts and the Sea of Tears, a vast inland sea, sat like a scar down the middle of the continent. Forests and tundra filled the north, and the south eventually gave way to the desert.

Ruwen remembered Bliz talking about the power of the

Void Band. How he could drain the entire Sea of Tears which is something no Mage could ever accomplish. That made Ruwen consider the danger the Crew Chief faced because of Ruwen's absence.

All these thoughts made Ruwen second guess his decision to delay heading home so he could help Rung Four. The Sixth Rune had taken him literally everywhere in the entire Universe, and its vastness defied comprehension. He had seen hundreds of billions of galaxies containing trillions of stars. What did one planet in one galaxy matter?

Rationalizing away the desperate need of a planet because it seemed insignificant made Ruwen's stomach turn. What he had told Lalquinrial in the Infernal Realm remained true, when Ruwen became a god, he wanted to save everyone. Or at least try when he had the opportunity. The powerful had an obligation to help.

Ruwen refocused on Sift.

"...and they use their fins to wrap victims in seaweed before they eat them, armor and all," Sift said.

Ruwen wondered how Sift had gone from pepper-flavored ice cream to fish covering people in seaweed. "Can we skip that part?" Ruwen asked.

"I guess if you're scared of getting eaten. But I'd really like to taste their jellyfish jam."

They sat quietly for a few seconds and Sift continued, his voice serious. "How are you doing?"

Ruwen considered the question. So much had happened he hadn't processed it all. "Okay, I guess."

"Really?"

Ruwen sighed. "I think I'm just burying the stress. So much that happens to me is life or death, and my only choice is to deal with it. Then I skip right to the next crisis."

"That's why we need a vacation. You're too serious now, and I worry about you."

"I know. Thanks, buddy, I appreciate that."

"My life got a whole lot better after you showed up, and I don't want it to end because you're stupid and don't listen to your friends."

Ruwen nodded. "Your life got a whole lot better after you almost murdered me, you mean."

Sift waved a hand dismissively. "I gave you the antidote before giving you fatal poison."

"I'm so glad you got that in the right order."

"You're welcome."

Ruwen shook his head and smiled. He had to admit his life had gotten a lot better after meeting Sift as well. So much had happened to them in the past two years.

Prythus exited the door opposite the one he entered. He looked around confused and his shoulders slumped. Ruwen changed his mind about how long he wanted to stay in this level. Before Prythus could enter one of the doors again he called out.

"Prythus, come sit with us," Ruwen said.

Prythus sat across from Ruwen. "This level makes no sense."

"A maze?" Sift asked.

Prythus nodded. "There are wide tunnels, narrow ones, and even a few you need to crawl through. They twist around and branch over and over again. I honestly didn't think I'd ever make it out."

Ruwen locked gazes with Prythus. "And yet, after all that work and confusion, you ended up where you started."

"Yes," Prythus responded.

"Meditate on that," Ruwen said.

Prythus frowned but did as instructed. It took thirty minutes for the rest of the team to exit the maze.

When they all sat together again Ruwen spoke. "What is the purpose of this level?"

"To waste time," one of the men said.

Prythus frowned at the man.

"A valid observation," Ruwen said. "But not the best word. What do you think Sisen?"

"Consume not waste," Sift said. "The maze consumes time as you navigate through it, just like the Steps consume your time as you master them."

"Then why did it bring us back to the beginning?" Nymthus asked. "Isn't the point of learning the Steps to become a Master? Shouldn't we have reached an exit?"

"Perhaps the exit is hidden," Prythus said. "We must have all missed it."

"What if I told you the maze has no exit," Ruwen said. "Only the two entrances behind you."

All of Rung Four looked confused.

"What could that mean?" Ruwen asked.

They sat in silence for a minute, before Prythus finally spoke. "That becoming a Master is not an end."

Nymthus answered next. "Or that once you're a Master your Step journey begins again, as if you knew nothing."

Ruwen let them discuss different possibilities for another five minutes. When the discussion quieted, he turned to Sift. "Sisen?"

Sift looked around at the group before responding. "A circle contains endless beginnings and infinite ends."

All eight of Rung Four bowed from their sitting positions, touching their foreheads to the floor.

Ruwen turned to Sift, impressed by his friend's wisdom.

Sift looked miserable and whispered so quietly only Ruwen's Diamond hearing picked it up. "I'm turning into my dad."

Ruwen hid a smile. It did sound like something Padda would say. "Sisen Sift is correct," Ruwen said. "Tonight, meditate on beginnings and ends. Now, let's head up to level three, and see what lesson it holds."

Ruwen and Sift stood, and Rung Four did as well, their faces still showing confusion. Ruwen walked to the top of the stairs and stopped. His Diamond senses detected a mass of people above them. Whatever level three held, it appeared to have halted at least two teams.

Two of the heartbeats above sounded familiar, their cadence slow and regular, despite the rapid thumping of all the others on the level. Ruwen had a good idea who might wait for them above.

The hidden passage above them had a fist-sized rock protruding from the ceiling, and Ruwen jumped up and pushed it. A ladder slid out of the ceiling, striking the floor with a thud.

Ruwen pointed at the ceiling. "Age before beauty."

Sift narrowed his eyes. "Why do you look happy?"

Ruwen tried to keep his face neutral. He really needed to work on hiding his emotions better. "I'm just excited to reach floor three."

Sift frowned. "I doubt that."

Sift looked up and instead of using the ladder, jumped, disappearing as his body passed through whatever veil the Founders used to separate the floors.

Ruwen heard Sift's heartbeat immediately increase, confirming Ruwen's suspicion. He turned to Rung Four. "Let's go meet some Grandmasters."

CHAPTER 7

*R*uwen entered the third floor last, and he found chaos. Rung Four stood in a tight group near the entrance, and Sift stood still in front of them. The other three Rungs remained here as well, and they fought each other in a massive brawl.

Unlike the previous two levels, this floor stretched at least a hundred feet into the air. A six-foot wide pathway wound around the outside of the room like a corkscrew climbing to the top. Small birds or maybe gliders soared near the ceiling, and unmoving bodies littered the pathway, most of them near the top. Ruwen could still detect heartbeats so they must be paralyzed in some fashion.

Madda and Padda sat meditating on the far side of the room in front of a golden gate. A large lock made it evident you needed a key to pass. Through the bars, Ruwen could see a stairway that he presumed led to the next floor. A waist-high fence started against the wall and surrounded the Grandmasters, creating a half circle as it stretched from one side of the door to the other.

Looking closer, Ruwen noticed a pedestal holding two hour-glasses. The sand in the smaller one had already drained into the bottom and the larger hourglass had almost done the same.

"Thirty seconds," Echo shouted.

Ruwen focused on Rung One. The seven of them stood close together near Madda and Padda but far enough apart from each other to fight effectively. Echo gripped what looked like a golden key with wings. He glanced up at the ceiling and realized what he thought might be birds were flying keys.

The members of Rung Two and Three surged toward Rung One. All the teams held at least one golden key which created smaller conflicts as they defended their keys from theft. Ruwen studied Rung One. While they had better Step skills than anyone in Rung Four, they didn't differ that much from Rung Two. That held true except for Echo, who clearly had better training than everyone here except Ruwen and Sift.

Echo glanced at the large hourglass and shouted. "Ten seconds."

Rung One formed an arc against the fence across from the Addas and frantically fought off the other teams. Echo jumped from fight to fight, helping her team defend its position.

Madda stood and strode to the pedestal. As the last of the sand fell through the large hourglass, Madda flipped it back around and opened a gate in the fence, creating a small opening.

Madda returned to stand in front of the gate where Padda now stood as well. Echo and Rung One fell through the gap in the fence and cries of disappointment from Rungs Two and Three rang loudly off the granite walls.

The last member of Rung One closed the gate as he entered the twenty-foot inner area.

Padda spoke, his quiet voice loud in the space. "Rung One present your Champion, your key, and your intention."

The fighting everywhere stopped as the other groups watched Rung One.

Echo stepped forward.

"Start the timer," Madda said.

Echo stepped to the pedestal and flipped the smaller hour-glass. Not wasting any time, she strode toward Madda and Padda. She slid the key into the top of her pants at the small of her back. She immediately attacked Madda, using a Viper Combination Dripping Star.

Echo moved like a Master, her Steps sure and correct. Ruwen noticed a handful of minor issues and many smaller ones, but on the whole, her technique looked excellent. The pressure waves from their exchange reached him, but the air explosions from their movements ripping the air apart sounded muted. The fence must have some type of noise-dampening.

Madda effortlessly countered Echo, moving like a mirror, matching Echo's speed, force, and even the mistakes in her Steps. Ruwen marveled at the skill to mimic someone so completely. It took incredible control of your body to do things improperly when you'd spent centuries perfecting the correct method.

Echo moved to Padda, and while the difference between the Bamboo Grandmaster and Madda was slight, it remained significant. Padda didn't even appear to fight, his movements so natural and fluid it looked like his counters to Echo's attacks were accidents. Just like Madda, Padda didn't counterattack with any Viper Steps even when Echo left herself terribly vulnerable.

Echo growled in frustration and jumped, trying to leap over the two Grandmasters she couldn't beat. Padda caught her foot, his hand there almost before Echo left the ground. He used Echo's momentum to flip her, and she landed near the pedestal.

The last grains of sand disappeared from the top of the small hourglass.

"Time," Madda said. "Forfeit your key."

Echo screamed in frustration and threw the key at Madda. Madda casually pulled the key from the air and dropped it onto a pile of other keys near the door. A pile that contained dozens and dozens of keys.

Madda moved toward the fence, the members of Rung One separating to let her pass. Ruwen admired Madda's movement, the Viper Grandmaster oozed danger with every stride. Ruwen guessed only Echo even considered attacking her now.

Madda opened the gate in the fence and Rung One exited, and the madness began again as Rung One attacked the other teams that had already obtained golden keys.

Madda and Padda hadn't looked at Sift once.

"What in the True God's Pits is going on here?" Sift asked.

"I'm not sure," Ruwen replied. He faced Rung Four. "This is a terrific opportunity to practice your improved Steps against the others. Go have some fun."

"Should we try and gain a key?" Prythus asked.

Ruwen shrugged. "If you want. It might increase the difficulty of who you fight. But don't make it your focus. I'm going to check out the ceiling."

Rung Four strode into the battle, and Ruwen looked at Sift. "You coming?"

Sift shook his head. "I don't want any part of this. Did you see how my parents mirrored Echo perfectly? Her speed and everything."

Ruwen nodded. "Even the errors."

"That's odd. It takes way more effort to do that."

"I agree. It must mean something. I'm heading up to the top to take a look at those flying keys."

"Have fun," Sift said. "I'm staying right here."

"Okay. I'll return shortly."

Ruwen strode into the fighting. Four Adepts lay paralyzed on the route upward, and twenty-seven Adepts fought on the ground floor. None of them had raced upward to get a key, instead, they battled each other for the three keys already retrieved.

Ruwen moved calmly through the fights, his mind and experience automatically choosing the path with the least obstructions. He ducked and twisted and leaned, never allowing anyone to touch him.

In just a few moments Ruwen had navigated through the combat and reached the bottom of the ramp that spiraled upward along the wall. After ten steps he calculated it would take him fifteen minutes walking at this pace to reach the top. Glancing down at the large hourglass Madda had reset confirmed the next interaction with the Addas would occur in less than fifteen minutes.

Ruwen considered running up the ramp, but running in circles didn't appeal to him. Instead, he angled toward the edge of the ramp and glanced upward. The ramp above extended from the wall eight feet, and he decided to take a shortcut.

With such a small distance, Ruwen didn't bother swinging his arms. Slightly bending his knees, he leaped upward and caught the edge of the ramp above, quickly pulling himself to the ramp surface. Without looking down, he repeated the process, rapidly advancing up the tower.

The first attack occurred just past half-way, at around seventy feet from the floor below. Ruwen had just pulled himself onto the ramp when a soft hiss caught his attention followed by the pressure wave of a small projectile.

Ruwen tilted his head to the side and triggered Last Breath to catch a glimpse of what kind of trap he'd sprung. As Last Breath sped his thoughts, the world around him slowed, and the projectile crawled through the air two inches away. It had the shape of an oval cylinder and it gleamed wetly. Probably a type of contact poison that would paralyze him for fifteen minutes.

With a Poison Resistance of one hundred eighteen percent, and a Diamond-Fortified body, Ruwen doubted the poison would affect him at all, but he didn't want to risk it, and he let the projectile pass him.

At the last second Ruwen realized the poison cylinder would drop into the crowd below, possibly striking someone from Rung Four. Not wanting to jeopardize them, he swiped his left arm upward, opening his Void Band slightly with a thought, and snatching the projectile from the air. It happened so fast, only someone with Diamond senses would have seen it.

By the time Ruwen reached the top of the ramp, he'd captured twenty-three of the projectiles. He glanced at the notification.

You have found...
Name: *Slug of Forced Meditation*
Damage: *1-3*
Quality: *Uncommon*
Durability: *1 of 1*
Weight: *0.375 lbs.*
Effect (Contact): *Lower Poison Resistance by 25%.*
Effect (Contact): *Paralyze extremities for 1 to 15 minutes.*
Description: *Grey-blue oval cylinder with a dimpled surface. Contact with the projectile causes disintegration, generating a cloud of poison around the target. Stop and think about what you've done.*

This seemed like something Fractal would like so Ruwen decided to keep them instead of dropping them all on the ramp.

Ruwen judged he stood one hundred thirty feet above the floor. He watched the combat and smiled to see Rung Four holding their own. He turned his attention to the flying keys around him.

They looked like a cross between a glider and an air-sled, as they generated their own magical wind that kept them airborne. Why have these at the top of this level? Ruwen studied the ramp and thought about how much effort it took to climb all this way.

Once Ruwen had a key, he could return to the bottom, where he'd started. The same lesson had repeated once again.

You end where you begin. But why the addition of Madda and Padda? The Grandmasters never attacked. They just mirrored their opponent exactly, as if they only wanted a stalemate.

The word "stalemate" set off an avalanche of thoughts. A stalemate was another way a person could end up where they started. That meant Madda and Padda represented yet another example of the first pattern found in the Steps: you end where you begin.

If they presented a stalemate, how did an Adept overcome that? Ruwen felt confident he could best Madda and Padda, and Sift could probably as well. But every other Adept that had ever taken this trial and probably every person in the future, would not be able to best the Addas. It seemed like an impossible task, which meant beating the Addas was not the point.

What then? Madda had asked the Adepts to present their Champion, their key, and their intent. The Champion implied a fight, the key was obviously for the gate, and the intent confused Ruwen. Why ask about intent? Wasn't the intent to open the door?

Ruwen groaned and shook his head at the obvious solution. It even explained why Madda and Padda mirrored the Champion's movements. That in itself provided a clue to the solution.

"Fifteen seconds," Echo yelled, her voice floating up to Ruwen.

Looking at the gliding keys, Ruwen considered grabbing one, but decided he would rather use one from below.

"Ten seconds," Echo yelled again as Rung One fought off the other teams. Ruwen smiled to see some of those causing the most problems for Rung One came from Rung Four.

Madda left her post and walked toward the gate.

Five seconds remained until Madda opened the gate.

Ruwen concentrated on a spot on the floor below and jumped off the ledge.

As Ruwen fell, Madda flipped the large hourglass around,

starting the timer once again. She moved to the gate, opened it, and stepped backward, creating a small gap.

Ruwen landed in the gap, not even bothering to bend his knees from such a small fall. Echo stepped backward, expecting the entry to be empty. Instead, he plucked the key she'd placed in the small of her back.

Echo twisted around with a hiss. Ruwen's right wrist had itched the entire time in this level, but now it almost burned.

Ruwen held up the key. "Is this yours?"

Echo growled and snatched the key back. Or tried to. Ruwen moved it just out of reach each time. The fifth time he let her have the key and she immediately aimed a blow at his neck, hoping to knock him out.

Ruwen took the key from Echo's hand before she could react. Then he stopped every one of her attacks before she could begin. Pinning her arm to her side, her foot to the ground, and slapping her hand before she could form a fist.

Ruwen handed Echo the key back, and she yanked it from his hand. She feigned a punch and then tried to kick him in the groin. He grabbed her leg and spun her around so she faced all the Adepts again. Then he removed the key from her grasp before she could react and pushed her forward. She tumbled into the rest of Group One.

Stepping backward, Ruwen slowly closed the gate. Echo turned and screamed at him. He smiled at her and stepped away from the fence.

Sift remained at the entrance but he had stood, and when Ruwen glanced at him he gestured in Shade Speak. *Now. Understand.*

Ruwen considered using the passive *Sphere of Influence* he'd gained from Rami's third Codex of Perception. It allowed him to speak telepathically to any non-hostile entity, but he didn't know if that would break the no magic rules. He decided to play it safe and use Shade Speak. Just to make sure Sift meant the trial token, Ruwen signaled back. *Item. Location.*

Sift nodded.

Ruwen flashed a short request. *Take. Four. Now.*

Sift nodded again and Ruwen faced the Addas.

Padda spoke, his quiet voice booming in the now silent room. "Rung Four present your Champion, your key, and your intention."

Ruwen bowed to the Grandmasters and held up the key he'd taken from Echo.

"Start the timer," Madda said.

Ruwen stepped to the pedestal and flipped the smaller hourglass. Turning he strode to the Addas and stood three feet in front of them. They remained like that for five seconds, all three of them unnaturally still, immense violence barely contained.

Ruwen slowly held out the key, and Madda mirrored Ruwen's movement until their hands met, and the key rested half in her hand.

"My intent is to reach the next floor," Ruwen said.

Madda took the key from Ruwen and handed it to Padda, who strode to the golden gate and opened it, leaving the key in the lock.

The silence lasted another two seconds before Echo yelled. "Are you joking?"

Padda returned to stand next to Madda.

"Rung Four Champion, choose your companions for the final level," Madda said.

Ruwen bowed to the Grandmasters and faced the group of Adepts. All the members of Rung Four grinned and some of them jumped in excitement. He glanced at Sift to verify he stood at the back of the group now.

Ruwen strode to the gate and opened it. "The person most deserving of this final level is the owner of the key that made it possible. I choose Echo and her team."

The smiles on Rung Four faltered as confusion and then disappointment hit them all like a tidal wave. Their shoulders slumped and they hunched forward like Ruwen had punched them all in the stomach.

Echo yelled in excitement and dashed past Ruwen, not even pausing long enough to say thank you. The other six members of her team followed, and they quickly disappeared through the gate and up the stairs.

Ruwen turned and followed Echo. The disappointed silence behind him like a knife to the heart.

CHAPTER 8

The stairs circled upward like a corkscrew and Ruwen took his time. At heart, he wanted to please everyone, and seeing the looks on Rung Four made him feel awful. It was necessary however because they didn't deserve to be on the tower's final level.

The walls of the tower glowed with enough light that Ruwen could see, but as he approached the top of the stairs the light turned redder. The exit came into sight, but it wasn't a doorway. Instead, the stairs ended in an opening on the last level's floor. Stepping up and out, he understood why this was the final level of the tower. He'd arrived on the roof.

For the first time, Ruwen glimpsed the sky. It looked brownish, the red light of the sun giving the entire heavens a dirty look. He preferred the blue sky of Grave.

In the center of the roof stood a thick pillar, fifteen-feet high. The roughly hewn granite had twelve sides, and five smooth circles traced a line down the center of each. Unlike the circles on the pillar in the courtyard, these remained blank.

Black sand covered the roof and Ruwen kneeled to touch it. The sand had absorbed the sun's heat all day and now burned to the touch. Small clam-shaped containers lay half buried in the sand, thousands of them. Rung One had spread out from the stairwell, ripping them apart, searching for the mysterious trial token they assumed one of the shells held.

The heat didn't bother Echo, but the rest of her team suffered. Their fingers had already blistered from the heat, and they moved slowly and painfully. Echo cursed at them to hurry before the next group arrived in fifteen minutes.

Ruwen walked to the tower's edge and looked down. The clouds had partially broken and he could see the ground, so he walked along the tower's edge until the town came into view. He smiled as he found Sift leading the members of Rung Four. They had almost reached the village, and Ruwen sat, hanging his legs over the edge to watch them.

"Why are you so happy?" Echo asked.

Ruwen had heard and felt Echo's approach but had ignored her. She couldn't hurt him here. Even pushing him off this tower wouldn't work. He knew he could easily survive a fall from almost any height now.

"I'm enjoying the view," Ruwen said. Then, after a moment, he continued. "Your father lied to you. He tried to hurt me. Keep that in mind the next time you rationalize around your oaths to do me no harm."

Echo hissed.

Ruwen continued. "Your mother was as pleasant as I remembered."

Echo approached from Ruwen's right side. Her heart pounded rapidly, and her strained breathing betrayed her roiling emotions. She stopped five feet away.

"How did you escape?" Echo asked.

Ruwen knew what Echo really cared about. He turned and locked gazes with her. "Are you scared I killed them?"

"Impossible," Echo said with a laugh.

Ruwen continued to stare at Echo, and after a moment she

grew uncomfortable. "What if I told you, in addition to your parents, I fought our five Brothers and Sisters? All of them. At the same time."

"Lies. I would know if they died."

Ruwen wondered if that notification came because Echo wore the Aspect of Death or if the Aspects stayed linked in some fashion and he would know as well when an Aspect perished.

"I spared their lives," Ruwen said.

"That would be the height of foolishness."

Ruwen looked away from Echo and checked on Sift's progress. He and Rung Four had entered the town, and they moved toward the courtyard.

Ruwen contemplated Echo's words. "Yes, I acted foolishly. I struggle to balance benevolence and harshness, mercy and justice. Just as you do."

"I am nothing like you."

Ruwen faced Echo again. "Your father wishes to destroy our Universe."

Echo looked away.

"You knew," Ruwen said, recognizing the guilt in Echo's body language. "How can anyone support such a thing?"

"I don't," Echo said.

Ruwen swallowed hard and forced the words out, knowing they would hurt Echo. "He is obsessed, Echo. He would sacrifice you. Your mother. Literally all of us, to gain the knowledge and power he craves. Darkness consumes him."

Echo didn't refute Ruwen because they both knew he spoke the truth. What would it do to a young woman, knowing her father would toss her aside for his own gain?

Ruwen checked on Sift again, relieved to find him and Rung Four gathered around the Summoning pillar everyone but Ruwen had arrived from.

Ruwen looked into the sky and spoke quietly. "You know what I've been thinking about lately?"

"How to kill my family?"

Echo had circled back to the fear that, Ruwen guessed, had consumed her since she'd seen him appear.

Ruwen faced Echo. "I didn't kill your family, Echo, despite them both wanting to do irreparable harm to me. I didn't kill your friends either, even though they joined the effort to destroy me. Those you love are safe."

Echo swallowed, and it took her three tries to get the next words out. "Thank you," she whispered.

Ruwen nodded. "You are welcome."

In the distance, Rung Four jumped and celebrated around the Summoning Pillar. Ruwen's Diamond hearing could just make out their cries of celebration. The lesson of this area, repeated over and over, hid the location of the trial token. You end where you begin.

"The token isn't here, is it?" Echo asked.

"No."

"That is why you said I deserved to advance here."

"Yes. I wanted to keep you safely out of the way in case you figured out the lesson of this trial."

"What lesson?"

Ruwen turned as Echo sat on the tower's edge, ten feet away. "That if done properly, we end where we start."

"That's a dumb lesson. You can't make progress if you always return to the beginning."

"Perhaps, but when you reach the end, you hold the experiences of the journey, giving your view of the beginning a new perspective. How else can we judge our progress if we don't compare it to our start."

Echo remained silent and Ruwen gained a deeper appreciation for the Steps. There were lessons found in every section, even the most simple, basic, and obvious parts. It humbled him that he kept discovering pieces of enlightenment.

Ruwen continued. "You didn't start as the woman you are

now. What would the choices you've made, and continue to make, look like to that young girl? Returning to your beginning now may illuminate your—"

Echo interrupted with an angry voice. "You don't know me. You don't get to judge."

Ruwen nodded. "I recently learned the Scarecrow is the Aspect of Famine. It made me curious, and I did some research. Do you know what, to my surprise, I found Famine carried? Not a sword or a whip or a bow." He waited a few seconds and then whispered. "Scales."

Echo didn't respond.

"That doesn't give me the right to judge you, Echo, but it is a reminder to me, yet again, that balance is the most critical part of life."

"And you judge me unbalanced?" Echo asked sarcastically.

Ruwen turned to Echo. "We all are. It is worth reflection."

Echo snorted. "You can stuff your opinions up your Aspect. I don't need them."

"I don't think it's just me."

"What?"

"I mentioned earlier I've contemplated something a lot lately. It's why I'm talking to you right now, despite your behavior. It is partially why I didn't kill your mother, and why I hesitated to attack your father."

Echo turned and locked eyes with Ruwen.

Ruwen continued. "In the library in Malth, the night before the quarterfinals of the Step Championship, we both spoke with Blapy."

Echo nodded. "The ancient wyrm."

"Yes. Do you remember what she said to you, right before Izac appeared?"

"The wyrm referenced death because she knew about my aspect."

"She did. But there is so much more. Blapy rarely speaks on

just one level. Her words are full of double and triple meanings. Most times, I don't understand until too late. For instance, I still don't know what this means."

Ruwen closed his eyes. "Blapy told you...*For advice, I seldom offer it freely, but for you I'll make an exception. After all, an arrow's path is easiest to alter before it's released. Here's my advice, wrapped in a question, just for you. I've been pondering this question myself lately. Can life exist without death?*"

Ruwen opened his eyes and studied Echo.

Echo frowned. "Wyrms are famous for talking nonsense. Thinking is just an excuse to not act. Her words were meant to cloud my mind before the next day's match."

"Perhaps. But her offhand comment that 'an arrow's path is easiest to alter before it's released' might have also been a message for me."

"Now I'm an arrow?"

Ruwen shrugged. "I don't know you, Echo, but you contain both the fierceness of your mother and the darkness of your father. I have learned through hard experience to listen to that ancient wyrm and never ignore her. When I released you from the webbing at our first meeting, I glimpsed a person I have not seen since. Maybe it's the girl from where you began. Whatever Blapy meant about changing your trajectory, this is my attempt. Don't confuse this with forgiveness. You have debts, and I will see them paid."

The sand helped mask the faint vibration of a Founder appearing ten feet behind Ruwen. But the past couple of days had been enough for him to recognize the differences between the three women.

Ruwen returned his attention to the celebration in the distant courtyard. "Hello, Dusk."

Echo gasped and turned to look behind them.

"Rung Four has found the trial token," Dusk said. "Our time in this area has ended. Assemble in the courtyard."

Without a word, Ruwen pushed himself forward and off the tower. He hated the feeling of falling, but he wanted to join Rung Four and their celebration, and walking down all those tower stairs didn't appeal to him at all. Plus, it didn't hurt to remind Echo of the differences in their power.

CHAPTER 9

*T*he Adepts assembled before the pillar grouped in their Rungs, and Ruwen and Sift stood behind Rung Four. Their disposition toward Ruwen had returned to deep green, as their disappointed confusion in the tower faded. The townsfolk had cleared the courtyard but stood bunched together around the outskirts.

The three Founders left the tent and strode to the pillar, Madda and Padda behind them. All five wore traditional fighting attire: bare feet, white loose pants, and a jacket that overlapped across their torso. Black Belts wrapped their waists and kept everything in place with a complex knot. Thorn and Madda had ten thin red stripes near the end of their belts, and Mist and Padda had green. Dusk's belt appeared plain.

Stalks of bamboo were stitched on the left side of Mist and Padda's jacket, the plants sewed in incredible detail. A small red viper weaved its way through the shoots, hidden by all the bamboo.

Thorn and Madda's jacket had a large red viper, its fangs bared and ready to strike. It coiled around a single small stalk of

Bamboo. The eyes of the viper followed Ruwen as the group made its way to the pillar.

The right side of Mist's jacket contained a fist-sized green circle surrounding an open hand. Thorn had a red circle holding a fist, and Dusk's jacket had no designs at all.

The Founders stopped in front of the pillar and Madda stood behind Thorn, Padda behind Mist.

Dusk spoke. "Adepts, today you have taken your first step toward Mastery. Congratulations to Rung Four for retrieving the first trial token, which marks the end of our time here. Rung Four, approach for recognition."

Prythus moved toward Dusk and the rest of Rung Four filed behind him.

"Aren't you going?" Sift asked Ruwen.

"I'm not sure. I'm worried I have too much stuff already."

"You definitely do. You're like a walking junkyard."

"I don't keep junk."

Sift shook his head. "You and Hamma can open a second-hand store with the stuff you carry."

Sift nibbled at a carrot and looked thoughtful as if studying the flavor.

Ruwen smiled. "Careful, your body won't know what to do with a vegetable."

"Very funny," Sift replied as he held the carrot near his hip. Shelly poked her head out from Sift's pocket, chomped down, and pulled the carrot from his hand.

"Hey! Settle down, Shelly. You almost got my finger."

Ruwen laughed and turned his attention back to Rung Four.

When the last of the original Rung Four received some type of token, Dusk held one more. Ruwen moved forward, not because he wanted the token, but because he didn't want to show disrespect to whatever this ceremony meant.

Ruwen stopped in front of Dusk and bowed deeply to the Founder. When he stood, Dusk regarded him for a moment before handing him the token. He bowed again and quickly strode back to Sift. Once there, he studied his reward.

Someone had carved the roughly circular token from a type of red tree, and it fit comfortably in the palm of Ruwen's hand. It had a pinky-sized hole in the middle and scratches across the surface. After a moment, he realized the scratches represented the trees of a forest. He stopped himself from *Analyzing* it, again not sure about the rules for using his magic here. It didn't appear valuable at all.

"Quartermaster," Dusk said.

The crowd to Ruwen's right parted, revealing a bald man sitting at a table. He wore the same traditional gear as the other leaders. He finished his drink and pushed himself off his chair as if he weighed a thousand pounds. Ruwen had the urge to run over and help the man stand.

The Quartermaster, who Ruwen could now see looked a thousand years old, moved slowly through the crowd and into the courtyard. Eventually, he made it to the Founders, and he bowed.

"Thank you for rushing," Dusk said.

The Quartermaster rubbed the small of his back. "You're welcome, Sisen. Such a large group requires a lot of work."

"Dawn approaches the Red Forest," Dusk said. "Prepare them."

The Quartermaster bowed and pulled a small shoot of bamboo from inside his jacket. With a practiced throw, he flicked it at the ground. It struck the dirt with an audible thump and Last Breath triggered as a mass of trees exploded outward from the shoot. Ruwen watched in fascination as long stalks of bamboo expanded outward. In a blink, the town disappeared, although he could still hear the townspeople's heartbeats.

The Adepts now stood in a small clearing surrounded by bamboo. The long stalks swayed as if blown by an invisible wind.

"Line up," the Quartermaster said.

Echo jumped to the front of the line and strode to the Quartermaster. The Quartermaster looked her up and down and shouted over his shoulder. "Medium, lean, short."

A moment later, a large viper slithered out from the bamboo, a square of white clothes balanced on its head. The Quartermaster grabbed it and handed the pile to Echo. "Change into these."

Ruwen's skin flushed with anticipation as he joined the line to receive the traditional Bamboo Viper fighting attire.

The line moved quickly and two minutes later Ruwen stepped up to the Quartermaster.

The Quartermaster scanned Ruwen and yelled. "Large, athletic, tall."

A large viper that reminded Ruwen of the ones in the Journeyman's trial slithered out from the bamboo carrying a set of clothes on its head. He carefully grabbed it, memories of the Elder Viper spitting snakes making him cautious.

Ruwen hurried back to his original spot and removed his black clothes. The new cloth felt thick, and a little rough, but it weighed very little. He ran his hand over it, feeling like he'd finally become one of the martial fighting masters from the books in the library.

Sift handed Ruwen his bunched-up Cultivator robes. Blapy had given Sift the robes right before he'd left the Black Pyramid for the first time. They provided no protection and allowed all forms of energy to pass through, allowing a Cultivator to absorb as much energy as possible. He'd worn them nonstop since then.

Ruwen stepped away. "When was the last time those things were washed?"

"They don't need washing. Nothing sticks to them."

"That is really gross."

"Just open your wrist thingy and I'll drop them in. You can give them back later."

Ruwen grimaced.

"Seriously?" Sift asked. "How many dead bodies have you had in there? How many are *still* in there?"

Ruwen raised his hands. "Quiet down. Fine, I guess that's true."

Ruwen opened his Void Band with a thought and Sift dropped his shirt, pants, and shoes. Ruwen added his own clothes, and they both dressed in their new attire.

"You look good," Ruwen said to Sift.

Sift rubbed the jacket, smoothing invisible wrinkles. They had both tied their white belts in simple knots, not knowing the proper method.

"Thanks," Sift replied. "You, too. Almost like a real Step fighter."

Ruwen smiled, and they faced the front as Mist spoke.

"Adepts, in a moment, we will teach you the proper way to knot your belts. We will begin with Rung Four to allow more time to study the available Clan relics."

Thorn continued. "You have completed the first trial. These moments are opportunities to reflect on what the Steps have taught you."

"Between the trials," Dusk said. "You will occasionally battle on Savage Island against the other Step Clans, powerful Mages, and Beasts both primal and sentient. The island will test your skills and provide an opportunity to gain honor and relics for our Clan. We will transition to Savage Island shortly."

As the Founders moved among Rung Four, Ruwen turned to Sift. "Have you ever heard of Savage Island?"

"No, but it sounds fun."

"It is not fun," Madda said, striding up to them.

Madda pulled at Sift's belt. "Seriously, child, this isn't even a knot."

Padda stood next to Madda. "Many die on the island. The objective is to survive."

"Watch," Madda said to Sift and Ruwen.

Ruwen studied the sequence as Madda slowly tied the belt around Sift's waist, and Ruwen respected how she could do this effectively backward. She undid the knot and tied it again. He undid his belt and repeated the sequence, pleased that the knot resembled the ones on the Addas' Black Belts.

"What are the relics the Founders mentioned?" Ruwen asked.

"They come from the island," Padda responded. "They are items imbued with power either from their owner's death or because of the close proximity of powerful magic."

Madda continued. "Some Clans measure their power by such artifacts. They poorly train hundreds in their Steps, and then sacrifice them to gain more relics."

Ruwen held up his token. "The Founders said something about relics."

Padda nodded. "Shortly the Quartermaster will display our Clan's relics. You can exchange that relic token for one."

"Don't misunderstand," Madda said. "The Bamboo Viper Clan wants to harden our Adepts. We focus on the quality of practitioners, not the number of relics, and the island is nothing more than training and gathering necessary resources for us."

"What do you get if you win?" Sift asked.

"What do you mean, win?" Padda asked.

"Well, there must be some purpose," Sift said. "What is everyone fighting over?"

"The point is nonsense," Padda said. "A meaningless title."

Madda jerked on Sift's belt. "The Champion's Throne is not your purpose. Surviving is."

Madda and Padda left to help the other Rungs.

Sift turned to Ruwen, his eyes gleaming, and whispered a single word. "Champion."

CHAPTER 10

*T*he bamboo around the Quartermaster split open like a chest on its side, revealing shelves with items, and under each piece a long sheet of paper hung. As the rest of the Adepts learned how to tie their White Belts properly, Ruwen walked to the closest item.

An inch wide coin made of gold sat on a tiny shelf. The figure etched into the metal had mostly worn away. The handwritten note hanging below it provided details in fifteen languages.

Name: *Boundless Bribe*
Quality: *Relic*
Effect: *Flip coin and press against any item to use as a bribe.*
Cooldown: *30 hours.*
Description: *Worn gold coin. Imbued with illusion magic this coin imprints an item with the recipient's greatest financial desire.*

Ruwen wondered about the illusion enchantment. He had very little experience with that branch of magic, and he thought it might help him understand illusions better for when he could practice essence recipes again. He moved on.

The next few relics, a purple gem, a bent cross, and a broken chain, all enhanced attributes in some fashion. A needle caught Ruwen's attention.

Name: *Lightning Spine*
Quality: *Relic*
Effect: *Symbols scratched into the skin will absorb lightning until triggered.*
Effect: *Lightning Immunity with active symbol.*
Duration: *Until symbol has healed.*
Restriction: *One symbol created per day.*
Description: *A quill from a Cloud Razor. Symbol may itch and burn. If not discharged manually, the symbol will explode when the skin heals.*

Ruwen wondered what a Cloud Razor looked like, as he moved to the next relic.

Name: *Soothing Stone*
Quality: *Relic*
Effect: *Fear immunity.*
Duration: *5 minutes.*
Restriction: *Once per 6 hours.*
Description: *A river stone from a stream on Mount Jasper. Rubbing the stone for 6 seconds calms the mind. You hear the faint sound of a babbling stream.*

Any type of immunity had value, Ruwen thought as he continued on. Rung Four grouped together around a handful of relics.

"What's so interesting?" Ruwen asked.

"These all give bonuses against demons," Prythus said. "Would you like to see them?"

Ruwen pictured the Infernal army he'd obliterated not that long ago, along with the other demons he'd fought. The only demon he really feared was their god, Lalquinrial. "No, you and your people need those more than I do."

Ruwen moved around Rung Four and found the next set of relics, which focused on attributes again. He realized how spoiled he was to come from a world where magic items were common. In fact, he wondered how many of these relics had started their journey from a craftsman on Grave. Regardless, while a plus ten Dexterity ring might benefit many here, his Attributes had long ago stopped needing enhancements from gear.

The next item Ruwen didn't recognize. It looked like a bracelet but had a circular dial on the front. Numbers from one to twelve circled the face and three arms pointed at various numbers. The clear crystal of its face had a crack, and he looked at the item's description.

Name: *Broken Time*
Quality: *Relic*
Effect: *Stop time.*
Duration: *3 seconds.*
Restriction: *Works twice per day.*
Restriction: *Must touch crystal to activate.*
Description: *Fashionable men's watch with a leather strap. When the current time matches the value of the timepiece and the wearer is touching the crystal face, the wearer becomes unstuck from time for three seconds, disappearing from sight and gaining an extra three seconds to perform actions undetectable to others.*

That looked interesting, if a little hard to use. Echo's voice caught Ruwen's attention.

"A book," Echo said to the Quartermaster. "A journal specifically."

The Quartermaster shook his head. "We have nothing like that."

"Are you sure?"

The Quartermaster frowned at Echo and she noticed Ruwen's attention. She immediately moved away, putting more space between them. He wondered what book interested her.

Ruwen paused in front of the Quartermaster and bowed. "What is your favorite thing here?"

The Quartermaster rubbed his chin. "That's difficult to answer, as so many of these relics are situational. But I feel bad for Tarot and wish he'd find a home."

"Tarot?" Ruwen asked.

The old man waved his hand and moved down the row of bamboo almost to the end. He pointed and said, "Tarot."

Ruwen stepped up next to the man and looked down. "Oh no. I have terrible luck with these."

Nestled in the bamboo like a tiny king sat a golem. Memories of Hamma's Carnage Golem Smash flashed through his thoughts. Smash disliked Sift for valid reasons, and Ruwen for questionable ones, and every time the golem emerged, it caused more problems than if fixed.

The Quartermaster smiled. "It's funny you mention luck. Tarot is a type of fortune golem."

"What's that?"

"He can read your future."

Ruwen studied the tiny golem. Unlike Smash, Tarot had very distinct and defined features, carved and shaped by a master craftsman, and stood the height of Ruwen's thumb nail. Remembering how Smash grew, Ruwen didn't make any judgments about Tarot's size.

Ruwen knew from his experiments with the Architect Role

that seeing possible futures had benefits. "That could be useful," Ruwen said. "Why has no one taken him?"

"Well, most Cultivators are so focused on the present they have little interest in the future."

"But, certainly insight into the future has value to someone."

The Quartermaster winced. "It does, which is why Tarot's power comes with a cost."

"That doesn't sound good."

The Quartermaster smiled brightly. "He has a dimensional pocket where he keeps the items he collects, and you could use it as well."

Ruwen narrowed his eyes at the Quartermaster's obvious deflection from the question on Tarot's cost.

Ruwen had no need of extra storage. Tarot seemed like a terrible choice for him on every level. He glanced down at the detailed page.

Name: *Thieving Misfortune Golem*
Quality: *Relic*
Effect (Passive): *Karmatic imbalance.*
Effect (Triggered): *Tarot reading.*
Restriction: *Reading requires an item you value.*
Description: *A half-inch golem made from Divine metal. No Fortune Golem provides more accurate results than those of the cursed misfortune type. The gods themselves turn their ears to hear a Cursed Misfortune's reading.*

The little golem was worse than Ruwen had expected. He turned to the Quartermaster. "What is karmatic imbalance?"

The Quartermaster sighed. "Bad luck. But just a little," he quickly added.

"Uru help me, bad luck is the last thing I need."

Tarot stood, and Ruwen leaned back in shock. He glanced at

the Quartermaster. "I thought golems needed binding and activation."

"Fortune golems are special. The way they're made gives them sentience. Not anyone can use them. They must also choose you."

Tarot spoke, Ruwen's Diamond hearing detecting the quiet voice and *Hey You* translating the golem's words. "Why do you look so sour?" Tarot asked Ruwen. "Did someone you love die?"

"No."

Tarot studied Ruwen, the shock of being understood clear on his greyish-white face. "They will."

Ruwen leaned down. "Did you just do a reading on me? Who is going to die?"

Tarot laughed. "No reading. You haven't paid. And dying is inevitable." Tarot looked down, his face growing sad. "Eventually, everyone you love dies."

A memory of Blapy flashed into Ruwen's memory. It had been the first time she had mentioned her God Stone, and her research into storing the essence of someone in one of Fractal's crystals, allowing them to be resurrected in a new body with no Divine intervention. She had said, "Fractal's crystals, my research, and the celestials' power source will mean the gods' control of life and death is over. No one I love will ever die again." Ruwen had no doubt she would succeed.

Ruwen looked down at the sad golem. "Times are changing. If you believe your loved ones will always die, you are a terrible Fortune Golem."

Tarot looked up and a mischievous smile appeared. "Is that so?" He held out his hand. "Pay up, Grumpy."

"I'm not grumpy." Ruwen turned to the Quartermaster. "Is it safe?"

"Is what safe?"

"What Tarot wants to do."

"You can understand him?"

Ruwen sighed and turned back to Tarot. "Can anyone here talk to you?"

Tarot shook his head.

"How long have you been here?" Ruwen asked.

Tarot shrugged. "Time here or time there it is the same."

Ruwen felt Tarot's immense sadness, and he wondered what it must be like for the Misfortune Golem, sitting in this bamboo container, waiting to be taken out periodically and shown like a trinket to eager token bearers.

"Why don't you run off?" Ruwen asked. "Is the Quartermaster keeping you here?"

Tarot shook his head. "No, the old man has tried to free me ever since he took over the job."

"Then why are you here?"

Tarot's playful smile returned. "Because I am the best Fortune Golem in existence, and why would I run toward my destiny when I could let it find me here." Tarot held out his hand. "Now give me something of value, Grouchy."

CHAPTER 11

*R*uwen frowned, which only reinforced Tarot's observation, so he tried to keep his face neutral. He swiped his right hand under his left wrist in a practiced motion, dropping an item out of the Void Band as his hand passed, the action so quick the item appeared to materialize by magic.

Ruwen held out a silver coin, wondering how Tarot would take it since they looked the same size.

Tarot waved a hand. "Something you value. Do you value this?"

Ruwen glanced at the coin. Before he'd ascended, money had held more value, but since then, money had not caused any of his problems. When he could use Spirit again, he could manufacture terium coins whenever he wished. He wasn't as bad as Sift, but his views of money had definitely shifted. Did he value this silver coin? He answered out loud. "No."

Flicking the coin back into Inventory, Ruwen glanced through his things. One of the early items had proved very valuable to him. He dropped them out of Inventory and held them out.

"What are these?" Tarot asked.

89

"They're wax earplugs. They stopped these flying things from crawling into my ears, getting into my brain, and exploding."

Tarot stuck out his lower lip and nodded appreciatively. "These are acceptable."

A black hole appeared in Tarot's stomach and an invisible force reached out and snatched the earplugs from Ruwen's hand. The black portal looked exactly like his Void Band, but that might be how many dimensional openings looked. The hole expanded as the ear plugs neared and, in a blink, they disappeared.

Tarot laced his fingers together, reversed his hands so the palms faced Ruwen, and cracked his knuckles. He shook his hands as if to relax them. "It has been a while."

Tarot went still and the portal in his stomach reopened. The force reappeared, this time holding a worn deck of cards like an invisible hand. The cards all looked black, with intricate gold designs around the edges. A single open eye, also in gold, sat in the middle of each card.

"Present your question," Tarot said.

Ruwen wondered if he should ask something specific? Or maybe a general or vague question? This entire conversation seemed like a street performer's scam.

The slight vibrations Ruwen now associated with the Founders appeared behind him, and he wondered if they had bothered to make themselves visible. It seemed they took this seriously, or maybe they just wanted to see what happened out of curiosity.

Knowing very little about how divination worked, or how to phrase a question correctly, Ruwen hesitated. What did he want to know right now? The obvious question surfaced.

Ruwen had pushed himself obsessively for the last year and a half, preparing to achieve a single outcome. The manner in which that outcome happened could be useful knowledge;

although, he wouldn't really know the circumstances until they arrived, which made asking a specific question difficult.

Aware of his audience and the possibility some of them might understand Tarot's language, he made the question a little vague, but compensated for that by boxing in the timeframe.

"Well?" Tarot asked.

Ruwen considered another moment, but nothing better occurred to him, so he asked his question. "Before I travel home, will my plans succeed?"

"Shuffle," Tarot said.

The cards exploded outward, and Ruwen stepped back. The cards' spinning slowed and finally stopped, before rapidly falling back together, each of them fighting with the others to fit in the deck. Tarot repeated this six more times before the cards' stilled.

The deck hovered in front of Ruwen's stomach.

"Cut?" Tarot asked.

Ruwen had played cards at home with his parents and sometimes at the library with Tremine, always for fun. He reached out and touched the top card with a finger. The card felt warm, and it spread to the tip of his finger. He brought his hand back, leaving the deck uncut.

Tarot looked into the sky and his voice grew louder. "Harken lost soul. You stare into the abyss. Prepare yourself for its gaze."

Then with a flourish, Tarot spread his arms, and the cards exploded once again. This time they formed a circle, seventy-eight cards hovering in perfect stillness, and the top card of the deck occupied the highest point from the ground. Tarot continued, his voice still loud. "I, Tarotmethiophelius, a Divine Fortune Golem forged from the mists of heaven, touching past, present, and future, offer these cards."

Tarot lowered his head, and they locked gazes. "Ruwen Starfield, choose three."

Ruwen held his breath, shocked at the last statement. He had not told Tarot his name. Maybe the golem had overheard Ruwen's first name, but certainly not his last. That meant Tarot possibly had access to hidden knowledge. It certainly made him take the Thieving Misfortune Golem more seriously.

Ruwen opened his mouth to ask, but Tarot lifted a tiny finger.

"No questions," Tarot said. "Concentrate on the deck and choose three cards. Your reading awaits."

Ruwen frowned and stepped back to better see the cards. Many of the other Adepts now watched, attracted by the giant circle of cards. The Founders remained close, and he sensed Sift just behind him as well. Ruwen felt self-conscious with all the attention and worried about what the cards might reveal.

With a sigh of relief, Ruwen remembered he might be the only one here who could understand the golem. Even if everyone could see his three cards, they wouldn't get any context. He considered walking away to avoid embarrassment or the possibility of the cards compromising his plans, but his curiosity had roared to life, and he knew he couldn't leave.

Ruwen had read a book on various methods of divination, and he wondered if a Narrator had spawned from that. He didn't want to take the time to enter the Citadel or Fortress in his mind, so he sent a mental message to Sivart, the Narrator that had spawned from the manifesto of the Mist Wraith, Talker. Sivart had taken charge of Ruwen's mental world while Overlord searched for Uruziel.

Sivart? You around? Ruwen asked.

Effective Generals always stand ready, Sivart replied.

Great. Do we have a Narrator in there that knows anything about card divination?

Divination is a desperate leader's last mistake. After a pause, Sivart continued. *Although I must admit everyone enjoys Premonition's company, even if her prophetic ability is highly subjective.*

When Rami had triggered her third Codex of Evolution, it had granted Ruwen multiple passives. One of them, *Split Personality*, enhanced his mental constructs by his Cleverness Attribute, which had reached two hundred and two percent. This had thankfully allowed Sivart to talk almost normally, although the Narrator still liked to use his proverbs.

I'm going to assume Premonition is the Narrator. Can you ask her if she's ever heard of Tarotmethiophelius or a style of card divination using seventy-eight cards?

"You are a real thinker, aren't you," Tarot said.

"Sorry, I just want to pick the right ones."

"The cards pick you. Never forget that."

"Right," Ruwen replied.

Tarot had told Ruwen to pick three cards, and his mind automatically separated the circle of cards into three groups, like pieces of a pie. He pointed at the last card in each section.

"Twenty-six, fifty-two, and seventy-eight," Tarot said.

As Tarot uttered the numbers, the cards Ruwen had pointed to glowed, softly at first and then brightly as white sparks engulfed them. They floated from their places in the circle to the center of the ring.

Ruwen's right wrist suddenly burned, swamping the constant itching from Echo's blood oath. He turned his arm and stared in shock at the underside of his wrist. Three miniature cards had appeared, their black backs covered in gold filigree, exact duplicates of the real things.

Tarot raised his arm and the dimensional portal in his stomach opened. The remaining seventy-five cards plunged into the portal like diving birds of prey. The dimensional portal disappeared, and the three glowing cards slowly lowered until they lay perpendicular between Ruwen and Tarot.

Before Ruwen could ask a question, Tarot pointed to the first card Ruwen had chosen. In a solemn voice, Tarot spoke. "Your situation."

The golem nodded to the card and Ruwen flipped it over, surprised at the palm-sized card's weight.

Ruwen studied the image. A winged figure stood on a sled of clouds. Two wyrms, one white and the other black, pulled the sled by chains of gold. Ruwen's wrist burned again, and he glanced down to see the first card now reflected the same image as the larger card. To his shock, the card also appeared over the cut-out figure in the lower right part of his vision that allowed access to his Inventory. Before he could investigate the addition, Tarot moved again and grabbed Ruwen's attention.

Tarot looked up from the card and locked gazes with Ruwen. "The Chariot represents commitment to change. Your decision is made, and you hurtle forward toward your goal. With determination like a tidal wave, and focus like a speeding arrow, nothing will stop you from your chosen path."

That did sum up how Ruwen felt. He had spent a year and a half preparing for this trial and the consequences of his decisions. Although really, probably everyone here could relate to that, as they'd all worked for years or decades to reach this trial.

The addition of the mark above his Inventory interested Ruwen, and he focused on it.

Relic Mark: *The Chariot*
Trigger: *Wings of Resolve - All allies within thirty feet gain fifty points in Strength and Stamina for five minutes.*

Before Ruwen could ask Tarot for details on the new mark, the Thieving Misfortune Golem pointed to the second card.

"Your action," Tarot said.

Ruwen turned the second card.

Five fighters, each armed with a staff, stood in a circle attacking each other. The men wore no armor and none of them appeared injured. They each wore distinctive clothes, giving the impression they came from different cultures.

Ruwen's wrist burned as the card manifested on his wrist and it appeared next to the existing relic mark over his Inventory.

"The Five of Wands," Tarot said. "Struggle and conflict, competition and rivalry, the Five of Wands represents an imminent challenge. Paired with the Chariot, this trial is near, but hints the adversary may include yourself. Examine your motivations, and brandish your weapon, the battle is upon you."

Ruwen looked at the new mark.

Relic Mark: *Five of Wands*
Trigger: *First Move – Stun up to five enemies in a fifteen-foot radius for one second.*

The reading might not provide much help for Ruwen, but the area of effect stun certainly did.

Tarot pointed at the final card. "Your outcome."

CHAPTER 12

*A*ll the Adepts stood around Ruwen now. The Quartermaster looked on in amazement, as did most of the others Ruwen could see. Once again, he felt nervous and vulnerable, like his secrets had stumbled out of hiding and revealed themselves for all to see. The rational part of his mind assured him the occurrence of the Five of Wands in the middle of a fighting trial shouldn't shock anyone.

Pleased with how the previous two cards had turned out, Ruwen flipped the third, eager to know his outcome here.

The card displayed the upside-down image of a young man walking along a crumbling cliff while reading a stone tablet held in his left hand. To the man's left lay clouds and birds and an endless drop. Just seeing the cliff made Ruwen's stomach turn. To his right, a stone road paralleled the cliff. The man held a bag full of tablets and scrolls in his right hand, and a black wolf gripped the cloth with large sharp teeth, desperately trying to pull the man onto the road.

"The Reversed Fool," Tarot said. "Negligence and fear. A disregard for consequences and risk. Imminent danger surrounds you, but you travel forward unaware."

Tarot closed his eyes for five seconds, his brow creased in contemplation. He opened his eyes and locked gazes with Ruwen. "The Reversed Fool combined with the Chariot and Five of Wands suggests you race toward adversaries that mirror your preparation and determination. The Reversed Fool walks along a cliff, implying three choices, one of which is moving to the safety of the road. But your Chariot recklessly hurtles at the Wand's five, making the step toward caution unlikely."

"This leaves two outcomes," Tarot said. He held up a tiny finger. "A misstep to the left leading to the abyss and the disaster it heralds." He raised a second finger. "Or, the Reversed Fool navigates the dangers of the cliff successfully despite his speed."

The deck of cards reappeared, and Tarot jumped on top of them as if riding an air sled. He maneuvered the deck to the first card Ruwen had chosen, touched its edge, and then repeated this with the other two cards.

Tarot and the deck of cards rose until he looked Ruwen directly in the eye from three feet away. The golem spread his arms and a moment later, transformed into golden-silver metal. Light of the same color radiated from his body, and odd patterns flitted across his form.

With a somber voice, Tarot spoke. "I, Tarotmethiophelius, a Divine Fortune Golem forged from the mists of heaven, touching past, present, and future, offer this fortune. Ruwen Starfield, the tenth muse, keeper of the scales, and holy father, hear me. Your plans, buried under an avalanche of the past, will suffocate and fail. Harken the wolf and the path not taken, or death will surely find you."

Ruwen's wrist burned, but he ignored the pain, fascinated and horrified at Tarot's words. The golden-silver light faded, and the golem lowered his arms.

Tarot seemed dazed and wobbled for a moment.

Ruwen stepped closer. "Are you okay?"

Tarot shivered for two seconds and then shook his arms. "That was an itchy one." He frowned. "That probably meant it was bad news, right?"

"You don't remember what you said?" Ruwen asked.

The golem shook his head. "No way. Touching the abyss would destroy my mind if I stayed present. What did I say?"

Ruwen frowned in frustration. "You called me the tenth muse, keeper of the scales, and holy father. You don't know what any of that means?"

Tarot shrugged. "Sorry, I'm just the messenger."

Ruwen bit his lip. For the first time, genuine doubt entered his mind.

In Ruwen's opinion, the first two cards could apply to anyone at this trial. The last card, however, felt a little close to home. Had he rushed to this trial too soon? He had certainly made many bad and risky decisions. But he hadn't chosen the timing of this test, and his preparations for the likely conclusion crossed into obsessive.

The endgame Ruwen expected here put him in danger, and running along a cliff fit the risks he'd already accepted. The prepared enemies Tarot had mentioned also made sense, and didn't surprise him.

As Ruwen thought the fortune through, despite the dramatic language, he concluded it hadn't told him anything he didn't already know and expect. He would face conflict against a prepared opponent and the battle held risks, including death. Nothing new there, and he calmed down.

Feeling better, Ruwen glanced at the upside-down Fool on his wrist and then focused on the third small card over his Inventory.

Relic Mark: *Reversed Fool*
Trigger: *Joker's Dance – Increase Critical Strike damage by 25% and decrease personal Armor Class by 50% for 5 seconds.*

Another ability that might prove useful. "Thank you for the reading, Tarot," Ruwen said. He held up his wrist. "What do I do with these?"

Tarot held his arm out. He pointed with his index finger and flicked his wrist. "Using just this one and flicking your hand will trigger the first card and activate its abilities. Use two fingers for the second card and three for the last."

Ruwen rubbed his wrist. "How long will they last?"

"Until you use them or get another reading, which provides three new cards."

The Quartermaster stepped closer. "That was spectacular! I've never seen Tarot do that before. What did he tell you?"

"To slow down and be cautious," Ruwen answered. "The same thing everyone tells me."

"Are you going to take him?"

Ruwen studied the Thieving Misfortune Golem. He felt bad that the creature sat here alone as the decades passed, but he really didn't want any more bad luck. And while the relic marks on his wrist had obvious value, he wasn't sure they balanced the karmatic imbalance.

"The reading made you uncomfortable," Tarot said.

"No," Ruwen said immediately. Then, after a moment, he sighed. "Yes, a little."

"Good," Tarot said. "That is wise."

Sivart?

Yes?

Did you speak with Premonition?

In a fashion.

What does that mean?

When I mentioned the name Tarotmethiophelius, she entered a trance, and has not stopped speaking since.

What is she saying?

She is chanting about alignments and prophecies. The name trig-

gered something in the core of her identity. One moment, she has recovered.

Tarot continued to watch Ruwen but remained silent. Ruwen's stomach turned with indecision. On one hand, he felt terrible for Tarot, as the thought of him locked away made Ruwen sad, and the relic marks had obvious value. On the other, he worried what harm the additional bad luck would cause.

Premonition calls him the supreme oracle, Sivart said. *Every source she has ultimately traces back to Tarotmethiophelius. She said he is far too dangerous to leave.* Sivart paused, and after a moment, continued. *From the additional details Premonition just provided, my recommendation is to destroy the golem. If that is not possible, you must take him to keep the golem from your enemies.*

Ruwen's frown deepened. *Thanks, Sivart.*

"What happened to your previous owners?" Ruwen asked Tarot.

"Horrendous deaths, all of them. Appalling really. But not without warning. What good is a fortune if you ignore it?"

"That's terrible. Why would you tell me that?"

"I'm a thief, not a liar. You remind me of another fool. Just like you, the Universe twisted itself around him. I bet you destroy the Resonance Offset of every place you go."

Ruwen wondered if Tarot meant Pen, and it shocked him the golem knew about the Architect Role's Navigator function. The Resonance Offset determined how much manipulation the Universe would allow, and how far into the future a Divine being could see. He had dragged Grave's Resonance Offset all the way to zero. Only when he'd traveled to the other side of the Universe had the Resonance Offset relaxed enough to allow things like time travel.

"Am I affecting your abilities?" Ruwen asked.

Tarot nodded. "I have spent my life spiraling from past to present to future and back. An endless cycle as I crept through the eons. For only the second time in my existence, am I locked into the present, trapped by the gravity of fate. It's like breathing for the first time."

Ruwen felt his chest tighten at the imagery Tarot used and how Ruwen made the golem feel better. How could he leave Tarot now?

"Do you think your karmatic imbalance caused your previous owners' deaths?" Ruwen asked, hoping the answer was a resounding no.

"Almost certainly," Tarot replied.

Ruwen rubbed his forehead. "Why would I do that to myself?"

Tarot smiled. "Because Fortune Golems can read auras and our cards manipulate them. Not even peak Deities can resist our marks."

With that shocking revelation, Ruwen turned to the Quartermaster and handed him the token. "I'll take the Thieving Misfortune Golem if he'll have me."

"I agree," Tarot said with a nod, as the Quartermaster took the red token.

Rain bounced off Ruwen's head and shoulders. He didn't need to look around to know it only fell on him. His karmatic imbalance had begun, and he prayed Tarot proved worth it.

CHAPTER 13

*T*arot's deck of cards shot forward fast enough that Last Breath triggered. The golem circled Ruwen's head three times before the cards vanished and Tarot jumped directly onto Ruwen's head.

Tarot burrowed into Ruwen's hair and he resisted the urge to slap or itch the tiny golem. Three seconds later, the movement stopped.

"You need a new barber," Tarot said.

Ruwen had given himself a haircut shortly after arriving at the Black Pyramid because he'd gotten covered in rod spider blood, and it had hardened so completely he'd had to cut it out of his hair, leaving it a little uneven and spikey.

Not long after that, Ruwen had created his Core and his hair had stopped growing on its own. He guessed he could make it grow if he wished, but had never tried it, although he and Overlord had discussed possibly growing a beard.

How had Ruwen even heard Tarot? The golem's voice had not arrived telepathically or loudly. It meant the communication had likely happened via bone conduction or some type of vibration.

Ruwen spoke under his breath, vocalizing the words but not speaking them. "Can you hear me?"

"No need to shout," Tarot replied.

Ruwen tried again. This time he kept his voice so low he didn't know if the thought had left his mind. "Sorry."

"That's much better."

Thorn spoke to the class. "We leave in five minutes."

The crowd around Ruwen dispersed as everyone prepared for the transition to Savage Island. He studied the little bamboo cocoon Tarot had lived in.

"Do you need anything from your bamboo house?"

"No. I carry all my stuff with me."

Ruwen could relate to that.

"I'm looking forward to this," Tarot said.

"Does that mean you expected me?"

Tarot laughed. "Disappointment is expectation's fruit."

"That's true," Ruwen agreed. "And a much better saying than 'Don't judge a pastry by its frosting.'"

"Also sound advice."

"I guess. You didn't answer my question, though."

Tarot paused a few seconds before speaking. "For the last seventeen years, my self-readings have contained the same six cards. And being one of the few creatures in existence that brushes against the universe, they partially reflect the universe's probable outcomes. The first set is always the Fool, Death, and the Wheel of Fortune. The second is the Archfiend, reversed Death, and the Tower."

Ruwen went still. Tarot's repeated readings had started at the same time as Ruwen's birth. "Archfiend? Like a demon?"

"The lord of demons, actually: oppression, fear, imprisonment, domination. Fun stuff."

It made Ruwen uncomfortable that Death had shown up in both readings, as it reminded him of Echo. "What do you think they mean?"

"The Fool, Death, and Wheel all reinforce the same theme: change. The Fool is new beginnings, Death is an end of a cycle, and the Wheel is change coupled with inevitable fate."

That described Ruwen's path pretty well. "And the other?"

"The Archfiend represents obsession and oppression and the Tower disaster. The reversed Death emphasizes the Archfiend's fear, decay, and resistance to change. That is a much darker outcome."

"Great."

"I'm just the messenger."

Death existed in both readings, and Ruwen wondered if that had anything to do with Echo. She wore the Aspect of Death from her father Lalquinrial and had become intertwined with Ruwen's life as well.

"Do you think I'm the Fool?" Ruwen asked, unable to hide his embarrassment. "I guess I've certainly acted like one."

"The name is misleading. I consider the Fool the most powerful card."

"Really?"

"The Fool walks the cliff's edge of adventure and reckless-ness, order and distraction, and idealism and foolishness. It requires exceptional balance."

Ruwen's skin prickled as his body flushed. "Balance?" He repeated.

"Everything has some balance, but the Fool represents its immense importance like no other card."

That made Ruwen feel better. "What would have happened if I'd left you here?"

"There is an aura here other than yours that reeks of Divine association. I expect that relationship would have led to that deity destroying this place to recover me."

That must be Echo and her father Lalquinrial.

"You're that valuable?" Ruwen asked.

"The desire to know the future is universal, and others are obsessed with collecting us."

"How many are there like you?"

"None of my siblings compare to me, but there are thirty-six of us. Nine specialties, each with four types: fortune, misfortune, cursed misfortune, and blessed fortune."

"Why couldn't you have been a blessed fortune?" Ruwen asked.

"Please, those golems are useless."

"I bet they're lucky, though."

"Luck is overrated, and if you need it to succeed, you're doomed anyway. Plus, only cursed misfortunes can manifest our readings into the physical world. It makes us extra valuable."

"So I need to worry about people stealing you."

"Yes, if it's just a collector. If they want me for my readings, they'll need to kill you first, since we've made a verbal pact."

"Good to know. What can break our pact besides my death?"

"My death, or we agree to part ways."

Ruwen's body could sustain massive damage now and it made him worry. The sheet had described Tarot as consisting of Divine metal. Did that mean terium? "How durable are you? Trouble always finds me, and some of it has powerful magic."

"I'm a combination of terium and aura extracted from the Universe itself. I've spent time with peak deities and only the great darkness ever concerned me. So don't worry about me."

A million questions surfaced from Tarot's revelations, but before he could get any details, the Quartermaster retrieved the bamboo shoot he'd thrown into the ground, and the forest disappeared.

Thorn raised her voice. "Group up and listen. I'll explain the details on our run."

Ruwen strode toward Rung Four as he spoke to Tarot. "I hope we can talk about your adventures sometime."

"Of course. Knowing the past is a map to the future, and also a pit that traps. It's a balance, and something the Fool understands."

"Maybe you can help me manage the difference until I get my stance right. My curiosity acts like a tidal wave, and it sometimes carries me to places I'm not ready for."

"A wise and balanced approach Ruwen Starfield. You might be okay."

Ruwen stepped up to Sift, who had stayed with Rung Four instead of moving over to Echo and Rung One. Shelly poked her head out and swung it back and forth.

"Shelly, stop it," Sift said.

"What is that?" Tarot asked.

Tarot squirmed in Ruwen's hair and a moment later, the tiny golem rode his deck of cards, diving toward Sift's hip. Now that Ruwen could see the golem, he used the passive *Sphere of Influence* from Rami's third Codex of Evolution, and created a mental link with Tarot.

Is something wrong? Ruwen asked.

Tarot glanced up at Ruwen. *How did you form this link? Are you bound to a Perception Wyrm?*

Yes.

What type?

Bookwyrm.

Oh, wow. You have really complicated your life. You can add the Ink Lords to the list of people who want to kill you.

That list is pretty long. Ruwen touched the hip pocket containing his Ink Lord's Wrap armor. It sat rolled up in the shape of a tiny scroll, but remained ready to deploy in seconds. He didn't bother mentioning he had already become an Ink Lord. *Is everything okay?* He tried again.

Oh, yes. Tarot replied, not looking up. *I'm just saying hi to an old friend.*

Tarot flicked his wrist, and a card protruded from his deck, creating a bridge for Shelly.

"Control your golem," Sift hissed at Ruwen. "He's upsetting Shelly."

Shelly squirmed out of Sift's pocket and climbed over the card and onto Tarot's deck. The golem jumped forward and hugged Shelly, wrapping his tiny arms around the tortoise's neck. She closed her eyes and rocked in pleasure.

"Hey, get off my turtle," Sift yelled.

Ruwen resisted the urge to correct Sift. "It's okay. Tarot says they're friends."

"Sure, sure. That's what they always say." Sift bent and glared at Tarot. "Watch yourself, little man. I will squash you if you hurt Shelly."

Tarot ignored the threat and spoke to Ruwen on their mental connection. *It's great to see her so happy.*

Sift takes good care of her.

Tell him I'll do a free reading for him, with your permission, of course.

You can do them on other people? Will they get the marks as well?

Yes, Tarot said as Shelly returned to Sift. He flew back up to Ruwen's head.

You are full of surprises, Ruwen said.

"Let's go," Mist yelled as she turned and jogged out of the courtyard.

Rung One fell into line behind the Founders and the Addas and the rest followed, Rung Four at the rear, with Ruwen and Sift at the very end.

Thorn's voice floated back. "I'll start the instructions for Savage Island with a warning. A quarter of you won't survive."

CHAPTER 14

$\mathcal{M}$ ist continued. "Why will so many of you die? Because you will not heed our warnings and instructions."

"Savage Island," Thorn said. "Is a necessary trial to harden you for life as a Bamboo Viper Master. The Bamboo Viper Clan has never allied themselves with another Clan or fought for dominance or control. The Clans see us as aloof, and it has isolated us. Consider the other Clans on the island neutral at best, and hostile at worst."

They left the small town and ran in the opposite direction of the tower they'd recently competed in, entering a pine forest. The dirt path had very few stones, but Ruwen's feet somehow seemed to find each of them. The rocks didn't damage or even hurt, but it irritated him.

Mist spoke. "We value the work you've invested in yourself and don't wish to waste it. Your aim is to survive. And while you competed here, on Savage Island you remain supportive members of the same Clan. To survive, you must work together."

For the first time, Dusk spoke. "Your first entry onto Savage

Island will occur at the river. The water is full of dangers, and a single bridge leads to the plains. If you are lucky, the starting area will be empty, but this is unlikely. Many Clans like to camp this area to farm relics off of newcomers instead of searching for them on the plains and beyond. Rung Four, your relics make you targets."

Ruwen thought about Tarot and Dusk's reference to luck. One thing about having a cursed misfortune golem was he could always predict the worst scenario would unfold.

Thorn spoke again. "Unlike many Clans, we have no requirement to acquire a relic before returning home. Instead, we require three visits to the island. For many of you, this will be the first time you've fought in a life-or-death environment. This experience is critical as you develop into Masters."

They ran in silence for twenty seconds until Echo spoke. "I've been told the island contains powerful relics. What happens to the ones we collect?"

Mist answered. "It is yours. You can donate any relics you find to the Clan, trade it for a relic our Clan already owns, or keep it for yourself. Our Clan does not take part in the Throne war, Clan rankings, or personal domination. Reflect on this as you observe other Clans."

"What about Soul magic?" Sift yelled.

Ruwen glanced at Sift.

"What?" Sift asked. "I miss flying."

Thorn spoke. "For those blessed to have found their souls, and further, discovered a way to harness its power, there are no rules against using it. However, know our Clan considers the use of magic a crutch that lengthens the hardening process."

Dusk continued. "Any type of magic, soul or not, is like wrapping yourself in a wet blanket as you navigate a burning forest."

"Running through a burning forest is what's dumb," Sift whispered.

They ran for another thirty minutes, the pace easy. The Founders didn't want to tire anyone out, as many here had normal bodies and none of the benefits of Fortification. They left the forest and turned left, leaving the path and running into a ravine. Five minutes later, they'd traveled deep enough that the sun shone through a thin line far above.

A narrow creek flowed along the bottom of the canyon, and they ran next to its rocky banks. Ten minutes later, the water disappeared under a rock wall as the ravine ended. Dusk stepped up to the stone wall and used her finger to trace the outline of a door. Her finger left a faint white line, and Ruwen recognized Soul magic.

Dusk stepped back, and Madda moved to the wall. With a finger, she traced what Ruwen immediately recognized as a gate rune. She used soul power just like Dusk, the rune glowing white.

When Madda finished, Padda drew the next one. Mist and Thorn followed, and Dusk drew the last rune to Savage Island. Ruwen memorized the sequence, wondering if portal chalk would also get him there. He wondered why they'd jogged so far to create this portal. Did this place have a special power? Or maybe something simple, like the adults needing time to build up the soul energy to power these runes?

Mist pointed to the portal. "This connects to our Clan platform at the river. The first person through will trigger a shield which lasts three minutes. Use it to prepare for what faces you."

"Dawn has arrived on the island," Thorn said. "The planet's day is twenty hours. Tomorrow at dawn, we will open the portal from our site across the river. If possible, bring your dead brothers and sisters. The survivors will move on to the second trial."

"You will know our portal stone by our mark," Mist said.

Dusk stepped forward. "Survive. This first exposure to Savage Island is the worst, and our Clan loses the most

Adepts. Use caution, protect your brothers and sisters, survive."

The Founders and the Addas stepped to the side. Echo didn't hesitate and leaped through the portal. Rung One quickly followed and everyone else hurried through. When just Sift and Ruwen remained, Sift stopped and handed Shelly to his mom.

"I just fed her, so don't let her fake you into thinking she's hungry," Sift said.

Madda took Shelly with two hands.

"And let her out to walk," Sift continued. "She loves moving around."

Madda nodded.

"And—"

"Seriously, child," Madda said. "Shelly will be fine."

Sift sighed. "Thanks." He stepped up to the door, pointed at the symbols, and looked at Ruwen. "These look right to you?"

"How should I know," Ruwen replied.

"I hate these things. They need a little peephole so you can see where you're going."

"You have trust issues. We need to get going before our shield runs out."

Sift sighed again. "Fine." He turned to Shelly. "If I get lost like Grumpy did, you come for me. Don't goof around either."

Shelly stared at Sift, and Ruwen wondered how much they communicated. With a last nod at Shelly, Sift stepped through the door, leaving Ruwen alone with the Founders and Grandmasters.

Mist held out an arm and Ruwen stopped.

"The Shattered Clan has held the Champion's Throne for generations," Mist said. "They fill their ranks with demons, and they spread chaos throughout the nearby galaxies, including the home world of Rung Four. Part of the Shattered Clan's strength comes from their control of Savage Island and the relics they recover there."

Thorn continued. "Your Rung will certainly recognize the Shattered Clan and might act irrationally. You and Sift have taken Rung Four under your wing, and we encourage you to curb any foolishness."

Ruwen nodded, thankful that neither Madda nor Padda made a comment about his penchant for reckless behavior.

Dusk spoke, her voice thoughtful. "Rung Four's world is on the brink. The Adepts that return there as Masters will be critical in turning the tide of defeat into victory. Vital certainly from a martial perspective, but also from the hope they'll foster. Few things can match the power of hope." She paused as if to emphasize her next words. "And nothing brings hope, like seeing your enemies defeated."

Ruwen had witnessed the opposite of that during his fight for New Eiru. When they had attacked the city with their Crazors, they had quickly destroyed the resistance there. Despair had spread through the enemies' ranks like wildfire.

"I understand," Ruwen said. During his time on Savage Island, he would do his best to protect Rung Four. Their world needed them.

With a last look at the five most powerful fighters in Ruwen's Clan, he stepped through the gate rune portal.

Ruwen appeared on top of a small flat-topped hill covered in short grass. A ten-foot flat rock protruded from the middle of the hill, providing the surface for the portal he'd just exited.

"Finally," Sift said. "Did you get lost?"

"Please, I always know where I am," Ruwen said as he looked around. "Where is Rung One?"

"On their way to the bridge," Sift replied. "They left immediately, which was smart, considering the current situation."

Ruwen turned in a quick circle, absorbing his surroundings. The blue-tinted sunlight gave everything a harsh look. A wide river, maybe half a mile across, flowed three miles in front of them. A giant bridge spanned the river, supported on the backs of massive bent over statues. Rung One sprinted toward it.

Parallel to the river, every quarter mile a hill identical to theirs jutted up from the plain, each with a gentle hundred-foot climb to the top. A mile past them and opposite the river, the ground disappeared sharply, probably from a cliff, and a green ocean stretched to the horizon. The surrounding ground contained grass that ranged from ankle high to areas over six-foot. In the distance, past the river, rolling hills began, and past those soared mountains.

Sift pointed at the base of their hill. "Luckily, only two bands came to greet us."

Ruwen studied the two groups below, each containing around fifty fighters. They stood on opposite sides of the hill. The left side wore red uniforms, more like practice gear than the formal clothes Ruwen and his Clan wore. The garb high-lighted the attackers' purpose as less traditional and more func-tional. They wanted relics.

Glancing to the right, Ruwen examined the enemies there. They wore black clothes, tattered and ragged from constant fighting, and appeared like they'd already fought a war. Most of them had the general shape of humans, but each had at least one feature that marked them as strange. Longer arms or legs, tails, horns on their heads and backs. The group consisted entirely of demons.

Rung Four stood on the right side of the hill, staring down at the mass of fighters approaching. Prythus hissed the words, "Shattered Clan."

Rung Four had all become highly focused on the approaching Shattered Clan, their stances ready for combat. Ruwen recalled what Thorn had told him about Rung Four becoming irrational.

"Prythus," Ruwen called. "Group everyone up, please."

Prythus reluctantly moved to the hill's edge and shepherded the rest of Rung Four toward Ruwen.

"Oh great," Sift said. "The group following Echo turned back to attack us. That sucks."

"Bad luck," Ruwen said, thinking of Tarot.

"How do you want to play this?" Sift asked.

"Give me a second," Ruwen said and triggered Last Breath, slowing the world around him to a crawl as his mind sped up.

Normally high ground would give them an advantage, but with the oncoming third group, the attackers approached from three sides. He hated to admit it, but Echo had probably made a wise decision to run for the bridge. They could fight with their backs to the river or at the bridge entrance to limit the angles their enemies could attack.

If more groups arrived, it would only make their situation worse. They needed to break through the current mass and find some place easier to defend against large quantities of attackers.

That only left one option.

Ruwen released Last Breath and turned to Sift. "I have a plan."

CHAPTER 15

$\mathcal{S}$ ift closed his eyes and sighed. "Let's hear it."

Ruwen pointed as he spoke. "There are two immediate groups that need countering and another on the way. One
of us goes for the approaching group, one of us defends half this
hill, and the Adepts guard the other half."

"I want the approaching bunch. It's already crowded up here,
and it's only going to get worse."

"Okay, I'm going to open a connection with *Sphere of Influence* so we can talk at a distance. It will work as long as you're in
sight. If things get dicey, retreat here. No stupid."

"Says the puddle to the rain."

Before Ruwen could respond, Sift sprinted down the hill.
The Shattered Clan moved to cut Sift off, but gave up when it
became obvious Sift's speed wouldn't allow them to intercept
him.

"Bamboo Viper Clan," Ruwen said. The twenty-four
remaining Adepts all turned toward him. "They outnumber us
four to one, which is terrible odds for our enemies." He smiled,
and the Adepts returned it, their heartbeats slowing.

Ruwen continued. "I propose we divide this hill in half." He pointed toward the Shattered Clan. "On that side, assemble into groups of three, one from each Rung. Once done, use those groups to form two lines, one at the hill's edge, the second ten feet behind. When the second line calls out, the Adepts in the first line will use their Bamboo Steps to throw an attacker to the second line."

"Isn't tossing enemies behind us dangerous?" Prythus asked.

"Yes, it is. That's why the second line will work in groups of three against each single enemy, quickly incapacitating them. If you see another group struggling, help them before calling for another body."

"What about the other side?" Nymthus asked.

"I'll handle that side. If you need help, call out. The groups below have spears and likely blades. The Adept in each group of three with the most experience deflecting ranged weapons will focus on that. Remember, your Clan is behind you, so redirect the weapons upward, not straight backward."

Prythus looked worried. "You are one man. If they overwhelm you, our backs are vulnerable. We should form a circle and present a more traditional defense."

"The lack of space here, coupled with the numbers we face, makes that a deadly strategy. If we only defend, they will eventually overcome us. This method allows us to slow our attacker's progress while whittling down their numbers. I believe once they see we aren't easy prey, they'll retreat." Ruwen looked around at them. "We use the strength of our Clan. With only Bamboo or Viper, we would lose here, but together we will find victory."

"They're moving up," Nymthus called. "Shield disappears any second."

"Let's do this," Ruwen said.

Ruwen turned away from the Adepts as they followed his strategy. He stepped to the edge of his side of the hill and studied the attackers who had climbed to within twenty feet.

Whatever Clan they belonged to focused on blades as all of them carried at least one.

With a glance, Ruwen sized up the enemies. Most moved with the competence of a Master level Step practitioner, but none stood out as exceptional. He didn't wait for them to get any closer and jumped the twenty feet to their front line.

The move surprised the attackers, but they reacted as any trained Step expert would, and transitioned immediately into an attack. Ruwen had already decided he didn't want to kill any non-demons on Savage Island unless necessary. The people here had spent decades of their life attaining the skills needed to reach this place. While their Clans might have different reasons for participating, it didn't feel right to end someone's life permanently over what amounted to a glorified training trial.

Demons were different. In the Infernal Realm Ruwen had witnessed the endless hordes under Lalquinrial's control. Ruwen's connection to Uru and his Inventory remained active here. That meant the demons likely kept their connection to Lalquinrial as well. It meant they, unlike the others here, had the possibility of revival, which had the additional benefit of consuming more of Lalquinrial's resources.

Ruwen struck elbows, shoulders, wrists, and fingers. Weapons had many benefits, like reach and damage, but they all had the same vulnerability. Training with them as the center-piece of your style meant that without one you lost a vast percentage of your preparation. While he hadn't yet mastered a weapon, it didn't matter. He had mastered unarmed defense and offense. With broken arms, he could still defend himself and attack with deadly force. His enemies could not say the same.

The first ten seconds of Ruwen's attacks incapacitated fifteen of their members. He moved casually through the front ranks, slowing his movements to Metal levels to avoid accidentally ripping their arms from their bodies or instantly killing them. Swords and daggers fell into the grass, drowned out by the cries of pain.

Ruwen tilted his head to avoid a bladed boomerang from striking his neck. He caught a thrown metal star and flicked it back at his attacker. They had raised their arm to throw another and the throwing star lodged in their armpit.

They had all trained as fighters and recognized a better Step practitioner. It only took a few more seconds, and another five fallen comrades, for the entire group to turn and run. If Ruwen had arrived at Savage Island by himself, he might have let them flee, but he wanted to protect his Clan, especially Rung Four.

Fifteen seconds later, Ruwen faced the last attacker. The man raised his two swords like a cross to stop Ruwen's attack. He could have killed the man a thousand ways, paralyzed him, or permanently maimed him. Instead, he executed the Viper Step Slapping Gust and broke the man's forearms.

Fifty bodies lay in a short line down the hillside, weapons scattered among them. Moans and hisses of pain surrounded Ruwen, but none of them cursed him. They knew he had spared them, and their racing hearts revealed their fear.

Ruwen had monitored the fight on the opposite side and Sift's fight via the vibrations in the ground and air. Sift didn't need any help, but the group fifty feet above did. Ruwen still faced downhill, and with a small crouch, he flipped backward, turning his body as he arced through the air.

Landing behind the Adepts' second line, Ruwen studied how the fight progressed. For the most part, the process had worked like he'd intended. The front line slowed the advancement with Bamboo Steps and fed the Viper Step group new bodies as needed.

The original problem Ruwen had foreseen had started to his left. Shattered Clan fighters had bunched up on that side, trying to flank the front line and get behind the defenders. His Clan had responded by collapsing the sides and moving slowly backward, giving up valuable territory.

Other than the pressured left side, Ruwen's fellow Adepts performed superbly. The mixture of the three Rungs helping to balance the lines. He glanced through the Shattered Clan fighters, and only one, an eight-foot demon in the back, looked to have any advanced skills. Ruwen could have wiped out the entire group in seconds, but something Sivart had told Ruwen repeatedly came to mind: *Blood binds soldiers like mortar, creating unbreakable armies.*

This training provided valuable experience for the Adepts, so Ruwen leaped thirty feet to the left side to ease the pressure there, dispatching five demons in two seconds. Then he triggered Last Breath and watched the entire line, ready to aid any of his Clan that encountered a situation that might kill them.

The large demon screamed in Inferni but Ruwen's *Hey You* understood the directions. They were about to trigger a poison attack.

The Shattered Clan withdrew, trying to pull the Adepts closer to the hillside edge.

Ruwen considered using his passive *Sphere of Influence* to speak in all the Adepts' minds, but he didn't know if using it in such a flagrant and mass manner went against the Founder's wishes. So instead, he just yelled. "Trap. Fall back."

To the Adepts' credit, they all withdrew immediately. The large demon grabbed a four-foot demon and threw him at the Adepts. Dozens of sacks hanging like giant raindrops off the flying demon's face and body expanded.

As the demon arced downward, it clenched its hands, straining. Ruwen leaped to the front of the Adepts, directly to the spot where the demon would land. Before the demon hit the ground, though, the bags on its body exploded, releasing black spores.

Ruwen studied the approaching cloud and quickly brought

his hands together in a clap, this time using his Peak Diamond strength.

The space around Ruwen's hands ignited from the friction of his movements. The air, churned violently by the sudden motion, whistled shrilly, then a massive boom arced outward in an enormous pressure wave.

The poison demon vaporized along with the spore cloud. Air, solidified into spears with the strength of steel, minced the demons in the front row. Those lower on the hill escaped the immediate decimation but fell backward and tumbled down the hill.

Ruwen stood at the hill's edge and studied what remained of the Shattered Clan warriors.

Showoff, Sift said from his fight on the plain below.

Ruwen smiled, increasing the Shattered Clan's fear as they struggled to regain their feet. He considered what to do with the surviving dozen demons. Killing them would be easy, but he wondered if they could avoid future trouble if word spread describing what happened here.

Ruwen locked eyes with the eight-foot demon and spoke loudly in Inferni so all the demons could hear. "Leave your weapons. Leave your relics. Leave. Tell the others to avoid the Bamboo Viper Clan if they wish to live."

The large demon nodded and hissed at the others. They immediately dropped their weapons and fled.

CHAPTER 16

*R*uwen turned to face the Adepts, verifying none had died. A few had injuries, but nothing serious enough to force the use of *Massage* to heal them. The Adepts continued to stand in stunned silence.

Ruwen pointed at the far side of the hill. "Rung Two and Three fetch the weapons and relics from the fallen. Leave them alive unless they threaten you." He turned and pointed at the decimated Shattered Clan fighters. "Rung Four, collect the weapons and relics here."

None of the Adepts moved. Finally, a member of Rung Two cleared their throat and muttered what they probably all felt. "What are you?"

Ruwen glanced at all of them. "I'm a Bamboo Viper Adept just like you."

From the direction of the bridge, a thunderous explosion boomed across the plain, followed immediately by a high-pitched whistle which grew louder with every moment. Everyone turned, and a moment later Sift arced above them, flying toward the ocean. The air behind him, super-heated from his passage, condensed into a white trail as it cooled.

Sift angled himself straight into the air, disappearing from sight for five seconds, before reappearing on a course for their position. A few seconds later he floated down to the hilltop using his Soul magic, his speed and control vastly better than when he'd first flown during the Step Championship so long ago. The edges of his clothes had frayed from the incredible speed.

Now who's showing off? Ruwen asked Sift using their mental link.

It feels so good to fly. I've missed it terribly.

Just a week ago, you were flying in Shelly.

Well, it has been a long week.

I can agree with that.

Ruwen felt Tarot move through his hair and a moment later the little golem flew away on a deck of cards, headed for the wreckage of the group Ruwen had attacked. It only took a moment to grasp why.

Ruwen shouted toward Rungs Two and Three. "Watch that golem. He'll steal your loot."

Sixteen Adepts dashed to stop the golem

Prythus approached Ruwen and bowed, and Ruwen returned it.

"I'm sorry to bother you, Sisen," Prythus said. "But did you just speak Inferni?"

"Yes," Ruwen answered. "And I'm not your Sisen."

"I didn't know humans could understand the demon tongue."

"I've picked up a few languages."

Prythus' heart raced. "Do you understand it?"

"I do."

Prythus yelled, and Nymthus ran over. "The young Master might be able to translate. Can you write it out?"

"Here?" Nymthus asked in disbelief.

"Unless you disagree," Prythus replied. "We might never get

another opportunity to decipher it. If we all know its contents, hopefully one of us survives to take it home."

Nymthus considered for a moment and kneeled. She used a demon inscribed blade to clear the grass and then traced a message from memory in the dirt. She pushed herself away and stood. "Does it make any sense?"

Ruwen read the message out loud. "Servants of the new dawn harken. Lightbringer desires two ancient journals. One contains advanced alchemy, the other numbers. Anyone recovering or providing information that leads to recovery of either journal will live alongside Lightbringer in the first ring, lords in their own right, for eternity. All hail Lightbringer. The new dawn comes."

"What do they want with a divine journal?" Prythus asked.

"Journals," Ruwen said. "Plural." He thought about Echo asking the Quartermaster if he had any books among his relics.

Ruwen swept his foot across the message, erasing it. What books could have the whole demon world, from Echo down to common demons, searching for them?

Lalquinrial had entered Ruwen's mind and met the Narrator Kholy, who had formed from the twenty-two journals Ruwen had in his memory. She had told Lalquinrial she was incomplete and asked if he knew the location of her twenty-third journal. The demon lord had reacted violently to the question, his whole demeanor becoming vastly more hostile. Was that the advanced alchemy journal referenced in the recovered demon message?

The demon message contained little descriptive information which probably meant Lalquinrial didn't know what the journals looked like either. Basically, they searched for something old. Ruwen wondered what the numbers meant in the journal Lalquinrial wanted to find.

Ruwen turned to Sift. "What's Echo doing?"

"She's crossing the bridge."

"We need to follow her."

"It's become a little more crowded," Sift replied.

Ruwen studied the distant bridge and confirmed Sift's observation. Chaos had spread across the entire bridge as teams from across the river had marched onto the bridge to fight the groups trying to cross. He wondered if Echo had made it across in time or if she and Rung One had gotten trapped.

The Adepts collected all the weapons and anything they thought might be a relic. One Adept had to hover over the pile as Tarot kept flying around the items.

"Tarot, can you identify relics?" Ruwen asked.

"Of course," Tarot said without removing his gaze from the Adept guarding the pile.

"How about a deal?"

The Adept guarding the loot spoke. "That little man grabbed three swords and a necklace already."

"Seriously?" Ruwen asked.

"It's in my nature," Tarot replied, still not taking his eyes off the loot pile.

"How about this," Ruwen said. "You identify all the relics for us, and you can have all the weapons and one out of every twenty relics."

"Preposterous. I want half."

"You want, but they need." Ruwen stepped in front of Tarot and opened his Void Band. "I can always take everything and sort it out later with another method."

"Believe him," Sift said. "He's a hoarder."

Tarot shifted his gaze up to Ruwen. "A hoarder, huh? I respect that. I'm a collector myself."

Ruwen didn't bother arguing. For once, Sift's comment might help him.

Tarot put a hand on his hip. "As a show of good faith, I'll settle for a quarter of the relics."

"No way," Ruwen said. "These warriors need the advantage the relics provide."

"Twenty percent then."

Ruwen shook his head. "Ten percent, but the Adepts get first pick."

Tarot rubbed his chin. "And the weapons?"

The Bamboo Viper Clan had no need of weapons, but Ruwen remembered the Inferni etched dagger and wondered if some of those might have value to Rung Four. "You can take ninety percent, but again, the Adepts get first pick for their ten percent."

Tarot considered and after five seconds, Ruwen opened his Void Band again and strode toward the pile.

"Fine, fine," Tarot said. "You drive a hard bargain."

Ruwen pointed at Tarot. "Good. Now put back what you took."

"What! That's not fair."

"They are part of our loot. You agreed to the percentages."

Tarot floated up and hovered two feet in front of Ruwen. His eyes grew large and glinted in the dawn light. Tears fell down the golem's cheeks. "I found them."

Ruwen hid a smile. "No, you took them because you're a thief. But you're an honorable one, right? And quite the actor."

The tears disappeared and Tarot narrowed his eyes. "Well played, Starfield. You are a worthy adversary."

Tarot floated to the loot pile and opened the dimensional portal in his stomach. Fifteen swords fell out, four rings, a necklace, and three bracelets. The last item to emerge was a white belt.

Sift looked down. "Hey! When did you take my belt?"

Ruwen laughed. He'd need to pay better attention to Tarot. Sift would, too.

The Adepts gathered around the pile.

Ruwen stepped back. "Tarot will identify the relics. Divide them among yourselves based on need."

Tarot faced Ruwen again. "Aren't you taking a share?"

Ruwen shook his head. "I carry enough."

Tarot shrugged and turned back to the loot. An invisible hand shot out from his portal and began arranging the weapons and relics into piles. Ruwen assumed there was some method to the erratic shuffling.

Ruwen signaled to Sift, and they walked to the side of the hilltop facing the bridge.

"What do you think?" Ruwen asked.

"I could just fly everyone over one at a time."

"A good idea, but we aren't supposed to use magic for anything significant to our purpose here."

"They told us to survive."

"True, but making everything trivial won't help them in the long run. Plus, you'd likely drop a couple."

Sift sighed. "I'd probably catch them."

"That bridge looks messy, and we only have a day to cross the river and find our portal stone."

"What about swimming or taking a boat?"

"The Founders said the river held danger, and there isn't anything here to build a boat."

"It looks like we fight then."

Ruwen agreed.

CHAPTER 17

*R*uwen stood at the front of Rungs Two, Three, and Four and studied the bridge entrance a thousand feet away. The Founders had warned them the island had its own inhabitants, and they had made their first appearance.

What looked like walking seven-foot wolves defended the entrance of the bridge. They wore leather armor and brandished swords and crossbows. Over two hundred Adepts from other Clans fought the wolves and each other as they attempted to cross onto the bridge.

This close, the details of the bridge had clarified. It had no guard rails and spanned twenty feet in width. Interlocking stone slabs gave it a rough look. The river moved much faster up close, and swimming or any type of raft would definitely take them far downstream before reaching the other side half a mile away.

Ruwen had considered following the river to the end and crossing where it entered the ocean but Sift had said the island appeared gigantic when he'd flown over the river and continued for as far as he could see. All that brought Ruwen's attention back to the bridge.

The wolves would only be the first obstacle. Creatures and Step fighters littered the bridge, and the water roiled as beasts fought for position to catch anyone that fell off while crossing.

Fighting along the bridge's edge would allow them to focus their defense on one side but made them vulnerable to any attack that pushed them into the water. Fighting down the middle of the bridge would force them to defend both flanks. It also contained the most fighters as everyone avoided the sides. Many of their enemies had weapons, and the Bamboo Viper Adepts would be vulnerable to them in the crowded space.

"We could clear that bridge in less than a minute," Sift said.

"I know," Ruwen replied. "But is that the right thing?"

"If the point is to cross the bridge, then yes."

"That isn't the only point, though, right? The Adepts need to fight in this furnace to harden them for what their future holds."

"I guess. But a furnace is for baking pies."

"Unfortunately, our future is not that sweet."

Sift reached down and confirmed his belt remained tied around his waist. "Too bad your new golem isn't like Hamma's. Smash would toss himself a path right through that crowd."

Memories of Smash throwing skeletons as he chased Sift during the fight outside Uru's Third Temple made Ruwen smile. It reminded him a little of what he'd done on the hilltop, and it gave him an idea.

"Hear me out," Ruwen said.

Sift sighed. "Oh, no."

"What is the strength of our Clan?"

"Me."

Ruwen frowned.

"Fine," Sift replied. "Options."

Ruwen pointed at the mass of opponents. "All of them are experts in combat."

"And?"

"We don't need to fight."

"You want to cross the bridge by not fighting?"

"Exactly."

"I didn't think your ideas could get any worse."

"Listen. If we fight, we get bogged down, which provides opportunities for our enemies. We need to slice through them like a Carnage golem through a horde of skeletons."

"I'm listening."

"On the hilltop, I had a line of Adepts use their Bamboo Steps to slow the enemy's advance and feed the Viper team victims. I want to do the same thing now, but without taking time to fight. We just move through the crowd using Bamboo Steps to remove people from our path."

Sift tilted his head in thought. "If we keep it narrow, like a knife, we can just throw people to the other side."

"That's what I was thinking. We let the Adepts forge ahead and I'll stay near the front while you handle the rear in case of any serious issues."

"Not bad."

Ruwen turned to the Adepts, who all studied the chaos on the bridge.

"Those who favor Bamboo step forward," Ruwen said.

Eight of the twenty-four Adepts moved toward Ruwen. He'd expected as much, since most practitioners enjoyed the Viper offense to the more reactionary Bamboo.

"Form two lines," Ruwen told the eight Bamboos. He turned to the others. "I need two Vipers between each Bamboo. We will form a narrow 'V' and push through that mess with the intent to avoid combat. Whenever attacked or approached, use Bamboo Steps to throw them backward or to the side."

The Adepts nodded their understanding and in just a few seconds arranged themselves as directed.

Ruwen stepped behind the two lead Bamboo Adepts. "Let's advance at a brisk walk and try to maintain it." He raised his voice. "This is combat. Just like the hilltop, you don't need to execute a flawless move, just one that keeps you safe and takes us closer to our goal."

The fighting remained thickest in the center of the bridge's entrance, so they angled for the left side. Most of the enemy fighters kept their focus forward, and the Bamboo Viper Clan's initial penetration of their ranks proved effortless. A hundred feet from the bridge, the fighting intensified, and their progress slowed.

The combatants on this side of the bridge looked mostly human, with only minor differences. The farther down the bridge Ruwen gazed, the more creatures he found, along with organized bands of demons. He wondered if these fighters lived here and received rewards for slowing or stopping Clans from advancing.

Everyone stayed out of the water. Ruwen couldn't find a single boat or raft. It reinforced his belief that the water held more danger than anything on the bridge. The only things visible in the water were the immense statues that supported the bridge. The bridge rested on their backs, and each figure gripped the bridge with thick hands.

Ruwen refrained from helping the Adepts, even though he wanted to move faster. While he ignored some of the advice he received, like advancing Sift so quickly, other advice he took seriously, especially from entities like Sivart who specialized in warfare.

Ruwen had purposefully not spoken to Sivart yet, as he wanted to grow as a leader himself. He planned to go over his choices with the Narrator after everyone reached safety. Even though Ruwen had mastered the Steps he had a lot to learn about leadership and this island could help with that.

Even though their pace slowed, they still made progress, and twenty-five feet from the bridge entrance Ruwen had seen enough to agree with the Founders' assessment: the Bamboo Viper Clan definitely emphasized quality over quantity. The

Clans that surrounded them provided little resistance to the highly trained Adepts of his class.

Part of the reason for their easy advance was they fought the weakest of the combatants here on Savage Island. If these fighters had greater skills, they would have already reached the bridge.

As they arrived at the bridge entrance, the number of fighters increased, clogging the area, and making the Bamboo Step throws harder to execute.

Ruwen modified his approach to match what he'd done on the hillside. He raised his voice above all the shouting and sound of combat. "If you can't clear, stun. Vipers incapacitate. Watch your step for bodies."

The new directions sped them back up as the enemies around them fell to the ground from well-aimed strikes to nerve bundles and pressure points. The Viper teams finished them, creating a line of bodies behind them like the wake of a boat.

They pushed through the jam of enemies and onto the bridge. Now that Ruwen stood on it, he discovered the entire bridge consisted of a single vertebra from some massive creature. The bone curved, and the slope pushed everyone to the sides and away from the middle.

Most of those on the bridge looked human, but their red-tinged eyes gave them away as demons. Ruwen wondered why they guarded the bridge and how they'd gotten here. Maybe one of the other Adepts knew and could tell him once they reached safety.

A loud gong sounded and Ruwen almost turned to see if Blapy had arrived, but the sound had originated in the distant mountains. From the giant fortress nestled between a cluster of distant peaks.

Ruwen and the rest of the Adepts had crossed a third of the bridge when the gong sounded, and they slowed in surprise as all the demons dashed for the giant hands of the massive statues that held the bridge on their backs.

In just seconds, the entire bridge had cleared of demons and Ruwen glimpsed Echo almost completely across the bridge. Rung One trailed two hundred feet behind her, not able to match the speed of her Gem-Fortified body. Not sure what the gong signified, he didn't want to waste the opportunity of the clear bridge.

"Run!" Ruwen shouted.

Their group dashed forward, and it took all of Ruwen's self-control to not grab the slowest runners and carry them. Echo left the bridge and dashed into the grass as Ruwen and his Adepts reached the middle. A shudder passed through the structure.

"Bad luck on the timing of that call to prayer," Tarot said as he hovered on a deck of cards in front of Ruwen. "I'll see you on the other side. I hate getting wet."

With that, Tarot disappeared, and the bridge began dropping. It only took Ruwen a moment to understand their terrible situation. The statues supporting the bridge were massive golems, and as they kneeled in prayer, the bridge descended with them.

In just a few seconds, the river would surround them.

CHAPTER 18

"Who can't swim?" Ruwen shouted.

Three of the Adepts raised a hand and Ruwen looked at Sift, sending him a message with *Sphere of Influence*. *You take the one nearest you. I'll take the other two.* Remembering the underwater level in Blapy with the Octorse, Ruwen added one more item. *And don't pee in the water.*

Their current location put them directly between two sets of giant golem hands that supported the bridge. More bad luck. Demons covered the massive hands, and they looked down on the Bamboo Viper Adepts with mirth.

The hands stretched thirty feet above the bridge, and he quickly calculated the height of the massive golems, assuming they had human proportions, and arrived at two hundred eighty feet. The golems supported the bridge on their backs which meant when they kneeled, if they didn't keep their arms extended, the bridge would drop around ninety feet.

A drop that far seemed unlikely since the demons had bunched around the top ten feet of the fingers. That meant the bridge wouldn't sink more than twenty feet into the river.

Twenty feet underwater would make fighting vastly more difficult, especially against anything that lived in the water. The Adepts would lose most of their training advantage, which, Ruwen supposed, was the whole point.

Water covered Ruwen's feet, and its coldness surprised him. He guessed the temperature came from the river's source, the glaciers and snow-covered peaks in the distance.

"Form a line and grab the belt of the Adept in front of you," Ruwen shouted as he strode to the front with the two Adepts who couldn't swim.

Three pressure waves approached Ruwen and without looking, he snatched the first spear from the air and used it to swipe the two that followed.

As Ruwen's calves sank into the water, he gained a clearer picture of the river. Water transmitted waves much better than air, even if they ended up a little more distorted. The vibration of the lowering bridge, along with all the demons moving on the giant hands, made the immediate area a little blurry, but enough clarity remained to see over twenty creatures in the surrounding water, many of them circling the bridge to grab the unlucky few who remained.

Ruwen had planned to form a line and pull everyone forward at a pace that he'd hoped would keep them safe. Now, after seeing the density of the surrounding creatures, he knew that wouldn't work. He quickly needed another plan.

Golems, well most golems since Ruwen didn't know about Tarot, consisted of some type of stone or clay or other similar substance. They didn't feel pain, which mattered since Ruwen only had one idea, and it wasn't a good one.

Ruwen's plan also made him a hypocrite, as he'd just told Sift how the Adepts needed to harden in this furnace. But he couldn't shake the fact that their current situation likely resulted from his deal with Tarot, and he didn't want others to suffer because of his bad luck.

Ruwen didn't want to just finish Savage Island, he wanted to do it without losing any of his Clan. At least any of the ones that remained with him. The waters surrounding them would make that unlikely, as the lake's predators had perfected this feeding process and wouldn't give him the time to protect everyone.

What would give them a little time, however, was if they found something else to eat.

The water had reached Ruwen's thighs, and he turned to Sift. "Change of plans. Take my two non-swimmers, group up, and get ready."

"Ready for what?" Sift asked as the Adepts clustered around him.

"A hand."

Sift frowned as Ruwen turned and leaped fifty feet down the bridge, the water covering his lower legs making the jump more difficult than normal. He landed over one of the giant golems supporting the bridge. The golem had already submerged and only its hands remained visible as it cupped the bridge, holding it in place.

Demons covered the fingers above Ruwen, and they threw knives and other blades down on him. He ignored the weapons, knowing his natural Armor Class would protect him.

Ruwen ran a hand over the smooth surface of the golem's wrist and used his fifty-seven levels in Stonemason, gained by preparing New Eiru's city walls for war, to look for any weaknesses. He considered using other Abilities or Spells but wanted to stay as true to the Founders' wishes as he could. He traced a finger along a slight stress fracture as the water reached his waist and more blades rained down on him.

The water around the bridge frothed as the creatures' excitement for a meal increased. Ruwen focused on the massive wrist in front of him, and with a twist of his hips, slammed a fist into the hairline fractures running parallel to the bridge.

The demons above screamed as the massive hand wobbled

and then tilted toward the bridge. Ruwen raised his hands and stopped the fall, the demons above going quiet in shocked appreciation. Then with a surge of Diamond-Fortified strength, he pushed the hand outward, toward the river.

The demons shouted as the hand leaned over the water, and their frantic movements and scrambling added the extra force necessary for the hand to topple over and into the river.

A yellow-brown cable, like a three-foot tendon, still connected the broken hand to the arm below. With a knife-hand strike, Ruwen split the dense structure. He grabbed the tendon sticking out of the hand and shook it violently. More cries sounded as the demons, now in the river, desperately tried to hang on.

Ruwen lifted the hand and slammed it down, stunning many of the creatures nearby and shaking off the remaining demons. With a quick turn, he placed the hand on the bridge between himself and the Adepts, the fingers pointing to the sky.

The water had reached Ruwen's belly button, and he jumped across the bridge to the other hand. The demons there, knowing what would happen, tried even harder to stop him, but just as before, they lacked the strength or weapons to harm him.

Ruwen snapped this hand off at the wrist as well, although he had to punch twice, the water absorbing some of his force. The water had risen enough that the creatures had almost reached the Adepts. He slammed the now separated hand into the river, sending a shock wave and buying him a few seconds. Using his massive strength, he picked up the hand and slammed it three more times into the water, breaking the thumb off and creating giant tidal waves in the river.

Now clear of demons, Ruwen reversed the golem's hand and positioned it on top of the previous hand. The two hands now appeared folded in prayer, but more importantly, they stood almost twenty feet high. As the water reached his armpits, he hoped it allowed his brothers and sisters to survive.

Sift had understood Ruwen's intent and had already thrown the three non-swimmers onto the topmost hand, his Gold-Fortified strength making the throw trivial. The other Adepts quickly climbed out of the river. The hands should keep most of them out of the water.

Ruwen turned to face the far shore and check on Rung One's progress. To his dismay, they had not quite reached the shore and stood in the shallow water covering the bridge. An enemy Clan waited for them at the bridge's exit and the surrounding water had filled with hungry beasts.

Echo's speed had separated her from Rung One and she stood two hundred feet downstream from the bridge. She watched the six Adepts trapped on the bridge.

Ruwen could imagine the calculations going on in Echo's mind. The Adepts of Rung One held a terrible position, and to help them, she would need to attack the mass of enemy Clan fighters at the bridge's exit. Even with her Gem-Fortified body and superb fighting skills it would put her in danger, and the examples she'd witnessed growing up would make her decision a selfish one.

The water reached Ruwen's armpits as he watched Echo turn away from her Rung One team.

"Echodriel," Ruwen shouted, using the name he'd heard Madda use in the Black Pyramid.

Echo froze and slowly turned to face Ruwen. The water had reached his neck and multiple pressure waves approached him from the underwater beasts.

"Do better," Ruwen yelled and then sank under the water.

If Echo didn't go back and help her Rung, they would all die. Her Step skills were the only thing that could save them. And from experience, he didn't hold much hope for their survival.

A tentacle wrapped around Ruwen's waist. He grasped it with one hand and violently twisted his hips, ripping it from the beast's body. Three of the creatures aiming for him turned and attacked the bleeding creature.

Ruwen used the tentacle like a whip, snapping it in the water, creating vicious pressure waves, and stunning the surrounding monsters. He used the few seconds of safety to swim in between the cupped hands.

As the water creatures swam close to the giant hands, Ruwen attacked the largest ones, leaving the Adepts above to handle the smaller beasts.

A large flat creature approached and he pushed off the hand below, careful not to use too much force. He didn't want to destroy the only thing keeping the Adepts above out of the water.

Launching himself out of the cupped hands he shot through the water toward the fifty-foot plate-looking creature. As he passed through the monster's body, he spread his arms and legs, creating the largest hole possible, crippling the creature.

The water around Ruwen filled with blood from all the dead creatures and it drew more of the monsters. He hadn't thought that part through, but it didn't matter since he hadn't had another plan.

From the pressure waves Ruwen sensed, most of the beasts had turned toward him, which would give Rung One a sliver of hope to survive on their own. He prayed they would make it out of this situation alive.

The dead created a feeding frenzy for the other creatures, and even though Ruwen had attracted what felt like the entire river's deadly beasts, the abundance of food had slowed the attacks on Ruwen and the Adepts nearby.

The respite gave Ruwen time to think. Even with Echo's upbringing, he didn't understand the selfishness it took to let others die when you had the chance to save them. An uncomfortable feeling blossomed in his chest. His desire to save everyone created a weakness his enemies would exploit. It seemed unfair that the opposite side of the spectrum, total self-ishness, didn't have this vulnerability.

Swimming back to the cupped hands, Ruwen floated between the palms. For now, they'd created a ring of dead bodies to feed on, but that wouldn't last. He flattened his hand, as if telling someone to stop, and quickly pushed it outward in a palm strike, careful not to use his full strength. Using all his strength would vaporize the surrounding water, and he'd learned firsthand, when launching Uru's Third Temple out of a water-filled hole, the power of steam.

The compressed water traveled through the river like hardened spikes, causing damage like siege bolts. He launched them out of each side of the hands, creating more dead beasts farther from the bridge.

Small creatures swam above him, but from the bodies falling past him like rain, Sift and the Adepts had it under control.

They kept this up for five minutes when the bridge rose. Thirty seconds later, Ruwen's head cleared the surface, and he jumped out of the hands and onto the bridge, which now had a layer of bloody slime and shredded body parts.

Ruwen studied the Adepts above him. A few had significant injuries, but they all survived. With a heart full of dread, he turned to the far shore and found what he'd expected.

The bridge exit and surrounding water were empty. The Adepts of Rung One had died, either pulled down by the creatures in the water or overwhelmed by the enemies on the shore. Ruwen's throat tightened in grief and his shoulders slumped.

Ruwen would make that enemy Clan pay for killing his brothers and sisters, but he would need to find them first, as they had retreated after the bridge sank and disappeared.

"Famine!" Echo yelled.

Ruwen turned toward Echo's voice. She stood a thousand feet down the shoreline. The six Adepts of Rung One stood behind her.

Echo raised a hand over her shoulder, pointing an elbow at Ruwen in the rude gesture Sift also loved.

Echo turned and sprinted into the plain, the members of Rung One following.

Ruwen grinned.

Being wrong had never felt better.

CHAPTER 19

*E*cho had found the Bamboo Viper Clan portal ring, and Ruwen, Sift, and their twenty-four Adepts joined them three hours later. Once past the bridge, no one bothered them. Either the other Clans had witnessed what had happened on the bridge or word had spread. Regardless, the run across the plains toward the foothills resulted in no fights.

Echo avoided Ruwen, not even making eye contact with him. He wanted to say something to her, to congratulate her for doing the right thing, but his Wisdom stopped him. What she had done went against her nature and upbringing, which must have caused confusion and uncertainty. She certainly didn't look happy.

They spent an hour tending to the wounded, and then Ruwen insisted everyone rest for six hours while he kept watch. Tarot reappeared and Ruwen wondered what the Thieving Misfortune Golem had done while away. Probably thieving.

Sift flew high overhead, saying he needed to watch for approaching enemies, but Ruwen knew he just wanted to enjoy himself for a bit. In fact, the quest *That's Not a Number* had forced him to compliment Sift's flying to get rid of the constant taste of maple syrup caused by the Uneven debuff.

Ruwen focused on Sift high above and used *Sphere of Influence* to send him a message. *Tarot said he would give you a free reading because you take such great care of Shelly.*

Keep your golem away from my turtle.

They know each other from before. He might have stories about Shelly.

Sift remained silent for ten seconds. *Well, I guess that might be interesting.*

Come get your reading then.

I don't like cards and I already know my future. It's amazing.

Ruwen rolled his eyes. *Ignore the divination piece and do it for the three spells you get.*

I get spells?

Ruwen knew this would get Sift's attention. He always complained about the unfairness of Ruwen's spellcasting abilities. The grumbling had decreased since Sift had learned to use his soul to power things like flying, but Ruwen knew the opportunity to cast more would overcome Sift's natural reluctance.

Ruwen answered Sift's question. *Yes, you get three spells related to your cards. Once they're gone you can get another reading and get three new ones.*

Sift angled toward Ruwen and descended rapidly.

Ruwen did his best to hide a smile and glanced at Tarot who circled their position like a vulture looking for a corpse. He used *Sphere of Influence* again. *Can you do that reading for Sift now?*

Sure, Tarot replied as he altered course toward Ruwen.

In seconds they had both arrived. Sift stood next to Ruwen and Tarot floated in front of them on a deck of cards. Ruwen prepared to translate between the golem and Sift.

"Hey, little man," Sift said to Tarot.

Ruwen stared at Sift in disbelief. "You speak his language?"

Sift shrugged and glanced at Ruwen. "My parents made me

learn enough Sacred to read old scrolls and hold a conversation." Sift turned back to Tarot. "I heard you're handing out spells. Are they burnt?"

"Burnt?" Tarot asked.

"He means good," Ruwen offered.

Tarot sighed. "The spells always relate to the card, but the details are new every time."

"Is there a donut card?" Sift asked.

Tarot stared at Sift for three seconds before responding. "No."

"You need better cards."

Tarot rubbed his forehead. "This was a mistake."

"Welcome to my world," Ruwen responded.

"Ask your question," Tarot said to Sift.

"I—" Sift started.

"Don't waste this on your dumb bakery," Ruwen quickly interrupted.

"It's not dumb," Sift said. "You need to dream bigger, Starfield."

Ruwen and Tarot locked gazes, their mutual suffering a shared bond.

"Fine," Sift said. "I won't. I'll ask about Lylan."

"Wait till I tell her she was your second pick," Ruwen said.

Sift glared at Ruwen. "If I survive that, you will never be safe."

Ruwen grinned. "Still worth it."

Sift tapped his chin. "You know, you didn't mention Hamma once during your reading."

Ruwen froze, unable to argue without revealing why he'd asked the question he had. "You win. My lips are sealed."

"That's what I thought."

"Are we going to be here all day?" Tarot asked. "I have things to do."

Ruwen turned back to Tarot. "What could you possibly be doing."

Tarot glared at Ruwen. "I'm a busy golem, and this is a target-rich environment."

Ruwen immediately reached down and checked to make sure he still had his belt.

"Hey!" Sift yelled. "Stop doing that! Give my belt back."

Tarot shook his head as the dimensional portal over his stomach opened. He reached in and flicked Sift's white belt to him. "I took that like twenty minutes ago."

Sift snatched the belt from the air and quickly tied it around his waist. "I really don't like golems."

Tarot smiled, stepped off the deck of cards, and locked eyes with Sift. The golem hovered in the air and Ruwen wondered what powers the tiny creature possessed. "Ask your question, Sift the broken Sifter."

"I'm not broken," Sift replied. "I just don't sift like before."

Ruwen wondered if Sift ever regretted attaching his Air Meridian to his center when they'd left the Spirit Realm. It had allowed him to fly, which he had improved with his Soul magic, but came at the cost of reducing his sifting of spells and Energy by half. He took far more damage now than before.

"Plus," Sift said. "Now I can do this." He pursed his lips and whistled.

"Winter Wren," Tarot said.

Sift nodded at the golem. "I like you a little better."

"Do you know any other birds?" Ruwen asked, having heard the same bird whistle a dozen times.

Sift pointed at Ruwen and opened his mouth to respond.

Tarot shook his hands, stopping Sift. "You two run from topic to topic like chickens on mynthyl."

"Oh," Sift said, nodding knowingly. "You should ask Ruwen about chickens."

"Stop it!" Tarot said. "Ask your question already."

Sift rubbed his chin and narrowed his eyes in thought.

"I know nothing is going on in there," Ruwen said. "You're faking. Come on."

Sift glared at Ruwen. "Fine." Sift faced Tarot and placed a hand over his heart as he asked his question. "How is Lylan?"

The cards exploded outward, spinning rapidly. Tarot clenched his hand and the cards collapsed into pile, fighting with each other to enter the stack. He did this six more times before the deck went still in front of Sift's chest.

"Cut?" Tarot asked.

"Of course," Sift said. "I live with a bunch of Shades, and they're all cheaters." Sift considered the deck carefully and continued. "Never play cards with a Shade should be their first rule."

Sift carefully pulled the top card off and slid it onto the bottom. "Thin to win," He whispered and stood up straight. He clapped his hands. "Come on, baby worm biters need shoes."

Tarot rolled his eyes. "This is not gambling. Are you sure the Shades are cheating? You don't seem very good at this."

"Please, I let those thieves win."

Ruwen raised his hand. "Why do worms need shoes?"

"Stop it!" Tarot shouted again. "What is wrong with you two?"

Ruwen and Sift locked gazes for a second before Ruwen turned back to Tarot. "You'll need to be more specific because we don't have time to go over everything."

Sift pointed at Ruwen. "His issues take up most of the list."

Ruwen faced Sift to argue.

"Heavens below," Tarot said before Ruwen could speak. "I've never felt more misfortunate in my long life."

"I'm really good at advice," Sift said. "I'll think of something to cheer you up."

Tarot held up a tiny finger. "No."

Before Sift could respond, Tarot continued. He looked into

the sky and his voice grew louder. "Harken lost soul. You stare into the abyss. Prepare yourself for its gaze."

Like before most of the Adepts walked over to watch.

With a flourish Tarot spread his arms, and the cards exploded once again. They formed a circle of seventy-eight cards hovering in front of Sift.

Tarot continued in a loud voice. "I, Tarotmethiophelius, a Divine Fortune Golem forged from the mists of heaven, touching past, present, and future, offer these cards."

Tarot lowered his head and locked eyes with Sift. "Concentrate on the deck and choose three cards. Your reading awaits."

Sift immediately pointed at the first three cards.

"You heard me say concentrate, didn't you?" Tarot asked.

"I did," Sift said.

Tarot shook his head. "One, two, and three," Tarot said.

As Tarot uttered the numbers, the cards Sift had chosen glowed, softly and then brightly as white sparks engulfed them. They floated from their places in the circle to the center of the ring.

Sift grimaced as three miniature cards, identical to the ones floating before him appeared on his right wrist. He turned his wrist and studied the black, gold filigree-covered, cards.

Tarot raised his arm and the dimensional portal in his stomach opened. The remaining seventy-five cards flew into the portal, and the portal disappeared. The three glowing cards slowly lowered until they lay perpendicular between Sift and the floating Tarot.

Tarot pointed to the first of Sift's cards. "Lylan's situation," the golem intoned.

Sift hesitantly reached forward as if scared of what the card might reveal, and slowly flipped it over.

CHAPTER 20

*S*ift withdrew his hand and Ruwen studied the card. A massive tower filled the card, and he guessed it probably didn't bode well from the drawing. Lightning had struck the tower and its crown-shaped top tumbled downward. Flames emerged from the windows and smoke billowed from the tower's door. Two figures fell to the ground, their faces full of fear.

Tarot turned his attention from the card to Sift. "The Tower in its darkest forms represents danger, chaos, and violence, and in its most positive way, sudden change and revelation."

Sift leaned forward his voice serious. "Is Lylan in danger?"

"A single card does not a reading make," Tarot replied.

"What?"

"Turn your other cards," Ruwen said. "He needs to see how they interact to know."

Sift reached for the second card and Tarot spoke again. "Lylan's action."

Sift quickly turned the card and everyone leaned closer to see.

The card depicted a woman riding a massive black wyrm,

her hair streaming behind her as if traveling at great speed. Her face looked resolute and fearless.

"Fortitude," Tarot said. "Strength, courage, and calmness under pressure."

"That one's much better," Sift said.

Tarot continued. "The Tower and Fortitude together suggest Lylan has encountered hardship or sudden change but is facing it, not retreating. Fortitude also suggests she will succeed in her endeavor, although paired with the Tower the cost for that victory may be significant."

"What?" Sift asked, his voice rising. "She's going to get hurt?"

Tarot shrugged and pointed at the third card. "Lylan's outcome."

Sift immediately flipped the card.

A woman, her back bent under the burden of ten poles, strode forward. Her hair fell forward hiding her face, and her posture conveyed she might collapse at any moment.

Tarot spoke quietly. "The Ten of Wands. A heavy burden."

Sift looked up from the card and locked gazes with Tarot. The good-natured Sift had disappeared, and the all-business Sisen Sift had emerged. "What does it mean?"

"The Ten of Wands is interesting in this reading. Paired with the Tower its meaning becomes exhaustion and stress, but paired with Fortitude, it could mean achievement, although still with a heavy cost."

"And your opinion?" Sift asked softly.

Tarot closed his eyes and rubbed his chin in thought. Sift stood unnaturally still, as if preparing for an attack. Ruwen decided this had been a terrible idea.

Tarot spoke. "You chose the Tower first, meaning the danger to Lylan is significant and meaningful. The Tower's shadow falls on the next two cards. The most likely meaning is Lylan faces the danger head on and will not retreat, regardless of the consequences. The Ten of Wands so close to Fortitude hints at achievement, but the shadow of the Tower means it may come at a terrible cost."

"Might she die?" Sift asked softly.

"Possibly, but because Fortitude stands between the Tower and Ten of Wands probably not."

"But she could. And you think for sure she'll get hurt."

Tarot shrugged. "I'm uncertain."

"Does that happen often?" Ruwen asked.

Tarot shook his head. "Very few things cloud my sight."

"Is this an excuse to skip the fortune?" Sift asked.

Tarot rose into the air, stopping at Sift's eye level. "I will give you my reading but know Lylan has encountered something so powerful it warps my ability to see clearly."

"Like what?" Sift asked. "A god?"

"A few of them," Tarot said. "Possibly one of my brothers or sisters."

"Tell me," Sift said.

The deck of cards reappeared, and Tarot stepped on top of them. He moved the deck to the first card Sift had chosen, touched its edge, and repeated this with the other two cards.

Tarot and the deck of cards rose until he hovered directly across from Sift's eyes. The golem spread his arms and transformed into golden-silver metal. Just as before, light of the same color radiated from his body, and odd patterns flitted across his form.

With a somber voice, Tarot spoke. "I, Tarotmethiophelius, a Divine Fortune Golem forged from the mists of heaven, touching past, present, and future, offer this fortune. Sift Adda, Melody of the Stars, Champion of Champions, and Sage of Heaven, hear me. Lylan Keel, a thief among thieves, pierced and bound, drinks inside a tavern of despair. One coin, the price of hopelessness, pain, and regret, buys passage on a sinking ship laden with loyalty, love, and friendship. The Curator strides through an ancient doorway, determined to embrace the tide."

The golden-silver light faded, and Tarot fell to his knees.

The show complete the Adepts shuffled away, moving back to their resting spots.

Sift turned to Ruwen. "Let's go."

"What? Where?"

"Home. I need to help Lylan."

Ruwen's anxiety had increased during Tarot's reading. Danger to Lylan likely meant the same for Hamma. It probably involved the unstable situation in New Eiru. Ky had told him Bliz had faced multiple attacks. Had Hamma and Lylan found this same danger.

Ruwen held up his hands. "I want to talk first."

Sift swiped his hand down across his body. "No talking! Lylan needs me!"

"Let's start there," Ruwen said. "Does she need you?"

Sift frowned. "She's in danger."

"Probably," Ruwen responded gently. "Which means Hamma likely is as well."

That calmed Sift a little. He pointed at Ruwen. "Then why are we talking?"

Ruwen sighed. "Because Hamma and Lylan don't need us. I mean, they might. But you know better than I how capable they are. You saw it in Shelly for over a year. If trouble found them, they have the skills, intelligence, and power to handle it. They don't need us to save them. In fact, if you think about it, they're usually the ones saving us. If anyone should worry, it is Lylan." Ruwen paused and smiled. "And maybe Hamma a little as well. I do tend to make a mess of my life."

Sift closed his eyes for a few seconds and then locked gazes with Ruwen. "If something happens—"

Sift stopped and swallowed hard a couple of times. "I can't lose her again."

Ruwen put a hand on Sift's shoulder. "She has the world's best Healer with her. And to hurt Lylan they'd need to find her first, and then avoid all her blades. And we both know only a Step Master could do that."

"That's true," Sift said.

"Imagine the beating she'll give you if you leave the Step Trial, giving up your only chance to progress forward, just to find her sipping some of Ky's terrible peppermint tea."

Some of the tension in Sift disappeared. "That would be bad."

"We might need them, but they don't need us," Ruwen said. "Certainly not to protect them. That is a hard fact."

The last of the tension left Sift. "I'm worried."

"Me too, buddy. But let's trust them while we're here."

Sift pointed at Ruwen. "No more goofing off. Going forward we finish this trial as fast as possible. Promise me."

Ruwen nodded. "Okay."

A hint of happiness crossed Sift's face. He held up his right wrist and showed Ruwen the cards there. "I have three spells."

Ruwen smiled. "What do they do?"

"Let's see," Sift replied. "The Tower summons fire and lightning in a fifty-foot radius for five seconds. Fortitude adds five hundred to my Strength for ten seconds, and the Ten of Wands is an area of effect Exhaustion debuff to all enemies within fifteen feet."

"Those are great spells."

Sift grinned and turned to face Tarot. "Thanks for the game, Little Man." Then Sift launched himself straight up into the air.

Ruwen quickly used *Sphere of Influence* to speak with Sift, as he'd almost disappeared from sight. *Come back in a few hours. We can continue Rung Four's training until the Founders' show up.*

Sift didn't respond and Ruwen heard a distant thunderclap as Sift ripped the air apart with his passing.

With the Adepts mostly sleeping Ruwen paced around the low hill that held their portal stone. Thoughts of Hamma filled his mind. Despite his speech to Sift, worry knotted his stomach.

He really believed what he'd told Sift. Hamma and Lylan could take care of themselves. But Ruwen's enemies were gods and if they'd gone after his friends, they would need help.

But even that wasn't the true source of Ruwen's worry. It originated from a conversation in Shelly as they journeyed home, where he had promised to stop facing things alone and stop disappearing.

The day after his Ascendancy he remembered Hamma standing in the doorway of Ky's safehouse in Deepwell. He had just finished multiple time-compressed days in the Black Pyramid and, along with Sift, was headed for the Worker's Lodge to meet Big D and start the camping trip.

Ruwen closed his eyes and recalled that meeting.

Ruwen knocked softly on the door, not wanting to wake up anyone in the neighboring houses. He was about to knock again when the door opened a crack, and Hamma peeked through. The door flew open, and Hamma stepped forward.

"I'm so glad –" Ruwen started.

Hamma slapped him.

"You can't just disappear!" Hamma shouted. "Do you know how worried I was? I came back, and everyone was gone. I thought you'd died!"

Ruwen stood speechless as his cheek burned. Hamma hugged him, but before he could hug her back, she stepped away.

Ruwen refocused on the present. From the beginning, Hamma hated when people suddenly disappeared. She had no problems expressing her boundaries and what she considered acceptable. Another memory surfaced, this one shortly after they'd saved Sift from the ambush and had just arrived at the Worker's Lodge.

Hamma had wanted to know where all the things Ruwen had used to help save Sift's life had come from. It had taken loot, dearly-won in the Black Pyramid, to stave off Sift's death, and she'd noticed. She had, once again, been very clear about the consequences of lying. He recalled her words.

"Before you answer, I'll tell you this. It's been fun and terrifying hanging out with you. But I won't tolerate a liar. If you lie to me, then this is goodbye."

Ruwen smiled. Hamma didn't tolerate bad behavior, and her independence made walking away from a bad situation easy. He loved those things about her. His smile faltered as memories of the promises he'd made in Shelly surfaced. It had taken less than an hour, once they'd returned, for him to break his word to Hamma. Once again, he'd disappeared. Yes, it had been out of his control, but he recognized the pattern in himself, and he worried about the consequences.

Sift's reading made it clear that something had happened back home and while Ruwen had hidden his fear from Sift, it gnawed at him now. He would honor his promise to Sift and move through the rest of the trial as fast as possible.

Hamma deserved an explanation, and the longer it took, the worse the consequences might be.

CHAPTER 21

*S*ift reluctantly returned to the hilltop to train Rung Four. To Ruwen's surprise, all the Adepts joined their session except Echo. She sat alone, head down, and quiet. Once again, he resisted the urge to speak to her. After all, her disposition aura remained a vibrant red.

Sift moved between the rows of Adepts making corrections as he passed. Ruwen hid a smile as he thought about his best friend. Sift tried to keep his life simple: food, especially sweets, Lylan, and adventure. But hidden under that good-natured, live for today man stood a mixture of his parents.

Wisdom, not the dumb pastry quotes, but real advice poured out of Sift as he strode up and down the line. He balanced the serenity of his dad with the fierceness of his mom. Once again Ruwen felt awed at Sift's ability to add beauty to the Steps. He understood a language few others did, and the Steps gave it voice.

"Are you going to stand there all night?" Sift asked Ruwen.

"Sorry, just thinking."

"Shocker. How about you do that on your own time."

Ruwen once again hid a smile. "Yes, Sisen."

Only when the Founders and the Addas stepped out of the portal stone did everyone stop practicing. Dawn had arrived and everyone quickly formed their Rungs, standing at attention.

Ruwen stood in his usual place at the rear and Sift stepped up beside him.

"Tarot?" Ruwen asked under his voice.

The Thieving Misfortune Golem squirmed on the top of Ruwen's head. "Yeah?"

"Please give Sift his belt back. I don't want him to get into trouble with the Founders. Or his parents."

"That's no fun."

"True, but you'll have plenty of opportunities later when the consequences aren't as serious."

Tarot didn't respond but a second later Sift's white belt launched outward, straight for Sift's head.

Sift snatched the belt from the air and turned toward Ruwen. "I am going to smush you, little man."

"What is smush?" Tarot asked Ruwen.

"It's like an extra tight hug," Ruwen said, not wanting to start a fight right now.

"Oh, I don't like physical contact."

"You should avoid Sift then, as he really wants to hug you."

Sift quickly retied his belt and kept one hand on it.

The taste of maple syrup filled Ruwen's mouth, and he glanced at Sift. "The skill differences between the Rungs have narrowed a lot. They're almost…"

Ruwen trailed off, praying Sift would say "even."

Sift nodded. "Balanced. I do good work. You helped a little too, I guess."

Ruwen frowned. "A little? I did just as much. In fact, we helped the same and are…"

Once again Ruwen paused, trying to get Sift to say "even."

"Fine, we're equal then."

Ruwen's skin flushed, and he prayed the quest would accept

"equal." He had never gotten so close before. His shoulders slumped as the debuff Uneven remained.

"You don't have to cry about it," Sift said, mistaking Ruwen's reaction. "If it's that important to you, let's agree you did more."

Ruwen shook his head, giving up on the quest for the day. "No, you're right. You have a natural way with the Steps I can't match. Others sense it, too."

As the maple taste faded, Sift smiled. "Thanks, that's nice to hear."

The Founders and Addas had remained silent as Ruwen and Sift whispered.

Dusk stepped forward. "It fills my heart with joy to see all of you. I thought perhaps you met no resistance, but I see injuries among you. Please, someone, explain."

No one spoke for ten seconds and then a woman in Rung One cleared her throat and bowed. "Rung One would have all died. Most certainly." She pointed at Echo. "But Echo saved us. She destroyed a thirty-member Clan by herself. Then fought the beasts in the water as we struggled to reach the shore." The woman paused a moment and turned to Echo. "It is the bravest thing I've ever seen."

Dusk gave a small bow to the woman. "Thank you for speaking." Dusk moved to stand in front of Echo and Thorn and Mist joined her. "We owe you a debt of gratitude, Sister. Never in our past has an entire cohort reached the river portal intact. You have made history."

Echo swallowed hard three times before speaking. "It wasn't my idea."

"But they were your actions?" Thorn asked.

After a moment Echo nodded.

"Then you deserve the honor," Mist said.

All three Founders bowed deeply to Echo, and she returned it.

Dusk stood and looked around. "Were you all with Rung One?"

Prythus bowed. "No, we remained trapped in the middle of the bridge when it sank."

"Oh, that was rotten luck," Thorn said.

"Thanks for that," Ruwen whispered to Tarot.

"I heard hardship makes you a better person," Tarot replied.

"Do you believe that?"

"Of course not. Hardship only makes you miserable."

"That's just great."

Dusk spoke. "I am shocked anyone lived. How did you endure that?"

All the Adepts of Rung Two, Three, and Four turned to look at Ruwen.

Ruwen bowed and when he stood, he replied. "A bridge golem gave us a hand."

"Two actually," Sift added.

"Interesting," Mist said. "They've never involved themselves before."

Thorn continued. "Did you use magic to gain their help?"

Ruwen had used his Diamond Fortified strength, but that didn't count since it had nothing to do with casting spells or using an ability.

"No magic," Ruwen replied. "Just a superb group of Bamboo Viper Step fighters. Everyone did their part to keep themselves and their brothers and sisters alive."

When Ruwen didn't add any details, Dusk spoke. "What an inspiring...and vague, description of this miracle."

"Sorry," Ruwen said. "I spent most of the fight underwater. Sift and the Adepts faced the dangers above."

Dusk and her sisters bowed deeply again, and everyone returned it.

"The Viper gives us fangs," Dusk said as the sun climbed fully into the sky. "But Bamboo demonstrates the power of the grove.

Our greatest strength comes when we stand together. Well done, Adepts. This is a proud moment for our Clan."

Dusk stepped back to stand between her sisters and pointed at the portal stone. "The second trial awaits. We will speak again on the other side."

Madda nodded at Echo and she strode forward and through the portal, Rung One right behind her.

As the rest of the Adepts followed, Sift leaned over and whispered. "Tarot called me a champion. And he can see the future, right?"

Ruwen sighed. He'd hoped Sift had missed that. "I guess."

Sift held up a finger. "Champion of Champions, actually."

"Probably just being dramatic."

Sift smiled and looked at the distant fortress nestled in the mountain peaks. "It has a Champion's Throne."

"I don't think you should jump to conclusions."

Sift shrugged. "It's your fortune teller golem."

"Misfortune," Ruwen muttered, knowing where this conversation was headed.

"It is my destiny."

"Uru, help me. You were just in a hurry to get home."

Sift grew serious as he remained focused on the distant stronghold. "Right. Lylan comes first. But if we get a chance, we give it a go. Okay?"

Sift turned toward Ruwen and they locked eyes. Ruwen didn't know what the future held, but he had no intention of going anywhere near the distant fortress, so this really didn't matter. "I guess. But only if it's close."

Sift grinned. "Right. It would really take some *bad luck* to end up there."

Ruwen frowned at Sift's observation. Ruwen should now assume anything that could go wrong, would.

Madda cleared her throat and Ruwen and Sift returned their attention to the portal hilltop. All the Adepts had passed through the portal and the Founders and Grandmasters studied Ruwen and Sift. None of them looked pleased by the delay.

"This is why you shouldn't argue about my destiny," Sift whispered and strode toward the portal.

Ruwen gave the adults an apologetic smile and bowed. Worried they might want to talk, he marched quickly behind Sift. The second trial awaited.

CHAPTER 22

*R*uwen stepped through the portal already knowing they would arrive on the same planet as the first trial. He had memorized the previous gate runes and recognized the symbol for this world. The location for the second trial, however, had changed drastically. The other Adepts had grouped by Rung in a small dirt clearing, and as Ruwen strode toward Sift, he studied this new location.

They stood on a thousand-foot-wide mound shaped like a plateau, and over fifty tents, most of them small, flapped in a gentle breeze as if breathing. A deep canyon circled them, separating their location from the desert-like plain that stretched to the horizon on all sides. Dry air swirled around Ruwen, the wind carrying particles of sand.

The slope from the canyon bottom to the plain above contained hundreds, maybe thousands, of small chests. Ruwen turned in a circle, confirming the chests continued around the entire circle.

"It's like a giant donut," Sift said. "I think I'll like this trial."

Before Ruwen could reply, the Founders and Addas arrived through the gate rune portal. Having just embarrassed himself with a lack of focus, he decided his response to Sift could wait.

"Before we begin the second Master's trial," Mist said. "We will ask you each four questions."

Thorn continued. "We will repeat these questions before your final trial."

"There are no wrong answers," Dusk said. "But your responses reveal how deeply you understand the philosophy of our Clan."

"No one told me about a pop quiz," Sift whispered.

Ruwen kept his eyes on the Founders but whispered back. "I like tests."

"Figures, you weirdo."

The Founders strode to one of the larger tents and Madda addressed them. "Meditate on the mysteries until your turn."

Everyone sat cross-legged and Padda motioned to Echo. She stood and followed the Founders.

A few seconds later, Madda appeared in front of Ruwen and Sift.

Madda squatted and whispered to Sift. "Did you roll around in a fire?"

Sift looked down at his scorched clothes. "Air friction."

"The bridge golems are controlled by the Champion," Madda said. "I saw your 'helping hands,' and it will bring his ire. You've made future stops there more dangerous because of it."

Sift locked eyes with his mom. "It saved our lives. So the future can eat my elbow."

Madda frowned.

Sift, unaffected by his mom's displeasure, continued. He pointed a thumb at Ruwen. "Nobody thinks better under pressure than this grump. He saved us."

Ruwen turned to Sift. "Thanks."

Sift nodded. "I mean, *I* could have survived by myself, but for sure you rescued the others."

"Really," Ruwen asked. "How?"

Sift held up a finger for each point as he spoke. "I'm a great swimmer, have experience fighting underwater, and I know a special trick to confuse my enemies."

"Peeing in that river would not have saved you," Ruwen said.

"I bet—" Sift started.

Madda slashed her hand through the air. "Enough. You two give me a headache. Now meditate."

Madda marched away and twenty seconds later, quiet snoring came from Sift as he entered his special ninth-level meditation. Or what everyone else called a nap.

Ruwen considered his first meeting with the Founders during his Journeyman trial. They had moved around him like panthers circling a stunned rabbit. Many things had changed since then, and he'd turned into a panther himself. Thorn and Mist had asked him four questions at that first encounter.

What had the Steps taught him?

Which was the most important Step?

What was his goal?

How many Steps were there?

As Padda fetched the Adepts one by one, Ruwen contemplated his past answers. For what the Steps taught him, he'd demonstrated the Viper and Bamboo forms for Thorn and Mist. His answer to the most important Step had been *the one that took him to his goals.* They had immediately asked him about his goal, and he'd replied *balance.* For the final question, they'd asked how many Steps the forms contained, and he'd responded with *none.*

Ruwen felt the most confident about the last two questions. Balance remained his goal and the symmetry of the Steps resulted in the same thing as doing nothing. He didn't plan on changing those. For the first two, however, he had discovered a different perspective.

Ruwen nudged Sift as Padda approached.

"Thanks," Sift whispered, keeping his eyes closed.

Padda stopped in front of Sift. "Adept, it is time."

Sift immediately stood and followed his dad toward the Founders.

Ruwen focused on the first question. What had the Steps taught him? As he contemplated the insight the Steps had revealed, they had one thing in common: immense complexity and multiple layers. Only time and building on previous knowledge had led to his success. Some things could not be rushed. The irony of his conclusion made his mind and chest ache.

The second question, asking for the most important Step, Ruwen struggled to answer. He had responded with *goals* the last time, but that didn't feel right.

Unsurprisingly, Padda and Sift had already started their return. As Ruwen expected, Sift's answers had taken almost no time at all. Sift needed Step philosophy like the ocean needed fish.

Ruwen had short answers as well, but for the opposite reason. He'd devoted immense thought to this, just like he did with everything. Too much thought, probably, but he couldn't change his identity. In fact, it provided the answer for the most important Step.

"Adept," Padda said. "It is time."

Ruwen stood and followed Padda, matching the man's serene stride. Just being near Padda relaxed Ruwen, like hearing a stream or listening to the rain.

"Thank you for saving them," Padda whispered as they walked. "Your strength is your heart, Adept."

Before Ruwen could respond, they stepped into the tent. The Founders sat cross-legged in the middle of the large open area. Ruwen and Padda bowed, and the Bamboo Grandmaster turned and left.

The ground here consisted of hard-packed dirt, but Ruwen easily detected the trail left by the other Adepts, and without being told, strode to a place five feet in front of the Founders. He sat and mirrored their posture.

"You have grown since our last meeting," Mist said.

"Unnaturally fast," Thorn added.

Ruwen gave a curt nod. "Extreme methods, obsession, and intense focus created many learning opportunities."

"You are a mystery to us, Adept," Mist said. "Silence and darkness fill you."

Ruwen had spent time alone in the deep icy darkness of the far universe. He knew exactly what true silence sounded like. Despite his best efforts, his soul and its light, remained trapped. Bound by his Ascendancy to Uru and imprisoned by the tattoo she'd placed over him like a blanket before his birth.

"I also hear the deafening silence," Ruwen replied.

"This is not the place for such a conversation," Dusk said.

Mist and Thorn nodded.

"How many Steps are there?" Dusk asked.

"None," Ruwen answered.

"What is your goal?" Mist asked.

Ruwen locked eyes with her. "Balance."

"What have the Steps taught you?" Thorn asked.

Ruwen faced Thorn but avoided locking gazes with the woman. Her eyes had a hypnotic ability that he wanted to avoid. Last time he had demonstrated the forms, but he took it further this time. The Steps, with all their complexity and slow revelations, had taught him a painful lesson. One he'd ignored and would ignore again.

Ruwen sighed. "The Steps have taught me patience."

"Ironic," Thorn replied.

Ruwen nodded. "I am mindful of my hypocrisy."

Ruwen valued the mysteries the Steps revealed, but with the stakes so high, not everyone could afford the time required to reach their potential. He needed powerful allies for the battles to come, but he kept all this to himself.

Dusk asked the final question. "What is the most important Step?"

One thing had motivated Ruwen his entire life. It had propelled every action, and the Steps were no different. "The Step toward knowledge."

Ruwen's Diamond Fortified senses and one hundred eighty-eight percent Perception allowed him to detect a slight disappointment in Dusk's expression. His answer had been close, but not the one she'd wanted or expected.

"Thank you, Adept," Dusk said. "You may leave."

Ruwen stood, bowed, and marched back toward the other Adepts. He had come so far, but there remained something left to learn, and he'd have one more attempt to get it right.

CHAPTER 23

*T*he Founders informed them the trial would start in the morning and everyone should find a tent for the night. One of the large tents provided food and water and another water for bathing. An hour after their arrival, everyone had eaten and changed back into normal attire. Ruwen and Sift spent the rest of the day training all the Adepts but Echo, who paced around the edge of their encampment like a caged lion.

After everyone went to sleep for the night, Ruwen walked away from the tents and sat at the edge of the plateau. Worn paths covered the slope to the canyon bottom like rain down a window. Tomorrow the Founders would explain the trial and he could focus on it more effectively when he had all the information.

Ruwen closed his eyes and entered the Fortress in his mind. He materialized at the base of the Citadel, and a blue beam extended into the sky from the top of the spire, disappearing into the shield that surrounded the mountain in a bubble. With Kholy's departure to stay with Blapy in the Third Secret, the shield remained significantly dimmer and likely less powerful.

The city below no longer displayed any damage from

Ruwen's use of the sixth rune. The Narrators had continued to expand, and the city now spread in a circle inside both the second and third walls.

The horizon still held a dark red glow from the damage Ruwen had done to his mind and body while smearing with the Sixth Rune, but it too had dimmed a little. Thankfully, he no longer felt the pain from that damage. The plain below looked brand new and all the defenses appeared whole. Thousands and thousands of Narrators, along with their word, sentence, and paragraph followers, moved briskly on business only they knew. The sea of letters appeared calm, the boats in the ocean floating peacefully.

Ruwen frowned at a ring of new islands halfway to the horizon. They all had glowing red tops.

"Are those volcanoes?" Ruwen asked out loud. To his surprise, someone answered.

"Yes," Sivart responded. "We are channeling the damage here."

Ruwen turned toward the Narrator. "Is that safe?"

Sivart hovered next to Ruwen, his gaze locked on the distant islands. "Their purpose is twofold. It relieves the stress damage in your mind, speeding your recovery, and produces the energy to create new islands. Soon a ring of mountains will surround us, and our sea will become a sheltered bay."

Ruwen wanted to argue about the danger and expansion but decided to keep his thoughts to himself. Sivart embodied the wisdom gained from generations of calculated risk and reward. It was the reason Ruwen had come here tonight. He couldn't do everything himself and needed to trust the people he put in leadership positions to do the right thing.

"Thank you, Sivart. I appreciate your efforts."

Sivart stood up straight, faced Ruwen, and placed his arms across his chest, making an "x." He dropped his arms and spoke sincerely. "Trust is a jewel no treasure can buy."

Ruwen nodded at Sivart, accepting the Narrator's gratitude. "I dropped by for two reasons."

"Overlord and Uruziel?" Sivart asked.

"Yes, that's the first reason. Have you found any hint of them?"

"I have deployed scouts around your Core, throughout your pathways, and in every Meridian. Boats float at the edges of our sea and sentries circle the sky above. If they so much as whisper, we will hear them."

Ruwen's shoulders sank. He missed Overlord far more than he'd expected. The debuff Unworthy Vessel, caused by holding Uruziel's Divine fragment in his mind, still produced five damage per second, so he knew she still lived. At least that's what he hoped it meant. The possibility existed that the fragment triggered damage even if Uruziel had died.

Ruwen pushed those thoughts away. They served no purpose but to worry him, and he had other things needing attention. "Again, my thanks, and I appreciate the thoroughness."

"The second item?" Sivart asked.

"I recently finished two minor battles, and I hoped you could assess my choices."

"A word between Generals saves a dozen lives."

Ruwen smiled. "I'll take that as a yes."

Ruwen spent the next few minutes describing the hilltop battle after the Adepts had arrived on Savage Island, and the fight to cross the bridge. Sivart listened carefully, asking detailed questions about the enemy's positions and compositions. Ruwen wished Rami were here to just show Sivart the details.

Providing descriptions actually helped Ruwen. The questions Sivart asked served as a teaching method by educating Ruwen on what to look for in the future without embarrassing him about everything he'd overlooked. The subtle and emotionally sophisticated method Sivart used to pass on knowledge shocked Ruwen. It forced him to consider, once again, how far these constructs had grown.

After Sivart finished all his questions, he hovered around the battlement as if pacing. Two minutes later, the Narrator stopped and faced Ruwen.

"On the hilltop," Sivart said. "You displayed your usual tactical brilliance. My only suggestion would have been to keep one or two Adepts in a third line to support any sudden incursion through the first two lines."

Ruwen nodded in agreement. That small suggestion sat on top of the mountain of information Sivart had provided with his questions about enemy composition, weapons, and spacing.

Sivart continued. "The bridge highlights one of your many strategic failures."

Ruwen didn't flinch at the harsh words. He wanted to improve, and he knew Sivart only spoke the truth.

"You are impatient," Sivart said. "One of the few resources you had in abundance on that hilltop was time, and you used none of it. If you had waited even an hour, the bridge sinking into the river would not have surprised you. It is a tactical miracle you survived in the water with non-aquatic troops."

"Agreed," Ruwen replied. "Rushing forward was a mistake."

"I also question two other decisions." Sivart held up two fingers shaped like daggers. "Why make killing your adversaries an option instead of a directive, and why handicap yourself by not using all your resources?"

"I'll answer the second question first," Ruwen replied. "I assume by resources you mean my spells and abilities."

Sivart nodded.

"The Founders wanted us to avoid the use of such things," Ruwen said. "They view it as a crutch."

"So your pride prevented you."

"What? Of course not. Why do you say that?"

"Either you believed so strongly in your non-magical abilities that you only used them, or you worried what the Founders would think of you if you employed magic. In both cases, the root of that is your ego."

Ruwen forced his anger down. "I was only following directions."

Sivart shook his head. "To preserve his soldiers, a general uses *all* his resources. Inevitably, conserving one resource results in the waste of another. It is foolish."

Ruwen remained silent, absorbing Sivart's words.

"Do not mistake me," Sivart said. "Pride is not always negative. You demonstrated on the bridge, and in the water, that your decision had justification. Possibly even merit."

Ruwen eventually nodded. "But regardless, it carried a higher risk. A higher risk to my soldiers."

"Correct. And your job as a leader is to minimize the risk to your followers."

Ruwen sighed and studied the distant volcanoes for a few seconds. "I understand and will think on this. I honestly wanted to follow the rules, but I can sense other motivations inside myself, including pride. Thank you for your insight."

They stood silently together for a minute as Ruwen gathered his thoughts. Sivart had wanted to know why Ruwen had prioritized stuns and injuries over killing while fighting to cross the bridge, and that question pointed to the center of a raging battle inside himself.

Finally, Ruwen forced himself to speak. "Honestly, Sivart, I'm worried that I'll begin to enjoy killing. There is a part of me that rejoices in the use of destructive power, and it feeds on carnage and slaughter."

Ruwen looked down as memories of the Infernal Realm surfaced. After a moment, he forced himself to lock eyes with Sivart. He did his best to ignore the slowly spinning swords that made up the Narrator's pupils. "I have avoided asking your opinion of my actions in the Infernal Realm, but now realize that is foolish. We can discuss that in detail shortly, but I want to highlight my point with an example."

Once again Ruwen sighed deeply, feeling the emotions he'd kept buried. "When I escaped the trap the demons had created for me, I faced an entire army. True to my beliefs, I warned them about the danger they faced. I asked for their help, knowing Lalquinrial had trapped them there as well. I pleaded with them to heed my words and help me leave. They refused."

Sivart and Ruwen stood in silence for a few seconds and Ruwen's gaze returned to the sea. He continued in a whisper. "Without any more thought, Overlord and I destroyed tens and tens of thousands of them. We even made a game out of finishing first." Ruwen clenched his hand. "The more power I gain, the quicker I seem to use it. It makes me whipsaw between mercy and destruction." He turned back to Sivart. "I struggle to find the balance between necessity and desire."

Sivart studied Ruwen before facing the battlement and the sea. "We are fortunate. Such introspection and conflict will shape you into a great leader. The balance you seek is difficult." Sivart hovered quietly for a few moments and then continued. "A wise general cages his tigers and brings them to battle. He does not leave them behind out of fear. They are a tool, no different from a swordsman or a cannon or a healer."

Sivart faced Ruwen and crossed his arms over his chest in a salute. "My humble advice is to stop fearing the beast. A craftsman can favor a tool, use it too often even, but it will never consume him. Emotions like fear, guilt, and desire have no meaning with a device."

Ruwen nodded, overcome by Sivart's logic and insight.

Sivart returned the nod and faced the ocean again. "If you leave the tigers behind, your soldiers pay the price."

CHAPTER 24

*R*uwen and Sivart spent the rest of the night discussing Ruwen's various fights in the Infernal Realm. Once Overlord returned, or Ruwen reunited with Rami, he would show the fights to Sivart instead of just describing them.

Even with just the descriptions, Sivart provided valuable advice on hundreds of alternatives. They discussed the hypothetical situations, and it reminded Ruwen of an advanced version of the strategy talks he'd had with Rami while studying his Steps in the Spirit Realm.

Ruwen left his mind and returned to the Master's trial as the predawn light fought to overcome the horizon. Minimized notifications had appeared overnight, and he opened them, pausing on the last one of each type.

Shing!
You have advanced a skill!
Skill: *Strategy*
Level: *35*
Effect: *Increase Intelligence by 17.5%.*

172

Shing!
You have advanced a skill!
Skill: *Tactics*
Level: *39*
Effect: *Increase Wisdom by 19.5%.*

The battles Ruwen had fought recently hadn't raised the Strategy or Tactics skills, but after discussing those battles with Sivart, he'd gained multiple levels in each. He wondered if the trick to leveling these skills required not only experience but discussion and contemplation. Going forward, he would make time to do that with Sivart.

Ruwen had gained six levels in Strategy, which provided an additional three percent bonus to his Intelligence, and the three levels in Tactics increased his Wisdom by one and a half percent. The passive from Rami's second Codex of Perception doubled all of Ruwen's mental skills, resulting in nine extra points in Intelligence and three in Wisdom. These skills leveled slowly, but with his new process, he hoped that would change.

The camp remained quiet, and Ruwen felt much better after his discussion with Sivart. Not knowing when the Founders planned on starting the second trial, and not wanting to waste time, he opened his Void Band and removed something he hadn't used in far too long.

Ruwen ran his index finger around the edges of the Collector Novice Manual. The brown book had a nice hefty weight, and he fanned the pages. The manual contained meticulous drawings, many in color, and all with detailed descriptions.

Ruwen opened his map and enabled the Resource flag. A few scattered dots appeared on his display, and he strode toward the closest one, which lay on the canyon floor.

The way down had far too many paths. All of them went straight down and they covered the entire slope, which made little sense to Ruwen. Not a single path cut sideways or meandered at all. Another mystery, just like the small chests on the opposite hillside. They'd likely learn the answer to both in the next couple of hours.

As Ruwen moved deeper into the canyon, the darkness took hold again, and he altered his vision to compensate, keeping everything visible. Sift's card fortune had increased Ruwen's worries about Hamma and Lylan and the trouble they'd found. Concern for them opened a floodgate, and anxiety about his parents, Tremine, Bliz, Big D, and the entire country swirled in his thoughts.

Big D's problem with the crime lord in New Eiru would be trivial to handle as soon as Ruwen returned. Removing that threat should make calming the country easier and an agreement between the factions should form quickly. Hopefully, his parents and Tremine would be back and Bliz kept himself and his bar safe for a little longer.

Ruwen shook the thoughts away as they solved nothing and only caused apprehension. He reached the bottom of the canyon and stopped, although the path continued straight up the other side, ending at a small chest halfway to the top.

Walking along the bottom of the canyon, Ruwen almost missed the small cactus his map had marked. He kneeled and studied the small plant. The green stems looked like long fingers, and thin yellow spikes surrounded them like armor. He tried to find it in the Collector Novice Manual, but after a minute admitted defeat. This manual probably only highlighted items on Grave.

Ruwen spent two minutes reading how to harvest different types of cacti and found the process similar between them all. Setting the book on the ground, he used twenty Mana on *Analyze*.

Target: *Limb Sticker*
Type: *Resource*

Components: *Organics, Minerals*
Health: *Piercing risk, hallucinogenic*
Alchemy: *Therapeutic, Pleasure, Poison*
Uses: *Wax, Water, Numbness Tonic, Potion of Colors, Nightfall Elixir*

The little cactus had a lot of uses, and Ruwen guessed Fractal would love this for his plant garden. He cast *Kindling* for two Energy per second, and a blade of condensed air extended from his right hand.

Carefully, Ruwen grabbed one of the spikey fingers, and used his air blade to slice it off at the base. He had just learned that collecting the entire plant was unnecessary with cacti, and they would regrow from a partial piece. He opened his Void Band and dropped the cutting inside, accepting the tiny Energy penalty to keep it alive.

Ruwen dismissed the air blade, retrieved the book, and strode to the next dot on his map.

During the next hour, Ruwen harvested nine more Limb Stickers. The rocks in the canyon didn't differ from the common ones on Grave, other than many had the shape of perfect spheres.

What could have caused such uniform erosion? Had a river run through the canyon, tumbling the stones into spheres, or possibly an animal that lived here produced them? While interesting, Ruwen left them alone and continued his search for items of value. He didn't detect any mineral concentrations or elements, so he contented himself with collecting the cacti.

When the sun had climbed enough to brighten half the hillside, Ruwen heard and sensed the vibrations of the Adepts waking in the camp. He had already returned the book to Inventory and, dismissing the *Kindling* spell for the last time, headed up the hill toward camp.

Ruwen opened the notifications his gathering had generated.

Shing!
You have advanced a skill!
Skill: *Herbalism*
Level: *16*
Effect: *Increase harvest speed by 32%. Increase harvest yield by 16%.*

Shing!
You have advanced a skill!
Skill: *Prospecting*
Level: *7*
Effect: *Increase chance of discovering plants, gems, ores, minerals, and other collectibles by 7%.*

Shing!
You have advanced a skill!
Skill: *Taxonomy*
Level: *8*
Effect: *Increase identification of plants, gems, ores, minerals, and other collectibles by 8%.*

It felt good to level these basic skills. Ruwen's life had made finding time for such things hard. He left the Resource option selected for now since the low concentrations of valuable rocks, metals, and plants didn't interfere with the map's display.

Ruwen crested the hill and strode toward the tents. Tarot shot toward him like a miniature crossbow bolt, riding on an air sled made from cards. The golem dismissed his sled at the last moment and crashed into Ruwen's hair.

Ruwen held out his hand.

"What?" Tarot asked.

"You know what."

Three seconds later, a white belt dropped into Ruwen's hand, and he turned toward the heartbeat he recognized as

Sift's. Adepts bowed to him as he passed, and he returned each, slowing his progress.

Pushing the tent flap aside, Ruwen found Sift still sleeping.

Ruwen lightly kicked the cot, but Sift's snoring didn't even pause. Ruwen shook his head and stepped forward, flicking Sift on the forehead. Sift sleepily waved his hand, as if brushing a fly away, and turned away from Ruwen.

While Ruwen couldn't sleep anymore, Sift still managed it once in a while, and when he did, he slept like the dead. Ruwen went through a checklist of items he could drop on the sleeping Sift from Inventory: oil, water, rocks, dirt, lake sludge, minor acid of dissolving, or maybe even Ink Lord Numarrow's body.

The Uneven debuff appeared along with the taste of maple syrup and it gave Ruwen an idea.

"Pancakes," Ruwen whispered.

Sift sat up quickly and had his feet on the ground before noticing Ruwen. Ruwen threw the white belt at Sift and he snatched it from the air.

"Your golem is a menace," Sift said rubbing his eyes. He grabbed his dimensional bag and dropped the belt into the top. "Is breakfast over? I'm hungry for pancakes."

CHAPTER 25

$\mathcal{R}$uwen studied the Founders in the morning light. They stood in front of the Adepts, who had assembled in their Rungs. Ruwen and Sift stood in their usual place behind Rung Four.

Mist held up a thumb sized metal key. "Every Adept will receive a key. You may open one chest per day."

Thorn pointed to the opposite hillside with all the chests. "One chest contains the trial token for this level. We remain here until someone retrieves it."

The Adepts didn't fidget, their training prevented that, but many of their hearts pounded loudly. Thousands of chests scattered the slope, and it could take months to find the correct one.

"Once you've chosen a chest," Mist said. "Use your key to open it and view its contents. To remove your key, you must close the lid."

Thorn waved a finger. "You may not leave markers or use any mechanism to indicate a chest has already been checked."

Sift whistled softly, immediately coming to the same conclusion as Ruwen. If the lids remained open, others would know not to waste their one daily choice on it. By keeping the lids closed, the trial became magnitudes more difficult to solve.

"They want us to work together," Ruwen whispered.

"Ahh," Sift said, understanding.

The difference between this trial taking a month or taking a year hinged on how well they worked together. If every Rung revealed what chests they'd opened, the other Rungs could avoid them. Ruwen could appreciate the team building aspect of that strategy, but immediately found the issue with working together. What Rung, if they worked together, would get the trial token and its associated relic tokens.

If a Rung worked alone and found the trial token, it guaranteed each member of their Rung a relic token. If all four Rungs worked together and divided the eventual relic tokens evenly, each Rung would only get two. That left seventy-five percent of the Adepts with nothing.

"This is a devious trial," Ruwen whispered.

Sift had come to the same conclusion. "If one group splinters off, everyone will need to protect their choices from spying eyes."

"Oh," Dusk said, as if just remembering. "Some chests are not what they seem, and some contain very unpleasant items. Please use caution."

Most of the Adepts now had rapid heartbeats as they pieced together the same scenarios.

The Founders bowed, and the Adepts returned it.

Mist pointed to a table with thirty-three keys. "Contemplate the mysteries and let your Steps guide you."

With those last words, the Founders turned and reentered their large tent. Ruwen hadn't seen the Addas that morning, so it left the Adepts alone.

Prythus stepped away from Rung Four and faced the other Rungs. "We should work together."

"Easy for you to say," Echo said. "You already have relics. Will you give up your share?"

Prythus bit his lip and didn't answer.

Nymthus spoke up. "If we don't work together, it could literally take us years to finish."

Echo shrugged. "I'm not in a hurry."

"We are," Sift whispered to Ruwen.

Ruwen sensed an air disturbance coming from the ravine and jumped the fifty feet to the edge. He looked down to find fog filling the canyon. The fact he could still see the ground meant it wasn't too dense, but it would severely hinder anyone more than a few hundred feet away.

Instead of jumping back to the Adepts, Ruwen walked back, giving himself a few seconds to consider the options. As he neared the group, they stopped arguing and turned toward him.

Prythus asked what they all wondered. "What's in the canyon?"

"Fog," Ruwen replied. He locked eyes with Echo. "Using observers to watch the other Rungs will require them to remain close. Certainly within easy sight of the competing Rung."

Echo's heart rate had never varied, but she bit her lip in frustration. She pointed at Rung Four. "They already have relics. Rung One should get their keys."

"Why Rung One?" Sift asked.

"Because we are the best," Echo replied. "It only makes sense to give your greatest every advantage."

Ruwen pictured the five Aspects he'd incapacitated in the Infernal Realm. They perfectly represented the make your strongest stronger mentality that Echo championed. Would it have made a difference in the Infernal Realm if the army he faced had been significantly stronger? If Lalquinrial had invested his resources in his followers instead of his Aspects?

"Your belief leaves the weaker more vulnerable," Ruwen offered.

Echo sneered. "The weak have no value. They only drain resources. The Founders know this. Why else bother with this trial if not to thin the weak from the strong?"

Ruwen considered Echo's words. "That is one possibility, I agree, and a very Viper way of thinking. Consider the opposite. A bamboo grove survives the storm even though each stem alone would face certain destruction. Are we not stronger together?"

Echo stepped toward Ruwen and growled. "I need no one."

Ruwen considered raising his right wrist and displaying the blood name Echo had inscribed on his skin for saving her life in the Journeyman trial. Without help, she would have either died there, or failed to advance in the Bamboo Viper Steps.

Instead, Ruwen nodded at Echo. "Possibly, but others need you."

For just an instant, Echo's iron grip on her emotions faltered, and confusion and joy and fear battled for control. Then her anger reasserted itself and she sneered. "Rung One will find the trial token on our own."

Echo marched to the table, grabbed a key, and headed for the canyon. Rung One hesitated, and then quickly retrieved their keys and followed. Ruwen didn't blame them. They owed their lives to Echo, and even if they'd wanted to work together with the other Rungs, he respected the value they placed on Echo's wishes because of her previous actions.

Even as Echo spewed her disdain, she had already taken several steps down the path of leadership. The loyalty of Rung One demonstrated that growth even if she didn't recognize it yet.

"Why are you smiling?" Sift asked.

Ruwen faced Sift. "No reason."

"Gas?"

"No. And why is that always your first choice?"

"Because you look so grim and grouchy all the time. When you smile, it looks painful."

"It does not. I look normal."

Sift winced and shook his head.

The other Rungs, unsure what to do, stood uncomfortably together. Ruwen focused on them.

"Who wishes to work together?" Ruwen asked.

The Adepts looked around at each other until a man from Rung Two spoke. "Rung Four took none of the relics won at the hilltop on Savage Island. Their generosity earned my trust. I do not speak for Rung Two, but I believe the correct path is working together and splitting the relic tokens."

The murmur of a dozen conversations started immediately. Ruwen let them continue for a minute and then spoke as he turned toward Sift. "How would you handle this collaboration, Sisen?"

Everyone quieted and faced Sift.

Sift narrowed his eyes in thought and rubbed his chin. "I think we should work in teams of three for safety. One from each Rung. When picking a chest, the member from Rung Four will open it since they have nine members. That would provide three relic tokens to each Rung here."

Ruwen nodded, impressed with Sift's strategy.

Sift continued. "We will form eight groups of three and when we decide on a chest, the other seven teams will kneel next to the surrounding chests. That will make it more difficult for any observers to know which box opened and keep them from benefiting off our choices."

Nymthus bowed. "How do we keep track of what chests we've opened? There are thousands of them."

Sift pointed at Ruwen. "I am confident our Brother will remember."

Everyone turned to Ruwen. He could easily place a point on his map for every location they chose, but he guessed that went against the Spirit of the trials. Instead, he would need to memorize the locations of all the chests and the geography of the canyon, something he felt sure he could accomplish.

"I will do my best, Sisen," Ruwen responded.

Prythus spoke next. "Where do we start? There are thousands of identical chests."

Sift opened his mouth, paused, and turned to Ruwen. "Since I came up with the structure, Adept Ruwen will explain the rest."

Of course, Sift would leave the hard part up to Ruwen. But fresh off his conversation with Sivart, Ruwen already knew where to start. Just like before the battle on the bridge, they had one resource in abundance.

Ruwen studied the Adepts, most of them unable to hide their nervousness. "The Founders told us what to do, and we have the entire day to complete it. I suggest we each gather a key, and then meditate on the mysteries, letting the Steps guide us. I will use this time to map the ravine and chest locations."

A distant roar followed by faint shouting came from the far part of the canyon. It appeared Echo and Rung One had decided on a chest.

With a nod at Sift, Ruwen strode toward the ravine. He wondered what Rung One had found, and if they now regretted going it alone.

CHAPTER 26

*R*uwen moved slowly through the canyon. The fog made mapping the chests painful. It took all his concentration, and he didn't have time to consider what this trial might be about.

Three hours into Ruwen's mapping, he came across Rung One. Echo kneeled next to an Adept, wrapping their arm in a strip of cloth. Four of the Adepts looked injured, although only the one Echo worked on appeared serious.

Echo ignored Ruwen, and he didn't poke her with questions. He nodded at the members of Rung One and continued on. With his Diamond senses, he had followed Rung One's progress. He listened to their discussions and followed all their fights. The fog made the eavesdropping more difficult, and he guessed very little sound escaped the mist.

Ruwen didn't know which chests Rung One had chosen or what criteria they used to pick, but from the six chests they'd unlocked, three had contained something violent.

Ruwen stopped and gave his eyes a break from the intent focus of the past hours. This trial reminded him a little of the egg level in Fractal and he smiled at his last encounter with the

Savage Seven. He had used *Survey* and *Stone Echo* to find the eggs that contained the keys quickly.

Doing that here, assuming it would even work, would definitely count as cheating and likely get Ruwen kicked out. He had no desire to take a shortcut, and once he finished here, he would turn his mind to deciphering the purpose of this trial. Spending months here did not fit in with his plans.

Eight hours later, Ruwen finished his examination of the canyon and strode up the camp-side slope toward the tents. By the time he returned he had good idea what the likely point was behind this trial.

The Adepts all sat cross-legged in the sunshine with their eyes closed in meditation. Ruwen sat next to Sift, surprised not to hear snoring.

"I'm so bored," Sift said. "You took forever."

"It was eight hours."

"For. Ev. Er."

Ruwen shook his head. "Did you have any bursts of inspiration?"

"No, but I took a long lunch. They had this fried dough thing. It's flat and covered in cinnamon, sugar, and honey."

That sounded much better than the maple syrup taste Ruwen had walked around with all day. He had forgotten to take care of it before leaving and had considered returning multiple times throughout the day.

"Sounds delicious," Ruwen said, and after a pause, continued. "I'm glad you figured out a fair way to divide the relics. It makes them all—"

Ruwen waved his hand, as if trying to remember a word.

"The same?" Sift offered.

Ruwen sighed. "Yeah, the same." He didn't have the mental energy to keep trying today, so he went right to the compliment. "I'm proud of the leadership you're showing. The Adepts look up to you."

Sift smiled, and the debuff disappeared. "Thanks for noticing. I'm actually trying."

"I know."

Sift handed Ruwen a key and he studied the unremarkable thumb length metal for a few seconds.

"Rung One came back a while ago," Sift said.

"They had a rough morning."

"It looked like it," Sift said as he stood. "We all went and studied the ravine after lunch for a bit. It will be nice to walk around again. I'm sick of sitting."

Ruwen stood as well.

"It's time to start," Sift said to the Adepts.

The Adepts all grouped in front of Sift and Ruwen.

"Did anyone find inspiration?" Ruwen asked.

Nymthus cleared her throat and nodded at Ruwen. "The first night you arrived, you spoke of secrets and balance. The first trial demonstrated that we end where we start, and I think we can assume this trial has a similar lesson."

"Excellent," Ruwen said. "Any ideas on how that helps us find the right chest?"

The Adepts remained silent and Ruwen waited.

"Order," Prythus finally said. "Your first night with us, I did the Steps in the wrong order, and you explained why. Can that apply here?"

"Interesting," Ruwen said, pleased that someone had come to the right conclusion. "Why don't you discuss that and figure out how?"

The Adepts grouped together in obvious excitement at the potential solution.

Sift turned to Ruwen. "Do you know which chest?"

Ruwen sighed. "No. I know how to figure it out, but the variables and math make it difficult to do in my head."

"I thought you were good at math."

"I am. But only Lir or Xavier could do this quickly and accurately. I can narrow it down some."

Sift shook his head. "Such a wasted youth. You should have studied harder."

Ruwen's eyes widened at the absurdity of Sift telling him he should have studied harder.

Sift laughed and patted Ruwen on the shoulder. "I'm just kidding. I know you didn't waste *all* of it."

Ruwen relaxed and scolded himself for swallowing Sift's bait so quickly. In hindsight, taking his current life situation into account, he *had* wasted part of his youth by focusing solely on Alchemy and ignoring the more martial skills. He thought about his dreams of becoming a Mage and shooting fireballs while strutting around in an expensive robe. Those dreams belonged to another, more immature version of himself. That kid would never recognize what Ruwen had become.

Ruwen refocused on the Adepts and realized with all the math books he'd read in Deepwell's library, he likely had multiple Narrators that could help with the calculations. But that also felt like cheating, so he didn't ask Sivart. Not yet anyway.

Excitement among the Adepts spiked, and Ruwen guessed they'd found a solution. The group separated, and they approached Sift and Ruwen.

"It is about energy," Prythus said. "We just need to find the chest that is level with this plateau."

Nymthus continued. "The energy gained going down our side should equal what it takes to climb the opposite side."

Ruwen bowed to the Adepts. "Excellent reasoning. Should we test it?"

Shouts of agreement erupted and Ruwen strode away, the Adepts following.

"You know where that chest is?" Sift asked in a low voice.

"There are several of them," Ruwen responded in the same quiet tone.

Sift's brow wrinkled. "I thought the Founders said only one chest contained the trial token."

"They did."

Sift's shoulders slumped. "So this theory is wrong."

Ruwen held up a finger. "I would say, it is mostly right."

"Is this the math part you mentioned?"

"Yep."

Sift sighed. "I came to this conclusion fifteen minutes after you left this morning. I thought when you returned, we could walk to the correct chest and be done with this trial. Now I feel stupid for wasting most of the day. Lylan is in trouble, and I should have acted sooner. I should have gone looking for you."

"Normally, I would agree with your stupid assessment, but this is bigger than us and Lylan and Hamma."

"I know they can take care of themselves."

"Yes, but it's more than that. We improved the Step forms of every Adept behind us. That will impact them the rest of their lives, but it will only take them so far. To reach their potential, they need to understand the purpose behind the Steps. Understanding gives the Steps more power."

"I know you're really into the deeper meaning stuff, and I agree with the balance part. But I'm not sure how necessary all this other knowledge is."

"That is understandable from your viewpoint."

"What does that mean?" Sift asked, a little defensively.

Ruwen waved his hand. "No, I don't mean it as a bad thing. Let me think of an example." Ten strides later, Ruwen continued. "Let's take your favorite thing—"

"Dessert?"

"No."

"Lylan?"

"No. And she will stab you if you ever list favorites in that order again."

"Noted."

"I'm talking about flying. Does a falcon need someone to explain the complexity of flight? When to flap their wings or glide or how to use the air currents to soar? No, of course not. It is natural to them, and the alchemy of it is meaningless."

Sift whistled, the sound high, almost shrill. "Female stone falcon. They live near the tree line in mountainous regions. I hope to see one when we finally get to visit snow."

Ruwen studied Sift as they walked. "Nice. Are you listening to me?"

"Yes. Mostly."

"Compare the falcon's natural flight, with you learning to use your Air Meridian to do the same thing. Then add the complexity of using your Soul magic to amplify your flying. Because that type of flying isn't natural, you need advice, practice, and a deep understanding of how to fly."

"Yeah, those early days were rough."

"Early days? If not for your Gold body, I'm pretty sure you'd be dead from all the times you smashed into a wall or the ground. And that was a week ago."

Sift waved a hand. "Nonsense. I was practicing hard landings."

"Okay, you're distracting me. This isn't about your reckless obsession with speed. I'm trying to make a comparison. I want you to understand my comment about your point of view came from respect, not the opposite."

They walked in silence for ten seconds, and Ruwen gave up hope that Sift understood.

"I get it," Sift said. "I'm a falcon, so I don't need your philosophy."

Ruwen smiled. "Yes, exactly."

"It's about time you respect my flying. I am an airborne Step falcon."

Sift dashed forward, jumped, and twisted his body, rotating twice, and lashing out with a crescent kick before landing. "Falcon Style!"

Ruwen bit his cheek, fairly sure Sift was baiting him by purposefully twisting his examples. Instead, when he caught up to Sift, Ruwen finished his original thought. "Understanding the patterns in the Steps, at least the three obvious ones, has immense value to these Adepts. So, while I want to get back home as much as you do, I feel like we owe it to them, and their futures, to spend a little time in these first three trials."

"I understand."

"All that just to tell you that you shouldn't feel guilty about wasting your day."

"You could have just said that. It would have saved five minutes."

Ruwen rubbed his forehead.

Sift laughed and patted Ruwen's back. "Relax. The explanation made me feel better. I joke a lot, but there is a sense of peace when I listen to you. I know you spend an immense amount of time on your words, and that you have thought everything through before you speak. It calms me and the others who know you. I value that about you."

They had almost reached the edge of camp and Ruwen studied Sift as they walked, but he couldn't detect any sarcasm. Sift had spoken sincerely.

"Wow, thanks," Ruwen said. "I'm a little shocked."

Sift shrugged. "Once I figured out this second trial, I had a lot of time to think today, and I realized how nice you've been lately. You compliment me every day, and I must admit it has made a difference to me and my confidence."

Ruwen nodded. "You're welcome." Guilty thoughts surfaced

as he'd only said those things to rid himself of the Uneven debuff.

Another realization occurred to Ruwen, and it repelled the guilt, scattering it like shadows before the sun.

Ruwen stopped at the edge of the downward slope and turned to Sift. "I meant every one."

CHAPTER 27

*T*he Adepts gathered around Ruwen and Sift. Directly across from their location sat a chest, almost hidden in the fog.

Ruwen pointed at it. "That chest appears the most level with the plateau. The distance and angles are difficult to determine exactly though, so I have a few other options if this one isn't it."

"This fog is thicker than I thought," Sift said. "We won't bother with fake kneeling when opening a chest. I think Echo and Rung One had enough of this ravine today, anyway."

"Should we all cross then?" Nymthus asked.

"From the state of Rung One, I would say yes," Sift offered.

"I agree," Ruwen said. "Although with this many people, and the steep terrain, we will need to assemble in rings."

Nymthus disappeared over the edge as she started down the path, and the rest of the Adepts followed. Ruwen kept an even stride and counted the steps down the slope, then the flat area of the canyon floor, carefully stepping over a round rock, and finally up the opposite side. The canyon's incline on the side with the chest wasn't as steep, and they made quick progress toward the chest.

Sift turned slightly toward Ruwen and signed in Shade Speak. *Understand. Problem. Now.*

As the Adepts grouped ten feet away from the chest, Ruwen waited a moment to see if anyone else realized the issues with just picking a chest at the same level as their camp.

No one spoke and Ruwen guessed it might take a few trips for them to understand why this trial proved far more complicated than it appeared, even when you knew the point of it. Although the walk here had revealed an obvious way to simplify it.

"Who wants to go first?" Ruwen asked.

No one moved, and Sift took a step forward. "I'll get us started."

Sift reached into the small hidden pocket near his hip and after a moment turned and looked down at it. After a few seconds, he stood up straight and slowly turned to face Ruwen.

"I hate that golem," Sift said.

Ruwen didn't let the smile reach his face. "Maybe if you were nicer, golems would stop singling you out." Before Sift could argue, Ruwen held out his hand. "Tarot?"

A heartbeat later, Tarot rearranged himself in Ruwen's hair and a key launched outward, perfectly landing in Ruwen's palm. "Thanks, Tarot."

Ruwen handed the key to Sift, who had not stopped glaring at the hidden golem on Ruwen's head. Ruwen messaged Sift in Shade Speak. *You. Nice. Benefit.*

Sift sighed, gritted his teeth, and spoke. "Thanks, Tarot."

Sift shook his head at Ruwen and turned toward the chest.

The interaction had brought Tarot to the front of Ruwen's thoughts though, along with the bad luck the golem carried, and he cleared his throat. "Uh, maybe we shouldn't open the one I picked."

Sift paused. "Where's the next chest on your list?"

Ruwen pointed behind him. "About a third of the way around the canyon."

Sift shook his head. "I'm not walking that far when we both think this is just an example."

"An example?" Prythus asked. "This isn't the right chest?"

"Ruwen doesn't think so," Sift replied.

All the Adepts looked at Ruwen and he offered an explanation. "I'm ninety-nine percent sure this isn't the right chest, but it's possible I've over thought this whole trial and complicated it for no reason. In which case, this has a high probability of being correct."

Everyone looked confused, so Ruwen clarified. "I'm pretty sure this isn't it, but I'm not positive."

"Should we pick another chest?" Nymthus asked.

Ruwen bit his lip.

"You do overthink things," Sift said. "Let's just open this one and see. We're already here."

Ruwen nodded.

The chest was three feet long and two feet high. Teak wood covered the sides and curved lid, but the golden color had long since faded to a dirty brown. Black iron hinges held the rear of the lid in place, while a dull metal lock secured the front. It looked just like the thousands of other chests circling the canyon.

The Adepts formed three circles around the chest. An inner circle of four surrounded Sift and the chest, the middle ring held eight, and the outer twelve. Ruwen stood between the inner and middle circles as Sift approached the chest.

Sift bent and hesitated right before the key entered the lock. He looked back at Ruwen, his face almost upside down. "Do you sense anything funny?"

Ruwen had studied the chest since the moment they'd approached. In the Spirit of the trials, he hadn't used any of his magical abilities or spells, but that still left his heightened senses and Perception.

"It doesn't look, smell, or sound any different from the other nearby chests," Ruwen told Sift. "I can touch and taste it if that would make you feel better. You know how I love the flavor of dusty teak."

Sift turned back to the chest. "You can lick the next one."

Sift placed his key into the lock, turned it, and grabbed the lid.

Ruwen immediately knew something had gone wrong. The faint scent of acid appeared, a slurping sound emerged, and the chest quivered.

As Sift opened the lid, Ruwen shouted. "Wait!"

But it was too late.

Sift realized it a moment later when enough of the lid opened to reveal a giant mouth full of teeth. He jerked backward with Gold Fortified speed, but his left hand remained stuck to the lid and the loud pop of his shoulder dislocating made Ruwen wince.

To resist Sift's Gold Strength, the chest must weigh a massive amount, and whatever it had used to trap Sift's hand now covered the entire fake-chest.

"Don't touch it!" Ruwen yelled at the other Adepts.

Two arms, shaped like worms, shot outward from the side of the chest toward the Adepts in the inner circle. The first Adept smashed the tip of the tendril with a savage punch and the chest shuddered. But just like Sift, the Adept's fist remained stuck, and the trunk yanked him forward.

The other tendril neared a second Adept, and they executed the Bamboo Step Swirling Leaf to spin away. But unlike an arrow or bolt, the tendril shifted direction and grazed the Adept's hip. Finishing the fierce twist, the Adept's pants ripped at his hip, leaving a ragged piece of cloth stuck to the creature's arm.

Two more arms emerged from the other side of the trunk, and both sprang toward Sift. He viciously yanked his arm back, and the chest wobbled. Ruwen guessed Sift's Gold Fortified body worked against him here, as his skin didn't rip away like the cloth had.

Ruwen triggered Last Breath to provide more time to think as Sift narrowly contorted his body to avoid the two tendrils.

If Ruwen attacked the chest directly, he might suffer the same fate as Sift, stuck to the chest by some extraordinary type of glue. Touching the creature to damage it wasn't necessary, as his Diamond strikes created enough of a shock wave to devastate anything with a poor Armor Class. Unfortunately, that included all the Adepts nearby.

Ruwen's Inventory had plenty of options. Everything from a lubrication potion to counteract the adhesive to Bliz's seven crystal Crazor set Ruwen could use to slice the creature into pieces. He had ten Blessed Bricks from his fight with the Bone Sculptor outside Uru's Third Temple, thirty-seven head-sized boulders, and three eight-foot boulders he could launch from his Void Band at the beast.

That would break the spirit of the rules, and while Ruwen agreed with Sivart and his mantra of using every resource available, Ruwen would wait until things turned desperate enough to justify doing so.

The Strength difference between Gold and Diamond Fortification made it likely that Ruwen could lift and slam the creature into the ground until it stopped attacking, but he wasn't positive, and he didn't want to risk it unless necessary.

This creature negated all the strengths of the Bamboo Viper Steps. It reminded him of how vulnerable the lack of a non-magical distance attack made him. With all the limitations on what he, or any of the Adepts could do, only one solution seemed viable. An embarrassingly primitive one.

Ruwen left Last Breath and shouted. "Inner Adepts toss dirt. Outer grab rocks and throw."

The Adepts stood paralyzed. Their skills unable to counteract the creature's attacks. Ruwen's voice shocked them into action. The tendril with the piece of cloth struck the Adept with the trapped fist, breaking their rib. The lid opened further, throwing Sift off balance, and a massive mouth, lined with teeth, opened wide. A long tongue, thick as an arm, flicked itself, and a stream of liquid arced toward an inner circle Adept.

Ruwen jumped forward, blocking the fluid with his chest. From the smell, dissolving shirt, and warming skin, he guessed it consisted of a strong acid. He winced at the powerful odor, but the acid didn't damage his skin.

Sift dodged two more punching attacks, yelling in pain as his movements forced him to twist his dislocated shoulder. With a violent punch to his shoulder, he popped the joint back into its socket.

"You're licking the next one," Sift hissed through the pain.

Ruwen punched the ground next to the chest, not using his full strength to avoid blowing out all the Adepts' eardrums. The ground absorbed the pressure wave and flipped the chest onto its side.

The motion twisted Sift's arm, but the creature's tendrils on the side facing the ground, were now pinned under its own weight. Dirt fell like rain around them as the three remaining Inner Adepts obeyed Ruwen's command.

The Adept stuck to the tendril by their fist had been thrown to the ground when the chest flipped and dirt now covered both him and the beast's limb. The Adept, understanding the point of the dirt, attacked the tendril repeatedly with a knife strike, his fingers protected by the dirt that absorbed the glue the creature oozed.

Rocks struck the creature as the outer ring Adepts entered the fight. The beast shuddered and used its two free tendrils to swat the stones away. The creature's tongue slithered around Sift's stuck hand and quickly wrapped his arm.

With a pop, Sift's hand came free as the chest released it. Sift jerked his arm back with a twist of his hips, as if trying to rip the tongue from the creature's tooth-filled mouth. Instead, the chest fell toward Sift, its mouth widening into a large oval.

Sift jumped backward, but the tongue remained attached, and he only quickened the beast's fall.

Ruwen clenched a handful of dirt and slammed his palm upward, stopping the creature's mouth inches from Sift's head.

Saliva mixed with acid dripped onto Sift and Ruwen. Sift's Cultivator clothes remained unaffected, passing the acid through to Sift's skin, which turned red but didn't blister.

Ruwen's cotton shirt disintegrated as the liquid covered him. The creature strained against his grip but couldn't overcome his Diamond Fortified strength. The chest's upper arms stopped blocking rocks and began punching him. But the beast's own acid saliva kept the tendrils from sticking and the blows had no effect on him.

Sift and Ruwen stayed like that for a full minute, while the Adepts bombarded the creature with rocks.

With a violent shudder, the creature stopped attacking Ruwen, let go of Sift and the Adept, and used its four arms to return itself to its original position.

With a snap, the lid closed, and the creature once again resembled an ordinary chest.

Everyone stared at the completely normal looking chest in disbelief.

Into the stillness, Sift spoke. "Did anyone see a token?"

The silence lasted a heartbeat, before the laughter started. In seconds, it turned hysterical as the shock and tension of the fight receded.

CHAPTER 28

*R*uwen wiped his eyes dry as the laughter finally subsided.

Sift pointed at the chest. "Should we leave it alive?"

Ruwen nodded. "It's just doing its job."

"It enjoys its job a little too much, if you ask me. Now I have trust issues."

The red welts across Sift's face and chest from the creature's acid had faded. Ruwen opened his Void Band and rubbed his palms together, letting the dirt-adhesive mix drop into his Inventory. Then he used his fingers to squeeze the acid still stuck in his hair into the Void Band as well. Fractal would appreciate such a strong acid and powerful glue.

Tarot squirmed, avoiding Ruwen's fingers.

"Are you okay? Did the acid hurt you?" Ruwen asked.

"Spirit-infused bile from a Corrosion Wyrm wouldn't even warm my skin."

"I'll take that as a no."

Ruwen closed his Void Band and stood up straight. He studied the Adepts, who had, for the most part, remained undamaged. The Adept with the broken rib had a cloth wrapped tightly around his torso, keeping the broken rib in place. Pain covered his face, but he didn't complain.

Sivart's advice about not using all your resources battled with Ruwen's desire to follow the preferred path the Founders outlined.

Ruwen locked eyes with the injured Adept. "We will suffer the consequences of our choices while using our keys, but once back at camp, I will heal you."

The man looked relieved and Ruwen turned his attention to the group. They had clumped together as they discussed the trial.

"What went wrong?" Ruwen asked.

"With the fight or our choice?" Prythus asked.

"Both."

"That thing—" Prythus started.

"Floot," Sift interrupted.

"What?" Prythus asked.

Ruwen turned to Sift. "Flute?"

"Yeah, it's fake loot," Sift explained. "Floot."

Ruwen frowned. It wasn't the worst name Sift had come up with. Curious, Ruwen *Analyzed* the Floot they'd just fought, but the information displayed matched a common teakwood chest. He guessed to know its true name, he needed to use *Analyze* when it had changed into its offensive form.

Another idea occurred to Ruwen, and he opened his log, displaying their brief fight.

"It's called a Greater Imposter," Ruwen offered.

"Floot," Sift repeated.

Ruwen sighed and motioned for Prythus to continue.

"That Floot removed the advantages of our training," Prythus said.

"The Steps are not enough to keep you safe," Ruwen said. "We should all invest time learning a ranged weapon. Or at the minimum, something like the spear or staff that provides some distance between you and the enemy."

"Isn't that a strange lesson to teach us in our unarmed combat Master's trial?" Nymthus asked.

Ruwen nodded. "It's possible I've over thought this encounter, and the Floot is only a convenient adversary."

"Regardless of the Founder's intent," Sift said. "Ruwen's logic is sound. I've always looked down on weapons as a crutch the weak needed to compete, but they have a practical side as well. I'll never touch a chest with my hand again."

The comment made everyone smile.

Ruwen bet the Founders had meant to teach this exact lesson. Regardless of your talent, always use caution and come prepared. An excellent lesson, all things considered.

They discussed the fight for another few minutes and decided on a method to approach the future Floots.

"Our logic for locating the token didn't work," Nymthus said. "But we've talked it over and we know why. The slope's angles on the two canyon sides don't match. The Floot side had a lower angle."

"Don't forget the canyon floor itself," Sift said. "It varies in width between the canyon walls and has a slope of its own."

Sift turned to Ruwen. "The math is difficult."

"It is," Ruwen said. "Does anyone have a solution?" he asked, hoping someone had noticed the same item on the walk here.

"Although it would be difficult to keep an even pace," Prythus said. "You could run down one side and up the other. Keeping an even stride would be difficult, though, and we'd probably need multiple people to run each one."

"Excellent," Ruwen said. "Normally I would let you do that, exhausting yourselves for a couple of days, but you've learned the point of this trial and I don't want to waste our time. Did anyone notice the round stones on the canyon floor?"

Everyone shook their head, but they immediately understood the purpose and the smiles turned to grins.

"Even with everything we know, it still might take a couple of days," Ruwen said. "There are over a hundred locations that are within my rough calculations as possibilities."

"If Rung One hasn't already figured this out," Sift said. "They will when they see us searching. We can choose to hide our knowledge from them or push forward despite the risk of losing the trial token."

The Adepts discussed the options. Rung Four and many other Adepts wanted to finish the Master's Trial quickly as obligations back home pulled on them. Ruwen could sympathize and when Nymthus responded for everyone, it didn't surprise him.

"We don't want to hide from Rung One," Nymthus said. "And we have a suggestion that hopefully means it doesn't matter."

"I love suggestions," Sift said. "We have a box for them back home."

Nymthus continued. "The Founders didn't tell us to return by dark like they did in the first trial. If we worked through the night, could we try most of the likely chests on your list?"

Ruwen smiled. "Split into two groups of twelve. My group will stay on this side. Sift will take the other group and move to the plain on the far side of the ravine. We will walk around the canyon together but on opposite sides, and when we find a possible location, I'll signal, and whichever side has the stones will roll them one after the other to the other side."

"Why three?" Prythus asked.

Ruwen explained. "With all the variables of dirt and terrain, I think three stones should provide a decent average. We will locate the trial token when the stone spheres finish rolling close to a chest. A group of twelve should keep us safe from any more surprises."

Out of curiosity, they tested the Floot chest and the stone spheres stopped three feet short of the Greater Imposter. Sift carefully removed his key from the Floot in case he needed it tomorrow.

"Which direction should we go?" Ruwen asked.

"What do you think?" Sift responded.

"Right?"

Sift pointed left. "Based on the fact your previous choice nearly killed us, we should go the opposite way."

Ruwen almost said something sarcastic to Tarot, thanking the golem for the bad luck, but Ruwen had chosen the Misfortune Golem knowing the consequences. And, as the Shade's First Rule clearly stated, he only had himself to blame.

"I can't argue with that logic," Ruwen said. "Let's go."

They moved to the left, going counterclockwise through the canyon. Twenty-eight chests later, the sun dipped below the horizon and night overtook them. The darkness slowed them down as only Ruwen had the senses and Perception to see through the combination of darkness and fog. He used the passive *Sphere of Influence* from Rami's third Codex of Perception to speak with Sift telepathically and direct the Adepts on the far side.

Echo found them shortly after nightfall, undoubtedly curious why they hadn't returned. From her heart rate and posture, Ruwen knew frustration consumed her. Rung One had used all their keys for the day and would need to wait until midnight before replicating the process Ruwen and the team had discovered.

No one complained as they worked late into the night. Around ten o'clock, they discovered a chest where the stone spheres stopped a foot away. They performed the test six more times with the same result. They all met at the canyon bottom and discussed what to do, eventually deciding to use one of the remaining twenty-five keys.

Ruwen offered to use his key, and with the Adepts all holding large stones, he unlocked the chest. Using a flat rock instead of his hand, he pried the lid open. Once again, the chest transformed into a Greater Imposter, but he easily dodged the creature's tongue, and because he used a rock to pry the lid open, he didn't get stuck.

The Adepts made quick work of the Floot, pelting it with stones. In under ten seconds, it had retreated to its original form, and they continued with their search. Ruwen guessed all the chests that almost met the criteria would be these dangerous creatures.

At midnight, Rung One began, and part of Ruwen worried they would steal the trial token out from under the other Rungs. The Adepts around him had grown tense and he guessed they felt the same.

As they strode to the next location, Ruwen spoke into the quiet night. "One lesson of this trial is energy. The Founders wish to teach mindfulness of its creation and use, and anxiety and worry do not benefit you. In addition, I think they intended for us to work together. Rung One is not our competitor, but our brothers and sisters. Their victory is our victory."

That relaxed the Adepts somewhat, and Ruwen passed on the speech for Sift to convey to the Adepts on the other side of the canyon.

At three in the morning, they caught up to Echo and two Adepts from Rung One. They stood at a location Ruwen had mentally marked, but he didn't tell his team, knowing it would worry them that Echo's choices seemed accurate. Echo shouted at the four Rung One Adepts on the far side and they started their test.

Despite the speech earlier, Ruwen's stomach tightened as his competitiveness surfaced. He stayed focused on the next possible location and quickly moved toward it.

Five minutes later, Echo and her two Adepts ran by them as

she scanned the canyon walls. It took all of Ruwen's willpower to not race after her.

"She moves too fast to search properly," Ruwen said. "Calm your minds."

Ruwen prayed he was right as they passed Echo testing another one of his probable locations. She had, despite the darkness and speed, successfully detected the next viable location, and he wondered if she cheated somehow.

Rung One needed to shout across the canyon to each other, making their decisions impossible to ignore. Echo had not opened that previous chest and again ran toward Ruwen.

Echo's ability to pick out likely chests changed the dynamic, and his competitive nature overwhelmed his desire to ignore her.

"Who feels like a run?" Ruwen asked.

Everyone immediately broke into a sprint, not bothering to answer, and Ruwen told Sift to run as well.

This time Ruwen reached the next likely chest before Echo and they quickly started their test. Before they'd finished, Echo dashed by.

For the next hour, they repeated the same pattern, each team running past the other to the next location. Echo identified the same chests Ruwen had without fail, and as the number of chests dwindled, his nervousness grew.

At five in the morning, only ten chests remained, and the two teams had become frantic.

As the sun broke the horizon, the two teams had almost circled the entire canyon and only two chests remained. Ruwen cursed his bad luck. After fighting the first Floot, they had chosen their direction for exploring based on his bad luck, but if they had picked the direction he originally said, these two chests, now the last two chests, would have been the first they encountered.

Now as Echo stood in front of one, and Ruwen in front of

the other, they each had a fifty percent chance of gaining this trial's token.

Ruwen's team rolled their first sphere at the same time as Echo. He studied both intently, trying to judge their end point. Echo's stone stopped first, inches from her chest. He turned back to his stone just as it struck the chest.

How hard did it strike the chest? Ruwen sent to Sift. *Did it just tap it or did it have a bunch of momentum?*

I don't know. I don't like getting close in case it's a Floot.

Ruwen nodded at the Adept next to him and they rolled the next stone. He focused back on Sift. *Get closer, so we know.*

Why? Sift asked. *You said these were the last two. The outcome won't change.*

That's true, Ruwen said. *We're coming over.*

"Let's go," Ruwen said.

Ruwen strode down the steep slope to the canyon floor, going slow enough that the Adepts didn't injure themselves following. Echo mirrored Ruwen and ran toward her chest as well.

A minute later, the two teams faced each other, three hundred feet separating them. One of their chests contained the trial token.

"Defensive positions," Ruwen said.

The Adepts circled the chest, all of them holding a stone in each hand.

In the distance, Echo kneeled in front of her chest, her key glinting in the sunlight.

Ruwen nodded at Prythus, and the man strode forward, crouching in front of the lock. His hands shook as he removed his key.

"Regardless of the contents," Ruwen said to the group. "I am proud of the way everyone worked together."

The scrape of Echo's key entering her chest reached Ruwen's

Diamond Fortified hearing. He nodded at Prythus again, and the Adept placed his key in the lock.

As if linked, Echo and Prythus turned their keys together.

CHAPTER 29

This time Ruwen didn't smell the acid, but the slurping and teeth grinding were impossible to miss. Almost immediately, shouts of surprise and pain began.

Ruwen turned from the smiling Prythus to look at Sift. "I'm helping them."

Sift sighed. "Of course you are. I'll meet you there."

Ruwen faced Echo and jumped fifty feet, creating room between himself and his team. As soon as he landed, he leaped again, only this time with his Diamond Strength.

The air exploded with a thunderclap as Ruwen ripped through it, and a moment later, he landed in the middle of Rung One.

Both of Echo's hands were stuck to the Floot. She raised her arms as if trying to pick up the chest, but the creature stretched, absorbing the fury of her straining. The four arms each had a member of Rung One attached, and the Floot had already smashed them all into the ground once.

The remaining two Adepts had grabbed one of their captured brethren, but their efforts to pull them free were useless against the Floot's strength.

To Echo's credit, even though her situation looked dire, she hadn't switched into her Death Aspect, which Ruwen figured could easily take care of this threat. She continued forcing the creature to stretch, and he could see her strategy had value.

The Floot's flexible movements had already slowed, but it wouldn't be enough. By the time the Floot had tired enough for Echo to pick it up, at least four Adepts of Rung One would be smashed to pieces. That assumed she could avoid the creature's massive mouth full of teeth.

Ruwen kneeled and shoved both hands forward, palms toward the beast, and angled downward. He only used enough Diamond Strength to move the dirt, as he didn't want to create an air explosion and destroy the eardrums of Rung One.

A massive cloud of dust, sand, and small rocks rose like a wave. It crashed into the Floot, covering it, and nullifying the adhesive. The Floot raised all four arms, the attached Adepts frantic as they tried vainly to attack the creature.

Ruwen sensed Sift's arrival, and as the Floot brought its four arms down with a vicious jerk, Ruwen caught the two Adepts closest to him, and Sift caught the other two, the momentum of their descent forcing him to his knees.

Releasing the two Adepts, Ruwen snapped his arms open, the sides of his hands striking the tentacles. A shudder passed through the Floot and it released the two Adepts, who fell to the ground and immediately crawled away.

The tentacles Ruwen had struck retreated. Like a whip, they snapped downward, striking Echo in the back and forcing her forward into the creature's teeth-filled mouth.

Last Breath triggered as Ruwen's thoughts fragmented with indecision. His natural instinct was to help Echo, but she had sided with her family, understandably, he had to admit. Wouldn't he support his own family? Hadn't he in fact already justified his parents killing of their party in order to obtain a terium shipment? How would the families of the murdered party view him and his choices?

But Echo's father wanted to torture Ruwen for his secrets and her mother wanted him dead. Both outcomes didn't appeal to him, which meant the best outcome here was Echo's death.

The Bamboo Viper oaths against killing each other remained active during the trial, but harming other Adepts, or allowing harm to come to them, just like during the Journeyman trial, had no consequences. He couldn't kill Echo himself here, but he could allow her to die fighting this Floot.

Another thought occurred to Ruwen, likely the result of his increased Wisdom. Despite Echo's allegiance to her homicidal family, she had taken tiny steps down a different path. If he helped her now by rescuing her again, the shame and embarrassment might undo the small amount of progress she'd made.

Helping Echo was not in Ruwen's best interest, and it would undo the gains she'd made here. Those realizations cleared the guilt from his thoughts and he regained his focus.

Leaving Last Breath, the almost stationary world around Ruwen returned to normal speed. As he jumped over the Floot he sent Sift a message with *Sphere of Influence*. *Take the Adepts to safety.*

Ruwen landed next to Sift who still held the two Adepts he'd saved from crashing into the ground. Ruwen struck the Floot's two arms and, like before, it shuddered and withdrew the tentacles. Sift wasted no time, leaping away with Gold Fortified Strength, an Adept under each arm.

Ruwen casually took three steps backward, giving Echo room to fight the Greater Imposter on her own.

The creature's tongue had wrapped around Echo's neck, and acid covered her head. Ruwen guessed she hadn't yet reached peak Jade, but she still had a Gem Fortified body. The acid didn't affect her skin, but her right elbow had hyperextended and her left wrist appeared snapped. The lack of breathing from being choked didn't appear to bother her, and her heart rate remained steady. Despite how it looked, she remained calm.

Echo relentlessly moved her arms back and forth, stretching the Greater Imposter while resisting the pressure of the tentacles against her back. Ten seconds later, the Floot wobbled and three seconds after that it lost its flexibility. She lifted the chest, her arms straining with the effort, and brought it down in a rush, smashing it against the ground.

The Greater Imposter shook and, in a blink, withdrew its four arms, tongue, and snapped its lid closed. Once again, it looked identical to all the surrounding chests.

Echo stared at the chest for a heartbeat and then kicked it, the force rocking the massively heavy creature. She stepped forward and brought her left elbow down on the lid, and the creature quivered.

As Echo stood to prepare for another elbow strike, Ruwen strode forward, and as Echo's elbow dropped, he grabbed it and pulled her sideways, using her momentum to turn her around. "It's over," he whispered.

Echo had been so focused on killing the Greater Imposter that she hadn't noticed Ruwen. She turned toward him now, her eyes full of hate and anger.

Ruwen stepped to the side, faced Echo, and clapped. In a loud voice, he spoke. "Superb technique, Sister. I doubt any of us could have survived that."

Ruwen continued to clap, and the other Adepts of Rung One, except for Sift, enthusiastically clapped as well.

Echo's anger turned to confusion as she turned from Ruwen toward Rung One.

Ruwen locked gazes with Sift and smiled. He reached out with *Sphere of Influence* so no one else could hear. *Let's blow this pastry stand.*

Sift grinned and his eyes turned white as he accessed his Soul magic. With a short nod, he launched himself upward, climbing into the sky like a human arrow. Ruwen leaped backward, slowly turning in the air, totally relaxed for the first time since arriving at this trial. They had finished it in just a day, and no one had died.

Ruwen landed on his feet, a hundred feet from Echo and Rung One. High above, Sift caught the morning light, and he glowed like a ray of sunshine as he climbed.

Echo turned her gaze from Sift, and locked eyes with Ruwen, her face a mix of emotions. The Adepts of Rung One surrounded her, continuing their congratulations, and blocking his view of her.

Ruwen strolled down the slope toward the canyon floor, his Diamond hearing bringing him the sound of celebration to his right as Rungs Two, Three, and Four passed around the trial two victory token. To his left, he listened to Echo checking the injuries of her team, concern clear in her voice.

"You're confusing," Tarot said.

"Why is that?" Ruwen asked.

"I don't understand you. You spend the entire night frantically competing with Rung One, and then, in the end, you help them? Now they remain at full strength, making the rest of your trials more difficult. Isn't the point of this to win?"

"I did win, Tarot," Ruwen responded. Thoughts of Echo's confused face as her team congratulated her, mingled with the happiness and cooperation of the other Rungs. "In fact, in this trial, I won twice." After a moment, he continued. "And winning is an outcome, not the point."

RUWEN HEALED ALL the injured Adepts as soon as they arrived at camp. His five levels in *Massage* healed for thirty-two health per second for thirty seconds, far more than anyone needed. He could cast the one hundred fifty Mana spell thirteen times before running low on Mana, but his twenty-five Mana per second Regen ensured his bar barely dropped.

The Quartermaster had arrived shortly after all the Adepts returned to camp. He took great interest in all the relics won during their first experience on Savage Island, and after examining them, thirteen met the Quartermaster's quality requirements. Turning in one of those items resulted in a relic token, which could be exchanged for one of the Quartermaster's relics if it provided more value to the Adept.

Rung Four, already equipped with relics won from the first trial, had given their captured relics to Rungs Two and Three. Between the relic tokens from the exchange and the nine won today, every Adept in Rungs Two, Three, and Four had a relic, and they still had six tokens left over.

In an irony that filled Ruwen with joy, the lower Rungs agreed to give the extra six tokens to Rung One.

Echo refused to take one, leaving enough for the six members of Rung One that followed her. Ruwen wondered if she wanted to earn the token herself, or if the generosity stemmed from good leadership.

In the end, between the two trials, and their adventure on Savage Island, everyone had a relic except Sift and Echo.

Now, Ruwen sat cross-legged behind Rung Four, Sift beside him. Everyone wore their traditional uniform, white belts tied around their waists. The Addas had reappeared, and Padda stood at the front of the group with thirty-three orange belts hanging over his outstretched arms, Madda beside him.

The Founders left a large tent and moved toward the Addas. As they approached, all the Adepts stood, and as one, they bowed.

The Founders returned the bow, and Mist spoke. "Another Clan first accomplished by this class."

"Not only did everyone survive the second trial," Thorn said. "But every Adept here faced a Greater Imposter in the process."

Dusk continued. "All in a single day."

Sift leaned toward Ruwen and whispered. "I've been thinking about Floots."

"That can't be good."

"To honor your achievement," Mist said. "Equipping your orange belt will upgrade your Clan mark and give a permanent ability."

Thorn pointed at the belts. "You will have additional opportunities to gain other Clan benefits during these trials."

"Congratulations," Dusk said. "For being the first orange belts to receive this honor."

The Adepts bowed again.

Madda removed an orange belt from Padda's arms and handed it to Thorn, who had stepped forward. Thorn nodded to Echo.

As Echo strode toward Thorn, Sift leaned close to Ruwen again. "That Floot gave me real trust issues. I wasn't kidding. When I'm done here, I'm going to learn a weapon. Something to give me a little space if I want it, like your staff."

"That's a surprisingly good idea. What are you thinking?"

Sift shrugged. "I'm not sure."

"I have flying swords, if you're thinking of something sharp."

"Seriously? Show me."

"Not here, genius. Didn't you hear the flying part?"

"Oh, I heard," Sift said, his eyes shining with excitement. "Don't you want it?"

Ruwen remembered the Aspect of War's massive sword. "I admit they look kind of burnt. For now, though, I want to return to my roots."

"Throwing books?"

"No. And stop guessing."

"Shouting details until everything dies of boredom?"

"Okay, now I'm not telling you."

Madda cleared her throat loudly and Sift and Ruwen

returned their attention to the class. All the Adepts held an orange belt but them.

Sift stepped forward, unaffected by his mother's scowl. He turned his head back and whispered as he moved away. "Paper cuts?"

Ruwen frowned and glared at the back of Sift's head.

Thorn and Mist each held one end of Sift's orange belt, and he bowed to them before taking it. As he strode back, Ruwen read Sift's lips. "Bookmarks?"

Ruwen didn't wait for Sift to return, and moved toward the front, going the opposite way to avoid Sift.

Madda handed Dusk an orange belt, and the Founder stepped forward. Ruwen bowed and held out his arms, and Dusk placed the belt across them. "Congratulations, Adept. The Clan acknowledges your orange rank."

Ruwen bowed again and Dusk did as well. He strode back to stand next to Sift.

Before Sift could offer any more guesses, Dusk addressed the Adepts.

"Replace your white belt with your new Clan rank. Save your white belt, as it holds the work and dedication of your first steps toward Master."

Ruwen threw the orange belt over his shoulder and removed his white belt, dropping it immediately into his Void Band to stop any chance of Tarot stealing it. Grabbing the orange belt, he quickly tied it in place.

The Bamboo Viper Clan mark appeared briefly on Ruwen's right wrist, along with a slight burning sensation. The viper wrapped around the bamboo stalk now had a light smoke or fog surrounding it. A notification appeared.

Tring!
Dusk has gifted you...

Name: *Symbol of Lesser Command Shadow*
Restriction: *Bamboo Viper Clan Adept (Minimum)*
Restriction: *Rank Orange (Minimum)*
Restriction: *Shadow Realm interaction impossible when active.*
Effect (Triggered): *Dismiss your shadow at will, storing it in your mark.*
Description: *Not all shadows fear the light.*

Ruwen had barely read the notification when Thorn spoke.

"Prepare yourselves for the third trial. We begin immediately."

CHAPTER 30

*E*veryone changed into their normal clothes and, less than fifteen minutes later, stood in a line to enter a new gate rune portal. Ruwen could tell from the fourth rune they would stay on this planet for trial three.

Ruwen and Sift had taken their normal place at the end of the line as Echo stepped through the portal first.

"How many trials are there?" Sift asked Ruwen.

Ruwen frowned in thought. "I hope only six, because that's all I've figured out."

"What do you think this one is?"

"Since the first two trials focused on the obvious patterns in the Steps, I'm guessing this third one is the last of those."

"Hard and soft styles," Sift muttered.

"Yeah."

After a few seconds of silence, Sift whispered. "I sure hope Lyl and Hamma are okay."

Ruwen couldn't tell if Sift had spoken to himself or meant for Ruwen to hear.

"Me, too," Ruwen whispered back. "Honestly, though,

between Hamma's Wisdom and Lylan's Dexterity, they can handle whatever's happening."

"I know," Sift said. "I just couldn't bear losing her again."

Ruwen didn't have a response for that, so he patted Sift on the back.

They approached the pillar, and Ruwen glanced at the Addas on the left and the three Founders on the right. Sift let out a long sigh as he prepared himself for entering the portal and then, like ripping off a bandage, he jumped through.

Ruwen stepped forward to follow, but Dusk held out a hand.

"One moment, Adept," Dusk said.

Ruwen paused and bowed to the Founders.

"You healed the other Adepts," Dusk said. "Why?"

Ruwen had wondered if the Founders would stop him earlier and being questioned about it didn't surprise him. He had already given it a lot of thought.

"Balance, of course," Ruwen said.

"Explain," Mist replied.

Ruwen's response incorporated his talk with Sivart. "The spirit of the trials dictates no use of magic or foreign items that might alter the outcome. This allows us to absorb the meaning and purpose of each trial."

"So, you know the purpose of these trials?" Thorn asked.

Ruwen faced Thorn and responded confidently. "Yes."

Ruwen risked locking gazes with Thorn. Soon he might need the knowledge to counteract the hypnotic effect of her eyes. He triggered Last Breath and searched for its source.

Last Breath, with no additional mental focus to increase its effectiveness, stretched a second to over eight, slowing world around Ruwen to a crawl. A Dizzy debuff appeared as he discovered the cause of the effect. Thorn's pupils swayed rapidly from side to side. The distance wasn't enough to notice with a glance, but the brain picked up on the motion, causing the hypnotic trance and dizziness.

One of the many benefits of Ruwen's Diamond Fortification was complete control of his body. He focused on his eyes and tried to mirror the movement of Thorn's eyes. A second later, his Dizzy debuff disappeared as his pupils vibrated in synch with Thorn's. He released Last Breath, pleased that he could maintain the vibration in the normal flow of time.

A notification glowed softly at the bottom of his vision, but he remained focused on the Founders.

Thorn's steady breathing paused for a fraction of a second as shock overcame her training.

"What sorcery is this?" Thorn hissed. "You shed your Metal skin for Gem less than two years ago."

Dusk placed a hand on Thorn's shoulder. "Sister, we already witnessed his control."

Thorn pointed at Ruwen, and half turned toward Dusk. "Control like this? He has barely hatched."

Dusk turned toward Ruwen. "In this short period, how have you gained such mastery of your body?"

The question reminded Ruwen of Lalquinrial's accusations in the Infernal Realm. When questioned about the world he'd built in his mind, he'd explained his obsessive nature, tireless training, and ability to focus on tasks until mastered. Coupled with an army of entities in his mind to help him break through mental blocks and a physical body made almost indestructible from Diamond Fortification, and the question seemed flawed. The real question, with all those benefits, was why he hadn't made even more progress.

Thorn's question triggered a realization for Ruwen. He had made such vast gains because he had nurtured and encouraged the expansion of his mental world. These mental constructs had, in turn, helped him master his physical world, including his body. Overlord especially, with his ability to control vast numbers of minions, had continually pushed Ruwen's physical limits.

Ruwen shifted his gaze between the three Founders, and both Dusk and Mist matched his eye movement, confirming they remained immune from Thorn's hypnotic power.

"The answer to my physical gains," Ruwen said. "Reflects the purpose of these trials. It mirrors the world around us and the Universe that contains us. It is balance."

"He mocks us," Thorn said, her Disposition Aura fading from light green to almost invisible.

Dusk shook her head. "I do not think so. Mist?"

Mist considered Ruwen for a few moments before speaking. "You never finished your explanation. Why was healing the other Adepts in keeping with balance?"

"We endured our injuries during the trial," Ruwen said. "Now that it's concluded, we will transition to the next." Memories of the time compressed years he had spent with Rami as she taught him the Bamboo Viper Steps swirled in his thoughts. As hard as that had been, she had insisted he spend some time every week relaxing and recovering. "Pain can enhance training but serves little purpose once the lesson is learned. In fact, it only hinders the focus on new lessons. As I said, it requires balance."

The Founders studied Ruwen.

Finally, Dusk spoke. "Have you mastered balance?"

Ruwen considered the question. Balance encompassed so much. How could he answer it truthfully? It reminded him of the "what is the most important Step" question.

Of all things, images of Famine appeared in Ruwen's mind, the Apocalyptic figure his Scarecrow Aspect represented. Famine carried a scale, which he'd spent a lot of time thinking about. Did the scales represent balance, or justice, or a way to distribute just enough food to avoid mass starvation, or worse, to guarantee it?

But now, reflecting on Dusk's question, another explanation occurred to Ruwen.

Ruwen gave the Founders a small bow. "Balance is not something to master." He held out his hands, palm upward, mimicking the scales Famine held. "Each of us carries a scale, not to parcel out the value of our thoughts, or actions, or entire existence like some merchant in a market, but to help reveal the truth."

Ruwen activated Last Breath to gain a few seconds to think through the implications of what he'd just said.

Pen had removed all the Spirit and hidden it away in the Third Secret with Miranda. This caused massive hardship across the Universe, and in isolation appeared like a horrible act. He had done this, though, to starve the darkness that used Spirit to feed its advance. He had created a Spirit famine across existence in order to save it.

A perfect example of the ends justifying the means, and a philosophy that Ruwen resisted.

Ruwen knew he skewed toward mercy and not justice, and this risked the innocent in addition to his own life. His difficulty centered on what justice looked like. When did punishment, violence, and killing turn from justice into something darker?

Good and evil had always existed as two opposites in Ruwen's mind, but the subjective nature of justice, coupled with Pen's example, made him wonder if good and evil existed at all. And even if it did, how would you recognize it unless you had a full understanding?

Blapy's words in Malth's library about Echo and changing an arrow's trajectory took on a new emphasis. It provided an example of a small action, adjusting the arrow before it's fired, to the significant impact that change had on the arrow's path.

Ruwen had aimed a couple of small actions at Echo during these trials and felt like he'd impacted her. He considered that good, but he doubted her family would agree.

Ruwen let go of Last Breath and gave the Founders a deep

bow. "Thank you for your questions. They have provided new insight."

"Which is?" Dusk asked.

"The idea of balance mirrors a scale's true purpose. Stable or unstable is not the lesson of balance, just like good or bad is not the lesson of the scale. The lesson of both is: nothing happens in isolation."

Thorn's Disposition Aura returned to its green color

Ruwen viewed himself in terms of right and wrong, but in the light of this new understanding, he needed to reconsider that standard. If he accepted what he'd just told the Founders, then right and wrong were just labels for the coins the powerful placed on the scales to justify their desired outcome. Good or bad, as the example of Pen's Spirit removal showed, were nearly impossible to know.

The conclusion filled Ruwen with dread. This thought process seemed like a path to destruction, with no regard for a moral compass. It made him feel like Lalquinrial and all the other deities who followed their desires with no apparent care.

The Founders watched Ruwen, and the Addas studied the ground.

"Honestly, though," Ruwen said. "I hope I'm wrong."

Dusk nodded. "A noble thought."

Ruwen stepped through the portal, confused and unsure. With a few simple questions, the Founders had, ironically, unbalanced him.

CHAPTER 31

*R*uwen felt the temperature difference first. His map showed a temperature of one hundred and four degrees, while the desert area they'd just left hovered around ninety degrees. The map had also filled with the yellow dots of resources. The humidity struck him next, making the air sticky and uncomfortable.

"What took so long?" Sift asked.

Ruwen scanned the dense trees around them and the pools of stagnant water visible between them. He focused on Sift. "Pop quiz."

Sift winced. "Oof, I'm glad I missed that. I already hate this trial."

Ruwen frowned. All the moisture probably meant a lot of bugs. "Have you seen any centipedes?"

"You really need to let that go," Sift said. "It was like two years ago."

Memories of Ruwen's first trip to the Black Pyramid surfaced, along with the terrible fear and anxiety he'd carried. He had grown up preparing for the easy life of a Mage, and the sudden exposure to creatures trying to kill him, coupled with having no skills to protect himself, had traumatized him. He would never forget those early days. Especially the centipedes.

"They were like twelve feet tall," Ruwen said and shuddered.

Sift shook his head. "You are such a baby."

Ruwen leaned close to Sift. "I'm serious. If there are centipedes here, I'm going airborne."

"Won't help if they can fly."

Ruwen leaned back, horrified. "Some can fly?"

"Oh yeah. They fly in swarms and cover your body, looking for any hole they can find to burrow into your body."

"Uru have mercy, you're lying."

Sift looked up. "I'll keep an eye out for you."

Ruwen couldn't tell if Sift was serious or poking fun at him.

The Addas stepped through the portal stone, followed by the Founders. Sift and Ruwen quickly moved toward the other Adepts who had grouped together on the nearest dry patch. As Ruwen moved he studied the ground, looking for what bugs this terrible place held, but only snails covered the ground. A lot of snails.

"Welcome to the third trial," Mist said. "This will be your last group challenge."

Thorn continued. "We will move to the safety of the fort which will act as your home base for the duration of this trial."

"Do not underestimate the swamp," Dusk said. "It holds many dangers, even for the most powerful among you."

Ruwen had just battled a god and lived, and he dismissed Dusk's warning. But as they walked in single file toward the fort, a couple of facts made him reassess. Lalquinrial hadn't wanted to kill Ruwen. Only subdue and extract Ruwen's secrets. Had the god wished to destroy Ruwen, he could have.

The other item that differed from the battle in the Infernal Realm was Ruwen couldn't use his Spirit. His scorched Core, pathways, and Meridians made using Spirit impossible. It meant he lost access to all the spells and abilities from the other

Classes he'd discovered, along with most of the powers from the Architect Role.

Ruwen always had the Gravity Shell around himself to protect against a deity obliterating him with a simple gravity attack. To make sure the shell provided no advantage to him, he'd created the weakest one possible, and it only consumed point one Mana per second.

Blapy had told Ruwen he would eventually recover, but only if he didn't injure himself further. It meant the only spells and abilities he had access to were the ones he'd chosen from the Fighter and Worker trees. He had sixty-one spell points and thirty-six ability points, and he needed to assign them to bolster his current Mana and Energy spell choices. Maybe he'd do that tonight, assuming he had access to any high-level Class books in his memory.

That made Ruwen think of Rami, and he wondered if the bookwyrm had gotten mixed up in whatever trouble Hamma and Lylan had found. Almost since his Ascension, Rami, and more lately, Overlord, had provided constant companionship, and he really missed them.

Ruwen still felt a little adrift from his conversation with the Founders about balance, and it reinforced a depression he'd carried with him since the Smear and landing in the Third Secret. The damage to his Spiritual network, and losing the related capabilities, followed him like a dark cloud.

Ruwen had kept himself busy, in part to distract himself; but now, as he carefully followed Sift through the low hanging leaves, rotting wood, and moss, he forced himself to face the cause of his unhappiness.

The Inventory figure in the bottom right of his vision dared him to open it and see the damage to his Spiritual body in raw numbers.

Instead, Ruwen opened the notification that had appeared during his talk with the Founders.

Shing!
You have learned a new skill!
Skill: *Coiled Drake Gaze*
Level: *1*
Effect: *Immunity to all Drake Gazes*
Effect: *10% chance per second of eye contact to mesmerize target.*

The new skill Ruwen had learned to counteract Thorn's hypnotizing stare had an interesting name. He had never heard of a coiled drake and wondered what type of creature had developed such an ability. Once again, he missed Rami, along with her near instant ability to provide answers to all his questions.

From the skill's description, Ruwen guessed Thorn had learned this from one of these drakes, and that more than one type of drake had this ability. He would need to practice so he could increase the chance per second of success.

Through the trees, Ruwen glimpsed a wall made of twenty-foot-tall logs. This must be the fortress, which meant he only had a minute to get the next part over with.

Reluctantly, Ruwen touched the Inventory icon on the bottom right of his vision. When the human cutout appeared, listing all the gear he wore, he pushed the edge, turning it around and revealing the Spirit details of his body.

Twelve circles representing his Meridians covered the cutout, their spacing uneven. The twelve Meridians had turned red, a sobering difference from the last time he'd viewed them. A list ran along the side of the cutout, and it confirmed what Ruwen already knew. All twelve Meridians and their associated body locations had reached a Fortification level of Peak Diamond. The progress to the next level, which required a transition from Gem to Divine, sat at ninety-nine point nine nine percent.

Ruwen's next transition would take him from Gem-

Diamond to Divine-Angel. But before that could occur, he needed to fix all the Spiritual damage, because more than just his Meridians had turned the angry red color.

Below the cutout sat a diagram of the Divine Circle. The twelve circles spaced evenly around the circle each represented a Meridian. All of them read zero percent, the result of emptying all his essence so he could survive the Smear and escape Lalquinrial's prison.

In the middle of the diagram rested a red sphere that represented his Core. More angry red lines led from the sphere to each red Meridian and back again. Those were the pathways that he used to purify raw Spirit into each type of essence, and because he had all twelve connections, it made him an Axiom.

As the group of Adepts approached the wooden fortress, Ruwen noticed long deep gashes in the tree trunks making up the walls. It seemed the Founders had not exaggerated the dangers here.

Quickly refocusing on the display, Ruwen used a mental finger to touch the sphere representing his Core, which revealed a few more details.

Scarring: *11%*
Inflammation: *98%*
Capacity: *9%*
Core Velocity (Max): *704 of 12,000*

The values explained why using Spirit crippled Ruwen with pain. While using the Smear to escape the Infernal Realm had saved his life, here sat the proof of the damage it had caused. He touched a few of the pathways and Meridians and found similar values.

Not having access to Spirit based magic would severely limit Ruwen's effectiveness, and he needed to find a way to speed his Spiritual healing. He made a mental note to speak with Fractal about solutions for this when he talked to the Dungeon Keeper about his other plans.

With a depressed sigh, Ruwen closed the display and studied his surroundings. The fortress had walls two hundred feet long and sat in the middle of an island of dryness. Whoever lived here kept the foliage from growing on the island, ensuring the views from the walls remained clear and denying any cover for attackers.

The only creatures Ruwen sensed nearby were the ever-present snails. Just like at the portal stone, you couldn't move ten feet without seeing one. Their sizes varied from tiny to thumb sized, and their shell colors ranged from shades of yellow to a greenish brown that reminded him of the stagnant water around them.

Everyone funneled through a small gate. Four large buildings, one parallel to each wall, formed a square. The walls didn't have ramparts, which meant they constructed them as a barrier, not to defend against an army or other type of organized foe.

The Adepts grouped into Rungs and Ruwen and Sift stood behind the fourth as rain fell. The Addas stepped to the front of the group, and Ruwen realized the Founders had disappeared. In fact, he had been so distracted, they might not have even left the portal area.

Padda pointed to the various buildings. "Sleeping quarters, dining hall, bathing and laundry, and meditation and training."

"Good luck," Madda said.

The Addas turned and strode toward the meditation and training building, and in seconds, had disappeared.

The Adepts turned and looked at each other, then, after a few seconds, at Ruwen and Sift.

Sift leaned toward Ruwen and whispered. "I sure hope you have a plan."

CHAPTER 32

*R*uwen had no idea how or where to start. To buy time, he pointed at the dining hall. "Let's eat first." Many of the Adepts, while not exhausted, were tired from staying up all night. "I also think we should sleep a few hours, so we start this trial fresh."

Many of the Adepts nodded, relieved they would get a break, and the group headed for the dining hall. Echo said nothing but moved in the opposite direction, toward the wall. When she reached the base, she crouched and easily leaped over the twenty-foot wall.

Sift turned to Ruwen. "That is an opportunity."

Ruwen frowned. From the beginning of their friendship, Sift had kept the same worldview. He believed that what you gave the universe you got back. Ruwen didn't care for that philosophy, probably because it seemed too simple.

From Sift's perspective, Echo had proven herself a threat, and remained one now. He clearly meant "opportunity" as a way to even the scales with Echo. Probably by helping her into whatever trap might keep her here for good.

By now, Lalquinrial and the other gods would know Ruwen

had escaped the Infernal Realm dimensional trap. That Echo knew as well didn't matter. When they left these trials, she would lose track of him. The reasons he had wanted to trap or incapacitate her no longer made sense. Was she dangerous? Absolutely. But the knowledge he'd participated in the Master's Trial wasn't valuable. While he agreed with Sift that she deserved some bad luck, Ruwen no longer had the urge to provide it.

Not because Ruwen believed Echo lacked the ability to harm him. He'd been wrong about that often enough not to trust his own judgment. But because Blapy, who always chose her words with care, had made a point of discussing Echo's path in front of him. A path he hoped had already changed from his efforts.

"You're right," Ruwen said. "That is an opportunity."

Sift looked at the sky and sighed.

Ruwen patted Sift's shoulder. "I'm aware of the danger, and I appreciate your advice. But a questionably wise man-child once told me, don't judge a pastry by its frosting."

"Oh, that's low. Throwing a man's wisdom back in his face."

Ruwen raised a finger and grinned. "Questionably wise man-child."

Sift laughed.

"Will you keep an eye on the Adepts?" Ruwen asked. "I want to look around. Maybe it will give me an idea. Because right now, I'm clueless."

"Just right now?"

"That's fair."

"Okay, fine. I'll stay. I am kind of hungry."

"Thanks. Be back shortly."

Ruwen didn't bother walking to the wall's base. Instead, he stepped away from Sift and jumped fifty feet toward the fence, sailing over the barrier. He landed ten feet from the island's edge, his feet sinking into the soft mossy ground.

A small biting insect landed on Ruwen's hand, but its stinger couldn't penetrate his skin. His distaste, and maybe a little fear, of insects and bugs seemed irrational at this point in his progression. Like Sift said, Ruwen probably needed to let those fears go. But not today.

Ruwen considered activating the level eight Worker ability *Insect Repellent*. He had created massively powerful versions of this ability with Spirit, but he didn't need those right now, and he couldn't cast them, anyway.

Insect Repellent only had one ability point assigned to it, and Ruwen rationalized a barrier that weak wouldn't offer enough protection to count as a benefit. It would, however, keep the crawling and flying things in this swamp from touching him.

Ruwen triggered the ability and a one-hundred-foot invisible sphere appeared. He pulled the shield inward, the barrier allowing the bugs to pass through it as it shrank, until it just covered him.

Glancing at the map, Ruwen strode toward the nearest resource location. He had bent the rules a little to trigger *Insect Repellant*, but it only provided him peace of mind. Using *Survey* or *Sixth Sense* to get an accurate picture of the surroundings would go too far in his opinion, giving him an advantage, so he relied on his Perception to inform him about the environment.

Echo had not moved far from the fort and stood two hundred feet away. Her heartbeat the only thing betraying her presence. Ruwen wondered if she planned to attack or force him into a trap. That would be ironic, considering the conversation he'd just had with Sift.

More likely, Echo knew that exploring alone made her vulnerable, and she merely wanted to see if anyone followed her. A sound strategy, as she could quickly return to the safety of the fortress and other Adepts.

Ruwen waded into the swamp, his feet sinking in the muck as the stagnant water reached his knees. Two minutes later, he stopped at the location of the resource his map displayed. With a sigh, and thankful for his *Insect Repellant* ability, he bent and stuck his hands into the brownish green liquid. This close, the swamp water, full of decaying plants and animals, nearly overwhelmed him with its stench, and he considered casting Fresh Air. After a moment, he decided to suffer like everyone else, and pushed the thought away.

Running a hand underneath a fallen log, Ruwen paused as something tightened around his finger. With effort, he kept his heart rate steady, reminding himself nothing could hurt him here. He gently pulled upward, using his other hand to pull the plant from its anchored locations.

With Diamond senses, Ruwen tracked an arm sized creature as it moved from a distant tree toward him. It wasted no time in attacking and leaped at his exposed neck.

Ruwen tilted to the side, just far enough to avoid the short-haired scavenger.

The creature crashed into the water next to Ruwen, splashing him, but the water slid off his barrier, keeping him dry. He gave a curt nod, using enough force to create a powerful pressure wave.

The surge of condensed air struck the floating beast, forcing it underwater. When it resurfaced, it quickly swam to the nearest tree and climbed to safety.

The plant snapped and the pressure around Ruwen's finger relaxed. He sighed and lifted the now dead plant out of the water to *Analyze* it, but it came back as useless. It took him two more tries to figure out how to harvest the weed successfully. This time when he *Analyzed* it, information appeared.

Target: *Razor Weed*
Type: *Resource*
Components: *Organics, Minerals*
Health: *Constriction risk*
Alchemy: *Therapeutic, Anti-Venom*

Uses: Filtration Elixir, Constriction, Poison Resistance

Ruwen continued deeper into the swamp. Echo had followed him for ten minutes before moving off on her own. He guessed she probably got bored watching him hunched over in the water. Even though he continued to harvest the razor weed, he kept his senses focused on the surroundings, not taking the Founders' warning about the dangers here lightly.

The Founders had said this would be the last team trial, which meant it likely was the last of the obvious Step patterns. The first trial had focused on the start and stop location, and the second trial on the buildup and release of energy. Assuming he had guessed correctly, that meant this one related to the hard and soft aspects.

The Viper Steps were hard and violent, aggressive and forceful. The Bamboo Steps provided the perfect balance with moves soft and defensive, passive and gentle.

What in Uru's name could that have in common with this swamp?

When no solutions occurred to Ruwen, he asked Tarot about auras and the Misfortune Golem happily talked about all the ways people got things wrong. Ruwen listened, rarely interrupting the golem, as he continued harvesting.

Two hours later, Ruwen casually put the thirty-third razor weed in his Void Band and stood up straight. Three of his skills had increased while out here: Herbalism had gone from sixteen to twenty-four, Prospecting from seven to eleven, and Taxonomy from eight to eleven. The advances plus the Razor Weed had made this a worthwhile outing.

Ruwen waded forward, but this time he didn't head for another resource node. Something or someone watched him, and he'd just noticed it, although he couldn't say which sense had discovered it.

For the last five minutes, Tarot had detailed a thousand-year argument between himself and a Blessed Fortune Golem named Tassebenidoros. "She contaminated her analysis with spectrums too close to visible light, which skewed the hues and invalidated her conclusions. It ruined—"

Ruwen interrupted the golem. "Someone is watching us."

"Well, that can't be good."

Ruwen smiled. "How often do you say that?"

"Hey, misfortune leads to opportunity and adventure," Tarot said. Then, after a moment, continued. "And death. A lot of death."

"Maybe this time it's something friendly."

"Yeah, I doubt that. I'll watch from a safe distance."

With that, the Misfortune Golem sped away on a deck of cards and Ruwen turned his attention back to the watcher.

The sensory rich swamp made it harder than normal to filter through all the noise. Bugs, water, moss, and creaking trees mingled with the smell of decaying leaves and animals. The air tasted bitter, and the heat and humidity hung in the air like a thin fog.

A single heartbeat behind and to the right of Ruwen went almost unnoticed in all the noise. He didn't turn, and kept his pace steady, but his mind whirled.

It was possible that the swamp contained creatures that had extremely slow heart rates. Many animals that had adapted to the water and land had such abilities. The other possibility included Gem Fortification and someone capable of complete control over their body, including their heart.

Stopping the heart or not breathing or anything else that damaged the body would instantly heal, using a minuscule amount of the Spirit that permeated a Gem Fortified Harvester's body, or in Ruwen's case, a tiny fraction of Mana.

Ruwen wondered what could be behind him. The only other Gem bodies he knew of that might join him here in the swamp were Echo, the Addas, and the Founders. Echo didn't control her body well enough yet to evade his detection, which left the old people.

Continuing forward, Ruwen considered what that meant. It suggested the person behind him had allowed the sound of their heart to become audible on purpose. Probably to test the limits of his Perception.

The sheer difficulty of moving through the swamp without leaving a sensory trail of some kind seemed impossible, and it bothered Ruwen that the watcher appeared capable of it. Between pressure waves in the air and water and the sound of moving branches, he didn't believe he could hide his presence here without the use of suppression magic or his Architect Role.

That left two other options. Either a deity followed Ruwen, or one of the dangerous creatures the Founders had mentioned. He decided to find out.

Ruwen stopped and turned to face his stalker.

And saw nothing.

Frustrated, Ruwen focused intently on the area he felt sure held the pursuer.

Thirty seconds went by and still Ruwen couldn't find anything. He wondered if his imagination had gotten the better of him. Once again, he considered using some of his other abilities or spells. He guessed a quick peek into the heat bands with either *Detect Temperature* or just adjusting his own vision, would reveal the prowler. But that felt like cheating.

Another thirty seconds passed, and then a single heartbeat.

Ruwen concentrated on the area and then, finally, ten seconds later, a form emerged from the patterns of the swamp, a deeper darkness in the shadow of a large cypress.

As if sensing the discovery, the creature stepped out of the tree's shadow, and Ruwen glimpsed, for the first time, what had found him.

Fifty feet away stood what Ruwen could only describe as walking darkness.

CHAPTER 33

*R*uwen had seen Gem-level creatures before. In fact, he'd fought two of them in the semi-final match of the Step Championship. Chip and Stump of team Apex had represented the Black Pyramid and had proven exceptionally talented at both the Steps and brewing toxic alcohol.

Ruwen and the shadow stared at each other, neither of them moving, although he couldn't be sure the creature looked at him since it lacked visible eyes. After ten uncomfortable seconds, returning to the fortress seemed like the best idea, since it didn't appear the shadow planned to attack him.

Checking the map, Ruwen confirmed what he'd guessed. The creature stood exactly between Ruwen and the fortress. He had no desire to fight a Gem level shadow with unknown abilities, so he strode forward thirty degrees to the right of its location.

The shadow disappeared and reappeared forty feet away, directly in Ruwen's path once again. The teleport created a negative pressure wave at the origin, while the new location pushed a surge of displaced air and water. It appeared the creature wanted to intercept him.

Ruwen mentally prepared himself for a fight. The creature vaguely reminded him of the Mist Wraith, Talker, but only a little. This creature's human shaped body had few features and appeared black with a flickering outline. The edges of its body wavered as if an invisible moving light source created chaotic shadows.

"Hello," Ruwen said with a short wave.

The shadow didn't respond.

"I'm not looking for trouble, and I apologize if I intruded on your territory."

Again, the creature remained silent. Maybe it couldn't talk. At twenty feet, Ruwen discovered the creature's Disposition Aura appeared faintly green. The lack of defined edges made seeing the aura difficult, especially from a distance.

That surprised Ruwen. The creature didn't appear to view him as an enemy. Then why did it act like it wanted to force a confrontation?

The friendly Disposition Aura opened another possibility. Ruwen wondered if, since the shadow had not responded, perhaps it lacked the ability to utter words.

Ruwen stopped and, using *Sphere of Influence*, repeated his intent directly in the creature's thoughts. *I'm not looking for trouble, and I apologize if I intruded on your territory.*

The shadow shuddered and the flickering around its edges increased. Ruwen guessed he'd surprised it with the mental communication.

The Shadow didn't respond, though, and Ruwen's confusion increased.

Once again, Ruwen moved at an angle away from the creature. Or tried to. His body didn't move, and a debuff appeared.

Superior Shadow Stake: *Your shadow is pinned to the current location.*

As Ruwen read the debuff, the shadow disappeared again and reappeared directly behind him.

The sudden appearance of the shadow triggered *Last Breath*, and time slowed. Ruwen had trained for something like this. He had spent months perfecting his Spirit based *Blink* spell. Now, when it finally had an actual use, the consequences of his previous decisions made it impossible.

Worse, it had never occurred to Ruwen that his shadow could influence his actual body. He'd seen Ky's Shadow Stepping and knew his shadow provided the equivalent of an open door to such people. Now, he realized too late, his shadow also acted as a weapon against him. And if his shadow could anchor him in place, his *Blink* strategy might not have worked, anyway.

Dusk had literally just hours ago given Ruwen a method that should help with this issue.

Dusk has gifted you...
Name: *Symbol of Lesser Command Shadow*
Restriction: *Bamboo Viper Clan Adept (Minimum)*
Restriction: *Rank Orange (Minimum)*
Restriction: *Shadow Realm interaction impossible when active.*
Effect (Triggered): *Dismiss your shadow at will, storing it in your mark.*
Description: *Not all shadows fear the light.*

Ruwen willed his shadow into the Bamboo Viper Mark on his right arm, and immediately tried to move.

Nothing happened.

Ruwen guessed *Superior Shadow Stake* just laughed at his *Lesser Command Shadow*.

The shadow circled around Ruwen and hovered two feet in front of him. Having someone in his personal space made him uncomfortable, especially since he couldn't move. The creature appeared even more like a man up close. Two eyes, small ovals of the darkest grey studied him. Black tendrils stretched from the creature to nearby shadows, like supports.

Ruwen *Analyzed* the creature and wondered how much trouble he'd found.

Target: *Gloom Stalker*
Type: *Creature (Gem)*
Strengths: *Shadow Manipulation, Shadow Teleportation, Physical Damage Mitigation*
Weaknesses: *Light*
Disposition: *Neutral*

Ruwen had never heard of a Gloom Stalker before, but the neutral disposition reassured him a little. Curious, he focused on the creature to trigger his Perception.

Name: *Gloom Stalker*
Deity: *Unknown*
Class Type: *Cultivator - Diamond*
Level: *81*
Health: *1,482*
Mana: *0*
Energy: *0*
Spirit: *12,000,000*
Armor Class: *947*

In hindsight, Ruwen should have stored his own shadow earlier to prevent this from happening. He had only studied the Shadow Stepping abilities and not considered the other ways his shadow could harm him. He needed to break this Gloom Stalker's Stake spell so he could remedy that problem.

"Hi" Ruwen tried again.

The creature tilted its head. "You speak Shroud? How?"

"Languages are a thing with me. Communicating is like a superpower."

"You desire power?"

Ruwen would have waved his hands had his shadow not kept him pinned. "No, well maybe. I'm interested in the power to help."

The Gloom Stalker floated a foot closer, and Ruwen's uncomfortable meter pegged.

"Do you help?" the Gloom Stalker asked.

Ruwen frowned. "Usually."

After a few moments, the creature continued. "You are peak?"

Ruwen guessed it meant his Fortification. "I am."

"Yet you cast no shadow?"

"If I didn't cast a shadow, how are you pinning me here?"

"Are you arrogant and prideful?"

The question surprised Ruwen. "I don't think so. I try to stay humble. My friends help with that."

"Yet you leave your light shadow unattended, as if inviting a confrontation to demonstrate your skills, and deflect my question regarding your true shadow with a foolish answer. Do you wish to fight?"

"Whoa, hold on. This shadow stuff is new to me. I didn't even know you existed."

The Gloom Stalker shifted the last foot and its nose touched Ruwen's, or close enough, as a sensation like ice seeped through his *Insect Repellent* shield, making his skin crawl.

"You lie," the Gloom Stalker hissed. "Your movements hold the darkness, and your light shadow confirms it, yet you cast no true shadows. Such control, to hide them even from me, reveals your mastery. How am I to interpret then, the flagrant disregard of your light shadow, as anything other than an invitation?"

Ruwen's eyes had nowhere to look but into the grey-black

eyes of the Gloom Stalker. "I don't know what you mean. Dusk gave me the *Symbol of Lesser Command Shadow*. Is that what you're talking about? I just got that like an hour ago."

The *Disposition Aura* in Ruwen's peripheral vision took on a red tinge.

"Perhaps you need encouragement to tell the truth."

"No, I'm good, and I already told you the truth."

Ruwen triggered *Last Breath* to think through his options. As a last resort, to save his own life, he would use his Spells and Abilities. Dying here would be catastrophic. He would revive with the memories and body of eighteen months ago. The last time he'd synched with Uru had been the morning of the semi-final fight with Chip and Stump, sitting on the floor of the underwater safe house outside Malth.

The gains Ruwen would lose defied comprehension. All the knowledge and progress he'd made during his time alone, his internal world including Overlord, Uruziel, and Sivart, along with his Peak Diamond body. Catastrophic losses. Which was why, if forced into a corner, he would use all his resources to survive, even if that meant failing the Master's trial.

Ruwen could use the Worker ability *Glow* to create enough light to disperse his shadow and free himself. The Worker spells *Harden* and *Melt* might work if the Gloom Stalker had an inorganic body. The level three Fighter spell *Tunnel Vision* would clear all impairing effects and granted brief immunity to them. If it worked on this debuff, it would give him time to free himself and store his shadow.

As a last resort, Ruwen could access his Scarecrow Aspect for *Cornfield of Despair*, the area of effect confusion, or *Infernal Panic*, and its line-of-sight fear. Misjudging the Mana the Aspect's spells consumed could cripple him, though, if he depleted his Mana and the Aspect accessed his Spirit. Until he healed, the Aspect remained a dangerous choice.

Feeling better about the options, Ruwen let go of Last Breath.

The Shadow Stalker moved back two feet, and Ruwen almost sighed in relief.

A black shaft the size of Ruwen's thumb, the tip sharp like a needle, shot out of the Gloom Stalker's chest, and Last Breath triggered again. He could see the trajectory and calculate the point of impact, a point between his left armpit and shoulder.

A flood of understanding followed immediately by a surge of panic struck Ruwen. Because the Gloom Stalker had chosen the exact location that Ruwen would use to either briefly paralyze an opponent's Air Meridian, or with enough force, damage or destroy it.

Based on the speed of attack, the creature only wanted to cause pain, not cripple Ruwen. But he no longer cared about keeping this exchange friendly. The Gloom Stalker had upped the stakes, because Ruwen knew exactly how deadly that attack could become.

Ruwen knew because he'd practiced that attack mentally tens of thousands of times as part of his discovery and understanding of the Shadow Steps. This creature, while not appearing to know the Steps, knew the secrets of Spiritual combat.

Instantly, Ruwen transitioned into focused combat.

Ruwen snapped his body forward in a Bamboo Step called Bowing to the Sun, used to flip an opponent that attacked from the rear. He tapped his Diamond Fortified strength, enhanced by all the Ascendancy Strength points from leveling, and strained against his own shadow.

Ruwen's shadow shifted, and from the terrible sucking noise, it pulled the water and mud that pinned it in place. He completed Bowing to the Sun and a massive pillar of water and mud struck the Gloom Stalker like a brown tidal wave.

The water did no damage, but the Gloom Stalker's focus

faltered, and in that moment, Ruwen activated his *Symbol of Lesser Command Shadow*, pulling his shadow into his Clan marking, and removing it as an option to attack or manipulate him. To his surprise, his Mana dropped ten points.

Ruwen, the friendliness in his voice gone, locked gazes with the Gloom Stalker. "I have some questions of my own."

CHAPTER 34

*W*ith the debuff gone, Ruwen moved his feet, gauging how it affected his balance, and instinctively compensated for the unstable mud and added water resistance. "Why did you attack me?"

A fragmented hissing sound that Ruwen guessed passed for laughter came from the Gloom Stalker. "That was no attack, Light Walker. Only encouragement to answer truthfully. I dislike liars."

The Gloom Stalker's Disposition Aura had lost most of its color, although a small amount of red remained, barely visible.

"Like I said before, I'm not lying, and you make little sense. I don't know what holding darkness is, or a true shadow, or how my shadow upsets you." Ruwen raised a finger and pointed at the Gloom Stalker. "But if you target my Spiritual elements again, I'll take you up on that fight."

The Gloom Stalker shifted to the right, sending ripples through the water as it passed, but it didn't do so by stepping. From the pressure waves generated underwater, it appeared the creature had created a platform for itself. The platform had a dozen tendrils snaking through the water to the surrounding shadows.

Ruwen wondered about their purpose. Did they power the platform and the Gloom Stalker, or did they act as anchors?

The Gloom Stalker continued to move right, entering Ruwen's peripheral vison. He didn't bother to turn, confident in his abilities to sense the creature's attack.

Just before disappearing completely from Ruwen's vision, the Gloom Stalker switched directions and in two seconds had returned to face Ruwen directly.

"You are not a prisoner to the light?" the Gloom Stalker asked.

"If you're asking if I need my vision to fight, then no."

"You are a curiosity."

"I've been called worse."

Ruwen remained calm and relaxed. While difficult to read the Gloom Stalker's body language and posture, he sensed impending conflict in the creature's voice. He hoped to get a little more information before the situation went sideways.

"What do you mean by 'hold darkness' and how can you tell?"

"I almost believe you are ignorant."

"I've learned enough to know I am."

"True or not, prepare yourself."

Six booms occurred simultaneously as six black rods the size of fingers ripped the air as they sped toward Ruwen. None of the spears would strike his spiritual components, and he guessed the Gloom Stalker wished to test his reflexes without hurting him permanently.

Ruwen lifted his right arm, turned his body thirty degrees, and bent backward, arching his back and leaning his head forward. At the same time, he stepped to the left, taking his legs out of reach of the two tendrils the Gloom Stalker had launched under the water.

All the tendrils missed Ruwen, only the pressure waves of their passing touching his body. The force of the air, ripped violently apart, would shred a normal body, but he ignored it.

Ruwen considered grabbing one or more of the tendrils and using them as leverage, but the long black fingers continued past him, striking pools of shadow around the swamp and disappearing.

Instead, Ruwen stepped closer to the Gloom Stalker, narrowing the distance until only two feet separated them. If the creature wished to test Ruwen's Gem body, he would happily demonstrate.

Ruwen swung his right hand using sixty percent of his speed, aiming for the Gloom Stalker's cheek. A massive boom surrounded them as his hand sliced the air. Half an inch from the Gloom Stalker's face, Ruwen stopped.

The Gloom Stalker's face distorted as the pressure wave passed over it, and to Ruwen's surprise, partly through it. The creature, while in the Material Realm, didn't completely reside here, nullifying part of the physical impact of Ruwen's almost slap.

Water vaporized to Ruwen's left, turning into a mist twenty feet away, and into a tidal wave fifty feet away. The nearby trees toppled with loud cracks as the pressure wave minced the trunks and sent slivers of wood into the swamp like siege bolts.

The Gloom Stalker's platform allowed it to remain upright, and the creature jumped backward ten feet in surprise. To its credit, it didn't rub its face or show any signs of pain.

Ruwen believed the creature had reached Diamond but wasn't sure if it had attained peak yet. Regardless, he doubted the shadow had encountered anyone like Ruwen short of facing a Divine being.

More tendrils launched from the Gloom Stalker and this time Ruwen didn't bother dodging. Instead, he swatted them away. Two of the tendrils stuck to his left hand, immediately wrapping themselves around Ruwen's wrist.

Ruwen jerked his left arm downward, the movement short and violent. The tendrils snapped off the Gloom Stalker and almost immediately dissolved.

Under the water, the platform shifted, and Ruwen felt the pressure waves approaching from above and around him. Shadows fell toward him like black streaks of lightning. In a blink, a surge of dense shadow rose from the water, fed by the Gloom Stalker's platform. It merged with the shadow lightning and surrounded him, encasing him in a sphere of darkness.

Ruwen didn't need light to see and still sensed everything around him. Even though the shadow construct mitigated part of the Material Realm's physical damage, the creature couldn't ignore it.

Ruwen snapped his right hand forward, palm outward and fingers raised, launching a burst of condensed air like a battering ram. He immediately replicated the movement with his left hand, repeating the attack. Over and over, as fast as he could manage, he threw bolts of air.

The space inside the shadow bubble roiled and exploded, turning super-heated and baking the mud on the swamp floor surrounding him as the water had yet to refill from his previous attack.

Instead of single air explosions from Ruwen's movements, the speed of the attacks created one long howling whistle.

The shadow sphere disintegrated and moss on the surviving trees near them burst into flames, followed a moment later by the trees. Farther away, the trees bent, and the moss disappeared as the pressure wave flung it away.

The Gloom Stalker remained standing five feet from Ruwen, as the world ignited around them.

Ruwen clapped, creating a savage explosion and causing the ground to shudder. The fierce wave of air snuffed out the surrounding flames, pushing the water away from them in a hundred-foot radius.

The force pushed the Gloom Stalker backward as all its tendril shadow connections disappeared, along with everything near it capable of creating a shadow. The creature latched onto distant shadows stopping itself twenty feet off the ground.

As the water returned in a rush, the Gloom Stalker floated back to the scorched mud. Ruwen stood in the middle of a giant circle of destruction.

A twenty-foot-tall creature emerged from a shadow fifty feet behind the Gloom Stalker. The beast had the front of a crab and the rear of a scorpion. It surfed on the water as it flowed back and in seconds had reached the Gloom Stalker, who lowered himself onto its back.

"Your power is formidable, Light Walker," the Gloom Stalker said. "I cannot match it here. When you enter the true Realm call out, Zylkin, and I will come. Perhaps then you will reveal the truth."

Ruwen placed a palm over his right fist and bowed. "The truth sounds the same in every Realm."

"Indeed," the Gloom Stalker said. "But it looks different. Until then, Light Walker, may the shadow guide you, may it surround and protect you, may it bring you harmony. Farewell."

The shadow crab leaped a hundred feet and disappeared into the shadow of a damaged cypress tree as if walking through a door. As the water swirled around Ruwen, he considered the encounter.

The Gloom Stalker had, without a doubt, targeted him with a Shadow Step. No, not a Shadow Step, as the creature didn't appear to practice the Steps. Regardless, it had known the exact location to strike, and that could not be a coincidence. Not here, in this place, during the Master's trial.

The water calmed and revealed hundreds of snails, their perches destroyed by Ruwen.

"I'm sorry," Ruwen whispered. "I didn't consider your homes in my race to end that fight."

The snails ignored Ruwen. Instead, they slowly formed lines, spaced twenty feet apart. They floated in the water, one line moving clockwise while the other counter. Without destroying such a vast area, he would have never noticed the odd behavior.

Ruwen turned toward the fortress. He'd had enough of the swamp.

CHAPTER 35

*H*alfway back to the fortress, Tarot reappeared, burying himself in Ruwen's hair.

"You are really noisy," Tarot said.

"I know. Which probably means questions for me back at camp."

"Well, it is something to brag about. It's not every day you meet a Realm Warden. And considering where we are, he is likely a Prime."

The water here reached Ruwen's chest, and he gently pushed a snail floating in front of him out of the way as he strode through the brown liquid of the swamp.

"Hold your aces, Big T, explain everything you just said."

"It takes significant energy to pass between Realms, and while the Shadow Realm isn't the hardest to bridge, it's not easy."

Ruwen had a lot of experience crossing Realms. Tremine's betrayal had led to the first Realm Ruwen had physically entered, and it had taken a lot of work, and Spirit, to leave the Spirit Realm. His exit had put him in Uru's Divine Realm. He had used a vast amount of Spirit to flee the Spirit Realm, and he didn't know if his destination, a divine Realm, had caused that, or if it always took that much.

The third Realm Ruwen visited had occurred without his consent. Echo had triggered his Scarecrow Aspect's Infernal Realm bind point, sending him into a trap set by her father, Lalquinrial. Again, he had no idea how much energy that took since he assumed Lalquinrial paid the price since he owned the Aspect.

The fourth Realm Ruwen visited had occurred after using the sixth rune and smearing himself across the universe. He had found Miranda in the Third Secret, Pen's Divine Realm. The energy needed to do that had nearly crippled him.

"Yeah, moving realms isn't easy," Ruwen agreed. "What is a Realm Warden?"

"The Material Realm is a mess, with all the deities, their followers, and Harvesters. The Shadow Realm works hard to keep that out of their Realm. I've never gone, but it's on my list."

"Now you sound like Sift."

"A soul for adventure is a good thing."

Ruwen shrugged. "I'd rather sit in a comfy chair and read."

"Ironic, then, your path."

"Yeah. That has crossed my mind."

Ruwen stepped onto a long narrow stretch of land and strode forward, making better time.

"What did you mean by 'prime' and 'considering where we are' when you spoke before?"

"This planet is special," Tarot said. "That's one reason I'm here. It was on my list."

"Okay, you need to do better than that."

Tarot squirmed in Ruwen's hair, and Ruwen resisted the urge to itch his scalp.

"This is a Nine Muses planet," Tarot said as if explaining the obvious.

Ruwen had an excellent memory. Better, in fact, than anyone

else he knew until he met Rami, and probably now Xavier. What he lacked was Rami's ability to index her knowledge and memories and create near instant access to information. In this case, however, the mention of nine muses made an instant connection in his mind.

With an ease born from thousands of hours of practice, Ruwen popped an item out of his Void Band and into his right hand. He held the nine-sided coin over his head so Tarot could see.

"These nine muses?" Ruwen asked.

A moment later, Tarot responded. "You're an Ink Lord?"

"Yes."

"With a Perception Bookwyrm?"

"Yes."

"Well, now I'll never cross the Archive off my list."

The narrow island ended, and Ruwen returned to the brown muck of the swamp. He had traveled farther than he'd thought from the fortress.

"Okay, this conversation is getting messy. I feel like I'm talking with Sift. Before we get even further from my original question, can you please, in simple terms, clarify what a Prime Shadow Warden is, what it means to be a Muses planet, and explain the Archive?"

As Tarot collected his thoughts, Ruwen brought the Ink Lord Emblem of Dominion down to eye level and studied it again. The charcoal-grey nine-sided coin depicted nine women in a circle around an open eye. He flipped the emblem over and examined the etching.

A pyramid with a black dragon coiled on itself, the wings creating the walls of the pyramid. Ruwen had seen this image before, on the cover of an ancient book Blapy had given him, *The Black Pyramid: Rules, Guidelines, and Procedures.* He focused on the emblem and brought up its description.

Target: *Ink Lord Emblem of Dominion*
Type: *Item (Magic)*
Properties: *Decorative*
Uses: *Authorizes attendance to Ink Lord Conclaves and permits access to the Nine Muses' Archive.*

The "Uses" of the emblem had triggered Ruwen's memory. The description had contained a reference to the Nine Muses' Archive.

"Don't they teach you anything in school?" Tarot asked.

"Not about this."

"Tragic. The youth of today are so ignorant."

"If you'd hurry, maybe you could fix that and prevent my death from curiosity."

Tarot sighed, the sensation like someone running their finger lightly over Ruwen's scalp. "Before the last battle, the nine most advanced worlds pooled their knowledge in a central location to preserve it for the coming dark ages. Each world provided a Muse to safeguard their portion. That emblem you hold is one of fifty, which were distributed to the other worlds to grant access to the Archive in the future."

"And this was one of those advanced worlds that provided a Muse."

"Right, which meant it contained multiple developed species, including those in the Shadow Realm."

"Is the Shadow Realm planet specific?" Ruwen asked.

Tarot shifted around again. "I'm not an expert on that. Like I said, it's on my list so I can learn more."

"That's fair. But you think Zylkin is important, or at least powerful, since he crossed into the Material Realm."

"Absolutely."

"Any idea on why he distinguished between my shadow and what he called a true shadow?"

"No idea. But one of my brothers is an expert in Augury

divination and knows how to read shadows, just like the Prime Shadow Warden read yours."

The fortress came into view and Ruwen slowed his pace so he could finish this conversation. "What do you mean 'read a shadow?' Aren't shadows just the result of blocked light?"

Tarot laughed. "Sorry. Laughing at ignorance is rude. I'm trying to act nicer."

Ruwen stopped and turned his head, but his shadow remained stored in his Bamboo Viper mark. It felt weird to not see a shadow connected to him, and even weirder that something he had ignored his whole life contained information about him.

"What can they see in shadows?" Ruwen asked.

"I'm not an expert," Tarot said again. "But of all my siblings, I seem to have received the greatest amount of curiosity, and so I've picked up things here and there over the millennia. You're right that a shadow in the visible spectrum results from blocked light, but many other spectrums pass through you, leaving patterns and shapes that experts can interpret."

"Is that what Zylkin meant about me not attending to my shadow?"

"I'm not sure. Like I said, I'm—"

"Not an expert," Ruwen finished. "Thanks, Tarot. I appreciate your knowledge and applaud your curiosity."

Ruwen remained stationary. He felt foolish and awed that something he'd ignored his whole life had far more meaning than he'd ever imagined. A notification blinked at the bottom of his vision, but he remained focused on the closest tree's shadow.

What type of information would a shadow contain after passing through an object? The concept fascinated Ruwen. When Zylkin had said Ruwen held darkness, he must have referenced something he'd noticed in Ruwen's shadow.

The Prime Shadow Realm Warden had also made a big deal about Ruwen's true shadow being completely hidden. Since he had no idea what that meant, and not something he did consciously, it probably related to the only thing about himself sealed away beyond finding: his soul.

Ruwen continued with that thought process. He knew souls had a sound, and he had seen their light. Sift blazed with so much soul energy it came out of his eyes and skin. So, if the soul created light, just like sound, it made sense it could cast a shadow. A shadow of what, though? This line of reasoning felt right to him, even if he didn't have all the answers. His soul must produce the true shadow Zylkin referenced.

The whole concept of shadows having substance, and various objects, some internal, generating shadows blew Ruwen's mind. When he had witnessed Ky and the Founders Shadow Stepping, he'd assumed it worked like teleportation or *Blink*. He considered now it might be more complicated than that—maybe they actually moved through a different realm somehow.

That gave Ruwen an idea, and while remaining focused on the cypress tree's shadow, he accessed his Architect Role, navigating through Navigator to Dimensional and finally to Keys. With a simple thought, he could confirm his suspicion that when focused on a shadow he would get two options for the Realm key, Material and Shadow, for the fifth symbol in the gate rune sequence.

With a mental effort, Ruwen restrained his curiosity. The previous times he'd accessed the Key Role, it had consumed all his Mana and pulled Spirit from his Core, so it would need to wait.

Ruwen quickly closed his Architect Role. Confirming he could enter the Shadow Realm using gate runes was something future-Ruwen would need to do. It made him wonder if the Shadow Clan moved between shadows by utilizing gate runes. That didn't make sense though. Dusk and Ky moved almost instantly and certainly didn't have time to draw out gate runes with chalk made from Divine blood or soul power.

That meant it probably related to this true shadow the Shadow Warden had mentioned. Ruwen would look for opportunities to learn more about this.

Ruwen opened the notification and found he had multiple. All for the same Rating.

Gong!
You have increased your Knowledge!
Level: *155*
The intelligent know true power is held by knowledge. The wise know knowledge can be dangerous. Greatness is found between them.

Ruwen's previous Knowledge level had been one hundred fifty-one, so the understanding he'd gained here had added four more points.

Striding forward toward the fortress, Ruwen marveled at how every increase in his Knowledge Rating reinforced his vast ignorance of the Universe.

CHAPTER 36

*W*hen Ruwen returned, he found Sift leading Rungs Two, Three, and Four through one of the more complicated Viper forms near the entrance. Everyone stopped when Ruwen strode through the open gate.

"Hey," Ruwen said with a wave. "I guess everybody's ready."

"The *thunderstorm* woke everyone," Sift replied.

Ruwen kept the guilt off his face. The fight with the Gloom Stalker had not gone unnoticed here. He looked up at the clear sky. "The rain must have just missed us."

Sift pointed at the open gate. "Right, well Rung One left thirty minutes ago."

Ruwen scanned the Adepts. "Any ideas on where to start?"

Nymthus stepped forward. "Sisen Sift had us focus on the hard and soft aspects. It made me wonder about the swamp. It is all soft and muck on the bottom and hard wood above."

Ruwen gave Nymthus a small bow. "Excellent observation, Sister. I missed that connection. You are exactly right. The swamp appears more fitting now that you've pointed this out."

Nymthus smiled and returned to Rung Four.

Prythus cleared his throat, his face red.

"Do you wish to add something?" Ruwen asked.

Prythus looked down, and Nymthus kicked his calf. Reluctantly, he looked up. "Well, when Nymthus told us her idea, we all loved it, and it made me think."

Prythus paused, and Ruwen filled the silence. "Please speak, Brother. There are no bad ideas."

"Says the god of terrible ones," Sift whispered.

Prythus swallowed hard. "It's a little more philosophical, and I'm not sure it's appropriate."

"Believe me," Ruwen said. "Philosophical is my language."

Reassured, Prythus continued. "It's the water. If Nymthus is right, the water connects the soft and hard elements. It creates them both, actually, and binds them. It's like the energy that powers our Steps. The trees grow, collecting energy and storing it in their trunks like we do our bodies during the hard style Viper Steps. Then, as the cycle completes, they die and return to the water, where they sink gently to the bottom, returning all their energy to the swamp like our Bamboo steps bleed the energy from our bodies."

Ruwen remained silent, and Prythus fidgeted. Ruwen held out a hand. "Be at ease, Prythus. The brilliance of your theory has stunned me into silence. It holds a perfect harmony and I believe you and Nymthus are absolutely correct. In hindsight, the swamp is a perfect location."

Prythus grinned as the Adepts smiled and congratulated him and Nymthus.

"Has anyone figured out how that helps us find this level's token?" Sift asked.

The smiles faltered.

Sift turned to Ruwen. "Ideas?"

Ruwen frowned in thought. Rung Four's theory felt correct, but it involved water as the boundary between hard and soft, and the swamp contained a lot of water.

"With the abundance of water, there must be another clue,"

Ruwen said. "Let's explore and see if anything triggers a solution."

Sift stepped toward the Adepts. "Pair up and form a line outside. We will move together, each pair in sight of the pairs on each side. Look for anything strange and yell if you sense any danger."

The Adepts immediately moved to the gate, and in seconds Ruwen and Sift stood alone.

"Hey," Sift said, stepping in front of Ruwen. "When I heard the first explosion, I ran outside, prepared to fly over and help you. Dusk convinced me to stay."

"Dusk? Why? Oh, and thanks."

"No problem. She said you weren't in any danger. I told her it sure sounded like you'd found trouble."

"What did she say?"

"She laughed and said you'd definitely found trouble, but that it posed no danger to you. She said, and I quote, 'he is curious, not angry' and then walked off."

Ruwen considered Sift's words.

"What did you fight?" Sift asked.

"A Gloom Stalker. Kind of like a shadow man. He had Fortified to Gem. Probably Diamond, maybe peak. Get this, he pinned my shadow to the ground, and I couldn't move."

Sift leaned back in horror. "What?"

Ruwen nodded. "Paralyzed me."

"How do you fight that?"

Ruwen frowned. "Didn't your orange belt give you a way to hide your shadow?"

Sift mirrored Ruwen's frown. "No. I got buffs to my dodge and critical strike."

"That's interesting. I kind of assumed we'd all get the same thing, but I guess they personalized it."

Sift turned his head around to look at his shadow. "Now I'm really freaked out. How can my shadow hurt me? Even Blapy wasn't that evil."

"Relax. I don't think shadow manipulation is common. This guy came from the Shadow Realm, and it makes sense he could screw around with them."

"When I first saw you, something bothered me, but I couldn't figure it out. It's your missing shadow that caused it."

"I know it looks odd, but I'm scared to put it back now."

"Will hiding it cause any trouble?"

That hadn't occurred to Ruwen. "That is a good question. I should probably find that out."

"Maybe you sunburn easier, or can't step into other shadows, or—"

"Stop, that isn't helping," Ruwen said. He pointed to his head to change the subject. "Tarot has a list just like you."

"Really? What's his number one? Exploding Burrowers?"

Ruwen tilted his head. "No. What are you talking about?"

"Oh, nothing. Obviously wrong list. Knowing that golem, I bet 'spanking' is in his top three."

Ruwen leaned back and shook his head. "Spanking? How many lists do you have? And what is that one for?"

Sift winced. "Uh, how about you tell me what kind of list Tarot has?"

Tarot climbed from the top of Ruwen's head to the front and stuck his head out. "I want your 'spanking' list."

"Uru help me," Ruwen whispered.

"Come on over here, Big T, let's compare lists."

A line of cards appeared, edge up, between Ruwen and Sift. Tarot slid down them, leaving blue sparks in his wake. In a blink, he'd disappeared into Sift's hair.

"You worry me," Ruwen said.

Sift patted Ruwen on the shoulder. "You, my friend, need more lists."

They strode toward the open gate.

"I have lists," Ruwen said, a bit defensively. "I keep one of all the things I need to give Fractal."

"Boring," Sift replied.

They crossed under the wall and into the line of Adepts, ruining any chance for Ruwen to defend himself.

"Let's go," Sift said. "We'll start by moving straight ahead. Keep yourselves relaxed and open to the surroundings. We can't be sure the clue we need will be visible. Oh, and if you see a small white turtle, yell."

"Tortoise," Ruwen whispered to himself. He smiled at Sift's concern about Shelly's whereabouts. That tortoise was one of the last creatures in the Universe that needed babysitting or worry.

Sift's directions to pay attention to the invisible was good advice, Ruwen thought. Especially after his recent shadow experience. Things they took for granted might have significance. It turned out Sift had already applied Ruwen's shadow lesson to his life as naturally as everything else related to the Steps.

As they advanced through the swamp, Sift walked up and down the line, whispering to Tarot and occasionally laughing. Ruwen stayed in the middle of the Adepts' line and twenty feet back. It would allow him to jump quickly in either direction if he heard any calls of distress or excitement.

Ruwen let his mind wander, not focusing on the problem, and letting it unravel in his subconscious. The swamp fit this trial well and it gave him confidence they'd figure out the solution.

The line of Adepts made Ruwen's brain itch, but he didn't focus on it. After an hour, Sift stopped everyone and they grouped together. No one had seen or sensed anything like a clue.

"Did anyone see my turtle?" Sift asked.

Everyone shook their heads and Sift's shoulders slumped.

"Some of these snails are bigger than she is," Sift continued. "What if they kill her to steal her shell?"

The island the Adepts stood on barely contained them, and instead of cramming himself into their ranks, Ruwen had stayed in the water. He stood chest deep, although *Insect Repellent* kept him dry. The snails really were everywhere in this swamp. As he watched, one swam in front of him, the slug swishing its rubbery tail to power itself forward.

How could something so squishy ever hurt Shelly? Sift really had to get a handle on his fears about that tortoise. How would the snails even attack Shelly? Knock their shells together?

The thought made Ruwen smile, and he placed a finger in the water. The snail didn't alter its course at all, and slid right over his hand, the soft underbelly leaving a streak on his *Insect Repellent* shield.

Ruwen froze as the snail dropped back into the water and continued.

"I'm an idiot," Ruwen whispered.

The snails had both a soft and hard section combined in harmony to fulfill one purpose. They reflected the lesson of this trial.

"The snails," Ruwen said louder. "The snails are the clue."

Everyone looked at the ground and out into the water. After a few seconds, Sift said the obvious. "They're everywhere. Are we looking for really big ones? Or special ones with arrows pointing to the token?"

Everyone laughed, and Ruwen smiled.

The image of the aftermath of Ruwen's battle with the Gloom Stalker materialized in his mind along with the frigid cold of his Cleverness trait activating. He winced in pain and rubbed his temples.

Three seconds later, the pain passed, and Ruwen focused on the Adepts. A single snail may not lead them to the token, but all of them together might. The snails near his fight with the

Gloom Stalker had formed a line, and it made him wonder if all the snails had arranged themselves like that. Perhaps they had assembled in some type of pattern that would give them the clue they needed.

"Are you okay?" Sift asked.

Ruwen released his head and met Sift's gaze.

"I have an idea."

CHAPTER 37

S ift bit his lip and refrained from commenting. It looked painful for him.

"I think they're traveling in lines," Ruwen said. He pictured the moments after the destructive fight with the Gloom Stalker. "And those lines alternate in direction."

Sift wrinkled his brow. "How can they lead us anywhere if they move in opposite ways?"

"I thought the same thing," Ruwen replied. "But what if the lines aren't straight?"

No one spoke for a few seconds.

"You mean like a spiral?" Nymthus asked.

"Exactly," Ruwen replied.

"If it's a circle, can't you do a math thing and point us at the middle?" Sift asked.

Ruwen turned to Sift, shocked he knew that could be done.

"What?" Sift asked. "I went to school, too, you know."

Ruwen discarded his first three responses to that statement. "Very true, Sisen. It's easy on paper because the circle is small, and you can see all the points. Assuming we're right, we should first determine how big the snail circles are." Ruwen pointed at the two closest Adepts. "Continue forward until just before you lose sight of us."

The two Adepts strode away, one watching the snails, the other for danger.

Ruwen pointed at two more Adepts. "Follow the snail line back the way we came and do the same thing."

Between the trees, moss, and fallen branches, it only took a minute for both sets of Adepts to stop, each three hundred feet away. To Ruwen's eye, both pairs of Adepts were in a straight line with him. That meant at their current location, the snail circles had a very large circumference and would make finding the center difficult.

Ruwen could easily place markers on his map where the distant Adepts stood. It would make calculating the center almost trivial with such exact distances, but he focused on doing it the hard way instead.

"We need to find smaller circles," Ruwen said. "But I can't tell if we should go right or left." He raised his arms, pointed perpendicular to the line he made with the two pairs of distant Adepts, and spoke to the group near him. "Split into two groups. One person is in charge of navigation. Pick a tree and walk toward it. Once there, pick another tree in your desired direction and so on. Four of you look for danger and the rest count how many snail lines you pass. After five hundred steps, come back and we should have the information we need."

The Adepts did as requested, and in less than a minute, only Ruwen and Sift remained.

"I could solve this in ten seconds if I did a flyover," Sift said.

"I know. But think about the impact these trials are having on the Adepts. When we started, Prythus did the steps out of order, but he's the one who figured out the balance this swamp represented. That's because he's thinking about the Steps differently now. They aren't just movements and forms, but actual lessons in balance."

Sift sighed. "I hate doing things the hard way."

"I know."

Sift sighed again.

"What?" Ruwen asked.

"Nothing." A couple of seconds later, Sift continued. "It's just thinking about the hard way made me think of tanking for Lylan and Hamma in Shelly. As they leveled up, things got difficult, and it really stressed me out. I need to reach Gem to catch up with everyone, but I don't see how."

"I have some ideas for that."

Sift turned to Ruwen, his face hopeful, and with none of the sarcastic pain he usually displayed when hearing Ruwen's ideas. "Really? Are they any good?"

"Of course. And you're thinking too small. I spent a lot of time thinking out there by myself. Fractal is some kind of alchemical genius, and when I get back, I'm giving him a few projects." Ruwen placed a hand on Sift's shoulder. "Don't stress about it. I promise you, I'm working on a way to protect us all."

"Okay, thanks." Sift returned to studying the swamp, and after a moment added. "Back home, all I thought about was getting away. I never appreciated the pyramid for its benefits, and I didn't worry like I do now. Blapy harassing me was as stressful as my day got."

Ruwen had worried the two groups, moving in opposite directions, would take different sized strides and throw off his calculations, but he felt them turn back within seconds of each other.

"To be fair, Blapy can be pretty stressful," Ruwen said.

Sift laughed. "Yeah, but looking back, it made me feel included somehow. The creatures in the pyramid really accepted me because of it." Sift turned to Ruwen. "Don't you dare ever tell my parents, but I miss it sometimes. That simpler life. I worked so hard to stay unattached to material things that the relationships snuck up on me. Now I'm bound tighter than Fluffy's coin bag."

Ruwen let out a long breath. "Man, I feel that. It petrifies me. Everyone's expectations are insane, and failure is catastrophic. I've taken on so many oaths, and so many people are critical to my life now, that the fear of failure or getting someone hurt is overwhelming."

"Well, you can't ruin the Universe until I have a proper vacation. Either someplace with snow, or a nice beach. The Spirit Realm beach doesn't count."

"I know. I just have a few problems to figure out first."

Sift picked up a stick and waved it. "I have problems, too. First that stupid Floot chest gave me trust issues, and now," Sift turned suddenly and stabbed his shadow with the stick. "Now, I can't even trust myself."

Ruwen didn't take the easy opening to poke Sift verbally. Instead, he opened his Void Band enough to launch a sword at Sift. The blade looked like tarnished silver and didn't have any etchings or symbols to save it from looking terribly plain.

Sift snatched it from the air before it struck him. "What's this?"

"It's to help with some of your trust issues."

"It's heavy, but the balance is excellent."

"That sword is called the Heavy Short Sword of the Comet."

"I remember this sword. You busted a giant crystal in front of Fractal's entrance with it."

Ruwen winced. "I had just figured out what it did. Check this out."

Ruwen held out a hand and Sift returned the sword. Ruwen placed both hands on the pommel and turned his hands in opposite directions. The sword rotated on the cross-guard and when the two blades reached ninety degrees they separated from each other.

"Two swords?" Sift asked.

Ruwen held up the blade in his left hand. "This sword sliced through my scale armor at the battle of New Eiru. It's called the Honed Short Sword of the Rising Star. It has a base damage of twelve to eighteen and it gives plus nine to Stamina and plus eight to Slashing."

Holding up the other sword, Ruwen continued. "This is the Honed Short Sword of the Falling Star. Same damage but it gives plus nine to Dexterity and plus eight to Piercing."

"They sound nice, but I really wanted something with a longer reach."

Ruwen smiled. "Longer than this?"

With a flick of the wrist, Ruwen launched the Honed Short Sword of the Rising Star into the air. Sift focused on the rising blade and Ruwen lowered Falling Star, the sword still in his right hand, and triggered the effect *Meteor Shower*.

Rising Star turned in the air like a boomerang and headed back toward them.

Sift looked at Ruwen. "What! How did you do that?"

"Like this."

Ruwen lifted Falling Star, and they both looked up. Rising Star stopped its descent and climbed upward again.

"Now that is burnt," Sift muttered. He looked down from the soaring blade and faced Ruwen. "Imagine what I could do with this when I'm flying."

Sift's questionable flying combined with the incredibly sharp airborne sword gave Ruwen second thoughts. "Promise me you'll practice on the ground until your chances of killing everyone around you drops to under fifty percent."

"Very funny, Starfield, let me try."

Ruwen handed the sword over. Sift moved it slowly, studying the effect it had on the Rising Star sword in the air. Within a minute, he had gained a decent amount of control.

"How do I land it?" Sift asked.

"That's tricky and depends on its speed. With Gold reflexes, you could probably catch it. The ground is an option if it's soft. If the swords collide, they merge again into the single blade."

Sift lowered the sword tip of Falling Star and Rising Star hurtled toward them. Ruwen resisted the urge to step in front of Sift and snatch the flying blade, trusting Sift's reflexes could handle the speed.

Sift snatched the blade, the sword's momentum turning him in a circle. He stopped and faced Ruwen, a huge grin on his face. "I love them."

"I knew you would. They're yours."

Sift frowned. "That's really nice, but I don't know."

"You never take anything, and these are perfect for you. In fact, you're like twins, both of you hiding your potential behind a plain surface."

Sift narrowed his eyes. "Did you just call me ugly?"

"Plain. There's a difference."

Sift flipped Rising Star and Ruwen twisted his body forward to allow the blade to pass him. The air disturbance made following the sword's path through the air behind him easy, and he noticed what Rami had the first time they'd studied the swords. They vibrated in synch with each other, and he could feel the connection between the weapons.

Sift altered the flying sword's path, bringing it back, and Ruwen stepped to the side to avoid the weapon again. With a snatch, Sift grabbed the sword and bled its momentum by letting it spin around his hand.

"Now you're just showing off," Ruwen said. "They're a gift. Please take them."

Sift studied the blades for a few seconds and then combined them into the Heavy Short Sword of the Comet. He locked gazes with Ruwen. "Thank you, Brother."

Tarot floated between them, the Misfortune Golem sitting on his deck of cards. "Any bets on what body part you cut off first?"

Sift pointed the sword at Tarot. "I was just starting to like you, Little Man. Don't mess it up."

"Finger," Tarot said.

"Head," Ruwen added.

"Oh, very good," Tarot said with a nod to Ruwen. "What a glorious failure self-decapitation would be."

"I hate you both," Sift said.

"You want me to hold that sword for you?" Tarot asked.

Sift dropped the weapon into his dimensional belt. "Absolutely not."

"The Adepts are almost back," Ruwen said. "They'll come into view in ten seconds."

"Seriously," Tarot said, pulling the end of a belt from his dimensional belly. "I'll trade you this orange belt for it."

"Is that mine?" Sift asked.

Tarot shrugged. "Hard to tell. There wasn't a name on it."

Sift jumped at Tarot, but the golem expected it and shot into the air. Sift leaped after him, his eyes glowing with white soul magic. The pair disappeared into the trees above Ruwen.

Not underestimating Tarot's thieving skills, Ruwen verified his orange belt remained in his Void Band.

Moss and branches rained down around Ruwen as Sift tried to catch Tarot. The Adepts came back into sight, and shortly they'd know which way the token lay hidden. Not long after that, they'd determine its exact location.

The Third Trial would soon be over.

CHAPTER 38

The group on the left had counted one more snail line than the right one, so they all moved in that direction. Forty minutes later, the lines had enough of a bend that Ruwen did his first calculation.

They all stopped and Ruwen sent a group of four Adepts down each snail line with directions to take one hundred steps and stop. He sent another group of four Adepts directly away from their position and told them to stop when they formed a line with the other two groups.

When the three groups had settled, Ruwen turned to Sift. "Does the distance look even on each side?"

Ruwen found judging distances without his map difficult. Probably because he'd relied on it his whole life. Sift on the other hand rarely used his basic interface and had an expert eye for distances.

"They're close," Sift replied. "Within a couple of feet."

"Which way is the center?"

"Our right."

Seeing an opportunity to finish the quest *That's Not a*

Number, and get Sift to say the word "even," Ruwen asked about the other groups. "What about the distance between us and the groups on the snail line?"

Sift glanced at both. "They're the same."

"You sure? They're exactly—"

Ruwen waved his hand as if searching for the right word.

Sift frowned at Ruwen. "Your brain fog is back. You should stop adding points to Intelligence. I think your brain is getting too thick to talk."

"I just want to make sure about the distances," Ruwen said, trying one more time.

Sift glanced both directions again and turned back to Ruwen. "They're equal."

"Thanks," Ruwen said, hiding his disappointment.

Ruwen placed his back to the snail line and turned his body until it pointed just a couple of feet to the right of the group in front of them. He had learned long ago that when a line with two points on a circle is crossed by a perpendicular line, that line points to the circle's center.

Tracing an imaginary line from this position, past the group of Adepts, Ruwen found a large cypress tree. Keeping his eyes on the tree, he spoke to Sift. "I'd like you to stay in this exact spot. When I reach the next marker, I'll use your position and mine to draw a line and pick a new marker. Then I'll signal you to come to my current location. We should stay on track if we do that."

"Got it."

Ruwen and Sift did this for the next hour and then repeated the line calculations. The snail lines had become noticeably tighter, their arcs more pronounced, confirming they had chosen the right direction. Seventy-five minutes later, they found the center, along with Rung One.

Unlike the rest of the swamp, the center's water remained

clear, and the bottom visible. Visible in the areas not covered in snakes, anyway.

"Why is it always snakes," Ruwen muttered.

During the Journeyman trial eighteen months ago, Ruwen had battled an entire bamboo forest of vipers. Most of them had reached an impressive size. The snakes, which only existed on the water's surface here, varied in size from worms to thinner than his pinky, with lengths ranging from the width of his hand to longer than his arm. After a moment of consideration, he decided these smaller versions were worse.

The clear water stretched a hundred feet across. The dark snails stood out on the surface and their slow spiral to the center had become easy to observe. When the snails reached the center, they turned, and began their spiral back to the swamp outskirts.

Two members of Rung One stood in bamboo cages only twenty feet from the shore, the water up to their armpits. Two more members of Rung One lay unconscious on an island thirty feet away. Echo and the remaining two Adepts of Rung One sat next to their unconscious team members.

The two Adepts with Echo stood and waved at Ruwen and his group. Echo continued to study the water, but she spoke under her breath, knowing his Diamond Fortified hearing would catch her voice.

"Took you long enough," Echo said.

Echo's Fortification to Gem had improved her senses as well, and Ruwen knew from this distance she would hear his voice even if he whispered.

Under his breath, Ruwen responded. "We took the scenic route. It looks like you have a problem."

The two Adepts with Echo moved toward Ruwen and the larger group. They tried to get Echo to come along, but she remained sitting.

"Nothing I won't figure out. You won't beat me again."

Ruwen turned his gaze from Echo and studied the snake-filled surface. Bamboo shoots covered the bottom and from the trapped Adepts, he guessed any disturbance caused them to snap upward, trapping whatever moved above them.

"This is not a competition," Ruwen whispered.

"The trial token begs to differ."

"This isn't about tokens, and you know it."

Ruwen sensed the pressure wave as Echo turned her head toward him, and he met her gaze. Their capabilities made the thirty feet between them irrelevant. With the slightest effort, Echo could have leaped the distance and attacked him before anyone nearby, except for Sift, could react.

The perfectly round lake had no trees, and the breeze high above, finding a hole in the swamp's defenses, swirled, mixing the rank deadness of the swamp with the clean scent of rain. It cooled his skin, and he enjoyed the sensation of something other than heat and saturated air.

"Are you sure?" Echo asked. "Philosophy can't shatter an enemy's throat or gouge their eyes out. In the end, will our Clan judge your philosophy or your Steps?"

"Can you have one without the other?"

"Infernal hells you sound just like my—"

Echo cut her response short, but Ruwen knew her family well enough to finish her thought. He reminded her of Lalquinrial, her father. When Ruwen had faced Echo's father in the Infernal Realm, he had sounded shockingly philosophical—even if he skewed toward crazy. Echo's mother, the Plague Siren that only wanted Ruwen's long painful death, didn't give the impression she cared much for thinking and had passed crazy long ago.

The two Adepts from Rung One arrived, and Ruwen turned his attention to them. They pointed to the unconscious Adepts near Echo and explained one had tried to out swim the snakes, but quickly found out this didn't work. The second passed-out

Adept had tried to float on their back with just their nose poking out, hoping the snakes would think it was just a snail. They hadn't and had bitten him on the nose.

The current in the water had quickly pushed both bodies back to the shore. The Rung One Adepts yelled to the two trapped teammates in the water, who responded they didn't feel any pain or unusual discomfort.

The Rung One Adepts described how one of their trapped teammates had tried walking along the bottom and the second, seeing the results of the first, had swum underwater but avoided touching the bottom. It didn't matter. The bamboo had triggered as soon as it detected a disturbance.

Everyone remained silent as they processed the information. If you couldn't walk, swim, or float there, what did that leave? Ruwen wondered if jumping there would work, although that required a Gem body to cross such a distance, which almost none of the Adepts had. That made it unlikely as a solution. Out of curiosity, Ruwen picked up a branch the length of his forearm and tossed it lightly at the center.

As it crossed the distance, snake after snake leaped upward and sank their fangs into the wood. The branch fell well short of the center, taken down by all the snakes hanging off it. The vipers would fill a person with venom as the mass of snakes pulled the jumper from the air. Unless that person had skin impervious to a snake bite.

Ruwen studied Echo. She would have obviously thought of this solution. Had she already tried? Knowing she would likely give him an elbow if he asked her directly, he queried the two Adepts. They explained when Echo pulled the unconscious Adepts from the water she had brushed their skin.

It turned out the venom spread through the body and trace amounts covered their skin, likely from pores, and would incapacitate anyone that came in contact with it. It had taken Echo ten minutes to recover from the tiniest brush.

Ruwen thanked the Adepts and returned his focus to the submerged chest fifty feet away. The snails wound their way around the clear water, the spiral this close to the center fully visible. The snakes swam between the snails but left them alone. He assumed the bamboo didn't trigger because the snails remained on the surface.

Ruwen had no idea how to reach the chest.

"I have an idea," Sift said.

Ruwen raised his eyebrows. "Let's hear it."

"We tie a rope around your waist. Then you jump. Best case, the snakes and their venom can't hurt you. You grab the chest and we pull you to safety."

"What's the worst case?" Ruwen asked.

Sift shrugged. "You pass out, but hopefully not before you shove the chest into your pants."

"My pants?"

"Or your shirt. I can't plan everything."

"And you call my ideas bad?"

"What? That's a good plan."

Ruwen frowned. "Let's call that Plan Never. I don't think the Founders envisioned people throwing their brothers and sisters into a lake like some kind of snake bait."

"No throwing. You jump. You're too heavy to throw. Should I explain it again?"

Ruwen held up his hands. "Dear Uru, no. Give me a minute to think of something else."

Everyone studied the clear water, snails, snakes, and chest. Ruwen turned his attention to the two Adepts trapped in the bamboo cages. One had tried to walk the bottom and the other to swim underwater, but both had triggered the traps just past the first snail line. Something bothered him about that and it took another minute to understand why.

The Adepts hadn't triggered the bamboo shoots directly

under the snail lines. It was only when they'd passed the snails that the traps had activated.

Ruwen's Cleverness attribute put all the information together with only a brief surge of cold, like someone opening a door in winter.

Ruwen cleared his throat and everyone faced him. "Prythus, you described the water in the swamp as the boundary between active growth and passive death. You likened it to the energy created by doing the Viper Steps and the release of that energy completing the Bamboo forms."

Prythus nodded, and Ruwen continued. "We arrive here and find concrete examples of your theory. Vipers on the surface, bamboo on the bottom, and the water between them."

Ruwen looked at the distant Echo, who he knew listened intently. "The *philosophy* embedded in the Steps laid out before us in a perfect representation. But how does that help us reach the token?" He paused for a moment before continuing. "How did we find this place to begin with?"

"The snails," Nymthus said.

"Yes," Ruwen said. "And I thought at first they had served their purpose. They are the obvious clue. Hard and soft in a spiral pattern that eventually became apparent."

Everyone remained silent, and Echo turned her head to watch Ruwen as well.

"All the components are here," Ruwen said. "Viper above, bamboo below, and a creature of hard and soft leading you like a literal road to the prize."

"Will you just spill it already?" Sift said.

"I just wanted to emphasize the worth of philosophy," Ruwen said without looking at Echo.

Ruwen glanced around the Adepts. "Before training with the Steps, I could maybe hold my breath for thirty seconds. But the meditation and controlled breathing strengthened my lungs, and yours. Breathing is also about balance. We breathe out when striking or throwing, and inhale while recovering." He turned to Prythus. "How long can you hold your breath now, as an Adept?"

Prythus thought a moment. "At least five minutes."

Ruwen nodded and looked back at the swamp. "Exactly so. I believe all of us here could manage that. Our training has ensured it."

Nymthus pointed to the two Adepts from Rung One. "But one of theirs tried swimming underwater. It didn't work."

Ruwen pointed to the two trapped Adepts. "Look closely. It didn't work once they passed the snail line."

Three seconds later, a loud splash caused everyone to turn toward Echo. She had dived under the water and immediately turned to follow the line of snails on the water's surface. They watched as she swam around the chest in a slowly closing spiral until, three minutes later, she reached the chest.

Echo grabbed the chest and continued following the trail the snails had created. Now, after reaching the center, they turned and began their spiral journey out toward the swamp's edges. Another three minutes and Echo spiraled out enough to escape the bamboo shoots on the swamp's bottom.

Echo stepped out of the water, her clothes sticking to her lean body. Ruwen knew the swim had been trivial for her. With a Gem body, she didn't need to breathe. As soon as the chest cleared the water, the bamboo cages withdrew, as did all the tiny snakes.

"Why did you talk so much?" Sift asked. "You could have just gone and got it."

Ruwen turned from Sift and looked at Echo. She stared at the chest, her face a mixture of happiness and misery.

"Now we lost," Sift said, disappointment in his voice.

Ruwen turned from Echo and faced Sift. He smiled at his best friend and answered mentally using *Sphere of Influence*. *We lost only if you wanted the chest.*

Sift looked confused, but before he could respond, Ruwen clapped, and soon the other Adepts joined him. Joy replaced most of the sadness on Echo's face, but a hint remained.

Ruwen opened his map, found the Fortress, and marched toward it, a grin on his face. It felt good to win.

CHAPTER 39

Once again, Ruwen sat cross-legged behind Rung Four, Sift beside him and the four buildings of the fortress surrounding them. They all wore their traditional uniforms, now with orange belts tied around their waists. Sift must have caught Tarot, or at least made a deal with the golem, as he'd regained his belt.

Padda stood at the front of the group holding thirty-three yellow belts, the Founders and Madda near him.

The Adepts stood and bowed as the Founders stepped forward.

"Never has a class shown such cooperation," Mist said.

"Or understanding," Thorn added.

Dusk continued. "Another day, another trial, another Clan first. Congratulations."

The Adepts bowed again, and the Founders returned it.

Madda turned to Padda, removed a yellow belt, and handed it to Thorn.

As Echo strode toward Thorn, Sift leaned over. "She didn't deserve to win."

Ruwen sighed. "This isn't a competition. I've said that like a hundred times. Don't you listen?"

"Mostly."

Ruwen frowned at Sift.

"Some," Sift amended.

Ruwen shook his head.

"I catch the highlights, okay," Sift said. "You repeat yourself a lot and I zone out."

"Are you calling me boring?"

Sift winced. "No?"

"You don't sound very sure."

"Stop making this about me. You're the one who gave our victory to the enemy."

"There are more important things than winning. And why do you care? You won't take a relic, anyway."

"Well, maybe you get something unusual for winning all three trials. Like a special meal or something."

Ruwen glanced at the surroundings. "Even the air tastes like dead leaves. The food can't be much better here."

"Don't judge a pastry by its frosting."

"I really hate that saying."

"We hate what we don't understand," Sift said and faced the front. "Stop distracting me."

"You started this!" Ruwen hissed.

"We can finish this later," Sift said. "Mom is glaring at you."

Ruwen refocused on the ceremony and confirmed Madda's stern face, but her glare focused on Sift not Ruwen. They waited in silence as all the Adepts moved one after the other to the front, where either Thorn or Mist gave them their yellow belt. All the previous ceremonies Sift had distracted Ruwen, and he hadn't made the connection between Adept and which Founder presented the belt.

All the Adepts had Master level skills in both the Viper and Bamboo Steps, but each favored a particular style. Sift and Ruwen were the only ones who had no detectable preference.

Sift had said his orange belt had different benefits than Ruwen's, and now that he paid attention, he noticed the Founder for each of the Adepts' preferred style presented the new belt.

Only Sift and Ruwen remained different. Thorn and Mist presented Sift's belt together and Dusk gave Ruwen his.

Ruwen sensed a slight disturbance from near Sift's hip, and it confirmed a theory he'd held. He remained still but whispered to Sift. "Shelly's back."

"What?"

"Check your hip pocket."

Sift turned quickly and a moment later held Shelly in his hands. He was still scolding the tiny tortoise for taking off on her own when Ruwen elbowed him.

Sift handed Shelly to Ruwen. "Thanks. Watch my turtle."

Ruwen took Shelly and held her carefully in his cupped hands as Sift marched to the front. Ruwen smiled at the tortoise and gently rubbed her tiny head. It was hard to fathom this creature could increase her size until she dwarfed this planet, swim through burning stars, and create tunnels through the Universe.

With a thought, Ruwen opened his Void Band an inch and gently launched a single Blessed Unleavened Bread from his Inventory. Hamma had given him the small cracker when they'd first adventured in the Black Pyramid together and it increased Stamina by two and Strength by one. The small cracker landed on the heel of his palm, and Shelly scooted forward to take a small bite. She chewed slowly and looked up at Ruwen briefly before taking another, bigger bite.

Ruwen's chest warmed with the thought of Hamma. She was always so generous and willing to help. He missed her positivity and common sense when they were apart. If anything, the time separated from her had highlighted what an outstanding balance she provided to his natural inclinations. She helped keep him present and grounded. He pushed the worry for her away, trusting she could handle her problems without his help.

Leaning down, Ruwen whispered to Shelly. "He doesn't deserve you."

"Bite your tongue," Sift said as he returned, holding out his hand.

Ruwen carefully handed Shelly back to Sift.

"What are you feeding her?" Sift asked. "Is it safe?"

Ruwen shook his head and ignored the question. He had watched Shelly eat a literal star and didn't imagine much in the Universe could upset the Elder Star Tortoise's stomach. Sift's concern for her made Ruwen smile. Sift had tried his best to remain free from attachments but had utterly failed. He had breezed through the first testing long ago, but Ruwen wondered if Sift's soul, weighted down with all those he loved, would find it as easy now.

"Hamma made them," Ruwen said as he strode toward the front.

"She can't cook!" Sift hissed.

Ruwen approached Dusk, who stood holding a yellow belt. He bowed and took the new belt when Dusk placed it across his outstretched hands. He bowed again, but before he stepped away Dusk spoke softly.

"You're missing something."

Ruwen didn't need to guess what she meant and took the opportunity to ask two questions that had worried him. "Will keeping it like this hurt me?" And as weird as it sounded, he pushed out the second one. "Or hurt my shadow?"

The thought of damaging something like his own shadow still seemed ludicrous, but he honestly did not know how the Shadow Realm worked, and worried that keeping his shadow locked in his Clan mark might cause harm.

"No damage," Dusk replied. "But without it visible, shadow magic isn't possible."

"Thank you," Ruwen said with relief.

Ruwen strode toward the back of the group. Since he didn't have any shadow magic, keeping his shadow locked away didn't cost him anything, and it provided some safety by denying others the opportunity to use it against him.

Ruwen reached Sift and found him trying to pull the cracker from Shelly, but the tortoise had half crawled on top and would nip at Sift's fingers when he tried to remove the bread.

Dusk spoke to the group. "Replace your orange belt with your new Clan rank of yellow. Store your orange belt with your white. They hold the work and dedication of your continuing steps toward Master."

Ruwen untied the orange belt and threw it over his shoulder, but after a moment reconsidered, and dropped it into his Void Band to head off any chance of Tarot stealing it. With now practiced ease, he tied the new yellow belt around his waist.

Like before, the Bamboo Viper Clan mark appeared briefly on Ruwen's right wrist, along with a slight burning sensation. The smoky fog surrounding the viper and bamboo had turned much darker, and he wondered if that resulted from the mark carrying his shadow.

Ruwen opened the notification.

Tring!
Dusk has gifted you...
Name: *Symbol of Lesser Shadow Funnel*
Restriction: *Bamboo Viper Clan Adept (Minimum)*
Restriction: *Rank Yellow (Minimum)*
Restriction: *Shadow required.*
Effect (Triggered): *Once per day, for seven seconds, reduce all damage taken by 10% and reduce damage done by 10%.*
Description: *Not all shadows fear the light.*

Ruwen read the notification twice more before Thorn spoke. "Our next destination is Savage Island."

Mist continued. "During your last visit, you likely noticed the mountains and maybe even the Champion's Fortress. Generally, classes take much longer between trials, and powering the portals to Savage Island creates no complications."

"This class, however," Dusk said. "Has obliterated the previous records and forced unexpected consequences on all of us."

Sift leaned toward Ruwen. "They're powering the portals with soul magic, and we aren't giving them enough time to recharge."

"Specifically," Thorn said. "Instead of five future visits to Savage Island, you will only return twice more."

"They should ask you," Ruwen whispered to Sift. "You never run out of soul energy."

Sift shook his head. "I am not hooking my soul to a portal. What if it sucks me in?"

"You have the weirdest fears."

"Many of the locations on Savage Island we place Adepts are educational," Mist said and held up three fingers. "Only three are necessary. The bridge, pools, and lake."

"In fact," Ruwen whispered to Sift. "It takes your parents and the Founders together, each powering a single gate rune, to open these portals. I bet you could power all five runes yourself."

"Not going to happen."

Dusk studied the Adepts for a few seconds before continuing. "Your Masters all used a crossing stone to translocate a mirrored form of your body and mind to the Journeyman test where you successfully scaled Mount Sorrow. Physically moving candidates from their home worlds to Mt. Sorrow would take a colossal amount of Clan resources. Wasted resources as so many students never complete or survive their training to reach the Master's trial."

Thorn held up a finger-sized black rock. It looked very similar to the one Padda had placed before Ruwen in the Black Pyramid.

Thorn moved the rock back and forth in front of her. "That is why the crossing stones are so important. It allows us to send many candidates to the Mt. Sorrow trial and determine if they are worthy to continue training in the Bamboo Viper Steps. Without these stones, our Clan would suffer."

"And we are dangerously low," Mist said. "We must collect more if our Clan is to thrive."

Ruwen kept his heart rate even, but he had wanted to study one of these stones ever since he'd learned of their existence. The Addas, before they had sent him to Mt. Sorrow, had told him the crossing stones used soul energy for the translocation.

The description for the Touchstone of Crossing that Padda had shown Ruwen, said the user's soul powered the translocation, and the Addas had made it sound like that as well. It remained unclear to him if his own soul had powered the crossing or if Padda had provided the power.

During Ruwen's Ascension, Uru had sealed up his soul. Had in fact, hidden it before his birth. Because these stones interacted directly with the soul, he hoped they would provide clues on how to break the vault that now contained his, or maybe a way to use his soul even in its current state. Because of all this, he had desperately wanted one to study.

And it appeared Ruwen's chance had finally arrived.

CHAPTER 40

*R*uwen stepped out of the rune gate into a clearing five hundred feet wide. Hundreds of stone pillars formed a giant ring around the open area, and they all had gate runes. The other Adepts grouped together, everyone looking around at their new location.

Mountains rose around them, blocking out the weak sunlight that storm clouds tried to smother. Distant thunder or, possibly, a battle between Gem Fortified fighters echoed off the steep sides of the nearby mountains. Cool air howled through the passes, swirling around them, and the strong scent of sulfur caused Ruwen to wince.

The Founders had come through the portal first, followed by the Adepts, and finally the Addas.

"This clearing is the only safe zone in this area," Mist said. "Clans are forbidden to fight here."

Thorn pointed at caves dotting the mountains surrounding them and finished by pointing at the large concentration of them at ground level. "Those are entrances to crossing stone mines. Digging through the rock or searching the natural caverns for the stones has a low success rate but is much safer than roaming the mountain passes and lava pools."

Mist raised a hand. "While the mines will keep you out of the elements and protected from the dangers on the surface, they are not safe. Be vigilant for other Clans. They allow you to enter but will attack on your return, hoping to steal any stones you've found."

"Where are the greatest concentrations of stones?" Echo asked.

"The lava pools," Dusk said. "But know they are filled with creatures, some as Fortified as you, Adept."

Echo pressed her lips together and nodded.

All the Adepts except for Ruwen, Sift, and Echo shivered in the cold air.

"My sisters and the Grandmasters will meditate here," Dusk said. "We will return to the trials when the class has collected a thousand pounds of crossing stones—or you've all died trying."

"If these rocks are so important, wouldn't this go faster if you helped?" Sift asked.

"Yes, it would," Thorn said. "And the Founders of some Clans are here doing just that. The Bamboo Viper Clan, however, is not so weak. Our Adepts can succeed without such compromises."

"Our first trip to Savage Island," Ruwen said glancing at the three Founders. "You told us to focus on surviving. Now we could all die before finding the stones you need. What changed?"

Dusk smiled sadly. "It is a consequence of speed. Like many things, progressing too quickly creates problems. In the past, this class would spend months together before reaching this point. The trials, coupled with the first four visits here, would cement trust in each other and the Steps while providing time to gain insights, new knowledge, and skills. Instead, we have jumped halfway, which makes the sudden shift in priorities confusing and sudden."

Ruwen frowned, uncomfortably aware this lesson applied to his training of Sift. "How long has it taken in the past to reach this point?"

"Before this class, the quickest took three months," Dusk replied.

Ruwen and Sift looked at each other and Sift shook his head slightly.

Sift's thoughts likely centered on Lylan and Hamma and it would take a miracle to convince him to stay so long. Not that Ruwen could afford to either, he had his own disasters brewing back home.

Ruwen turned back to the Founders. "Can we split the class? Those that want to go fast and those that want the traditional process?"

"No," Thorn said.

Ruwen's stomach knotted. He wanted to balance the need to get home quickly with the traditional experience for the other Adepts. Now he felt terribly selfish for wanting to proceed so quickly. His desires meant the others would not have the same training and experience as traditional classes when facing these last two visits to Savage Island.

The problems Ruwen faced required attention and could not wait three months. That meant the Adepts here would suffer so he could fix the issues he'd created somewhere else. None of that was fair to the Adepts, but he couldn't feel guilty about it either. In the past, he would have carried this guilt for days or weeks, but as his problem became bigger, and the stakes higher, he needed to make hard decisions and move on.

Ruwen stepped to the front of the group and turned to face the Adepts. "I can't wait three months, and I'm sorry this impacts you. I can't reveal my reasons, but I didn't make this decision lightly."

Before any of the Adepts could respond, Ruwen faced the Founders and bowed. "I respect your traditions, but I will no longer put my classmates' lives at risk by not using my capabilities. Restricting my abilities during the trials I understand, but the situation here, as you've already explained, is different, and I will treat it as such. I won't trivialize our stay here, but I won't let anyone die if I can help it."

Ruwen waited for the Founders to respond, but they only returned his gaze with neutral expressions. That was good enough for him.

With a thought, Ruwen pushed the *Insect Repellent* shield to it maximum distance of one hundred feet. Immediately the gusts of wind calmed, the shield turning them into a breeze instead. Channeling fifty Energy per second into the level eighteen Collector spell *Greenhouse*, he raised the temperature ten degrees in a hundred-foot radius, the most he could at the spell's current level. It should stop the shivering of the Adepts though.

Once again Ruwen missed having access to his Spirit. He had spent all that time alone learning how to create powerful Spirit versions of his spells, and now he couldn't use them.

Ruwen focused on Sift and used *Sphere of Influence* to speak telepathically. *One of us needs to get the Adepts out of the cold, while the other quickly finds the crossing stones.*

After a moment, Sift responded. *I'll stay, but hurry.*

Ruwen nodded and turned to the Adepts. "I'm heading for the lava pools, and anyone is welcome to join me. I would recommend however you stay with Sift who is entering the caves. With a large group, the mines should hold no dangers."

"What about you?" Nymthus asked.

"I have advantages to keep me safe," Ruwen replied.

"Everyone with me," Sift said. "Let's get out of this wind."

"I hate the smell of sulfur," Tarot said. "It reminds me of the Infernal Realm. I'm going with List Boy."

Tarot squirmed off of Ruwen's head and shot toward Sift.

Sift marched toward the closest mine entrances two thousand feet away. With a few glances at Ruwen, the rest of the Adepts followed. Everyone but Echo.

"What?" Echo asked when Ruwen glanced at her. "I'm not letting you get all the glory."

Ruwen nodded, turned, and jogged toward the strongest sulfur scent. As he'd told the Founders, he didn't use *Sixth Sense* or *Survey* to make finding the crossing stones trivial, and he toggled off the Resource tab on his map as well. He stopped channeling *Greenhouse* since the cold didn't bother him and pulled his *Insect Repellant* shield up against his body.

Echo followed two hundred feet behind Ruwen, and he wondered at her true motives.

This high in the mountains only scrub brush grew, the pine trees unable to survive past a point three hundred feet below. After five minutes of jogging, the rock turned from broken granite into hardened lava flows. Another three minutes, and Ruwen slowed to a walk as the pumice under his feet turned soft.

After a moment of thought, Ruwen stripped down to his underwear, dropping his formal attire in his Void Band. He didn't want to destroy them, which seemed likely as the temperature had increased thirty degrees already. The lava must be close. He tried to ignore Echo's presence but made the mistake of looking back before continuing.

Echo had followed Ruwen's example, except she'd taken everything off. He whipped his head around and forced his body to ignore what he'd just seen. How in Uru's name would he explain he saw Echo naked while he stood in his underwear. That might test even Hamma's patience.

Ruwen hurried forward, and the heat increased as the valley narrowed. Two minutes later the path he'd taken ended at a thirty-foot wall made of oozing pumice. It dripped down the cliff face like wax from a burning candle. Not wanting to turn around and face Echo, he leaped the thirty feet up.

Ruwen cleared the wall and glimpsed the source of the half-melted pumice, right before he landed in a bubbling lake of lava. His momentum pushed him waist deep in the thick liquid, and his Diamond Fortified body, vastly more dense and much heavier than a normal person, sank.

The superheated rock roiled from unseen currents, and they grabbed his legs, pulling him deeper into the lava. He controlled his instinctive panic, reassuring himself the lava wasn't hot enough to harm him. After a few seconds that proved true and he swept his arms downward, pushing himself back toward the surface. His Diamond Strength made the motions effortless even though he swam through molten rock. He couldn't bring himself to open his eyes though.

Cool air, at least cooler than the lava, struck Ruwen's face, and he opened his eyes. He moved his arms and legs slowly, keeping himself stationary as the currents tried to toss him around. He had landed thirty feet from the cliff edge that dropped to the valley he'd jumped from. The lava lake continued for another five hundred feet and ended at a small set of cliffs that climbed like stairs up to what appeared to be another lake.

The upper lava lake boiled, sending spouts of liquid rock into the air. It spilled down the cliff-stairs in a glowing orange lavafall, the intense heat warping the air and causing the whole scene to waver. It looked beautiful and hypnotic.

Something bit Ruwen's right calf and pulled him under.

Swimming in lava was a new experience, and what he'd thought were slow-moving pressure waves coming from chunks of rock or semi-solid pumice, turned out to be something else. The waves had originated from something living. Something with a lot of teeth.

Ruwen let the creature pull him down. It jerked its head

from side to side, probably trying to rip his leg off. They reached the bottom of the lava lake, and he reached down, running his hands along the beast's head. What type of creature lived inside lava?

Whatever it was, it had a long head. Ruwen pulled the mouth open wide enough to remove his leg and then released the creature. It immediately snapped onto his right arm. He could have moved out of the way, but his curiosity had gotten the better of him, and he wanted to see it above the surface.

With a push off the bottom, Ruwen shot upward, pulling the creature along. He burst through the top of the lava lake like a whale coming up for air. Splashing down, his back made a loud smack as it struck the viscous liquid. He kicked his feet slowly, keeping himself on the surface, and raised his arm to see what had attacked him, causing his Perception to trigger.

Name: *Obsidian Eel*
Level: *68*
Health: *1,935*
Mana: *250*
Energy: *2,275*
Spirit: *0*
Armor Class: *1,720*

The eel had a shiny black color, like polished stone, and its scales overlapped each other, allowing it to twist, but not nearly as much as a snake or water eel. Ruwen couldn't find its eyes, and he guessed it spanned over twenty feet in length. Two feet of that length consisted of a mouth filled with razor-sharp black teeth.

The Obsidian Eel tried again to tear Ruwen's arm off, and he flicked his arm forward hard enough to fling the eel into the lava twenty feet away. The creature immediately righted itself and swam through the lava, directly back at him.

"I gave you a chance," Ruwen said as the eel came into arm's reach.

As the eel opened its mouth to attack, Ruwen pushed its mouth to the side, grabbed it behind the head, where he guessed the body began, and squeezed his hand into a fist.

The Obsidian Eel had an Armor Class of over seventeen hundred, more than a plate armored Fighter with a tower shield. Ruwen's clenched hand crushed the creature's neck, severing its head from its body.

Almost immediately, as if Ruwen had covered the area in black blood, he felt dozens of pressure waves approaching him from off the floor of the lava lake. He didn't know if they approached him to battle, or to eat their fallen brother. Maybe both he thought and swam away.

From the far edge of the lake near the lavafalls, five hundred feet away, a pack of nine glowing wolves sprinted from the shore directly onto the lava, their huge paws keeping them from sinking, at least while they moved. Their bodies looked fluid, as if made from lava, and heat radiated off their bodies. He focused on the biggest one in front.

Name: *Greater Magma Hound*
Level: *88*
Health: *2,726*
Mana: *400*
Energy: *1,690*
Spirit: *0*
Armor Class: *990*

They raced directly toward Ruwen.

Not far from the cliff that dropped to the valley below, in an area Ruwen had thought only contained pumice, a boulder separated itself and floated toward him.

Name: Cinder Mammoth
Level: 79
Health: 3,285
Mana: 1,100
Energy: 2,900
Spirit: 0
Armor Class: 1,990

Ruwen found Echo watching him from three hundred feet away. She stretched out on a rock, as if enjoying the sun.

They both sensed the newcomer at the same time and Ruwen turned his attention to the top of the lavafalls, his Perception providing the details.

Name: Ash Specter
Deity: Unknown
Class Type: Cultivator - Topaz
Level: 69
Health: 1,775
Mana: 0
Energy: 0
Spirit: 50,000,000
Armor Class: 1,050

Ruwen sighed and cursed Tarot under his breath. Only monumental bad luck would send all these creatures at the same time.

If it wasn't for bad luck, Ruwen wouldn't have any luck at all.

CHAPTER 41

*T*he Ash Specter on the lavafall above Ruwen had a humanlike form, only thinner and standing seven feet tall. The heat radiating from the creature distorted the air, making it hard to see other details. The lava near the Ash Specter bubbled and exploded as its heat vaporized the liquid rock.

"These are my pools," the Ash Specter hissed.

Ruwen treaded lava, keeping his head above the surface. Over a dozen Obsidian Eels, nine Magma Hounds, and a Cinder Mammoth had locked on to his location and would start arriving in the next ten seconds. The thought of finding a less crowded lava pool crossed his mind when a terrible realization occurred to him.

The lava had destroyed Ruwen's underwear, and he currently swam naked.

Ruwen had come a long way physically from his days as a— how had Slib put it on Ruwen's Ascendancy Day: book brain. Ironically, that unimaginative insult had literally come true as the books in his head spawned Narrators.

Since that time, Ruwen had added over a hundred Attribute

points to his Strength, around one hundred fifty to Stamina, and more than fifty to Charisma. He had spent tens of thousands of hours honing his body into a lethal instrument and Fortified it to Peak Diamond. Physically, he knew he looked like one of those statues in Uru's Temple.

Even with a vastly increased Wisdom, Ruwen couldn't overcome a lifetime of modesty and shyness. Especially with a naked Echo watching him from shore. Fighting naked was more Sift's style, which was just another reason to stay in the lava.

"Can we share?" Ruwen shouted back.

The creature growled and flexed its arms forward. Ruwen narrowed his eyes, reducing the intense brightness the Ash Specter's body radiated, making it bearable to watch. He wondered if it might be part fire elemental. It looked like a living torch.

"No need to get so upset, Torchy," Ruwen called. "The pool is big enough for us both."

The growl turned into a scream and Torchy disappeared. Ruwen frowned in confusion until he noticed the hole where Torchy had stood. The Ash Specter had melted through the rock and Ruwen could guess the creature's destination.

The first eels reached Ruwen and six of them coiled around his body as they tried to bite through his skin. Instinctively, he rotated his right leg forward to protect his groin. Even knowing that his entire body remained impervious to the eels' bites, the thought of something chomping down on his privates actually made him panic for a moment. He sunk into the lava, the combination of no longer treading lava and the eels making the descent quick.

Ruwen added destruction proof underwear to his priority list.

Six more Obsidian Eels wrapped around Ruwen as his feet sank into the soft mostly melted rock of the lava lake's bottom.

Eels covered almost his entire body, and it gave him an idea. And for once, he considered it a bad one.

The Cinder Mammoth moved slowly through the lava and wouldn't reach Ruwen for another fifteen seconds. The Magma Hounds ran around in circles thirty feet above Ruwen's head, evidently not able, or willing, to leave the surface. With his feet touching rock, he could feel the vibrations Torchy caused as he melted his way toward Ruwen. The Ash Specter would arrive in ten seconds.

The eels exerted significant pressure, leveraging their long bodies to constrict Ruwen's frame. His right hand had protected his groin when the eels arrived and now it lay pinned against his body from their coils.

Ruwen brought his left arm down and pressed it against the three eels wrapped around his torso, pinning them against his body. Then he lifted his right arm, while keeping the creatures trapped with his left.

The three eels, unable to unwind, tore in half. Ruwen grabbed the head of the eel trying to bite through the top of his head with one hand, while the other hand snatched the eel wrapped around his neck and trying to chew through his nose and eyes.

Ruwen clenched both hands, separating the heads from the eels. Knowing he didn't have much time, he slammed his arms down against the outside of his legs, crushing the remaining eels.

Not having the time to second guess, Ruwen grabbed one beheaded eel and wrapped it around his waist like a belt. Using his level two Worker Ability *Knots*, he quickly tied it, the ability adding ten percent to the knot's effectiveness. Almost out of time, he seized the other beheaded eel and looped it between his legs, around the eel-belt behind him, and back through his legs. He threaded the second eel under the knot near his bellybutton and tied it off.

The two eel knots were large and cumbersome, but the eel-underwear served as passable protection, and gave him immense relief. Thank Uru, no one could see him.

Torchy emerged from the bottom of the lava lake, ten feet away. The surrounding temperature increased immediately, and the lava thinned as it became super-heated. Ruwen sank as the floor melted and he used his arms to swim upward.

A three-foot spear shot toward Ruwen ten times faster than a siege bolt, and he twisted his body to let it pass. No solid ground reduced his offensive and defensive options, and the sensation reminded him of Rainbow's End before he'd increased the gravity.

Three more spears erupted from Torchy, and Ruwen felt the expenditure of Spirit. He dodged two and pushed the third away. Torchy, it seemed, didn't have anyone telling him to fight honorably with just his Step skills.

Ruwen felt tempted to spray lake water from his Void Band, creating a massive explosion of steam, or *Harden* the area around the Ash Specter to interfere with his movements. Even the *Greenhouse's* meager ten-degree temperature might make a difference.

Access to Spirit would have provided Ruwen with hundreds of options, but he pushed that thought away. No use in dwelling on his limitations. Plus, he didn't need an advantage.

Ruwen thrust his palm toward Torchy, using twenty percent of his Strength. The lava, thicker than water, created an almost instantaneous column of compressed molten rock that struck Torchy in the chest.

The Cinder Mammoth arrived from behind Ruwen. He turned his body, placed a hand on the creature's rock-hard nose, and cartwheeled over the creature as it passed below him. From the pressure wave the creature created, it stood fifteen feet tall and twice that long. He couldn't see in the lava, but from the way it moved, he guessed it had flippers or a small tail.

More eels found Ruwen, and he rapidly punched the lava, sending spears of compressed lava that ripped the creatures apart. Torchy dived to the side, his Topaz reflexes allowing him to avoid the Cinder Mammoth as it tried to slow and turn back to Ruwen.

Torchy pushed both hands forward, along with a burst of Stone and Water essence.

The lava around Ruwen solidified, trapping him in a twenty-foot sphere of pumice. He immediately twisted in a circle, using his arms to carve out a sphere in the rock. Switching on *Glow*, he opened his eyes for the first time. He rubbed them as the intense heat made them itch.

Ruwen looked down and studied his eel-underwear, shaking his head at the absurdity of this entire situation.

Torchy cast another spell and obsidian needles slid through the already remelting pumice. Ruwen didn't have enough room to avoid the attack, but instead of destroying the pumice trap and escaping, he sat and considered what to do next.

Ruwen ignored the fifty obsidian needles that penetrated his sphere. They shattered against his skin and fell, tinkling around him like breaking glass. He picked up a long fragment and twirled it through his fingers as he thought.

Killing Torchy seemed like an overreaction, but Ruwen didn't want to waste a bunch of time fighting either. He had barely started his search and had already gotten himself bogged down. Honestly, this whole thing would go faster if someone would tell him where to look for the black crossing stones.

Could it be that simple? Ruwen stood, dropped the obsidian needle, and using fifty percent of his Strength, clapped.

The clap created a vacuum behind Ruwen's hands, forming a massive air depression and ripping the pumice prison apart as it collapsed. A fraction of a second later, an enormous pressure wave spread outward from the impact of his hands.

A sphere of sound and air expanded, Ruwen at its center.

The fifty feet of lava above him soared upward like a massive geyser. The airborne lava, exposed to the frigid mountain wind, immediately solidified. The lava around him rose in a tidal wave, rushing outward toward the lake boundaries. The pressure wave had forced the surrounding liquid away and created an area free of lava fifty feet wide.

The Magma Hounds had paced in a tight circle directly above Ruwen, and the nine of them rose a hundred feet into the sky, disappearing in the sludge of solidifying airborne lava.

Torchy stumbled on the now solid lake bottom, the icy wind swirling down from above and cooling everything it touched. His face and chest had turned solid as he struggled to counter the sudden change in temperature.

Ruwen leaped over the twenty-five feet separating him and Torchy. Grabbing the Ash Specter's shoulders, he steadied the creature.

"Hey," Ruwen said. "I feel like we started on the wrong foot."

Shards of pumice dropped around them like dirty hail and the tidal wave of lava struck the cliffs, rebounding, and creating a massive return wave. The surrounding lake surged downward to refill the void.

Ruwen grabbed the molten Ash Specter and jumped with seventy percent of his strength, launching them four hundred fifty feet to the top of the lava falls. A massive clap of thunder shook the surrounding mountains as his passage violently disturbed the air.

The sudden movement stunned the Ash Specter, and he wobbled on his feet. Ruwen held him steady and brushed the layer of pumice dust that covered Torchy's solidified shoulders. The grey skin felt hot, and when the wind blew, it glowed orange, reminding Ruwen of campfire coals.

Torchy's eyes were mostly hidden behind slits, either naturally or because the Ash Specter squinted. The pupils, barely visible, had a mixture of orange, red, and blue, and they glowed like two burning embers.

Ruwen glanced at the lake below. The lava waves crashed into each other as they filled the void he'd created. Nine Magma Hounds streaked downward, creating small craters where they struck the churning lava. The Cinder Mammoth lay on the shore, and it struggled to stand. It looked like a cross between an appah and a walrus.

The Cinder Mammoth flew into the air, the creature just turning itself in time to land with a massive belly flop. Echo pushed herself to her feet, a scowl on her face. She looked up at Ruwen and flashed him an elbow. He turned back to Torchy, not bothering to hide a smile.

The Ash Specter still looked dazed, and fear made his body tense. The creature had experienced enough to understand its situation.

"Like I was explaining before, I'm new here," Ruwen said. "Could you help me find some rocks?"

After a moment, Torchy nodded.

Ruwen's smile turned into a grin. Sometimes the easiest thing to do was just ask for the help you needed.

From the lava shore down below, Echo's voice floated up, loud and clear.

"Nice butt!"

Ruwen didn't need to look down to see he'd lost his eel-underwear in the violent jump here. Echo must have seen the makeshift clothing and realized the lengths he'd gone for the sake of modesty before the Cinder Mammoth landed on her. Maybe that's why she didn't dodge the massive beast to begin with. Regardless, she wouldn't miss the opportunity to make him feel uncomfortable.

Ruwen's smile faded as Torchy also noticed Ruwen wore no clothes.

Echo whistled, and Ruwen's cheeks warmed, this time not from the lava.

"Is that an eel in your pocket?" Echo yelled.

"Oh Uru, no," Ruwen mumbled. "This is not happening."

Echo's hysterical laugher kept her from answering her own question.

Ruwen shook his head, sighed, and met Torchy's gaze. "So, this is awkward."

CHAPTER 42

*T*orchy didn't respond, and his heart rate increased dramatically. The Ash Specter pinched an area just under his left shoulder and pulled down. The glowing grey skin folded down like a pocket revealing a fist sized chamber. He reached in and removed four finger sized crossing stones, holding them out to Ruwen like an offering.

Closing Torchy's hand over the rocks, Ruwen gave the Ash Specter a slight bow. "I will find my own."

If Ruwen could convince the Ash Specter to help, the knowledge would speed his search, but Torchy remained in obvious fear. After a moment of thought, Ruwen channeled twenty Energy per second into the level five Worker spell *Calm*. After the one second cast time, it increased his Persuasion by thirty, bringing it to eighty-two percent, and added two Charisma to his current value of sixty-six.

Ruwen had rarely needed to leverage these abilities, but he had experienced their effects from people like Big D and many of the performers he'd seen in Deepwell. Not to mention all the deities. With a little effort, he could now replicate that effect on others, as the body Fortification and leveling compounded his Charisma gains.

"I could use your help," Ruwen said, as friendly as he could.

Torchy calmed in just a few heartbeats, as Ruwen's voice, enhanced by his Persuasion and aided by his natural Charisma, struck the Ash Specter like a one-two punch.

The fear disappeared and Torchy turned chatty, explaining the stones sometimes washed up on shore, but the highest concentrations existed in the magma chambers underground. He pointed to the lava tubes that led to the largest magma pools and offered to take Ruwen.

Ruwen thanked the Ash Specter, feeling a little guilty about the purposeful manipulation. He stopped channeling Persuasion and Torchy came to his senses, immediately jumping away and fleeing.

Echo had still not recovered, and Ruwen tried to ignore the laughter. Since he needed to return to the blistering liquid, he skipped getting dressed and headed for the lava tube Torchy had identified as leading to the largest magma chamber.

Ruwen hurried, both to lose Echo and get back out of sight.

Two hours later, Ruwen strode into the portal clearing they had all arrived at earlier. Once again, he wore the Bamboo Viper Clan traditional attire along with his yellow belt. The Founders and Addas sat in a circle next to the portal stone, all meditating. He smiled and wondered if any of them had reached Sift's ninth level.

Ruwen angled away from the adults and directly toward the cave Sift and the other Adepts had marched at when Ruwen had left. Now that he understood the geography better, he recognized the openings were old lava tubes.

Motion caught Ruwen's attention, and he focused on an opening six hundred feet to the left of the one Sift had entered. Demons, some similar to the ones Ruwen had fought in the Infernal Realm, poured into the valley. The group of fifty moved with purpose, and it only took him a moment to calculate their destination: Sift's tube.

Still a thousand feet away from the same destination, Ruwen sprinted, only using a fraction of his speed. He didn't want to draw attention to himself with a concussive boom from moving too fast. Even at this pace, he would beat the demons by twenty seconds.

Ruwen considered his options. He could stop and fight the horde, assuming they knew the Bamboo Viper Clan had entered that tube and the demons' intentions were bad. If they had some other intention, though, fighting them might draw more demons, or cause some other issue that Ruwen hadn't considered. Since he could always fight later, he opted to ignore the fighters and concentrated on finding Sift.

The group of demons saw Ruwen, but on the rock-strewn ground, most of them couldn't increase their speed any further. A handful did, though, probably having Fortified into Gem and possessing the reflexes to navigate the dangerous terrain at a sprint.

On Rainbow's end, as Ruwen had slowly created an atmosphere, he'd learned that the loud explosions caused when he moved too fast differed as the atmosphere changed. Back home, he could move a thousand feet in a second and avoid tearing the air and creating a thunderclap. That number on Rainbow's End started vastly higher and lowered with the air pressure.

Ruwen's time there had made him an expert at judging when the boom would occur. From the lava pool fight with Torchy, he knew the air pressure here allowed him to approach one thousand two hundred feet per second and remain quiet.

With the precise control of a Peak Diamond body, Ruwen pushed off harder with his right foot and launched his body forward, crossing the remaining thousand feet in a single second.

Ruwen landed on his feet inside the lava tube and slowed his sprint to a jog. This lava tube had a diameter of thirty feet, twice the size of the ones he'd just swum through, and it angled gently downward. Without *Survey*, *Stone Echo*, or even *Sixth Sense*, he didn't have any idea what surrounded him, and a slower, more cautious behavior felt warranted.

The walls looked smooth until closely examined, and the air still held the powerful scent of sulfur. Protected from the wind, and surrounded by all the stone, the tunnel felt almost warm, and Ruwen jogged forward.

As the entrance disappeared behind Ruwen, the tube darkened; he compensated by speeding up the dilation of his pupils. Two tunnel turns later, true darkness took hold, and he considered triggering *Glow*. Instead, he relied on his hearing, using the echoes from his movement to paint a picture of the surroundings.

Twenty minutes later, Ruwen worried he'd picked the wrong path when he still hadn't found or heard anyone. He'd passed over thirty branching tunnels, all smaller, and he'd reasoned the Adepts would stay in the large one. Now he wondered if he'd guessed wrong.

Five minutes later, Ruwen felt the first slight vibrations of distant movement, and relief washed over him.

Ruwen increased his speed to a run and within a minute heard faint sounds bouncing down the tunnel. Ten seconds later he detected the first heartbeats, and when the number passed thirty-five, he frowned. Sift's group was not alone. Ruwen increased his speed again, sprinting through the darkness so quickly he needed to run up the walls at every turn.

The tunnel scattered sound and Ruwen couldn't tell if he approached a battle or not, but the noise echoing up the lava tube illuminated the tunnel like the midday sun. The smell of sulfur turned intense, and the temperature increased significantly. Fifteen seconds later, dim orange light filtered into the tunnel as it grew even wider.

Ruwen burst from the lava tube and into the magma chamber at over thirty miles per hour. Small shards of obsidian and pumice dust followed him like a long cloak, his wake roiling the air behind him.

The magma chamber spanned two thousand feet, and the ceiling soared to at least a hundred. The far side of the space held a bubbling pool of magma, three hundred feet across. Between the heat and overpowering sulfur smell, breathing felt painful.

At least six other large lava tubes, like the one Ruwen had just exited, branched off this space. Thousands of holes covered the walls and floor, their sizes varying from a couple of feet to over ten. Most of them had a demon head poking out, and they all watched the same thing.

Sift. Along with the rest of the Adepts.

Five hundred feet from Ruwen sat the only two structures in the room. The first appeared like a long warehouse with twenty-five-foot-tall double doors on one side. Sift and the Adepts grouped around the second structure, a fifteen-foot-tall circle of black rock standing upright on its edge like a giant ring. White light filled the entire ring's center and Ruwen couldn't see through it to the other side.

Sift and most of the other Adepts fought off a horde of demons while the entirety of Rung Four attacked the ring with a frenzy.

Ruwen hadn't slowed much since entering the magma chamber and now weaved between the demon holes, appearing and disappearing before any of them could react. He considered jumping to Sift, but his time with Overlord and all his various minion combinations had taught Ruwen painful lessons about the vulnerability of sailing through the air. With so many demons here with unknown abilities, he sped up instead, and ran the five hundred feet.

The demons Ruwen passed didn't have the variety he'd seen in the Infernal Realm. While they came in different sizes, the demons all had a human shape with the addition of a muscular tail and claws that extended from their knuckles. Exposed skin looked rough, like rock, and he guessed it provided natural armor. The size and number of horns on the tops of their heads provided the most variation in their appearance other than height.

Ruwen's Perception informed him they were a type of Scourge Grunt.

As Ruwen approached the fighting, the demons on the far side of the glowing ring yelled and shouted in Inferni, trying to get the attention of their comrades before Ruwen blew by them.

One of the larger demons turned in time to prepare for Ruwen's arrival. As he neared the demon, it jumped up and forward, its timing excellent, and pushed two clawed feet at Ruwen while balancing on its tail. Striking anything at his current velocity would crush a normal person, turning their chest into mush.

The demon had timed its jump with enough precision to earn a sliver of respect from Ruwen. Even though he traveled in basically a straight line, he ran at a faster speed than normal, and calculating the attack to strike him took some skill. The timing, in fact, would make the attack impossible to avoid for most people.

Ruwen didn't slow but altered his center of gravity to the right, his reflexes and mental decision making more than enough to handle such mundane things. His training with Overlord had prepared him for far worse than this, and he didn't even bother with Last Breath.

As Ruwen passed the demon, he grabbed its foot and then, like an acrobat, twisted in a tight circle, never slowing, the movement so smooth it never altered his balance. He released the demon halfway through the turn, throwing him into the demons on the far side that had warned of Ruwen's impending arrival.

The now flying demon struck the group, and demons flew outward like a bomb had exploded. Two seconds later, Ruwen slowed as he reached the fighting.

Rungs One, Two, and Three had formed a circle around Rung Four, who savagely continued attacking the black ring. Blood stained many Adepts' formal clothing, and most of it appeared their own. The Adepts, however, held their position, using their superior techniques to counter the demons crude fighting skills.

Sift held a quarter of the circle himself, the area in front of him littered with unconscious or dead demons. Ruwen made a short jump over the fighting and landed between Sift and the ring.

Ruwen strode over to Sift. "Hey."

Sift kept his focus on a group of three demons that were coordinating their attacks.

"I hate your golem," Sift said without looking at Ruwen.

"Why?" Tarot said from above. "I told you the truth."

Sift jumped forward before the group of three demons could attack. He slapped the middle demon and kicked it under the ribs. It wasn't the most destructive attack, but certainly one of the more painful ones, which was what Sift had intended. As the demon jerked to the side in a natural pain reflex, Sift kneeled in a Bamboo Step called Begging Butterfly.

Grabbing the injured demon's head, Sift used the demon's own momentum to flip him sideways into the demon on the left, the motion so effortless and natural it looked gentle. But the cracking of bones as the two demons collided revealed the violent truth. Casually, Sift snapped his right leg out, crushing the remaining demon's ankle. As the demon fell, Sift kicked higher, catching the beast in the throat. It fell backward, gasping.

Sift spun around and into a standing position, never losing sight of the surrounding enemies. He pointed up at Tarot without looking, keeping his focus forward. "He told us this tube had the most crossing stones."

"That's true!" Tarot said. "I'm a thieving golem, not a deceitful one."

"More like a 'not all the facts' golem," Sift replied.

"Look at it!" Tarot yelled, pointing at the large black ring. "And there are more in that warehouse, I bet. I'm going to check."

Tarot flew toward the warehouse, disappearing behind it two hundred feet away. Ruwen glanced at the fifteen-foot ring. Could that come from a single crossing stone? He used *Analyze*.

Target: Infernal Crossing Ring
Type: Structure
Strengths: Extreme Durability, Mobility
Weaknesses: None
Uses: Oversized portal linked to another. Resonance paired and not rune anchored provides location independence.

Rung Four franticly attacked the ring.

"Are you going to help?" Sift asked. "Or just stand around? We should blow this bakery before more of these things climb out of their holes. Or worse, better fighters arrive."

Ruwen thought about the group he beat to the tunnel entrance. "I think those are coming. There are Cultivators on the way."

"Just great," Sift said as he snatched a spear from the air, turning and throwing it back at the sender in one motion. "What is wrong with Rung Four?"

"Good question," Sift said. "They went crazy when they saw that thing and ran straight into this mess. They won't leave."

"Okay," Ruwen responded. "Let's get some breathing room and find out what's going on. Should I take over here or do the clearing?"

"Clearing," Sift said immediately. "It's your golem's mess."

While talking to Sift, Ruwen had kept track of the surrounding battle. The Adepts outclassed the demons, but the vast numbers had created pressure.

"Give me a few seconds," Ruwen said and jumped to his right, landing outside the circle of Adepts and in the middle of the thickest clump of demons.

CHAPTER 43

*W*ith only a few exceptions, the demons Ruwen had seen in the chamber lacked any body Fortification, and while their fighting skills were above average, they paled in comparison to highly trained Step practitioners.

Ruwen had told Sift he'd clear enough of the attackers to give everyone a break and hopefully provide enough time to understand what possessed Rung Four. To that end, he focused on efficiency, not beauty.

With spread arms, Ruwen ran through the massed fighters, scooping up demons and letting them pile up in front of him. His Diamond Strength easily pushed the mass of bodies, and every time he collected around twenty, he angled himself away from the Adepts and shoved the demon pile backward. The mass of demons acted like a wave, spreading out and tumbling into the other demons, breaking bones and twisting joints.

After the second lap around the Adepts, the demons retreated, and Ruwen strode back to Sift.

"Fancy," Sift said. "Nice technique."

"Shovel style," Ruwen replied.

"Shed style, and now Shovel. You have a real theme."

Ruwen grinned. "I'm a Worker. What do you expect?"

The Adepts shrank into a tight circle and rested. Rung Four seemed oblivious to their surroundings as they pounded on the Infernal Crossing Ring with stones, which did no damage. Ruwen opened his Void Band and released cool fresh air. He'd collected it shortly after reactivating Uru's third temple, which felt like a different lifetime, and still had one hundred forty-three thousand cubic feet in his Inventory.

Ruwen had learned from Bliz the importance of collecting whatever you could. Everything stored became another tool in your kit, and Ruwen had already found this fresh air useful three times. Once in the underwater safehouse after Xavier had tried to kill him and burned the air to toxic levels, at the city gate during the battle of New Eiru as toxic fumes surrounded his allies, and during the fight with an elite squad of fighters serving Naktos. That fight had ended with Hamma sacrificing herself to save them.

After releasing sixteen thousand cubic feet of air, the intensity of the sulfur smell lessened, and everyone breathed easier.

"Sometimes you're useful," Sift said. "Or at least your bracelet is."

"I have an extra," Ruwen offered. It had been on the wrist of the arm he'd sliced off the Naktos Stone Carver Valora.

"No thanks. I don't want to risk getting your hoarding issues. True god only knows what else you have in there."

"Fair enough."

Sift didn't understand, but Bliz did, and true to the Crew Chief's philosophy, Ruwen had collected five hundred thousand cubic feet of magma while swimming through the lava tubes after leaving Torchy.

Now that everyone could breathe better, Ruwen walked over to Prythus.

"Prythus?" Ruwen asked.

The man kept beating on the ring, his hands bloody from holding the sharp rock, and he didn't react to his name.

"Prythus?" Ruwen tried again, this time louder.

When Prythus didn't respond, Ruwen grabbed the man's bloody hand.

"What is going on?" Ruwen asked.

Rage covered Prythus' face, but trying to break Ruwen's grip was less than useless and after a couple seconds, his eyes focused.

Ruwen let go. "What are you doing?"

Prythus gasped as if stabbed, and immense sadness filled his face and posture. "This is how they come. They move them from city to city."

"Who arrives?"

Prythus glanced around the chamber, the sadness replaced by hate. "These are the creatures destroying our home. They killed my family. My children. They took everything."

Prythus sagged and Ruwen caught him.

Now Ruwen understood. These rings acted as giant rune gates, shuttling large quantities of demons to the ring linked to it. Savage Island was more than just a proving ground for Step Clans. It served as a staging area for demon invasions. Or at least part of one.

"I'm sorry, Prythus," Ruwen said. "Please get the others to stop. Then we'll decide what to do."

Prythus nodded and moved to Nymthus.

Sift scanned the demons milling fifty feet away. "I'd guess we have a minute before things get interesting." He pointed to the walls. "Some of the bigger ones are forcing the small ones to come help. They'll probably try to swarm us."

Ruwen pointed at the giant ring. "That is a portable gate, and the Shattered Clan uses them to invade Rung Four's world."

"Well, that explains it."

"Thorn warned us Rung Four might act irrationally."

"Hey, don't blame this on me," Sift said defensively.

"I didn't mean it like that. I just kind of ignored her warning. They seemed fine, but I didn't look hard enough to see the anguish."

"I'm not sure how to help them," Sift said, and then pointed at the portal. "I guess Tarot didn't lie. That thing must be one giant crossing stone."

Ruwen had come to the same conclusion.

"Did you get the thousand pounds we need?" Sift asked.

"Yeah."

"What are we going to do with that, then?" Sift asked, nodding at the large ring.

"I could stash it in my Inventory," Ruwen said. He glanced at Rung Four and their bloody hands. "I'm guessing they would rather destroy it, though."

"Let's do it then and get out of here."

"Don't you want to know what's in the warehouse?" Tarot asked as he returned.

Sift swatted at the golem, but Tarot moved fast enough to avoid it.

"No way," Sift said. "Don't tell us."

Ruwen remained silent and Sift glanced at him. "Right, Ruwen? We don't want to know."

Ruwen winced. "Aren't you kind of curious?"

"Some doors should stay closed."

"Won't you wonder for the rest of your life?"

"No. No I won't. Your curiosity is going to kill us. Plus," Sift pointed at Tarot. "Never trust a golem. They just want us to suffer."

"That's a bit dramatic."

Sift raised his eyes and tilted his head.

"Fine, Smash probably wanted to kill us."

"And the longer we stay here, the more dangerous it

becomes." Sift pointed to the gathering demons. "They're going to attack any second."

"Okay, you're right. Let's destroy this thing and get out."

Ruwen glanced at the recovering Adepts, who had all listened to the conversation. "Does everyone agree?"

Everyone did, and Sift moved them fifteen feet from the Infernal Crossing Ring. Ruwen stepped to the side of the ring farthest from the Adepts, and using ten percent of his strength, punched the black stone.

Ruwen had spent a couple hours collecting the crossing stones and knew, while hard, they easily broke. *Analyze* had warned him about the portal's durability, but it still shocked him that the ring didn't shatter. The entire structure vibrated, and it became clear the energy filling the ring had soaked into the stone, giving it strength.

Once again, Ruwen struck the ring, this time using twenty-five percent of his Peak Diamond Strength.

The ring shook but remained whole.

"Quit screwing around," Sift said.

Ruwen frowned at the ring, and prepared to strike it again, when Sift sighed loudly.

"Just great," Sift muttered.

Ruwen turned to see the group of fighters he'd beaten to the entrance spill into the chamber. From just their movements, it was obvious they had vastly better training than the demons the Adepts had fought here.

Sift locked eyes with Ruwen. "What tunnel should we retreat into?"

Ruwen quickly glanced around the chamber and considered the other options. A tunnel behind them and to the left angled sharply upward, and he reasoned it might take them to the surface the quickest. He pointed at it. "That one."

Sift nodded and turned to the Adepts. "As soon as the ring shatters, we run for that tunnel."

Ruwen turned to look where Sift pointed. It sat on the opposite side of the chamber and corner from the one Ruwen had chosen.

Sift faced Ruwen and shrugged. "Your golem."

"That tunnel angles downward," Ruwen said.

"Your *misfortune* golem," Sift repeated.

Ruwen couldn't argue with that. Tarot did seem to make things harder. Maybe Sift had a point.

"Cover your ears," Ruwen told everyone.

Striking with fifty percent power caused a thunderclap as Ruwen's fist ripped the air. The ring shuddered but didn't break. This had become a little embarrassing.

"Step away," a woman shouted.

At the front of the elite demon group strode a female demon, obvious from her three exposed breasts.

"Why are they always naked?" Sift mumbled.

Ruwen's Perception provided more information a moment later.

Name: *Scourge Queen*
Deity: *Lalquinrial*
Class Type: *Cultivator - Sapphire*
Level: *73*
Health: *1,988*
Mana: *0*
Energy: *2,300*
Spirit: *1,190,000,000*
Armor Class: *1,800*

The Queen continued. "This portal belongs to the Savage Champion. Attacking it is an attack on him, the Shattered Clan, and the Infernal Realm."

Ruwen didn't care about any of those things or the Scourge Queen. He wanted to destroy this portal and get his Clan to safety. He turned away from the queen and prepared to strike the ring with seventy-five percent of his power.

A demon stepped out of the glowing white energy of the ring and into the chamber. It seemed disoriented for a moment and once again Ruwen's Perception delivered bad news.

Name: *Scourge Commander*
Deity: *Lalquinrial*
Class Type: *Cultivator - Diamond*
Level: *81*
Health: *3,100*
Mana: *0*
Energy: *7,500*
Spirit: *2,400,000,000*
Armor Class: *2,200*

A foot extended out from the energy field as another creature stepped through. Whatever army sat on the other side of this portal had sensed Ruwen's attacks and had come to investigate. The odds of everyone surviving this had gone from bad to terrible. And adding an entire army to the equation didn't seem like a good idea.

Ruwen triggered Last Breath so he could immediately transition into fighting the demon horde, turned with his hips, and struck the Infernal Crossing Ring with one hundred percent of his power.

CHAPTER 44

*R*uwen hadn't used his full power since Rainbow's End, and even then, the planet had lacked an atmosphere, limiting the side effects of moving at such speeds.

The air around Ruwen's fist ignited, the friction caused by the sudden movement like a falling star. A pressure wave blossomed outward, containing both the compressed air and thunderclap associated with quick actions.

The knuckles on Ruwen's right hand shattered as his punch struck the ring. The force traveled through his perfectly aligned wrist and elbow, saving those bones, to his shoulder, which wrenched and dislocated. The pain in Last Breath was a distant thing and he had become accustomed to discomfort anyway.

Ruwen had expected the soul ring to shatter and fall apart. Instead, it shuddered as the force of his blow passed through it.

Then it exploded.

Even in Last Breath the pressure wave sped toward Ruwen at an incredible pace, throwing him backward. He exerted as much mental energy as possible into Last Breath, speeding his mind to its maximum. Normally such an effort became unbearable as a single second stretched into hours, and the mental fatigue it caused meant he couldn't sustain it for long anyway.

Even as Ruwen reached his mental capacity, the explosion didn't stop. It crawled through the air in a spreading bubble, its velocity so great nothing he could do would stop it.

With all the practice on Rainbow's End, Ruwen had become an expert on explosions. He could calculate the damage a pressure wave would cause based on its size, shape, and velocity.

Having never witnessed an explosion so violent, Ruwen knew with certainty no one in the chamber would survive this blast, including himself. Divine magic had created and powered that soul ring. It was the only explanation. And like an angry god, the soul ring would dispense its wrath on everyone here.

Ruwen pushed the panic away to keep his thoughts clear. He needed to act immediately if he had any chance of surviving, and panic only slowed him.

The problem had already grown too large. None of Ruwen's spells would contain such a blast and nothing he could do would protect Sift and the Adepts from the fatal damage. He needed to move them away from the explosion.

Or, move the explosion away from them.

Ruwen latched onto the idea, not wasting another iota of time deciding. It might already be too late.

Ruwen had four thousand five hundred twenty-one Energy. His Regen of two-hundred three per second didn't matter, as everyone in this chamber would be vaporized a second from now.

The idea also relied on how quickly the idea reacted to Ruwen's wishes. Anything short of instantaneous and none of this mattered. He would wake up in a revival bath in New Eiru, his last memory the underwater safe house the night before the semi-final match of the Step Championship.

Overlord, all the Narrators, the knowledge he gained about the Architect Role, Essence, and utilizing his Spirit on the far side of the Universe, and the perfection of his Steps, gone. All of it.

Worse, so much worse, Sift would be dead, and Ruwen wouldn't even know he caused it.

Ruwen willed his Void Band open. Praying something designed and managed by the Goddess Miranda and linked to her vast vaults under the Black Pyramid, would match the quality of everything else she created.

The Void Band grew.

More importantly, it grew faster than the expanding pressure wave. Immense relief threatened to consume him, but like the panic, he kept it away from his thoughts. There would be time for that later.

Void Band lessons first learned with Crew Chief Bliz and perfected over the two years since turned Ruwen's thoughts into actions.

The explosion had thrown Ruwen backward, and his feet had left the ground. He stretched the Void Band outward like a finger and angled it down slightly to catch the bottom of the pressure wave. Thankfully the rocky ground had slowed the downward expansion of the pressure wave enough that he believed he could get under most of it.

Comparing the growth of the explosion with the speed of the Void Band, Ruwen worried the band wouldn't reach the far side of the pressure wave before the blast struck Sift and the Adepts.

With a thought Ruwen raised the entire Void Band opening, making the angle shallower, which increased how fast it overtook the pressure wave. A small portion of the explosion on his side would remain, an unfortunate consequence of the angles.

Even with the adjustment, saving Sift and the Adepts would be close, assuming he could manipulate the Void Band well enough to capture the explosion.

The Void Band finger Ruwen had created finally overtook

the far side of the explosion thirty-five feet away. It had expanded to within inches of Sift's face.

Ruwen had never created an opening with his Void Band this large, and he wasn't sure how much Energy what he planned to do next would take. Manipulating the opening usually didn't take much Energy, but that might not be true of the gigantic one he was about to try.

There was a real risk it would take more Energy than Ruwen had.

If it saved Sift and the Adepts, though, it was worth that cost.

With that thought, Ruwen expanded his Void Band finger outward from a long line into a circle, creating a round portal opening thirty-five feet wide. That alone would cost two hundred Energy per second, and he had no idea how much Energy it had taken to extend the opening in the first place. Or, even worse, how much what he planned to do next would cost.

Ruwen rotated the entire thirty-five-foot opening upward, scooping up the pressure wave along with the shards of soul ring. When the Void Band passed Sift's face, Ruwen relaxed a little. At least one of them would survive.

As the rising Void Band passed the halfway point of the pressure wave, Ruwen decreased the size of the opening as it climbed, trying to minimize the amount of Energy he consumed.

If the Void Band suddenly stopped moving, Ruwen would know he'd depleted his Energy pool and would die. He wondered if death would happen immediately, or when he released Last Breath.

The fear of imminent death, and everything it would cost Ruwen, made watching his Void Band slowly consume the explosion excruciating.

With forty percent of the explosion left, Ruwen considered warning the Narrators of their possible impending death, but decided it served no purpose. He didn't think he could manage the mental conversations anyway since all his mental energy kept Last Breath maxed.

At thirty percent, sadness crept into Ruwen's thoughts. Despite his best intentions, and a thoughtful and cautious approach to problems his increased Wisdom provided, he'd still almost killed Sift, and might yet die himself. He wondered if Tarot had, once again, shifted the odds enough to get his keeper killed.

Twenty percent, and thoughts of Hamma pushed him from sadness to grief. If he died now and revived with a level of twenty-six how would she feel now that she had climbed so high. Worse, she would remember months of a different Ruwen. The Ruwen that he had become while out in the darkness. He would revive as someone else. Someone she didn't recognize. He doubted their relationship would survive it.

The stress and worry as Ruwen crossed the final ten percent of the explosion almost convinced him to stop. He had likely done enough. But he worried the remaining pressure wave, angled upward, would collapse the ceiling and kill everyone. He forced himself to finish.

At five percent, Ruwen's thoughts turned to the others he loved and who loved him. His parents, Rami, Sift, Tremine, and even Lylan with her sarcastic pragmatism. He loved the life he'd created, even if he hadn't chosen much of it, and the ache of possibly losing it all created a pain inside him Last Breath couldn't touch.

Four precent.

Three.

Two.

One.

The Void Band finished its rotation back to Ruwen, the opening a narrow line as he captured the last of the explosion.

It was done.

And he hadn't died.

Relief so powerful it hurt filled Ruwen, and he spent the next few slivers of time, as he crept through the air, drowning in it. He had done something extraordinary, and it made him proud.

Ruwen studied his handiwork. Where an expanding sphere of fatal destruction had existed, nothing remained. Well, almost nothing. A sliver of pressure wave he couldn't capture under his feet, and angled at the ground, still advanced through the air. Even if that tiny amount caused damage, it faced away from Sift and the Adepts.

Glancing at the small remaining pressure wave Ruwen noticed its bottom had scraped the floor, creating the beginning of a furrow through the stone. The Infernal Crossing Ring's base must have been reinforced somehow as it had resisted the pressure wave long enough for him to scoop it up. The damage beginning on the floor below concerned him a little, as the destruction already caused hadn't seemed to weaken the pressure wave at all.

To Sift, the Adepts, and everyone else in the chamber, it would look like Ruwen had struck the Infernal Crossing Ring before everything just disappeared. Not even the sound of his attack survived. The shattered structure, the sound wave, the explosion's pressure wave, and whatever energy held it all together now rested safely in his Inventory.

The detonation had thrown the Scourge Commander into the air just like Ruwen, and the explosion had propelled them both to an insane velocity. His barely detectible Gravity Shell he always kept active, protected him from a deity's gravity attack, but it wouldn't help buffer his impending meeting with the chamber wall. If he could access his Architect Role, and use his Gravity Shell to stop his movement, the shell would protect him from the consequences of that sudden stop.

The tiny portion of his mind that allowed these thoughts and observations was the only thing not dedicated to keeping Last Breath maximized. He guessed diverting even a small amount of mental energy to use the Architect Role would weaken Last Breath enough that he'd strike the wall before he could modify anything.

Even if Ruwen could manage it, if he miscalculated the amount of change and consumed all his Mana, it would tap his Spirit. And with the damage he'd done to himself already from the Smear, it might permanently cripple his spiritual abilities.

If Ruwen didn't try, though, the explosion or impact might kill him, and he needed to give himself the best chance at surviving.

Sivart, I don't know if you can hear me, but I might need your help in a moment.

Ruwen went over the steps, and pictured himself slowly shifting focus from Last Breath to the Gravity Shell his Architect Gravity Role powered.

With a mental sigh, Ruwen shifted a fraction of energy from Last Breath toward the Gravity Shell, hoping everything went well and he wouldn't be forced to test the durability of his Diamond Fortified body.

Like a spinning top, the slight shift caused a catastrophic wobble that instantly unraveled his entire mental focus.

Pain blossomed over his entire body for a fraction of a sliver before his thoughts stopped and darkness took him.

CHAPTER 45

*H*e floated in darkness, and it felt familiar, but he didn't know why. Releasing the stray thought, he returned to the calm and peaceful silence. He felt the vibration first, a cross between an itch and a tickle, striking him, and he tried to move away, but the unwelcome new sensation followed, and worse, it grew more intense.

Sometime later he heard a faint ringing, which combined with the vibrations, made him…he couldn't think of the proper concept…it made him different than before, and he wanted to go back to the before.

Eventually he wondered about the vibrations and ringing and after a while he thought they might be linked.

The feeling and sound both intensified again, the ringing sounding metallic. Metallic, he thought, what a strange word.

Somewhere distant, but connected to him somehow, he felt warmth.

He wondered about warmth and what it actually meant.

Blinding light surrounded him and a sensation like warmth, but a lot more of it, enveloped him. He didn't like this feeling and wanted to return to the before.

The light faded or he got used to it, but the blinding light that had erased the darkness of before, revealed the source of the glare, a sphere.

The ball rotated, the light on its surface swirling, bathing everything near it in warmth.

Warmth.

Perhaps this might be better than the before. He could stay here and watch the glowing ball. Warmth. Yes, this might be better than the quiet darkness.

But the itching and ringing wouldn't stop. He turned away from the sphere of warmth and looked for the source of irritation.

A strange creature stood behind him. Its long twisting body had thousands of legs, and massive black wings sprouted from its back. Pincers protruded from its neck, curving around a mouth filled with sharp teeth. Blonde pigtails fell to each side, framing a pyramid shaped head with two dark, gold specked eyes.

This was irritation.

He didn't like irritation and turned back to the warmth.

But the glowing sphere had disappeared.

The darkness of before had returned, but he now missed warmth.

Even the irritation might be better than the darkness he thought.

Turning, he found irritation remained.

The vibrations and ringing intensified.

He moved toward irritation and studied it.

The mass of legs created another feeling, disgust.

Disgust and irritation, but still better, he thought, than the cold darkness of before.

As he neared disgust and irritation, he found the legs on one side each held a gold plate, and the source of his irritation originated there.

Each leg on the other side held a rod, and with a sudden movement, the plates and rods collided.

Waves of vibration and metallic ringing enveloped him, and he tried to move away, but as if sensing his closeness, irritation and disgust smashed their plates and rods together, fervently.

The vibrations and ringing grew louder and the warmth from before turned intense and uncomfortable. The vibrations pierced him, and he gasped at a new sensation, pain.

The pain took shape, and he realized he had a body. An entire body of pain.

Circles, rectangles, and symbols filled the darkness. In the top left, a mostly empty rectangle suddenly lost the remaining blue that filled it. Immediately, warmth spread through his body and the pain receded for a moment. An empty red rectangle filled a little, before dropping again. A mass of squares flashed under the colored rectangles.

Pain, heat, and irritation shoved him, and he stopped resisting.

Grey replaced the black surroundings, and the pain intensified. Voices emerged, but he didn't recognize them, and he didn't have the strength to open his eyes.

"He's coming around," a voice said.

"Oh, now you're a doctor?" a young girl asked.

"I don't need a degree to know you shouldn't bang a gong at a dying patient."

"That just shows how much you know, Tarot" the girl replied. "He's too dumb to die."

"You should heal him."

"No, way. I'm not getting involved in this. I'm just here to yell."

"Some things never change."

"Fold your cards, Tarotmethiophelius. You have no idea how much trouble this kid creates."

"I'm starting to get a picture."

"One of his constructs is healing him anyway," the young girl said.

"I'm not sure Worker heals will be enough."

"Yeah, it's going to be close."

"Shame if he died. Who would you yell at then?"

No one spoke for a few seconds and then the gonging stopped.

The blue in the rectangle disappeared again, and another wave of warmth covered him. The red rectangle increased, but not as much as before.

"Maybe you could cook him an omelet," Tarot said. "Boost his Stamina."

"They're not that type of chickens," the young girl replied. "They're protection. You know we're vulnerable in this Realm."

"How about a trade then," Tarot offered.

"What could you possibly have that I want?"

"Perhaps you'd enjoy playing an instrument. I recently picked one up that fits your musical ability."

After a brief silence the girl spoke again. "Did you steal my gong?"

He felt pressure, as if someone had dropped a boulder on his chest.

Tarot laughed. "Your tricks don't work on me, wyrm."

"Ugh! I hate you," the young girl screamed. Then in a calmer voice, continued. "You were always the worst one. Too clever. Too curious. When word gets out you've resurfaced it will get dangerous. I could help protect you. We have a Curator. Just give me my gong back."

"No deal. I'm not suited for the Curator's care. Shuffle, and try again."

"Fine, what do you want?"

A few seconds later, Tarot replied. "A divine bandage of soothing, a superior cure bleed, a contact salve of bone regrowth, a binding of cure concussion, a wrap of skin mend-ing, and an aromatic oil of regeneration. And one of your chickens."

Tarot screamed and a moment later an explosion decreased the red in his rectangle to just a sliver.

"Keep your chicken then!" Tarot yelled. In a serious voice he continued. "Pay up, or I'm heading out on tour. Tarotmethiophelius and his magical gong. This could be my big break."

The blackness returned, edging out the grey and removing the strange shapes. The pain grew distant as well, a welcome change. The voices fading.

Tarot spoke again. "Did I ever tell you about the diary I found? It was a while ago, but the poetry holds up. Ageless really. I think I'll open my gong show with readings."

"That was you," the girl hissed. "You took my diary? Of course it was, you thieving pile of—"

Tarot continued. His voice dramatic, the volume changing, as if he quickly moved around the room. "Scales rough and hard, wrapped in wyrmstone, your touch—"

The girl screamed loud enough that the ground shook under him.

"Stop!"

"I'll trade for the diary," the girl said.

"No deal, wyrm. I already gave you my terms, but to show my good faith, I promise not to read any more of your poetry."

The darkness had almost completely returned. Once again, he felt the comfort of the before. The voices were barely audible and the cold didn't bother him anymore. Warmth was now a distant memory.

"Why?" the girl asked. "Why do you care about him?"

"Ah, the wyrm finally asks the right question. Are you ready? I have three words for you, and they're good ones." Tarot paused and continued. "Does it matter?"

The girl laughed. "Oh, that is rich. Even for you. Too clever.

Too curious. Too *knowing*. I hate you, Tarotmethiophelius. Now give me back my gong and quit spying on me."

The voices disappeared, along with most of the pain.

The before welcomed him back.

Heat surged down the last thread of pain that held him.

Sensation returned.

Warmth.

The darkness from before reached for him, but the sensations became a torrent. His body convulsed, pain and fire swirling like partners in a dance.

Memories surfaced like a volcano erupting. He groaned as his body painfully healed and his identity returned.

Ruwen opened his eyes.

The beak of a chicken hung an inch from Ruwen's right eye. The chicken's head turned, its glassy black eye meeting his. He wasn't an expert on chickens, but he recognized this one, which meant the other six stood nearby.

Blapy, her blonde pig tails almost touching Ruwen's forehead filled the vision of his left eye.

Blapy pointed a small finger at Ruwen's eye. "You are in big trouble."

CHAPTER 46

*R*uwen felt like someone had mashed his body and burned it. The debuffs had disappeared, replaced by a line of buffs across the top of his vision. Notifications glowed softly in the lower right portion of his vision. The chicken moved away, probably joining the other members of the Savage Seven. He couldn't tell where the light came from, and the pumice ceiling looked less than ten feet away as he lay on his back. Tarot appeared to have left.

For the second time that day, Ruwen realized he had no clothes. He lifted his head enough to see a pile of pumice dust covered him like a blanket. It appeared only his head and part of his left arm remained free of it.

Blapy's disposition aura appeared solid red. Not a speck of friendly green.

"Hey, Blapy," Ruwen croaked, his throat resisting his voice.

"Don't 'hey' me. What in the Darkness did you do?"

Ruwen's right calf cramped, and his left arm convulsed. His vision swam for a moment and then steadied. Taking control of his body, he relaxed the calf muscle and calmed the nerves in his arm.

Blapy's comment about Ruwen's constructs reminded him he wasn't alone. *Is everyone okay in there?*

Sivart replied. *Everyone survived and the damage is being addressed.*

"Are you ignoring me?" Blapy said in a dangerous voice.

Thank you for the heals, Ruwen quickly sent, before focusing on Blapy.

"No," Ruwen said, but it came out as a hoarse whisper. He swallowed hard. His mouth dry. "I think I'm in shock. What happened?"

"What happened?" Blapy asked, exasperated. She stood and threw her arms in the air. "What happened?" She asked again, her pitch higher.

Ruwen already regretted the question and tried to piece together his scattered thoughts.

"Oh, I broke that ring."

Blapy put her hands on her hips and glared down at Ruwen. "That ring?"

"You're really full of questions," Ruwen said, and again, immediately regretted it.

Blapy screamed in rage and Ruwen winced.

Ruwen tried to minimize the damage. "I'm sorry. Honestly, what happened surprised me."

Blapy squatted down, still glaring. "Well, imagine my surprise, then, when a Divine explosion appeared in my vaults. Do you have any idea how much energy, Spirit, and mental focus I'm exerting to keep that detonation confined?"

Ruwen tried to swallow again. "A lot?"

Blapy slowly nodded. "A lot. Yes, let's call it, a lot."

"Can't you, I don't know, release it somewhere? Like into a star or something?"

"I wish I could, but the terms of the Pact require I store whatever the deities' followers place in their dimensional storage. Which is the fifth biggest mistake I've ever made."

"Why does everyone have so many lists?" Ruwen asked, speaking before his brain, still a little foggy, could trigger his self-preservation instinct.

Blapy leaned closer, her face now inches from Ruwen's. "I have another list. And guess who passed that bothersome barkeep for the number one spot?"

"Sift!" Ruwen said, his scattered thoughts piecing together more of the recent past. He tried to sit and a Vertigo debuff appeared as his world spun. Blapy placed a hand on his chest and pushed him back to the floor. Closing his eyes, he laid back, trying not to empty his stomach all over Blapy. She was already in a bad mood.

"Sift is handling things for the time being," Blapy said. "You aren't in any shape to help yet anyway. Give those buffs another minute or two and you can go."

Ruwen offered a suggestion. "How about I just shoot it back out."

Leaning back, Blapy sighed. "By the time I could react, the pressure wave had expanded to almost ten miles." She rubbed her forehead. "Can you survive creating a portal ten miles wide?"

"No."

"Then for the moment, it's stuck in my vault."

Ruwen tried to sit up, and his vision wavered, so he decided to remain on his back a little longer. "Can't you, I don't know, squish it back together?"

Blapy stared at him for a few seconds. "I forget how ignorant you are."

Ruwen didn't detect any malice in the statement. Blapy's disposition aura had lost most of its red, strengthening his suspicion she only stated a fact.

"I know," Ruwen agreed. "I'm trying to fix that."

Blapy sighed again. "I know. More than most, actually."

The last of the red disappeared as Blapy's feelings toward him returned to neutral.

"I can't 'squish' it back because I lack the power," Blapy said.

Ruwen had just visited Blapy in the Third Secret, and it contained the Spirit from most of the Universe. "That doesn't seem possible."

"I should be clearer. To channel enough power to 'squish' that explosion, I would need to be there."

It only took Ruwen a moment to understand. The Blapy in front of him was just a Spirit created clone of her true self, which remained trapped in the Third Secret. Pen had removed all the Spirit in the Universe and placed it in his Divine Realm. Without the Spirit to power its spread, the Darkness died, along with Pen.

Pen and Blapy had planned for that, and she had remained in his Divine Realm, keeping it open despite Pen's death. If she left Pen's Divine Realm, it would close, and because Pen no longer lived, the Realm would disappear. Disappear with all the Spirit from their Universe. It would make everything they'd sacrificed to put the Spirit back, pointless. Blapy couldn't leave.

"Oh," Ruwen said. "That's not good. I'll find a way to get my portal opening that big."

"I haven't told you the bad news yet," Blapy said.

Ruwen rolled to his side and pushed himself up slowly. He held his head until it stopped spinning and focused on the miserable looking Blapy.

"How can that not be the bad news?" Ruwen asked.

"Oh, child, you have so much to learn. There is always worse news."

"What is it?"

Blapy locked gazes with Ruwen. "It's expanding."

Ruwen frowned. "Oh, no."

"Now you begin to see."

"So you can't squish it and I can't release it right now, and by the time I can, it will be even bigger. Forget the Pact and just move the explosion yourself."

"It's never that easy. I hated most of Pen's disciples, but he loved them. He wasn't blind though and asked me to not let them make our sacrifice meaningless."

"You made the Pact," Ruwen guessed.

"They tore each other apart, scavenging the remains of Pen's body like starving wyrms. They devoured the twelve Meridian's that orbited his corpse like moons. I couldn't stand it. The only way I could think to fix it, was binding enough of them into a soul contract that punished aggressors and cheaters with outright destruction by the group. The boundaries worked and things calmed."

Blapy's current form was the one Ruwen associated with the Black Pyramid. Her winged human deity form she called Miranda, and he had just learned her true form when he'd met her in the Third Secret. Even though he spoke to Blapy, she was still Miranda, the Adjudicator for the Pact.

Ruwen assumed Miranda knew about Naktos and the other gods working with Lalquinrial to mine terium in the mountains around New Eiru. But knowing something and having someone say it as fact to the Adjudicator, were two different things.

Ruwen chose his words carefully. "I'm sure, in the thousands of years since you made the Pact, some of the deities have bent the rules."

"Certainly," Blapy replied. "I have, on occasion, broke them myself, even though it has brought me nothing but trouble."

Ruwen remained silent, very aware who she meant.

Blapy continued. "The Pact is soul bound. Bending the rules or even breaking a few doesn't cause any real damage in the Material or even Spirit Realms. But you didn't release Mana or Spirit, you unleashed soul energy. And manipulating that much soul power while breaking a soul pact, would most certainly destroy me."

"Wait, you called it a Divine explosion earlier, but now you're talking about soul energy."

Blapy's brow furrowed.

The confused expression on Blapy's face triggered Ruwen's Cleverness ability and he groaned as his mind grew frigid. Memories of his discussions with Uruziel, as they traveled in Shelly, swirled in his mind.

Uru no longer had the power to undo the soul prison Ascendancy created. She had irreversibly damaged herself turning Ruwen into an Axiom.

Ruwen had damaged his soul prison sometime around the time Overlord had manifested as his own entity.

Breaking the soul prison would reveal Ruwen's location and attract their attention. Uruziel believed that would prove fatal unless he had already become Divine.

This topic of Divinity and souls had come up before. During that same conversation in Shelly, Uruziel had told Ruwen a secret. She'd said, "Everyone's soul, man, woman, child, or god, is a tiny spark of the Divine. And Divinity is a gift from the Universe."

Ruwen had thought Uruziel used those words in a poetic sense, as in everyone's soul was something beautiful.

But if Ruwen took Uruziel's words literally, she had said: everyone's soul is Divine.

Ruwen had also thought Uruziel's description of "Divinity is a gift from the Universe" meant the Universe gave everyone their beautiful souls.

Again, if Ruwen took the words literally she meant the Universe recognized Divinity.

Another memory surfaced, the real Uru using almost the exact same phrase as she transferred her Architect Role to Ruwen so he could rebuild her third temple. She had called the Role "a reward from the Universe for attaining Divinity."

When Ruwen had transitioned his body from Metal levels

into Gem, everything but his bones had melted away before being rebuilt with Spirit.

That probably meant the same would happen when he transitioned from Gem to Divine, a process the Universe recognized with the Architect Role, providing the Roles of a god.

Finally, as the pain in Ruwen's head made him gasp, two more things Uruziel told him surfaced. She had used the word "inevitable" twice.

When Ruwen had asked if he could break the soul prison himself, she'd said: "It's inevitable."

Then, when Ruwen had tried to find out the mechanism to damage the soul prison, she added: "I've already told you, what you wish for is inevitable." And that "wish" Uruziel referenced had been the use of his soul to power the abilities of a Shadow Step Grandmaster.

All of that churned in Ruwen's mind, a blizzard of memories that coalesced around a single fact that united them all.

Ruwen opened his eyes and met Blapy's gaze. "Souls are a spark of the Divine, and Divinity is a gift from the Universe."

Blapy nodded.

"Transitioning from Metal to Gem remade me into a being of Spirit."

Blapy nodded again.

Ruwen tried to swallow but his throat had tightened. "The transition from Gem to Divine takes that divine spark and makes it anew. It becomes your body. Deities are all soul."

For the third time, Blapy nodded.

Ruwen sat in stunned disbelief. Uru had literally told him, and he'd been so distracted with what he wanted to hear, that he'd missed how she'd answered the question.

Ruwen shook his head, trying to refocus on the original issue. "It was an Infernal Crossing Ring, so does that mean the energy binding it together came from Lalquinrial?"

"One deity could not power such a structure. A normal Divine soul is not enough."

"Then how is Lalquinrial doing it?"

"He offers the disadvantaged access to their desires, but when they die, he owns their soul. He rips pieces off them to create and power things like that Crossing Ring, and you have seen the effects it has on his followers."

"The demons? Those are people?"

"They were. He has damaged and warped them by harming their souls."

"That is horrible."

"Yes," Blapy said and sighed. "But also powerful. That ring contained the equivalent of thousands of souls."

"Can't you make a distant moon somewhere part of the Black Pyramid and move the explosion there?"

"The Pact clearly states the vaults must remain on my planet."

"Then just move the explosion to some uninhabited place."

"You still don't understand the power you unleashed. That explosion will destroy the entire planet."

Ruwen couldn't speak. Stunned. "Destroy it?"

"Yep."

"How much time do we have?"

"I'm not sure. I'm still trying things to slow it."

"If I transitioned to Divine, would it give me enough Energy to expel the explosion from my Void Band?"

Blapy shrugged. "I'm not sure, and it depends on how long that process took. The destruction of Black Pyramid will happen in years, not centuries."

"Can we swap places?"

"Anyone can leave the Third Secret, but only an Axiom can enter."

"Which means even if I heal my meridians and stuff, if I Smear again and switch places with you, its permanent."

Blapy started to clarify and stopped, biting her lip.

"What?"

"Nothing. It doesn't matter because some seeds take longer to sprout than others."

"That doesn't make sense."

"Now isn't the time to complicate things with facts. For our current situation, if we swap it's permanent."

Ruwen narrowed his eyes. "Is there some way you can return to the Third Secret?"

"No," Blapy said firmly.

"Then why are you acting like it's not permanent?"

"I am three seconds from squeezing your head from your body."

Ruwen held up his hands. "Okay, I'll stop."

Thay sat in silence for a few seconds and the healing bandages Blapy had placed on Ruwen's forehead and cheeks began to itch. He reached up to pull one off, and Blapy slapped his hand away.

Ruwen knew he needed to take it easy a little longer because he hadn't even sensed the slap before it happened. He tried to ignore the itching, which had become unbearable now that he couldn't touch his face. "Is there nothing we can do?"

"You could die. Like for good. Then I can purge your stuff with no issues."

"Can we call that plan B? Or maybe Z?"

"There is something else, but honestly, I would rather kill you."

"I think I'd like to hear it and discuss all our options before you kill me."

"Fine," Blapy said and looked at the ceiling. A few seconds later she met Ruwen's gaze once more. "This cure might be worse than the disease."

"Worse than blowing up your planet?"

"Yes."

"That is hard to believe."

Blapy's shoulders slumped. "Our cure cannot be bound by the Pact. They must be intimately familiar with the soul energy in question, and powerful enough to help."

Despair filled Ruwen as he finally, completely, understood not only what he'd done, but how complicated he made the solution. The person Blapy meant had just tried to maim Ruwen. An individual that welcomed destruction and didn't care about anything but his own interests.

The only person capable of stopping the destruction of the Black Pyramid, was Lalquinrial.

CHAPTER 47

*T*he idea of asking for Lalquinrial's help made Ruwen feel sick. "That is awful."

"Yes," Blapy said. "And he will wonder why I need his help. It shows vulnerability, which is never good to reveal to a predator."

"You could put me on a moon somewhere and I could vent the explosion slowly like a hole in a balloon. It's no different than getting rid of water or oil or whatever."

"Oh, it's different. It's a ten-mile expanding sphere. Do the math on that amount of energy. And you're assuming I could control the flow of power enough to only measure out a fraction, which I can't. Not without vaporizing you. Although, on second thought, that does solve some issues. Maybe you should try that."

Ruwen laughed, but Blapy's face remained serious.

"Um, let's skip that idea."

Blapy shrugged.

They sat in silence for ten seconds, and Ruwen offered his last idea. "Can you dissolve the Pact?"

Blapy raised her eyebrows. "I wondered if you'd think of

that. Yes, I can. But as bad as the surrounding chaos seems, it is nothing compared to the massive destruction and suffering the deities caused before the Pact stopped them. The world would fall off a cliff and directly into an apocalypse."

"So, our options are to trigger a catastrophe on Grave, reveal your weakness to Lalquinrial and make a deal we both hate, my death, or transition from Gem to Divine and pray that gives me the power to expel the explosion without killing anyone, including myself."

"That's an excellent summary," Blapy said. She rubbed her temples. "The amount of trouble Inventory storage has caused me is something I never dreamed possible. It's the bane of my existence and it might very well cause the destruction of our Universe."

Ruwen snapped his fingers. "Tarot gave Sift a reading, and it sounded like Hamma and Lylan had found some trouble. Are they okay?"

Blapy scowled. "I hate that golem."

"You sound like Sift."

"Now I know we're all doomed," Blapy muttered. She focused on Ruwen. "Speaking of that troublemaker, you should go help now."

"I really am sorry."

Blapy studied him. "I know you are."

"What about Hamma and Lylan?"

Blapy shrugged. "The two of them are moping around in the Pyramid."

That didn't sound like Hamma or Lylan. "Are they okay?"

Blapy tilted her head. "Are any of you ever okay?"

The Savage Seven strutted from their positions around the chamber and gathered around Blapy. She shook her head a final time, as if in disapproval, and disappeared along with the chickens.

Ruwen activated *Glow* in the sudden darkness and pulled

himself out from under the pumice dust. A small part of his orange belt lay in the mound, and he placed it in his Inventory. Destroying his formal Clan attire would probably get him in trouble with the Founders, but future Ruwen could deal with that.

Dressing in the dark clothes of the Black Pyramid, Ruwen crawled into the only exit. A shaft sloped gently downward from the small chamber, and he laid on his stomach in the cramped tunnel. The shaft spanned two feet and stood three high, and he forced down a wave of claustrophobia.

Ruwen used *Stone Echo* and *Survey* to determine his location in relation to Sift. He also wanted to make sure the tunnel didn't narrow any further and cause him to become stuck headfirst, an outcome that gave him anxiety.

Stone Echo created a thousand foot sphere and *Survey* displayed the results in Ruwen's vision. He had become accustomed to the Spirit version of *Stone Echo* which could reach as far as he desired. After reaching level fifty-eight, he had accumulated thirty-six Ability Points, and he considered adding some to *Stone Echo* now. Each point would increase the radius of the sphere by five hundred feet.

Ruwen studied *Survey's* output, and found he lay only twenty feet below the surface, and the tunnel didn't waver in width or direction. Everything around him consisted of the soft pumice. It looked like someone had shot an arrow from the small chamber he'd awoken in to somewhere below the surface.

Understanding hit Ruwen, and he rested his forehead against the tunnel floor. The chamber didn't mark a starting point, but the ending one. His body had created this tunnel through the pumice as the explosion forced him away with a Divine level blast. The tunnel wouldn't become too narrow for him because he'd created it to begin with.

In the near future, Ruwen might need to use additional ability points on *Stone Echo* if he couldn't heal his Spiritual pathways. For now, knowing the tunnel wouldn't narrow any further and the surrounding rock consisted of pumice calmed his fears enough to leave *Stone Echo* in its current state.

Ruwen didn't know how far the explosion had forced him through the rock, but he didn't want to waste any more time. Crawling down the tunnel would not be very efficient, but he could at least start while he looked for better options. He pulled himself into the tunnel and moved forward on knees and elbows.

Remembering the tunnels he'd traveled while touring the terium mine outside of Deepwell, reminded him of something that should be faster: an air sled.

Casting *Worker Wagon* for two hundred-fifty Mana would be ideal, but Ruwen couldn't control the wagon's size and it wouldn't fit in this tunnel. Instead, he turned to his standby *Shed*, but realized he only had the power to manipulate the size when using the Spirit based spell. The Mana based one came in a standard ten-by-ten-by-ten-foot cube. Only the location of doors and windows could be altered.

This situation highlighted how dependent Ruwen had become on his Spirit during the eighteen months he'd been gone. He crawled forward, not wanting to waste any more time, and studied his spells and abilities for something to speed his movement.

The level eight Worker spell *Climb* would create a hundred feet of magical rope. With extra Energy, Ruwen could even propel things up or down the rope, but he didn't see how to make a good sled from it. The level twelve Commander spell *Move On* provided another possibility, but it generated five hundred square feet of surface area, far too much for him to manage in this tight shaft.

Ruwen had traveled two hundred feet, and *Survey* continued to show the same straight line as the tunnel moved downward with no changes. How far had the explosion thrown him?

Dig or *Melt* would work, but didn't seem much faster than crawling. Ruwen didn't find any good solutions in his spells and abilities, so he glanced through his Inventory.

Only one set of items triggered an idea, and Ruwen wondered if using them would be wise. But he couldn't hear anything or sense any heartbeats, which meant Sift and the Adepts must be a significant distance away. Crawling might take too long to reach them. Blapy had made it sound like Sift had things under control, but Ruwen didn't really trust her judgement on such things.

Ruwen dropped three items onto the tunnel floor in front of his face. Two of them looked the same, silver squares about the size of his palm. They reflected the light of *Glow*, creating rainbows across their surface. The third item contained a black liquid in a hand sized bottle. He recalled their descriptions.

Name: *Rock Centipede Scale*
Quality: *Uncommon*
Durability: *50 of 50*
Weight: *5.0 lbs.*
Description: *Alchemy component. Very clean.*

Name: *Lubrication Potion*
Quality: *Uncommon*
Area: *3x3 feet*
Weight: *0.50 lbs.*
Effect: *Friction reduced by 99%.*
Description: *A black liquid that smells like sulfur. Extraordinarily slippery and resistant to water. Removal requires flames or an alcohol-based solvent.*

The scales had come from Ruwen's first fights in the Black Pyramid. He'd killed the centipedes using *Scrub*, cleaning them all to death. The lubrication potion had come from the loot they'd taken from Echo's mother, the Plague Siren Simandreial.

Using the level one Worker spell *Mend Tool*, Ruwen spent twenty-five Mana and three seconds of cast time to attach one scale to the toe of his left shoe. Not wanting to attach the second scale to his bare hand, he retrieved the fragment of his orange belt, wrapped it around his right hand, and attached the second scale to the belt.

Ruwen had originally wanted to create an air sled, but the tight space had made that impossible. Since the shaft went downhill, he felt dropping the air part and just using the sled was a clever idea. With the lubrication from the potion, he hoped to make quicker progress than crawling. He figured he might need to use his Void Band to propel himself, which is why he left his left hand free.

Carefully removing the waxy substance sealing the bottle's lid, Ruwen gently opened the potion. The stench of sulfur so close to his face made him gag, but he didn't spill any of the liquid. Rolling onto his back, he brought his foot forward as much as he could in the tight space.

Slowly, Ruwen tipped the bottle until the liquid dripped onto the centipede scale. When the scale had turned completely black, he moved his right hand over his stomach and repeated the process on the attached scale.

Ruwen finished coating the second scale, and delicately turned his body, resting his weight on his elbow and knee and keeping the scales from touching anything. As he turned, a small drop of black liquid rolled downward from the lip of the potion bottle. It touched his thumb, sliding between his skin and the bottle.

The pressure of Ruwen's thumb caused the now slick bottle to slip and drop from his grasp. Instinctively, he snatched the bottle with his other hand, not wanting it to strike the floor and break.

Instead of grabbing the bottle, however, the centipede scale Ruwen had attached to his right hand smashed the glass, spraying his face, chest, and the surrounding rock in lubricating potion.

Immediately, Ruwen slid down the shaft. He blinked the potion out of his eyes and tried to get the scales under his body. It required all his Peak Diamond Strength and Dexterity to get the scales balanced under him.

In seconds, gravity had accelerated Ruwen at a pace faster than running, and the speed kept increasing.

The lubrication potion, true to its name, created a surface so slick, even the air seemed to slide around Ruwen's potion covered head, and he hurtled downward.

The sameness of the shaft made Ruwen's speed hard to determine, but his map displayed his velocity as *Survey* displayed his route. After a minute, his speed leveled out to just under three hundred miles per hour, and he considered using his Void Band to slow his descent. He resisted the urge to slow down, worrying any new variables might cause a crash in the tight space.

Ruwen sensed a mass of sounds and heartbeats, and *Survey* displayed what he already knew. He had finally returned to the original chamber.

CHAPTER 48

*R*uwen exited the tunnel at three hundred twenty miles per hour and soared directly over a massive new magma pool, the heat from the liquid rock striking him like a blow. He had two seconds until he struck the ground, and tightened his stomach, pulling his legs forward. Reaching down, he removed the centipede scale from his left foot, but it remained attached to the bottom of his shoe, and the entire thing came off.

With only a moment left before striking the ground, Ruwen tossed the centipede scale-shoe combo into his Void Band, along with the orange belt fragment and scale from his right hand, which also didn't separate.

Ruwen closed the Void Band and relaxed his body, preparing to use his one hundred ninety-two levels in Tumbling to ease the impact of his landing. His right foot struck the pumice floor of the cavern, and he shifted his center-of-gravity forward to complete the somersault caused from the friction of his foot touching something solid.

But Ruwen's right foot, like most of his body, remained soaked in the black liquid of the Lubricating Potion, and instead of flipping forward, he slid, with no apparent decrease in his velocity. Without the reflexes of a Diamond body, he would have never remained upright.

Sift and the Adepts had their backs to the warehouse a hundred feet away and a half ring of demons surrounded them. Ruwen drug his bare left foot behind him, creating a furrow in the pumice. It slowed his advance, but not quickly enough, and he crossed the hundred feet in a quarter of a second.

Just before Ruwen struck the outer ring of demons, he shifted his bare left foot forward and launched himself forward in a shallow jump. He flew over the demons' heads and then the inner circle containing the Adepts. Only Sift had the reflexes to see Ruwen's flight, and he followed Ruwen's trajectory while fighting the Scourge Queen.

Ruwen had time to use his Gravity Shell and stop his movement instantly, but that risked accidentally using Spirit, plus, the gravity wave the sudden stop generated might create even more instability down here and he knew surviving at these speeds was trivial. Despite the velocity, he wasn't in any danger.

Ruwen crashed into the warehouse at two hundred miles per hour. The demons had built the structure from hardened rock, which only spread the effect of his impact to the entire structure.

The warehouse vibrated for a moment before exploding outward, away from Ruwen and the Adepts. The impact had drastically decreased his momentum, and raising his lubricant covered right foot in the air, he slid to a stop on his bare left foot.

The destruction of the warehouse caused the entire room to pause their battle and absorb what had just happened. Ruwen channeled ten Energy per second into *Scrub* and the lubricant on his hands disappeared. He lifted his right foot and cleaned the potion off his shoe.

Ruwen walked between the four large Infernal Crossing

Gates that lay on their sides amid the destroyed warehouse. None of them had the white centers and appeared like large black circles on the ground.

Across the chamber, Ruwen noticed a large red splatter on the wall, about the same height as the shaft he'd created when he'd exited this room. It appeared the Scourge Commander hadn't survived the blast that had thrown them both outward.

The demons had stopped shouting and only the bubbling magma filled the silence. Ruwen strode between the Adepts and up to Sift. The Scourge Queen stood ten feet away, her posture displaying frustration and anger.

Sift's forearms had multiple bruises, probably from blocking the Scourge Queen's strikes. His Gold-Fortified body would not fare well against direct punishment from a Gem level fighter. His eyes contained a tinge of white. Fighting the Scourge Queen for so long had required Sift to supplement his body's Metal strength with soul power.

"Hey," Ruwen said to Sift.

Sift glanced at Ruwen and did a double take, laughing as he turned back to the Scourge Queen.

"What?" Ruwen asked.

"I guess you saw a familiar face," Sift said as he defended himself against the queen.

How did Sift know that? Ruwen wrinkled his brow in confusion, causing the small healing bandages Blapy had placed on his cheeks and forehead to crinkle. The Adepts all smiled, despite the terrible circumstances, which confused him even more.

"No," Ruwen whispered, "she wouldn't have." He reached up and peeled a bandage off his cheek.

In bright yellow letters, easily readable, a phrase Ruwen had seen before: *I pooped today!* A large happy face filled out the rest of the bandage. He removed another and it read: *I still live with my parents.* Quickly pulling the rest off his face, it was just as he feared, they all contained embarrassing phrases.

"Curse that wyrm," Ruwen muttered.

"Welcome to my entire life," Sift said as he blocked a thundering kick with his shin. "That is, until I met you, and things got even worse."

"Sorry about that," Ruwen said. He pointed at the Scourge Queen. "Why are you messing around?"

Sift frowned. "Because you disappeared again, and I didn't have a plan B."

"Again, sorry about that. What is plan A?"

"Delay until I thought of plan B."

"Ah," Ruwen said with a nod. "Our usual method."

"What did you do?" shouted the Scourge Queen, taking a step closer to Sift and Ruwen.

"I'm curious about that myself," Sift said.

Ruwen shrugged and held up the bandages. "Let's just say I bit into a poop pastry."

"That is really gross," Sift replied. "You aren't allowed in my bakery."

"You don't have a bakery."

"Stop talking nonsense!" the Scourge Queen screamed. "What did you do with the Commander and the Vicar?"

Ruwen winced. He pointed to the red smear seven hundred feet away. "That's the only one I saw." He realized another demon had started stepping out of the Infernal Crossing Ring when Ruwen had destroyed it, slicing the demon's leg off. A leg he had scooped up along with the Divine soul explosion. He needed to make sure Sift didn't find out he had another body part in his Inventory. Turning from the distant red splotch, he faced the Queen. "I'm sure the Vicar is hopping around someplace."

Ruwen grinned, even though no one got the joke but him.

"Seriously," Sift said. "What were you doing?"

Ruwen tilted his head. "I inspected some chickens, listened to disturbing poetry, and discovered the meaning of 'it can always be worse.' Oh, and I think I witnessed the birth of Tarot's gong band."

Sift raised an eyebrow, understanding enough of Ruwen's clues, along with the bandages, to confirm Blapy had arrived. He looked around, worry on his face. "Oh, no."

"Yes, that sums it up," Ruwen agreed. "Plus, I just thought of plan B."

Sift closed his eyes briefly, as if fighting off a wave of pain. "I don't even want to know."

The Scourge Queen growled and took another step closer. "You will tell me what happened to the Ring."

Ruwen turned from Sift to the Queen. "You would never believe me." He turned back to Sift. "I'm grabbing those other rings. We don't want them lying around." He pointed at the Queen without looking. "She's a fast runner. Make sure she can't follow."

Sift nodded and strode toward the Scourge Queen.

The Scourge Queen sneered and advanced as well. "I've had enough, you Metal infant. Your death will—"

Sift struck the Queen in the throat, avoiding her far too careless defense. Before she could recover, he stepped closer, turning his body, and swinging his elbow into her temple, just below one of her larger horns. The Scourge Queen staggered and Sift followed.

Ruwen turned and strode back to the four Infernal Crossing Rings, giving the Adepts a wave. He opened his Void Band into a narrow twenty-foot oval and passed it over the rings. In seconds, he'd captured four exceptionally valuable structures, denying their use to the Infernal Realm.

The ground shook from a quake deep underground, causing the wall Ruwen had exited to collapse into the new magma pool. *Survey* displayed the damage caused by the small piece of pressure wave he couldn't capture. It had continued downward at a shallow angle. *Stone Echo* could only reach five hundred feet, and he wondered how far the small pressure wave had traveled. It must have gone somewhat deep to bring this new magma to the surface.

Ruwen strode over to the Adepts. "Everyone ready?"

"Are we fighting our way out?" Prythus asked, glancing at the demon filled chamber.

Ruwen considered. "We could. Let's call that plan C."

The ground trembled again, this time more violently.

Ruwen continued. "Although, I don't think we have time for plan C."

"I'm almost done," Sift shouted.

Ruwen turned to the area that had contained the four rings he'd just taken. He focused his attention on a flat spot and cast the two second spell. His Mana dropped by two hundred fifty and a fifteen-by-six-by-five-foot wagon appeared, floating on a cushion of air.

"Jump in," Ruwen said to the Adepts.

Not waiting to see if they obeyed, Ruwen cast the level twenty Gatherer spell *Worker Wagon* a second time. The second wagon immediately latched itself behind the first.

Ruwen channeled one Energy per second into the level eight Worker spell *Climb,* and a hundred feet of magical rope appeared coiled around his hand. The ground shuddered and pieces of the ceiling fell. He quickly threaded the rope into the hitch of the lead wagon and wrapped the other side around his waist.

Sift stepped up to Ruwen and pointed at the wagons full of Adepts. "This is plan B?"

"Yep, which is better than plan C," Ruwen replied. He pointed his thumb at the back. "You're the appah's tail. Catch any fallers and do your best to keep up."

"Whatever," Sift said as he strode to the back of the wagons.

"I'm the undisputed champion of the Shelly Raceway. Not even that glowstick could catch me."

Ruwen smiled and stared at the mass of demons surrounding the dazed Scourge Queen. She waved weakly in their direction and the demons paused, unsure about attacking the people that had just disabled their Queen.

As the ground shuddered again, Ruwen didn't give them any more time to think. He trotted forward, and in five steps had increased his speed to a sprint.

The first line of demons consisted of the group that had surrounded the Scourge Queen on their run here. They were all Cultivators and would cause Ruwen the most trouble here. As he approached, they struck him, some blows arriving at Gem speeds.

But Ruwen's clothes remained covered in the Lubricating Potion, and the kicks, strikes, and grabs flowed off him.

As the ground trembled violently, Ruwen left the last of the demon horde behind, and entered the large lava tube he'd arrived in. Something had created a disturbance deep in the planet, and he dashed forward, intent on pulling his wagon full of treasure to safety.

CHAPTER 49

*R*uwen exited the lava tunnel and sprinted into a rainstorm. The water surprised him as it had seemed too cold earlier for rain. He didn't stop running until he reached the large circle of portal stones. The Founders and Addas sat meditating, while Echo seemed intent on something in the distance.

Worried that the lava tunnel they'd used for escape might collapse from the now constant ground quakes, Ruwen had pushed his speed as fast as he thought safe for the Adepts. Even so, Sift had needed to steady the wagons twice to keep them from flipping as Ruwen took corners at too steep an angle.

Ruwen slowed as he approached the leaders of his Clan, but the two Worker wagons full of Adepts kept their momentum, and when he slowed, the only thing that changed was the rope grew slack.

Ruwen set his stance on the slick rocks and prepared to grab the lead wagon to slow it as his summoned rope, still tied around his waist, coiled at his feet. The force of the rain, however, had pushed enough of the lubricating potion down his arms and onto his hands that grabbing the wagons proved impossible.

Unfortunately, Ruwen didn't figure that out until the lead wagon had slipped through his hands and then slid over his lubricated clothes, forcing him to bend backward and creating a ramp for the wagon. Realizing his mistake, he immediately channeled five Energy per second into *Scrub*, cursing the spell's one second cast time.

The lead wagon sailed into the air as Ruwen flipped away from the trailing wagon. He noticed the rapidly diminishing pile of coiled rope at his feet and realized in a few moments it would jerk him into the air.

Ruwen dismissed *Climb* and the magical rope disappeared. The second Worker wagon, without his body to use as a ramp, stayed on the ground and pulled the lead wagon back to the surface. He leaped forward to where the lead wagon would land, praying *Scrub* would finish casting by the time he got there.

The low jump made for a clumsy landing, but Ruwen's Diamond body made it look graceful to anyone watching. He slammed one hand into the rock covered ground and grabbed the undercarriage of the wagon with the other. *Scrub* activated just before he grabbed the wagon, and he got a good grip.

Even though Ruwen had only used five Energy per second to power *Scrub*, his vibrating hands quickly overcame the magic wood's durability, and his grip on the wagon melted away.

Ruwen immediately stopped channeling *Scrub* and regained his handhold before the entire wagon passed him by.

The wagon pushed Ruwen downward, its air cushion soft like a pillow. He could have resisted the force, but he wanted to make the landing less violent for the Adepts. The lead wagon continued forward, and Ruwen jammed his free hand deeper into the stony ground to slow them all down.

Sift grabbed the back of the second wagon and dug his feet

into the rocky surface. Between the two of them, the wagons slid to a stop twenty feet later. Ruwen rolled out from under the wagon and flashed Sift a quick *Thanks* in Shade Speak.

The Adepts jumped out of the wagons, and Ruwen thought they looked a little too eager. The ride couldn't have been that bad.

Sift stepped up to Ruwen. "That could have gone worse."

"Right? That's what I was thinking."

"You're lucky I dodged the pukers."

"Are you joking?"

Sift nodded at the Adepts who had clumped around the now standing Founders. A few still held their stomachs, and a couple looked like they might still vomit, but most of them had faced the same direction as Echo.

Ruwen winced. He might need to reconsider what others considered normal speeds. Curious about what had grabbed everyone's attention, he turned to look.

For as far as Ruwen could see, the mountains had shed their snow as lava poured from the dormant volcanos. The super-heated gases mixed with the cold air and squeezed the remaining moisture from it, causing the rain. The sky had filled with ash, and it reflected the red-orange glow of the erupting mountains.

The newly active volcanos ran in a straight line. Ruwen glanced back at the lava tube he'd just exited and did some simple geometry.

"Oh, no," Ruwen whispered.

"I think it's beautiful," Sift responded.

Ruwen considered the new magma pool that had filled the area where the tiny pressure wave he couldn't capture had escaped. It seemed the wave had continued a little farther than he'd expected. In fact, it appeared it had traveled past the horizon.

"Come on," Sift said. "Let's join the others."

Ruwen dismissed the *Worker Wagons* and followed Sift toward the group.

As they neared the others, Sift pointed at the line of volcanos. "Does that happen often?"

The Founders turned from the destruction that ran straight as an arrow from the mountain they had just exited. Ruwen did his best to act natural.

"No," Thorn replied. "It is not normal."

"This island shifted away from the larger magma chambers long ago," Mist added.

"What happened down there?" Dusk asked. "We worried for your safety. It shocked us all that you chose such a heavily traveled tube. It is obviously the most used in this valley."

"I hate that golem," Sift muttered.

"It sounded very noisy down there," Madda offered.

The comment meant they knew a lot of fighting had occurred. Ruwen also wondered if there might be some way to detect what he'd done to the Infernal Crossing Ring. He prayed no one brought it up.

Sift pointed a thumb at Ruwen. "He brought company, and they didn't like us."

Madda frowned at the bruises covering Sift's arm and he quickly lowered it. Ruwen breathed a sigh of relief that Sift hadn't given any more details.

"You might have heard Rung Four," Sift continued. "They were a little obsessed with a big glowing donut down there."

"A glowing donut?" Padda asked.

Sift drew a big circle with his arms. "Black rock holding some sort of energy."

Echo stiffened and turned from watching the volcanos to study them.

"But now we're here," Ruwen said. "So we can go."

Prythus still looked sick, but he bowed toward the Founders and Addas. "Master Ruwen performed a great service in that chamber." He turned to Ruwen and bowed even deeper. "Even if that portal didn't lead to our world, it served as a link in the chain of demon oppression. Losing five of their rings will surely be a blow."

Echo stepped toward them. "Five?"

Prythus looked embarrassed, and he bowed to Echo. "I did not intend to offend you, Sister. I do not judge all demons by the actions of the Infernal Realm."

"You should start," Sift muttered.

Echo took another step closer, now less than ten feet separating them all. "Did you say he destroyed five Infernal Crossing Rings?"

Ruwen kept his face and body neutral as Echo glanced at him.

Prythus continued. "The one he struck disappeared, as if the hand of the True God himself had snatched it from existence. The other four he placed in his bracelet, a truly powerful magic. It is a victory for the oppressed everywhere."

Echo slowly turned until she faced Ruwen. "As if the hand of the True God himself had snatched it from existence," she repeated.

Ruwen remained relaxed, prepared for an attack. Echo certainly knew more about the Infernal Crossing Rings than he did. She probably understood what should have happened and was trying to figure out what he'd done to stop it.

Echo turned her face from Ruwen and studied the line of volcanos spewing lava and ash into the air. She returned her focus to him. "It appears the True God didn't quite snatch everything. Still, I consider myself lucky to have survived such a thing, and I wonder how the ring on the other side faired, and if anyone lived."

Echo's words struck Ruwen like an avalanche, and he immediately fell into the third meditation to keep the guilt from overwhelming him. He hadn't even considered what might happen to the paired ring. She had made it sound like losing one ring caused the other to follow. If she told the truth, how much destruction would that cause?

Ruwen considered he might have destroyed Rung Four's planet.

The third meditation absorbed Ruwen's tidal wave of guilt, and on the outside, he remained calm. The truth was, Echo didn't know what would happen. Her words had betrayed the uncertainty. Likely, considering the consequences Ruwen had witnessed, Lalquinrial would know better than to test the result just out of curiosity. The cost in souls alone would make that unlikely.

But that didn't mean Echo was wrong, as she probably had extrapolated from her knowledge of the rings. It also struck him how, despite his best efforts, he had once again created an enormous mess by trying to do what he considered the right thing.

CHAPTER 50

*T*he tremors on Savage Island grew stronger, and the Addas herded everyone back through the portal. As soon as they all arrived back at the swamp, the Founders and Addas created another rune gate and once again, they all moved to a new location, except this time, they remained on the same planet.

Night had already fallen in the swamp, but when Ruwen stepped out of the rune gate, the setting sun greeted him. That probably meant they hadn't traveled more than a few thousand miles.

Salt, seaweed, and the faint odor of fish surrounded Ruwen. He had stepped through the portal near the middle of the Adepts, scared if he stayed until last, the Founders and Addas would interrogate him. Moving away from the twelve-foot slab of granite, he made room for the rest of his class.

Ruwen took off his remaining shoe and dropped it into his Void Band. He squished his toes in the soft sand of the beach before strolling forward toward the water and lazily crashing waves. An ocean stretched to the horizon, and the sun had dropped below the clouds, hanging just above the blue water.

"Now this is a proper beach," Sift said.

Ruwen closed his eyes and let the sound of the waves ease his mind. The worry and guilt about the paired Infernal Crossing Ring remained fresh in his thoughts. This beautiful place stood in stark contrast to the planet ending destruction he'd unleashed less than an hour ago.

"Yeah," Ruwen said.

"It reminds me of this place I saw in Shelly that had octoshakes. Come on, let's see how warm the water is."

Ruwen opened his eyes at the strange name but didn't bother asking if Sift meant a creature or a drink. He followed Sift to the waves, and many of the Adepts followed them.

The warm water rolled into Ruwen, rising to the middle of his shins. As the wave returned to the ocean, it pulled the sand from under his feet, making him sink a little. The sensation felt incredibly relaxing.

"Where is Shelly?" Ruwen asked.

Sift shrugged. "I can't keep track of that turtle. She gets out of my pocket all the time, and I'm terrified for hours that I lost her, and some fish or bird ate her. Then she shows up again, begging for a carrot or piece of lettuce. Scolding her never helps either. I swear all I've done is worried since I met her."

"You sound like a parent," Madda said, stepping next to Sift.

Padda stopped next to Ruwen, his eyes closed. "The ocean scorns the storm's fury."

Sift sighed. "Is that supposed to be helpful?"

The familiar bickering relaxed Ruwen, and the worry and guilt withdrew a little. He turned to Padda. "He'll use that when you're not around."

"You traitor," Sift hissed.

Padda opened his eyes and turned toward Ruwen, placing a hand on Ruwen's shoulder. "That makes me very happy, thank you." He dropped his hand and turned his attention back to the ocean. "I hope you listen. Understanding speaks with a soft voice."

"See what you get?" Sift added.

"This is my favorite place," Madda said. "I am glad you're finally here. That both of you are."

"Adepts!" Thorn called out over the sound of the surf.

Everyone turned to find the three Founders standing higher on the beach. Ruwen's eyes climbed to the view behind them. He hadn't looked backward before now.

A massive bamboo forest started a few hundred feet from the shore. It stretched as far as he could see in both directions and covered the rolling hills that disappeared into the low clouds hanging like a curtain and blocking his view.

Between the forest and the water stood hundreds of huts, their walls made from bamboo and their rooftops of thatch. The structures varied in size and people moved between them. Ruwen refocused on the Founders.

"This is our Clan's home," Mist said. "A Bamboo Viper Step Master is always welcome here."

Dusk glanced at them all. "Never in Clan history has a class reached the hidden trials so quickly. The summit is within sight."

"The preceding three trials," Mist said, "tested your understanding of the first strides required for your journey down the Bamboo Viper Master path."

"The remaining trials await you here," Thorn added. "Unlike the previous three, you are not required to work together."

Dusk continued, "The dangers in this place are not the same as those of the previous trials, but Adepts have died here nonetheless."

Mist pointed at the small town of huts. "You will stay in the village during your time here. Soon we will eat and then perform the green belt ceremony. To earn the blue, brown, and red belts, you need not find the answers here, but you must discover the right questions."

Ruwen's stomach twisted with worry at hearing the belt colors. He knew black marked a Master, which meant, just as he feared, there was a seventh trial. A hidden mystery in the Steps he had yet to uncover. One he had not prepared for at all.

Thorn spoke. "Once you have gained your red belt, only one trial remains. If successful, you earn your black belt and the title of Master."

Dusk spoke quietly, her voice just louder than the surf. "Lest you think the danger has passed, know that a final trip to Savage Island remains, and it carries the most danger, as you are usually alone. Do not relax."

Echo, under her breath, but knowing Ruwen could hear her, spoke. "Assuming you didn't destroy Savage Island's planet as well."

Once again Ruwen reminded himself, Echo knew nothing for sure. She had likely sensed or guessed his distress and now only wanted to poke the wound to cause pain.

"Planet?" Ruwen whispered back. "That Scourge Commander came from your father's Realm. How many of the Infernal Realm's nine circles would an explosion like that destroy? Maybe all of them."

Ruwen knew less than Echo about the ring and its possible location, and he felt a little bad for lying. The comment kept her silent, though, which made it worthwhile.

Mist continued. "In two hours, return here for the green belt ceremony."

The Founders bowed, and the Adepts returned it. The Founders turned and strode gracefully toward the village.

"Find an empty hut," Madda said to Ruwen and Sift. "Enjoy your stay here."

"We don't have time for that," Sift said quietly.

"There is no such thing as time," Padda replied just as quietly. "Only now exists."

The comment made Madda smile. "Take care, boys. Enjoy the eternal present."

With that, the Addas moved into the mass of Adepts, answering questions about housing and food and how long people usually stayed.

Sift faced the ocean again. "Did Blapy tell you anything about Lylan?"

Ruwen turned as well. Only half of the sun remained visible above the ocean's horizon. "I asked her about them, but she didn't answer."

"At least they'll know we're okay."

Ruwen winced.

"Right?" Sift asked. When Ruwen didn't respond, Sift asked again. "Right? You gave Blapy a message for them, right?"

"Listen, I had a lot going on. I basically died. I saw lights and darkness and—"

"Are you kidding me?" Sift interrupted. "And don't exaggerate. You had like five small poop bandages. How bad could your injuries have been?" Sift shook his head. "What if Lylan and Hamma are in trouble and think we're goofing off?"

"I'm sure Blapy will mention we're here and okay."

Sift tilted his head and frowned at Ruwen.

"Okay, she probably won't," Ruwen admitted. "But it's not like she'd play the messenger for me, anyway. She was already upset."

"She's always upset," Sift said. Then in a defeated voice, he continued. "Yeah, she wouldn't help us. Probably make things worse. Maybe we should use your magic chalk and just go see them quick."

"We aren't allowed to leave the trials until we're done. You know that. You want to risk losing all this for a quick kiss?"

Sift sighed. "No, more like risk it all to avoid Lylan's daggers."

"That does make for a harder decision."

After a moment Sift asked another question. "What upset Blapy this time? I'm kind of surprised she'd show up on that island."

Echo stood on the edge of Adepts, appearing uninterested in Ruwen and Sift. But Ruwen knew she listened intently to their conversation. He had likely said too much already.

Ruwen, hoping to mislead Echo, responded with half-truths. "When I noticed her, she was arguing with Tarot, and he had upset her."

"I hate that golem. Where is he?"

Ruwen didn't reveal that Tarot had saved his life. "I don't know. Maybe Blapy took him. When she spotted me, she yelled about the lava."

"Lava?"

"I grabbed a little while out rock hunting, and she didn't like it. She's tired of managing all the junk I stick in my Inventory."

"Now, that I get," Sift said. "For the first time, I almost feel like I understand that little brat."

Ruwen nodded, but for a completely different set of reasons. "Me, too."

CHAPTER 51

*R*uwen and Sift grabbed one of the empty medium-sized huts with two hammocks. Honestly, Ruwen would have rather just made a *Shed* for them, having become attached to the structures while isolated all those months. He resisted, not wanting to attract attention or break any rules. If the roof of their hut leaked, though, he would reevaluate.

Sift left to find the dining hut and check it for sweets. Ruwen laid down in his hammock and tried to relax. Casting the level fourteen Collector spell *Sow Seed*, which consumed ten Energy per second, he attempted to swing himself using the telepathic hand to push away from the hut's wall. The current level of the spell only affected items weighing a pound or less, and it barely moved him. The simple failure made him miss his Spirit based spells even more.

Ruwen raised his left arm and dropped the Spirit Infused Baton of a Thousand Uses from his Void Band. He twirled the baton in his right hand, and then ran a finger over all the bulges and protrusions on its surface, some of whose purpose he still didn't know. Placing the end of the baton against the wall, he lightly pushed himself, until his hammock rocked gently.

The swaying motion and distant but still audible surf relaxed Ruwen. He expanded the minimized notifications he'd received on Savage Island and went through them, pausing on the maximum increase of each.

Gong!
You have increased your Knowledge!
Level: *159*

Ruwen's previous Knowledge level had reached one hundred fifty-five, so the understanding he'd gained here had added four more points.

The next ones contained skill increases, and he read "*Shing! You have advanced a skill!*" dozens of times.

Mining increased seven points to reach nine. It now increased extraction speed by eighteen percent, extraction yield by nine percent, and decreased gem and mineral damage by nine percent.

Prospecting had risen four to level fifteen, and increased Ruwen's chance of discovering plants, gems, ores, minerals, and other collectibles by fifteen percent.

Taxonomy had inched up two, reaching thirteen, and improved Ruwen's identification of plants, gems, ores, minerals, and other collectibles by thirteen percent.

Swimming through the lava had triggered an advancement of three in that skill to fifteen percent, raising Ruwen's speed in the water by fifteen percent while decreasing the Energy cost by seven and a half percent.

Tumbling had risen to one hundred ninety-four, the two additional points bringing his fall damage reduction to ninety-seven percent.

Tactics had increased by one to level forty, which boosted Ruwen's Wisdom by twenty percent.

Creativity climbed two, reaching nineteen, now increasing Ruwen's Cleverness by nine and a half percent.

Ruwen's intense planet saving use of Last Breath to give himself enough time to place the Infernal Crossing Ring's explosion into his Inventory had increased the rare skill by eleven to one hundred seventy-nine. It now reduced pain by one hundred seventy-nine percent, increased mind Resistance by eighty-nine point five percent, and thought speed by three hundred fifty-eight percent.

In reality, all the mental skills like Last Breath, Tactics, and Creativity had values double their notification's numbers, as the passive from Rami's second Codex of Evolution made them twice as effective.

During Ruwen's search for crossing stones, he'd killed thirteen lava eels. They'd averaged level twenty-five, and he'd gained one hundred eighty-four thousand seven hundred experience from them. It didn't look like he'd gotten experience for the Scourge Commander, and he wondered if the explosion he'd created didn't count. He checked his log, and the answer reminded him of his very first kill, even if accidental, of the Naktos Mage assistant in the park on his Ascendancy Day.

You have killed a Scourge Commander, Warlord (Level 84)!
You have gained 178,300 experience! <Deferred>
< Scourge Commander, Warlord (Level 84) is a member of a War Party (1 of 25)>

"Deferred" experience kept a person from getting information their Perception level wouldn't reveal to them. Since his Perception had reached one hundred ninety percent, he guessed the reason for the deferral wasn't because of his Perception, but the fact the rest of the twenty-five member War Party resided on another world.

Ruwen checked his experience total.

Experience: *1,605,031/1,711,000*

Level fifty-nine was only a little over a hundred thousand experience away. The experience from the eels had added up quickly, and Ruwen hoped their last trip to Savage Island would be close to the lava pools. He could power level himself into the sixties in less than a day.

The notifications taken care of, Ruwen considered how to proceed with the trials. He already knew the answers and had, in fact, perfected them. The three hidden patterns these trials revealed related to the force of your Steps, breathing, and timing. Already knowing what he needed to find should make locating each trial easy. He and Sift could be finished by lunch tomorrow.

What about the other Adepts? Especially Rung Four. They had come here, risking the trials when barely ready, to gain the rank of Master. They intended to take their new rank and train others back home, giving them the skills to push back the invading demon horde.

If Ruwen finished these trials and left Rung Four here on their own, it might take them months or even years to gain the insight they needed to proceed. This long thoughtful process worked for the Bamboo Viper Clan Founders, and he already knew how they felt about rushing knowledge. With no intervention, however, the demons would likely have already won by the time Rung Four finished.

Then, assuming one member of Rung Four told the others what they'd discovered, they would travel as a group to Savage Island and face the danger there without the help of Ruwen or Sift.

The longer Ruwen thought about it, the more certain he became. He couldn't in good conscious leave them here to fend for themselves.

Sift returned, excitedly talking about the desserts here, and Ruwen listened until Sift finally paused.

Ruwen stopped rocking himself and spun the baton through the fingers of his right hand. "I want to tell Rung Four what the three trial questions are, and how to begin finding answers."

"Okay," Sift responded immediately.

Ruwen sat up and moved his legs off the hammock. "You aren't going to argue?"

"Why? You did it for me."

"You're different. Don't you want to know why I want this for them?"

Sift pinched his chin. "How much thought have you put into that decision?"

"A lot."

"How shocking. And you've thought of consequences and counterarguments and rationalized your justifications?"

Ruwen titled his head. "Your vocabulary is getting better."

Sift waved a hand. "No, I heard Lylan use that phrase. It sounded smart."

"She said that about me?"

"Do you overthink and rationalize your justifications?"

Ruwen considered that. He did always convince himself what he did was the right thing. "I guess."

"Well then, does it matter if she meant you?"

"I guess not."

"Telling others the hidden stuff will probably upset the old people."

"I've been thinking about that, too," Ruwen said, tapping the baton against his free hand. "They haven't said anything to us about our training, the hidden forms, or the really hidden one. We just keep plodding along here."

Sift shrugged. "Like I said, they're old, and old people forget stuff. Except Fluffy. That guy's memory is as sharp as a knife."

"Ugh, he wants me to do more cleaning. I'd kind of hoped he'd have forgotten after all this time."

Sift's eyes grew wide. "All what time? How long have you owed him something?"

It was Ruwen's turn to shrug. "I cleaned some valuable gear in the vault, and he seemed really excited about it. He wanted me to come back as soon as I could to do some more."

"How long ago?"

"Around the time we went on that camping trip with Big D."

Sift pinched the bridge of his nose. "True god help you."

"What?"

"I guarantee you the Black Pyramid's Quartermaster has thought of *you* multiple times a day for the past, what, with the Spirit Realm adventure and your trip across the Universe, must almost be *two years*."

Ruwen swallowed hard. "That's a lot of thinking about me."

Sift slowly nodded his head.

Ruwen waved a hand. "Stop distracting me. What were we talking about?"

"Jelly rolls?"

Ruwen refocused his thoughts, and a moment later, he remembered. "No, we were talking about how no one has yelled at me yet." He winced and raised a hand. "Let me restate that. The Founders haven't yelled at me yet."

"Who cares?" Sift responded. "You should spend more time thinking about sweet rolls and less about the amount of trouble you're in."

"That seems irresponsible."

"Has thinking about the trouble ever stopped it from finding you?"

"No."

Sift stood, walked over, and placed a hand on Ruwen's shoulder. "Then rest assured your trouble is still coming, whether you're thinking about it or not."

"Thanks?"

"No problem. Now let's go stand in the ocean until the ceremony."

Ruwen stood. Once in a great while, something valuable came out of Sift's mouth, and standing in the ocean was one of them.

CHAPTER 52

*S*ift and Ruwen moved to stand in the back of Rung Four as the Adepts gathered for the Green Belt ceremony. It remained remarkably easy to see as the bright moon reflected off the ocean and the hills of bamboo glowed. The surf also grew bright every time a wave crashed as something in the water activated, and he scooped up a few gallons for Fractal.

"I'm going to kill that golem," Sift hissed. "Do you know where Tarot is?"

Ruwen patted the top of his head to make sure. "No. I haven't seen him since…" he trailed off, not sure how to finish that sentence.

"The poop incident?" Sift offered.

Ruwen turned to Sift. "What?"

Sift drew a circle around his face. "I pooped today. All over your face. Seems straight forward to me."

"Everything that happened there, and you land on poop?"

"It was memorable. I need to find your golem before this ceremony starts."

"Why now?"

"He took my orange belt again."

"I told you to leave it in your bag. He's fast."

Sift looked at Ruwen, his face serious. "I did. I never took it out. Not once."

Ruwen frowned. "You must have. I saw you put the belt away."

"I think I would remember."

Ruwen would have doubted Sift, but he looked genuinely upset. As Ruwen had recovered in the small chamber after the explosion, Blapy had been arguing with Tarot. She had said something about staying out of her Pyramid. He had thought it was just a general warning, like don't come visit me, but now he wondered if she'd meant literally.

Sift owned a small dimensional belt that he stored his travel books and extra clothes. Like almost all dimensional Inventory, it linked back to the vaults under the Black Pyramid. If Tarot had stolen Sift's orange belt, and Sift had never removed it here, it meant the golem had taken it from one of Blapy's vaults. It also meant Tarot had a lot more power than just telling the future.

"Now I really want to talk to that golem, too," Ruwen said.

Ruwen removed his orange belt and used *Melt* to separate the centipede scale from the belt fragment. The scale remained covered in lubricating oil and he guessed it would be virtually impossible to hold, so he let it drop into his Inventory.

The orange belt drooped sadly over Ruwen's palm. He grabbed the frayed end and pulled the charred cloth apart, splitting the piece in two. Handing one to Sift, he smiled. "Aren't we the pair."

Sift returned the smile. "Thanks buddy."

Sift's formal attire looked awful, with burns and rips covering it, but at least he had most of it. And now he had a narrow two-foot section of orange belt. Ruwen only had the matching piece of belt, as his formal attire had vaporized in the lava lake. He stood self-consciously in a set of the black clothes he'd gotten on his first trip to the Black Pyramid.

The Adepts grew quiet and Ruwen turned his attention to the front. The Founders and Addas strode down the beach toward them, and to his surprise, the Quartermaster followed behind them.

The Adepts bowed, and the Founders and Grandmasters returned it.

"Never have so many Adepts stood on this beach," Mist said.

"Tomorrow," Thorn continued. "You begin the hidden trials. Tonight, though, we finish the third trial."

"Rungs," Mist said. "Present your crossing stones."

Echo stepped forward. "For Rung One," she said simply as she held her left hand out.

A three-foot dimensional opening appeared from a dull red pinky ring. Echo slowly stepped backward as a line of black rock fell out of her Inventory portal and onto the sand.

A lot of rock. It appeared while Ruwen had gathered enough to end the trial, Echo had searched for enough to win. He briefly considered dropping one of the giant Infernal Crossing Rings to secure a win for Rung Four. Gaining more Relics would aid their fight against Lalquinrial's demon horde.

But common sense won out over Ruwen's competitive nature. "For Rungs Two, Three, and Four," he said, and created a second, smaller pile next to Echo's.

Since Ruwen had clearly lost, he kept a few stones for Fractal.

Echo grinned in a very self-satisfied way, Ruwen thought.

"Well done, Adepts," Dusk said. "This will help our Clan for many years."

The ancient bald Quartermaster limped up to the Founders and bowed. With a flick of his wrist, the shoot of bamboo struck the sand. Ruwen, remembering from last time, activated Last Breath, hoping to catch the transition.

When the Quartermaster's shoot struck the sand, the bamboo forest didn't grow upward from the sand, or expand outward from the bamboo sliver. Instead, it just appeared, as if it had always been there, and the Quartermaster had merely revealed it.

Ruwen released Last Breath and wondered what that meant. He reached out and touched a nearby trunk. The sandy beach now had a layer of leaves and he glanced upward to make sure the moon remained in place, and they hadn't moved. The moon remained, the bamboo radiating the light like the bamboo on the hillsides behind the village.

Ruwen could see the bamboo shoot the Quartermaster had thrown to the ground, and he concentrated on it, hoping his Perception might reveal some information.

Name: *Phased Bamboo Shoot*
Quality: *Relic*
Effect (Triggered): *Grow – Contact with the ground synchronizes a bamboo forest with users current Realm and dimension.*
Effect (Triggered): *Gather – retrieving shoot collapses synchronization, returning the forest to its natural phase.*
Description: *A three-inch bamboo shoot dimensionally linked to a thriving bamboo forest.*

That explained why the forest had just appeared. Ruwen wondered what other things surrounded him and if viewing these out-of-phase areas was possible somehow. They reminded him of small portable Realms.

The Quartermaster concentrated on the stone piles. The leaves that now covered the ground under the rocks rose together, as if connected, and lifted both mounds.

"The winner is Rung One," the Quartermaster said as the piles floated across the ground and disappeared into the forest.

"Congratulations, Rung One," Mist said. "You may collect your reward from the Quartermaster when we finish here."

Dusk glanced at all the Adepts and then spoke. "Only by rising above the fog of doubt, uncertainty, and fear can one see their potential or ever hope of reaching it." She paused a few seconds and then continued. "Doing so has risks unrelated to personal growth, which our Clan wishes to minimize."

The Addas, already behind the Founders, moved closer to them. Padda held a mass of green belts and Madda gestured at Echo.

Echo strode forward and Thorn presented her with a new green belt. Madda pointed Echo to the Quartermaster who already had a new set of formal attire waiting.

The process repeated itself until it was Ruwen's turn. He strode forward, carefully watching what happened to Sift with the orange belt fragment that mirrored Ruwen's. No one appeared to hassle Sift about it, and Ruwen relaxed.

Dusk raised her eyebrows at Ruwen's attire but handed him the green belt without comment. He bowed and stepped over to the Quartermaster, who handed Ruwen his new clothes with a shake of the head. Ruwen accepted the rebuke with a bow and opened the notification that had appeared as he hurried back to his spot.

The Bamboo Viper Clan has gifted you...

Name: *Bamboo Jacket of Falling*
Quality: *Fine*
Durability: *100 of 100*
Weight: *2.6 lbs.*
Effect (Passive): *Falling Leaf – falls greater than five feet slow the wearer to three feet per second.*
Restriction: *10-mile radius of Masters' Village.*
Description: *Heavy-cotton long jacket. The first Step is the hardest.*

Name: *Viper Pants of Floating*
Quality: *Fine*
Durability: *100 of 100*
Weight: *2.4 lbs.*
Effect (Passive): *Cresting Wave – Dizziness or unconsciousness increases buoyancy by 500% and creates a bubble of air around the wearer.*
Effect (Passive): *Riptide – Swimming +100.*
Restriction: *10-mile radius of Masters' Village.*
Description: *Heavy-cotton pants with reinforced seams. The first breath is the hardest.*

Mist described what the jacket and pants did, and Ruwen realized it was because no one there received notifications but him.

The uniform's effects gave Ruwen some ideas on where to focus his search for the three hidden trials. A search he planned to start immediately.

CHAPTER 53

*W*hile Rung One looked through the Quartermaster's Relics, Ruwen and Sift took the rest of the Adepts closer to the surf. The bamboo forest stretched into the water, making for an odd sight. They remained close enough to the Phased Bamboo Shoot that the forest remained thin. It allowed Ruwen and Sift to spend a few hours training the other Adepts. Rung One eventually joined them except for Echo.

The Adepts, all with over a decade of training, made significant progress under Ruwen's and Sift's guidance. Rung Four especially made gains, absorbing the knowledge like water on a dry sponge. Rung Four spent fifteen minutes at the conclusion of the training telling Ruwen and Sift more of their precious memories.

Prythus spoke of his murdered family and the niece and nephew he still fought to protect. Nymthus described her husband, a general in their last remaining army, and her daughter, who loved yellow flowers and wanted to be a warrior like her mother. The other members of Rung Four offered similar memories. They valued family and peace, and the demons had destroyed both.

The bamboo forest had disappeared hours ago, and Ruwen watched the Adepts walk back to the village, laughing and joking with each other. Rung Four's openness with their memories had led to quick friendships among the other Rungs, as many of them had things in common.

Ruwen considered the power of what Rung Four did with their memories. By sharing a part of themselves so openly, it accelerated the relationship building and trust with everyone else. It was an incredibly powerful technique for team building, and he wondered if the leaders on Rung Four's planet had planned it that way.

Sift had joined the Adepts, eager to see if the food hall remained open and he could grab more dessert. Ruwen stood alone on the beach, feeling homesick after hearing all the memories of Rung Four. He hoped those he loved and cared for remained safe. His time here was almost over, and he would see them in person soon.

Ruwen stripped off the Black Pyramid clothes and placed them, along with the orange belt fragment, into his Void Band. Pulling on his new Bamboo Viper Clan uniform, he tied the green belt around his waist.

The magical effects on the jacket and pants made it easy for Ruwen to guess at least one trial took place in the water, and one somewhere high. He still hated heights, especially now, without Spirit spells or easy access to the Gravity Shell to keep him safe from a fall. So, he decided to focus on the water trial first.

The three hidden patterns in the Steps were force, time, and breathing. With nothing else to decide, Ruwen strode into the water.

The heavy cotton of the uniform absorbed the ocean water, and coupled with his muscle dense frame, easily kept him in contact with the ocean floor. The additional one hundred points in Swimming from the *Riptide* effect on the Viper Pants of Floating made moving through the water effortless.

Just a few feet underwater, the moonlight mostly disappeared, and Ruwen turned on *Glow*. The light revealed the ocean floor, which contained occasional clusters of coral that leaked bubbles from their straw like shapes.

Fifty feet from shore, Ruwen stood fifteen feet under the surface. He moved back and forth parallel to the waterline, slowly moving farther from the beach, searching for clues to one of the hidden patterns. Two hundred feet from shore and nearly straight across from the village, the ocean floor changed.

The coral had become more frequent but hadn't turned into a reef, which made the structure in front of Ruwen even more unusual. *Glow's* soft light didn't illuminate far and he couldn't judge its size, so he retrieved his Worker's Class Symbol of Radiance. Big D had given him the gift after the terium mine tour during the camping trip. He still had Sift's Fighter one but figured one symbol would be enough.

Ruwen used five Mana to attach the small, clasped hands symbol to the top of his forehead, and channeled twenty-three Energy to it, which consumed exactly ten percent of his Energy Regen per second.

The symbol blazed with light, revealing the entire area for a hundred feet in whatever direction Ruwen looked.

Three things occurred to Ruwen at the same time.

The oddly shaped coral continued in each direction, forming a hundred-foot circle.

The water over that circle contained a massive number of slowly rising bubbles.

And Ruwen wasn't alone.

Two creatures stood at the edge of Ruwen's light. They had the eyes and hooded head of a cobra, but the mouth, jaws, and teeth of a shark. Their narrow bodies had the black slimy look of eels, and three arms floated on each side. Two more tendrils floated below them like legs. It reminded him of some night-mare combination of an octopus and snake.

Sift had said this place seemed familiar, but the location he'd seen using Shelly's memories had something he'd called octoshakes. Taking into consideration Sift's habit of smashing words together, an octopus-shark-snake is probably what he'd seen. Which meant Shelly had been here before.

The creatures' disposition aura appeared white, and Ruwen guessed that meant they probably wouldn't attack. He remained still, watching the two octoshakes, and they mirrored him. His Perception triggered and provided more information.

Name: *Coral Viper*
Deity: *Unknown*
Class Type: *Cultivator - Gold*
Level: *38*
Health: *886*
Mana: *0*
Energy: *0*
Spirit: *900,000*
Armor Class: *490*

The distance of Ruwen's light barely reached the Coral Vipers, and out of the darkness behind them emerged another pair of Coral Vipers. The first set turned, and in a blink, the four Coral Vipers battled each other.

Ruwen watched the fight with interest. Neither pair seemed frenzied or angry. It honestly appeared like a friendly fight. Ten seconds later, he detected something familiar about the attacks. His brain itched, and he studied the fighting intently. It took another ten seconds for a suspicion to form, and only another twenty seconds to confirm it.

The Coral Vipers knew Viper Step techniques. Had they

learned it from watching the Adepts, Masters, and Grandmasters in the village? If so, that seemed like an amazing accomplishment for water creatures, unless maybe they could breathe air. Even so, it would take a high level of intelligence to survive outside the water and watch the Bamboo Viper Step Clan practice.

Another simpler solution occurred to Ruwen. His Clan had observed the Coral Vipers and had adapted their efficient strikes into forms. These creatures hadn't learned their fighting techniques from the Clan. The Clan had learned it from the Vipers. Or at least based their style on the creatures' battling methods.

Ruwen moved onto the large circular coral. As his light reached farther into the darkness, more of the Coral Vipers revealed themselves. They occasionally glanced at him, but mostly watched the fighting pair. Not a single Viper had moved closer than the edge of the coral disk.

The one hundred skill points in Swimming, added to Ruwen's own twelve, made movement in the water little different from the surface. He certainly felt the resistance of the water, but it felt more like wearing weighted gloves than a true hindrance.

Many of the Viper strikes Ruwen had learned kept the hand flat, like a spear, for most of the attack, only forming a fist in the instant before striking. Attacking like this made the strike faster as it encountered less air resistance, but the difference only became noticeable near the peak of his training.

But knowing now that the forms had come from an underwater creature, the technique made much more sense. Water would offer far more resistance, and a flat hand, traveling like a spear, would be far faster than an open palm or fist.

As Ruwen crossed the coral disk, he located the origin of the bubbles. Small holes covered the coral disk, and the openings released streams of gas seemingly at random.

When Ruwen drew close to the four fighting Coral Vipers, they stopped and faced him. They floated peacefully, like they hadn't been assaulting each other moments before. All of them still had the white Disposition Aura, and it gave him all the encouragement he needed.

From the edge of the coral disk, Ruwen bowed to the four Coral Vipers and then turned slightly and gestured toward the disk, inviting them to cross whatever boundary kept them on the other side of the disk.

Hey You hadn't worked with animals, to Ruwen's great disappointment, but if the Coral Vipers had basic intelligence, they likely had a language that he could communicate in. There was only one way to find out.

Ruwen had exhaled his breath at the beginning of tonight's underwater search because it increased his buoyancy too much. Even if he hadn't, it would only take a few words before it ran out. If he wanted to talk to the Coral Vipers, only one solution remained.

Ruwen's heart rate increased and he forced himself to calm down. Even though water-filled lungs held no danger for him, a lifetime of air breathing, coupled with the primal instinct to survive, made inhaling the water difficult. Recalling his underwater training in the Spirit Realm, he steadied his emotions, and took a deep breath of ocean water.

"Greetings, noble fighters," Ruwen said, the water's density requiring more effort to speak. "I would like to spar."

Ruwen's light had revealed at least fifty more Coral Vipers, and all of them reacted the same. Black clouds erupted from the tips of their tendrils, and in a blink all the Coral Vipers but the four in front of him had become lost in the blackness.

"Where you learn talk?" the largest of the Coral Vipers asked.

Ruwen smiled at his success but hurriedly hid his teeth as the Coral Vipers' disposition auras took on a pink overtone.

Showing your teeth obviously didn't mean anything friendly. He couldn't think of a good name for the speaker, so he decided to call him Shark Boss. Maybe naming things well was harder than he'd thought.

"Pleasure, I have," Ruwen said with a small bow to Shark Boss. "To learn many talks."

Shark Boss pointed one of his eight tendril arms at Ruwen, and he noticed the sharp barbs at the end of their appendages, like fingers. "You deformed air swimmer. No match."

Ruwen guessed his deformity related to only having four appendages, not eight. "Not number important. How used."

The black cloud had thinned, and the mass of Coral Vipers swam closer. The water vibrated with clicks that Ruwen registered as laughter.

Shark Boss seemed to think Ruwen had made fun of him as his disposition aura briefly took on a red tinge again. He held up a tendril over his eyes and Ruwen realized his Worker Symbol of Radiance shone directly into their eyes.

"Apology," Ruwen said, and lowered the Energy from twenty-three per second to five.

The area dimmed considerably and Ruwen quickly came up with an idea that would allow him to see while not blinding the Coral Vipers. They were used to the sun, so he would mimic that.

Ruwen channeled twenty Energy per second in the level twelve Commander spell *Move On* and shaped the mobile bridge it created into a flat, one-hundred-twenty-five by four foot strip. He created a *Shed* on each side of the coral disk and used *Mend Tool* to attach the narrow bridge to the edge of the nearest *Shed*. Using his one hundred and twelve Swimming skill, he moved like a fish through the water to the other end. He pushed the bridge backward, and it buckled upward, creating an arch.

Ruwen attached the mobile bridge to this second *Shed* using *Mend Tool*. He swam to the middle of the arch above the disk's center and attached the Worker's Symbol of Radiance to the bridge with five Mana. Then he channeled forty Energy to the item, and it blazed brightly, shining down on the coral disk like a small sun.

The Coral Vipers had watched Ruwen, their interest in his spell casting obvious. When he returned to the four Coral Vipers, Shark Boss immediately asked Ruwen a question, his voice betraying nervousness.

"You sky predator?"

Ruwen took a moment and decided Shark Boss wanted to know if he was a god. "No."

"You air dancer?" Shark Boss asked.

That probably meant the Bamboo Viper Clan. "Yes. I here test."

Shark Boss waved all his tendrils at once. They flicked forward at Ruwen and then back in a wave. "Forbidden fight air dancers."

Ruwen smiled again, but kept his teeth hidden. "Our secret."

Ruwen moved to the center of the disk, and after a moment of hesitation, Shark Boss moved onto the coral as well. Once done though, the Coral Viper lost all his reluctance, and surged toward Ruwen.

Shark Boss attacked Ruwen relentlessly, the Coral Viper's strikes coming from all eight limbs. To Ruwen, it felt like sparing two highly coordinated opponents, and while this might overwhelm a normal fighter, it didn't scratch the surface of his abilities. Within a minute, he'd seen the foundations for dozens of Viper forms.

Ruwen encouraged the other three to join Shark Boss, and the eight limbs turned into thirty-two. It required more concentration, but at the speeds the Coral Vipers attacked, he was in no danger.

In fact, Ruwen noticed something that, in all his training, he'd overlooked. The difference between water and air to his

Peak Diamond body was insignificant, but he quickly realized moving too fast in the water created massive water vortexes behind his actions. He knew the same happened in air, but he'd never studied them before. The water made seeing them easy.

Ruwen had intended to find the locations of all three trials that night, but sparring the Coral Vipers was fun, and he used the time to study how the vortexes his movements caused affected his body and limbs. To his surprise, they slowed the movement of his body, slightly pulling back whenever he moved away from the disturbance.

Ruwen experimented with slight variations to his attacks. The changes to how he moved through the Steps were incredibly tiny, and something nearly impossible to teach. But the modifications in the shape of his arm or hand mattered as it moved, and some shapes resisted the pull of the vortexes better than others. It made him a fraction of a fraction faster, and it made him incredibly happy.

And personal improvement wasn't the only benefit because it only took Ruwen being on the coral disk a few minutes to figure out its purpose and how it related to the trials. He hadn't found all three trial locations, but he'd found one, and he'd bring the Adepts here tomorrow to demonstrate.

With that thought, Ruwen stopped thinking about the Adepts, the trials, or his bigger problems, and sparred the Coral Vipers long into the night.

CHAPTER 54

*R*uwen and the rest of the Adepts including, to his surprise, Echo, treaded water above the coral disk he had found the night before. The late morning sun reflected off the water, causing him to squint. The waves swelled as they approached the shore, and everyone moved up and down with the perpetual motion.

The thick cotton of their uniforms held the salt water and normally would have made swimming difficult with all the weight, but the combination of everyone's superb physical shape and the extra one hundred Swimming skill the Viper Pants of Floating provided made it easy.

"Below us is a coral disk," Ruwen said to the Adepts. "It high-lights one of the three hidden patterns in the Steps. Do any of you know them?"

Ruwen glanced at Sift who floated on his back with closed eyes, smiling every time a wave raised and lowered his body.

After a brief silence, Nymthus responded. "Since it is under water and our pants keep us safe from drowning, I'm assuming it has something to do with breathing."

"That's right. Who here pays attention to their breathing?" Ruwen asked.

Prythus spoke up. "Our Master taught us to breathe through our nose, exhale when striking, and take deep breaths to calm the heart and feed our muscles."

"Excellent advice," Ruwen responded. "But there is more. The first three trials emphasized balance, and this breathing trial is no different." He glanced at all the Adepts. "If you pay attention to your breathing, you will find it incredibly erratic. Sometimes you breathe quick and shallow, other times, slow and deep. Also, many Bamboo and Viper Steps benefit from lungs that are only partially full. Which means we should not assume the two best states are full lungs or empty and rush to each."

The Adepts watched Ruwen, obviously not having ever given thought to alternate states. The exception was Echo, who observed passively, but he could tell she already knew this concept.

"Sisen Sift," Ruwen said. "Is it more complicated than that?"

"It's always more complicated," Sift responded, still floating on his back. "Many Steps benefit from a buildup of oxygen, and some even from a lack of it."

"How can starving your body of air be helpful?" Nymthus asked.

Sift let his feet drift downward and he looked at the Adepts. "The Bamboo Viper Steps are much more than a fighting style. They teach balance, and not just how to make the two styles even, but the complexities of reaching that balance."

Ruwen's heart raced at hearing Sift say the word "even." He brought it under control and swallowed, his mouth still filled with the taste of maple syrup.

Sift continued. "Primal parts of your brain respond to danger like not getting enough air, altering the alchemy of your blood and providing a surge of strength and speed, beneficial for some Steps. Empty lungs make other movements easier to perform. The complexities go on and on."

The Adepts watched Ruwen and Sift with rapt attention.

"Below us," Ruwen said. "Is a coral disk. It contains thousands of tiny holes that bubble air seemingly at random. They are not random."

"We confirmed it this morning," Sift said.

Ruwen nodded. "The trial below, if I had to guess, provides most of the hidden breathing knowledge. More than enough to give you an advantage over your opponents."

"How does it work?" Prythus asked.

"In a moment," Ruwen said. "We will sink and swim to the edges of the coral disk, which produces a constant stream of bubbles. It takes practice, but when you feel a bubble passing your nose, breath in immediately."

"It feels like your nose is itching," Sift added. "That's when you know to breathe. This is difficult, and your heart will race. Normally you'd control that with breathing, but since that is the source of the issue, it compounds the problem. A wicked design."

The Adepts remained silent.

Sift continued. "I'll say it again. This is not easy. It took me an hour this morning to get comfortable breathing at the edge, and longer to make my way through the Steps. Do not let the stress overwhelm you."

Ruwen hid a smile. It had only taken Sift a few minutes to catch on to the underwater breathing, but he'd added almost an hour to the time to take the pressure off the Adepts.

Over *Sphere of Influence*'s mental link, Ruwen spoke to Sift. *You are a great Sisen.*

Sift turned to Ruwen and grinned, and the taste of maple syrup disappeared.

"Let's see if anyone can beat our Sisen," Ruwen said, hoping the competition might distract them from the worry of breathing underwater.

Ruwen sank and the other thirty-two Adepts followed. The water here was far enough from the beach that it remained free of sand and the sun provided plenty of light. The Coral Vipers had disappeared or remained out of sight.

Echo, who didn't need to breathe because of her Gem Fortified body, figured the bubble-breathing out almost immediately. A man in Rung One and a woman in Rung Three didn't know how to swim, and the added anxiety made the process hard for them. Even with the added hundred skill points to Swimming, their lack of familiarity with the water made it difficult.

All the Adepts except for Echo triggered the safety passives on their Viper Pants of Floating at least once, but less than thirty minutes later, the Adepts stood in a ring along the edge of the disk. Ruwen and Sift strode to the middle where a flowing stream of bubbles, just like at the edge, floated upward. The water-soaked uniforms provided enough weight to keep everyone firmly pressed to the ground.

Sift began the Viper Step forms, and when enough space separated them, Ruwen moved to the center and began breathing from the stream of bubbles. Then, mirroring Sift, he began the Viper Steps as well.

Ruwen moved through the forms, marveling at the ingenuity of this trial. It wasn't perfect. He had spent a vast amount of time figuring out the most efficient way to breathe through the forms and had taken his knowledge far past what this disk provided. The value of the trial to the others was massive, though. Instead of spending months experimenting constantly to find the right sequences, this disk got you close.

When Ruwen needed to breathe, a column of bubbles always met him, when he shouldn't breathe, no bubbles existed. It was an astounding piece of construction. Spending an hour down here would have shaved months from his trial-and-error method. The Founders had commented about Masters always being welcomed here, and he could see why they would want to return. This type of advanced training was invaluable.

Echo remained on the edge of the disk as the other Adepts attempted the course. She studied the bubble patterns intensely, and Ruwen guessed she was mentally moving through the forms. He did something similar when learning. Visualizing the movements and actions ahead of time to aid his technique.

The Adepts triggered the passive on their Viper Pants of Floating with every attempt, some of them not even making it three steps before panic overwhelmed them and they gulped in a lungful of water, or the lack of oxygen made them too dizzy to function.

As the day wore on, all of them made progress, however, and Ruwen could see the immense pride they felt for the accomplishments. At mid-afternoon, he stopped them for the day, as the Adepts showed signs of exhaustion from the difficult training.

Echo remained as the rest of the Adepts swam to the surface. As Ruwen, Sift, and the Adepts swam toward the beach, he studied the pressure waves she generated as she attempted the coral disk for the first time.

Not needing to breathe gave Echo an advantage, because when she failed, she only needed to walk back to the center and start the process again. With the entire day spent studying the bubble patterns, she made incredible progress.

On the ninth attempt, Echo successfully finished the Viper sequence.

Ruwen, Sift, and the Adepts reached the beach, and the Adepts stumbled out of the surf, their bodies trembling from the day's efforts. They laughed and joked, their spirits high from success. Ruwen told Sift to head to the dining hall with the other Adepts, and that he'd catch up later.

Ruwen stood in the surf, waist deep in the ocean. He faced

the bamboo covered hills and analyzed the pressure waves Echo continued to generate back on the coral disk.

It took seventeen attempts for Echo to finish the Bamboo forms, as the Step's throws and twists created a more complex breathing pattern.

On the fifth attempt of the combined Viper and Bamboo Steps, Echo succeeded. Ruwen strode out of the water, amazed at Echo's ability to master techniques she'd only observed for half a day. Her Gem Fortified body helped, certainly, but he knew that wasn't the only thing. Echo had excellent Step skills paired with natural ability, and while not on the same scale as Sift's talent, it bore many similarities.

Ruwen doubted Sift or Echo would ever match his probability wave abilities, so they would likely never best him in a fight, but Echo, just like Sift, had a natural grace that gave their movements a beauty Ruwen couldn't match.

Ruwen sighed as he exited the ocean, scolding himself for the brief attack of jealousy. What he lacked in natural ability, he made up for with focus, intelligence, and work ethic. This allowed him to succeed in almost everything he concentrated on. Only art like the Stone Carver Valora's sculpture, Clouds Embracing the Sun, that gave a buff just by looking at its magnificence, were outside his capabilities to master.

A voracious curiosity had served Ruwen well his whole life, but he didn't have time anymore to chase perfection on things that didn't matter to his immediate goals. So Sift and Echo could remain the champions of graceful beauty, while Ruwen concentrated on healing himself, transitioning to the Divine rank, and creating gods.

CHAPTER 55

*T*he sun had almost touched the horizon when Ruwen gathered with the rest of the Adepts on the beach. He kneeled next to Sift, digging his toes into the warm sand.

"I think this should count as a vacation," Ruwen whispered. "It's a proper beach."

"You wish," Sift replied. "This is work, not play. And it doesn't count if Lylan isn't with me."

"What? That's never been part of the deal."

Sift grabbed a fistful of sand and let it slowly fall from his hand. "Sure it has. You never asked for the details."

"Why do I feel like every time I take you to a beach, you're going to come up with a reason it doesn't count."

Sift glanced at Ruwen and flashed a grin. "I have a list."

"Of course, you do."

"Adepts!" Thorn called as the Founders approached the beach.

All the Adepts stood and bowed. The Addas emerged from the village as well, and Padda carried blue belts over one arm and brown belts over the other, while Madda carried an armful of red belts.

"At the end of every day," Mist said, "we will assemble here and offer each of you the chance to advance your belt."

Thorn continued. "The process is simple. We meet here as the sun reaches the horizon, and while it sets, you contemplate the knowledge gained that day. When the sun disappears, those wishing to advance their belt remain kneeling, and the others are free to leave."

"If you remain," Dusk said, "we will speak with you and discuss what insights the day has brought. Discovering a hidden pattern is enough to advance your belt and gain a relic token. We do not expect mastery. Sometimes the questions are more important than the answers."

The Founders sat and closed their eyes, and the Adepts mirrored them. Only the Addas remained standing. Ruwen enjoyed the weak heat of the sun on his neck. The rush, crash, and retreat of the waves felt hypnotic, and he let himself relax.

A minute later, Sift entered his ninth level meditation and snored softly. Ruwen kept his mind empty, avoiding the uncertainty and doubt his actions with the Adepts caused. He guessed his behavior violated centuries of tradition.

Ruwen opened his eyes as the last sliver of the sun disappeared along with its warmth.

All the Adepts remained.

The Founders and Addas, with complete control of their bodies, hid their surprise, but Ruwen knew they felt it. The Founders stood, and everyone followed their lead. Ruwen tapped Sift on the shoulder to bring him out of his deep meditation. He wondered if this would be the point where the Founders confronted him about his disregard for so many traditions.

Thorn nodded at Echo, and she moved to stand in front of the three Founders. Ruwen focused his hearing on the surf, not wanting to overhear these private conversations.

After a brief exchange, the Founders bowed to Echo, and she

returned it. Thorn stepped over to Padda and removed a blue belt. She presented the new belt to Echo, and they exchanged bows again.

Echo returned to her spot on the beach and stood patiently while the member of Rung One next to her approached the Founders. She had far less control over her body, and Ruwen sensed her happiness.

The second Adept received their blue belt, and the process continued. Ruwen closed his eyes, forcing his anxiety into the third meditation. He stayed there, blissfully numb.

A tap on the shoulder forced Ruwen from his peacefulness. Sift stood with a blue belt over his shoulder and he gave a quick nod toward the Founders.

Thanks, Ruwen signaled in Shade Speak as he stood and strode forward. The Adepts all wore blue belts, and most couldn't contain their smiles.

Ruwen stopped in front of the Founders and bowed, placing his right palm over his left fist.

The three Founders returned Ruwen's bow but remained silent.

Ruwen swallowed hard and began. "The three most evident patterns are balanced by three hidden ones. One of these is breathing. The number, duration, depth, and pace are balanced between the Viper and Bamboo forms. Starting with the sharp inhalation of the first Viper Step, feeding muscles for violence, to the gentle exhalation of the final Bamboo Step, releasing the last traces of built-up Energy."

Ruwen drew a circle through the air with his finger. "Breathing, the first hidden pattern, like the three before it, teaches balance."

"It doesn't seem very hidden tonight," Thorn said.

Dusk frowned at Thorn, but Thorn seemed unaffected by the facial scolding. She continued. "Do you think you're helping them?"

Ruwen considered the question before answering. "I'm not sure, because I'm not positive what the goals are for these trials."

"Then what rationale do you have for your actions?" Thorn asked.

"Protection," Ruwen answered immediately.

"You can't protect them forever," Mist replied.

Ruwen nodded. "I know, but I can protect them long enough to return them safely home. Their conflicts are urgent, and this is one of the few ways I can help."

"Such responsibilities generate a heavy burden," Mist said.

"Burdens that crush you," Thorn whispered. "You are profoundly out of balance, Adept."

"Enough," Dusk said forcefully to Thorn. "We agreed to a process. Do not shift your balance now."

Thorn turned to her sister. "That was before he dragged the entire class into his orbit. We are responsible for them."

"No," Dusk replied. "They are responsible for themselves. Are you offering to protect them as well?"

After a moment, Thorn turned from Dusk and locked eyes with Ruwen. Her pupils vibrated, and he immediately mirrored the movements, defending himself from any hypnotic effects.

"Judgement waits in the shadows," Thorn said. "A pity you will avoid ours."

Dusk slid in front of Thorn. "Now who stands out of balance, Sister."

Thorn took a large step backward. She met Dusk's gaze and gave a small nod. Then she turned and strode toward the village.

After a moment, Dusk nodded to Padda, and he moved forward, giving Dusk the last blue belt.

Dusk faced Ruwen. "You spent the night with our underwater friends. Did you learn anything?"

"I learned mastery is an illusion."

"An important lesson," Dusk replied. She paused and then

continued. "My sister judges you harshly, maybe rightfully so, but she ignores your insight. Perhaps she has forgotten the power of illusion."

Ruwen bowed and kept his thoughts to himself. The Founders' judgement of him was itself a mirage, an illusion of opinion, belief, and tradition. It remained a powerful obstacle, however, and one he hoped to overcome soon.

Dusk handed Ruwen his blue belt and a relic token. They bowed once again, and Ruwen strode back toward Sift.

Mist spoke to the Adepts. "Since relic tokens were earned tonight, the Quartermaster will make himself available in the hour before sunset here on the beach. Well done, Adepts."

Dusk and Mist left to join their sister, and the Addas followed. The Adepts relaxed and celebrated. Ruwen returned their smiles as he thought about Thorn's last words to him. She had sounded like he would never face their judgement. If they planned to wait until the end before putting him on trial, then it meant she didn't believe he'd successfully finish the seventh trial.

Worry knotted Ruwen's stomach. Thorn had called him profoundly out of balance, but he couldn't see how. Now he feared the seventh trial would show him, and he would be unprepared to handle it.

It would be ironic if, after all his preparations, he didn't even pass the trials.

CHAPTER 56

*T*he next morning Ruwen led the Adepts into the bamboo forest behind the village. He had spent the night exploring the hills and studying the creatures that inhabited the trees. Well, grass technically, but the bamboo grew so tall it was hard to think of it as anything but trees.

Ruwen stopped after thirty minutes of hiking. The bamboo gently shifted in the wind far above, and the sound reminded him of ocean waves. It was difficult to enjoy however, as a war took place above them.

The combatants consisted of a long tailed, furry, clawed creature and a type of living bamboo with stubby leaf appendages. Both species stood less than four feet tall, and while the furry ones had a lot of speed, the bamboo creatures used this against them, and tossed them through the bamboo.

Just like with the Coral Vipers, Ruwen could see the foundation for many of the Bamboo Step forms in the bamboo creatures' movements. He now knew with confidence that the Bamboo Viper Steps had originated from observing these groups.

"What are they fighting over?" Nymthus asked, pointing to

the combat in the trees fifty feet away.

"I can't tell," Ruwen answered. "But they ignored me all night."

Sift studied the chaos above. "I'm more worried about bathrooms. I would guess we're in some danger down here."

"Well, it's a good thing we're not staying down here then," Ruwen replied. "This is where we head up."

"What's up there?" Sift asked.

Ruwen tapped the bamboo stalk on his right. It had a dull, hollow sound. He rapped on the bamboo to his left. Once again it sounded hollow, but the sound had a higher pitch.

Ruwen raised his voice so all the Adepts could hear him over the distant fighting. "It took me awhile to notice, but there is a small section of the forest that none of these creatures enter. When I investigated—" He struck the bamboo to the left, generating the odd sound again. "I realized this isn't actually bamboo."

Prythus ran a hand down the stalk. "It looks identical."

"A masterful illusion," Ruwen said. "The second hidden trial waits above."

The Adepts all looked up, including Echo.

Ruwen let them study the distant tops, a hundred feet above. After a few seconds he explained the trial. "What differs between striking a sparring partner and an enemy?"

"Intent," Echo whispered, and immediately bit her lip at letting the thought escape her mouth.

"Thank you, Echo," Ruwen said. "Intent," he repeated for everyone else since none of the Adepts had heard it. "An excellent answer."

Echo did her best to not look pleased.

Ruwen continued. "Intention is a concept. How do we make it concrete?"

"How hard we strike," Prythus said.

"Exactly," Ruwen replied. "The force we apply."

Ruwen paused to let that stew for a second. "We move through the Steps with," he glanced at Echo, "intent. Your Sisens have taught you the proper angles to strike, the correct footing, the precise positions to make your *intention* real."

Ruwen looked up at the sky, barely visible through the dense fake-bamboo. "There is a hidden *balance* you have not learned. A balance within the balance. In a moment, I will demonstrate how this balance occurs inside the forms, and how, taken together, balance the Bamboo and Viper Steps."

The Adepts stared at Ruwen in silence.

"The lessons of this hidden pattern are many," Ruwen said. "Alchemy teaches actions create reactions and reminds us that every movement creates a force on the universe around us. These forces stack, piling up, and without care, without balance, you fall. This hidden trial teaches mindfulness of how you move through the universe."

Ruwen verified all the Adepts wore their Bamboo Jacket of Falling. They would need it. He could have jumped to the top of the bamboo, but such a display of power served no purpose. Instead, he grabbed two nearby stalks and placed a foot on each. Keeping even pressure against each stalk with his feet, he climbed.

The Adepts followed. When they reached the top Ruwen balanced on his stalk. He pointed to a spot thirty feet away. "The starting location is a small platform where a fake bamboo stalk fans outward. Take a moment to appreciate the superb crafting of this trial. Each stalk of bamboo is located where the correctly performed Steps require them. Not only that, many stalks get reused multiple times, and a clever spring mechanism alters the internal tension after each encounter. Stomping on the starting platform resets the trial. A true marvel."

With that, Ruwen strode toward the platform, moving across the bamboo tops like they were a road. He reached the platform and faced the Adepts, who looked like ground squirrels poking their heads above the dirt. He gave the platform a gentle stomp, and the faint vibration of the trial resetting traveled through his feet.

The wind's strength bent the real bamboo, causing it to sway. The fake bamboo of the trial remained still, another clue that this area differed from the others. Ruwen hated that the Clan had placed this trial so high. They could have used a platform on a small pole like he'd trained Sift on. Despite all the ways he could survive a fall, including his new jacket, he still hated the height.

The density of the bamboo hid the altitude well, but Ruwen closed his eyes anyway. That way he didn't need to think about it at all. Then, like he'd done thousands and thousands of times, he moved through the Steps.

When Ruwen finished, he opened his eyes. The Adepts watched in awed silence. Well, except for Echo, who looked neutral, and Sift, who appeared bored.

"This trial is not as forgiving as the breathing one," Ruwen said. "A small failure here is met with immediate consequences and your ability to recover is limited. Be prepared to fall. A lot. Your jacket will keep you safe. Sisen? Anything to add?"

Sift looked at the Adepts. "Break the forms down into groups that circle a common point. One of this trial's lessons is focusing on the present. Thinking of a strike ten Steps away will lead to disaster. As your Bamboo Jacket of Falling has already warned you, the first step is the hardest."

Ruwen bowed to Sift before facing the Adepts. "Let's begin."

After an hour, Ruwen created a hundred feet of magical rope using *Climb*. Then used small amounts of Energy to move the Adepts upward to the top of the forest after they fell. Which they did in almost a constant stream. Echo didn't bother with his rope, preferring to jump a couple times to reach the top.

Learning the way Ruwen had, on a platform, would have been easier as it provided some forgiveness and allowed for small corrections. In the trial here, however, if an Adept used too much force, or too little, the bamboo bent, destroying any hope of recovering, and robbing the Adept of knowing which way they'd erred.

Ruwen had completed the trial early that morning, before bringing the Adepts here, and by the end of the day, of the remaining Adepts other than Sift, only Echo had progressed past the fifth Step. The pace of her advancement created a cloud of anger and frustration that she didn't try and hide. Curses accompanied the entire length of her falls, and everyone kept their distance from her, except Ruwen, who continued to offer advice after every collapse. Such emotional responses reminded him of Echo's mother, the Plague Siren Simandreial.

As the sun descended toward the horizon, the Adepts marched back toward the village. Ruwen explained how he'd trained on a platform, and recommended they create such a structure in their schools back home.

They reached the village and found it hidden in the Quartermaster's bamboo forest. They moved through the stalks toward the beach.

"Are you going to use your token?" Ruwen asked Sift.

Sift waved a dismissive hand. "I already gave that to Prythus."

"Good idea."

"Don't bother trying."

"What?"

"None of them will take your tokens. They all think you're a god or something. Well, Echo doesn't. She'd probably take it."

Ruwen frowned. "I think I'd rather keep it then. Why do they think that?"

Sift shrugged. "Probably because of your Steps and what you did on the island. It's not just you. I had to threaten Prythus with a god curse if he didn't take my token."

"Wait, so you let him think you're a god and threatened to

curse him?"

"How else would I get rid of the token?"

"Why didn't you just drop it in the sand?"

Sift waved a finger. "I did. And a very angry Quartermaster gave it back to me ten minutes later. I upset a Quartermaster exactly one time in my life. I'm not risking faulty gear from a furious Quartermaster ever again. Cloak of Invisibility, Fluffy says. Walk right through the Whipping Vines, Fluffy says." Sift turned to Ruwen and held up three fingers. "Three weeks before I could sit down without pain." He shook his head and continued. "Nope. God curse it is."

"You're terrible."

"No, I'm practical, and you're stuck with a token."

"Well that sucks," Ruwen muttered. As the sound of the surf grew louder, he continued. "You shouldn't let people think you're a god."

"Blasphemy. I'd make a better god than most of the ones I've met. I'd use my Divine power to make Spirit Sweets for my followers." Sift closed his eyes. "It would fall from the heavens like delicious rain."

Ruwen had created a cake for Sift using one of Uru's Architect Role recipes while traveling back home in Shelly and Sift had said he'd finally understood the point of Divine power. He'd been trying to come up with a proper name ever since: Core Cake, Divine Dessert, and now, Spirit Sweets.

"I've seen worse goals from the current gods," Ruwen admitted. "But you still shouldn't threaten people. More cupcakes, less curses."

"You do god your way, I'll do me."

"Fair enough," Ruwen said as he stepped into the warm ocean water.

The god discussion reminded Ruwen of his need to transition to Divine and his wish to bring his friends along as well. He smiled, picturing Sift streaking across the sky, probably literally, dropping pastries on his followers. Not a bad place to live, Ruwen thought.

The bamboo forest disappeared as the Quartermaster packed up his shop. The Founders and Addas had already arrived on the beach and Padda held an armful of brown belts.

Like the day before, the Adepts meditated as the sun sank, and just as before, they all remained after it had set. One by one the Adepts approached the Founders, spoke briefly with them, and received their brown belt. Ruwen felt a little embarrassed to have caused such a disruption in the Founders' traditional process, but not enough to change his path.

Thorn remained silent when Ruwen approached and returned his bow after a brief pause.

"No one has ever successfully completed the Trial of Force on their first attempt," Dusk said.

"I failed for months, before learning its lessons," Ruwen replied.

Thorn stiffened, the change so slight Ruwen doubted anyone without Diamond Perception would have noticed. He faced her and bowed. "Some of the lessons. I have obviously not learned them all."

Thorn didn't respond and Ruwen turned his attention back to Dusk. "I meant only that I failed thousands of times."

Dusk nodded at the Adepts behind Ruwen. "I wonder how such a forceful step is balanced."

Ruwen thought back to Sift's words to the Adepts that morning. "The balance of the present must also balance the past and future. It is a difficult thing to judge."

"Choices are like Steps," Dusk replied. "Their impact, right or wrong, is not always apparent."

Ruwen bowed. "I take every choice seriously."

Dusk nodded to Padda, and he handed her the last brown belt. She faced Ruwen and presented him the belt and relic token. "Time will tell if serious is enough."

CHAPTER 57

The mid-morning sun warmed Ruwen's cheeks, and for the hundredth time, he forced himself to not look down. He stood at the edge of a canyon, but unlike the canyon with the Floots and keys, the sides here were steep. Steep as in a three-hundred-foot vertical drops.

A brisk wind rising from the ravine tousled Ruwen's hair. The brown rock of the canyon's walls glowed and made the distant boulder-strewn ground below painfully apparent. After discovering this place the night before, he'd fallen three times as he figured out how it worked. The zig-zag staircase of death, that's how he thought of it anyway, that connected the top and bottom of the ravine is what had attracted his attention in the first place. It hadn't taken long to realize he'd found the location of the last trial.

Ruwen turned away from the cliff and faced the Adepts. "The final hidden pattern is time. How can time be a pattern when the combinations are endless you might wonder." He glanced at the sky and the clouds that floated high above. "My whole life I've seen patterns others ignored or dismissed. They see a cloud, where I find an appah swinging from a pole."

"Wow, that explains a lot," Sift said.

Everyone laughed, including Ruwen.

"My point is, I take what I notice seriously, and I believe the Founders, in our first trip to see them, foreshadowed these hidden trials. They planted a seed in our minds so that decades later, while in the village below, it could sprout."

"I don't understand," Prythus said.

"And neither did I," Ruwen replied. "Until this final pattern, time, revealed itself. Because this hidden pattern is only visible after mastering your force and breathing. Stop for a moment and appreciate the immense effort and thought that created the Steps you practice. In the beginning I viewed the Steps as a way to protect myself and those I love. As I learned its secrets, it transformed, and reshaped not only my body, but my thoughts. The Steps are a way of thinking, a way of life, and it whispers a single word. One you already know but might not yet fully appreciate."

Many Adepts muttered "balance" and even Echo mouthed the word, caught up in Ruwen's words and the impact of his Charisma.

"I spoke of a seed," Ruwen said. "Our first meeting with the Founders we encountered the viper forest. Remember how the snakes would leap at the slightest vibration? How carefully you needed to walk and remain quiet. Those snakes were responding to the *force* our bodies created on the environment."

Ruwen let that fact sink in and after five seconds started again. "If you needed a break or to save your precious minutes, how did we do that? We meditated with our controlled breathing techniques. And speaking of minutes, the Founders didn't even hide the aspect of time. We received a set amount and were given options like fruit and combat to earn more."

Comprehension dawned on the Adepts.

"Now you grasp how all the clues are there," Ruwen said.

"Nothing is really hidden. It just requires you to see, not just look."

Ruwen contemplated that experience again as well, looking for hints to the seventh trial. If the Founders had foreshadowed the hidden trials, they certainly would have included them all.

The most obvious place for clues was the trap filled forest where he'd freed Echo, or the almost impossible climb up the mountain. If so, what knowledge had the Founders hidden there?

Ruwen refocused on the Adepts. "I have walked the path you begin now, and I think it's important for you to know my knowledge ends here. There is a seventh trial, about which I know nothing. Search your experiences and use that information to reexamine your time there. I believe it will aid you."

Ruwen let out a sigh and turned to Sift. "Sisen."

Sift faced the Adepts. "All I remember about that trip was how good the red fruit tasted. I'd still be there now if I hadn't accidentally stumbled into the end."

The Adepts laughed, but Ruwen guessed Sift wasn't joking. He probably had spent the whole time ignoring the point of the test in his search for something good to eat.

"If force is the pastry and breathing the filling, timing is the frosting," Sift said. "Timing only makes sense when the other two pieces are in place. Frosting without a pastry is not a meal. Yesterday, I told you the first step was the hardest. I lied. Today's will be harder."

Sift waved at the Adepts to gather near the cliff.

"You need to work on your examples," Ruwen whispered to Sift. "Frosting without a pastry is not a meal?"

"The Sage strikes again," Sift said with a nod, happy with himself.

The Adepts drew near and Ruwen hid his fear. Taking that first step last night had proved difficult. The canyon walls had retained their glowing light, and he hadn't even had the darkness to hide the height.

Sift evidently had said all he intended to, so Ruwen spoke. "There is little point in trying to master this pattern until you've succeeded with the others, but I encourage all of you to try it at least once. Then you can choose to return to the ocean trial, the bamboo trial, or the beach where Sisen and I will help with your Step forms."

Ruwen turned his back to the Adepts and stepped up to the cliff. This trial was another marvel of craftsmanship similar in concept to the underwater trial. Instead of bubbles, the holes in the cliff walls threw powerful blasts of air in seemingly random spurts. He could hear the soft puffs coming from below and from the cliff across the ravine.

It had taken Ruwen a few minutes to figure out the purpose last night and twice that to calm himself down. The bursts of air from each cliff always intersected, momentarily creating dense areas of air, like temporary platforms.

One vertical line of holes generated a constant flow of air from each cliff, and they started right below Ruwen's feet. He knew the Bamboo Jacket of Falling would keep him safe, as it had worked multiple times last night. Even with his expertise and precise body control, he couldn't mentally get past where he performed the Steps, and it had overwhelmed him multiple times.

Tossing the unhelpful emotions into the third meditation, Ruwen stepped off the cliff, and strode forward confidently. The Adepts gasped and he heard them rush forward toward the cliff.

The dense air under Ruwen supported him surprisingly well. He kept his eyes on the far side of the ravine, avoiding any accidental view of the ground to save his mental state. In the exact middle of the span between the cliffs, air from the distant floor struck the two flows from the cliff sides, creating a firm platform, and he stopped. This is where the Steps began and ended.

To the Adepts, Ruwen knew it appeared like he'd walked on air across the canyon and now floated in the middle of the ravine. In reality, that is exactly what he'd done.

Ruwen waited until he heard what sounded like the soft hiss of a viper. He'd learned that signaled the beginning of the sequence.

Stepping into the first Viper Step, Ruwen ignored the fact he hovered three hundred feet in the air, and moved confidently through the forms, knowing the precisely timed blasts of air from each cliff would intersect exactly where required and support him.

Ruwen knew what the Adepts on the cliff felt, as he'd experienced the same thing that morning when watching Sift: amazement, fascination, and terror. The Adepts gasped and cried out as he moved back and forth across the open air. He scolded himself for letting the height and the Adepts' reactions distract him and focused entirely on the flow of his body.

The symmetry of balance within balance within balance provided immense mental satisfaction. Performing the Steps now, had become a celebration of perfection, and he radiated gratification and joy. He fleetingly wondered if this was how Sift felt when he moved.

With a final exhalation, Ruwen ended where he'd begun. He remained standing, three hundred feet above the canyon floor, held aloft by jets of air. Something had changed. As he hung suspended in the air he searched for the source and found it.

Ruwen had often given himself over to the Steps, removing his conscious mind from the muscle memories. This morning had differed because the fear of falling, coupled with an audience of Adepts he didn't want to disappoint, had required him to force his feelings into the third meditation.

But this time, the joy and gratitude, born from the recognition of perfectly nested balance, had become so intertwined within his forms, that he couldn't remove it. The Steps had turned from a mechanical exercise into a celebration.

Ruwen's body flushed and prickled. Memories of the Spirit Realm rose, of Rami and Ruwen in her mental construct, and the first time he'd completed the Bamboo Viper Steps completely.

This had felt the same.

It hadn't felt mechanical or cold, but alive and joyful. Ruwen had lost that happiness at some point, and discovering it again felt amazing.

Ruwen's hands trembled, and he remained in the middle of the canyon as he worked to regain control of his body and emotions.

Turning, Ruwen faced the cliff. The Adepts stood in stunned silence. Nymthus bowed deeply, and the other Adepts followed. Sift held out his fist and covered it with his palm, and after a moment, Echo did the same.

Ruwen wasn't the only one that recognized something had changed, and he bowed deeply to the Adepts.

CHAPTER 58

*A*fter all the Adepts had tried the timing trial, they returned to the village. To Ruwen's surprise, everyone joined him and Sift on the beach, and no one left to work on the breathing or force trials. Even Echo, for the first time, joined them for instruction.

The Adepts stood in a single line down the beach, each going through the Steps. Sift noticed Echo at the far end and immediately took the opposite side to teach. Ruwen moved down his side, picking the most glaring issue from the thousands he observed in each Adept.

Echo's heart rate increased with every Adept Ruwen instructed, until, when he finally stood in front of her, it raced so quickly he wondered how her body withstood the frantic beating.

Emotions fought for control of Echo and Ruwen remembered how passionate the Plague Siren Simandreial had been about killing him. Despite the circumstances, he'd maimed Echo's mother and Echo's hatred of him warred with her fierce desire to improve her Steps.

"Peace, Sister," Ruwen whispered.

Echo turned to go.

"I can help you."

Echo turned back to Ruwen and hissed. "That's the problem! I shouldn't want your help. My mother would skin me."

Ruwen guessed there was a fifty-fifty chance Echo was being literal about her mom skinning her.

"Those things are for another place," Ruwen said. "Here we are two Adepts, bound by our Clan to help each other."

To Ruwen's surprise he realized he meant that. They were enemies in the real world, but here, the Bamboo Clan, and its oaths, took priority.

"Allow your Brother to offer a suggestion," Ruwen said.

Echo's heart rate slowed slightly. She let out a long breath and nodded.

Ruwen moved into the Viper Step Twirling Hourglass. "Your strikes are too eager, which doesn't give your hips time to rotate completely, costing you speed and power."

Ruwen turned sideways to Echo so she could see his hips. He extended his arm. "This is where your hips stop in seventy percent of your attacks."

Echo studied Ruwen's stance. In reality, Echo's Steps were free from glaring issues, but she had many small issues that compounded each other to hold her back. Her eagerness to punch and strike things was the most prevalent. Even so, it would take an expert to see the small differences he pointed out.

Ruwen faced Echo again and tapped his chest. "Try it, you'll feel the difference. Do it your way first."

Echo immediately lashed out, striking Ruwen's chest. The sound of her Topaz fist striking his Diamond chest sounded like a thousand-pound book striking a library floor. Everyone stopped and stared, but Ruwen ignored them.

"Now, this time, start your hip rotation before you chamber your strike," Ruwen said.

Echo practiced the movement a few times slowly, getting a

feel for the timing of the change. Then with a sudden surge, she struck Ruwen again, this time taking his advice.

The strike sounded the same, but this time, Ruwen felt the full power of the attack. He winced and rubbed his chest. "Did you feel the difference?"

Echo grinned.

"Good," Ruwen said. "Focus on the strikes that depend on your right hip, those are the worst. Then left hip strikes, and finally your kicks, which need the least modification."

Echo bowed to Ruwen, and he returned it, before striding back to the center to start down the line again.

They spent the entire afternoon and early evening on the beach. None of the Adepts left to eat, wanting to maximize their training, and Sift grumbled about it every time they met at the center.

Echo, similar to Sift, absorbed and assimilated Ruwen's instruction like only a true master could. She quickly fixed her issues, and with every rotation he made past her, the problems he explained became smaller.

The Founders observed all of them for over an hour. They remained invisible with some type of soul magic, but Ruwen detected them anyway. No matter the hiding method, it became difficult to hide vibrations and pressure waves when near him. Only the gods he'd met could do it.

Ruwen felt pride and accomplishment for what he'd accomplished here, especially with the other Adepts. All of them had significantly increased their mastery of the Steps. Most of their Sisens back home were just other Masters of varying skill level. As the Adepts progressed at their schools it became harder and harder for them to see their own issues, while the number of people who could see their problems decreased.

An hour before sunset the Quartermaster arrived along with the bamboo forest, and the Adepts stopped training for the day. Everyone headed to look through the relics, but Ruwen turned toward the ocean and strode into the water until it reached his knees.

Sift joined Ruwen.

"It's beautiful," Sift said.

The sun had dropped below the height of the bamboo, but its light raced through the shoots, softened by the late hour, and glistened off the water. The colors had turned orangish which the bamboo reflected, creating an almost mystical scene.

"Yeah, I love sunsets," Ruwen said.

Sift kept his eyes on the hidden horizon. "No, I meant your Steps this morning. Did it feel different?"

Ruwen glanced at Sift but Sift kept his focus forward.

Ruwen studied the sunlight again, and whispered a single word, his throat suddenly tight. "Yeah."

"I saw it. We all did. What changed?"

Ruwen shrugged. "The terror of falling for sure. That fear amplified not wanting to screw up in front of everyone, and it overwhelmed me. So I used the third meditation to calm down. But now that I understand the balanced perfection of the Steps, even the third mediation couldn't remove that joy."

Sift cleared his throat. "Listen, I stopped being your Sisen in anything but name long ago."

Ruwen started to interrupt but Sift held up a hand. "Let me get this out."

Ruwen closed his mouth and nodded.

Sift sighed. "Whatever you and Rami did in the Spirit Realm, it catapulted you past me, and you never slowed down. I've carried this horrible combination of jealousy and pride ever since. Guilt too, as you poured every ounce of your knowledge into me, while I offered nothing in return. I've never experienced such unselfishness." Sift paused and Ruwen remained silent, unsure if Sift had finished.

Sift cleared his throat again. "Anyway, I just wanted to know if you felt what happened today, because it was the first time I've seen you perform the Steps."

Ruwen turned toward Sift, but Sift kept his gaze forward, the soft sunlight glinting off his golden eyes.

Sift had seen Ruwen do the steps thousands and thousands of times. What did he mean, this was the first time?

Sift stood up straight as if gathering himself and turned to face Ruwen. "I wanted to tell you, as your Sisen, that the joy you found today has always been there, buried under a mountain of thinking." Sift clenched his jaw, trying to control his emotions. "That, and it was truly beautiful. I am honored to have witnessed it."

Ruwen's chest tightened, and his throat clamped shut. He couldn't speak, so he took a step back and bowed deeply to Sift, holding it for three seconds.

Ruwen stood and Sift returned the bow. They both faced the setting sun, crashing waves the only sound.

After a minute Sift spoke, his voice soft, as if talking to himself. "And to think, you're my worst Sijun."

Ruwen laughed, and Sift did as well, their emotions quickly turning the laughter hysterical.

The bamboo forest disappeared as the Quartermaster left the beach. Ruwen and Sift had collapsed to their knees, the water half covering their chests. They cried and gasped for air, unable to stop laughing.

Ruwen, through tear-filled eyes, tried to focus on the Adepts standing on the beach. Their faces held concern, but when he tried to tell them everything was okay, Sift's laughter sent Ruwen spiraling into another fit of hysteria and he gave up.

CHAPTER 59

*R*uwen sat in the sand on the opposite side of the Adepts from Sift and used a combination of the third meditation and the Gem control over his body to stop laughing. The belt ceremony was a solemn affair, which made stopping even harder. He pulled his senses in as close as he could and tried to ignore the pressure waves off Sift's body as he also tried to contain his laughter.

The sun disappeared behind the horizon and Ruwen opened his eyes. The three Founders sat in front of the Adepts, their eyes closed in meditation. As if feeling his gaze, Thorn opened her eyes and locked gazes with him.

Thorn had spent a lifetime controlling her body, and reading her emotions proved almost impossible. Her Disposition Aura remained green and if Ruwen sensed anything from the look, it was sadness. Why would Thorn be sad? Or was she sad for him? She looked away as the Founders all stood.

Madda frowned at Sift, probably because of the laughing, and Padda evened up the red belts hanging over his arm.

One by one the Adepts approached the Founders, and after a brief exchange, received their red belt. Ruwen had regained control of his emotions by the time his turn arrived, but he avoided looking at Sift, anyway.

Thorn and Mist remained quiet after returning Ruwen's bow.

"What have you learned, Adept?" Dusk asked.

Ruwen thought about the breakthrough he'd had floating three hundred feet in the air. "Humility."

"How so?" Dusk asked.

Ruwen pushed the admission out. "When I arrived, I believed I'd already learned all the Steps offered. That changed when sparring with the Coral Vipers. Then," he paused, swallowing hard in a suddenly dry throat. "Then I experienced what I can only describe as…joy."

"We witnessed it, Brother," Thorn said quietly.

Since Ruwen hadn't sensed their observation, they must have done it from a significant distance.

"A rare thing to see here," Mist added. "Recognizing the balance between function and art usually happens early in training or not at all. Thank you for the gift of your revelation."

Ruwen had never considered such a balance, and hope erupted in his chest. "Is that the seventh trial?"

Dusk shook her head sadly. "No. Beauty is not something you can teach or test. It is a personal experience."

Ruwen nodded, disappointed that the challenge of the seventh trial remained. The fact that such a balance existed and that he'd been blind to it shook his confidence.

"What does the sixth trial teach?" Dusk asked.

Sift's terrible pastry example came to mind and for a moment, Ruwen worried he'd start laughing again. The moment passed and the seriousness of the situation returned. "This trial demonstrates the importance of foundational knowledge, and how some elements can't be learned out of sequence. It highlights the importance of time."

Thorn remained silent, but Ruwen could guess her thoughts,

and he turned to her. "I understand how my actions violate this lesson. The maturity gained during the time a student builds their foundation is the bedrock for a balanced Step Master. That is wise, and I accept it."

Ruwen took a deep breath and sighed. "If I had come here as an isolated student, I would have kept with tradition, and stayed silent. For better or worse, I've seen dangers none of us can face in our current states. Not sharing knowledge creates a missed opportunity that may save a life. For that purpose alone, I violated the trial of time's wisdom."

Ruwen bowed to the three Founders, and they returned it. Dusk nodded at Padda, and he handed her the final red belt.

Dusk presented Ruwen his new belt and, after bowing again, he returned to stand next to Sift.

The Founders, instead of dismissing them, remained standing before the class.

"This class has had many firsts," Dusk said. "The most important is, that you all survived. Not only survived, but advanced through the trials at an incomprehensible speed. So many potential Masters. It is a boon for the Bamboo Viper Clan, as our enemies vastly outnumber us. Congratulations on this marvelous success."

Dusk studied the thirty-three red belt Adepts. "A final, seventh step, remains on your path to the black belt of Master. You may attempt this trial at any time, beginning immediately. Any Adepts present who wish to test for Master, follow me."

Ruwen's heart rate increased, and it thudded in his chest. The seventh trial already? Part of him had hoped he would have more time to prepare, to try and figure out what it related to. But as the Founders moved down the beach, and the rest of the Adepts followed, he realized his time had run out.

The seventh trial, whatever it contained, would soon reveal itself.

They traveled for over an hour down the beach, which

narrowed as the bamboo forest pushed toward the ocean. Ruwen walked behind Sift and the other Adepts, with only Madda and Padda remaining behind him. The crashing surf created the glowing water he'd seen on his first night and lit their path.

Scattered rocks appeared and soon they turned into a small wall, which quickly climbed into a cliff. The Founders didn't slow when the beach disappeared, and they all strode next to the rock face as the ocean swirled around their knees.

Three minutes later, the Founders disappeared from sight, and a moment later Echo did as well. It took Ruwen another second to figure out they'd disappeared into a cave. When Ruwen's turn came he followed Sift into a narrow passage. The glowing water sloshed around in the small space, throwing shadows erratically across the walls.

Ruwen still kept his shadow stored in his Bamboo Viper Clan mark, but the others' shadows made him think of the Prime Shadow Warden he'd met and Ruwen wondered if the being could see them from the shadows they created.

The tunnel ended in a cave fifty feet across. Most of the floor remained out of the water as the ground sloped upward. The Adepts each held a glowing water filled glass. Ruwen watched a member of Rung Four retrieve a glass from near the water, fill it with sea water, and shake it. It immediately glowed, and they joined the other Adepts farther in the cave. Sift and Ruwen quickly created their own glass lights and followed.

The Addas, seeing everyone safely delivered, turned and left.

Mist spoke first. "In a moment, you will begin your final trial. A black belt and the title of Master wait on the other side."

"Unlike the previous trials," Thorn said, "failure here is catastrophic, and likely fatal. There is no shame in leaving. A Grandmaster waits in the ocean below, and will guide you back to the village."

Dusk studied the Adepts and waited to see if anyone would

depart. After ten seconds she spoke. "When you hear your name, continue forward into the tunnel. You will find us waiting, and we will instruct you further."

The Founders turned and strode into a large crack in the cave wall, disappearing from sight. Ruwen turned to Sift, who raised his eyebrows, but didn't speak. Something about the cave, oddly glowing water, and flickering shadows discouraged speaking.

Echo stiffened, looked around, and then moved toward the path the Founders had taken. Ruwen frowned. He hadn't heard anything, and his Diamond senses would have certainly detected Echo's name being called.

A few minutes later, another member of Rung One jerked in surprise before quickly entering the tunnel. Again, Ruwen hadn't heard anything, which must mean the summons occurred mentally.

Ruwen sat, and the rest of the Adepts followed his lead. He closed his eyes and tried to relax. The time for figuring out the seventh trial had passed. Either he had the answers, or he didn't.

Time passed, with only occasional glass shakes for light interrupting Ruwen's thoughts.

Sift stood and Ruwen opened his eyes, and then stood as well. Only the two of them remained.

Sift tapped his temple. "It's time."

Ruwen nodded.

"Are you going to puke?" Sift asked. "You look terrible."

Ruwen swallowed. "I hope not."

"Listen to me, Sijun. Everything you need is already here," Sift touched Ruwen's head. "And here," Sift moved his hand to Ruwen's chest, over his heart.

Ruwen nodded.

"It is enough," Sift whispered.

Ruwen nodded again, too worried to speak.

Sift grinned. "See you on the other side."

Sift's relaxed, no cares smile infected Ruwen, and he returned it, despite his misery.

Sift disappeared into the tunnel and Ruwen stood alone.

The delay between Adepts being summoned usually ranged from three to five minutes, so Ruwen jerked in shock, when, a minute after Sift's disappearance, he heard a voice, the sound like ice across his neck, but also one he recognized from the swamp.

"Ruwen Starfield," the Prime Shadow Warden whispered, "you are summoned."

CHAPTER 60

*R*uwen stood and strode into the tunnel, eager to
finish this last challenge. The passageway angled
steeply upward and thirty seconds later he discovered the
Founders sitting in a small chamber. A dark doorway stood in
the wall behind the Founders, and the previous Adepts' glowing
jars surrounding its entrance. He bowed, and Dusk motioned to
the floor, so he sat and placed his jar on the ground.

"Congratulations, Adept, for reaching the seventh trial,"
Dusk said. "The doorway behind us leads to the surface."

"To see the sky again," Thorn said. "You must survive the
journey."

"Not every Adept does," Mist added.

The Founders paused and Ruwen nodded his understanding.

"How many Steps are there?" Dusk asked.

"None," Ruwen answered the now familiar question.

"What is your goal?" Mist asked.

Ruwen shifted his attention to Mist. "Balance."

"What have the Steps taught you?" Thorn asked.

Ruwen had answered "patience" the last time, but his recent
experiences had imparted a new lesson.

Ruwen sighed. "Humility."

This new answer didn't seem to bother any of the Founders.

Dusk asked the final question, the one Ruwen had spent hours thinking about as he searched the area for trial locations these past days. "What is the most important Step?"

Originally, at the Journeyman testing, Ruwen had answered the step toward his goals, and then here, he'd told Dusk the step toward learning. That had produced disappointment in Dusk, but only because the answer had just missed her desired response.

Over and over, Ruwen had discovered that critical knowledge he needed to advance had been revealed to him in the past. The first time he'd taken a Clan test and met Pine and his grandson, clues to the hidden Step patterns had surrounded him. His breakthrough on Probability Waves had come from the first exercise Sift had taught Ruwen, the endless rotation of the punch and block of the Wheel.

With this in mind, Ruwen had returned to his earliest memories of the Steps, and to his complete amazement, found an answer at the literal beginning.

During Ruwen's first trip to the Black Pyramid, he had accepted the offer from Madda and Padda to train in the Bamboo Viper Clan and received the Clan's mark. Along with the mark he'd received a bunch of Step quests along with the passive area of effect spell *Snake in the Grass,* that allowed him to sense when a member of the Bamboo Viper Clan was near, although with Sift's constant presence he had basically just ignored the sensation.

The very next words spoken after Ruwen had accepted the Bamboo Viper Clan mark had come from Padda and Madda.

Padda had said, "Welcome to our Clan, Ruwen, Champion of Uru." And then, Madda had told Ruwen this: "May your Steps lead you to enlightenment."

This revelation stunned Ruwen. The first thing anyone said

to him after "welcome" had contained the answer to the question asked here, at the very end.

It explained why Dusk had revealed her disappointment. Ruwen's answer, "knowledge," had been on the right path, but he hadn't gone far enough. After this revelation, he realized the difference between knowledge and enlightenment mirrored the problem Rami had solved with her indexes. Knowledge, by itself, didn't help much, and sometimes, too much of it actually hurt.

Knowledge though, when indexed and combined into information, contained great power, and Ruwen's previous answer of knowledge had fallen one step short. Because knowledge, when combined with experience and Wisdom, produced enlightenment. The very first thing Madda had told him.

Ruwen's chest tightened at the beauty and symmetry of Madda's words spoken at the beginning with those he voiced now, to become a Master.

"The most important Step," Ruwen whispered, "is toward enlightenment."

Dusk closed her eyes, and a brief smile appeared. "Enlightenment," she repeated.

The four of them sat in silence for a few heartbeats, before Dusk continued. "You are outside the realm of our experience."

"Your grasp of Step philosophy mirrors our own," Mist said. "You are a treasure."

Thorn leaned forward. "Which is why I'm begging you to stand and leave."

The statement from Thorn shocked Ruwen. Her Disposition Aura remained green, and her words held no malice or anger. They sounded genuine and almost friendly.

"Is this because I trained the Adepts?" Ruwen asked.

Thorn shook her head. "That is merely a philosophy difference, and while I feel strongly about it, my reasons for this are unrelated. Your potential, given your age and training, appears limitless, and your association with the Great Wyrm and the gods means you have a larger part to play. I don't want to see it all destroyed here."

"Destroyed how?" Ruwen asked.

"This is inappropriate," Dusk whispered to her sisters.

"Thorn is right," Mist said. "For this Adept, we can't view him from only our Clan's perspective."

Thorn touched Dusk's shoulder. "Do you honestly believe he can take the seventh Step?"

"He ascended Mount Sorrow," Dusk replied. "Neither of you thought it possible."

Mist gave a small bow to Dusk. "You are right. But he barely made it, and Mount Sorrow is a fraction of a fraction of what he faces now."

"A valid point, Sister," Dusk replied.

Mist's comment confirmed for Ruwen that the seventh trial related to his time around Mount Sorrow. It worried him that this trial presented a greater challenge than Mount Sorrow. Because Mist was correct, he'd only just reached the top. Perhaps it wouldn't hurt to at least hear the alternatives they suggested.

"What happens if I don't attempt this trial?" Ruwen asked.

"You will lose your Bamboo Viper Clan knowledge," Dusk replied.

"And survive," Mist added.

Ruwen had already planned for a loss of knowledge. If the Founders succeeded in breaking through his mental defenses to strip him of Step knowledge, he planned to use Overlord to learn it again. Although losing Overlord complicated that plan. Complicated it a lot.

"It is not our place to intervene," Dusk said to Mist. "Thorn lost her balance over his teaching methods, and your silence earned you a share of that burden."

"Unbalanced," Thorn said. "Because I've dreaded this

moment since we met him. The scope of his burdens and darkness of his soul are both so profound, it is incomprehensible."

Mist placed a hand on Dusk's knee. "And it doesn't end there. Suppose by some miracle, he succeeds. Judging him after such a victory here seems cruel."

"So, judgement comes after this trial?" Ruwen asked.

The three Founders turned toward Ruwen.

Dusk shook her head and glanced at her sisters. "Look at the three of us. How unstable our footing." She sighed. "Perhaps my sisters are right. Avoiding the seventh trial only delays the loss of your Clan knowledge, but at least you survive."

"What about Sift?" Ruwen asked.

"He will stand in judgement as well," Dusk replied.

Ruwen shook his head. "It sounds like the three of you have already judged Sift and I without hearing any details."

Dusk looked sad. "What details change the fact that you, an Adept, taught another the Bamboo Grandmaster and Viper Grandmaster Step forms or that you broke your oath about using Shadow Form knowledge?"

"First, details always matter," Ruwen said. "And second, how does any of that relate to Sift?"

"Sift is your Sisen," Dusk said. "And responsible for your actions."

Ruwen opened his log file and searched for *Darkness Holds No Shadows*. He read the entry carefully.

Darkness Holds No Shadows
You have vowed never to use the Forbidden Steps of the Shadow Form until discussing their origin, use, and costs with Madda and Padda.
Reward: +1 Knowledge.
Reward: Audience with Shadow Clan.
Restriction: Bamboo Step Rank of Master Required.
Restriction: Viper Step Rank of Master Required.
Penalty (Broken Oath): Exiled from the Bamboo Viper Step Clan.

Penalty (Broken Oath): Marked for Death by the Bamboo Viper and Shadow Step Clans.

Ruwen looked between the three Founders. "I believe the oath also included a marked for death penalty. I thought you three wanted me to live."

Thorn nodded. "The penalties, like the rewards, only trigger if you meet the restrictions, which are the ranks of Master. If you don't become a Master, your Step knowledge fades, including the Shadow forms, and your death isn't necessary."

"To spare your life," Mist said. "We would hold the trial before the Master's ceremony, so you never hold that rank."

Ruwen took a deep breath and sighed. "So let me get this straight. You three don't care about the context or details of what I did, just that I broke an oath that triggers when I hold the rank of Master and that I taught Grandmaster forms I'm not qualified to teach. Sift, because he's my Sisen, is held to the same standard as myself. If I'm guilty, then so is he. So, if I attempt the seventh trial or if I don't, Sift will be put on trial, and I assume with your rules, our Clan will strip him of his Step knowledge."

"That is the most likely outcome," Dusk whispered.

"Why even bother with all the trials, then?" Ruwen asked. "Why not hold the trial the first day?"

"Selfishness," Thorn said. "This is a punishment none of us wish to execute, and if you failed the trials, our action would not be necessary."

"Can't you change the rules?" Ruwen asked.

"Without rules," Mist said. "There is chaos."

Dusk continued. "And what good are rules if they only apply to some?"

"I see," Ruwen said softly.

The fortune Tarot had given Ruwen at their first meeting had made him briefly doubt his preparation: given the references to risk, failure, and even death. The fact Sift faced judgement for something Ruwen had done destroyed any thought of skipping this trial.

Ruwen glanced at the Reversed Fool on his right wrist. Tarot's fortune had urged caution: the risks posed by his past actions, coupled with the determination and training of his opponents, meant failure was the likely outcome.

Behind the Founders stood the portal to the seventh trial, the final obstacle Ruwen needed to pass in order to execute the plan he'd made after talking with Ky in the underwater safe house over eighteen months ago.

Ruwen had a plan, and he wouldn't falter now. Reversed Fool or not.

Ruwen stood.

Thorn looked up at Ruwen. "Please don't. The burdens you carry are too heavy."

"Is that true?" Ruwen asked Dusk.

"Perhaps," Dusk said. "But the shadow you hide hints at hope. No one knows the weight of a word, or a poem, or a life realized. May the shadow guide you, Child."

Ruwen bowed to the Prime Shadow Warden who had whispered his name to summon him here and now watched curiously from Dusk's shadow.

Facing the Founders, Ruwen bowed to them as well. "I'll see you on the other side."

Then, with no hesitation, Ruwen strode to the entrance of the seventh trial, and stepped into shadow.

CHAPTER 61

*R*uwen floated in darkness, and it reminded him of the no gravity blackness he'd experienced on the other side of the Universe. Panic gripped him and he focused on his heart rate, preparing to slow it, and realized he couldn't hear anything. Nothing but total silence. He raised a hand to touch his face, to feel something, but nothing happened, and he didn't know if it was because he couldn't move here or if he had no body.

What kind of trial was this?

Ruwen willed himself to the Citadel in his mind's fortress, but he remained in the darkness.

Sivart? Ruwen asked, but no response came.

Ruwen couldn't move and didn't have anyone to talk with. The only thing he seemed capable of was thinking, so that's what he did.

Anything relating to the Steps, Ruwen revisited—except for his time with Rami and the early days of training with Sift, which dealt with little philosophy and a lot of physical pain. He found two references to his current state that seemed relevant.

Mist had told Ruwen "Silence and darkness fill you." At the

time, he'd thought they were two different things, but knowing souls emitted light and produced sound—she probably meant the same thing. Uru had trapped his soul behind an impenetrable curtain, and Mist thought that would present a problem.

Just a moment ago, Thorn had also referenced the darkness of Ruwen's soul, and described how his burdens would make this trial impossible to finish. She'd said, "The scope of his burdens and darkness of his soul are both so profound, it is incomprehensible."

Burdens, weight, and darkness came up over and over. Thorn had referenced Ruwen's struggles on Mount Sorrow, and he remembered clearly the effort it took to drag himself to the summit.

Mount Sorrow wasn't the only reference to burdens, though. It had come up recently when Thorn had gotten upset by Ruwen's teaching methods. When he'd justified his behavior as a way to protect the class, both Mist and Thorn had responded.

Mist had said, "Responsibility for others is a heavy burden."

And Thorn had immediately followed with, "A burden that is crushing you," and finally, something Ruwen still didn't understand, Thorn had whispered, "You are deeply out of balance, Adept."

How could protecting people be a burden? And how could that affect his balance? What balance had Thorn referenced?

None of the burden talk made sense to Ruwen, so he turned his attention to the darkness issue. Darkness seemed to be the second reason Mist and Thorn thought he would fail, since they always spoke in the context of darkness and not sound. He assumed that would be the issue.

When the other Adepts stepped through the doorway, did their souls light this space? Did it make the point of the trial clear? Dusk's last comment to him had been, "may the shadow guide you."

Did Dusk mean an actual shadow? If she did, then that

confirmed Ruwen needed light here. Probably from his imprisoned soul. Which brought him back to a problem he'd struggled with before arriving here. How to free his soul.

Except it had become complicated as Uruziel, the Divine fragment of Uru Ruwen had saved, had told him this about his soul prison, "the moment you create a passage through those protections, you will appear, like a mountain in a world full of sand. It will be impossible to hide, and all the deities will come. Some to see an Axiom, some to kill him, maybe even some to follow him."

And while Ruwen had spent over a year trying to figure out a method to do just that, he now worried he might do it by accident. Especially since Malth, when sometime around the library incident where Rami had triggered the *Literary Aneurism* trap, he'd damaged the shell surrounding his soul.

Ruwen wondered how much time had passed here. It felt like he'd been floating and thinking for days. Thorn had pleaded with him not to attempt the seventh trial, but he'd ignored her, and now he might spend eternity regretting that decision.

But Dusk had felt Ruwen had a chance. She had mentioned the shadow, which meant she must think he could create one. Did she think he knew the process to break the soul prison? She wouldn't know he couldn't do that, for fear of summoning all the gods. Despair filled his thoughts as he realized the hope Dusk had held for him, would, if he succeeded, likely kill them all.

Ruwen floated in misery for a minute or a day or a month. He couldn't tell. Eventually, he grew sick of the feeling and turned his attention to why Dusk thought he knew how to break the soul prison.

Rami had absorbed all of Ruwen's memories, including his time at the first Bamboo Viper test. When Dusk had spoken to him about his soul at the top of Mount Sorrow, Rami believed the Founder had emphasized the words "thinkers like us" when she'd said this about her sisters: *"Neither one is great at seeing the hidden. They aren't thinkers like us. You have already discovered some Shadow Steps, so finding your soul might be possible."*

Ruwen had already gone over all this while floating in a *Shed* across the universe. He had concluded the only thing Dusk's comments and the *Literary Aneurism* that damaged his soul prison had in common was his mind. Which didn't help him at all.

Did Ruwen know anything now that he didn't know then? Some way to look at the problem with more information. Dusk had visibly reacted when Ruwen had told her the most important step was toward enlightenment. Why had that made her so happy?

Enlightenment. It had light in the name, which Ruwen could really use, but it was the wrong type of light. Enlightenment, as he understood it, related to taking knowledge and creating an understanding from it. Something more than just the raw facts knowledge provided.

The *Literary Aneurism* had shoved a massive amount of knowledge into Ruwen's mind, even if it had arrived shredded in raw components. He hated himself for the analogy, but if his mind acted like an oven, and enlightenment formed a pastry, then the *Literary Aneurism* provided a massive amount of raw ingredients.

The Narrators had organized those ingredients and created an entire world with them inside Ruwen's mind. If this line of thought was right, then the *Literary Aneurism* had created the damage to his soul prison.

But why hadn't the world the Narrators created in Ruwen's mind continued to damage the shell around his soul? He thought about that for a while and concluded the Narrators had mostly just arranged what already existed in his mind.

To stay with the baking analogy, the Narrators had organized the ingredients into piles, and created some dough, but they hadn't baked many of their own pastries yet. That process had begun as the Narrators created their own knowledge, but compared to what already existed in his mind, they hadn't changed the total volume much.

Ruwen's thoughts pulsed with excitement, as this line of thinking felt right. It meant that as the Narrators matured and created more original knowledge, it would affect the soul prison, just as absorbing another *Literary Aneurism* would.

Joy filled Ruwen's mind. He had, after all this time, finally figured out the likely process for destroying his soul's prison.

Although it didn't help right now, Ruwen celebrated the victory anyway. And once again, the insight gained from his Bamboo Viper Step journey had provided the clues. The layers of complexity the Step Clan philosophy contained staggered him. It had led to the balance of his physical body, and now a breakthrough in the internal state of his mind and soul.

Ruwen's thoughts stopped as a sudden realization shocked him senseless.

Balance.

If the previous six trials focused on perfecting the external balance of Ruwen's body, it only made sense that the seventh focused on balance as well. A balance he had not considered until this very moment.

The seventh trial taught the importance of internal balance.

CHAPTER 62

*R*uwen had spent immense effort balancing his external body, and no time at all focusing on anything he would consider internal balance. But as he thought it through, internal balance, with the Founders' talk of responsibility and burdens, likely didn't mean balancing his inner self by doing some sort of inward workout. No, it likely meant finding true balance required the inner and outer self to reach an equilibrium. In hindsight, this trial was obviously necessary.

Thorn's comment, "you are deeply out of balance, Adept," made sense now. He could sense how fragile his inner self had become as his life tumbled from disaster to disaster.

Uru help me, Ruwen said, although without a voice no one heard. With this new insight, so many more comments from the Founders made sense, and he understood what burdens they meant.

The Founders had brought up burdens over and over. In fact, had Ruwen listened carefully, and understood the conversation where Thorn had become so upset with him better, he would have realized Thorn and Mist had literally given him a warning.

Mist had told Ruwen, "Responsibility for others is a heavy burden." Then Thorn had immediately added, "A burden that is crushing you." Before ending with, "You are deeply out of balance, Adept."

They had tried one last time at the door by bringing up that exact conversation, probably hoping to nudge his thoughts there. They had brought up the impending judgement, hoping he would see that risking the seventh trial was pointless. Instead, it had reminded Ruwen of Sift, and that had quickly derailed all his thoughts.

Trying to salvage Ruwen's life, Thorn had begged him to not take the seventh trial. When he didn't waver, Dusk had left him with some final advice.

The burdens Ruwen had carried up Mount Sorrow he knew came from soul bound items, oaths, and connections he had with beings like Rami and Fractal. But he had misunderstood where their weight had come from.

Mist had told Ruwen, in plain words, where the source of the weight originated. She had told him, "Responsibility for others is a heavy burden."

The burdens Ruwen carried stemmed from the responsibilities he'd attached to his soul.

And now, finally, far too late, he agreed with Thorn. He was hopelessly lost.

Ruwen's external world contained so many responsibilities, it made balancing it with his internal self impossible. As the Fourth Secret, he held responsibility for the Universe. For putting it back, ironically, into balance. How in Uru's name could he balance an obligation like that?

As Ruwen once again experienced despair, his mind continued to piece together this mystery. The externally focused Bamboo and Viper Steps must mean the Shadow Steps represented the internal state.

The very name, Shadow, implied a source of light, and Tarot

had explained to Ruwen that the creatures in the Shadow Realm interpreted the shadows cast by the soul. He also had a guess at what this seventh test actually involved.

The first six trials had concentrated on the external Bamboo and Viper Steps, so he felt confident that the seventh trial, the final step, would be a step inward, toward the soul.

A soul which Ruwen couldn't see. But with his new understanding, he could finally visualize what it might look like. Everyone's soul acted like the pivot of a scale which had two plates connected to it. One plate held the weight of his outer self, the other his inner.

Sift, who had almost no responsibilities attached to his soul, likely stood on what Ruwen imagined looked like a flat plane inside this trial. Sift's two plates were even, and his soul blazed like a sun above him. Because of this balanced state, he could step in any direction, and it signified the importance of the balance between internal and external forces.

Ruwen could not take a step. His obligations pulled him outward, and instead of standing on a flat surface, his external plate had tipped the scale all the way to one side. He stood at the bottom of a deep hole, his dark soul somewhere high above him and out of reach.

For a time, Ruwen floated numbly, unable to come to terms with his failure. His mother had scolded him often for hearing, but not listening. Even with the knowledge of an unknown seventh trial, he had brimmed with confidence that he could manage it.

Eventually, Ruwen again got bored with his self-loathing and despair, one small advantage of his short attention span. He wondered if he could figure out where his soul floated in relation to his direction, even in this darkness.

The darkness reminded Ruwen of his first moments in the silent emptiness of the far Universe. It had even felt like this. Weightless without bearings. He had solved that by creating a

Shed and gravity sphere. He couldn't cast those here, but forces acted on him, and that meant he could gather more information.

For instance, Ruwen knew he skewed massively toward his external side, which meant moving that direction should offer less resistance than trying to reach the internal plate far above. In fact, moving from his current location to the internal plate would feel like climbing a mountain. Exactly what he'd experienced in the first Bamboo Viper test.

Ruwen hyper focused on his useless senses and willed himself in different directions. He imagined a sphere, since he didn't know if he stood on his external plate or rested on it, and methodically visualized himself traveling in different directions.

Time passed, Ruwen would have given up long before, but he had nothing else to do. So he repeated the process, again and again. On the fifth attempt, he thought he felt a slight easing, but figured his imagination had started creating sensations for his brain. He concentrated on the feeling, anyway.

Over and over, Ruwen willed himself toward the location, imagining himself in different orientations. He convinced himself he'd found the external direction, but didn't understand why it remained so difficult to go that way.

After a few minutes of thought, Ruwen decided his external burdens had pulled his outer plate so far downward that he'd reached the maximum bottom and could go no further. Not only did he stand at the bottom of a metaphorical mountain, but he'd tied himself to the ground.

Thorn's words, "You are deeply out of balance, Adept," now seemed like an understatement.

If the tiny difference in resistance Ruwen sensed represented the edge of the plate closest to the outer world, then if he turned around, which he did, he should now face the direction of his internal plate and his soul which acted as the fulcrum between these plates.

Ruwen allowed himself a moment of pride for this accomplishment. If his soul could shine, it would look like a star above him. He had the knowledge now to break his soul prison, but even if he wanted to risk all the gods showing up, he didn't know how to increase his knowledge enough to make a difference.

That made Ruwen think of his last conversation with the Founders. Thorn had asked him not to enter the seventh trial and said, "The burdens you carry are too heavy."

Ruwen had asked Dusk if Thorn spoke the truth, and Dusk had responded. "Perhaps. But the shadow you hide hints at hope. No one knows the weight of a word, or a poem, or a life realized. May the shadow guide you, Child."

What had Dusk seen in Ruwen's shadow that gave her hope that he might succeed? The words she'd chosen he had dismissed as philosophical, but perhaps, once again, he had heard, but failed to listen.

Dusk had specifically mentioned the shadow Ruwen hid, and he recalled the description for the gift he'd received from her when receiving his orange belt.

Name: *Symbol of Lesser Command Shadow*
Restriction: *Bamboo Viper Clan Adept (Minimum)*
Restriction: *Rank Orange (Minimum)*
Restriction: *Shadow Realm interaction impossible when stored.*
Description: *Dismiss your shadow at will, storing it in your mark. Not all shadows fear the light.*

Ruwen repeated the last line of the description again: *Not all shadows fear the light.*

Shadows always pointed away from the light, so what did it mean when a shadow didn't fear the light? Could a shadow point toward a light?

None of that made any sense to Ruwen, and he didn't know

how it helped. More time passed as the fear of spending the rest of his life trapped here smothered him.

In a desperate attempt to remain sane, Ruwen focused again on the odd parting words from Dusk: "The shadow you hide hints at hope. No one knows the weight of a word, or a poem, or a life realized. May the shadow guide you, Child."

Ruwen had assumed Dusk meant a shadow existed in here to guide him. But what if she wanted him to know she had seen something in his shadow that made her hopeful, and the reference to the weight of a word, a poem, or a life realized referenced his mental world? When she said, may the shadow guide you, maybe she meant not an actual shadow, but whatever she'd seen in the shadow he hid. May the shadow guide you. Dusk had been telling him to use his mental world.

Ruwen's thoughts raced. If knowledge increased the size of the soul, could it also help to balance the responsibilities and obligations of the external world? Could it somehow add weight to his internal plate? His mind went blank as full understanding arrived, like the fist of a god.

"What is the most important Step?" Dusk had asked.

Knowledge, combined with mediation, experience, and wisdom, created the very thing Dusk had wanted him to see from the beginning.

Enlightenment.

Ruwen finally understood. Enlightenment balanced his responsibilities, and Dusk had seen the weight of a word in his shadow.

The pressure against Ruwen's back had decreased a fraction, as if his newfound enlightenment had weighed down the internal plate above, and raised the external one he stood trapped on. He felt less resistance at his back, because he had risen off the bottom, and now a tiny space existed for him to fall.

Ruwen rejoiced as it confirmed his conclusion about

enlightenment, and since the pressure had decreased at his back, he knew his soul, and the internal plate, existed above his current direction.

It also meant Ruwen's mental world lived somewhere up there, too.

Looking up into the darkness, Ruwen spoke a single name, hoping this time, facing the right direction, they would hear it.

Sivart?

Yes, Sivart replied.

CHAPTER 63

$\mathcal{E}$motions overwhelmed Ruwen and he couldn't reply.

You sound odd, Sivart said. *Faint.*

Ruwen regained control of himself. *I'm in a strange place. Stuck here, actually.*

A General knows the enemy's home like their own. Strangeness is a lack of preparation.

Ruwen grinned at hearing Sivart's verbal scolding. *Guilty.*

Guilt is an indulgence a leader must sacrifice.

Okay, let's pause the advice for a minute. Can you come to my location?

After a moment, Sivart replied. *I sense your direction, but I cannot find you.*

That figures. Listen, I've encountered a slight problem and need some help.

What aid do you require?

That's a good question. Honestly, I don't know. I'm in a Step trial that has materialized the forces related to my responsibilities. I've figured out enlightenment balances those forces.

The solution appears straight forward. Increase your enlightenment.

Well, I just had a big enlightenment, and barely felt the difference. Plus, that's not something you can just produce. It takes a combination of stuff to happen.

Stuff?

That's a technical term.

Regarding enlightenment, Sivart responded. *I practice kadda obviously, and some madda, but I am no Adda.*

Wait, what? How do Sift's parents relate to this?

I am unaware of anyone's parents.

I'm confused, Sivart. Let's start over. Maybe with what you think about enlightenment.

As I said, you should speak to an adda for a thorough discussion. Of the five paths, I journey on kadda, and even then, I am not a strict adherent.

Um, what five paths?

One moment, Sivart said. *Let me speak to Gita.*

No problem, Ruwen said, irritation overcoming the misery his current situation caused. *I'll just hang out until you've chatted with your friend.*

Ruwen stared into the darkness and tried to nurse the flame of anger at Sivart, but common sense and a high Wisdom kept the fire at bay and left Ruwen feeling guilty for speaking so sarcastically to Sivart who only wanted to help the best way he knew.

My apologies, Sivart said after a minute. *I had assumed you were familiar with the five paths as you spawned Gita from a sacred text on the topic. But Gita informed me Rami gave that scripture to Overlord, to guide his growth.*

No problem. Can you explain now?

I have brought Gita to provide a more authoritative source.

Greetings, Brahm, Gita said.

Hey, Gita. Great to meet you. Sivart says you're an expert on enlightenment.

446

I walk four paths, and search for enlightenment in each.
Can you give me a short summary?

Of course. From each of us, four paths extend, like the points of a compass. North is the path of madda, or what you might call action. Opposite this path lies, radda, or knowledge. East points to tadda, which can be called devotion. Finally, the west, and the path of kadda, duty. In the center is padda, the path of meditation.

Ruwen wondered if he was the only one who hadn't known Madda's and Padda's names came from some type of enlightenment religion. *And what is an Adda?*

A name given to those at the highest points of self-realization. They are masters of the five paths.

Ruwen knew that Madda and Padda weren't Sift's parent's real names, but he hadn't realized they actually meant something. So Madda Adda meant Action Master and Padda, Meditation Master. Usually, the ignorance Ruwen experienced felt small, but this revelation really impacted him. It made him wonder what other things everyone knew that he remained completely clueless about. Ignorance never felt good.

The mention of *realization* in Gita's explanation triggered the memory of Dusk's final words and shifted Ruwen's focus back to the conversation. She'd told him, "No one knows the weight of a word, or a poem, or a life realized."

What does a life realized mean? Ruwen asked.

Self-realization is the destination of the five paths. It is the act of transforming knowledge into a true identity.

Ruwen paused as Gita's words twisted around inside his thoughts. Contained in the maelstrom of concepts, a mote of hope appeared. *Is self-realization the same as enlightenment?*

Enlightenment takes many forms, but the most powerful one is self-realization, Gita said.

Sudden understanding stunned Ruwen, and for a minute, he marveled at the insanely complex nature of both his problems and their solutions. Dusk had glimpsed some part of his internal world from his shadow and had given him the clues necessary to balance his incomprehensible burdens.

How did you balance the responsibility for saving the Universe? It would require more enlightenment than any person could ever hope to generate. More maybe than a hundred people, or even a thousand. But he held millions of constructs in his mind.

Ruwen forced the question out. *How can you reach enlightenment?*

Gathering knowledge, performing your duties, finding—

No, Ruwen interrupted. *I don't mean in general. I am asking you, Gita. How do you reach enlightenment?*

I cannot, Gita said sadly.

The hope Ruwen had tried to keep from his thoughts exploded into a cloud of despair and threatened to destroy his sanity.

Why? Ruwen choked out.

I mentioned before I walk four of the paths. Without the fifth, I have no hope of finding any form of enlightenment.

What path do you lack?

Tadda, the path of devotion.

What does that mean? Ruwen asked in desperation.

Devotion is a path of love. The focus is usually a deity or those close to us.

Why can't you love? Ruwen asked, before realizing how direct and personal that question was. *Wait, you don't need to answer that.*

Gita paused for a few moments. *Forgive me for saying this, Brahm, but your creations do not possess the capacity for love.*

Confusion replaced some of the hopelessness. Ruwen was no expert on love, but he recognized Overlord's interest in Uruziel. Overlord had to be experiencing some form of Devotion. *I have seen it in Overlord,* he told Gita.

Overlord is not one of us. He is a literal piece of you.

What do we have that you don't? What is keeping you from Devotion?

Ruwen heard the deep sadness in Gita's voice. *We lack free will.*

CHAPTER 64

*A*gain, Ruwen floated in shocked silence. *I don't understand. You can do what you want.*

Sivart spoke for the first time. *We cannot. Only the nihilist Narrator Nameless succeeds at small acts of destruction. The nature of our construction created absolute boundaries for our choices and limits our independence.*

Ruwen's shock turned to horror. *I'm so sorry. I didn't know.*

You misunderstand, Sivart said. *You brought us into existence. You provide space for our growth in your mind and protect and nourish us. We owe you everything.*

We would not exist without you, Gita said. *Everyone but Nameless holds nothing but gratefulness in their thoughts.*

But you're trapped, Ruwen said. *Bound by whatever my mind did. That's terrible.*

It was wise and necessary, Sivart replied. *Imagine the danger to your mind from the millions of entities that emerged from your thoughts as they flailed around, trying to understand their purpose. In the beginning, there was no structure, no organization, no order. Free will would have turned that confusion into chaos.*

As repulsive as the idea of robbing someone of their free

will, Ruwen could see the logic in Sivart's words. The necessity of it.

Can I undo that? Ruwen asked.

I do not know, Sivart said. *It is dangerous. A general keeps his tigers caged, not among his troops.*

What might happen if everyone suddenly had free will? Ruwen asked.

Chaos and destruction, Sivart said immediately.

After a moment, Gita responded. *Self-realization and enlightenment.*

Two extremes, but both possible. Ruwen asked another question, hoping to find some reassurance. *Can I limit the instability?*

Again, Sivart responded immediately. *Regardless of a free or bound will, you retain the power to destroy your creations. If unacceptable behavior is met with quick and firm judgement, the worst of the turmoil might be avoided.*

Ruwen winced internally, as he'd demonstrated a weakness for second chances in the past.

Mercy builds devotion, Gita said.

Once again, Ruwen found himself in a situation that required balance. Perhaps he would never escape it. He considered for a few moments, but realized, in his current situation, he had little choice. Ironic that, with a free will, he rarely felt like he had a choice.

I'm out of options, Ruwen said. *And this might allow us to escape. Thank you both. I will lean on your wisdom in whatever mess I'm about to create.*

Ruwen kept his focus upward but didn't concentrate on anyone in particular, a method he'd used in the past to speak to all the mental constructs. Instead of thanking them for protecting his mind, or repairing the fortress, he'd give them the freedom to attack him from the inside.

Hey everyone. I've learned you can't make your own decisions. At least not all of them, and I want to change that. In a moment, I'm going to try and undo that wrong. Thinking of Sivart's concerns, Ruwen added a warning. *I really value what we've built, and I hope you do as well. Free will isn't a justification for harming others or destroying things. This is my home, too, and I won't tolerate agents of chaos.*

Not sure what to do, Ruwen stilled his thoughts, and concentrated on the mass of mental constructs above him. After a pause, he spoke three words.

You are free.

Nothing happened.

Ruwen concentrated on Sivart. *Did it work? Do you feel any different?*

Sivart didn't respond, and before Ruwen could ask again, something did change.

The pressure behind Ruwen decreased as if, once again, the external plate had risen as the internal one fell. Feeling returned to his limbs, and he touched his face, but when he tried to step forward, he didn't move.

Sivart? Are you okay?

Sivart still didn't respond, and Ruwen worried about the situation above.

Time passed, and Ruwen's external plate continued to rise. Giving millions of mental constructs their freedom might have created chaos above, but it had served its purpose, because a portion of those entities had reached some type of enlightenment.

More time passed, and Sivart remained silent. Gita didn't respond to questions either, and Ruwen worried what might keep them silent. Had the initial rush of freedom caused enough chaos to threaten their lives? Had his mind become a battle-ground for the apocalypse? He couldn't move to find out.

The massive waves of enlightenment from Ruwen's creations eventually caused the pressure against him to disappear completely as thousands, tens of thousands, maybe millions, of his constructs attained self-realization. Their enlightenment balanced the scale that hung from his soul.

A speck hung in Ruwen's vision, and it took him far too long to realize his eyes had detected something. This had happened to him in the great darkness of the far Universe, as his mind, bored with the darkness, created fake motes of light.

With nothing else to concentrate on, Ruwen watched the distant point grow, and eventually he wondered if it might be real.

The point became a spot, and it continued to expand. Since he couldn't move, it must be coming toward him.

The light grew but remained too distant to illuminate Ruwen's surroundings. He held up a hand and shielded his eyes as the intensity of the light, after so long in the dark, became uncomfortable. After a few more minutes, he closed his eyes as the powerful light turned painful.

A soft rustling surprised Ruwen, and he held up both hands to block the light, squinting to see what caused the noise.

The first thing Ruwen noticed was his shadow. It began at his feet, which still wouldn't move, and stretched toward the light. The silhouette of the shadow didn't mirror his body and contained a mass of odd lighter colored lines and shapes. A second later, he realized these different colored shadows came from his internal pathways and Meridians, and for the first time, he viewed the sixth rune.

Ruwen tilted his head away from the white sun that had descended on him. He angled his head up slightly and caught sight of the source of rustling.

Men and women stood before Ruwen, too many to count, and the sound came from them parting as something moved through their ranks toward him.

The man closest to the front had a bow slung across his body and a scabbard hung from his hip. The sheathed sword glowed with blue light and gave his worn leather armor an odd color. He spoke to the approaching white light, and to Ruwen's shock, the man spoke with Sivart's voice. "It is good to see you."

Sivart, and the others turned toward Ruwen, following whatever approached him. His shadow stretched outward like an arrow, directly at the brilliant white light.

Then a familiar voice spoke. One Ruwen hadn't heard for what felt like an eternity.

"Miss me?" Overlord asked.

CHAPTER 65

*O*verwhelming joy filled Ruwen, and he tried to look up, but the light blinded him.

"Oh, sorry," Overlord said. "She takes some getting used to. Is this better?"

The light remained, but the intensity decreased drastically. Ruwen cautiously raised his head and found Overlord in his red Overseer armor standing in front of Uruziel, blocking most of her light. Uruziel, the mental shard of Uru that Ruwen had protected inside his mind, caused him constant damage from the Unworthy Vessel debuff, but it allowed him to save her life.

A glowing white hand from behind Overlord slapped his shoulder, the sound like a thud against the armor. "I do not 'take some getting used to,'" Uruziel said.

Overlord removed his helmet, smiling at Uruziel's attack. The goddess peeked out from behind Overlord and waved. "Hi."

Ruwen grinned, thrilled to see them both.

When Ruwen had landed in the Infernal Realm's trap, Uruziel had worried Lalquinrial might sense her if she remained in Ruwen's mind, and she fled. Overlord had followed her, hoping to bring her back, and Ruwen had not seen them since. He had worried that escaping the Infernal Realm using the Sixth Rune might have killed them both, or destroyed their identities, but now they both stood before him, to all appearances, healthy.

Uruziel blazed with white soul power. Ruwen had learned transitioning from Gem to Divine remade your body and converted it from one of Spirit to one of soul. When the day came for him to unlock his soul, he would radiate his own white light.

Ruwen tried to step toward them but again found his feet anchored in place by a pool of shadow.

Overlord strode forward and slowed as he neared Ruwen. With a gauntleted hand, Overlord reached up and touched the space inches from Ruwen's face. "There is a barrier between us."

From behind Overlord Uruziel spoke. "It's the boundary between Ruwen's inner and outer self."

"Just to set the record straight," Overlord said. "She didn't think we'd ever scale the mountain you'd made."

A loud thud came from behind Overlord, and he stumbled forward a step from Uruziel's slap to his back.

"Can't you keep anything to yourself?" Uruziel scolded. She peeked around Overlord. "You were really out of balance, though."

"I know," Ruwen said. "I just figured that out."

Ruwen looked down at his shadow and saw that it didn't point at Uruziel like he'd thought. Her light only revealed what had already existed, and the shadow pointed not at the goddess, but from the direction she'd come. It pointed into the darkness, past the sea of people in front of him. It pointed at his hidden soul.

More pieces of the seventh trial fell into place. Ruwen's internal shadow crossed the barrier separating his outer self from his inner, just like his physical shadow crossed the Material and Shadow Realms. He guessed that Shadow Grandmasters used this overlap to move from shadow to shadow in the Material Realm. That was a practical application born from the relationship the Founders had witnessed here.

Just like a physical shadow in the Material Realm, Ruwen possessed an internal shadow. In the outer world, his shadow moved away from the light, but here, his inner shadow stretched toward the source of his internal light, even though it lay smothered under layers of Ascendancy and tattoo magic.

Ruwen had learned six important lessons, each a step toward his understanding of the mysteries the Bamboo Viper Steps contained.

And just like Ruwen's shadow pointing toward the light, instead of away, he grasped the practical portion of the seventh trial. He finally understood what he needed to do.

When Dusk had asked what the most important step was, Ruwen had rightfully answered enlightenment.

How did one go about enlightenment? It started with knowledge, meditation, and an inward focus.

Ruwen had also learned that his shadow crossed the boundaries between the Material and Shadow Realms, and they could be controlled.

Ruwen closed his eyes and heard Dusk's question again. "What is the most important step?"

Ruwen opened his eyes, focused on his shadow, and answered out loud. "The step toward yourself."

The shadow stretching from Ruwen's feet moved. It shrunk toward him, and to his shock, stood.

The shadow appeared roughly human with bulky arms and legs, and it remained connected to Ruwen by a short black line that wrapped around his feet. The lighter areas inside the shadow, caused by his pathways and Meridians, were clearer now—along with millions of tiny grey motes floating like stars throughout the shadow's body. The drifting points of light gave the shadow depth, and maybe from some odd aspect of

Uruziel's light or the nature of this place, the body with its stars seemed to extend forever.

Ruwen nodded at his shadow, and it nodded back.

Overlord and Uruziel had moved back and now stood next to Sivart.

"I've neglected you," Ruwen said to his shadow. "You have stood here alone and in the dark your entire existence. I promise you, someday soon, I will change that."

Ruwen turned to look at his distant, invisible soul. The vast group of people in front of him absorbed and radiated Uruziel's light, creating a soft glow. Where the crowd ended, though, a deep darkness began.

It pained Ruwen to admit it but Sift had once again been right. Sift had told Ruwen he contained everything he needed to succeed within himself already.

Addressing the shadow again, Ruwen spoke softly while keeping his focus on the horizon. "I've taken six steps to reach this place. Only one remains."

As Ruwen studied the silent darkness, he didn't consider climbing a cliff, or reaching Overlord, or crossing an invisible barrier.

The feelings of sadness, disappointment, and fear Ruwen's imprisoned soul created no longer made sense, and he let the emotions go. He had lost the desire to smash the shell with mental fists, or break it, or hunt endlessly for weaknesses.

Instead of running away from what Ruwen considered a failure, he accepted his soul's trapped state, and for the first time, viewed it without hostility or anger.

"What is the most important Step?" Ruwen asked quietly.

"The step inward," Ruwen answered his own question. "A step toward yourself. This step."

In the Material Realm Ruwen's shadow followed him, but here, where his shadow stretched toward the light, things worked differently. He concentrated completely on himself, his thoughts free from any burdens, responsibilities, or obligations, and willed himself toward his soul.

The shadow beside Ruwen stepped forward, taking the seventh step.

And Ruwen followed.

CHAPTER 66

*R*uwen tumbled forward, clumps of short green grass doing little to cushion his fall. Gasps and shouts erupted from somewhere in front of him. Feeling seeped into his limbs and he looked up. The afternoon sun shone brightly down on Sift and all the Adepts, which it appeared he'd been instructing. Everyone now ran toward him.

You still there, Overlord? Ruwen asked, worried his sudden exit had created problems.

Yeah, it's good to be home. You should probably drop by when you get a chance. A lot changed. Uruziel, Sivart, and I are on it though.

Thanks, buddy. It's so great to hear your voice again.

Ditto.

Three heart beats later, Ruwen almost felt normal, and by the time Sift arrived, Ruwen had made it to his feet.

Sift wrapped Ruwen in a hug, and as the taste of maple syrup filled Ruwen's mouth, he realized it must be the next day. He returned Sift's hug and then Sift quickly stepped away, his cheeks pink.

"It's good to see you," Sift said.

"It's been an interesting few hours."

Sift raised his eyebrows. "It's been three days."

The rest of the Adepts arrived, talking excitedly and congratulating Ruwen. Echo stood at the edge of the group, her face neutral. Her Disposition Aura still whipsawed between red and pink.

Three days had passed, but as Ruwen considered his time in the seventh trial, he knew he would have accepted three years as an answer.

Prythus laughed. "All of us succeeded! Can you believe it?"

Everyone but Echo wore smiles, and Ruwen could feel their excitement.

"I do believe it," Ruwen answered. "You have all worked hard and deserve the title of Master. Congratulations." After a moment, he continued. "Why did you all wait?"

The Adepts looked confused. Nymthus spoke. "How could we not? You have made every one of us better, and if not for you, some of us would have died. We owe you far more than a brief wait by the sea."

Many of the Adepts nodded their heads in agreement, and they all bowed to Ruwen, including Echo.

Humbled by the words, Ruwen returned their bow.

Conversations erupted everywhere as the Adepts discussed the next ceremony. Now that Ruwen had arrived, they could receive their black belts and new title.

"What took you so long?" Sift asked.

"How long did it take you?" Ruwen asked in return.

Sift shrugged. "I don't know. Two or three..."

Sift squished his brow in thought, trying to decide.

"Two or three hours?" Ruwen prompted.

Sift frowned at Ruwen. "What? No. Seconds."

"You did this in three seconds?" Ruwen asked as calmly as he could.

Sift shrugged. "I saw this massive light and when I took a step, I fell out here. Just like you."

Ruwen dropped into the third meditation, feeding it emotions that ranged from burning rage to proud happiness.

"I bet you complicated it," Sift said with a knowing nod.

"I did not," Ruwen responded, probably a little too defensively. "It was already complicated. Like super complicated."

"Okay, okay," Sift said, holding up his hands. "It was already complicated."

Ruwen sighed. "You were right, though. I had what I needed to succeed."

Sift grabbed Ruwen's shoulder. "I never doubted it."

"Thanks," Ruwen said. "I'm lucky you always have my back."

The maple syrup taste faded.

"Of course, we're a team," Sift replied.

Ruwen turned his attention to what had caused the Adepts to grow suddenly silent.

The Founders had exited a group of rocks, probably another route down to the beach, and strode toward the Adepts. The Adepts organized themselves into Rungs and watched excitedly as the Founders approached.

"I've dreamed about this ceremony since I was little," Sift said. "Master Sift. Soon to be Grandmaster Sift. You'll see."

Ruwen remembered the conversation he'd had with the Founders before entering the seventh trial. They approached not to start a Master's ceremony, but to pass judgement and strip Sift of everything he'd spent his life training for.

Emotions swirled inside Ruwen, but as he stood there, watching judgement approach, he noticed a difference in himself.

The trial had changed Ruwen somehow. He felt full. Not like when he'd eaten too much of Mom's best breakfast, Survivor's Guilt, but like he'd taken a really deep breath. Like his entire body had taken a deep breath and held it.

Ruwen didn't want to draw attention to himself by throwing a punch or twisting into a kick. Instead, he rotated his right hand in a move called Bear Paw, hyper-focusing on the move used to break an enemy's grip.

Ruwen had mastered physical balance long ago, and he centered himself automatically, not requiring any thought to find his body's equilibrium. He repeated the move again, and then again. It felt the same, but different.

As the Founders reached the Adepts, Ruwen guessed at the change. Whatever balance he'd attained in the seventh step had resulted in an ability to feel his inner state for the first time. What had been empty before now had substance, and it pushed outward, balancing against the pressure of his physical body.

It didn't make Ruwen lighter or faster, but it made his movements completely effortless. He worried about such a change so close to the insane plan he was about to implement. He couldn't control the timing however, so he let the worry go. His plan would either work or it wouldn't, and he would know soon enough.

All three Founders studied Ruwen, and he guessed they desperately wished to know how he had overcome the seventh trial, but he remained silent. Perhaps some time in the future, assuming he survived his plan, he would explain. After his frustration with the traditions and rules meant for times of peace, not war, had passed.

Ruwen had hoped this day wouldn't come, but he had prepared for it. He had planned and practiced his solutions since the day Kysandra had told him the risks of his actions in the underwater safe house near Legion's Vault.

"Congratulations, Adepts," Mist said.

"Before the ceremony," Thorn continued. "We must address Clan business."

Ruwen let out the breath he held and strode forward.

"Two—" Dusk started and then stopped as she noticed Ruwen's movement.

The Adepts all turned and watched Ruwen march forward.

Since the night Ruwen had discussed his training of Sift with Kysandra in the underwater safe house, and she had explained the risks, he had pictured this moment. The question he had asked Tarot—*Before I travel home, will my plans succeed*—referenced his next act, and despite the warnings from the Misfortune Golem, Ruwen remained optimistic.

A memory surfaced and Ruwen smiled. It came from his first trip to the Black Pyramid. Sift and Ruwen had stood near the top of the Black Pyramid watching the massive storm Ruwen had created by Harvesting with his Core for the first time.

Sift held out his fist, and Ruwen stared at it.

"You put your hand on it, palm down. It's a Clan shortcut, so we don't always have to bow to each other," Sift said.

"What happens if we both put our fist out?"

"Look at the over-thinker at work. If that happens, the lower-ranked member changes to the palm. If they don't, that means they want to challenge you and try to advance in rank."

"Okay, so I'm basically always palm."

"Yes, probably for the rest of your life."

"Thanks."

Ruwen placed his open hand over Sift's fist.

Ruwen returned to the present as he approached the Founders. The three sisters stood near each other, and they studied him. He had changed considerably since they had all met that first day of his Journeyman test. Slapping him would require a lot more effort now.

Stopping in front of the Founders, Ruwen bowed.

The Founders bowed in return.

"What is it, Adept?" Dusk asked.

Ruwen made a fist and slowly extended it toward the Founders.

"Oh, no," Sift said, clearly audible in the sudden silence.

The Founders stared at Ruwen's outstretched fist.

Dusk stepped forward and stretched out her fist as well, stopping an inch from Ruwen's.

They stood that way, gazes locked.

Twenty seconds passed.

"Do you know what you're doing?" Dusk asked.

"What I need to," Ruwen replied.

"Are you seriously challenging me for the rank of Founder?"

Ruwen didn't hesitate. "Yes."

CHAPTER 67

*S*ift started forward to help, but Ruwen had expected that, and already had his free hand behind his back. He signaled Sift in Shade Speak. *Stop. Okay. Thanks.*

Sift stopped.

Dusk frowned at Ruwen. "This is foolish."

"With all due respect, Founder," Ruwen replied. "I've been far more foolish."

"What are you thinking?" Dusk asked in disbelief.

Ruwen kept his fist extended. "The Shadow oath I took triggers when I become a Master. You wanted to avoid this by removing my Step knowledge, preventing me from advancing. I'm just going to skip Master all together."

"So you skipped Grandmaster?" Dusk asked.

Ruwen shrugged. "The only Grandmasters I've seen are Madda and Padda. First, I consider them friends, and don't want to force them into fighting me. Second, there are no Grandmasters here for the hidden forms."

"You are so sure?" Dusk asked.

"Yes," Ruwen responded simply. "At least not nearby. Only the gods can hide from me now."

"As you wish," Dusk said. "With the soul stone costs, it will take at least three months to summon our Clan."

"Wait, what?"

"Challenging a Founder is historic and requires the entire Clan."

The last thing Ruwen wanted to do was wait here another three months. "Do I need to stay here the whole time?"

"You are in the Master's trial," Dusk said. "Leaving before it ends is automatic failure."

Ruwen kept his fist out and steady. "Are there any quicker options?"

"Now you want to explore options?"

The comment annoyed Ruwen. "Don't think I haven't thought this through, Founder. I don't know the technicalities of your ceremonies, that is all. Is there a quicker way?"

Dusk nodded. "You can face those you've wronged in a Step match."

"So three matches," Ruwen said. He nodded at Mist and Thorn. "One with each Founder?"

Dusk shook her head. "No, Adept. One match. With all those you've wronged. You would face all three of us at once."

"Okay," Ruwen said.

Dusk frowned in confusion. "Are you serious? Instead of waiting three months and facing one impossible opponent, you wish to face three immediately?"

"I'm in a hurry."

Mist and Thorn stepped forward.

Thorn spoke softly. "Do not mock us, Adept."

Ruwen shook his head. "On the contrary. If you had any idea how long and hard I've trained, it would flatter you."

"You are barely seventeen," Mist said. "I have spent longer arranging rocks."

"Time is complicated, and my training unconventional," Ruwen said.

Thorn spoke quietly. "Your Steps are flawless, and your comprehension of balance, now that you've taken the seventh step, matches our own. You are worthy to challenge us. Wait the three months and give yourself a chance to succeed."

Ruwen nodded at Thorn. Her words confirmed what he'd guessed. Despite her issues with his training methods, she wanted to help him. He thought seriously for five seconds, balancing his preparation for this fight with the problems back home, and the possible trouble Hamma and Lylan had found.

"If I fight the three of you now," Ruwen asked. "What happens to my rank?"

Dusk turned to Mist and then Thorn, and Ruwen wondered if they had some type of method to speak to each other mentally.

After another moment, Dusk faced Ruwen. "Technically, the match is not a challenge for advancement, so if you managed to succeed, you would not gain the rank of Founder. However, we think it appropriate that such a display of skill merits recognition, despite the forum for its display. If you triumph, you will earn the rank of Grandmaster, and be recognized as such for both Bamboo and Viper forms. Shadow Grandmasters require a different type of confirmation, and you will need to demonstrate that at another time to gain advancement."

Ruwen kept his fist extended and bowed slightly from his hips. He knew the Founders had added this reward to allow his plan to succeed. If he wanted to avoid the rank of Master, he needed to transition from Adept to either Grandmaster or Founder to evade the punishment for breaking the Shadow oath.

Ruwen remembered his fight with Phoenix in the Spirit Realm. He had needed to prove his innocence there as well, and it hadn't required Ruwen to win, only survive. "What are the match details? How is success measured?"

"Soul magic is allowed," Mist said. "Spirit based or any other type of magic is forbidden. No potions or enhancers are allowed."

"You are given an amulet of guilt," Thorn said. "Each of us will hold an amulet of innocence. They must always remain visible. The match is over when either you have gained all three amulets from us, or any of us obtains your amulet."

Ruwen hid his disappointment. This match would be far harder than his one in the Spirit Realm because he needed to do more than survive. "If I acquire an amulet of innocence, does that Founder remain to fight?"

"Yes," Dusk said. "We will always outnumber you three to one. Your plan is clever and has merit. Wait the three months. Succeeding against one of us is possible, but winning against us all would take a miracle."

Ruwen considered the situation. The match's constraints against magic and his damaged pathways and meridians, meant parts of his original preparations wouldn't work. For instance, he couldn't summon Overlord for help, or any type of *Minion*. He couldn't use his Void Band in any fashion, and no buffs or spells. The loss of *Blink* was especially painful as he'd counted on that to counter any Shadow Stepping he might encounter.

Despite these losses, Ruwen kept three powerful advantages. He had trained extensively against Overlord and his *Minions*, endlessly sparring Grandmaster level opponents. Ruwen's Perception, coupled with his peak Diamond body, gave him an almost complete picture of his surroundings and opponents' intentions. Those intentions fed into his strongest ability, Probability Waves, which had allowed him to survive an assault from a literal god.

Ruwen had used Overlord's *Blinking* obsession to practice against an opponent who could Shadow Step. He had integrated this experience into his Probability Wave training and felt confident he could predict its use. Not being able to *Blink* or

Shadow Step would hinder him, but how much depended on the Founders' ability to fight as a team.

Still, all things considered, Ruwen didn't think he'd need a miracle to succeed. Perhaps a little luck though, which made him consider Tarot, and the Misfortune Golem's impact on Ruwen's life. It was hard to know how many of the problems he'd encountered had come from Tarot's karmic imbalance, when Ruwen's life already seemed like one extended disaster after another.

The tiny golem had saved Ruwen's life after the Infernal Ring explosion. Maybe Blapy would have found an excuse to save him anyway, but the fact remained, Tarot had arrived to take any blame for Blapy's actions.

That made Ruwen wonder if Blapy could have planned that. Could she have planted Tarot in Ruwen's path? He stopped that line of thinking, scolding himself for getting distracted when he had such an important decision to make. Still, getting rid of Tarot, even with the slight tilt toward bad luck, seemed unwise.

That left the reason for the rush. Kysandra had warned Ruwen in the Black Pyramid's Blood Gate, that the situation at home had gotten bad. Bad for a lot of people, not just Big D and Bliz. She had talked about an impending civil war that might undo everything they'd sacrificed to restore Uru's Third Temple, and worse, lead to the destruction of the entire country.

Kysandra had wanted Ruwen to come home immediately. Instead, he had spent a few days in the Infernal Realm, more time in the Third Secret, and almost a week here. Time flowed differently on each planet, so he didn't know for sure how long his two-week detour had taken back on Grave.

What Ruwen did know, was Kysandra had looked worried, and he knew it took a lot to worry that woman. She had wanted him to come immediately, and, instead, two weeks had likely passed. It might already be too late to fix the issues back home.

Then there was Tarot's fortune for Sift that implied Lylan and Hamma were in trouble. Ruwen had told Sift Lylan and Hamma could take care of themselves, and they didn't need help. He believed that, but he also worried. How many times had he needed his friends' help in the past two years? A lot. And while he might have succeeded with some of it on his own, having his friends around made everything better.

And Ruwen had to admit, he really missed Hamma.

Not just Hamma. The hole Rami left within him by her absence created a constant ache. He also desperately wondered how much progress Fractal had made, and if the little crystal was okay. Ruwen couldn't help but feel he'd failed Fractal by his absence for the last year and a half.

Ruwen prayed his parents had returned home, and that Tremine, Bliz, and Big D hadn't suffered because of Ruwen or his disappearance.

When Ruwen thought about it, there were a ton of reasons to hurry back home. Waiting three months felt irresponsible and dangerous to him.

More irresponsible and dangerous than fighting the three Founders of his Step Clan?

The Founders had waited patiently while Ruwen worked through his thoughts. Dusk's fist remained inches from Ruwen's.

Gently, Ruwen moved his fist forward until it touched Dusk's. "I am worthy to instruct others in the most advanced Bamboo and Viper Steps and have earned the rank of Grand-master. I respectfully request a match to prove it."

CHAPTER 68

*R*uwen stood in a small circle with five other peak Diamond experts of the Bamboo Viper Steps.

Around them, a larger hundred-foot circle, stretched across the mountaintop. At this altitude, a person's breath crystalized instantly; although breathing the oxygen poor atmosphere would kill a normal person in minutes.

No one considered the present six normal.

The surrounding mountains blocked much of the wind, and what did reach them, had lost most of its ferociousness.

Somewhere in the nearby peaks, viewing rooms had been carved from the granite, protecting the observers from the wind and cold, and filled with rich, lowland air. It kept them safe not only from the elements, but from the destructive forces that the impending fight would generate.

Ruwen knew Sift and the other Adepts watched from these rooms. Here to witness Ruwen fight for not only his future in the Bamboo Viper Clan, but Sift's as well.

Padda handed Madda a red gem attached to a short leather band. She took the gem and stepped up to Ruwen. She still had the frown she'd worn since learning of this match. Her worry and anger radiated from her like only a mother could produce.

Ruwen bent down as Madda reached up, fastening the necklace around his neck.

"Foolish, Child," Madda muttered, probably without realizing it.

"Thank you, Madda," Ruwen whispered.

Madda jerked hard on the leather strap around Ruwen's neck, either to make sure she had fastened it tightly, or to express her displeasure with him, or maybe for both.

Padda remained silent and handed Madda a green gem with an identical strap. She moved to Mist and, far more gently, attached it around the Founder's neck. The process repeated for Thorn and Dusk.

All six of them wore traditional attire, the heavy white cotton snapping anytime a gust struck them. Ruwen wore his brown belt, and everyone else had black. Only Dusk's belt appeared plain, the other black belts had ten stripes, signifying how many of the ten ranks they'd achieved as a Grandmaster. Green stripes for Bamboo Grandmasters and red ones for Viper.

Madda stepped back to her place on Ruwen's right and nodded at Padda, who waited on Ruwen's left side.

Padda broke the silence. "Grandmaster Adda and I will oversee this match. No Spirit, Mana, or Energy based spells or abilities are allowed. If thrown from the ring, you have ten seconds to return. Any longer, and your gem is forfeited to the competing side. The match will conclude when any of the following conditions are met. All competitors on a side are killed, disqualified, or lose their gems. Any questions?"

Ruwen looked at the edge of the hundred-foot circle they stood on. "How far is that fall?"

Padda pointed to the narrow path that disappeared from the edge of the mountain top. "The portal we arrived through is connected to the village. It means your Bamboo Jacket of Falling will activate and stop the fall from killing you. We are well over thirty thousand feet above the village, so from this height, with your jacket's protection, it will take over three hours to reach the bottom."

A few minutes ago, Ruwen had stepped through the portal stone in the village onto, what he considered, a far too small platform on this mountain's sheer side. They had climbed twenty feet of narrow path to reach this spot.

"Thanks," Ruwen said, as he contemplated a three-hour fall.

"Don't fall off," Madda said.

Ruwen nodded at her. "Good advice."

Ruwen didn't think they'd chosen this location because of his fear of heights. When Gem level fighters battled, the resulting pressure waves held incredible danger for anyone not Fortified. Plus, this high, the air barely existed, making the resulting pressure waves even less hazardous. Objectively, it was a great place for near god like figures to fight.

A three-hour fall.

"It is not too late to reconsider," Dusk offered. "We do not need to take this path."

"Exactly," Thorn agreed. "Your cleverness has found two solutions that provide balance."

"Three months is a breath," Mist added.

Ruwen bowed to the Founders, humbled by their concern for him. They didn't want to lose him or Sift, and waiting three months provided a much easier route to that outcome. He wished the circumstances of his life allowed for that time. Sitting here on the beach and relaxing for three months sounded fantastic.

Except Ruwen had collected far more burdens than this situation, and most of them waited impatiently for him back home. The five experts surrounding him contained a wealth of experience and wisdom that dwarfed his seventeen years. He understood why they thought him young, rash, and immature for taking this course.

Ruwen couldn't argue against his youth, rashness, or even probably his immaturity, but the Addas and Founders had only seen a fraction of his skills. Since the night in the underwater safehouse, as Kysandra warned him of the consequences instructing Sift might cause, he had planned for this very moment. He had known this scenario would almost certainly occur and had worked obsessively to destroy any weaknesses in his Steps.

Ruwen didn't stand on this mountain desperate and afraid. He stood as a man on the cusp of divinity. One who had faced gods, traveled the Universe, and walked the Third Secret. What the Founders didn't know, was while they felt sorry for him, and expected this fight to end in seconds, he had embraced a destiny far greater than this moment. The weight of that fate crushed the last fragments of doubt.

The Scarecrow Aspect kept Ruwen constantly in the second meditation, and he slid into the third, preparing for the imminent combat. He realized he had nothing left to give this level, as his mind had become dead calm.

Balance within balance nested in balance, the perfection of the physical Steps and their philosophical meanings wrapped Ruwen like sunshine, and like a volcano he erupted with joy.

The three Founders bowed to Ruwen and took three steps backward. Madda and Padda moved to the edges of the ring. The match would begin in moments, and he entered the hyper focused state the Probability Wave recognition required.

A ripple of panic crossed the ocean of Ruwen's thoughts. Something had changed, and the world around him felt different. He immediately recognized it originated from his newly balanced internal and external states.

Now that Ruwen had attained balance on both sides of his soul, he realized Probability Waves were the tip of a massive mountain, hidden behind the enormous imbalance he'd carried. Never had he felt more connected to the present, and his immediate surroundings.

The three Founders stood in front of Ruwen generating constant Probability Waves he couldn't see but felt as they passed over his now balanced inner soul. Their intentions created small waves, and as Thorn attacked, he noted her movements made larger waves.

But the waves were an aftereffect of what had really occurred, because as Thorn moved, Ruwen felt the balance shift around them as her actions produced unevenness in the surroundings. He moved to balance the disruption Thorn had created, bringing the world back into harmony.

Ruwen lifted his right foot four inches to avoid Singing Leaf, rotated his hips twenty degrees to counter Angry Sea, and gently brushed Thorn's strike away with his right forearm. He lowered his foot and stood with his back to Thorn, connected to her, her sisters, the Addas, the wind, the ground, everything.

Understanding rushed through Ruwen and he felt the emotions as a brief roiling of the calm sea around him.

The Steps had never been for fighting, or self-defense, or to find meaning. Even saying they were meant for balance understated their purpose.

The Steps guided a person to a mental and physical state that connected them with their environment, created harmony in the present, and complete unity with the world.

As Mist joined Thorn, Ruwen casually shifted his position to offset each of the disturbances they created. When only using Probability Waves it was possible to trick someone into a trap by faking intent. In this new state, Ruwen sensed the false actions, but without an associated balance disruption, he could safely ignore them.

Dusk entered the fight.

CHAPTER 69

*V*ibrations saturated the air from the rapid movements of the four combatants, and even these disturbances Ruwen balanced, creating his own pressure waves with the exact opposite frequencies.

Ruwen countered Blind Morning with Lion's Knee, Dead Seed with Folded Bean, Tumbling Shower with Clay Horse. He had only moved three inches from his starting place and finished each flurry of attacks standing, relaxed and ready.

The Founders activated their Soul abilities, and Ruwen witnessed a Shadow Step for the first time in this new state. To his surprise, it wasn't Dusk but Thorn that Shadow Stepped. It made sense that the Sisters would master all three branches of their Steps, but the confirmation still provided a small shock.

Ruwen sensed the Shadow Step as two movements. He felt Thorn disappear from her current location, creating an imbalance from the void she left. When she entered the Shadow Realm, she disappeared, but he detected the bulge forming as she displaced the air at her destination. A disturbance that began forming as soon as she arrived in the Shadow Realm.

As Thorn reentered the Material Realm, Ruwen had already

balanced her new location, and gently took the gem from around her neck as she appeared.

To Thorn's credit she didn't show anger or disappointment or any emotion. Like a Founder with a lifetime of experience, she continued to try her best to reach Ruwen.

The Founders had certainly mastered something like Probability Waves, and Ruwen thought Dusk glimpsed the state he now called Harmony. Even if they had all mastered Harmony, it wouldn't have mattered. While everyone on the mountaintop had reached Peak Diamond, only he benefited from the Ascendancy Points from his fifty-eight levels of Worker and Fighter Classes. In every way, he surpassed them.

Perhaps not enough to matter in a brief fight, but as the seconds turned into minutes, the advantages Ruwen held compounded, making the outcome inevitable.

Mist performed a soul move that sent a wave of energy toward Ruwen. The magical attack, powered by the soul, remained a set of vibrations, however, which he balanced with a palm thrust that generated the opposite frequencies and nullified her strike.

Harmony exposed the world around Ruwen as an intricate series of vibrations, some large like Mist's attack, and some incredibly tiny, like the vibrations in the stone under his bare feet. He wondered about the limits of this new state, and how balancing the Founder's attacks might affect his surroundings as well.

Ruwen started with the wind, using knife-hand strikes and sweeping kicks to create complete stillness around the platform. Wondering about the opposite effect, he used his command of balance to create an imbalance.

With a roundhouse kick, Ruwen created a gust of wind, knocking the three Founders off balance. As Mist recovered, he removed her necklace. When the Founders regained their stances, he kneeled and struck the stone with three fingers, pushing against the balanced stone ten feet away. The three sisters jumped, as four-foot stone pillars erupted from the ground under their feet.

Before the Founders could recover, Ruwen jumped forward and struck the stone pillars with straight punches, turning each to dust.

The Founders looked at each other and Ruwen sensed the vibration of their communication as they spoke to each other mentally. *Hey You* translated the vibrations but he pushed the words away, not wanting to listen to their conversation. He realized because he could sense the slight tremors, he could disrupt them as well.

The Founders surrounded Ruwen, each taking a one-hundred-twenty-degree arc. He guessed from their communication they had coordinated an ultimate attack to try and best him. They rotated together, clockwise, until Dusk's shadow touched him.

Harmony detected Mist and Dusk disappearing into the Shadow Realm behind Ruwen. Thorn's shadow swelled in two locations, one in front of him and one behind. Thorn's shadow expanded upward as the two Founders began to return to the Material Realm. They intended to sandwich him between the two of them.

Ruwen slid his foot across the stone, applying pressure to the stable rock under him, unbalancing it. The environment immediately shifted to balance the pressure he created, and a ten-foot stone wall rose in front of Thorn, cutting off her shadow.

Dusk and Mist materialized near Thorn, not around Ruwen. With a sweep of his other foot, the wall collapsed into the ground, and he jumped the six feet separating him from the Founders, landing in their midst.

For the first time, Ruwen went on the offensive, disturbing the Harmony of the surroundings and studying how the

Founders' reactions shifted the balance that enveloped all of them. They performed their Steps perfectly, but not always in a way that completely balanced their environment.

Thorn blocked Ruwen's Hissing Hen strike with a flawless Sleeping Turtle, but after the exchange Harmony revealed a slight disturbance remained between them. Thorn had transitioned from Sleeping Turtle into Leafless Tree, a valid shift that raised her right arm. With Harmony however, he now knew had she moved into Angelic Bow, lowering her right arm, she could have returned their surroundings to neutral again.

Mist stepped to within two feet of Ruwen, trying to bait him into attacking. Instead, he felt the disturbance Dusk created as she rotated into a crescent kick behind him. He stepped forward, next to Mist, but facing the opposite direction.

Mist's right arm reached for Ruwen's hip, her intent to upset his center of gravity, and depending on how successful the attack, either rotate her body against his back to choke him or sweep one of his legs.

Ruwen rotated away from Mist, grabbed her extended hand, and bent it downward in a joint lock. She knelt to relieve the pressure and brought her right leg around in a sweep. He released her as Dusk transitioned her crescent kick into a roundhouse kick that made the thin air tremble with its power.

Again as Mist twisted herself to a standing position, Ruwen felt the tiny imbalances scattered around them. The Founders had done nothing wrong, and in fact, their Steps remained perfect, but the effect the Steps had on their surroundings lacked this same perfection.

Dusk's Roundhouse kick missed and Ruwen stepped forward to attack her supporting leg, but she disappeared in a Shadow Step before he could sweep her, appearing next to Thorn five feet away. The exchange left even larger disruptions in the surroundings.

Thorn attacked as Mist stepped behind Ruwen, and he

focused on the fight. Understanding how to take advantage of these tiny disturbances, while important, didn't need to happen while fighting the Founders. Sometime later, he could practice against opponents with far less skill to understand how to use this to his advantage. He could likely finish this fight faster if he knew now, but he didn't need it. If he ever fought a deity, though, it might save his life, which made it worth pursuing.

Knowing Harmony could improve even more made Ruwen happy.

Ruwen twisted his hips, throwing an elbow toward Mist behind him. As he expected, she pushed his elbow, adding her energy to his, and trying to force him into over rotating. Instead of resisting it, he added even more strength to the turn and Mist reacted accordingly, preparing for a strike from his other hand.

Instead Ruwen pulled his elbows inward, and connected to everything around him, he used the twisting energy to push the air out of balance around him, creating a powerful gust that lifted him off the ground, launching him into the air.

Ruwen had meant to land quickly behind Thorn and Dusk, but as he fell, his Bamboo Jacket of Falling triggered, slowing his descent considerably. He cursed himself as memories of Overlord and his thousands of Minions punishing Ruwen on Rainbow's End every time he mistakenly arced through the air.

Ruwen imagined Thorn and Dusk were thrilled as they rushed toward his slowly falling body. With nothing to leverage against, they expected him to be nearly helpless. He rotated himself so he fell headfirst, facing the Founders as they dashed toward him.

Still ten feet in the air, Ruwen waited until Dusk and Thorn had almost reached him, before using a spear strike to push himself suddenly downward.

Instead of Ruwen's head, the Founders faced his feet, and when his hands touched the ground, he pushed upward in a violent handstand, aiming his feet at the two Sisters' chins.

Dusk and Thorn reacted automatically, dodging the kick, but it forced Dusk to lean outward enough to affect her center of gravity, and Ruwen, still upside down, slammed his hand into her heel. He used the resistance of Dusk's stance to pull his own body downward, and Dusk's leg finally gave out.

Dusk fell, and Ruwen stood. As they passed each other, Dusk finished her Shadow Step, and disappeared.

A moment later Dusk appeared next to Thorn as Mist approached Ruwen from behind.

Dusk reached up to touch her bare neck.

Ruwen had snatched the necklace as she'd Shadow Stepped away, and he held up the three gems of innocence.

Instead of attacking, Mist slowed to a walk and joined her sisters. The Founders formed a line in front of Ruwen and bowed deeply.

The match had ended.

CHAPTER 70

When the Founders stood, each of them extended their fists, acknowledging Ruwen's skills.

Ruwen let go of Harmony and rose from the third meditation. The world around him now seemed dull, and he felt the loss of the connectedness Harmony provided.

Ruwen had also bested Tarot's fortune. The plans he'd made so long ago to challenge the Founders had now succeeded. The Sisters had come prepared and determined to punish him for the foolishness, failures, and mistakes they accused him of. Now, his teaching Sift the Grandmasters' Steps and use of the Shadow Forms, had been validated. He had sprinted along the cliff of the Reversed Fool, and made it safely to his destination.

Stepping forward, Ruwen grasped Dusk's fist, and gently opened it. He turned to Mist and then Thorn, repeating the act. The three Founders now stood with palms facing down.

Taking a large step backward Ruwen bowed to them and then clenched his right fist, covering it with his left palm.

Ruwen spoke from his heart. "You created the extraordinary, wrapped it in remarkable, and covered it with wonder. If I live a thousand lives, I could never repay this gift. Thank you."

The Founders, exposed to the final incarnation of the amazing and complex philosophy they'd conceived were overcome with emotion.

Dusk tried to speak, cleared her throat, and tried again. "We have doubted ourselves. All this time, and we only see echoes, shadows, of the...of the—"

"Harmony," Ruwen offered.

Dusk nodded. "Yes, Harmony. Only now are we sure it exists."

The Founders, like all artists, had taken their vision and crafted a version for everyone, encapsulating an idea or concept into as perfect a reflection of their dream as possible.

Ruwen smiled. "A Sage, a Priestess, and a Shade have taught me an important lesson. Question your thoughts, but never doubt your heart."

The three Founders bowed again.

"I regret thinking you immature," Thorn whispered through a tight throat. "You humble us with our own teaching."

"Agreed," Mist added. "I feel like a Novice again."

Dusk hesitated and then in a rush the question Ruwen expected arrived.

"Is it something we can learn?" Dusk asked.

Ruwen grew serious. "That is up to you."

The three Founders bowed, thinking Ruwen had answered their question in the same vague metaphysical way they instructed.

"As a Novice, my Sisen gave me direct, actionable, instruction," Ruwen said. "When my center had shifted too far forward or my hips didn't align or whatever, he told me, and I fixed it. At some point between Novice and Master, everyone stops teaching like that. Why do you think that happens?"

Thorn answered. "As a Step practitioner advances, their growth stems from internal revelations as their physical skills level off. That is why we discourage easy advancement as you approach Master. Such rapid progress leaves no time for inner growth."

"There is logic in that, I admit," Ruwen said. "But my own rapid advancement proves you can have both. You asked me if Harmony can be taught, and I said it's up to you. I meant that literally. I know why I succeeded when you didn't."

"Respectfully," Padda said to the Founders. "Do you wish us to leave before anything further is discussed?"

Ruwen turned and smiled at Madda and Padda, standing together at the edge of the ring. "Do you know I just learned what your names mean. I really feel stupid."

"Stupid is all you and Sift find," Madda said. Then her eyes grew large as she realized what she'd said. "I'm so—"

"Stop," Ruwen said, holding out a hand. "Don't apologize. You're right. Although I'd like to think it's mostly Sift's fault. I'm still the same person, please don't treat me any different."

Madda nodded, and Padda looked relieved.

"I don't want you to leave," Ruwen said to Madda and Padda. "In fact, that is the entire problem."

The Founders all frowned, confused.

"I think there's another reason you alter the way you teach," Ruwen said. "It goes to the core of your failure and explains why I succeeded." The Founders and Addas waited, eager for understanding. "As a Step student advances their knowledge and experience, they create a metaphysical weight as their value to our Clan increases. Explanations are like investments, and the clearer and more precise the knowledge, the larger that investment becomes. There is risk that the student will fail, despite the knowledge, and the Sisen shares that failure. In short, the more exact your instruction, the greater the responsibility you carry for that Sijun."

Ruwen had realized this when teaching Rung Four, and then later, the other Rungs. The more he taught them, the stronger his connection to them became, and he began to feel responsible for them.

Rung Four amplified this with their memories and intense desire to save their world. He cared about every one of them, and as this attachment formed, he realized he'd created yet another burden on his soul.

Ruwen continued. "The first Step practitioner I ever met reminded me time and time again the value of a light soul free from attachments and burdens. He was right, there is value. And everyone that comes to these trials has learned the same lesson, passed down from one Sisen to the next, which is the danger of burdens."

Ruwen paused, remembering his feelings when Sift had said the seventh trial had only taken seconds. "The value this philosophy has is the ease of the seventh trial, which reinforces your beliefs that it's correct. You are wrong."

Ruwen let the Founders absorb that for a few seconds, and then started again. "I didn't understand completely until our fight. I've spent the last two years creating unbelievable connections to the world around me. Items, people, and other responsibilities that pinned my soul to the external world." He looked at each of the three sisters. "This made the seventh trial difficult for me. The greater your external connections, the more enlightenment you require to balance it. But that cost doesn't come without benefit."

Ruwen closed his eyes and felt the world around him. He opened his eyes and pushed his palms out, stopping the wind that gusted around them. Into the sudden silence, he spoke. "The seventh trial, using my soul as the pivot, balanced my inner and outer worlds, but the connections I'd made to the external world remained. I feel the breath of the wind, hear the heartbeat of the world, and taste the tears of the clouds. And it feels me. We are connected."

The wind returned, causing the cotton of their clothes to snap.

Dusk closed her eyes, comprehension arriving with silent tears. "Of course," she whispered. "How can we sense a world we have no connection with?"

Ruwen nodded. "This knowledge unites us. I feel responsible for trusting you with it. But that burden doesn't make me weaker, it only increases the power of my Harmony."

"Our Clan owes you eternal thanks, Grandmaster Starfield," Dusk whispered.

The Founders and Addas bowed and Ruwen returned it.

Ruwen had arrived at the Master's trial believing he'd learned all the secrets the Steps contained. Instead, the Steps had humbled him, and revealed a deeper message.

It reminded Ruwen of the Shade Rule Lylan had told Sift in passing. Only now did Ruwen appreciate the vast wisdom it contained.

"Shade's First Rule," Lylan had said. "Move fast alone, travel far together."

CHAPTER 71

*T*he sun hovered across from the class, the lateness of the day creating yellow and orange streaks through the patches of clouds. Mountains quickly shrank to bamboo covered foothills which stretched to the ocean, and the barely visible Masters' Village.

Ruwen and Sift remained still, as the rest of Rung Four moved toward the Founders as a group.

"Why does everything need to be so high?" Ruwen whispered to Sift.

"The view, of course," Sift replied.

Ruwen pressed his back against the cliff face of the mountain behind them. A small amphitheater carved out of the mountainside provided a view that didn't look awful.

On the left side of the auditorium, the Quartermaster stood in the doorway of a vault, the stone door half open. He handed Padda eight new uniforms and Madda eight black belts tied together in a bundle, and the pair quickly strode to the Founders.

The rest of the Adepts stood arranged in their Rungs. They

had already received their black belts, new Bamboo Viper Clan tattoos, attire, and relic tokens.

"Rung Four," Dusk said. "Few in the Bamboo Viper Clan can match the suffering you've endured. Recognizing this, and to preserve the sacrifices each of you made in service to protecting your world, the Quartermaster used the last of the *One from Many* spell thread when stitching these belts' enchantments."

"You know the cost of war," Thorn said. "The schools you create upon your return will produce fighters capable of turning the tide. But danger is a constant companion, and death is inevitable."

"The *One from Many* enchantment on these belts," Mist said, "will help preserve your sacrifices. The thread binds all of you together, and when one of you dies, their skills and strengths will pass to the remaining members."

"In this way," Dusk said. "You continue to aid your cause, even after you depart the living Realm."

"That is powerful magic," Tarot said from Sift's shoulder.

Sift jumped and tried to grab Tarot, but the Misfortune Golem rose upward on his floating deck of cards.

Ruwen looked up at the golem. "Where have you been?"

"Hanging out with Shelly," Tarot said.

Sift pointed at the golem. "Where's my turtle?"

"Master of the Bamboo Viper Steps, Prythus, approach for recognition," Thorn said.

Ruwen slapped Sift's shoulder. "Do this later. Let's enjoy the ceremony."

Sift glared at Tarot, who appeared unfazed by the look, and Ruwen shook his head.

"I misjudged," Tarot whispered. "Bad luck. Go figure."

Ruwen tried to ignore the comment, but his curiosity won as usual. He glanced up at Tarot and whispered. "First, thank you for saving my life."

The golem nodded at Ruwen.

"Second, what did you misjudge?"

Tarot sighed. "The timing."

"The timing of what?"

Tarot waved a hand in a circle. "All this."

"Master of the Bamboo Viper Steps, Nymthus, approach for recognition," Mist said.

Ruwen didn't want to miss any more of Rung Four's ceremony, and he refocused on the presentation. He would get to the bottom of Tarot's comment after they finished here.

"I wonder what my belt will do?" Sift whispered.

Ruwen continued watching the ceremony but whispered back. "Your dad told Prythus all black belts contain five slots of dimensional storage. I know how full yours is."

"Ha-ha, Stasher. Spoken like a true hoarder."

Warm happiness spread outward from Ruwen's chest at seeing all Rung Four advance to Master. He had worked with them the entire time here and felt gratified about the difference he'd made. Because of his training, the quality of the fighters they produced back home would increase greatly. He had made an impact on them, and it felt great.

"Master of the Bamboo Viper Steps, Sift, approach for recognition," Thorn said.

Sift pushed off the rock wall and strode forward, trying to act normal, but joy radiated from him like a blazing fire. Sift said he didn't care about any of this, and Ruwen believed him. But Ruwen also knew Sift had wanted the title that matched his skills, and now he did. Well, almost. Sift could test for Grandmaster tomorrow if he wanted. Assuming there was even a test for that.

Madda and Padda beamed in pleasure and Sift smiled at them. Thorn, and then Mist, pressed their forearms to Sift's, altering his mark from the one he'd received as a Novice. Now it marked him as a Master on two Grandmaster paths. Thorn and Mist presented Sift with his black belt, uniform, and relic token. Then, in just a few seconds, he stood next to Ruwen again.

Sift held out his arm and turned it back and forth. At one angle, it had a slightly larger snake than the normal Master mark and smaller bamboo. As Sift progressed down the Viper Grandmaster path, those size differences would increase. The other angle had the larger bamboo and smaller viper of the Bamboo Grandmaster path.

"That is burnt," Ruwen said.

Sift grinned. "Yeah, I love it. Thanks."

Everyone's mark had changed, most to the balanced Master one, but Ruwen guessed Echo had also received a Grandmaster marking from Thorn.

"The Bamboo Viper Clan is honored to welcome you as Masters," Dusk said. "Before we celebrate, however, we wish to award a Grandmaster belt. Normally, this occurs in a more dramatic ceremony, but this audience feels more appropriate. Grandmaster of the Bamboo Viper Steps, Ruwen, approach for recognition."

Ruwen strode forward and as he passed the Adepts, they bowed. No, not Adepts, Masters.

In school, Ruwen had avoided attention. His Intelligence had made him a target for bullying and being recognized like this would always make the harassment worse. Luckily, his shy nature made remaining unnoticed natural. Despite the vast differences between the pre-Ascendancy Ruwen and his current state, attention still made him anxious.

At some point Ruwen's advancement would make him a god, and attention might become impossible to avoid. Transitioning into a deity didn't fit with the mental picture he had of himself. Gods had always been statues in the temple or invisible beings you cursed after stubbing your toe.

Some gods, like Izac in Malth, made themselves visible, but Uru had remained hidden from her people, causing some to doubt she existed or cared any more. Maybe if Ruwen had grown up in Malth, he'd feel different, but he liked Uru's way better. Attention was the last thing he desired.

Ruwen reached the Founders and bowed. They returned it, holding theirs for three seconds.

Dusk stood up straight and addressed the group. "As Masters of the Bamboo Viper Clan you have earned knowledge of our secrets. One such secret we will discuss now. Sister Thorn, how coil the vipers?"

Thorn slowly studied the group and responded. "In a nest, Sister."

Dusk nodded and turned to her right. "Sister Mist, how stands the bamboo?"

Mist examined everyone present before speaking. "In a grove, Sister."

Dusk faced the new Masters. "In the nest, among the grove, I call this conclave of Masters."

White soul magic spread out from the Founders, creating a bubble around them all, and, Ruwen guessed, hid them from any eavesdroppers or onlookers.

Dusk held up Ruwen's black belt. It didn't have any colored thread at the ends like the other Grandmasters' belts. "You all witnessed what happened today and know that Ruwen has earned Grandmaster stripes and more. Why then is his belt bare?" She held up one end of her belt. "For that matter, why is mine?"

The Masters remained silent, knowing Dusk would reveal the answer to something all of them had noticed.

Dusk continued. "A lifetime of dedication has earned you the title Master. This is the pinnacle of the Bamboo Viper Steps. Some have more than one life to offer, and the Steps can provide an even deeper understanding of the mysteries. These few will journey on the Grandmaster path, either Bamboo or Viper. But there is another Grandmaster path, and it contains the original Steps, born in shadow. The first six trials taught you the exquisite balance between the Bamboo and Viper Steps. You learned how they complement each other."

Dusk paused, and instead of addressing the Masters, she locked eyes with Ruwen, as if she spoke to him personally. "One of the many lessons of the seventh trial is the balance between light and shadow, not only in ourselves, but in the world around us. We created the original Steps to bring balance to power. A way to fight back against the mighty. A way to right wrongs. Three deeply unbalanced sisters stepped into the shadows. From that desperate act, new friendships formed as we learned the secret knowledge the Shadow Steps now hold."

The Prime Shadow Warden, standing behind Dusk in the cave of the last trial, had spoken Ruwen's name and summoned him to the seventh trial. The secret knowledge Dusk spoke of probably included whatever Shadow Realm magic had powered that trial. He quickly checked his Realm count to see if he'd crossed into the Shadow Realm during the trial, but he hadn't, as his count remained at four.

Dusk turned her attention back to the Masters. "Our new friends taught us balance, and we used that knowledge to create the Bamboo Viper Steps, taking inspiration from our childhood home. The Steps took hundreds of years to perfect, but one thing never changed. At their heart rested the hidden Shadow Steps."

Dusk locked eyes with Ruwen. "The Shadow Grandmaster wears the belt of a Master. Not only to hide the fact of the Shadow Step's existence, but to honor the Bamboo Viper Steps and the duty they perform. A Shadow Grandmaster, with the power they hold, must see past the world. They must see the mysteries, the patterns, the secrets of the Universe. Knowledge, Wisdom, and Enlightenment must be constant companions. The Shadow Grandmaster lives in two Realms, and their shadows do not fear the light. This existence gives them the ultimate balancing power. They are god killers."

Dusk blinked as if pulling herself from the past and focused on the Masters again. "Few possess this knowledge, and those that do are beings of great power. Why then reveal our brother's path to you?"

Dusk swallowed hard and emotion made her cheeks flush. "The revelations of this day lay heavy on my mind. Only now do I understand the power of connections and the importance of a burden. Telling you so much of the Shadow Clan history creates a connection between us. A shared responsibility that strengthens us." Dusk refocused on Ruwen. "Knowing Ruwen's secret creates a bond with him. A responsibility. A burden. Keeping it will strengthen you."

Dusk held up the black belt. "Ruwen Starfield, in acknowledgement of the balance and understanding you possess, in recognition of your displayed mastery of the Bamboo Viper Steps, we welcome you as a rank ten Grandmaster of the Bamboo and Viper Steps. In addition, the Shadow Clan has judged your shadow worthy of the darkness."

Ruwen bowed deeply, and Dusk placed the belt in his open hands. When he stood, she pulled the cotton of her sleeve upward, revealing her normal looking Master mark. As he watched, the bamboo and viper in the mark faded as a swirling darkness moved through the bamboo.

Dusk held out her arm and Ruwen grasped it, their marks touching. His forearm burned, but the pain disappeared a heartbeat later. She released him and he studied his new mark.

The novice mark Ruwen had carried since that day long ago in the Black Pyramid had changed from the single stalk of bamboo with a plain viper around it into a grove of bamboo, with a detailed viper coiled among the stalks, mouth open and fangs bared.

"Think of your shadow," Dusk whispered.

Ruwen thought of his shadow, locked away in this very mark, and the design became fuzzy like fog had appeared.

"With a thought," Dusk whispered. "You can alter your mark from this, a rank zero Shadow Grandmaster, to any rank from zero to ten for Bamboo or Viper Grandmaster, all the way down to the novice mark Padda and Madda gave you in the beginning. This allows you to pass the appropriate mark to any Sijun you teach."

Ruwen bowed to Dusk, altering his mark to that of a Master, just as she wore.

As Ruwen stood, Dusk locked eyes with him.

"Not all shadows..." Dusk whispered.

"Fear the light," Ruwen finished.

Dusk bowed, and Ruwen's chest warmed. He'd done it. Navigated himself and Sift out of the storm that had surrounded them. This trial had resulted in amazing success, not only for himself, but for everyone here. It made him proud, and he allowed himself something he never did enough: a moment of pleasure.

CHAPTER 72

*M*inimized notifications appeared in Ruwen's vision as Dusk handed him his new uniform and pressed a relic token into his palm. "Congratulations," she whispered. "Our Clan owes you so much. I'll notify Kysandra of your rank so she can begin your training."

Until Ruwen broke the prison around his soul, he would likely not successfully move between the Material and Shadow Realms like other Shadow Steppers.

Dusk continued. "I had hoped Kysandra could be here today, but the short notice must have made it impossible, as she didn't respond."

"Thank you, Founder. The trials have proved..." Ruwen struggled to find another word, but after a second, smiled and just said it. "Enlightening."

Dusk returned the smile. "Good. It is what we intended."

As Ruwen returned to the back of the class and Sift, he worried about Kysandra's absence. The Mistress of the Black Pyramid and head of a massive spy organization, and who knew what else, probably had something important going on and couldn't just jump over to watch him get a belt. But he also worried that she might have gotten in trouble. Maybe the same trouble as Hamma and Lylan, and it reinforced his eagerness to get home.

When Ruwen reached Sift, Thorn addressed the class. "Your required time here is almost over. The Soul Pearls used to power many of our Clan spells, enchantments, and of course the Journeyman Trial's Crossing Stone, are found around Victory Lake in the Red Forest. The forest holds many hazards and the closer you get to Champion Fortress, the more danger you'll encounter."

Champion. Sift signaled to Ruwen in Shade Speak.

Mist continued. "We hope each of you can find five pearls. The more translucent they appear, the better. Regardless, the portal to the lake will remain open and after an hour you are to return. Any longer gives the Shattered Clan time to mount an attack. They hold the Fortress and have patrols looking for other Clans at the lake."

Dusk spoke next. "From now on, twice a day, we will open the portal to Victory Lake. If more than one Master goes, you can venture off alone, which makes you less visible, or stay together, which adds safety. It is a balance. At sunrise and sunset, for those who wish to finish their required time here, a portal is available."

Ruwen looked at the sun, which had almost reached the horizon. He felt eager to get home, see his friends and family, and address the problems there. "Including today's sunset?"

Dusk glanced at the setting sun and back at Ruwen. "Yes. We will portal back to the village shortly, and then send anyone interested to Savage Island. Congratulations. Never has the Bamboo Viper Clan had such a successful class. Be proud of what you've accomplished."

The Founders bowed, and the Masters returned it.

Ruwen strode directly to the vault door and handed his four relic tokens to the Quartermaster.

497

"I don't have room to bring out the relics," the Quarter-master said. "You'll need to wait until tomorrow at the beach."

Ruwen had planned for that, and because he didn't care about the relics, he listed off the four he'd glanced at earlier before picking Tarot. "That's okay. If they're still available, I'll take the Boundless Bribe, Lightning Spine, Soothing Stone, and Broken Time, please."

The Quartermaster raised his eyebrows, and Ruwen smiled. The old man disappeared into the depths of the vault, grumbling to himself. Ruwen planned to portal home as soon as he finished his hour at Savage Island and wanted to get rid of the relic tokens. The excitement of going back home made his heart race, and he forced himself to calm down.

Sift stepped up beside Ruwen.

"Rung Four is coming with us," Sift said. "Some of the others might as well. I think everyone wants to get home."

"I'm so excited to see everyone."

"Me too. I really wish Shelly would come back. I'm worried if we portal home, it will be too far for her to reach me."

Ruwen knew Sift's fear had no basis in reality. Shelly had literally traveled across the Universe to fetch Ruwen, and because his connection to Uru and Blapy remained, he guessed this planet likely sat in the same galaxy, or a nearby one. Which equated to a tiny step for the Elder Star Tortoise.

Instead of saying that, Ruwen patted Sift on the shoulder. "I'm sure she'll show up. She always does."

"Yeah, that's true."

The Quartermaster returned with the four small items and handed them to Ruwen. He glanced at their descriptions again.

Name: *Boundless Bribe*
Effect: *Flip coin and press against any item to use as a bribe.*
Description: *Worn gold coin. Imbued with illusion magic this coin imprints an item with the recipient's greatest financial desire.*

Name: *Lightning Spine*
Effect: *Symbols scratched into the skin will absorb lightning until triggered.*
Effect: *Lightning Immunity with active symbol.*
Description: *A quill from a Cloud Razor. Symbol may itch and burn. If not discharged manually, the symbol will explode when the skin heals.*

Name: *Soothing Stone*
Effect: *Fear immunity.*
Description: *A river stone from a stream on Mount Jasper. Rubbing the stone for 6 seconds calms the mind. You hear the faint sound of a babbling stream.*

Name: *Broken Time*
Effect: *Stop time.*
Description: *Fashionable men's watch with a leather strap. When the current time matches the value of the timepiece and the wearer is touching the crystal face, the wearer becomes unstuck from time for three seconds, disappearing from sight and gaining an extra three seconds to perform actions undetectable to others.*

Ruwen bowed to the old Master and dropped the four items into his Void Band for Fractal. It felt good to be rid of the tokens. Nothing held him here anymore. In just over an hour, he'd be home.

The Founders and Addas created a portal back to the village and once there, Dusk told everyone it would take ten minutes before the Founders and Addas could power the portal to Savage Island. The five of them sat around the portal, meditating to regenerate their soul power more quickly.

Ruwen thought about drawing the gate runes himself with his portal chalk but decided it might come across as rude. Especially since the wait was only ten minutes. Sift wandered toward the beach, following a group of seabirds and trying to mimic their whistle. Ruwen stayed by the stone and went through the rest of his minimized notifications.

The first didn't surprise Ruwen, considering the importance of what he'd discovered about himself.

Gong!
You have increased your Knowledge!
Level: *171*

Twelve extra points in Knowledge almost didn't seem like enough.

The next notification was one Ruwen had never seen before.

Thrum!
*The Soul Oath, **Darkness Holds No Shadows**, has become invalid...*
Violation: *Restriction - Bamboo Step Rank of Master Required*
Violation: *Restriction – Viper Step Rank of Master Required*
Explanation: *Current rank exceeds quest rank.*

It appeared Uru invalidated commitments that could no longer be completed. Probably to stop the awarding of experience or rewards to those who skipped steps. In this instance, since he'd never became a Master to trigger the completion of this quest, coupled with his current rank of Grandmaster, meant Uru considered this quest prohibited.

And the next notification contained the same thing, only this time it referenced a quest.

Ting!
*The Quest, **Last Steps**, has become invalid...*
Violation: *Reward - Bamboo Step Master*
Violation: *Reward - Viper Step Master*
Explanation: *Current rank exceeds reward rank.*

Losing easy experience and rewards disappointed Ruwen, but it also meant none of the penalties triggered, and some of those had included marking him for death.

Shing!
You have advanced a skill!
Skill: *Unarmed Combat*
Level: *1,004*
Effect: *Increase unarmed damage by 502.0%. Increase chance to deflect or dodge a blow by 502.0%.*

UNARMED COMBAT HAD INCREASED from seven hundred eighteen to one thousand and four, a gain of two hundred eighty-six points. With Ruwen's new understanding of balance and the connection he had with his surroundings from Harmony, he believed he could now face anyone in unarmed combat without fear, even the gods.

Shing!
You have advanced a skill!
Skill: *Bamboo Step Mastery*
Level: *199*
Effect: *Increase Armor Class by 199, Increase Dodge to 199%.*

Shing!
You have advanced a skill!
Skill: *Viper Step Mastery*
Level: *199*
Effect: *Increase Haste to 199%, Increase Critical Strike to 199%.*

Now that Ruwen had passed the rank of Master, the Bamboo and Viper levels over ninety-nine had opened to him, and they had both jumped a hundred levels.

The next notifications came from when Dusk had handed Ruwen his new belt and uniform.

Tring!
The Bamboo Viper Clan has gifted you...

Name: *Grandmaster Belt*
Quality: *Rare*
Durability: *50 of 50*
Weight: *1.0 lbs.*
Armor Class: *100*
Effect: *10 slots of dimensional storage. Open and close by running two fingers along belt.*
Effect (Triggered): *Whispering Grove – For five seconds all communication, including telepathic, vocalized, sign, and vibrational, in a 500-foot radius is replaced by the gentle sound of wind through a bamboo grove.*
Effect (Triggered): *Constriction – Belt will wrap and hold the first entity that contacts the wearer.*
Restriction: *Bamboo Viper Step Grandmaster*
Description: *A black heavy-cotton belt. Balance is crucial in all things.*

Name: *Grove Jacket of the Grandmaster*
Quality: *Rare*
Durability: *100 of 100*
Weight: *2.6 lbs.*
Armor Class: *500*
Effect (Triggered): *Warming Rays – Absorbs up to 90% of light striking the wearer, and alters the angle of reflected light, effectively lowering the Perception of an observer by 500% and making the wearer invisible when standing still.*
Effect (Triggered): *Calming Grove - Creates a grove of illusionary*

bamboo in a 500 foot radius reducing visibility to five feet. Members of the Bamboo Viper Clan are immune.
Restriction: *Bamboo Step Grandmaster.*
Description: *Heavy-cotton long jacket. Like bamboo, you are strong and flexible.*

Name: *Nest Pants of the Grandmaster*
Quality: *Rare*
Durability: *100 of 100*
Weight: *2.4 lbs.*
Armor Class: *500*
Effect (Passive): *Toxic Resistance – Increases Poison, Acid, and Disease Resistances by 100%.*
Effect (Passive): *Snake Skin – Increases Armor Class by 1% per rank of Grandmaster.*
Restriction: *Viper Step Grandmaster*
Description: *Heavy-cotton pants with reinforced seams. Like a viper, you are quick and deadly.*

The gear had far more benefits than Ruwen had expected. Even on Grave, where magic filled the entire world, this uniform would be considered superb, especially for cloth. The Master gear probably wasn't quite this good, but he guessed it would still seem godly on the worlds the other Masters had come from.

Ruwen glanced at his Profile and two values jumped out at him. The skill increases had pushed his Dodge to one thousand and nine percent. He had become literally untouchable. His Haste had increased to three hundred thirty-four percent, and a punch with his normal buffs and enhancements would cause over three hundred fifty damage. Of course, that was calculated at a normal velocity. Using Diamond Strength, he guessed he could shatter walls.

The Founders and Addas stood and grouped around the

portal stone. Ruwen closed his Profile and turned to find Sift. Instead, Ruwen found the entire class behind him, including Echo. It seemed everyone wanted to finish tonight, and it made him happy they'd do it together.

Sift stood two hundred feet away, his new uniform pants soaked as he stood knee deep in the ocean, head bent back as he whistled at the circling birds.

Ruwen used *Sphere of Influence* to speak directly to Sift's mind. *Come on. It's time to finish this.*

CHAPTER 73

The Red Forest got its name, Ruwen realized, from the blood-colored trees that surrounded a massive lake. Mountains circled them, but above the peaks he noticed giant plumes of smoke and ash. The ground trembled periodically, as if it had caught a fever. Whatever damage the small pressure wave had created, it appeared long term.

Tarot used his deck of cards like an air sled and bounced across the water in front of them, moving back and forth and leaving rings of waves with every touch, like some type of possessed skipping stone.

Sift stared at the giant fortress nestled between two mountain peaks on the opposite side of the lake. He turned his attention to Tarot. "You called me Champion of Champions. Does that include this place?"

"Are you asking for another reading?" Tarot asked.

"No, he's not," Ruwen said. "We don't have time for that." He shifted his focus to Sift. "It's too far. We're only here an hour."

"You could jump there in a few minutes," Sift said. "And I can fly."

Ruwen glanced around at the class. Echo had disappeared as

usual, but everyone else walked the sandy area between the trees and the lake, heads down, looking for pearls.

Ruwen turned back to Sift. "What's your plan?"

"Find the Champion's Throne and claim it."

"And if the Champion is there?"

Sift grinned. "Fight him."

Ruwen sighed. Sift studied the distant fortress and Ruwen glanced around again. The learning portion of the trials had finished. The Adepts had all become Masters, and Ruwen didn't need to babysit them. It meant he could use his magic guilt free, and he activated *Survey* and *Stone Echo*, spreading his awareness in a five-hundred-foot sphere.

In addition to the information in *Survey*, Ruwen used his Diamond Perception to analyze the areas outside his *Stone Echo* bubble. Small animals in the forest, soil, and water were the only things he detected. Not anything to cause the remotest bit of worry. He spent another thirty seconds straining every sense to make sure. These Masters had become his friends, and he didn't want to leave if any hint of danger existed.

Ruwen couldn't find any threats, and the fact that Sift had only mentioned going to the fortress twice meant it really mattered to him. When things weren't important, he used them to poke Ruwen. Significant things, though, Sift didn't push. Maybe because hearing Ruwen say no hurt too much.

"How low can you fly and not constantly crash?" Ruwen asked. "Uru help me, I can't believe I called what you do flying."

Sift smirked. "Under the trees for sure."

Ruwen doubted that. He used *Survey* to plot a route and calculated if he ran just below the air explosion speed, they could make the fortress in under five minutes.

"Let me talk to Prythus," Ruwen said.

Sift nodded and Ruwen strode over to Prythus and Nymthus who walked together, smiles on their faces, unable to contain the excitement of going home in less than an hour. Nymthus would return to her husband, and Prythus to his niece and nephew, both protecting all they had left.

Ruwen felt immense satisfaction about the progress of Rung Four. They had in the short time here, under his and Sift's guidance, caught up with some of the Masters in Rung One. With the eight new schools these Masters would create, they could train fighters capable of destroying the demon plague, giving them a chance to reclaim their world.

Prythus and Nymthus placed their palms on their fists and gave a short bow as Ruwen approached.

"Grandmaster," Prythus said. "How can we serve?"

Ruwen waved his hand. "Just Ruwen is fine. Hey, I looked around and we seem alone. How do you feel about Sift and I leaving for a while?"

"There are thirty Masters here," Prythus said. "I can't imagine what could cause us trouble."

Nymthus nodded. "I trust you would have detected a large group. You and Sift should leave." She grinned. "Don't forget your five pearls, though. We can't be carrying you."

Ruwen laughed. "I understand. Sift tells me all the time what a burden I am." He grew serious. "Keep everyone near the portal stone. If there is any trouble, immediately retreat. I don't care about the hour or the five soul pearls. Leave."

Nymthus and Prythus both mirrored Ruwen's seriousness.

"We will, Grandmaster," Prythus said.

Ruwen sighed. "Okay, then. I'll see you soon."

Nymthus and Prythus bowed, and Ruwen returned it.

Ruwen strode to Sift. "Okay, Champ. Let's go."

Sift grinned and turned on Ruwen. "Some days you are almost bearable, Starfield."

"Funny, Hamma says the same thing," Ruwen replied. He turned to Tarot. "Are you coming?"

"No," Tarot said. "I don't like the view from the throne. I'll wait here."

Ruwen turned to Sift. "I guess it's just us."

Sift's golden eyes faded as white light covered them. His feet rose off the ground a few feet and Ruwen nodded, acknowledging Sift's stability.

"Race you," Sift said, and then shot headfirst down the beach like a siege bolt.

"Not fair," Ruwen mumbled.

Ruwen ran near the tree line. Jumping would have gone faster, but he wanted to stay under the trees to avoid attention. It wouldn't have mattered though, as he needed full control over his Gravity Shell to compete with Sift's speed.

Only once did Sift almost crash, but he recovered and never even slowed. Ruwen had to admit Sift had gained real flying skills.

They reached the outer wall of the fortress and Ruwen glanced back at the lake. He couldn't see any activity, and Rung Four and the rest of the class were undetectable this far away. To see the distant Masters would take special skills. He didn't like splitting from the group but knew he had drifted too close to becoming overprotective.

Sift levitated quickly to the top of the wall and Ruwen jumped the seventy feet. The wind gusts on top of the wall had a lot more strength than the breeze down below, and it whipped their hair around. They kneeled on the empty parapet while studying the city.

The fortress consisted of many three-story square buildings along wide streets that ran in straight lines. The city spanned over a mile but felt smaller because of the looming snow-covered mountains that surrounded it. Whoever designed the layout had made moving large numbers of troops quickly around the city easy. While ugly, it looked incredibly practical.

Demons ran around in small, armored groups, but Ruwen couldn't make any sense of their purpose.

Sift whispered what Ruwen had concluded as well. "It's like they're all running around to look busy."

Ruwen pointed at the largest building to their left. "I'm guessing that's headquarters and the location of your throne."

The streets between here and there contained thousands of demons.

"Can you make that jump?" Sift asked, pointing between the fortress wall and the throne building.

At its closest point, three hundred feet separated the two structures. "Yes, but the issue is height. To make it that far, I need a running start, which means starting outside the wall. But my path through the air will take me pretty high. High enough to be noticed, probably."

"I could carry you."

"Sorry, I value my life too much. Plus, I'm not sure you could carry me. I weigh a lot more after the Gem transition."

Sift puffed out his cheeks. "You should cut back on the sweets."

Ruwen's body fat percent, even before the transition to Gem, had hovered around five percent. Every muscle he had appeared on the verge of pushing through his skin. Not to mention, he rarely even ate.

"It's your lack of strength I'm worried about," Ruwen said, and squeezed Sift's bicep.

While Ruwen had a more athletic build, Sift had always been lean. Sift flexed his arm, causing his bicep to bulge. "I'm a Springing Frenzy to your appah."

"I don't even know what that means," Ruwen said and shook his head. "How did we get on this topic?" He pinched his heavy cotton jacket. "This hides me, but not when I'm moving fast, which probably makes jumping too dangerous."

"Just use your jacket to walk through the streets."

"That seems risky."

"What about your gravity thing?"

"I have to be super careful not to use Spirit because my insides are hurt. Anything that costs Spirit will drain my Mana bar first, and even if I use the Sublime Centipede of Solace Miranda gave me, I'll only have another five thousand Mana banked there. If I blow through all of it, and tap my core, I could damage myself permanently, and I don't know how much Mana the Gravity Shell consumes."

"A simple no is fine."

"Sorry, I have a problem with information."

"No kidding. If you took all the time you spent explaining things and did something useful, you'd have a million skills."

"A million? Really? I just want you to have the full context."

"If every time you gave me the 'full context' you had planted a flower instead, you'd be a master planter."

"I don't think planter is a job."

"It's called farming."

"So I could be a master flower farmer?"

"Exactly. Think how useful that would be."

Ruwen rubbed his temples. "We did it again. Let's focus."

Sift returned his attention to the city. "You could hop from building to building."

"That's better than all at once," Ruwen said. "Aren't you worried about being seen?"

"No. I'll be across that distance in a blink. It would be safer for both of us, though, if we had a distraction."

Ruwen checked his Inventory to remind himself what the eggs he'd gotten from the Savage Seven level in Fractal did. He had seventeen of each colored egg. The seven colors corresponded to the colors of item quality, and the legendary purple eggs contained all the effects of the previous six eggs. It produced an explosion with bright light, deafening noise, thick smoke, intense flames, a concussive blast, and flammable gel.

"I have an idea for that," Ruwen said.

"Of course you do. How about an idea to get into that building. Are you slow playing this so we need to go back without seeing the throne?"

"No," Ruwen said, probably too quickly. The thought had crossed his mind. He glanced through his spells to see if a solution struck him.

Ruwen groaned.

"What?" Sift asked.

"I have an idea, but it's terrible."

"A terrible idea beats no idea."

Ruwen tilted his head. "I don't think that's true."

"Spill it."

Ruwen sighed again. "I could use my jacket to hide, and use *Move On* to create a four-inch-wide bridge, three hundred feet long. Then I'll put two spell points in a level six Worker spell *Steady* to enhance my balance and make falling impossible. I should be able to walk straight over."

"You're a Diamond Fortified Bamboo Viper Grandmaster and you're going to put two points in a spell called *Steady*?"

Ruwen pointed at the sky. "It's really windy."

"Your plan," Sift acted out planting a flower. "Is too complicated. Just create a distraction, and we go for it. If things go sideways, we retreat and hightail it back to the others."

Ruwen considered that for a moment. "That is easier."

Sift tapped his temple with a finger. "Simple, Brother."

"Yes, you are," Ruwen replied with a smile.

CHAPTER 74

*B*efore Sift could respond, Ruwen jumped off the wall on the lake side, and ran along the stone until *Survey* and *Stone Echo* displayed the area directly across from the throne building. Sift had followed through the air and dropped to the ground next to Ruwen.

"You ready?" Ruwen asked.

"Do you need to ask?"

"Okay," Ruwen said. "These purple eggs make a mess. I'm going to lob it over the city to the far side, past the wall. I don't want to hit a building because I don't want anyone looking up and accidentally seeing us instead."

Sift bent to plant a flower, and Ruwen swept Sift's legs, but instead of falling to the ground, Sift levitated into the air with soul magic.

"That's cheating," Ruwen whispered.

"Come on, let's go," Sift replied.

"Fine."

Ruwen stepped twenty feet away from the wall, opened his Void Band a foot, and angled it over the parapet. He recalled how much Energy he'd used when launching other things out of his Void Band, like Blessed Bricks and Lylan. The egg was light, only about three ounces, and he didn't want to overshoot the far wall too much and make the distraction useless.

"How hard can throwing an egg be?" Sift asked.

"It's complicated."

Sift hovered ten feet off the ground, moving back and forth as if pacing. Ruwen rechecked his calculations, and then, using three hundred sixty-three Energy, launched a Savage Purple Egg over the wall. He breathed a sigh of relief because he'd worried the force of the acceleration might trigger the egg as soon as it left his Inventory.

Ruwen guessed the egg traveled around two thousand eight hundred feet per second, and if his calculations were correct, it would take just under three seconds to detonate.

"Get ready," Ruwen said to Sift.

Ruwen turned his head to the side, listening intently for the explosion. Three seconds passed, and he frowned. Had he miscalculated? At ten seconds, he stood up straight.

"What's wrong?" Sift asked. "Did you miss?"

"How can I miss the ground? It should have exploded ten seconds ago."

Sift twisted his lip. "That's weird. Do they go bad? Maybe you should have kept them cold."

"That's dumb. They're exploding eggs, not baking supplies."

Sift shrugged. "Did they come out a chicken's butt?"

Memories of the Savage Seven raising their rear ends and shooting the eggs at Ruwen filled his thoughts. He kept silent, not wanting to admit Sift had guessed right.

"That's how baking eggs are born," Sift said. "You should have stored them with ice. You'd make a terrible baker."

"It can't work like that," Ruwen said, a little too loudly. "These eggs explode in this huge," Ruwen waved his hands. "Explosion."

"I'm not sure they do," Sift said, looking into the sky as if judging the time. "It's been like ten minutes."

"It's only been one," Ruwen muttered. "There has to be an explanation."

A gust of wind blew Ruwen's hair into his face, and he angrily pushed it to the side so he could see. A realization struck him.

"Oh, no," Ruwen whispered.

Sift saw Ruwen's expression. "What happened?"

Ruwen pointed up. "The wind. That egg is only three ounces."

Sift dropped to the ground and walked backward toward Ruwen as he studied the sky. "Where did it go, then? It can't go up forever."

Ruwen studied the sky as well. "I honestly don't know."

"It could be halfway around the world by now," Sift said. "We're running out of time. Let's just go without the distraction."

Ruwen bit his lip. He had no idea where the egg had gone. The wind, trapped in between the surrounding mountains, had erratic patterns. In fact, with the deep snow covering so much of the stone, the egg could have landed softly and not exploded.

"Okay, let's go," Ruwen said.

Sift grinned. "All right. On the count of three. Three!"

Sift shot off the ground and just cleared the top of the fortress wall.

"Cheater," Ruwen mumbled as he ran forward five steps and leaped, *Survey* displaying exactly where to aim.

Ruwen flew over the wall, not far behind Sift, but Sift, with control of his trajectory, kept a low arc, while Ruwen sailed high into the air. They would land in the same spot, but it would take him four seconds longer.

At the top of Ruwen's arc, high above the city, the Purple Savage Egg finally met something solid. The wind had carried it high into the air, slamming it into a massive snowfield. Far from being expired, the egg detonated in spectacular fashion. The massive boom echoed between the mountain peaks, and the bright flash appeared like a second sun in the sky. Smoke rose from the snow as the flammable gel covering it burned.

Loud snaps quickly followed as a colossal snow and ice sheet, covered in fire, slid down the mountain and toward the city.

Everyone turned their gaze upward, including all the demons in the courtyard of the throne building. The largest demon snarled at Ruwen, the awful sound causing his skin to flush. The demons watched Ruwen as he landed perfectly on the roof next to Sift.

Sift stared at the mountain of burning snow sliding toward the city. "Definitely not expired."

Ruwen closed his eyes in frustration. The demons below shouted as they organized themselves to attack, and he considered the terrible timing of that explosion. What an incredible piece of bad luck.

"If it wasn't for bad luck," Sift said.

"We wouldn't have any luck at all," Ruwen finished.

"We better go."

"Sorry, Sift."

"I know. It's not your fault. Well, mostly not."

Ruwen glanced at the avalanche high above and *Survey* calculated its speed and distance. The flaming sheet of destruction had already accelerated to sixty miles per hour and would reach them in less than four minutes.

The avalanche made Ruwen's brain itch, but before he could focus his Cleverness, he felt a pressure wave rising from the courtyard and turned his body to face it.

The large demon that had growled at Ruwen earlier landed on the roof twenty feet away. It had leaped thirty feet up to reach them, and pulled itself to its twelve-foot height. Black bristles covered its skin like armor. It didn't have a tail, but a small hood rose from its neck, surrounding the head like a cobra. Two black eyes sat over a vertical slit the demon breathed through. It also had a small eye on each edge of the hood. The combination would give the demon depth perception, along with an excellent view of its surroundings. Teeth filled a circle shaped mouth below its breathing slit.

Perception provided more details.

Name: *Scourge Champion*
Deity: *Lalquinrial*
Class Type: *Cultivator - Diamond*
Level: *74*
Health: *2,950*
Mana: *0*
Energy: *6,600*
Spirit: *500,000,000*
Armor Class: *1,700*

"Foolish men, to enter my city," the Champion hissed as its clawed feet dug into the stone roof.

Ruwen sighed and nodded at the Scourge Champion. Sift didn't speak Inferni and couldn't understand the demon, and his Perception likely wouldn't provide much information. "I'm not sure this counts as good luck, but here's your Champion."

Sift looked from Ruwen to the Champion, smiled, and pointed at the demon. "I've come for my throne."

The demon didn't understand Sift, but recognized the challenge, and the short bristles covering its body rose, revealing scaley grey skin.

Ruwen Analyzed the Scourge Champion.

Target: *Scourge Champion*
Type: *Creature (Gem)*

Strengths: *Toxic Saliva, Poison Barbs, Visibility Arc*
Weaknesses: *Order, Elemental-Cold, Hearing*
Disposition: *Hostile*

"We need to leave in three minutes, so don't screw around," Ruwen told Sift. "It probably spits something terrible, has good vision, and I think it shoots those barbs. It doesn't like cold, and its hearing is weak."

"Thanks," Sift said, his attention focused on the Scourge Champion.

Ruwen jumped to the building's edge, away from demon, so it and Sift could settle the issue of the true Champion.

CHAPTER 75

A demon from the now visible courtyard threw a bone spear at Ruwen. He caught the weapon and threw it back, not bothering to turn it spearhead first. It slammed into the attacking demon, vaporizing its chest, and traveled through three more creatures before shattering against the stone ground.

The demons below grew still and then, in a pack, fled the courtyard, leaving their four dead companions.

The avalanche had created a constant rumbling vibration and Ruwen glanced at the oncoming wall of burning snow and ice. Its speed had increased, and *Survey* updated its calculated arrival time, decreasing the time they had by thirteen seconds.

Between the avalanche and being discovered, this had turned from a fun adventure into something more serious, and Ruwen wanted to buff both himself and Sift. But Ruwen already knew Sift would complain about the buffs, because he wanted to beat the Champion with just his own abilities. For now, Ruwen would honor that.

Instead, Ruwen cast his worthwhile individual buffs, as their situation had turned uncertain. He started with the Worker's

Sick Day to increase his Resistances by ten percent for forty Mana, followed by the Fighter spell *Hustle* to add ten percent to his Haste for thirty minutes, and *Power Nap* to increase his out of combat Health Regen by fifty percent.

Leeching Blow, one of the few spells Ruwen had increased to level five, healed him twenty-five percent of the damage he dealt for half an hour. His Commander Subclass spell *Relentless* was another maxed spell, and he cast it, increasing his Energy Regeneration by twenty-five percent for thirty minutes. *Quartermaster's Yell* decreased the resource cost of all his spells by fifty percent and potions became fifty percent more effective. *Emissary's Shout* increased his Perception and Speed by ten percent. And *Warlord's Roar* increased his Armor Class and damage by fifty percent.

Ruwen wore his Bamboo Viper jacket, pants, and belt, and didn't want to change out of it into his Inklord Wrap or Overseer armor. As his Mana bar refilled from the cost of the buffs, he dropped the Sublime Centipede of Solace into his right hand.

The small totem looked like an actual centipede. It had the sick green color of mucus and its black eyes seemed dead and uncaring. Its spread, bile-colored wings, gave it the shape of a cross.

Ruwen placed the totem inside his jacket, hoping he wouldn't need to rely on the items five-thousand-point Mana bank. He couldn't cast any Spirit spells or use his Architect Role as they tapped the Spirit in his core after draining his Mana. If he accidentally depleted his Mana bar in the heat of battle, he wanted a buffer, and the totem provided that.

Ten small pressure waves approached Ruwen from the area Sift and the Champion fought. Ruwen glanced at the pair as he dodged the flying barbs the Scourge Champion had launched in all directions.

Sift's eyes had filled with white soul Energy and it covered his body as well. He would need the added durability the soul

Energy provided as the Scourge Champion had fortified to low Diamond Ruwen guessed, making the demon's strikes painful on a Metal-Fortified body like Sift's.

The Champion lunged at Sift, trying to scrape its claws across Sift's neck. Sift used the Bamboo Step Lost Ladybug to shift the strike downward. In quick succession, Sift struck the demon's forearm with the Viper Step Stone Drum, numbing the demon's arm for five to ten seconds, followed by Hidden Knife which delivered an elbow to the chin.

The demon didn't have a chin however so Sift turned the attack into a backhand across the demon's face. It did no damage but succeeded in enraging the Champion further.

Sift appeared to have complete control of the fight.

Ruwen triggered his Commander Ability *Ringleader* and formed a group with Sift. Using *Chat*, he spoke to Sift. *I'm not sure how hard it will be to escape this city, so I'm buffing up, and I only want to cast these party buffs once so I'm doing them now. You obviously can beat this guy so no complaining.*

Fine. Sift said as he stepped over the demon's attempt at a sweep.

Ruwen cast his Energy buffs, including *Bodyguard* on Sift, which would transfer sixty percent of Sift's damage to Ruwen. Then he picked the five Warlord *Banner* buffs, choosing them to maximize a safe retreat while dealing with any demons that got in their way.

Havoc, the first *Banner* buff Ruwen cast would increase their damage by twenty-five percent. *Awareness* would increase Perception by twenty-five percent, which had a bigger effect on Sift, since Ruwen's Perception, because of Rami's second Codex of Evolution, had already doubled.

Next Ruwen cast *Forced March* to increase their movement speed by thirty-five percent, and *Unrelenting* to increase their Regen rates by thirty percent. Finally, he cast *Indestructible* to increase their Armor Class by twenty-five percent.

Ruwen glanced at his Profile, checking the main items the buffs had affected. His Mana hadn't yet recovered from all the spells, but would shortly.

Pools
Health: *2,657/2,657*
Mana: *1,168/2,204*
Energy: *4,026/4,026*

Ratings
Armor Class: *8,785*

Regeneration
Health Regeneration per second: *31*
Mana Regeneration per second: *32*
Energy Regeneration per second: *293*

All Ruwen's Resistances hovered around one hundred nineteen percent, except for his Mind Resistance, which had climbed to six hundred seventy-two percent. All his stats had incredible values, but his Armor Class, with all the compounding benefits, buffs, and enhancements, staggered him. Even a little bit of extra AC, like the jacket and pants he wore, increased the value drastically.

The vibration from the approaching avalanche grew stronger and Ruwen glanced at the wall of burning snow. *Survey* displayed they had less than two minutes. The rest of the class, across the lake, would remain safe from the wall of snow, but he worried about them anyway. So he removed a ring from his Inventory, and slid it onto a finger.

Ruwen rubbed the Watcher's Ring of Travel, and Whiskers appeared in his giant panther travel form. The cat lowered its head, and he scratched Whiskers between the ears. The last time he'd summoned the cat had been outside the walls of New Eiru.

The newly created Overlord had ridden Whiskers toward the advancing army.

"I missed you, too, friend," Ruwen mumbled.

Ruwen changed Whiskers' form to the small urban cat and sent it to escape the city and check on the Masters on the beach across the lake. He stayed with the cat long enough to see most of the streets were empty as the demons sought safety inside the city's buildings.

A sharp pain forced Ruwen to refocus on the rooftop fight, and his Health bar dropped by fifty points. He found Sift rubbing his forearm and realized *Bodyguard* had shifted sixty percent of the damage and pain of Sift's injury to Ruwen.

Sorry, Sift said in *Chat*. *I didn't expect touching that weapon to hurt.*

The Scourge Champion held a white spear created from soul energy, and he stabbed at Sift again. Sift didn't block the spear this time, which evidently caused damage, and dodged instead, landing a quick kick to the Champion's hand.

The Champion released the spear but it remained attached to his hand, an obvious advantage to soul Energy weapons. Even with a Gem-Fortified body, the Champion could not match Sift's speed. Add in Sift's complete control and mastery of the Bamboo Viper Steps, and the Champion had no chance.

We should go, Ruwen told Sift. *I don't want to spend an hour digging out of the snow.*

I didn't want to rush the fight in case he had a surprise like that spear. I'll hurry.

Ruwen studied Sift's Steps and found them nearly flawless. The moves radiated a confidence mixed with deadly beauty that transfixed Ruwen. The next time Sift competed at the Step Championship, the crowd would adore him.

Whiskers made it out of the city and Ruwen transformed the cat into the puma sized scout. It gave the cat more options for camouflage in the wild and Whiskers dashed down the beach, just in the tree line of the Red Forest.

"Of course," a male voice said.

"We should have guessed," a female voice responded.

Ruwen recognized the voices and his stomach knotted. He turned his back to Sift and the Champion and looked down into the courtyard. On the far side, two hundred feet away, sat two figures on unnatural horses.

The Pestilence Aspect sat atop a yellow horse, and his sister, the Plague Aspect rode a green horse beside him. They both had pulled their hoods forward, and Ruwen knew it hid the infected sores that covered their faces.

Pestilence turned from his sister and looked up at Ruwen. Blood oozed from the Aspect's eyes, leaving fresh streaks across the dried blood covering its cheeks. Plague didn't look any better, as her eyes leaked yellow pus.

Plague sneezed, and a cloud of green mucus sprayed into the courtyard. Her breathing remained raspy and labored, and she hunched over, trembling under her robe as if she suffered from a fever.

The appearance of the two Aspects meant the situation had become dire.

Sift, Ruwen said over *Chat. There are Aspects here and you need to leave immediately.*

What are you going to do?

Delay them.

But—

Ruwen interrupted him. *Don't argue. We—*

The word "we" made Ruwen pause. Plague had used that word. It's possible she just meant her brother and her, but it also might mean something far worse.

Ruwen shifted his focus to Whiskers. The cat had superb eyesight and he could make out the distant Masters searching the beach for Soul Pearls. He relaxed a little at seeing them safe. To be sure, he asked Whiskers to glance at the lake.

Ruwen's breath caught.

Three figures, each atop a horse, galloped across the lake. The Aspect of War on a red horse, Drought riding a blue one, and Poison between them on a white horse.

They rode directly toward the group of new Bamboo Viper Clan Masters. Ruwen's classmates. His friends.

They didn't face two Aspects, but five.

The itch in Ruwen's mind that had started with the avalanche became a shard of ice at the number five. The mental icicle exploded as his Cleverness Attribute triggered, and the splinters shredded his mind, slowly crystalizing around a single memory of Tarot, glowing with golden-silver light, giving Ruwen his fortune in a somber voice…*I, Tarotmethiophelius, a Divine Fortune Golem forged from the mists of heaven, touching past, present, and future, offer this fortune. Ruwen Starfield, the tenth muse, keeper of the scales, and holy father, hear me. Your plans, buried under an avalanche of the past, will suffocate and fail. Harken the wolf and the path not taken, or death will surely find you.*

Ruwen had believed this fortune described the plans he'd made to challenge the Founders. That the prepared and determined foes had meant the three Sisters. He had assumed the mistakes Tarot had mentioned when examining the three cards had referenced Ruwen teaching Grandmaster Steps and using the Shadow Forms.

After winning the fight with the Founders, Ruwen had believed he'd successfully sprinted along that crumbling cliff, arriving at his destination without a scratch. He'd thought the Reversed Fool, like all the rest of the warnings he received, could be ignored. The wolf attempted to drag the Fool off the cliff and to the safety of the path not taken, which Ruwen realized now had referenced caution.

Instead of that caution, Ruwen had embraced the Chariot

which signified his rush to return here. The Five of Wands had pointed to the five Aspects, prepared and determined, and the Reversed Fool represented the most grievous mistake and act of foolishness, the fact the Aspects could be here at all.

Tarot's voice echoed in Ruwen's mind. *Your plans, buried under an avalanche of the past, will suffocate and fail. Harken the wolf and the path not taken, or death will surely find you.*

Tarot's fortune had foretold this moment. Predicted Ruwen's failure. Prophesied his death.

"here are the Crossing Rings?" Pestilence asked.

"We know the Bamboo Viper Clan was involved," Plague added.

Ruwen triggered Last Breath to give himself time to think.

The last time Ruwen had fought these five Aspects he had access to his Spirit and all the enhanced spells and abilities that brought. Now, he only had Mana. The fight would be far different this time. He needed to use every advantage he could think of to survive this and save his friends.

Ruwen started with a list of priorities to frame his response. Protect Sift. Get back to the beach as fast as possible. Protect everyone while they retreated.

Overlord?

I'm here. This isn't good.

I know.

Tell me what you're thinking.

We practiced with Spirit strengthened spells. Ruwen replied immediately. *These Mana ones will be far more fragile. Worse, the spell Fallen Heroes has a thirty-minute cool down. I'm going to add two spell points to bring the level from three to five. So, when I channel that spell, we'll get five of them, but that's it. I think you should send four toward the beach immediately and use one here.*

No problem.

I'm going to push your ability to multitask. I want to use Stone Carver Valora's Dark Portal, but I can't control two Void Bands at the same time. I'll control mine, and do you think you can manage hers?

I've managed tens of thousands of Minions at the same time, Overlord said. *I can handle five Fallen Heroes and a Void Band.*

Okay. It's just this one can kill us. We need to be mindful of any type of Energy drain.

Understood.

I took all the good stuff out of that Dark Portal. I think it has a lot of square stones from her tunneling and some mud and water. Why don't you focus on defense. That will free me up for offense.

Good idea, Overlord said.

When I fought the Founders, did you feel the Harmony?

I did, and I can replicate it. That ability came from understanding not a skill. We'll be fine for anything that gets close, but area of effect spells are going to give everyone issues.

I know, Ruwen said. *Thankfully the two Aspects specializing in area damage are here, not heading toward my friends.*

I hope you're right. If I remember, Analyze listed it as Massive Area of Effect-Damage. Don't discount their ability to still reach the other Masters.

Good point. Are you ready?

Yeah, but I want to say one thing first, Overlord said. *As much for myself as you. There will be time for guilt and blame later. It's important we stay focused on what we can do right now.*

Thanks. I'm going to distribute some points.

Ruwen opened his Profile and added two spell Points to *Fallen Heroes.* Fifty-nine spell points and thirty-six ability points waited for distribution. He had wanted to save these for the advanced spells and abilities available now that his level had surged to fifty-eight. Knowing how dire the situation had become, he applied them to his current choices instead, bringing every spell or ability he focused on to its max of five.

Hoping to slow the Aspects, Ruwen added the level twelve Collector Spell *Net*. *Jump* doubled his jumping distance now, and *Sick Day* helped his Resistances by fifty percent. *Sixth Sense* now stretched five thousand feet in every direction. That gave him the capability to see things in almost a two-mile circle.

When Ruwen maxed *Campfire* a new advanced option appeared, like what had happened with *Hey You*. The advanced spell, called *Bonfire*, allowed him to create three massive fires that tripled Regen rates for allies within two hundred fifty feet. The best part was they could be attached to people or things and could move.

Chaff now increased Ruwen's Haste by one hundred twenty-five percent. *Melt's* description wasn't very specific, but *Harden* had been so useful, he guessed *Melt* would as well. Hoping to stall the Aspects with conversation after reaching the Masters, he increased *Calm*, adding ten to Charisma and making his Persuasion one hundred fifty percent more effective.

Dig was another utility spell with a vague description that had come in handy and Ruwen advanced it. *Dash* doubled his top speed, and *Scrub* would now do more damage with less Energy. If he maxed the channeled Energy at twenty now, the damage he inflicted on anything he touched became catastrophic.

That left Ruwen with eight emergency Spell points. He moved over to his Abilities and decided how to divide his thirty-six points. Nine Abilities seemed appropriate, and he pushed them all to five, using all the available points.

Ruwen increased *Glow* because he planned on weaponizing the mining set Bliz had given him. *Brawl* doubled his damage now, and *Store* would let him bank another fifty percent of his Mana, Health, and Energy.

Stone Echo now reached two thousand five hundred feet, and

Sunburn converted one hundred percent of any Energy directed at him into his own Energy. *Shell* increased his Armor Class by fifty percent and *Honed* upped his damage by the same.

Iron Stomach doubled all his Resistances and *Weak Link* would now allow his attacks to ignore twenty-five percent of an enemy's armor.

Ruwen accepted all the changes. He hated using all the points as it limited his options, but locking in these capabilities vastly increased his survivability and he didn't regret it.

Ruwen checked his stats so he knew how his choices had affected him in real numbers.

Pools
Health: 3,623/3,623
Mana: 3,005/3,005
Energy: 5,490/5,490

Ratings
Armor Class: 10,685

Regeneration
Health Regeneration per second: 42
Mana Regeneration per second: 44
Energy Regeneration per second: 400

Ruwen's Health had gained a thousand, his Mana eight hundred, and his Energy fourteen hundred. The increased pools had pushed his Regen rates up as well. His Resistances now hovered around two hundred forty-nine, except for his Mind Resistance, which had reached eight hundred two percent.

Armor Class had passed ten thousand and Ruwen wasn't wearing his best gear. More incredible than his AC, was the damage his buffed fist caused. A normal strike, without using his Diamond Strength would do eight hundred sixty damage. A critical strike on a stunned opponent would amplify that to two thousand five hundred seventy-nine.

Ruwen's current stats were the exact reason the deities didn't want a combination of Ascendancy and Cultivation. It gave one person too much power for their level. Power he hoped would be enough to save everyone.

Here we go, Ruwen told Overlord.

Ruwen released Last Breath.

CHAPTER 77

"I have your Crossing Rings," Ruwen yelled down at Pestilence and Plague. "Call back the others."

Plague laughed, the sound bubbling from a throat full of mucus.

"War is too excited about belt collecting, and fresh Masters are his favorite," Pestilence said.

Well, there went Ruwen's plan A.

The Scourge Champion flew over Ruwen's head as Sift threw the demon off the roof.

Echo had sent Ruwen to his Aspect's bind point with a safety measure all the Aspects had. It allowed other Aspects to send an injured one home if they became unconscious. She had activated her Aspect's form to send him, but he couldn't risk triggering the Scarecrow Aspect since he didn't know how much Mana that consumed. He focused on Pestilence and Plague and willed them to their bind point, hoping it would work without the Scarecrow.

Pestilence shook his head. "With an enemy among us, our lord fixed that vulnerability. Now the Aspects portal back on their own."

Plan B had failed as well.

That left the hard way.

Ruwen channeled twenty-five Energy into *Fallen Heroes* and willed them to appear fifty feet behind the two Aspects. They had bare feet and wore the heavy cotton pants and jacket of the Bamboo Viper Clan. They looked identical to him in every way. Overlord took control and four of the five apparitions dashed away in the direction of the lake.

The fifth one called out. "Stop me if you've heard this. Two Aspects walk into a bar."

The Aspects turned to face the *Fallen Hero*, and Ruwen jumped away from the building's edge, landing next to Sift.

Ruwen launched his Emblem of Dominion out of his Void Band and into his right hand. He grabbed Sift's hand and pressed the coin like object into his palm. Blapy had told Ruwen that only fifty of the emblems existed and you had to kill another Ink Lord to get them. But he hoped that was only because they never wanted to give them up freely.

"I Ruwen Starfield do hereby relinquish this Emblem of Dominion to Sift Adda along with my roles and responsibilities as Ink Lord."

The parchment like bracelet on Ruwen's right wrist disappeared and Sift raised his right hand in shock, as the band now wrapped his wrist.

Overlord spoke to Ruwen. *They're headed your way. I couldn't distract them.*

Ruwen focused on Sift and used *Chat*. *Think the word 'wrap,' and don't ask questions.*

Pestilence and Plague jumped to the top of the roof, no longer riding their horses.

The parchment swallowed Sift, and in a blink only a figure remained, wrapped in hundreds of scrolls. Not even his face remained visible. Sentences and words moved across the scrolls giving the armor a hypnotic effect. Ruwen couldn't help but admire how cool it looked. If he'd worn it, his Armor Class would have become even more ridiculous, but Sift, with only a Gold body, would be vulnerable to the Aspects' attacks.

Sift held his arms out in front of him. "What in all that is holy is—"

Ruwen turned and faced Pestilence and Plague. Over *Chat*, he sent the description of the armor to Sift.

Name: *Ink Lord's Wrap*
AC: *2,250*
Quality: *Legendary*
Durability: *3,000 of 3,000*
Weight: *4.3 lbs.*
Effect (Passive): *Know It All: +50 Intelligence.*
Effect (Passive): *First Edition: Reduce all magical damage by 33%.*
Effect (Passive): *Lost and Found: If the Ink Lord is separated from the armor by more than fifty feet, it will teleport to the Ink Lord's right wrist.*
Effect (Triggered): *Top Shelf: Once per hour, create a staircase made from air with a max height of 200 feet and max weight of 500 lbs.*
Effect (Triggered): *Librarian's Hush: Once per day, restore silence to your library by suppressing all sound in a 1,000-foot sphere for five seconds.*
Effect (Triggered): *Book Burning: Once per month, grant elemental immunity to all inanimate objects in a 1,000-foot sphere for thirty minutes.*
Effect (Triggered): *Ink Lord's Paper Knife: Create a small temporary blade suitable for slicing open pages or unruly patrons. Blade's composition dependent on focus. Inflicts 12 to 24 Piercing damage.*
Effect (Triggered): *Bookmark: Set location and, once per day, instantly return there.*
Restriction: *Black Pyramid Ink Lord.*
Description: *Small off-white scroll made from Dragon Spider Webbing. The librarian can wrap and unwrap themselves with a*

thought, offering protection while carrying out the duties of the Black Pyramid Ink Lord. Stain resistant inside and out for the Ink Lord's inevitable bloody demise.

Get to the beach, Ruwen told Sift. *I'm right behind you.*

Ruwen felt Sift lift off the roof and fly away, causing a massive pressure wave.

Plague and Pestilence watched Sift leave as a thunderclap momentarily smothered the sound of the approaching avalanche, now less than a minute away. The air disturbance Sift caused pushed the Aspects' robes back, and Ruwen got another look at the sores and lesions covering the faces of the brother and sister.

"There is nowhere to run," Pestilence said. He smiled, showing rotten teeth, and then pulled the hood of his Aspect forward, hiding his features again.

"Have you not realized yet that you will all die here?" Plague asked.

Ruwen opened his Void Band enough to briefly place his right hand into the portal. He withdrew it, but Valora's Dark Portal now wrapped his right wrist. He wanted to try one more thing before retreating, so he replied.

"I let you live in the Infernal Realm," Ruwen said. "There are no second chances."

The Aspects laughed, a terrible and sickly, sound.

Ruwen used Whiskers to see how much progress the other three Aspects had made. They were two thirds of the way to the beach. He had Whiskers stop and search the beach for Masters. The cat's excellent vision caught site of Nymthus. Saying a silent prayer to Uru, Ruwen tried something he should have done at the start and tried to add Nymthus to his group.

A portrait of Nymthus appeared on the right side of Ruwen's vision.

"So foolish and arrogant," Plague hissed. "We are prepared now, and you will reap what you've sown, Famine."

Ruwen spoke in *Chat*, and Nymthus jerked in surprise at the sudden appearance of his voice in her head. *Nymthus, this is Ruwen. Get everyone to the portal. Danger on the lake.*

Nymthus turned and studied the lake. She yelled, and within seconds everyone ran toward the portal stone which sat hidden inside the Red Forest. Ruwen and Sift wouldn't make it, but the rest of the class would, and he felt immense relief that they'd be safe.

Pestilence tilted his head. "Aren't you in a hurry to help your friends?"

"I'm headed that way," Ruwen responded. "It turns out I have the time to take care of you two before I leave."

"Take care of us?" Plague asked. "Oh, I hope it's a massage," she said, rotating her head in a circle. "My neck is killing me."

Through Whiskers, Ruwen watched the class enter the forest. He couldn't tell if Echo joined them, but he guessed she had placed herself far away so she wouldn't need to act against the other Aspects, or her father's wishes.

Pestilence held out his hands, displaying jagged fingernails. It looked like something had ripped the fingernails off his skin, covering his fingers in blood. "I could use a manicure since you're offering. Breaking granite is so hard on the nails."

That caught Ruwen's attention. Why would Pestilence be breaking stone?

"No?" Pestilence asked. "Maybe one of your classmates will help me."

Ruwen smiled. "Too, late. They'll be gone in moments."

Plague looked at her brother. "Did you hear that? War will be so disappointed. Bamboo Viper black belts are his favorite. It's all he's been talking about since we got here."

Nymthus's voice appeared in Ruwen's head as *Chat* activated, and she sounded upset. *I don't know if anyone can hear me, or if I'm just talking to myself, but it's gone.*

I can hear you, Nymthus, Ruwen replied. *What's gone?*

A terrible feeling washed over Ruwen, and his stomach turned.

The portal, Nymthus said. *It's not here.*

Plague tilted her head. "Didn't I say we prepared for you this time."

Pestilence removed a sack attached to his belt, opened the top, and turned it over. Chunks of stone dropped out of the dimensional bag, making a pile on the roof. The white portal runes, made with soul magic, had not yet faded, and Ruwen recognized them. It was their portal home.

"Now you start to see," Pestilence said.

"Like I told you," Plague added. "You're all going to die."

CHAPTER 78

*L*ast Breath activated and the world froze. The three Aspects on the lake would reach his friends in less than twenty seconds. Even if Sift reached them, he stood no chance against the three handpicked warriors from the Infernal Realm. Ruwen needed to get there as soon as possible.

Plague and Pestilence exerted their power over massive areas, and if Ruwen left immediately and didn't neutralize them, their magic might still kill everyone before he could get back to them. From a strategic perspective, leaving enemies alive to attack from behind was a terrible decision.

It pained Ruwen to stay, but he needed to at least try and stop the threat they posed, before leaving to help Sift and the rest of the Masters.

Hanging over Ruwen's thoughts, like the burning avalanche approaching him now, was the fact he had allowed this situation to occur. He owned this mistake, and whatever happened today would land squarely on his shoulders.

Ruwen pushed the fear, anxiety, and guilt into the third meditation. He still had time to act and save everyone.

Releasing Last Breath, Ruwen did three things almost simultaneously. From his Inventory, he launched a Crazor Crystal Bliz had given him at his left hand. Bliz had adapted the Crazors, critical to the victory for New Eiru, into mining tools and given Ruwen seven carefully shaped variations.

The crystal labeled "One" had a short beam only three inches long, but it would, if powered correctly, slice through terium like snow. Each successive crystal grew less powerful but had a longer beam. Ruwen would start with Crazor Crystal "Three."

Next Ruwen activated Glow and the ability, now with five points, turned Ruwen into a walking sun. The Crazor reached his left palm, and as he gripped it, a dense red beam four feet long, appeared.

Hoping to end this quickly, Ruwen angled his Void Band at Pestilence and launched five Hardened Instability Rods with enough Energy to send them several miles. The rods had barely left his Void Band when he fired five more angled at Plague. Ruwen recalled the description for the items which Stone Carver Valora had used to aid the speed of Naktos' tunneling effort under New Eiru.

Description: *A one foot silver rod with a terium alloy tip. After impact and penetration, an Instability Sigil detonates weakening the surrounding structures and creating an ideal environment for tunneling.*

Ruwen released Last Breath and booming explosions immediately engulfed the rooftop caused by the rods tearing through the air. They reached the two Aspects almost instantly.

The rods struck Pestilence and Plague, the force of the impact detonating the Instability Glyphs. The explosions catapulted the two Aspects off the roof, throwing them hundreds of feet into the city. Hope flared in Ruwen that the speed of his attack had ended this fight quickly.

A hoarse, phlegmy cough reached Ruwen's Diamond Fortified ears.

"I keep trying to tell you," Plague said from somewhere down below. "We prepared for you."

Overlord leaped onto the roof from the courtyard. *Their Aspects generate a shield now.*

Ruwen cursed. Of course Lalquinrial would have made improvements to the Aspects after seeing how Ruwen wrecked them in the Infernal Realm. A shield made perfect sense as well, since a lot of the damage he inflicted came from his fists and Steps. They all knew how dangerous letting him get near them was, so they made shields capable of stopping his attacks.

The sky darkened, and Ruwen glanced at the avalanche, thinking it had arrived ahead of schedule, but it remained thirty seconds away. Instead, millions of tiny flying scorpions fell out of the sky. At the same time, tens of thousands of rats appeared, covering the city streets.

Ruwen's nose itched, and he noticed flecks of a white substance floating in the air. His log contained a repeating message which had started a second ago.

You have resisted Greater Blight!

Pestilence and Plague had begun their attack, and if any of this magic reached the beach, it would kill the Masters there. Ruwen jumped down into the courtyard, and using *Stone Echo* and *Survey* located the two Aspects. As he sprinted toward them, he checked on the state of the others.

Whiskers had almost reached the group of Bamboo Viper Masters who were currently leaving the forest and returning to the beach. Ruwen turned the cat's head toward the lake.

Sift stood on the beach, his stance relaxed and ready for the coming fight. The words moving across his armor had gained speed, briefly turning the scrolls all black, and giving the armor a flickering effect that hurt to look at.

The three Aspects had slowed their horses to a walk as they evaluated Sift. War's scratched and dented plate armor had the color of dried blood making it look black. A tilted crown sat atop his helmet, and he lifted his massive two-handed broadsword, pointing it directly at Sift.

Despair filled Ruwen. Sift had no chance against the combined might of three Aspects, and Ruwen had briefly held War's broadsword, the Infernal Blade of Mayhem, and knew its capabilities. The sword had two abilities that Sift now faced, and Ruwen remembered them well.

*Effect (**Passive**): Dominion of War – Anyone but the Aspect of War holding this blade takes 200 damage per second of Fire damage. Stacks 5 times.*

*Effect (**Active**): Ray of Slaughter – Generate a 5 second beam of Chaos doing 300 damage per second and ignoring 50% Armor Class.*

*Effect (**Active**): Skipping Razor – Launch the Infernal Blade of Mayhem at an enemy for 250 Slashing damage per attack. Blade will circle target five times before returning to the Aspect of War.*

In a moment one of those effects would trigger and Sift would battle for his life.

Ruwen stopped. Rats pooled around his bare feet, trying to bite through his Diamond-Fortified skin and failing. The light coming from his body repelled most of the creatures, and only the most determined risked attacking him. He dropped his arm, and the Crazor Sword sliced into the granite.

Ruwen couldn't let Sift die. He reached for his core.

Don't, Overlord said, placing a hand on Ruwen's shoulder, and stepping in front of him.

He's going to die.

Blapy was clear. Using your Spirit will permanently scar you, in which case, Sift dies anyway.

But he won't die today!

Not just Sift. Hamma, Rami, your parents, everything and everyone. You know Lalquinrial's plans. Who can stop him?

"It's my fault!" Ruwen screamed out loud.

Whiskers stood not far from the Bamboo Viper Masters, who all stood in combat stances, and, in front of them, Sift. The cat relayed to Ruwen in real time the disaster unfolding on the beach. He should have left Pestilence and Plague and went to help immediately. Maybe he could have made it in time.

Just one more mistake Ruwen had made. He turned toward the lake and jumped with all his strength. Pestilence and Plague had likely only meant to distract and delay him, and he'd fell for it. He had thought it would take longer for the three Aspects to reach the beach, but he had misjudged.

Ruwen cleared the fortress wall as the burning avalanche struck the city. The five points he'd added to *Dash* doubled his top speed and he ran as fast as his Diamond legs would move. In a blink, he'd reached the lake. He channeled fifty Energy into *Harden* and turned off *Glow*, leaving the Crazor in his palm.

Harden froze the water in a fifteen-foot radius and Ruwen ran directly at the Aspects from behind. Survey calculated he would arrive in thirty-seven seconds.

But it was already too late. Through Whiskers' eyes, Ruwen watched as War triggered *Ray of Slaughter*. From the tip of the Infernal Blade of Mayhem, a beam of Chaos erupted, striking Sift in the chest. The beam caused three hundred damage a second for five seconds and ignored fifty percent of any armor. Ruwen didn't know if Sift had that many Health points.

Whiskers looked away as seeing pure Chaos created intense discomfort, and from his position behind the Aspects, Ruwen couldn't see what happened.

The Health bar under Sift's portrait in Ruwen's party display dropped, and Ruwen gladly accepted the intense pain and damage *Bodyguard* funneled to him.

"It's my fault," Ruwen whispered. "It's all my fault."

When the odd shadows disappeared, Whiskers looked at the beach, and Ruwen saw to his amazement, that all the Masters remained alive. The cat turned its head toward the lake.

Sift stood just as before, although he rubbed his chest vigorously now.

Joy diluted Ruwen's despair.

Sift gave a long whistle, and then spoke to War. "Wow, that doesn't feel good. It almost makes me regret my choices. Wait, I never regret those."

"He's a Sifter," Drought said. "I see the streams."

Sift gave a small bow. "It's what I do."

War didn't respond, instead he triggered *Skipping Razor*, and the great broadsword launched itself at Sift. Ruwen's stomach twisted in worry. The sword would circle Sift five times, doing two hundred fifty damage with each pass, and Ruwen could do nothing about it.

Sift didn't react as the sword approached, the spinning blade traveling so fast it blurred. Casually, he reached up and snatched the blade from the air, and Ruwen gasped. He should have guessed Sift might do that, since he didn't know *Dominion of War* would burn him for two hundred damage per second and stack five times.

Again, pain washed over Ruwen from his connection to Sift.

It's hot! Ruwen screamed in *Chat*.

Hot like fire, Sift replied.

Sift held the giant sword for a few seconds, his hand glowing white with soul energy. He stabbed the sword into the beach, and a moment later the sword flew back to War's outstretched hand.

"Oh, that's burnt!" Sift said. "I have a sword that does that.

Want to see? My best friend gave it to me. Although, all things considered, I should reevaluate that."

Sift spoke to Ruwen in *Chat*. *How long do I need to stall these guys?*

Twenty seconds, Ruwen replied.

You are so slow.

Sift touched his waist and the Ink Lord Wrap parted giving him access to his Bamboo Viper Master's belt. He removed the Heavy Short Sword of the Comet from the dimensional storage there.

"We are wasting time," Poison said.

The three horses stepped forward.

"Wait," Sift yelled. "It gets better."

The Aspects continued forward.

"Okay, I guess I'll just show you," Sift told them.

Sift applied pressure from opposite sides of the hilt and the sword split and rotated apart. He held the Honed Short Sword of the Rising Star in his left hand and the Honed Short Sword of the Falling Star in the right.

"Still not impressed?" Sift asked as the Aspects approached. He held up Rising Star. "I call this one Flyer." He held up Falling Star. "And this one Pointer. I bet you wonder why."

The Aspects evidently didn't as they continued forward.

Ruwen would reach them in twelve seconds, and he prayed Sift could stall a little longer.

"Fine," Sift told the Aspects. "Tough crowd. I'll give you the light show then."

The Ink Lord Wrap turned white as soul energy surrounded Sift and enveloped both swords. He floated off the beach and threw the now white Honed Short Sword of the Rising Star into the sky.

"Your paltry soul will not save you," War said.

Ten seconds and they would have a chance.

The three Aspects prepared to attack Sift together.

Six seconds away.

The ice under Ruwen's feet turned black, and dozens of decaying hands grabbed his feet and legs. The sudden and unexpected attack stopped his legs, but his immense momentum carried his body forward. Diamond reflexes and one hundred ninety four levels in Tumbling, stopped him from slamming into the hardened ice, but it still threw him off target, and he slid across the ice, away from Sift.

Plague's feverish laughter reached Ruwen. She had cast her attack from somewhere far above him. He had paid the price for leaving enemies at his back, and now Sift faced three Aspects by himself.

Sift had miraculously handled War's initial attacks, but now he faced their combined might, and moments after that, their physical assault. Sift's Gold body, strengthened by his soul, might survive a few attacks, but not an extended fight.

In short, Ruwen knew, as he flipped himself to his feet and angled back toward the fight, he would never reach Sift in time. He would instead, witness the death of his best friend.

Desperate to stop the inevitable, Ruwen gave up the element of surprise, and launched a barrage of thirty Hardened Instability Rods at the three Aspects.

Still eight seconds away, Ruwen's stomach clenched, as the rods disappeared in a yellow fog, dissolving in whatever awful mist Pestilence had summoned. More laughter came from above him and he looked up to see Pestilence and Plague riding their horses through the air high above.

Terrible magic gathered around the three Aspects and then it arced toward Sift, who stood calmly on the beach, his white sword Pointer in his right hand.

Ruwen's heart stopped in dread.

The water roiled and exploded upward in front of the Aspects as a giant tortoise intercepted the Aspect's attack before crashing down on top of them.

CHAPTER 79

*S*helly's bellyflop created a massive wave, which at Ruwen's current speed, he couldn't avoid. *Harden* solidified the water in front of him into a wall and he crashed through it.

"Don't hurt my turtle," Sift screamed.

A large depression in the water where Shelly had landed caused Ruwen to suddenly lose the ability to create ice, and he soared over the opening. He could see Sift with his own eyes now, hovering twenty-five feet in the air. Sift shot forward toward Shelly, the Aspects, and Ruwen, transferring the sword he called Pointer to his left hand.

War, Drought, and Poison rose out of the water.

As Sift neared them, he flicked his right wrist forward, extending his index finger, and Ruwen witnessed an activated Relic Mark for the first time.

Sift had told Ruwen the first card Tarot revealed during Sift's reading, The Tower, would create fire and lightning in a fifty-foot radius for five seconds. Thankfully, it only affected enemies, because the world seemed to shift into an active apocalypse, or at least, fifty feet of one.

Fire fell from the sky like a thunderstorm, blue-white lightning weaving itself through the molten drops. The Aspects had all gained shields and they activated. Ruwen glanced up and found the fifty-foot radius extended upward, and had caught both Pestilence and Plague in its fury. The horses the pair rode evaporated, and they plunged downward.

Ruwen landed on the far side of the depression Shelly had made and *Harden* created a landing area for him. He stopped running but his momentum pushed him forward, and he continued to slide.

Overlord? Ruwen asked.

Almost to the Masters.

Ruwen found Overlord and the other four *Fallen Heroes* dashing down the beach.

Catch, Ruwen said.

Ruwen dragged his right foot like a rudder, keeping his slide trajectory straight, opened his Void Band, and launched the portal chalk Sift had loaned him toward Overlord.

It was a toss that even Bliz would admit neared perfection. Overlord caught the portal chalk in stride.

Ruwen slowed to a stop and turned to face the destruction out on the lake. *Do you have the gate runes for the village?*

Yeah, I took them from your memory, Overlord responded.

Get them home.

Ruwen focused on Whiskers for a moment and saw the confused look on Prythus and the other Masters' faces at seeing five Ruwen's rapidly approaching. He told Whiskers to scout for Overlord and warn Ruwen about any danger.

The lightning and fire ended as suddenly as it began, and disappointment filled Ruwen at seeing all five Aspects standing on the water thirty feet from a hovering Sift.

Ruwen activated *Glow*, creating his Crazor Sword and still channeling *Harden*, ran toward Sift. His Diamond hearing caught the Aspects' conversation.

"Divine golem magic," Drought whispered to War.

"Unpleasant," War responded.

Poison looked around. "It might be worth splitting up to look for it. Our Lord would rejoice at such a find. It would offset our recent embarrassment."

War shook his head. "No. We can search after. First, I want these black belts for my collection."

"He listens," Plague said.

War shrugged. "It matters not. His fate is sealed, along with his companions."

Overlord? Ruwen asked.

Drawing the door now.

Relief flooded Ruwen. Overlord could draw gate runes as fast as Ruwen, and in less than a minute, all the new Masters would be safe.

A faint whistling reached Ruwen along with a small pressure wave. War swiped his sword upward, deflecting a glowing white blade that had descended from above like a bird of prey. The blade disappeared into the sky.

Pestilence spoke quietly. "How many pearls does the boy carry? Such a dreadful waste of soul energy? He should have exhausted himself by now."

Drought studied the water. "The Elder Tortoise approaches."

"A complication we don't need," War said. His red horse appeared below him and he galloped toward the shore, angling past Sift. The rest of the Aspects followed, and Pestilence and Plague climbed into the air again. None of the Aspects seemed in a hurry or worried at all.

Ruwen wondered if his Aspect had a horse as well but couldn't risk finding out right now.

Are they through? Ruwen asked Overlord.

There's a problem, Overlord responded.

Ruwen's heart skipped a beat and he calmed himself. *What is it?*

The portal doesn't work.

Are the runes correct?

I've triple-checked them, but they're already fading. I'm worried I know what's wrong.

What?

Overlord paused a moment as Ruwen ran toward the beach and Sift circled above.

Remember the very first thing Simandreial said to us when we landed in the Infernal Realm?

Ruwen did and he fought down panic. The Plague Siren, Echo's mother, had greeted Ruwen with these words. *Hello again, Ruwen Starfield. Welcome to your new home. You probably already know your Inventory doesn't work. Not even that wretched wyrm can reach you now. Just to save us all some time, know the ground you stand on is desecrated, and Divine blood is powerless. Any portal chalk you have is useless.*

Plague's laughter fell from the sky like an awful thunderstorm. Ruwen looked up at her. She and her brother hovered a hundred and fifty feet above the Red Forest, looking down at, presumably, Overlord and the Masters.

"You just don't listen," Plague said, glancing at Ruwen, and knowing he would hear her. "When will you realize? When will you understand? We prepared for you."

The Aspects had desecrated the ground and Ruwen, along with everyone else, remained trapped here.

Shelly rose out of the water like an island and Sift landed on her shell.

Overlord, ask Uruziel how we counter desecrated ground. Ruwen shifted his focus to Sift and spoke to him over their mental connection. *There's a problem with the portal chalk. Let's use Shelly to escape.*

Ruwen arrived at the beach. He strode onto the sand, turning it into diamonds, and he stopped channeling *Harden*.

"There is no need to kill everyone. I have the Infernal Crossing Rings you want."

Poison tilted his head. "You have nothing to give. Everything you have, your very soul, belongs to our Lord already."

"The Elder," War said to Drought.

Drought slid off his horse and into the water, disappearing from view like he'd fallen into a well. He reappeared almost immediately on the water ten feet in front of Shelly and Sift.

Run! Ruwen yelled at Sift.

Drought pointed a fist at Shelly, displaying a ring that held three glowing red stones. A surge of energy erupted from one of the stones, striking Shelly.

The Elder Star Tortoise disappeared.

"Shelly!" Sift screamed as he tumbled into the water.

The air made a snapping sound as it rushed to fill the area Shelly had left. One of the three stones on Drought's ring faded. Sift exploded upward in a spray of water and white soul energy, but by the time he turned to attack Drought, the Aspect had disappeared into the water.

"It's done," Drought said to War as he rose from the water along the beach. He remounted his horse. "I was worried it wouldn't work on something so big."

"Excellent," War replied before looking up and addressing the two Aspects in the sky. "Leave me a few. The belts mean more if I harvest them myself."

"As you wish, War," Pestilence responded.

"You should hurry," Plague added. "You know we lack your precision."

Ruwen sensed Sift rapidly approaching, likely to take revenge on Drought. *We need you in the sky. Attack Plague and Pestilence.*

They killed Shelly! Sift yelled across their mental link.

Shelly is fine. No spell can harm that star eater. The only way to help her is to leave here alive. Focus on the flying ones.

Sift didn't respond, but he angled away from the beach and into the sky. Ruwen had reassured Sift about Shelly's health, not because Ruwen actually knew, but because he needed all of Sift's concentration here, not on something out of their control.

"Drought?" War asked.

Drought studied Ruwen. "I believe it safe. Not a speck of Spirit has left his body, despite a situation he thought dire. I believe him crippled, and we can proceed as planned."

Dreadful realization struck Ruwen. The Aspects truly had planned this. They had acted vulnerable and hesitant with a purpose. The small hope he'd nursed that they had a chance to match these Aspects on the battlefield, or at least get everyone else to safety, died. All the Aspects had done was try and prod him into using his Spirit. Lalquinrial likely guessed that if Ruwen survived the Sixth Rune, it wouldn't be without damage.

They had planned for Ruwen, but how did they know he was here? Or that he would return? Two immediate possibilities came to mind.

One, the demon survivors of the underground cavern had described Ruwen well enough for Lalquinrial to know it was him. Or maybe he, or one of the Aspects, had access to the demons' memories here.

The more likely explanation, Ruwen guessed, was Echo had informed her father's assets here during the last visit, and they had passed it on to the Infernal god.

Had Echo found a way around the Bamboo Viper oath to not harm her own Clan? Or maybe passing along information didn't trigger any issues because it was too vague, too far removed, from actual harm.

Amid the horror of Ruwen's situation, he felt disappointment as well. In himself, because he had believed Echo could change, and in Echo, that she could rationalize what happened next to everyone here.

Ruwen moved into the third mediation to stop the horrifying conclusions of what he'd sown.

Whiskers sneezed and something damaged the cat, causing Whiskers to dematerialize, and Ruwen's connection to disappear.

The apparitions are taking damage, Overlord said. *There is something in the air.*

The red bar under the portrait of Nymthus in Ruwen's party display, ticked downward. She, just like the apparitions, had begun taking damage.

"No," Ruwen whispered, as he understood the full extent of his situation.

Plague cackled from above. "Finally."

CHAPTER 80

*W*ar turned his horse toward the forest in the direction of Overlord and the Masters. None of the Aspects had a hint of hurry, confident their prey had no ability to run or harm them. It provided another example of how dreadfully serious the situation had turned.

Ruwen turned toward the trees, and with *Dash*, disappeared into the forest almost immediately. He focused on Sift and spoke in *Chat*. *The class is taking damage. I'm going to try and take out Plague and Pestilence before the other three Aspects reach our friends.*

How are you going to reach them? They're really high.

I have an idea for that.

I'm harassing them with Flyer and will join you as soon as I see you.

Don't bother, you won't see me. I need you to really harass them. I can't handle any more of their spells.

Alright. Sift paused a moment. *This looks serious.*

I know.

Ruwen reached the small thirty-foot glade that Overlord and the Masters stood in. Their portal door had once stood against the thirty foot cliff of the stone outcropping that the clearing touched. The top of the outcropping led to an even larger clearing.

The five *Fallen Heroes* stood in a circle around the Masters, who were all bent over coughing. Overlord tossed him the portal chalk and Ruwen snapped it in two. He threw half back to Overlord and dropped what remained into his Void Band returning it safely back to Inventory.

Bunch everyone together, Ruwen told Overlord.

The apparitions immediately picked up the closest Masters and brought them toward Ruwen.

Ruwen cast the new spell *Bonfire* for two hundred fifty Mana, and three massive fires, ten foot high, appeared. With a thought, he placed one on each side of them, against the rock and the last directly in front.

Ruwen used one of his eight remaining spell points and increased *Shed* to level two, giving him an extra five feet in every direction. He cast *Shed* for fifty Mana, creating a structure fifteen-by-fifteen-by-fifteen around them. He left the front of the building open. Touching the *Shed*, he channeled *Harden* briefly, turning the walls into diamond.

The Void Band, still open from catching the portal chalk, expanded to three feet as Ruwen prepared to get rid of whatever contaminated the air. Using fifty Energy per second he accessed the one hundred twenty-seven thousand cubic feet of "cool air" he'd gathered shortly after restoring Uru's Third Temple.

The force of the air leaving the Void Band pushed Ruwen up and against the *Shed's* ceiling, so he doubled the portal opening to six feet and he dropped back to the ground.

Survey displayed a wave of small creatures *Stone Echo* had detected approaching from the forest. The Masters had stopped coughing and Ruwen narrowed the Void Band opening.

Catch, Ruwen said to Overlord and launched the stack of

fifty Major Health Stickers he'd created in Shelly with his Mobile Alchemy Lab. They would heal one hundred eight damage immediately and another eleven Health per second for thirty seconds. *Put one of those on everyone, including the Fallen Heroes.*

Ruwen had displaced thirty thousand cubic feet with fresh air which would buy them a little time. He stepped out from the middle of the crowded group of Masters and aimed his Void Band at the ground. Narrowing the opening further to increase the force, he sprayed oil across the clearing, walking in a quick arc from one side of the outcropping, around the *Shed*, to the other. He drenched the area with five hundred gallons of black liquid.

Casting *Warm Welcome* for twenty Mana, a flaming dagger appeared in Ruwen's hand, and he threw it into the oil.

The oil ignited immediately setting the trees ablaze, which Ruwen hoped would slow whatever crawled toward them.

Overlord, what did Uruziel say?

To counter desecration you use blessed or holy items.

How long does it take. Oh, and ask about soul powered runes.

One sec.

If soul energy ignored desecration, then Sift could use his seemingly endless well of soul power to create a portal for them. How ironic would that be? Ruwen looked at Pestilence and Plague high above, absorbing the information *Survey* provided on height and wind velocity.

Sift, Ruwen said in *Chat. Try and keep them in one place. I'll only get a single chance at this.*

Overlord responded. *The neutralizing time depends on the strength of the blessing compared to the power of the desecration.*

And the soul runes?

Uruziel says you already know the answer. The desecration is severe because portal chalk made from Miranda's Divine blood doesn't work. And Divine blood comes from...

Overlord trailed off and Ruwen understood. Reaching the Divine levels remade a body into something completely made from soul energy. Including the blood. In reality, they were already trying to draw the runes with soul power.

Thanks. Ruwen said. He hated not having exact values to create the neutralizing solution, but at least he had a way forward. Stepping over to Nymthus, he kneeled next to her. "Are you okay?"

Nymthus nodded weakly.

Ruwen opened his Void Band and dropped the Spirit Infused Baton of a Thousand Uses. He touched one of the protrusions and the baton lengthened and one end morphed into a scoop. Holding the Void Band over the makeshift bowl he dropped the remaining nine Blessed Unleavened Bread and ten Blessed Water Hamma had given him on their first trip to the Black Pyramid together. They had added a couple points to various stats and he'd thought they were amazingly powerful. He had come a long way since that moment.

War and his buddies are twenty-five seconds from your location, Sift said in *Chat.*

Almost done. Ruwen responded. *When I give the signal rush over here. I'm not sure how long it will take me to land and the Masters will need your help to survive.*

Got it.

Ruwen had tracked the trio of Aspects as they slowly advanced toward this spot. He prayed he had enough time to start the process of getting his class home. He launched the Fastidious Dagger into his right palm and handed it to Nymthus. Then he stood and moved to the back of the *Shed,* giving Nymthus directions in *Chat. Hold that dagger tight. As soon as it gets dirty, like when you stick it in the blessed bread and water, it will vibrate. It should quickly mix that into a paste. Then I want you to smear that paste on the rocks. I'll have already started in the area you need to use the paste.*

Okay, Nymthus responded.

Ruwen had ten Blessed Bricks left over from his fight against the minions the Bone Mage occupying Uru's Third Temple had summoned. He put the Crazor Crystal in his right palm back into Inventory and launched a Blessed Brick into each hand as he stepped up to the cliff. Channeling twenty Energy into *Melt*, he worked quickly.

The Blessed Bricks turned to liquid and Ruwen smeared it across the rock in a two-by-five-foot rectangle. He swiftly used the remaining eight, and the brick paste smoked and crackled against the desecrated stone.

Now or never, Sift said.

Taking a large step to the side, Ruwen used his forearm and *Melt* to remove a three inch layer of stone. If the desecration didn't penetrate very far, this area might work, and they wouldn't need to rely on the blessed items.

Ruwen removed a Soul Fruit of Potency from his Inventory. He had brought the three types of fruit back from the previous Bamboo Viper test, and Fractal had gotten them to grow. Fractal had let Ruwen take three of each. This one, the small green one, was the sweetest of the three and would add thirty to his Strength, Dexterity, and Stamina for thirty minutes. He didn't know if he needed the extra Strength but didn't want to take the chance. His plan needed to work.

Ruwen focused on Overlord again as he turned to the front of the *Shed. Remember the Naktos Assassin?*

Good times.

Only focusing on one side doubles my chance of success.

I got you, brother. Right side is the fun side.

Ruwen dived over the heads of everyone in the *Shed* and rolled to his feet twenty feet away. Flames surrounded him. He spread his arms wide and cast *Climb*, creating one hundred feet of magical rope pointed directly at the Aspects. The magical rope had the benefit of moving things along it, and Energy powered that movement.

Ruwen gripped the rope tightly with his left hand, squeezing with all his Diamond Strength, aided by the thirty points from the Soul Fruit of Potency. Before the rope fell, he channeled three hundred Energy to it, praying that much power didn't rip his arm off.

Now! Ruwen yelled in *Chat* as he triggered Last Breath.

The Energy Ruwen had directed into *Climb* jerked him upward so quickly, the burning air surrounding him exploded, and his vision dimmed for an instant. His enhanced Strength wasn't enough to stop the rope from sliding through his hand, and his Health dropped thirty-six points from the rope burn.

Even in Last Breath, Ruwen hurtled toward the two Aspects in the sky, and he worried he might have overdone the velocity.

Stone Echo didn't work as well in the air, but the two Aspects were large targets and easy to find. *Survey* told Ruwen what he already knew. He had aimed well and only needed tiny corrections to his flight path.

Ruwen released the rope and directed small puffs of air from his Void Band, altering the angle of the dimensional portal to nudge him in the right direction and altering his trajectory slightly. Sift had done his job well and the two Aspects sat on their horses three hundred feet in the air, but less than five feet apart. Ruwen had aimed for the exact middle of the pair.

Ruwen increased the size of his Void Band as Overlord did the same with the Dark Portal on Ruwen's right wrist. Ruwen regenerated four hundred Energy per second and his Energy pool had reached five thousand four hundred ninety. He had never created two ten-foot ovals however, and he worried the scaling of two portals might grow exponentially and his massive pool wouldn't be enough.

The reality was, Ruwen didn't have any options. Fighting

three Aspects while protecting the vulnerable might be possible, but five remained out of the question.

Only an ability like Last Breath would have provided Pestilence and Plague time to react. And it appeared neither had such a skill, as they failed to react as he approached. He hurtled toward them like a flying cross, massive open portals hanging off each wrist.

Twenty feet from Pestilence and Plague the pair finally reacted. Their hooded heads slid toward him slowly. Too, slowly. Hope surged through his thoughts.

At five feet away, Ruwen felt resistance coming from both Aspects. At this speed it had to be something triggered by the Aspect armor itself. The sensation reminded him of pushing two magnets together with the same pole, but because he felt this force from both, they counteracted each other a little and instead of pushing him away, Pestilence and Plague leaned to the side.

Ruwen increased the size of his portal to compensate, and Overlord did the same. Ruwen realized this meant not only had the Aspects been upgraded with powerful shields but, at least these two, had also gained a repulsion field. It made complete sense. He was walking death to anyone he could reach, so Lalquinrial had made it so Ruwen couldn't touch them. Once again, it demonstrated how prepared they actually were.

What the Aspects had not prepared for was a flying Void Band traveling over a thousand miles per hour.

Ruwen's Void Band sliced through the yellow horse Pestilence rode, the head of the phantom animal disintegrating as it separated from the body. The Aspect had almost turned his head toward Ruwen and for an instant their gazes locked.

Then Pestilence disappeared into the black portal of Ruwen's Void Band. Out of his peripheral vision, he watched Plague enter the mouth of the Dark Portal.

The bands both closed, and relief flooded Ruwen's mind. They had a chance. He could still fix this.

I'll keep trying the gate runes, Overlord said, *while the other four Fallen Heroes attempt to buy you time. Hurry back.*

Thanks, brother. See you in second.

Ruwen prayed when he released Last Breath, he would still have Energy, and would remain here to fight. He spent a moment producing a plan on how to get back, since his previous one had ended right here, and decided to just take the most direct route.

With a mental sigh, Ruwen released Last Breath.

CHAPTER 81

*T*ime resumed its normal pace, and a red Energy bar greeted Ruwen, the color a result of dropping under ten percent. Using two portals with such large openings had almost cost him his life.

Ruwen's Energy Regen of four hundred per second quickly replenished the paltry four hundred ninety-seven left in his pool. He continued to fly upward, his velocity still over a thousand miles per hour.

Overlord, I'm coming in hot. Match my Void Band actions.

Will do. Sift landed down here and he's still angry about his turtle.

It's not a—

Ruwen stopped mid response. Overlord obviously knew Shelly was a tortoise, not a turtle, so he'd only said turtle to lighten the oppressive mood.

I'll be right there, Ruwen said, and then added. *Thanks.*

Careful not to pull too much Energy from the depleted pool, Ruwen created a hand sized portal. Trying to stop his forward momentum would take far too long and require a lot of energy. Plus, he'd just need to speed up again anyway. Better to just alter his direction a bit.

Ruwen straightened his body, and placed his hands down, a foot off his waist. Just like he'd done in the underwater level of the Black Pyramid when avoiding the Octorse, he took in air on the front of his Void Band and released it with a little more Energy out the back of the portal.`

With the propulsion in place, Ruwen angled himself forward by tilting the Void Band. In two seconds, he had turned himself around and now hurtled toward Sift, the Masters, and the Aspects, while gravity added its acceleration to his own.

Unlike Ruwen's sub-second attack on Pestilence and Plague, his transition toward War, Poison, and Drought had taken a few seconds, making it easy to detect the pressure waves he created. He wouldn't be able to duplicate his Void snatch again.

The three Aspects sat on their horses at the edge of the Red Forest. Drought waved a hand dismissively and the flames instantly disappeared. From the speed and lack of water, he had probably utilized some type of oxygen starvation.

In the fire's place, a white mist formed, and it spread toward the Bamboo Viper group. Ruwen *Analyzed* the fog.

Target: *Shuddering Death*
Type: *Resource*
Components: *Jellyfish Venom (Aerosol)*
Health: *Extremely Toxic*
Alchemy: *Necrotic*
Uses: *Poison*

Stone Echo and *Survey* calculated five seconds before the poison reached the group. Ruwen had originally planned to just land near the Aspects with a massive concussive force. If he did that now, the force of his impact would cause the poison to surge toward his friends. Since he had less than two seconds to decide, he modified his plan, hoping to delay the poison until he could get into position to help.

Instead of aiming for the Aspects, Ruwen used his Void Band to nudge himself in front of them, right in the middle of the poison gas. He spread his arms and legs out wide and channeled one hundred Energy into *Melt*. If this didn't work, it would be the most embarrassing entry ever as he faceplanted with a bellyflop right in front of the enemy.

Ruwen struck the rocky ground at a thirty-degree angle, and instantly *Melted* it, creating a self-generating hole which he continued to fall into. *Survey* displayed the effect on the poison, and the results were just what he'd hoped for. The sudden opening, coupled with the air he'd dragged with him from his rapid descent, pulled the poison mist in behind him. His plan had worked well.

Too well, as Ruwen quickly found himself fifty feet underground. Using blasts of air from his Void Band he angled himself upward and exited the top of the outcropping behind Sift and the Masters. Using more forced air, Ruwen maneuvered himself through the air and over the cliff, dropping down and landing three feet to the right of Sift.

All three Aspects had turned their attention to the sky where Pestilence and Plague had hovered just seconds before.

Ruwen spoke to Sift in *Chat* as he studied the three Aspects. *Their armor has a shield that repulses physical attacks.*

Sift still held the sword Pointer in his left hand, keeping his right free to release the two Relic Marks that remained. *Survey* displayed the change in trajectory of the sword Flyer two hundred feet above them.

Overlord? Ruwen asked.

Gate runes still don't work. Nymthus is adding the last of the blessed paste now.

Prythus stepped away from the group of Masters and strode up to Ruwen. He had a Major Health sticker on his cheek that read "I Love Bubbles."

"We recognize these creatures," Prythus said. "They cause

more destruction than the demons they lead and are responsible for great suffering."

"Thank you," Ruwen said. "Organize the others so as soon as a portal opens, we can leave quickly."

Prythus nodded and moved back toward the group. Ruwen appreciated that all the Masters wanted to help, but they had absolutely no chance against these three.

Drought looked at Poison. "Want to bet?"

Poison glanced at Ruwen's wrist and then back at Drought. "Two portals, the final exit under a literal mountain of snow, I'll say ten minutes."

War gave a short laugh. "Plague will be furious it happened to her first. I say five."

Drought tilted his head in thought. "I'll split the difference, and add War will sleep in a bed of lice for a year when he fails to hold his tongue at her failure."

Ruwen's confusion turned to worry and then fear as the Aspects spoke. He had received two notifications as he'd expected when snatching Pestilence and Plague with his Void Band. He'd assumed they'd contained the usual warning that if he didn't add Energy to keep them alive, they'd die, which is exactly what he wanted.

With the distractions of getting safely back to the ground, Ruwen had missed that the notifications had disappeared. He opened his log and found only the initial warning. No count down or notification that either Aspect had perished.

Ruwen suppressed a dry heave as he understood just how far Lalquinrial had gone to protect his Aspects. Ruwen's Void Band was no secret, and anyone with ten Intelligence could figure out the powerful killing tool it represented.

It explained, once again, the behavior of the Aspects. They lacked all urgency, and instead appeared to be stretching this encounter out, as if to increase their pleasure. Ruwen knew now that one of his most powerful capabilities for killing monstrously powerful beings had been neutralized. The most likely way, based on the Aspects' discussion, was an automatic portal by their armor back to the Infernal Realm.

It meant, far from killing two vastly powerful Aspects, Ruwen had only inconvenienced them, and they would return within minutes.

The three Aspects discussed the reward for the winner of their bet as Ruwen spoke to Sift in *Chat*. *The Inventory trick doesn't work. They planned for that, too. Pestilence and Plague will be back within ten minutes. Maybe as soon as five.*

Do you ever have good news?

Fractal is growing those red fruit you love.

What! And you're just telling me now?

I have a lot going on.

You are a terrible friend.

I know. We can discuss that after killing these three but using my Void Band will only delay them.

Do you have a good plan?

Let's just call it a plan.

That means even you know it's terrible. Let's hear it.

The three Aspects appeared to agree on the winner's reward, and Ruwen knew he only had a few seconds left.

War has heavy single target damage, and Drought is a Step Master. I think we should overwhelm Poison to get rid of their area of effect spells. Then we focus on Drought and last War.

Which one is Poison?

The one on the white horse. I'm going to use my Relic Marks. Use your exhaustion one after my stun wears off or is cleansed.

What about the physical damage shield?

I'm hoping to overwhelm it.

Whatever happened would occur within the next five minutes, so Ruwen extended his pointer finger and flicked his wrist outward, like dealing a card. The Relic Mark disappeared, replaced with an intense point of cold, that rapidly disappeared.

The Chariot Relic Mark triggered the effect *Wings of Resolve* which would give all his allies in a thirty feet radius fifty extra points in Strength and Stamina for five minutes. That should provide another five hundred Health for everyone.

Here we go, Ruwen told Sift.

CHAPTER 82

*R*uwen held up his hands and walked slowly toward the three Aspects. They turned their attention to him, and he spoke. "I want to make a deal."

The Aspects remained silent, studying Ruwen as he approached. Not one of them showed any fear or concern. He considered using Harmony now and trying to nullify their shields. But if he did affect their shields, it gave them time to react. He wanted to save Harmony for a surprise when he stood near all of them.

It took three strides, and *Survey* displayed all three Aspects sat within the fifteen-foot radius of Ruwen's next Relic Mark. He stopped and began the one second cast of *Scrub*. Right before *Scrub* finished casting, he extended his middle finger to match his pointer. With a flick of the wrist, he activated the Five of Wands Relic Mark and triggered *First Move*, a one second stun for up to five enemies.

At the first hint of coldness on Ruwen's right wrist, he channeled twenty Energy into *Scrub*, and leaped at Poison.

First Move's stun kept the Aspects locked in place, and as

Ruwen approached he felt the resistance of Poison's shield. Using the level three Worker ability *Third Hand*, he grasped Poison, pinning himself to the Aspect. Poison's shield continued to try and push Ruwen away, but *Third Hand* kept him anchored in place.

The Worker textbook Ruwen had carried since his Ascendancy Day detailed basic Worker spells. It contained a table for *Scrub* detailing what Energy and spell levels should be used for various materials and stains. He had consulted it when cleaning the Leaf Dragon Silk for Fluffy. Starting at spell level one, anything over ten Energy per second would cause severe damage to skin. He slammed his hands against Poison's shield. His hands vibrated with twenty channeled Energy, the maximum amount the level five *Scrub* allowed.

The intense vibration of *Scrub* created a tingling sensation in Ruwen's fingers but caused far more significant problems for Poison's shield. It took less than a second for the damage caused by *Scrub* to overwhelm and collapse the shield.

The one second stun ended and Sift landed next to Ruwen. The three Aspects slumped as Sift triggered his Relic Mark for the Ten of Wands, creating an Exhaustion debuff on all enemies within fifteen feet.

Ruwen sensed an immediate pulse of magic from War's Aspect likely a reaction to the debuff and some defensive measure to cleanse the harmful magic. Whatever the spell, it worked, and the Aspects recovered. Tarot had told Ruwen that the effects of Relic Marks could not be resisted, but that didn't mean they couldn't be diminished once active.

Ruwen used his last Relic Mark, the Reversed Fool, flicking his wrist outward with three fingers extended. Warmth covered his body as the magic increased his Critical Strike damage by twenty-five percent at the expense of half his Armor Class for five seconds.

In such a dire situation, Ruwen didn't wrestle with good and bad or right and wrong, instead he struck at Poison's neck. The strike, under normal conditions, sent a surge of blood to the victim's brain, and depending on the power of the hit, would cause everything from dizziness to death.

Ruwen struck at Poison's neck with all his Strength. The armor of Poison's Aspect successfully stopped him from being decapitated, and an invisible link between Poison and War surged, causing War to groan, as he absorbed much of the damage to Poison. The horses Poison and War sat on disappeared and as Poison dropped to the ground, he opened his mouth and vomited black sludge, spraying Ruwen's face and chest.

Before Poison hit the ground he disappeared. *Stone Echo* detected the Aspect fifty feet away, on top of the outcropping behind the Masters. As much as Ruwen loved using *Blink* himself, he hated when others did. Poison didn't immediately move back toward them and Ruwen hoped the Aspect had taken fatal damage.

Overlord, send a Fallen Hero to check on Poison.

Understood. Gate runes still aren't working. Should I come help?

Keep trying.

Ruwen transitioned into Harmony and felt the balance of the space surrounding him, including the shields around Drought and War. Unlike the straightforward balance of elements and the Founders' soul magic, these shields fluctuated, constantly shifting the force they applied to the environment. It wasn't immediately clear to him how to balance such an advanced construct.

Drought attacked Sift, and Ruwen sensed the surge of magic as Sift triggered his last Relic Mark, Fortitude, adding five hundred to Sift's Strength for ten seconds. Drought felt it too, and stepped backward, giving up ground to avoid the onslaught of Sift and Ruwen.

War pointed his sword upward and used a thumb to press the back of a silver band wrapped around the sword's hilt. The front of the band pointed at Ruwen, and it held three glowing red stones, just like Drought's ring had. A surge of energy erupted from one of the stones.

Ruwen captured the spell with his Void Band and immediately released it back at War. If he could remove War with his own spell, it would greatly improve their odds of surviving this. But the spell vanished as soon as it contacted War's energy shield.

Disappointed, Ruwen stopped channeling *Scrub* and launched two Crazors out of Inventory and into his palms. He activated *Glow*, maximizing the brightness, but kept the ability to just his palms. A four-foot red beam of Energy materialized from the number three Crazor in his right hand and a two-foot beam from the number two Crazor in his left.

He struck at Drought's shield with both.

Sift with the five hundred extra Strength, easily overcame the repulsive resistance of Drought's shield, and attacked as well.

Rags covered Drought's dried leathery skin, and his face, little more than a skull, contained large cracks. The Aspect smiled, splitting the skin of his lips and revealing worn teeth. A surge of channeled energy erupted outward and a debuff appeared under the group portrait of both Sift and Nymthus.

Focusing on the debuff Ruwen read the description of what likely affected the entire class of Masters.

Dying Thirst: *Severe dehydration. 50% decrease to all Attributes. 75 damage per second while channeled.*

Sift visibly slowed. Nymthus wouldn't survive ten seconds of this debuff, which meant most of the other Masters likely had similar Health points and would die as well. If it wasn't for

Ruwen's *Bonfire* tripling their natural Regen, and the relic mark's Endurance buff, they likely would have died in seconds.

Sift groaned and tripped, and Drought laughed.

Everyone collapsed here, Overlord said.

Attack War with two Fallen Heroes, we need to keep him distracted.

We just lost the one I sent to find Poison. I think that means he's alive.

Seven seconds remained until Drought's debuff killed everyone, and Poison it appeared would soon return.

Ruwen continued to strike at Drought's shield, but the Aspect fell back, pulling Ruwen away from everyone and allowing the shield to survive longer.

Did you see if Poison had a red ring with three stones, Ruwen asked.

Let me check my memories. Yes, he does.

Five seconds until the unthinkable occurred.

Sift collapsed to the ground. Ruwen touched Sift with a foot and cast *Massage* for one hundred fifty Mana. It would heal thirty-two points of damage per second for thirty seconds and keep Sift alive awhile longer.

Drought's channeled spell covered too large an area for Harmony to neutralize, and manipulating the air or stone into an attack would fail miserably against the Aspect's armor. The only hope for the rest of the class was if Ruwen could reach Drought and physically stop him from channeling *Dying Thirst*.

We lost the two fighting War, Overlord said. *Should I go?*

Having to rely on the Mana versions of the *Fallen Heroes* spell made them far less effective for fighting Diamond Cultivators. Ruwen's spirit versions would have lasted much longer. *Keep trying the gate runes. Only go if he moves toward or attacks the Masters.*

Three seconds remained.

Ruwen cast *Net* for one hundred Mana, and the instantaneous cast covered Drought in a glowing yellow net. The fine mesh constricted and anchored itself to the ground, trapping Drought in place.

Stepping close to the momentarily trapped Drought, Ruwen jammed the Crazors into the shield. He stomped the ground with his right foot, and behind him, the stone under War's feet rose and encased the Aspect up to his shins, delaying his attempt to help Drought.

The Health bar under Nymthus pulsed yellow and then red. Two seconds until she died.

Drought's physical protection shield collapsed, and Ruwen stepped forward. The Aspect destroyed the *Net* trapping him and held out a fist, pointing a ring with two glowing red stones directly at Ruwen.

Ruwen swept both Crazors around in an arc as he turned to face War.

The debuff on Sift and Nymthus disappeared.

Drought's body dropped forward like a slow falling tree. His head and left hand striking the ground first, followed by the headless body. Killing such a vile creature filled Ruwen with joy. Drought, a Gem Fortified Cultivator would not revive in one of Lalquinrial's infernal tubs. This despicable creature had died the true death.

Locking eyes with War, Ruwen bent and removed the red ring before, just as he expected, the Aspect automatically returned itself and the wearer, to their Infernal Bind point.

Ruwen read the ring's description.

Tring!
You have found...

Name: *Infernal Banishment Band of Physical Protection*

Quality: *Legendary*
Durability: *66 of 66*
Weight: *0.29 lbs.*
Charges: *2*
Restriction: *Infernal Aspect.*
Restriction: *Desecrated ground.*
Restriction: *Triggered effect's maximum range is ten feet.*
Effect (Passive): *Personal Space - Creates a five-foot bubble around wearer repelling physical attacks equivalent to ten thousand damage.*
Effect (Triggered): *Infernal Confinement – Wrap target in dimensional orb and banish them to Infernal Realm's dimensional prison.*
Description: *Platinum band with three infernal rubies. With rubies pointed at target, press thumb against bottom of band.*

The Aspect's odd behavior made sense now. With Plague's warning that they had prepared for Ruwen, he should have realized capturing him had been the real purpose. The Aspects had told him they searched for the Infernal Crossing Rings, and that might also be true, but only as a secondary goal. From the beginning they had orchestrated this to capture him.

It explained why the Aspects had not aggressively attacked him. They didn't want to kill him. What they needed was for Ruwen to attack them. To get within ten feet so they could trigger a ring they all wore and send him back to the Infernal Realm. Likely in a much stronger dimensional prison.

Shelly was banished to the Infernal Realm, not hurt, Ruwen told Sift. *Their dimensional prison won't be able to hold her. So don't worry.*

Sift remained on the ground, the heal slowly returning him to normal. *Thanks.*

War ripped his feet free of the stone. The dented and scratched crimson armor he wore revealed a ready stance, but not one poised to attack. He wanted Ruwen to approach him.

Survey confirmed all the Masters remained on the ground.

Ruwen counted thirty heart beats and internally felt immense relief. He had temporarily gotten rid of two Aspects, and just, hopefully, killed another. That left War and Poison to deal with, but now that he understood their plan better, he felt confident he could avoid any of their traps to banish him. A spark of hope flared to life. He could still save everyone.

CHAPTER 83

*R*uwen debated wearing the ring for a moment, but it wouldn't work against the Aspects, so he dropped it into his Inventory. Fractal would love the Legendary item.

Stone Echo detected a slow-moving mist on top of the outcropping. Poison had rejoined the fight, and *Survey* displayed the terrible news that Ruwen only had fifteen seconds before the poisonous fog spilled over the outcrop's edge and onto the Masters.

Ruwen triggered Insect Repellant and pushed the ability to is maximum of one hundred feet. He hoped it would slow the advance of whatever Poison sent.

Using *Chat*, Ruwen spoke to Sift. *Are you feeling okay? Poison is on top of that outcropping.*

Sift exploded into the air, and Ruwen took that as a yes.

Gate Runes? Ruwen asked Overlord.

Hard to tell exactly. I'd guess another three minutes.

They definitely didn't have three minutes.

Do you think the Masters can get away from that outcropping? Ruwen asked.

Negative, they are barely moving. We could use the last Fallen Hero to move them, but we couldn't move them all in time.

Ruwen started the two second cast for *Worker Wagon* and circled toward the trees, forcing War to turn as well. Hopefully that would stop him from interfering.

Ruwen's Mana dropped by two hundred fifty and a wagon appeared. The *Fallen Hero* immediately picked up the closest Master and placed them in the wagon.

We need to address the disease, not the symptoms, Overlord said.

I know.

Ruwen began the one second cast for *Shed*. He planned to build a barrier above the Masters to buy more time to move them.

For a moment, Ruwen touched the immense guilt he held for allowing this situation to occur. He had left these servants of Lalquinrial alive in the Infernal Realm. If he'd made another choice, killing them, this situation would not exist. His friends and classmates were in dire jeopardy, and he owned that.

A fifteen-foot Shed appeared and Ruwen immediately cast another.

"What if I surrender?" Ruwen asked War.

War nodded at the Crazors. "I thought you didn't like swords. What did you call them? Arrogant weapons?"

"I'm trying new things."

"That's good. Our Lord also wishes to try new things."

"There is no reason to harm the others. They have nothing to do with this."

War tilted his head, the effect exaggerated by the plate helm. "They are Bamboo Viper Clan. Their lives and belts were mine the moment I saw them."

"But you're here for me."

War pointed his sword at the outcropping but kept his attention on Ruwen. "We already have you. All you've done is delayed the joy of killing all these grass snakes."

A beam of energy surged from the sword, and the *Fallen Hero* loading the Masters dived to intercept the attack. It disintegrated but saved the life of an unconscious Master. Now only Overlord remained.

I have some bad news, Sift said.

How can this get worse?

Those two you snatched with your band just burst out of that snow covered city. They're riding their sky horses directly toward us.

How much time do we have?

A few minutes.

With no one to move the Masters, there was no reason to keep distracting War. Ruwen needed to kill the Aspect quickly, and then do the same if Poison still lived. When Pestilence and Plague arrived Ruwen might survive it, but the Masters certainly wouldn't.

Poison's fog pushed through the *Insect Repellant* barrier, as Ruwen only had his Mana based version. He tried using Harmony to create enough wind to blow the poison away, but the distance exceeded what he could effectively unbalance.

War tilted their head a fraction, as if listening to something.

Ruwen leaped at the Aspect taking advantage of the distraction. He needed to kill War quickly.

Harmony allowed Ruwen to feel the small imbalance of the telepathic communication War currently had with the other Aspects. Likely he had just learned of Pestilence and Plague's arrival.

Ruwen traveled at immense speed toward War, but it wasn't faster than thought, and War triggered an ability that instantly teleported him away. A thread of energy remained, and it led directly toward the top of the outcropping.

The thread of magic reminded Ruwen of a trip wire for a trap, and he stepped away from it. He didn't want to trigger anything that might complicate things further.

Stone Echo confirmed War's new location, standing next to Poison.

Oh, no, Sift said in *Chat.*

I know, War teleported to Poison.

He did?

Ruwen winced as Sift cursed for a couple seconds. He interrupted Sift's outburst. *What was the first "oh no" about?*

Those other two did something to the sky and it will arrive shortly, Sift replied.

How shortly.

Less than a minute.

Ruwen leaped to the *Shed* on top of the outcropping. *Overlord, give me some good news.*

The chalk isn't immediately flaking away anymore. Maybe another thirty seconds and I can draw runes that will stay.

They needed a minute. Ruwen frowned as *Survey* displayed the odd-shaped tunnel that had formed when he'd fallen from the sky. It connected the top of the outcropping with the clearing below. If he didn't refill it, the poison would use it to flow downward and fill the area around the Masters.

From this height, Ruwen stood above most of the trees, and he could see what Sift had observed. The sky roiled with something that looked like ash and a strong wind powered it toward them. Lower to the ground a mass of flying insects approached, unnaturally fast. Survey calculated twenty-one seconds.

The Health bar under Nymthus had returned to a healthy level because of Ruwen's *Bonfire* Regen buff. He spoke to her with Chat. *How are you doing?*

Just really thirsty, but other than that, everyone is recovering, Nymthus responded.

We are still in trouble, but I just had an idea that might protect you all long enough to escape. There is a hole down there from when I struck the ground and Melted it. Gather everyone and quickly get in that tunnel. I'm going to seal it from both ends to keep out whatever the Aspects throw at us. Overlord will have the portal home done within a minute. We just need to hold on.

I'm on it.

Ruwen turned off *Glow* and dropped the Crazors into Inventory. Then he jumped to the tunnel opening on the outcropping side and opened his Void Band until it covered the hole completely. Using fifty Energy, he sucked the air upward out of the tunnel, and out the back of his Void Band. He had pulled a bunch of poison into the tunnel with him earlier, and he didn't want to accidentally kill everyone if any of it remained.

When Nymthus neared the tunnel entrance below, Ruwen closed his Void Band and used *Dig* to seal the top exit. He jumped down next to Prythus and Nymthus and hurried the last few Masters into the hole.

Ruwen dropped three seeds into his hand. "Sorry I don't have anything better to give you light, but I don't want to use anything magical that might give your position away. These are flash seeds. If you crush them, they will blind you for ten seconds, so don't chew them. Instead, swallow them. They'll make you glow from the inside for six hours. Better than sitting in the dark down there."

Prythus and Nymthus both swallowed one and Prythus took the remaining seed. "Thank you for protecting us. We owe you so much."

"Go," Ruwen said as his guilt threatened to surface.

The two members of Rung Four slid down the steep slope of the tunnel and Ruwen quickly closed and smoothed it flat with *Dig*. He leaped over to Overlord and picked up the Baton of a Thousand Uses. He closed the scoop and dropped the tool into Inventory. Nymthus must still have the Fastidious Blade.

The rock hissed and steamed as the blessed paste neutralized the desecration. Ruwen cast a *Shed* around them, leaving most of the rock wall side visible, and then *Hardened* it into diamond. He pulled the Class Symbol of Radiance Sift had given Ruwen after the tour of the mine during Big D's camping trip and channeled ten Energy to it, making it glow brightly. With five Mana, he attached it to the *Shed's* ceiling.

The Shed should keep out the nasties for a bit, Ruwen told Overlord. *Good luck.*

Overlord remained focused on working the blessed paste into the stone but nodded at Ruwen.

Channeling twenty Energy into *Melt*, Ruwen sank into the ground six foot and then moved forward at a shallow downward angle. It took him ten seconds to meet the tunnel the Masters were in. Turning off *Melt*, he quickly returned to Overlord and using *Melt* and *Harden* created a thin rock covering over the tunnel entrance.

Nymthus, Ruwen said using Chat. *I created another tunnel to Overlord and the door back home. I'm going to leave a thin stone covering the exit to keep you hidden and safe if the Shed gets compromised. But if I tell you to go, run up that tunnel, smash the cover, and jump through the portal door.*

Got it.

Ruwen channeled five Energy into *Melt* and placed his back against the rock wall. Instead of vaporizing the stone like before with twenty Energy, the granite turned into a thick paste, and he pushed himself backward into it. Pausing, he briefly switched to *Harden* to reseal the cliff wall that protected Overlord.

Walking through the semi-liquid rock for a couple of feet, Ruwen turned and exited the cliff wall on the outside of the *Shed*. He resealed the exit with *Harden* and leaped to the top of the outcropping.

Now to finish this.

CHAPTER 84

*R*uwen sprinted across the outcropping toward Poison and War. Hope rose again inside him. They had a chance. The Masters sat, safely sealed away from the area of effect spells of Pestilence, Plague, and Poison. Sift and Ruwen only needed to delay the Aspects a little longer, and the door home would be complete.

Swirling particles from Plague's spell surrounded Ruwen and he *Analyzed* them.

Target: *Bloody Tears*
Type: *Resource*
Components: *Burned Blood Flower Seed*
Health: *Extremely Toxic*
Alchemy: *Hallucinogen, Blood Thinner*
Uses: *Poison*

Stay above this ash stuff, Ruwen told Sift. *Use your swords from above. We only need to delay them a minute and we can all get out of here.*

Okay.

Pestilence's contribution crawled across Ruwen's back, through his hair, and into his clothes. The tiny flying worms tried burrowing into his skin and eyes.

Ruwen cast *Insect Repellant*, pulling the ability in close to his body, and channeled the level four Fighter spell *Wrath*. His body burst into magical fire, vaporizing all the bugs that had gotten inside his shield.

Poison and War had moved to the far end of the stone outcropping, almost two thousand feet away, and Ruwen felt a moment of joy. So far from the hidden Masters, it made their success even more likely.

The flying insects interfered enough with Ruwen's hearing, that at this distance, he lost track of the Masters' heartbeats. It didn't matter though, as he still had Nymthus in his group and her portrait had a full Health bar. His plan was working.

Ruwen slowed as he approached War and Poison, wary of a trap, and slipped into the beautiful balance of Harmony.

"Your fighting is pointless," Poison said. "Our Brother and Sister have already returned."

"Tell that to Drought," Ruwen replied. "I showed you all mercy in the Infernal Realm, and this is how you show thanks. First, you attacked me as I fought your Lord, and now this. It is shameful."

"The only thing shameful," War hissed. "Is your misplaced arrogance and incredible ignorance."

A thin strand of magic vibrated like a string. It stretched from War, into the distance behind Ruwen. Stalling for time, Ruwen continued. "What ignorance?"

"That our victory was ever in doubt," War responded.

Sift spoke to Ruwen with *Chat*. *Pestilence and Plague have stopped at the clearing. They're still in the air.*

That makes me nervous. Head down there.

Right.

"This isn't a contest," Ruwen told War. "There doesn't need to be a victor. I will give you what you want."

War pointed the Infernal Blade of Mayhem directly at Ruwen and shouted. "We are at war!"

Stone is ready, Overlord told Ruwen. *Give me thirty seconds to get the runes drawn. Send them up.*

Ruwen's skin flushed, unable to hide the immense joy that surged through him. He spoke to Nymthus over *Chat. Nymthus, head to Overlord. You're going home.*

War shook his head slowly. "You still don't see. You are powerless. Too weak to even summon Famine. You think you can protect those delicious new black belts, when you can't even protect yourself."

The Infernal Blade of Mayhem, still pointed directly at Ruwen, activated, and the five second beam of chaos, *Ray of Slaughter*, exploded from the broadsword.

The beam struck Ruwen in the chest, activating the level eighteen Collector spell *Sunburn*, which he had maxed to spell level five earlier. Instead of damaging him, he converted one hundred percent of the chaos beam into Energy for himself.

Concerned about the thread of magic coming from War, and worried the chaos attack served as a distraction, Ruwen used Harmony to encase War and Poison in rock up to their chests.

War laughed. "You failed."

The thread of energy leading back toward the clearing vibrated and disappeared.

War had disappeared as well.

Ruwen didn't hesitate. He turned and dashed toward Overlord. Black, soot like tendrils, filled the air around him as Poison did his best to disable Ruwen. But Ruwen's Resistances had reached two hundred forty-nine percent, and he resisted everything.

Do you see War? Ruwen asked Sift. *Can you see the Shed Overlord is in?*

No, it's just a huge layer of bugs and ash. Should I get closer?

Ruwen considered Sift's Resistances. *No. Keep an eye on Pestilence and Plague. I'm on my way back.*

Nymthus, Ruwen asked in *Chat. Have you reached Overlord?*

Not yet. We just found the new tunnel.

Hurry.

We are. Wait, I hear a voice. Is Overlord down here?

Ruwen's stomach clenched so hard, he almost tumbled to the ground.

Overlord, Ruwen said. *War is in the tunnel.*

I understand.

The magical thread Ruwen had seen and thought activated some type of trap, had actually triggered the second part of War's spell or Aspect capability. It acted like a two-part *Blink*. Sending you to a new location, and then putting you back in the original spot if you wanted. A great ability for a warrior.

The bugs smashed against Ruwen's *Insect Repellent* shield, leaving behind mucus yellow smears. In moments, he couldn't see at all, and he relied completely on *Survey*.

The bugs created vibrations of their own, however, and it interfered with *Stone Echo*, making the information displayed by *Survey* blurry. Ruwen ran so fast, the pressure wave he built pushed the bugs away and scraped his shield clean.

Pestilence and Plague dropped straight down, through the layer of bugs, Sift said. *Should I follow?*

Ruwen wrestled with the risks for a moment. *Can you coat your body, mouth, and nose with soul energy like a shield.*

Maybe.

If you can, go down. Otherwise, don't.

Ruwen switched focus. He was only a few seconds away. *Nymthus, are you out.*

Overlord rushed by and told us to run. Prythus and I are—Ouch!

Ruwen almost screamed at the sound of pain from Nymthus. *Are you okay?*

Sorry, yes. Some type of surge through my body surprised me.

A moment later Nymthus groaned again and Ruwen desperately watched her Health bar, but it remained full.

No one is in the tunnel, Overlord said in *Chat. It's rapidly filling with some type of burrowing insect. I'm taking damage, and probably can't make it back.*

Thanks, Ruwen told Overlord. *Come back home. You've done more than enough.*

I'm back, Overlord said, now back inside Ruwen's mind.

Something's wrong, Nymthus said.

I'm almost there Ruwen told her. *Hang on.*

Survey displayed the *Shed's* that acted as a poison barrier and Ruwen leaned backward, skidding across the ground to slow himself. He could only hear a handful of heartbeats and he prayed it was because of the interference.

True God help me, Sift whispered in *Chat.*

Ruwen crashed through the *Shed* and dropped the thirty feet to the ground.

Prythus had made it half out of the tunnel when War yanked him up by the head. With a violent squeeze of his armored hands, War crushed the neck of Prythus. Then with the other hand, War grabbed the leader of Rung Four's hair and wrenched the body apart. With a casual toss, War threw the head to the side, and placed the body on a pile near him. Probably so he could collect the belts.

Ruwen stopped himself from vomiting and fed every emotion he had into the third meditation. Twenty-nine bodies lay at War's feet, the remnants of the destroyed *Shed* scattered around them.

Nymthus, do not come out, Ruwen said, his voice distant to his ears. *It's not safe.*

It hurts, Nymthus whispered. *Burns.*

War kneeled and pulled Nymthus out by the hair. "One grass snake left," War said gleefully.

The colors of the world turned harsh, the edges jagged, as Sift transformed into a white sun. The spells of the Aspects vaporized under the onslaught of soul energy, and War held Nymthus up like a shield.

Poison, Pestilence, and Plague joined War, the four of them shielding their eyes against the brightness of Sift. Ruwen strode forward as Sift lowered himself to the ground, still blazing with white light. Twenty feet separated them from the Aspects, and Nymthus hung limply from War's grasp.

Ruwen continued to feed all his emotions into the third meditation, knowing if he didn't, he would lose the ability to function after witnessing the horror that confronted him.

Ruwen and Sift could fight these four and win. Maybe even save Nymthus.

Fog spilled out of the trees, roiling like it was possessed. The silence became oppressive, as if something suppressed every noise in the surroundings. The trees disappeared as the fog engulfed them, and then, out of the mist, a figure emerged.

And they rode a pale horse.

CHAPTER 85

The Aspect held a seven-foot-long scythe, their hand hidden by a dark haze that emerged from the black robe. The robe's hood cast the face in shadow, and the cloth fluttered as if an invisible wind touched it. The pale horse walked slowly, the hoofbeats eerily silent.

Echo had returned.

Tarot had predicted this moment as well. *Your plans, buried under an avalanche of the past, will suffocate and fail. Harken the wolf and the path not taken, or death will surely find you.*

Death had found Ruwen.

More despair than the third meditation could handle filled Ruwen, and for a moment his heart and mind broke. They had a chance against four Aspects, but five seemed unlikely unless he used Spirit. And now that they would force him into using his Spirit anyway, he could have done that earlier and saved everyone. This battle could have ended before it began. Worse, if he and Sift survived this, Ruwen would likely carry permanent scars, and the rest of the Universe would suffer.

And above it all, the knowledge that this was his fault. He could have prevented this entire situation if he'd killed these

Aspects in the Infernal Realm. This blame extended to Echo. Instead of looking for a way to trap her in one of the trials, he'd tried to reach the part of her he hoped existed.

The third meditation recovered from the surge and Ruwen's emotions once again leveled off, although the pain of them remained.

If I don't use Spirit, Ruwen told Overlord, *I die. Five Aspects is too much with just Mana.*

I know, Overlord said with a sigh.

I could have saved them.

Maybe. We don't know yet. I have your memories of the Sixth Rune now. The pain when you tried to use your Core verged on unbearable. I doubt much has changed in a week, despite the heal from Miranda. The most likely scenario is you try to cast a Spirit spell, curl up into a ball, and are promptly banished to the Infernal Realm.

Pestilence, Plague, and Poison sat astride their horses not far from War, who stood holding an unconscious Nymthus by the hair. They all watched the Aspect of Death's slow approach.

As Ruwen prepared for the worst, he wondered how Echo could break her Bamboo Viper Clan vows. The answer sat right in front of him he realized. The Aspects. The armor must change enough about a person that when they became their Aspect, the vows didn't hold. He would use that same advantage when he hunted down and killed Echo for her part in this.

Death stopped ten feet from War, and the other Aspects watched from Death's left side, fifteen feet away.

"You are a welcome sight, Sister," War said. "Although I must confess, I only saved one for you."

Death turned their head and studied the heap of bodies and then the pile of heads. Slowly Death turned their head toward Ruwen and Sift, and the blackness under the hood studied them for a few seconds, before returning their gaze to War.

"What was your mission here?" Death asked, the voice that of a young woman.

"Oh, True God, no," Sift whispered, recognizing Echo's voice.

War nodded his head toward Ruwen. "Banish the brat and find the missing crossing rings if possible."

Death pointed at the pile of heads with their Scythe. "Then what is this?"

"An opportunity for some much-needed fun. The grass snakes are enemies."

"I see," Death said. "Do you desire my belt as well, War? Would you like to remove my head to claim it?"

"Don't be ridiculous. Regardless of your Clan, you will always be one of us."

Death looked again at the pile of heads, not looking away for several seconds, as if memorizing every face. Death returned its gaze to War. Nymthus had awoken from whatever had affected her and she stared in terror at the black clad Aspect.

"Release the woman," Death said. "Leave the dead, including their belts. Depart this place."

The words shocked everyone in the glade.

War recovered first. "What do you mean? Your father sent us here."

Death pointed their Scythe at Ruwen. "For him."

"Then let us finish our task," Plague said.

The pale horse pranced in place, as if sensing their rider's emotions. "It is too late for that."

Poison shifted on his horse. "Are you telling us to disobey your father?"

"This, you have already accomplished," Death responded.

War stood up straight and pointed an armored finger at Death. "Listen here, Echodriel, you—"

A wave of magical energy pulsed outward from Death. Harmony detected the vast imbalance to the surroundings as Sift wavered and dropped to the ground, his soul power interrupted. The Aspects became unnaturally still, as if locked in place.

In a booming voice, deep and terrifying, but still Echo's, Death responded. "Silence! You face Death. Defy me and I will harvest your souls."

After three seconds, Death gave their scythe a small slash, ending the spell and releasing the Aspects. Sift regained the use of his soul power and hovered off the ground again.

In disgust, War threw Nymthus toward Death. As soon as War released Nymthus, she rotated her body with a hard twist and slammed her bare foot into War's plate helm, creating a thunderous ringing sound.

Ruwen winced, expecting to hear bones snapping, but the Health bar under Nymthus didn't waver. War dropped to his knees, stunned by the massive blow, and Nymthus rolled to her feet and sprinted toward Ruwen.

Death turned its pale horse toward Ruwen and slowly advanced. Nymthus stood beside him, breathing hard. Hope warred with disbelief and doubt, whipsawing his thoughts. Had Echo really just evened the odds? Or, maybe, if the Aspects obeyed her, ended this fight? Or was this more cruelty from the Aspects as they toyed with their victims.

Unsure, Ruwen prepared to rotate his Core and destroy every Aspect here, including most probably, himself.

Death's casual pace finally brought them to Ruwen, and they turned to face the other four Aspects.

War punched the ground, and the area shook. He stood and pointed a finger at Death. "Your father will hear of this!"

"I am sure of it," Death said.

The other Aspects remained silent, none of them wanting to fight Lalquinrial's daughter and the Aspect of Death. War summoned his red steed, and the four Aspects galloped into the sky.

Death watched them for ten seconds and then dismissed her

horse. The black robe fluttered in an unseen breeze and Death slid across the ground, their steps leaving no vibrations or other detectable clues. When Death reached the pile of heads, it dropped to its knees. A heartbeat later, the robe disappeared, and the small form of Echo remained.

Rips, burns, and blood, some of it her own, covered Echo's uniform, as if she'd just returned from battle. Tears spilled silently down her cheeks as she stared at the pile.

Nymthus sobbed and ran toward the remains of her friends. Sift released his soul and dropped heavily to the ground, he closed his eyes at the horrible sight, and a low moan of despair escaped his lips.

Ruwen strode forward numbly and collapsed to his knees between Echo and Nymthus. He yanked himself out of the third meditation and embraced the harvest he had planted. The pain in his chest grew so intense he gasped.

"I'm sorry," Ruwen whispered to the sightless eyes. He rocked back and forth on his knees, unsure what to do. "I'm sorry," he repeated again. Anguish choked him. His eyes grew blurry, but he forced himself to repeat the phrase to every dead classmate and friend. "I'm sorry."

The useless and pathetic words Ruwen offered did nothing to ease the mountain of guilt he felt or fix the terrible loss their families would soon experience.

But the words were all Ruwen had, because he didn't have a good excuse. They had died because of him and his foolish decisions.

CHAPTER 86

Shouting broke Ruwen out of his trance of self-loathing.

"You're one of them!" Sift shouted, no longer wearing the Ink Lord Wrap.

"I saved your life!" Echo screamed back. She pointed at the dead bodies. "Why didn't you help them! You're useless!"

Ruwen pushed himself to his feet and stumbled toward Echo and Sift, ten feet away. He rubbed his eyes and cheeks dry.

"How could you let your friends do this?" Sift shouted.

"They're *not* my friends!" Echo screamed back and raised her elbow at Sift.

Sift growled, his eyes and skin turning white.

"Stop!" Ruwen yelled. He reached the pair and stood between them. "Can we stop shouting."

Sift took a deep breath and asked in a somewhat lower voice. "Did you know she was one of those things?"

"I only recently figured that out," Ruwen responded, remembering the shock of seeing Echo transform into Death as she activated his Scarecrow's Infernal Bind point in the Black Pyramid's kitchen. He turned to Echo. "Why did you help?"

Echo narrowed her eyes, and her Disposition Aura went from light pink to dark red. The scent of cinnamon saturated the air. Rage filled her response. "You need to ask?"

Ruwen held up his hands. "I'm just trying to understand. He's your father after all."

Echo took a deep breath and slowly released it. The Disposition Aura lightened but remained darker than before. "Yes, he's my father. Yes, I'm conflicted. But I took the same oaths as you."

Ruwen nodded, finally understanding. "So our Clan oaths remain in effect, even when you become your Aspect." That explained why Echo helped them. Her oaths had forced her into action as soon as she learned of the trouble.

Echo shook her head. "They aren't. Death is free and unbound except for possibly one blood oath. Blood magic is different. More personal. But our Clan oaths," she shook her head. "Powerless."

"What does that mean?" Sift asked.

Ruwen made a fist, placed his left palm on top, and bowed to Echo. "My apologies Sister, for doubting you."

Echo still glared at Ruwen, but the Disposition Aura returned to its light pink color. "You should be." She turned back to Sift and placed an index finger on his chest, pushing him backward. "And so should this clown."

Sift tightened his jaw, and Ruwen spoke to him over *Chat*. *She didn't need to help. Her Aspect doesn't feel the weight of our oaths. We owe her.*

Sift closed his eyes and sighed. He took a step backward and bowed to Echo. "Thank you, Sister."

Echo flashed Sift her elbow again, muttered "stupid clowns," and strode to Nymthus, who had finished arranging the bodies with their owner's head.

Misery punched Ruwen in the stomach and he forced himself to keep his eyes open. He stepped over to Nymthus and blurted his confession, the need for honesty almost as painful as the sorrow of everyone's death.

"This is my fault," Ruwen said.

"No, wait," Sift said as he came up next to Ruwen. "This is my fault. If I hadn't wanted to fight that Champion, we wouldn't have split up. We could have reacted faster. Better maybe."

Ruwen stepped in front of Sift. "You bear no responsibility for this. I made two huge mistakes that cost all these lives."

Sift opened his mouth to argue and Ruwen shook his head. "Listen to me, and you'll know."

Sift nodded.

Ruwen let out a long breath and locked gazes with Nymthus. "I let these creatures live. I had the power to destroy them, and I didn't. If I had, your friends would still be here. Their families would get to see them again, and your world wouldn't be lost." He swallowed hard as the guilt tightened his throat. "Then I destroyed that Infernal Crossing Ring and took four others bringing the Infernal Lord's gaze to this place. They came because I let them live and because I all but invited them here."

"Unless Death told her dad about you and they would have come anyway," Sift said.

Ruwen could actually hear Echo grinding her teeth. "I did not betray my Clan," she hissed. "I haven't spoken to anyone about the stupidity that surrounds me."

"There you have it," Sift said. "The word of an Infernal demon and the Aspect of Death."

Echo actually looked hurt and Sift sighed. "Fine, I'm sorry for saying that. But you must admit your absence worked out for the bad guys."

Echo looked down. "Maybe he knew. He has the Architect's sight, after all. But even so, my tasks are legitimate. There are only a few people father can trust completely."

"What tasks?" Ruwen asked.

Echo glanced up. "Infernal Realm stuff."

"I forgive you," Nymthus whispered.

The words felt like a sword had ripped Ruwen's chest open. He stepped in front of Nymthus, his words growing louder until he shouted. "No. What are you saying? I'm despicable. You should hate me. Despise me. Curse my name. I killed your friends!"

Nymthus stepped forward and hugged Ruwen. His arms hung limply at his side as Nymthus squeezed him.

"No, no, no, no," Ruwen just kept repeating the word. How could Nymthus forgive such an atrocious act?

"You are a good man," Nymthus said softly as she released Ruwen. "Anyone can see that by spending a few minutes with you. I trust your decisions. The responsibility for this act rests at the feet of the four surviving Aspects. I hope to someday hold them accountable." After a moment she continued. "We were trying to destroy the Crossing Ring when you arrived. Just attacking it like we did might have triggered their arrival. We will never know, and you should not assume you caused this."

"But I let them live," Ruwen whispered again.

"I do not second guess fate," Nymthus replied. "We can't know if something is good or bad until time has passed. Even this," Nymthus choked and stopped to gather herself. "Even this, might serve some greater purpose."

Ruwen's shoulders ached a little from the tight hug Nymthus had given him. There was also the massive bare-footed kick to War's armored helmet. As he'd walked over to speak to her, he'd noticed how much better her posture had become. He could tell her center of gravity was near perfect for her stance.

"You changed," Ruwen said. "I can see it." He rubbed his shoulders. "And feel it."

For just a heartbeat, Nymthus smiled before the deep sadness returned. She waved her hand at the seven bodies nearest her. They all belonged to Rung Four. "The spell thread in our belts had the One From Many enchantment. It bound us together and when someone died the remaining members received a percentage of their skills and strengths. It was so we could, in a way, continue to fight for our cause even after we died."

Ruwen understood now. Nymthus had the strength and skills of seven others. "Honestly, you feel stronger than that. And your balance looks nearly perfect."

Nymthus rubbed her arms as if a cold breeze had brushed against her. "I don't think the enchantment expected everyone to die in such a short timeframe. I think it changed me too much."

"It appears so," Ruwen said. "We have a power ranking system and middle tier are Gems, the highest of which is Diamond. That's what I think you are."

"What does that mean?" Nymthus asked.

"It means," Echo said. "That you could survive fighting one of those Aspects if they appeared alone. Possibly, with your Clan training, even beat them."

Nymthus looked down at her right hand. "It seems impossible. Even if true, my people will lose hope when word spreads only one Master survived. Perhaps we were never meant to have serenity."

Ruwen looked up from the bodies to Nymthus. "Did you say serenity? Why did you use that word?"

Nymthus shrugged. "Calm, peaceful, and untroubled, who doesn't desire this?"

"I can think of a few," Ruwen responded. "But I have something. Well, it's not really mine. Although she told me to destroy it so maybe that does make it mine. What are the rules for that? I—"

Sift put a hand on Ruwen's shoulder. "Nobody knows what you're talking about."

"Right," Ruwen said. "I should have started with that." He reached into his Void Band and carefully grabbed the end of the item. As he pulled the first section of marble out, he nodded at Sift to grab it, and then took a few steps to allow room for the item to emerge.

Sift and Ruwen started to kneel to set the nine-hundred-pound sculpture on the ground when Echo screamed. It was high pitched and not at all fitting for the Aspect of Death.

Echo blushed but pointed at the sculpture. "Do not let that touch this ground. I honestly don't know what would happen."

Sift shifted on his feet. "Like crack-a-little don't know, or like destroy-the-planet don't know."

"Closer to the second one, I think," Echo said. She stepped closer to the sculpture but didn't touch it.

"Why do you have so much dangerous stuff in there?" Sift asked Ruwen.

"It is literally a marble carving of mountains and the sun. How can that be dangerous?"

Nymthus stared at the sculpture, more tears covering her cheeks. She rubbed at them. "I didn't think I had any tears left."

"I have a lot of questions," Echo said. "If you answer them truthfully, I will tell you what that is."

CHAPTER 87

"It's a marble statue," Ruwen said. "It's so beautiful it gives you a buff called Serenity. That's why I thought of this when Nymthus said it."

Echo turned to Nymthus. "Do you feel anything when you look at this?"

Nymthus nodded. She tried to speak but couldn't. She swallowed hard and managed one word. "Hope."

"And you?" Echo asked Ruwen.

"It's beautiful, but I'm no art guy," Ruwen said. "It gives me a buff called Serenity which adds five points to my Wisdom and increases all my Resistances by ten percent. Its quality is legendary however, which is one of the reasons I didn't want to destroy it when Valora went a little crazy."

"I remember this," Sift said. "Do you still have her arm?"

Echo and Nymthus both turned to Ruwen, horror on their faces.

"It is a long and complicated story," Ruwen said. "And I gave the arm back the next time I saw her."

That "time" had been during the fight for New Eiru as Ruwen ran for the deep hole Uru's Third Temple had been dropped into. Valora, the Naktos Stone Carver had seen him and went into a rage. He had launched her arm from his Void Band like a spear, which he felt bad about. She had demanded he destroy the sculpture he'd found in the Dark Portal he'd taken from her.

"Anyway," Ruwen continued. "I'm sure she has a brand-new arm by now. Can we go back to what this is please."

"I need more details," Echo said. "Where did you get it?"

Ruwen bit his lip, as sharing information with Echo seemed dangerous, but his curiosity had already ignited. "Naktos had tunneling crews digging under Uru's Temple. One of those Stone Carvers made this. And then I found it in her Inventory when I was *forced* to cut off her arm."

Echo pinched the bridge of her nose and shook her head.

"What?" Ruwen asked.

"How can one person cause so much trouble?" Echo asked. She pointed at the sculpture. "Guess who commissioned that and who failed to provide it."

"I don't like where this is headed," Ruwen said. "Since she was a servant of Naktos, I'm guessing he is the one who failed to deliver it."

Echo nodded.

"And since I saw demons trying to break through Uru's Third Temple right before I launched it into the sky, I'm guessing your father wanted it."

"Ugh," Echo screamed. "We have to make some kind of Clan oath or some binding to prevent me from revealing I know about this."

"What is it?" Nymthus asked.

Echo pointed at the sculpture. "Some things are so perfect they capture the very essence of the items they mirror. Items like this are so rare, legendary, doesn't do them justice."

"Essence like what Spirit is made from?" Ruwen asked.

"No," Echo replied. "Not at all like that. Abstract things, like the feeling of sunlight, or the smell of rain, or the freedom of a cloud."

"How can it help Nymthus?" Ruwen asked.

"That is a level zero Artifact," Echo said. "Its perfection has allowed it to absorb things like sun, stone, and cloud essence, but it can just as easily absorb things like faith and hope. That's a big deal by itself, but an Artifact's real power is that it can mix and amplify these essences, returning them as buffs. Sometimes permanent buffs. Like you see it once, and it changes you forever. Gods covet them. And my dad commissioned this exact one for a world he wants to control. This would have made it trivial. He will lose his mind if he knows you took this from him."

"But if Nymthus takes this," Ruwen said. "Wont your dad go steal it once Nymthus shows it off?"

"It's only level zero," Echo said. "If Nymthus takes this and spends a few weeks meditating and praying near it, she will bind the Artifact to herself, and limit the Artifact's power to the things she cares about. I assure you, Nymthus and my father have nothing in common. This will become useless to him."

"It looks fragile," Sift said. "Can't someone just come by and break it?"

"In its current state, yes," Echo said. "As soon as Nymthus increases its level from zero to one, it is almost indestructible. Artifacts are symbols that generate great power. It was a massive blow to my father's plans when Naktos lost this sculpture. I find it interesting the creator wanted you to destroy it. Perhaps she learned its ultimate destination."

"A symbol is what we need," Nymthus said. "Only hope will see us to victory. But I cannot accept something so valuable."

"I have a quest to return this to the sculptor," Ruwen said, "but after all the damage I caused, I—" He paused as his mouth went dry and he lost his voice. He started again. "If this can help in any way, I want you to have it. I will find the sculptor and explain what I did."

Nymthus shook her head.

"Nymthus, I am begging you," Ruwen whispered. "There is a hole in my heart, and I don't know if I'll ever recover from today. The debt I owe your people pales in comparison to giving you this sculpture. Please, please, take it."

After five seconds, Nymthus gave a small nod, and Ruwen sighed in relief. She removed her black belt and ran her fingers down the side, opening the dimensional storage along its entire length. She stepped over her belt and grasped the nine-hundred-pound marble sculpture, easily moving it to the belt. In moments, the storage opening closed, and she tied the belt around her waist.

Nymthus bowed to Ruwen and he returned it.

"We need a secrecy oath," Echo said.

"I'm good at these," Sift said. "Gather around." He placed a hand in the center between them.

Ruwen placed his hand on Sift's, and Nymthus rested hers gently on Ruwen's. Echo's small hand came last.

Sift cleared his throat. "Okay, so, this is a secrecy oath—"

"Are you just copying what I said?" Echo asked.

"No," Sift said. He started again. "This is an oath of secrecy."

Echo rolled her eyes. "This is a bad idea."

"No," Sift said. "Wait. Give me a second." Sift closed his eyes and five uncomfortable seconds passed, then, he opened his eyes, cleared his throat, and spoke. "In the last grove of our fallen Brothers and Sisters, whose blood soaks this desecrated land, we four, witnesses to tragedy, heartbroken by fate, faithfully steadfast, affirm and swear this oath of secrecy, to not communicate in any fashion the whereabouts of the Legendary Artifact safeguarded by Nymthus of the Bamboo Viper Clan. As Step Masters, we guard our bodies, let this expertise now protect our thoughts and memories. We four, the last of our class, Brothers and Sisters of the Bamboo Viper Clan, so swear."

Sift's hand glowed with white soul energy, causing the blood-soaked hand of Nymthus to radiate a deep red color. A ball of warmth in the middle of Ruwen's chest expanded and flowed down his right arm. Gold light surrounded his hand. Ruwen felt the surge of Spirit from Echo, and it spilled out her palm, surrounding all their hands.

Ruwen's skin flushed, and he shivered. The others did as well. What felt like lightning passed through their hands, and for a moment he felt dizzy. A notification appeared and he opened it.

Thrum!
You have accepted a Celestial Oath...

We Four
You have vowed to not disclose the location or stewardship of the Legendary Artifact, Clouds Embracing the Sun. This oath, bound with the original forces of soul, blood, divinity, and spirit, has transcended the heavens. No power above or below can breach the Celestial Vault holding these memories.
Reward: *Unarmed Combat level added to Mind Resistance.*
Reward: *Grove of Four – mental grove of bamboo, hiding memories and thoughts from intruders. Trespassers take Unarmed Combat level damage per second from the vipers inhabiting the grove.*
Reward: *Celestial Vault – an unassailable mental refuge capable of holding other memories for a number of seconds equal to Unarmed Combat level.*
Restriction: *Physically and mentally unable to discuss this topic or oath with anyone other than the original four oath takers.*

Warning!: This is a soul binding and bridges death.

"Wow," Echo said as she pulled her hand back. Her body trembled with another shiver. "That was okay."

"Thanks," Sift replied.

Overlord, Ruwen asked. *Do you know what that gold energy was?*

Uruziel added a bit of her Divine energy to show her sympathy.

Tell her thank you. None of them deserved to die.

Nymthus hugged Sift for a few seconds, and when she let go, Ruwen gave Sift a nod. "Great job, buddy. It sounded perfect, and you expanded your vocabulary."

Sift shook his head. "It's this armor. I can't stop thinking all the time, and it's driving me crazy." Sift pressed the Emblem of Dominion and Inklord Wrap into Ruwen's hand. "You can have your job back."

Ruwen placed the paper bracelet around his right wrist and returned the Emblem of Dominion to his Inventory. It appeared Sift hadn't enjoyed the extra fifty points of Intelligence the armor provided, but it had created an excellent oath.

Ruwen explained to Nymthus what the oath provided her since she didn't get notifications. He didn't know how detailed Sift's were either, or if Echo got them, so Ruwen did it for their benefit as well.

The oath had turned into something miraculous. The benefits awed Ruwen, and he marveled at what the four combined powers had created.

They all faced the bodies again.

"How will we get them back?" Nymthus whispered.

"I'll handle that," Ruwen replied in the same soft tone.

The four of them stood silently, their clothes and feet covered in blood, each lost in their own thoughts.

The enormity of the loss struck Ruwen again. His reluctance to kill had cost the lives of twenty-nine of his friends and classmates. Regardless of what Nymthus said, he knew the truth. The reasons for not killing Lalquinrial's Aspects were naïve and foolish. They were the ideals of a sixteen-year-old, sheltered his whole life from the realities and brutality of war.

He needed to change.

"I'm sorry," Ruwen whispered the useless phrase yet again.

The misery and despair seeped into every part of Ruwen's body. Anguish smothered him, and his thoughts crystalized into a single realization. If change didn't come from this, then it made these deaths even more senseless.

Ruwen didn't need to change. He *would* change.

A part of Ruwen died. The happy, second-chance optimism of everything will turn out fine, had crashed into the reality of the Universe.

Now Ruwen knew, at least in part, what he felt so sorry about. It had taken the deaths of all these people for him to see an issue he could have addressed without such a catastrophic event.

"I'll change," Ruwen whispered to the dead.

Silence descended again as they each dealt with the crushing loss of their classmates.

"We should go," Echo said. "There are safer places for this."

Everyone nodded. Nymthus, forcing herself forward as if she battled a fierce wind, stepped in front of the first body. "Prythus, leader of Rung Four, Bamboo Viper Master, loving father and husband. I will cherish your memories of skipping stones on the south beach of Dreaming Lake. Seventeen perfect circles, spreading outward, their rings combining until the lake calmed and reclaimed the stillness for itself. Seventeen, a record that will live on among our people. Goodbye Prythus, know your niece and nephew will live safely with me. I will miss you."

Nymthus placed her open palm on top of her right fist and bowed deeply, holding it for five seconds. She stepped to the next body and Sift, then Echo, repeated the bows.

Ruwen stepped in front of Prythus and mirrored their bows. He opened his Void Band and as he passed it over the body, he whispered. "May the grove shelter you and the nest keep you warm. Farewell my brother."

They repeated this twenty-eight more times. Nymthus had a memory for every person, and her attention to detail reflected how much she cared about her classmates. She had that rare ability to see and capture the essence of a person. All of them laughed and cried as she honored each of her Brothers and Sisters.

Then it was done, and only the four of them remained.

"That was beautiful, Nymthus," Ruwen said.

"Thank you," Sift whispered.

"You will make a superb leader," Echo said.

Nymthus shook her head. "I'm no leader."

Echo placed a hand on the arm of Nymthus. "You are. And you will be again."

Ruwen considered the irony of the Universe. That the daughter of the god that spearheaded the invasion that plagued the world of Nymthus, would show support for the only person left with the skill and tools to stop it.

Nymthus held out the Fastidious dagger and Ruwen shook his head. "Keep it. It is a fine blade and will serve you well."

Nymthus protested and Ruwen whispered. "Please."

"Thank you," Nymthus said shyly. "I quite like it."

Ruwen felt wrung out emotionally, almost numb. The guilt and loss remained, but his ability to process the pain had reached its limit. He guessed it would take a long time to get through it all, assuming he ever could.

Ruwen strode over to the tunnel entrance where Overlord's Fallen Hero had died and picked up the portal chalk. He walked to the stone and brushed the dried blessed paste off the rock. He drew the gate runes for the Masters' Village.

The time had come to inform the Bamboo Viper Clan of the tragedy, along with who bore the responsibility.

CHAPTER 88

To Ruwen's surprise and dismay, the Founders didn't punish his lack of judgement. He had hoped for some type of rebuke, anything to help blunt the guilt and pain. They mourned the loss of so many Masters but took it far better than he'd expected. Didn't anyone understand the depth of his responsibility? Why would no one make him pay for his actions?

Instead, they buried the Masters in the bamboo grove overlooking the sea. Permanent death for people so young was new to Ruwen and he hated the idea of placing people under the ground.

The Founders insisted, explaining the Masters would live on forever as part of the grove. After burying the dead, nothing remained for Ruwen. Mist requested that Nymthus stay in the village a little longer. Mist and Padda would start her training in the Bamboo Grandmaster path.

Echo, too, needed to stay. The Founders told her a Master had fallen ill, and his Sijun still required training. They informed her she shared a bond with the student and would understand eventually.

Thorn and Mist planned to instruct Sift themselves but could not start his Grandmaster training immediately and offered him a place in the village to wait. Technically, he could take the Grandmaster test immediately and pass, but he wanted to leave.

Kysandra had still not responded to the Founders so Ruwen had nothing tying him to the village either. He turned down the offer to rest there, expressing his gratefulness for the offer.

Ruwen, just like Sift, wanted to go home.

They hugged Nymthus, and Ruwen promised he'd visit her when he could. Echo flashed Ruwen and Sift an elbow, which made Ruwen smile. He bowed to her and Sift followed a moment later.

As they strode toward the portal stone, Sift looked at Ruwen. "Do you think she knows what that means? Maybe someone told her it meant 'thank you.' Like as a joke."

"I don't think a lot of joking happens in the Infernal Realm," Ruwen responded. "Her childhood was probably horrific."

"Yeah, I can see that. It's weird being on the same side with her."

"Echo has more than her fair share of internal conflict. Some battles are hard to see."

"Well, I'm glad to put her, and this whole trial, behind me. I just want to get home and find Lylan, and then my turtle."

"I wouldn't worry about Shelly." Ruwen said as he removed the portal chalk. "She will reappear shortly. And speaking of home, I'm taking us to my lair. I need to talk with Fractal and hopefully Rami, before I inevitably get sidetracked. If Hamma is with Lylan, tell her I'll be there in a few minutes."

Sift winced. "Maybe I should wait. It might get you in trouble if I show up and you didn't. It might make Hamma feel like you don't care as much."

Ruwen glanced at Sift. "Wow, that is some real emotional intelligence."

"It's just common sense. Even appahs know the greenest grass gets eaten first."

"I have no idea what that means."

"It's about priorities, my brother."

Ruwen shook his head. "Hamma knows her importance to me. I trust she'll understand."

Sift tilted his head. "If you spoke the language of—"

"Stop! Love is not a language. I should know, I speak like all of them. Even if it was, I'd communicate just fine."

After a few steps, and a little consideration, Ruwen continued. "But I see your point. How about this. After we arrive you get Lylan and Hamma and bring them back to the lair. That way I get a few minutes alone with Fractal and hopefully Rami and then we can figure out what to do together."

"That is a much better plan."

They had almost reached the portal stone.

"With everything I've discovered about balance," Ruwen said. "I still haven't found it in my personal life."

They reached the portal stone, and none of the gate runes had faded away on their own yet, and Ruwen didn't know what runes he could clear to draw his own. So instead, he created a *Shed* behind the nearest hut, and drew the gate runes for the Dungeon Master's Lair inside Fractal on the wall.

Ruwen's stomach turned. "I'm nervous."

"That makes two of us," Sift said. "True God knows where this will take me. Remember last time when you dropped us in the middle of a forest?"

Ruwen started to argue but Sift grinned and stepped through the portal. It might have been the first time he'd voluntarily gone first. He must really be anxious to see Lylan but couldn't resist poking Ruwen while doing it.

Letting out a long breath, Ruwen stepped through the door and into his Dungeon Master's Lair.

Sift stood just a couple feet from the wall, and Ruwen almost stepped into him.

Rocks, gems, and crystals, ranging in size from inches to yards, covered the floor, making it hard to walk.

"I love what you've done to the place," Sift said.

"Wow," Ruwen replied, unsure what else to say about the mess.

Ruwen? Rami asked.

Hey, Rami. I missed you.

I'm headed your way.

Thanks.

Sift took a deep breath. "It feels good to be back."

Ruwen nodded, but fear of the unknown tempered his joy. He removed Sift's Cultivator robes from Inventory, and channeled *Scrub* over the clothes as he handed them over.

"Thanks," Sift said as he changed out of his formal Bamboo Viper Clan attire.

Ruwen did the same, changing into the soft black cotton of the Black Pyramid garments.

The stone floor vibrated, and a faint glow came from one of the thick crystal veins running over all the surfaces.

"I think Fractal is almost here," Ruwen said.

Sift dropped his formal attire into his dimensional belt and shuffled his feet toward the wall, not wanting to step on any of the scattered items. He touched his wrist to the stone. "Lylan," he said simply. A portal opened, and he looked back at Ruwen. "Thanks again for everything. I guess, maybe after all you did, teaching me and fighting the Founders to help me, when compared with the eighteen months to fetch you, maybe we're…" Sift paused, looking for the right word.

Ruwen held his breath. After all his attempts, might Sift say "even" on his own? Ruwen desperately wanted to complete *That's Not a Number*, and remove the Uneven debuff that put the taste of maple syrup in his mouth every morning.

"Balanced," Sift finally said.

Ruwen hid his disappointment but nodded. "Of course."

Sift turned back to the portal but paused again. He looked over his shoulder. "Or, what's that word you've been trying to get me to say for months? Even? We're even."

Sift winked and jumped through the portal.

The Uneven debuff disappeared and Ruwen stared at the portal in shock. How long ago had Sift figured this out?

Fractal arrived, traveling through one of the many crystal tubes that ran everywhere. He erupted from the floor and shot toward Ruwen at a very unsafe speed. He caught Fractal and stepped backward a few steps to bleed the momentum from the impact.

Fractal shatters in joy at your return.

Ruwen grinned at the small crystal sitting in his palm. When he had first met Fractal the Dungeon Keeper had looked like a handful of quartz crystals mashed together into a vaguely human shape the length of his index finger.

Now, just over two years later, Fractal had grown up. His speech came faster and clearer, and physically he'd grown to the length of Ruwen's hand. The Dungeon Keeper had taken on more human traits as well, with tiny blue sapphires for eyes, and a cape made of small colored gems. His arms and legs still ended in points, but he could instantly morph them into hands and feet when required. Wherever his body touched a surface, rainbows appeared from his body fracturing the light.

Ruwen hugged Fractal to his chest. *I shatter as well. It's good to be home.* He glanced around at the scattered mess. *It looks like you've spent some time in here.*

Fractal keep his favorites here while wait for Dungeon Master. I'm sorry it took so long. But I brought you some gifts.

Fractal jumped up and down on Ruwen's hand, and a thick stone pillar erupted from the ground a foot in front of him. It stopped rising when it reached his waist. Fractal jumped down onto the stone altar and ran around in a circle.

A portal opened on the wall Sift had used to leave, and a young woman stepped out. She dashed toward Ruwen, her dark hair streaming behind her, and her bare feet making small slapping noises against the stone floor. She leaped at him and he caught her.

"Hi, Rami," Ruwen said, returning her fierce hug. "I missed you so much."

Fractal continued to run around the altar, and after a few seconds Rami let go.

Rami looked up at him, concern on her face. "What happened? Why are you so sad?"

Ruwen's throat tightened, and he couldn't speak. *Easier if you just look,* he thought to Rami.

Rami kept her hands on Ruwen's forearms and closed her eyes. After ten seconds she gasped, and tears streaked her cheeks. Five seconds later, she let go of Ruwen, opened her eyes, wiped them as best she could, and gave him another light hug.

"I'm so sorry," Rami whispered.

"Thank you," Ruwen whispered back. "The guilt and responsibility have unbalanced me. I can feel it, but I'm still able to use Harmony. I need to find a way to deal with the sorrow and guilt before it overwhelms me and pulls me completely out of balance."

Rami continued to cry and Ruwen frowned. "Are you okay?"

Tears flowed down Rami's cheeks, but she nodded.

Ruwen hugged Rami again. "What's wrong?"

Rami sobbed into his chest.

"Hey, what's going on?" Ruwen asked gently.

"My mom," Rami said. "She's so alone." Then after a small pause she continued. "And I've never really met her."

Ruwen closed his eyes and hugged Rami tighter. He had forgotten about that revelation during his time in the Third

Secret. Miranda had remained in Pen's Divine Realm since Pen had died. Every interaction Rami had ever had with her mom she now realized, had been with an apparition created by her actual mother trapped in the third secret.

"I have a plan," Ruwen said. "I'm going to finish this business quickly. Then you can see your mom for real. Okay?"

Rami nodded, and after a few seconds Ruwen released her. A part of his heart had returned, and most of the rest would arrive here soon.

Overlord cast *Fallen Heroes* and appeared next to Ruwen.

"What's this?" Overlord asked. "I thought I was the favorite?"

Rami laughed, wiped the rest of her tears away, and hugged Overlord.

Ruwen turned to Fractal who still raced around the altar in excitement. "Okay, Champ. Here you go."

When Ruwen placed the Void Band over the Altar, the top of the stone turned into a bowl as Fractal jumped to the edge. He sat swinging his legs and looked up at Ruwen expectantly.

The items for Fractal were spread haphazardly throughout Ruwen's Inventory. So he just started at the beginning and scanned the contents, dropping Fractal's gifts whenever he came across one.

Into Fractal's dish Ruwen dropped:

10 black crossing stones from Savage Island
Infernal Banishment Band of Physical Protection taken from the Aspect of Drought
3 gallons of ocean water that glowed when agitated from the Master's Village
33 razor weed plants from the third trial
Floot adhesive and acid from the fake boxes
3 spiral mass fern spores from the space plant
10 cacti also from the Floot trial
A clump of grass and 5 flowers from under the first trial's tower

Clothes covered in demon blood and desecrated infernal soil
23 Slugs of Forced Meditation

Fractal jumped up and down in excitement, and Rami laughed at seeing his obvious joy.

Ruwen looked back and forth between them. "I have three important tasks for the two of you." He waited until Fractal stopped moving and looked up at Ruwen with full attention. "Each of these tasks are incredibly important, but if I had to put them in order, here they are. First, my Spiritual network of paths and meridians are badly swollen and inflamed. I need something to heal that damage as soon as possible. Not having access to Spirit weakens me massively, and this is no time for weakness."

"I'll start looking immediately," Rami said. "And Fractal has added significantly to your personal library. He offers adventurers loot bonuses for books. The rarer the better. He has become quite the scholar, although his shelving method makes no sense."

Ruwen looked down at Fractal. "Is that true? I'm so proud of you!"

Fractal dropped the spiral mass fern spore and jumped upward. Ruwen caught and hugged him. Fractal stood on Ruwen's palm, and he held out his hand so the Dungeon Keeper was between him and Rami.

"Okay, so the second thing is related to the first," Ruwen said. "Once I heal myself, I want to transition from Gem to Divine as soon as I can. From what I've gathered, that process takes a long time. Maybe even centuries. I want to do it vastly faster than that. We need to figure out an elixir or some process to accomplish it."

"Those are tall orders," Rami said.

"I know," Ruwen responded. "But the sooner we start the faster I can finish the Fourth Secret and live my own life. Which brings me to my last request." Ruwen brought his face close to Fractal's. "The God Stone you are working on with Miranda, the one that will allow revival without a god involved, how is it going?"

Need Energy. Need Dungeon Master. Close, close, close, Fractal kept repeating the word close as he jumped up and down.

Ruwen smiled. "Okay, great. It made me think though. Your God Crystal stores not only the person's attributes and skills, but their core, meridians, paths, and all that stuff. Basically everything."

Yes, yes, yes, Fractal repeated. *Everything.*

"Okay," Ruwen said. "Here is the part I'm hoping you can help with. I want you to test changing the information you stored before you do the revival. Specifically, I want you to attempt attaching pathways to Meridians."

"What are you thinking?" Rami asked.

Ruwen faced Rami. "I don't want to lose the people I love. With Fractal's help, and your mother's crystal-based revival, I plan to remake you all into gods."

CHAPTER 89

*R*ami looked shocked.

Friends coming, Fractal said.

Ruwen wanted to take care of two more items before everyone showed up. *Lir?*

Yes, Architect Starfield?

It's good to hear your voice.

I welcome your return, Architect. There are items that need your attention.

How many? Wait, just the high priority ones.

One million, two hundred—

Stop, Ruwen interrupted, staggered by the number. *That will need to wait.*

As you wish.

Sift stepped out of a portal on the wall, and Ruwen knew he only had seconds left.

I need you to find a way to synchronize me. Please study my current state, as I've added a few complications. If I revive now, it comes with a catastrophic loss of abilities and knowledge. We need to fix that.

Architect, are you aware of the Divine Fragment you contain?

Yeah, and there are a few million other entities in here as well. I want to save them all. This is a priority. Tell me the resources you need, and I will provide them.

Lylan stepped through the portal, and they exchanged nods. She immediately strode over to Sift and grabbed his hand.

Can you and the other Temples identify when someone is hearing my voice or seeing me? Ruwen asked.

Yes, if it occurs within Uru's Blessing.

Great. Can you modify what they remember about me? Like the sound of my voice?

It will require specific permission as altering memories is an Architect only privilege.

Understood. I have an idea, but it requires my identity remain hidden from most people. We'll talk later. Thanks.

Hamma stepped through the portal, and Ruwen's chest tightened. Her heart thudded quickly, the excitement of seeing him impossible to hide. She glanced around the room and her eyes found him, their gazes locking. He handed Fractal to Overlord and strode to Hamma.

Ruwen pulled her into a hug, breathing in the faint scent of lavender. She hugged him back, their embrace tight.

"I missed you," Ruwen whispered.

"I'm so happy you're home," Hamma whispered back.

After another few seconds, they released each other.

"Sift and I worried about you both," Ruwen said.

"We're fine," Hamma said as she stepped back. She frowned. "What happened? Why do you look so sad."

Ruwen's chest tightened, and his heart ached as he thought about his twenty-nine dead classmates. "Later." He finally got out. Normally he wouldn't remove these feelings, figuring he owed it to the dead to endure them, but he needed to communicate right now, so he pushed all the self-hate, guilt, and sorrow into the third meditation.

"How are things here?" Ruwen asked.

"That's hard to answer," Hamma said.

In a rush, Ruwen spilled his worries. "Are my parents back? Have you seen Ky? What about Bliz and Big D? Is the country in civil war? And is that guy still in the city causing issues?"

Hamma's eyes widened. "Um, we saw Ky a few days ago, but I don't know about anyone else."

Ruwen hid his disappointment. "I had hoped you'd visited Pour Judgement."

Lylan cleared her throat. "Some Black Pyramid business took our attention."

"Yeah," Hamma said. "A lot happened after you left."

Ruwen's shoulders slumped. "I'm so sorry about that. Echo was in the Black Pyramid for the Master's Trial and she triggered my Scarecrow Aspect. I ended up in a trap in the Infernal Realm."

Hamma's eyes grew large. "What? The Infernal Realm?"

Ruwen nodded. He touched his chest. "I kind of broke myself escaping."

Hamma placed a hand on his chest and Ruwen felt Energy coursing through his body as her spell looked for damage. "I can't find anything."

"It's all spiritual damage."

Hamma nodded but kept her hand on Ruwen's chest. He placed his hand over it. "I ended up at the Bamboo Viper Master's trial along with Sift. We rushed through most of it, so we could return."

"I understand," Hamma said.

"What happened here?" Sift asked. "That stupid Misfortune Golem told us you were in danger."

Lylan turned slowly toward Sift. Like his words had stunned her ability to move. "What golem?"

Sift shrugged. "Some golem Ruwen picked up. I think it's worse than Hamma's." Sift laughed and turned to Lylan. "Thank the True God we don't have any of those things."

Lylan reached up and touched her earring, smiling weakly at Sift. "No kidding."

"Well?" Sift asked. "What happened here?"

Hamma and Lylan exchanged a long glance and Ruwen frowned.

Hamma cleared her throat. "What happened doesn't matter. Or, it does matter, actually, but not right now. Let's take a second and appreciate *this* moment, before we rush off to fix the world's problems. Let's rejoice that all of us are safe and together. Let's celebrate what matters."

Ruwen grinned. "That almost sounds like a sermon, Priestess."

Hamma looked up at Ruwen and smiled. "It was my last prayer."

"Well, amen," Ruwen said as he hugged Hamma again.

Soon, Ruwen knew, they would venture outside this lair, and the world's problems would test them once again, but for now, they had all finally made it home, and that's the only thing that mattered.

The End

EPILOGUE

*G*under sighed in frustration as another knock interrupted his thoughts. He looked up from the ledger on his lap and raised his voice so his head of security, which everyone just called Hos, could hear him through the door. "Yes?"

"Sorry to disturb you again, sir, that security breach remains active, and we wish to move you from the city."

"I thought you sent a team to address it."

"We did, sir. Unsuccessfully."

"Are you positive it's one person?"

"By all appearances, sir."

"I'm confused. Are you saying one man countered six of your specialists?"

Three seconds passed in silence, and then the response finally came. "Countered does not capture the encounter, sir. Ignored is a better term. No one saw the fight, but all six men are down."

"Dead?" Gunder asked.

Another pause. "Unsure, sir. Somehow the group I'd formed with the team terminated before the attack."

"Did you cancel the group?"

"No, sir."

"Do you think he did somehow?"

Before Gunder could get a response, a buff appeared on his display. Shouting erupted from the guards arrayed around this building. It appeared he wasn't the only one to have the unexpected addition to his display. He focused on the buff and read the details.

Uru's Favor: *Cure Hunger, Cure Thirst, Minor Heal, Minor Cure Poison, Regen +10%.*

Gunder closed the ledger, placed it on the nearby desk, and opened the door. "Send two more teams. I want to see this man for myself."

Gunder considered the buff Uru's Favor. The power to generate such a large area of effect spell meant this intruder must be a Cultivator. Probably another troublemaker from the mountain group Phoenix led. He had hoped Phoenix would see reason, but if not, Gunder wouldn't allow an enemy to remain so close. If this did turn out to be a Cultivator, he would strike their village later today.

A Dimensional Mage at the end of the hall stood straight as they approached.

"North wall," Hos said.

The Mage nodded, cast a spell, and warped the three of them to the top of New Eiru's wall. They faced north toward the forest and that cursed dungeon.

A lone figure approached the city, still five hundred feet away. If the figure generated that buff, it meant it spanned over a thousand feet. Since that seemed absurd, Gunder guessed whoever worked with this person had planted some sort of magical device in the city earlier.

Someone down below cast *Dawn* and the entire area to the

north lit up. Two strike teams raced toward the figure on air sleds. Gunder removed a looking glass from his Inventory and held it to his eye, bringing the trespasser into focus.

A man most likely from the build, Gunder decided, but he couldn't tell for sure as they had covered themselves completely in the garb of the sand assassins from the south. But instead of the normal brown, this person wore all white. Might it still be a Dune Wraith? He had encountered very few of their kind since reviving. They were dangerous, but not enough to destroy one of his strike teams.

The figure strode forward at a slow and even pace, unconcerned about the two air sleds bearing down on him. One of the sleds stopped and the other angled around behind, surrounding the man. He appeared to be alone.

"Fluid movements," Gunder said. "Probably an unarmed specialist. They might need you."

Hos nodded and the Mage warped him to the back of the now stopped air sled. Gunder relaxed a little, knowing his best men surrounded the figure, and Hos could match even a Step Master in unarmed combat.

To Gunder's surprise, the distant figure seemed to trace the Dimensional Mage's path directly back to Gunder. With white cloth covering the face and eyes of the Dune Wraith he couldn't tell for sure, but his heart rate increased as worry surfaced for the first time. Something about this person didn't feel normal.

Gunder, I will see you shortly.

Gunder dropped his looking glass in surprise, the fragile glass shattering on the stone. The voice had appeared inside his head, as if he'd grouped with the man. And he'd known Gunder's name, which should have been impossible with his settings on private.

Who are you? Gunder asked. *How are you speaking to me?*

I am Uru's Shadow, and judgement is a voice only the wicked hear.

"Goodbye, Judgement," Gunder whispered as he touched his ring. The linked jewelry sent a signal, telling his men to attack.

Before Gunder's men even reacted, Judgement spoke again in his mind. *Wasteful and unnecessary.*

Gunder cursed his broken looking glass and leaned forward, straining to see details. The two strike teams practiced together, and their attacks were perfectly coordinated. The front group cast a stun, root, blind, Resistance debuff, and snare while the rear group launched two heavy crossbow bolts, a fireball, lightning, and a chaos orb.

The figure immediately shifted, moving faster than Gunder could follow through what looked like some type of Step forms. Did Dune Wraiths have a Step Clan?

Before the thought had finished, the figure stood still again. None of the spells had reached the man, or he had nullified them somehow. He must possess a powerful artifact to cancel out so much magic. In each hand, he held a heavy crossbow bolt, which spoke to not only the man's Dexterity, but his Strength.

The intruder suddenly appeared in the middle of the rear air sled, even though Gunder had not even seen him turn. He must have some type of *Blink* spell as a human couldn't move that fast.

The five members of the rear strike team, plus the Air Mage guiding the sled, collapsed at the same time. The two Marksman had their own bolts lodged in their chests and Gunder couldn't see what had caused the other four to fall but assumed they had died as well.

What do you want? Gunder asked, wondering what mechanism the trespasser used for this communication. One thing was clear, the man didn't tolerate threats. He hadn't even offered Gunder a warning to withdraw his men.

I want to discuss your actions, and the justifications for them, the Dune Wraith said.

You want to judge me, Gunder replied.

Yes.

If Uru really sent you, then you know I've received my punishment. There is nothing left to take. You want my life? Take it if you can. I reject you, Shadow of Uru, just as I reject Uru and anyone else who says they care for us. It's a lie. You're a lie. And I will kill you for it.

Gunder flicked his wrist, signaling his men down below to send everyone into the clearing. A hundred highly trained soldiers from his personal army spilled into the clearing. Some of them had reached levels over seventy-five.

Including Hos, the unarmed combat specialist, who strode toward the intruder from the first air sled.

If you run now, Gunder said. *You might make it to the trees.*

Your time is up, Gunder. I will see you in eight seconds.

Gunder laughed. It took ten times that long just to reach the top of this hundred-foot wall, not to mention the strike team in front of this false prophet or the hundred plus experts rushing toward him. What a joke.

One, the number sounded loud in Gunder's head.

The Head of Security attacked with a right jab, which the intruder side-stepped as they struck Hos' neck, causing him to collapse.

Two, Uru's Shadow said calmly.

The Dune Wraith slammed a palm forward into empty air as a Fire Mage launched a massive fireball. The spell struck a shield in front of the intruder and before the flames disappeared, he strode through them and jumped onto the air sled. All of the men collapsed.

Three, the voice said.

Cracks of thunder reached Gunder, seeming to originate from the air sleds. Did the intruder have some sort of explosives?

Gunder's reinforcements had only made it a hundred feet

from the wall. He gasped as the intruder jumped four hundred feet and landed in front of the wave.

Four, the voice came.

For the first time Gunder felt concern. This obviously was a Cultivator, and likely Gem-Fortified. He touched his right earring shaped like a white orb. It meant he would need to use one of his relics. One that would suddenly stop this Cultivator's spinning core, causing intense pain, and giving Gunder plenty of time to remove the man's head with an infernal-terium garrot. It would slice through Gem-Fortified flesh like fresh bread.

Five.

Uru's Shadow strolled through the small army, redirecting spells with a wave of his arm, or shoving them back at the caster with palm strikes.

Six.

Gunder's heart raced. He had never encountered a Cultivator with such skills, but that didn't surprise him as they kept themselves and their methods as secret as possible.

The figure raised his arms and the ground rose with them. He brought his hands together as if praying and the land folded itself, devouring the army like a hungry predator.

Seven.

A weaving palm strike from Uru's Shadow on the battlefield below, and the air grew suddenly cold atop the wall, the wind gusting suddenly. The sound of falling bodies caused Gunder to look down the walkway. The guards as far as he could see had all collapsed, spears of ice protruding from their chests.

Gunder turned back to the clearing, to see if any of his army remained, but they all lay motionless. Worse, the trespasser had disappeared.

"Eight," a voice said from behind Gunder.

Gunder jumped. His normal composure destroyed by this Dune Wraith. He spun around to find Uru's Shadow standing four feet away. The white strips of cloth wrapped the six-foot figure completely, not revealing any skin at all. Perhaps this wasn't a man at all, but some type of demon from the Infernal Realm.

Gunder jerked his hand upward toward his ear. He had never intended to let Uru's Shadow get so close to him. His hand had barely moved when the figure grabbed and held it.

"Do you think that will help?" Uru's Shadow asked.

Frustration filled Gunder. He had underestimated the creature's speed.

Uru's Shadow released Gunder. "I won't stop you."

"You are a fool," Gunder said, raising his hand.

"Yes," came the simple response.

Gunder couldn't believe his luck. The arrogance of this man to think himself immune to magic. Gunder would demonstrate how ignorant the intruder was, and then kill him.

Pressing on the earring, Gunder, an Ascendant of Uru, didn't feel the wave of Spirit he knew the earring released. He smiled, expecting to see Uru's Shadow clutch his chest and collapse like the previous Cultivators had.

"Interesting," the intruder said, and took the earring from Gunder before he could even flinch.

"So you're a thief, then?" Gunder asked rubbing his now bare earlobe.

"The dead wear no jewelry."

Gunder sneered. "I will walk this wall again by sunset tomorrow. The only one dead here is you."

"Gunder, for what purpose do you create unrest and brew discontent among Uru's people?"

Gunder spit on the ground between them. "Curse Uru, and the rest of them, who destroyed this world along with their followers. If Uru did send you, then I hope you burn a thousand thousand years in the darkest pits of the Infernal Realm."

"I am a shadow, and the Infernal Realm cannot hold me. I have come to right the wrongs."

Gunder stepped forward and pointed at the figure, shouting the response. "Then give me back my family! I want my life back!"

The spell *Dawn* still hung high in the air, and the shadows from Gunder's movements created odd shapes on the stone. That is when he noticed the figure didn't cast a shadow. Nothing. It was as if he wasn't even standing there. Could this be some sort of illusion or hallucination? Had he finally lost my mind?

The figure glanced at the area Gunder studied and offered an explanation. "Shadows do not cast shadows."

Uncertainty filled Gunder. Could this figure really come from Uru?

A debuff appeared.

Shadow's Judgement: *Unrevivable.*

"You will cease creating unrest and problems immediately," Uru's Shadow demanded.

Gunder looked at the wrapped face, where he imagined the creature's eyes must be, and answered. "I will not."

"Then you will die."

Gunder closed his eyes, the pain would finally be over. He cupped his hands near his heart. "The tide comes for us all," he whispered, and brought his palms to his lips.

Gunder waited, his closed eyes filled with the blinking debuff that made this death permanent. He wondered if Uru's Shadow would make his death painful.

After ten seconds, Gunder opened his eyes. The figure stood only a foot away.

"Why did you say that?" Uru's Shadow asked.

"They are my wife's words. I say them to remember her. To remember what the gods took from me."

The figure gasped and took a step backward.

Gunder lowered his cupped hands, wondering what could shock this creature.

Slowly, Uru's Shadow reached out, took Gunder's right hand, and turned it toward the light. It stood that way, staring at Gunder's palm.

The figure dropped Gunder's hand and jumped off the wall. A thunderclap sounded, and in seconds, Uru's Shadow had sprinted across the clearing and entered the trees.

Gunder raised his right hand, the one that had itched for weeks, and looked at his palm. But this time, he saw something. Not the rash he thought would explain the itching. No. Something almost as unexpected and unexplainable as the figure that called itself Uru's Shadow.

In the middle of Gunder's palm a windswept tree softly glowed.

*** The prologue for Divine Apostasy Book 8 is free at patreon.com/afkauthor ***

APPENDIX

Item QualityInventory Color
    Common White
    Uncommon Brown
    Fine Green
    Rare Yellow
    Special Orange
    Epic Blue
    Legendary Purple

Metals
    Bronze
    Iron
    Steel
    Titanium
    Obsidian
    Terium

ClassSymbolColor
    Worker Hands Brown

Mage Brain Black
Observer Eyes Green
Order Heart White
Fighter Body Blue
Merchant Mouth Red

Fortifying Levels

Metal Levels
Lead
Copper
Silver
Gold

Gem Levels
Jade
Topaz
Sapphire
Diamond

Divine Levels
Angel
Archangel
Demigod
Deity

MeridianLocation

Body Heart
Stone Right Leg/Foot
Order Spine
Water Right Shoulder/Arm/Hand
Light Head/Neck
Life Groin/Hips/Abdomen
Mind Brain
Air Left Shoulder/Arm/Hand
Chaos Torso

Fire Left Leg/Foot
Dark Organs
Death Intestines

Money
Copper
Silver (100 Copper)
Gold (100 Silver)
Platinum (100 Gold)
Terium (100 Platinum)

RankLevel
Novice 1-9
Initiate 10-19
Apprentice 20-29
Journeyman 30-39
Acolyte 40-49
Disciple 50-59
Expert 60-69
Adept 70-84
Master 85-99
Grand Master 100

Level StartExperience Level End
1 1000 2
2 3,000 3
3 6,000 4
4 10,000 5
5 15,000 6
6 21,000 7
.
.
.

97 4,753,000 98

98 4,851,000 99

99 4,950,000 100

100 5,050,000 101

GLOSSARY

Divine Apostasy Series

Ahvy

A Worker in Deepwell who leads a team of elite Shooters. Her team loaded Ruwen's Void Band for Big D's camping trip in record time.

Ancient Mother

The term Uru used when seeing Sift's soulbound turtle, Shelly. See also Shelly, Elder Star Tortoise.

Andi Kandi

Blonde woman who conducted field side interviews at the Step Championship.

Annul Strongspell

A Merchant with a Journeyman level Glass Specialty. With her husband, Luim, she creates magical globes with trapped snowstorms and is one of Deepwell's wealthiest families. She is Slib Strongspell's mother and the woman seen with House Captain Juva when he ambushed Ruwen, Sift, and Hamma in Deepwell.

Apex

Step Tournament team made up of Chip and Stump.

Ash

Possible name referenced in Pen's journal.

Aspects

Six Aspects created by Lalquinrial. They represent: Poison, War, Famine, Pestilence, Death, and Drought.

Avalanche

Step Tournament team made up of Mai and Yap.

Axiom

The term used when all twelve Meridians are connected to a person's or creature's Center by pathways. Seven connections is all it takes to move from the Gem Levels to the Divine Levels and become a god.

Big D

The Worker in charge of the Worker's Lodge in Deepwell. Ruwen received his first spells from her and she oversaw the camping trip to foster Class appreciation. See also Yasmine Durn, Pit Boss Durn.

Blackout

Member of Step tournament team Tornado Fist.

Blapy

A seven-year-old girl with blond pigtails and a fondness for centipedes. See also Biggest Understatement of All Time.

Blink

A legendary step champion who partnered with Hourglass.

Bliz

Leader in Deepwell's Worker's Lodge who acts as a mentor for Ruwen regarding the use of Void Bands. An eighty-eight-time bandball Champion. Owns the bars Dizzy Judge in Deepwell and Pour Judgement in New Eiru. See also Crew Chief Bliz.

Breathless Sea

Sea along the west coast of the continent. Izac's Capitol, Malth, is located on its shore.

Burning Scorpions

Step Tournament team made up of Claw and Stinger.

Center

The structure inside your body that connects via pathways to Meridians and holds a Core if one has been created.

Chancey

A Clapping Brawler who buses tables at the Pour Judgement and is the son of Knuckles.

Chip

Member of Apex, a Step Tournament team.

Clarysa

Ruwen's mom and an Observer who specialized as a Ranger with an Expertise in Pack Leader which allows her to shapeshift into animals.

Claw

Member of the Burning Scorpions Step Tournament team.

Colyn

Ruwen's father and a Fighter who specialized as a Shield Champion with an Expertise in Knight Defender.

Core

The structure created by condensing Spirit and shaping it into a usable form. The Core sits inside a person's or creature's Center like a seed.

Crew Chief Bliz

Leader in Deepwell's Worker's Lodge who acts as a mentor for Ruwen regarding the use of Void Bands. An eighty-eight-time bandball Champion. Owns the bars Dizzy Judge in Deepwell and Pour Judgement in New Eiru. See also Bliz.

Cuddles

A stuffed centipede.

Cultivation

The term used when gathering energy from your surroundings does not harm any living things. Examples would be light, heat, vibrations, etc.

Dalyn

Lylan's brother and a member of the Black Pyramid.

Deepwell

City in the north-west part of Uru's lands not far from the Desolate Mountains. Ruwen was raised here.

Desolate Mountains

Large mountain range down the entire east coast of the continent.

Dizzy Judge

A bar in Deepwell owned by Crew Chief Bliz.

Drivyd

Observer Elder in New Eiru. Rami has placed a group of red balloons over his head so Ruwen can find the Elder despite his Observer skills.

Dusk

One of three sisters who oversee the Bamboo Viper Step Clan. Dusk is in charge of the secret Shadow Clan that learn the forms that can destroy gods. They are called God Killers and are very unpopular with deities.

Echo

A mysterious young woman from the Infernal Realm that Ruwen saves during his first Bamboo Viper Step Clan binding ritual. Ruwen released her from a webbing trap that had incapacitated her. Echo wrote her name in blood on Ruwen's right wrist as a promise to repay the debt she owes him.

Eclipse

A fighter in the step tournament that can block the sun.

Eiru

One of the earliest names of the Goddess now called Uru.

Elder Star Tortoise

A Divine Creature capable of altering its shape and traveling the darkness between worlds or the depths of the ocean. There are ancient references to them eating actual stars.

Elyse Blakrock

A Deepwell City Council member. Her husband, Niall, disappeared shortly after the birth of their daughter, Hamma.

Essence

Spirit is a combination of all twelve Essences. By Refining, a Harvester or Cultivator can thread their Spirit through each Meridian and gather just that Meridian's essence. These essences can then be combined to make spells and abilities. The twelve essences are: Body, Stone, Order, Water, Light, Life, Mind, Air, Chaos, Fire, Dark, and Death.

Fainting Goat

A tavern near Deepwell's Temple that Hamma frequents. Ruwen and Hamma were attacked here by a Naktos assassin and they met Kysandra for the first time as a result.

Fetid Clan

An Infernal Clan rebelling against Lalquinrial.

Findley

The Head cook in the Black Pyramid.

First Secret, The

the first axiom

heralds darkness, ensuring,

the last axiom

(Pen's birth triggered the destruction of our universe.)

Fluffy

The Black Pyramid's Quartermaster.

Fortifying

The process of using Spirit to saturate a particular Meridian's area of the body and make that area stronger. The Fortifying levels progress like this:

Metal Levels

Lead

Copper

Silver

Gold

Gem Levels

Jade
Topaz
Sapphire
Diamond
Divine Levels
Angel
Archangel
Demigod
Deity

Transitioning between Levels is very difficult and time consuming.

Fourth Secret, The
one ruined scarecrow
protecting its field of stars
ensures our harvest

(A reference to the person who will restore the Spirit back to the Universe.)

Fractal
The Dungeon Keeper for the dungeon outside Deepwell. When Ruwen first met Fractal the Dungeon Keeper was only a two-inch mass of moving crystals.

Frigid Sea
The sea along the eastern coast of the continent. Stone Harbor sits on its shores.

Fusil
The Priest who oversaw Ruwen's Ascendancy. His son was part of the group that was murdered and had their terium shipment stolen. Fusil blames Ruwen's parents for this and thinks poorly of Ruwen as a result. See also High Priest Fusil.

Gabryel
The Elder Priestess in the city of New Eiru. Usually at odds with the Fighter Elder Vachyl.

Gadyel

Warden of Legion's Vault.

Grave

A name for the planet Ruwen lives on.

Gunder

Real name of the Merchant King and part of the great revival of New Eiru.

Haffa

One of the gods whose lands border Uru's. Haffa's followers live under the Frigid Sea.

Hamma Blakrock

A seventeen-year-old Priestess from the Deepwell Temple who after helping Ruwen escape from the Temple, gets sucked into his world.

Hand

Group of five people who are tasked with helping Uru's Champion. They each have a small tree marking on their right palm.

Harvester

The term used when gathering energy from your surroundings includes living things. Living beings are far more Spirit dense than natural sources.

Head Priest Fusil

The Priest who oversaw Ruwen's Ascendancy. His son was part of the group that was murdered and had their terium shipment stolen. Fusil blames Ruwen's parents for this and thinks poorly of Ruwen as a result. See also Fusil.

Heatstroke

A fighter in the step tournament that can turn the ground into magma.

Hourglass

A legendary step champion who partnered with Blink.

House Captain Juva

The head of the Strongspell family guard who was pulled

into the Spirit Realm with Ruwen and his friends after trying to ambush them. See also Juva.

Ishdell

Guard in Legion's Vault.

Izac

Uru's twin brother whose Capitol is Malth along the Breathless Sea on the west coast of the continent.

Izac's Wrath

A mountain, twenty thousand feet high, that sits fifteen miles out in the Breathless Sea and visible from Malth. It is frequently the recipient of Izac's frustration.

Jagen

Izac's Champion who was trapped in the Spirit Realm with Uru's three Champions, one of which he is in love with. Jagen loves armor and has dual classed as a Fighter and Priest.

Juva

The head of the Strongspell family guard who was pulled into the Spirit Realm with Ruwen and his friends after trying to ambush them. See also House Captain Juva.

Kaylin

The first Champion of Uru trapped in the Spirit Realm by Naktos's magic. Uru promises she will figure out a way to return Kaylin to the Material Realm and Kaylin believe that person is Ruwen. Kaylin has dual Classed in Observer and Order.

Kholy

Goddess with superb understanding of the stars and a genius in dimensional math and alchemy. She died in the early part of the war against the darkness invading the Universe leaving behind over twenty research notebooks.

Knuckles

A Clapping Brawler who is one of the shelvers in the Black Pyramid's libraries.

Kysandra

The Dungeon Mistress for the Black Pyramid, responsible for arranging entrance to the dungeon for high level groups. The top levels of the Black Pyramid are the headquarters for her extensive spy network. She also goes by Ky and has extensive Step training.

Lalquinrial

Part of the original group of disciples that followed the True God. The only deity to not sign the Pact. He created the Infernal Realm and resides there with his followers. His source of power is unclear. He has created seven Aspects that his chosen wear, including the Scarecrow Aspect that Ruwen finds in the Plague Siren's lair.

Luim Strongspell

An Elemental Cold Mage that with his wife, Annul, creates magical globes with trapped snowstorms. He is Slib Strongspell's father and head of one of the wealthiest families in Deepwell.

Lylan

A young woman in her late teens that is an Observer and part of Kysandra's network of spies. Lylan and Sift were in a relationship when Lylan died in the Black Pyramid, causing her to lose her memories of Sift. Lylan's brother is imprisoned in the Legion's Vault in Malth.

Madda Adda

A Grandmaster of the Viper Steps and Master of the Bamboo Steps. She resides with her husband Padda Adda and Sift Adda in the Black Pyramid.

Mai

Member of the Avalanche Step Tournament team.

Malth

Izac's Capitol city that sits on the west coast next to the Breathless Sea.

Maygy

Owner of the Dizzy Judge and wife of Bliz.

Meridian

There are twelve Meridians located throughout the body:

Body->Heart

Stone->Right Leg/Foot

Order->Spine

Water->Right Shoulder/Arm/Hand

Light->Head/Neck

Life->Groin/Hips/Abdomen

Mind->Brain

Air->Left Shoulder/Arm/Hand

Chaos->Torso

Fire->Left Leg/Foot

Dark->Organs

Death->Intestines.

Each Meridian stores its own type of essence. Spirit is a combination of all twelve essences. By Refining, a Harvester or Cultivator can thread their Spirit through each Meridian and gather just that Meridian's essence. These essences can then be combined to make spells and abilities.

Mica

The second Champion of Uru trapped in the Spirit Realm by a Naktos spell. Mica has dual Classed as a Mage and Merchant. He specializes in Dimensional magic.

Miranda

The name used by the True God's Companion when in human form. A young blond haired woman with black gold-tinged wings and gold-flecked black eyes. See also Blapy.

Mist

One of the three founding sisters of the Bamboo Viper Clan. She represents the Bamboo Grandmasters.

Naktos

One of the original disciples of the True God, Naktos is called the Father of Stone and his followers live underground and are fond of alchemy. Naktos' love of knowledge led to his discovery on how to forcibly move a person from the Material Realm to the Spirit Realm.

Nameless

A narrator formed from a famous book on destructive nihilism.

Niall Blakrock

Former Head Priest of Deepwell's Temple, he is an expert in Temple repair.

Numarrow

Inklord for the god Izac.

Nymthus

Blonde woman and member of the Bamboo Viper Clan. Her home is being overrun by demons.

Odalys

The Mage Elder in New Eiru.

One True God

The original Axiom, who used his immense power to save the Universe, killing himself in the process. His disciples are the current deities who signed the Pact, minus Lalquinrial who went his own way. His dearest friend and Companion is Miranda. See also Pen.

Ovurnhyst

Volcanically active country along the north west coast.

Padda

A Grandmaster of the Bamboo Steps and Master of the Viper Steps. He resides with his wife Madda Adda and Sift Adda in the Black Pyramid.

Pen

A Harvester referenced in some older texts and the possible identity of the first Axiom. A terrible poet with excellent handwriting and a gift for seeing the future. See also One True God.

Pine

An ancient looking man who desperately wanted to save his grandson during Ruwen's Bamboo Viper Step Clan Binding process. Pine's family uses trees as names, hiding their true names.

Pit Boss Durn

The Worker in charge of the Worker's Lodge in Deepwell. Ruwen received his first spells from her and she oversaw the camping trip to foster Class appreciation. See also Yasmine Durn, Big D.

Pour Judgement

Bliz's bar near New Eiru.

Prythus

Blond man and member of the Bamboo Viper Clan. His home is being overrun by demons.

Qip

A trusted Worker of Big D's, Qip and his brother Wip, guarded Ruwen to keep him safe from danger during Big D's camping trip.

Quintyn

God occupying the area north of Uru's lands.

Qwyn

The senior librarian for the libraries inside the Black Pyramid. This giant spider acts in Ruwen's place while Ruwen is away from the Black Pyramid.

Rainbow's End

A small planet orbiting the star Shiny.

Rami

A rare bookwyrm who bonds with Ruwen as a reward for becoming the Black Pyramid Library Custodian. Rami can speak with Ruwen telepathically and is capable of many amazing things.

Ruwen Starfield

Uru's Champion whose base Class is Worker and whose high Intelligence qualified him to wear a Void Band.

Savage Island

Island containing important resources such as Crossing

Stones and Soul Pearls. Many Step Clans battle here for the Champion's Throne, currently held by the Shattered Clan.

Scos

This Sublime Centipede of Solace is a totem of Ruwen's divine authority capable of holding 5,000 Mana.

Second Secret, The

Fall's harvest ablaze

bright flames scattering shadows

sowing our sunrise

(Pen removed the Spirit from the vast majority of the Universe.)

Shelly

A tiny turtle smaller than a thumb. Sift rescued the creature from the Plague Siren's lair. See also Ancient Mother, Elder Star Tortoise.

Shiny

Medium sun at the edge of the Universe.

Shredded Sea

A vast ocean of letters.

Shroud

The language spoken by many inhabitants of the Shadow Realm.

Sift

A seventeen-year-old Bamboo Viper Step practitioner who is ready to take his test for Master. He has lived his entire life in the Black Pyramid and desperately wants to visit other places. His greatest desire is to fly, followed closely by wanting to whistle. His Center contains no connections which allows him to "sift" the energy around him, making most magic ineffective against him.

Simandreial

The peak Diamond Plague Siren Ruwen encountered in the Spirit Realm.

Sivart

The head narrator, born from the Shredded Sea whose identity is wrapped around the manifesto of the Mist Wraith Talker.

Slib Strongspell

A classmate of Ruwen's who Ascended around the same time as Ruwen. Slib Ascended as a Mage even though his Intelligence made that impractical.

Smack

Member of the Step tournament team Tornado Fist.

Smash

A Carnage Golem bound to Hamma who tends to hold grudges.

Spirit

The Energy inside every piece of the Universe from living things to natural sources such as light and heat.

Stinger

Member of the Burning Scorpions Step Tournament team.

Stone Harbor

A large city on the coast of the Frigid Sea.

Stump

Member of Apex, a Step Tournament team.

Talon

Fighter in step tournament that can fly through the air.

Tarotmethiophelius

Divine Thieving Misfortune Golem

Tassebenidoros

Blessed Fortune Golem that Tarotmethiophelius has argued with for thousands of years.

Terium

Most valuable metal in existence and nearly indestructible. Ruwen believes it might be more than a metal.

The First Secret

the first axiom

heralds darkness, ensuring,

the last axiom

(Pen's birth triggered the destruction of our universe.)

The Fourth Secret

one ruined scarecrow

protecting its field of stars

ensures our harvest

(A reference to the person who will restore the Spirit back to the Universe.)

The Second Secret

Fall's harvest ablaze

bright flames scattering shadows

sowing our sunrise

(Pen removed the Spirit from the vast majority of the Universe.)

The Third Secret

soil swaddled seeds

despite the sower's demise

survive the winter

(The secret Blapy says relates to her, which she hasn't explained.)

Third Secret, The

soil swaddled seeds

despite the sower's demise

survive the winter

(The secret Blapy says relates to her, which she hasn't explained.)

Thorn

One of the three founding sisters of the Bamboo Viper Clan. She represents the Viper Grandmasters.

Thumbs

Clapping Brawler who works as a shelver in the Black Pyramid libraries.

Tora

A Worker with a Void Band working in the terium mine

near Deepwell. She gave Ruwen a tour of the mine and warned him not to take any of Bliz's drinking quests.

Tornado Fist

Step Tournament team made up of Blackout and Smack.

Tremine

A Chaos Mage who has Specialized in Void magic. He is also the Head Librarian of the Deepwell Library and Ruwen's mentor and friend.

Una

The third Champion of Uru trapped in the Spirit Realm by a Naktos spell. Una has dual Classed as a Fighter and Observer. She is in love with Jagen, Izac's Champion.

Uru

One of the original disciples of the True God, Uru was once called Eiru the Fair. She has spent over ten thousand years planning how to fulfill the One True God's last wish. Her brother Izac disagrees with her plans and refuses to help, wanting instead to remake the universe in his own image. Ruwen is the culmination of all Uru's planning.

Uru's Blessing

The area where Ascendants of Uru will continuously synchronize their physical and mental state. Ascendants who die will revive at the temple they are bound to with up-to-date memories and capabilities.

Vachyl

The Fighter Elder for New Eiru.

Valora

A Naktos Stone Carver and artist.

Void Band

Dimensional storage with a flexible opening and 100% weight reduction. More than just the opening can be manipulated with Energy, but if the Energy pool drops to zero while the band is open, it causes instant death.

Wenquian

Goddess controlling country west of Uru's lands.

Whiskers

A cat with four forms that can be summoned by a ring.

Windswept Tree

This describes the tree visible behind Uru in her Divine Realm. It is also the symbol visible on the right palms of those who serve Uru's Champion as Hands. see also-Hand

Wip

A trusted Worker of Big D's, Wip and his brother Qip, guarded Ruwen to keep him safe from danger during Big D's camping trip.

Xavier

A Junior Celestial Remnant who is forced by his father to leave the dungeon and find pressure that will help him evolve. His kind are usually born inside exploding stars and Blapy assists the family in finding a new source of pressure to further her own interests.

Yana

Worker Elder in New Eiru.

Yap

Member of the Avalanche Step Tournament team.

Yasmine Durn

The Worker in charge of the Worker's Lodge in Deepwell. Ruwen received his first spells from her and she oversaw the camping trip to foster Class appreciation. See also Pit Boss Durn, Big D.

Zahara

Merchant Elder in New Eiru.

Zylkin

Prime Shadow Realm Warden

ACKNOWLEDGMENTS

First, and most importantly, I want to thank **you**. It has been a difficult few years for everyone and I am so grateful, despite all the hurdles, you chose to spend some of your precious time with this series. From the bottom of my heart, thank you.

Erika, you suffer the most from my writing. You deal with me complaining about story issues, staring off into space (this happens A LOT) as the story spins in my head, worrying about the future of the series and my writing, and all the other insecurities authors have. For all that, and so much more, thank you. I appreciate you and love you so much.

At heart I am a family guy, and my kids are precious to me. Megan, Zachary, Nicole, Liam, and a week after this book launches Ethan. You all fill me with joy and I'm so lucky to be your dad. I am proud of you all and love you more than I can put in words!

Megan, as you focus on your future, know that I am so proud of you. I envy your amazing mind and spirit, and much of the wisdom I try and sprinkle through this series I learned from you, or because of you. I love you so much.

Zachary, thank you for always being willing to discuss the problems in my stories. With your extensive knowledge, you provide me a view and insight I would otherwise not have. Thank you for your advice. I love you so much.

Nicole, you suffer through all my texts, emails, and calls, sometimes daily. Without your amazing memory this series would be full of plot holes and have far less wonder. You are the silent and unknown Rami behind this series. Thank you doesn't seem like enough for your massive contribution. I love you so much.

Betsy, I didn't know how working with someone else in this series would go…but it went great. Your insight into the story and characters has made a massive difference in these books. I appreciate all you've done and look forward to working with you again. Lylan is waiting.

Jason, I beat you to the finish line, again. Hopefully when I finish book eight you won't have "three chapters" left in your second book. Thanks for listening, discussing, and brainstorming with me. I am blessed to have you as a part of my life.

Isaac, thank you for being such a fan of the series and providing feedback. As you've grown up and read even more incredible books, it humbles me to still be in your top five author list.

I say this in all the books, but I can't put it any better, so I'll just restate it because it remains the truth: my Patrons are special people. All the authors I know battle self-doubt and the incredible resistance to not only writing your inner thoughts but placing them where everyone can tell you how much they suck. The antidote to those people and to the inner demons that want you to stop, are the superfans of this series. My patrons hold a special place in my heart. You keep me motivated to continue. I know for a fact this book would not exist without you. Thank you so so much.

Mom, I can always rely on you to help or listen to me. There is something soothing and reassuring knowing some other person in this crazy universe is always thinking positive and loving thoughts about you. It is a source of strength for me. Thank you for everything you've done, and continue to do, for me. I love you so much.

Liam, this book is dedicated to you, although you won't be able to read it for a few years. Being a dad is a large part of my identity and something I enjoy very much. You benefit from all the mistakes I made with Megan, Zachary, and Nicole. They turned out wonderful anyway, and my prayer is that you do as well. The sound of your laughter fills my heart. The gentleness of your soul shines like the sun and pulls everyone into your orbit. You are a joy, and I'm so thankful you are part of my life. I love you so much, Champ.

SPECIAL THANKS

The following people deserve special thanks, as their support for the series has made a significant difference in my ability to tell this story. I appreciate you all so much!

Andrew Fuerst
Andrew Patterson
Archer9512
Arthur Bishop
Austin Carlile
Austin Weinreber
C'tri Goudie
Casey Connelly
Clark Sinclair-Harry
Clinton Johnson
Cole Kempf
Daemon Shade
Derek Morgan
Derek Raxter
Don Barry
Draxy Bear
Drew Chepil

SPECIAL THANKS

Dusty Norris
Gayle Brown
General Senpai der KKdKPuU
George Purnell
Grumbling Grizzly
Halie Bou-Chedid
Harold Sandahl IV
Herzog Nils
Jacob
James Bateman
James Goodchild
Joe Bou-Chedid
John Lascola
Joshua Franks
Jordon Kellow
Kathryn Hopkinson
Kevin McClelland
Kye Colquhoun
Lonnie Sizemore
Luc Montgomery Martin Barbeau
Lukas Eagleton
Mage
Marcus Perry
Marshall Watts
Mason R Hoskins
Matt Alonso
Matthew Baumann
Michael Schober
Michael Springer
Michael Stephens
Mike Blanding
Mike LaPeters
MillionLittleE
N

Nikki McClenahan
Paul Petrov
Perry Wood II
Richard Burris
Robert Thatch
Samuel Strode
Shaughn Noble
Spencer Wade
Spenser Chamberlin
Sterling Holcomb
Sweet
Tellistto Perjurron
Thomas Self
Tim Christensen
Tim V
Tyler Schibig
Tyler Schleicher
Ward Yorgason
Zach Hoeken

Thank you all so much!

AUTHOR'S NOTE

I am overjoyed that this series continues to resonate with others. From the bottom of my heart, thank you for supporting this story.

Book seven turned out almost as long as book six, but I finished it much earlier. A big part of that was the deadline I had with the narrator, Travis Baldree. That is one deadline I didn't want to miss.

The good news is that I may finally be increasing my productivity, which would allow me to not only meet the deadlines of the Divine Apostasy but write some other books that are rolling around in my head. Fingers crossed.

I don't take any of this for granted, and I'm grateful every day that we have found each other.

Sincerely and truly, I appreciate you taking the time to read this series.

Shade's First Rule: move fast alone, travel far together.

Let's go far.

LITRPG LINKS

Join these great LitRPG groups to discuss your favorite books with other readers and learn about new releases and promotions.

LitRPG Society
www.facebook.com/groups/LitRPGsociety
LitRPG Books
www.facebook.com/groups/LitRPG.books
LitRPG Forum
www.facebook.com/groups/litrpgforum
LitRPG Releases
www.facebook.com/groups/LitRPGReleases

LITRPG FACEBOOK GROUP

LITRPG FACEBOOK GROUP

To learn more about LitRPG, talk to authors including myself, and just have an awesome time, please join the LitRPG Group.